RUSSET

KIRBY JONAS

Cover design by Birgitta Bright

Howling Wolf Publishing
Pocatello, Idaho

Howling Wolf Publishing
1611 City Creek Road
Pocatello ID 83204

For more information about Kirby's books, check out:

www.kirbyjonas.com
Facebook, at KirbyJonasauthor

Or email Kirby at: **kirby@kirbyjonas.com**

Manufactured in the United States of America—*One nation, under God*

Publication date for this edition: September 2018
Jonas, Kirby, 1965—

Russet / by Kirby Jonas.

ISBN: 978-1-891423-32-1
Library of Congress Control Number: 2018909425

To learn more about this book or any other Kirby Jonas book, email Kirby at kirby@kirbyjonas.com

Dedicated first of all to Mom, who gave me all the tools I needed to be a writer, and the time and freedom to perfect my craft. This book was written in the deep hope that it would please her.

Also dedicated to my grandfather,
former Bingham County Sheriff Archie Evan Hess,
my Uncle Burdette Hess, of the Calgary Stampeders,
and the spirit of the 1981 Shelley Russets,
Richard Hobbs

CHAPTER ONE

● *April, 1955* ●

How did a boy overcome the fact that his parents had knowingly—if lovingly—named him after a potato?

Simple. He embraced it. He became proud of it. He became the toughest, fastest, most agile spud that had ever lived. And he carried his boys to the opposing team's end zone—again and again and again.

Until he became a local legend.

James Russet Blevins, eighteen years old as of April second, and tough as bull rawhide, could have been like most other boys and gone by James, or Jim, or any of a dozen other nicknames his friends, coaches, and admirers had given him over all the years since he became obsessed with a piece of aerodynamic pig skin known fondly as a football. After all, he pretty much *was* the football team of the Shelley Russets in nineteen fifty-five. He could have chosen whatever name he liked best.

But Russet was different. It was remarkable. It was . . . symbolic. It was like he was the team mascot *and* its star player—which in Shelley, Idaho, in the 1950's pretty much meant being the most celebrated person in the entire town. That is, with one exception.

His father, Arch Blevins, stood six-foot-four and was the former chief of police and now the most famous and most beloved sheriff Bingham County had ever known. It was in the giant shadow cast by this legendary peace officer that Russ Blevins had grown to be a man.

● ● ● ● ●

April had swept over the little town of Shelley, and snowmelt had filled the ruts along Spud Alley, many of the town's gutters, and all the

low spots along the railroad tracks that ran by not too far from his house. The fingers of the wind picked through Russ Blevins's hair as he ran, far from home, out past the big sugar factory, past farms and fields, where cattle and horses grazed side by side and raised their heads to watch the unusual form of the lone runner flashing by.

With spring had come track, and like most of the other Shelley Russets, Russ had signed up. Unlike many of the others, however, he needed no coercion. To Russ, any method of improving his stamina, his speed, and agility was worth his effort. He had signed up to run the one hundred and two hundred yard dash, to throw the discus, and to perform the pole vault. He had quickly learned that the pole vault was not going to be his strong point, however. His thick, solid muscle, especially the meat in his legs, was a chore to get over that bar. Because of this fact he would stick with pole vaulting, because no sport was ever going to get the best of Russet Blevins.

Evening was coming on, and the air was getting chill. The thin sweat shirt he wore was not enough, especially soaked with sweat. But still Russ ran on. Track practice was over, and all the other athletes had gone home. But Russ would not quit. When fall came, he was going to have the weight of the Shelley Russets on his shoulders. If he couldn't run ten miles without stopping, then he didn't deserve the name Russet.

Behind him from the direction of town, Russ heard the hum of a motor, and he moved to the weeds at the road's edge but kept jogging. One more minute and he would sprint out again for another two hundred.

The car slowed alongside him and adopted his speed. Annoyed, Russ slowed even more and looked over. It was the sheriff's car, a fifty-three Ford Crown Victoria, white with black doors bearing the legend, ***Bingham County Sheriff.***

His father was looking at him with a grin, and he pulled up another fifty feet and stopped, leaning over to roll down the passenger window.

Russ sped up to reach the car, then stopped and leaned in, resting his big hands on the top of the door as he huffed for air.

"Hey, Pop."

"Hi, Son. You going to run all night?"

"I still got four miles."

"Mom's starting supper, and all the girls are going to be waiting on you too. How long does it take you to run four miles?"

Russ shrugged, glancing back the way he had come. "I don't know. Now that I'm tired, maybe thirty-five minutes."

"Really? You say you're tired but you can still go that fast? I'm impressed. You're more than four miles out from the house now, though."

"I know, but I was going to use another mile to cool off."

Sheriff Blevins laughed. "You're a hard charger, Son. I'll tell you what. Why don't you see some new country today instead of going back over what you see all the time? I've got to drive out to Sand Creek and serve a summons. How about heading out that way, as hard as you can, and then do your cool off, and I'll pick you up on my way back in."

"Wow, Pop—thanks! Sounds great."

"Then quit lollygagging," said the sheriff with a grin. And he sped off down the road.

● ● ● ● ●

Back home, Russ took time out to stretch against the side of the house while his father went inside to change out of his uniform. Russ was leaned far forward, with one leg out behind him, stretching his calf, when a voice startled him.

"Hey, Russ!"

Russ groaned inwardly. It was the voice of Isaac Thorpe, who for quite some time had gone by the nickname of Rusty, a name of whose origin Russ could only guess, because unlike most "Rustys," his hair was not red. But Isaac wore it proudly, which Russ had come to suspect was because it was so close to his own name. Russ may not have been completely in tune with other people's feelings, but the way little Isaac looked up to him was obvious to anyone.

Isaac was ten years old and lived not very far away down Park Avenue. He didn't seem to have many friends, although he was a sharp enough kid, and likable. For whatever reason, he had adopted Russ as his idol, and Russ hadn't minded, for a while. Who wouldn't be proud to have someone who admired him the way Rusty did? But it had gotten to where it seemed like every time he turned around—like right now—the boy was there. An eighteen-year-old man sometimes needed his space.

"Hi, Rusty," Russ turned and greeted his shadow reluctantly. Ike was a dark-skinned boy, with eyes that at first glance appeared to be deep chocolate, but on seeing them closer were more a mix of brown, green, and faint highlights of gold. His mouth was full and pink, and always ready to give up a shy grin, and his hair was the color of molasses. He was dressed in faded Levi's, red and white sneakers, and a light blue V-neck sweater over a white and black plaid shirt.

"What are you doing?" Isaac asked.

"Just stretching out from a run."

"Oh. Hey, have you heard about James Dean?"

"Who hasn't?"

Isaac chuckled, blushing. He kicked at the sidewalk. "Yeah, so everybody says he's pretty cool, huh?"

"Yeah, I guess. He's got long hair." Russ could claim that because unlike most of those at his school he usually wore a crewcut, so almost everyone else's hair was long compared to his.

Isaac raised a hand and ruffled the back of his hair. It was even longer than most, especially in the conservative little town of Shelley. It was every bit as long as James Dean's, and longer. He dropped his eyes. Russ caught on. "Hey! Sorry, I didn't mean it's so bad if you don't have a lighter, buddy. Just because most guys have shorter hair doesn't mean you have to."

"Aw, that's okay. I didn't take it bad. I'm hopin' my dad will let me get a lighter sometime."

Inwardly, Russ smiled at Ike's copying his use of the slang term for a short haircut.

"He won't let you? How come?"

"He said he doesn't want me lookin' like everybody else."

"That's what I said, right?" Russ thought the more likely reason was Isaac's family didn't appear to have a lot of extra money. He walked over to Isaac and ruffled his hair. "Hey, you don't look like everybody else anyway. You're a cool cat!"

Isaac grinned, and his deep dimples showed how that compliment pleased him. "In school, they call me Bundie."

"Oh, brother! Don't listen to them. I've seen plenty of longer-haired kids than you. At least you don't have a duck butt!"

Isaac giggled. That style of hair-do was not popular with the upper echelon of Shelley's school system. In fact, many of the tougher talking crowd had an even more derogatory name for it, often using the initials D.A.

The younger boy took a deep breath, and a hopeful look came into his eyes. "So what do you think about that movie James Dean's in, *East of Eden?*"

"Whatever. I don't have much time for movies. Besides, it's already gone, you know."

"From the Virginia," Isaac agreed. "But now it's at the Sky Vu—in Idaho Falls."

Russ chuckled. "Right! It's April. You going to go freeze to death in the bleachers at the drive-in?"

"It wouldn't be so bad."

"Well, what're you gonna do, walk seven miles, then seven back home? Besides, you got the jets to know your mom's not gonna let you go to that kind of movie—especially at the passion pit."

Isaac blushed at Russ's use of the colloquialism for a drive-in theater. His glance went to the forty-one Studebaker Champion parked in the Blevins driveway, the car Russ usually took any place he needed to go—that is, if he wasn't running.

The light green vehicle was rust-spotted and battered, and the trunk lid had sustained extensive damage well before Sheriff Blevins picked it up at a bargain price from some local woman whose son was going to the big house. But all that and trashed seats didn't stop young Isaac from seeming to think it was the coolest car in town. After a moment's scrutiny of the car, his eyes fell. "Well, uh . . . I don't really think she'd care."

"Better think again, buddy. I got a mother too, and I know how those critters think!"

Once more, Isaac kicked at the sidewalk. "Yeah, you're prob'ly right."

"Yeah, you know I'm right! You get your mom to call me and tell me you can go. I wanna see that!"

Isaac smiled, but Russ missed the sadness in the expression.

"Hey, bud, I gotta go refuel. I'm starved!"

Isaac looked toward the house, and there was a longing that this time Russ did not miss. But he wasn't about to be saddled with a shadow the rest of the evening, and there were times he couldn't pry Isaac away with a crowbar. He could be a real pest; the other Russets would call him a germ.

"Hey, Ike, you better put an egg in your shoe and beat it," said Russ, delivering a light punch to the boy's shoulder. The phrase might have been taken as rude in some cases, but he knew how Isaac would take it. "See you later, alligator."

The big dimples showed again, as Isaac crammed his fingers into his pockets. "After while, crocodile."

He turned to go, and Russ watched him amble down the sidewalk. He was halfway along the block, with Russ still watching him, when he started to cut across the street, to the side opposite from his house, which he had almost reached. The boy turned his head and looked surprised to see Russ watching him. His step faltered, as if he would turn back toward his house, but then he continued on, a little slower. Now, instead of crossing over as he had apparently intended to, he walked along the edge of the street, kicking up loose dirt and gravel. Russ noted that he made a point of not looking back again.

When Russ headed for his house, after his mother called him in to eat, Isaac had reached Elm Street, far past the walkway up to his own house.

The house was in a bit of an uproar—at least as much of an uproar as a home full of teenage girls and one pre-teen girl were willing to create—particularly in the home of Sheriff Arch Blevins, who appreciated his peaceful evenings.

Seventeen-year-old Doris, who shared the same grade in school as Russ, in spite of being fifteen months younger, said, "It's about time, jabber jaws! Thanks! Now the spuds are cold." She gave him a teasing look, and he knuckled the top of her head.

"Cool it, Betsy! I had to get rid of the germ."

Fifteen-year-old Annie frowned at her brother, but eleven-year-old Kathleen wasn't so quiet in her disapproval. "Hey! Why do you call him that?"

"Oh, give me a break! That's what all the guys call him. He's getting to be a real pest!"

"Russ, you know that boy adores you," his mother cut in with her usual attempt to mediate. "It's not everybody that can claim a young idol worshiper like that."

Russ grinned. "Jeez Louise, Mom! Don't you know the whole town worships me?"

Amid the groans and laughs of his sisters, Arch pounded his fist a couple of times next to his plate. "All right, cut it out. This is *all* going to be cold by the time I get you bunch of yahoos to hush. Let's eat." He grabbed hold of his fork.

"Arch," cut in Eleanor Blevins with gentle warning. "A blessing?"

"Oh, sure. Hey, Mr. Everybody's Hero, I suppose you're probably the only one important enough around here for God to listen to your prayer. Bless the food for your mother."

Russ grinned and shot a look at his mom, then bowed his head. His blessing wasn't twenty words long, and those few were strung together like one great big word he had invented. His dad knew he would be the most succinct, and that was why nine times out of ten he picked him to say the prayer. They had a good partnership going: his dad didn't have to pray, and he still managed to appease Eleanor with a good, brief blessing so he could get right to the all-important job of filling his gut.

As Russ raised his head and took his fork and knife in hand, he avoided the reproving look he knew his mother would be giving him. With a slight rustle of her strong shoulders under her dress, Eleanor pursed her lips and picked up her own fork, scrutinizing the mashed potatoes. Russ didn't look at her because he didn't want to give her any opening for preaching to him about his manner of prayer. His father had taught him well.

CHAPTER TWO

Helen James had long, lustrous chestnut hair with highlights that shone like a new penny. It reached to the middle of her back in natural waves artfully augmented with curlers, and framed an oval face set off by full, pink lips and eyes of the most sparkling bluish green Russ Blevins had ever seen in anyone's eyes. That hair which she was obviously so proud of was the longest in the school, as most of the other girls preferred the current shorter styles that were common now in Hollywood.

It was rumored that Helen was on the track team for one reason only—to keep her near-perfect figure toned. She didn't really seem to care about winning meets, and in the eight hundred she was always toward the middle—but always flashing the most wonderful smile on the team. With as little effort as she put into being average, if she had applied herself she might have ruled the field. That was about the one and only thing that bothered Russ Blevins when it came to Helen James: her lack of drive to excel.

"Hey, Custer!"

It was the voice of Coach Dan Nalder that snapped Russ out of his trance. Russ had been staring after the diminishing but still stunning figure of Helen, the only girl who could turn his head.

"Yeah, Coach!" he called back.

"You're not here to exercise your eyes—get back on the track. Five more minutes of wind sprints. Then come find me."

It was the only reminder Russ would need. Helen James aside, he was here to rule the grid iron that fall, not to ogle girls—not even Helen.

Taking a deep breath, he sprinted down the track.

At the end of practice that afternoon, everyone gathered together in their groups. Helen only had two girls in her entourage—two girls who, if possible, cared even less about sports than Helen did. Lonna Hansen and Bobbie Ketchum were both brunettes, the first one tall with bobbed

hair, the other one short, with medium-length hair curled under at the ends, and they had joined the track team only because of Helen, whose reason was vanity. Lonna and Bobbie were barely attractive enough to fit into Helen's group, yet plain enough to let her shine.

Toweling sweat off his face as his team members trickled in to surround him, Russ ogled Helen like the rutting buck watches a moist-eyed doe. "Get your eyes back in your head, Cus!"

A smile coming to his face, Russ looked over to see his second-best buddy, Peter Basso, grinning at him. Basso was a dark-eyed, good-looking boy whose parents had come over from Italy. In well-meaning humor, they all called him "Wop."

"What else am I gonna look at, Wop? You and your homely mug?"

The other boys laughed. "Go ask her on a date, Cus!" joined in Russ's best friend, Everett Morin. "She didn't run hard enough to break a sweat—she oughtta have enough energy left for some back seat bingo."

"Ah, knock it off," Russ chided. "Helen's a lady."

"Yeah, right!" one of the other boys chimed in. "A lady. We see the way she's lookin' at you. No lady makes eyes like that."

He felt someone punch him in the shoulder, and he grabbed the boy's wrist and looked over. By the big grin that met him, the hit was supposed to be a teasing one, but it still hurt. Shave-headed linebacker Charlie Braun, called Egg by all his buddies, because of his smooth white dome, was big and rough. He had no concept of hitting someone softly.

"Jeez, Egg! You trying to break my throwin' arm?"

"Toughen up! How you gonna make it through next season if a little love tap sends you cryin' to Mama?"

"Oh yeah? How about a challenge?" said Russ.

"Sure. What?" Egg wouldn't turn down a challenge—*any* challenge. Heaven forbid someone ever dared him to fly off the top of the Virginia Theater with paper maché wings.

"Race you to the fence. Winner gets to punch the loser as hard as he wants."

There wasn't even time for a reply before Egg's eyes got big and he took off sprinting toward the fence, only fifty yards away. Egg never was very bright. Russ caught up and passed him ten yards before they made it to the fence. Egg was slamming up against the chain-link as the other

boys jogged to catch up. A good punch to the shoulder wasn't something they wanted to miss—especially since Charlie was the one usually doing all the hitting.

Never one to weasel out of a deal, Egg walked over to Russ and offered a manly shoulder. As the boys gathered around, Russ hauled back and hit his friend, making him stumble back a couple of feet and clutch his shoulder in pain. "Dang, man! Holy crap! I owe you."

"Deal's a deal!" said Russ, laughing, and he felt someone dig him in the ribs.

It was Everett. "Hey, look, man!"

Russ followed the tilt of Everett's chin to see Helen and her friends watching. As she realized they were looking at her, she tossed her head, and the three of them started off the field.

"I'm tellin' you, buddy," Everett elbowed Russ in the ribs. "The time's ripe. Go on, chicken!"

With a sudden surge of recklessness, egged on by Everett's wink, Russ took off loping down the track. He sure wasn't going to brook being called a chicken in front of the whole team. He caught the three girls as they passed behind the bleachers.

"Hey, Helen."

She turned and eyed him up and down. "Hey . . . Russ."

Impatient, the other girls looked on.

"Can I talk to you for a minute?"

"Well . . . sure." She glanced to the left and right at her friends, then again massaged his senses with those incredible eyes.

Russ Blevins admired many things: a tough, fast football player, a fat baked potato, a juicy steak, a sharp, shiny hot rod. But there weren't many things in the universe that could turn his knees to jelly like the unblinking gaze of Helen James.

His glance bounced over at the other girls. "I mean just us."

"Oh." She looked again at Lonna and Bobbie. "Hey, just a minute, girls. I'll be right back."

She turned those eyes back to Russ, melting the rest of his body to jelly now too, and he started to walk off with her, very conscious that she was in step beside him.

Thirty steps away from the girls, and now back well within sight of the rest of the football team, she stopped. He was slow to react and had to walk a couple of steps back to her. "So? Talk."

"Hey, um . . . I was wondering if you might like to go grab a soda pop or something."

"But don't you always run some more after practice?"

"Well, yeah, but . . . Well, I could do that some other time."

"Are you serious? Wow. I'm flattered. People at school say you don't give up your extra run for anybody."

"Not *just* anybody." He felt his courage getting a little stronger. But he was glad he had already been sweating. Maybe she wouldn't know the new sweat on his cheeks was over her.

"I guess we could go sometime for some French fries or something," she said. "But hey—I need to say something right off. If you're looking for a make out or something, I'm not that girl."

Russ felt his face turn hot. "What?"

"A make out, you know. I'm not anybody's easy date, if you know what I mean."

He gathered his floundering strength. "No, Helen, it's nothing like that. I just . . . I like you. I think you're a lady."

She studied his eyes for a moment longer, reading him like a neon sign. "Huh. Okay. Yeah, let's go hang sometime. That'd be cool."

She graced him with a little smile, like a queen to her servant—not quite enough to make him think he was in like Flynn, but . . . *something.* Then she turned and sashayed back to her friends, leaving him standing there with his mouth open as he watched her poodle skirt sway.

The other boys, after hanging back long enough to let the girls disappear into the back door of the school, hurried over and surrounded him.

"What the?" asked Alvin Wheeler, another Russet linebacker, whose only conceivable sport in track was the discus, because his six-foot-four and two hundred thirty pounds didn't allow him any grace running down a track. Everyone tended to call the big boy Nash, after his locally infamous chariot. "So what happened?"

"She turn you down?" cut in Egg.

"Yeah, come on!" Mark Knaggs, the football team's center, a boy they called "Spit," because of his most visible habit, grabbed Russ's shoulder. "Give us the scoop, man!"

Everett stood beside his friend, suave enough to know when to shut up.

"Heck no, she didn't turn me down. She said yes!"

Everett now livened up and got hold of his friend's other shoulder. "She what? No kiddin'? She said yes? When? You goin' right now?"

"I don't know, man!" The fact that he really didn't know embarrassed Russ, who was used to being the star of the show. "She said something about me running after track, and I said I could do it later, and then . . . She ended up saying we could go for fries or something sometime. Then she just walked off."

"Yeah! We saw her walk off!" remarked Spit with a laugh. "And boy, what a walk!"

"Well . . . Maybe she's going to get cleaned up right now!" Egg suggested, hopeful for his buddy.

"Nah, I don't think so. No, the last thing she said is 'let's go hang sometime.' That doesn't sound like 'right now'."

Nash Wheeler stood there. Finally, he looked back down at his friend and clapped him on top of the head. "Don't sweat it, brother. You're still in—I think."

The other boys all laughed good-naturedly, threw a few jabs of pure jealousy at Russ, then started for the back door. When they realized Russ wasn't with them, a couple of them turned, and then they all did. "What's up?" asked Everett.

"Well, there's no reason I can't run now."

"You're nuts," said Ev. "Jeez, give your body a break sometime."

"It's okay. You guys go on. I'll just run a couple."

But to Russ Blevins, there was no "couple." If he was going to run, he was going to *run.* Two miles wasn't worth breaking back into a sweat.

His body packed once again with energy, but this time of the nervous variety, Russ went back to the track. He leaned down on his palms to stretch his calves, then stood and looked up and down the track. His eyes ran the whole length of it as he felt the cool April breeze rippling his sweat-damp, almost see-through white tee shirt. He was alone again. No

one else cared about football like he did—track either, for that matter. When the coach said they were done, they took that as a commandment. Russ, on the other hand, understood it as a mild suggestion, intended to be ignored.

With a deep breath, he took off at a good nine-minute mile pace, which he kept for half a mile. He came back to his mark and started into a brisk walk for half a minute. Then he took off and did once around the track at what could have been a four-minute mile, if he were able to sustain it.

This time, when he came back around, he saw a girl sitting up on the top bleacher on the west side. He tried to scrape the sweat out of his eyes, but he couldn't focus on her for a moment. Still, the short bob of her deeply chocolate hair and her blood-red sweater were a giveaway. And anyway, there was only one girl he could name right off the bat who would be here alone watching him run.

He lifted a half-hearted hand. "Hi, Edie."

Edie Russell, her eyes popping open wider because of his acknowledgement, waved and smiled. "Hi, Russ. You still trying to knock all the gravel off the track?"

Russ laughed. "Yeah. Still a little on there."

Edie smiled, the white of her teeth rivaling Helen's, but otherwise staggering deep in her shadow in the beauty queen department. "Yeah, I see that." She averted her eyes.

"Well, I've gotta run some more. I guess I'll see you."

"Oh. Okay." The girl seemed about to say something else, but Russ could not stay and risk losing his warm-up. He turned away and took off down the track in a long jog. He didn't want to be what they called an "actor" right in front of the girl—a show-off. She would be gone, soon enough, and he could pick up his speed again.

The first time he came back around the track, jogging fast, she was still there. He concentrated on the track in front of him and didn't look at her. He couldn't let her become a germ like Isaac.

The second time he rounded the track, he saw Edie trudging away, holding a handful of books to her chest, her head down. As he was about to turn back to the track and set himself to really run, the back door to the school opened, and Helen James appeared, bringing the sunlight with

her in her hair. Russ slowed almost to a walk. The two girls paused abreast of each other and seemed to be exchanging words. Then Edie continued on into the school, and Helen came on.

With a surge of energy, Russ took off. He made it all the way around the track in another minute and five seconds. When he came back around, glorying in the wind in his face, one of his wildest dreams came true.

Helen James, alone, was still standing there, watching him.

CHAPTER THREE

Russ slowed down and walked over to Helen, a little too conscious of his sweat-soaked shirt and face. "Hi."

"Hi."

"Sorry about the sweat."

"You were running fast!"

"Ha. Yeah, kind of."

"A lot faster and harder than I do." She smiled without showing her teeth.

Russ was at a loss for words. Why had she come back out?

"So . . . I thought we were going for fries or something."

A cold shock jolted Russ. "Yeah, but . . . I thought you said some other time."

"Oh, yeah. Well, I got thinking about it and wondered if you would really be willing to give up your run. My friends swore you don't give that up for anybody."

"Ha! Well, how would they know? Did they ever ask?"

"Okay. So . . . you're pretty wet."

"Yeah."

"This is the only time I had, though," she said.

Russ's heart fell, and his eyes leaped toward the back door of the school. "It would only take me maybe fifteen minutes to clean up."

"You'll still keep sweating though."

"Yeah, I guess." It embarrassed him that she would know that.

Without saying anything, she walked over and sat down on the second bleacher, putting her feet up. A breeze sauntered by and ruffled her hair, and she raised her face into it, closing her eyes and taking a deep breath through her nose. "Ooh. Smell the apple blossoms!"

Russ smiled. He wanted to sit. He realized that all his years of football had left him no time for figuring out how to act around a girl he actually liked. Most of them were little better than sisters to him, and he didn't care what they thought. Now it was different. Did he sit, or remain standing? Did he have to wait for an invitation?

"You can sit by me—if you want," Helen said, rescuing him from his quandary. However, he still felt the fool, as if he had never been near a girl before.

He walked over and sat down, keeping half a foot between them. Without saying anything, she casually scooted away until it was almost a foot. He felt himself blush and looked down at his shoes.

"Why does the team call you Cuss?" she asked. "Making fun of your name?"

He laughed. "The coach told me a story about General Custer one time, and how hard he fought, and how he led his troops to victory in the Civil War—way before he got killed by the Indians. He used to ride out in front of his men and inspire them to fight harder. So Coach nicknamed me Custer. And yeah, those guys. Jeez. Kids can't leave well enough alone, you know? So they shortened it to Cus, to rhyme with my name."

"That's funny." Helen raised a hand and ran it back through her hair, letting it tumble over her right shoulder. The wind shifted, and he smelled her perfume, freshly applied after her shower.

He got the courage up to study her out of the corner of his eye. She wore a white cashmere sweater and a Scottish plaid, pleated skirt. Her footwear was saddle oxfords, white with the stripe in red. The mid-fifties had changed it all for that all-defining fat middle stripe, which traditionally had always been only black or brown.

Russ had told Helen she was a lady, and he told himself he didn't care about anything else. But no eighteen-year-old boy—he liked to think of himself as a man—could miss the delicious curves of this girl, accentuated by the form-fitting, thin sweater. There were few things in

the life of Russ Blevins that could render him light-headed. Helen James happened to top the list.

"My father loves football, especially the Shelley Russets. He says you've been the whole Russets team for two years."

Russ swallowed. He smiled and looked down. "Naw, the other boys are good too. I couldn't do it without them."

"Maybe. But my father says if it weren't for you, all the things those other boys can do would be wasted effort."

"Really? Your dad said that?"

"Yes. He's really into ball."

Getting the strength to keep his eyes on her face, he happened to notice that her skin had no blemishes. But he couldn't help thinking about what she had said, even while engrossed in the purely scholarly study of her attributes.

"But you don't like ball much."

Helen shrugged, pushing her full pink lips into a thoughtful pouting shape. "I never thought about it much. I guess not really. Sorry."

Russ's heart fell. But it was okay. They must have things to talk about other than some stupid sport.

"You run pretty good," he commented.

"Oh, thanks. I'm not into it much. Coach hates me for it." She scrunched up her face, gazing out at the mountains to the east. "Russ, did you ever want to just . . . get out of here? Maybe run and run, way past those mountains, and never stop?"

He followed her eyes to the mountains, with Taylor Mountain rearing up over the rest of the Blackfoot range. Right now, the ridges and valleys were still more snow-covered than not.

Russ couldn't remember ever feeling anything like what Helen had suggested. He was happy with his life. He had recognition. People liked him. And he enjoyed the feeling that perhaps he really *was* carrying his team to victory. There sure were a lot of people in Shelley who seemed to believe that—so why not?

"No, I never thought anything like that."

Helen sat pondering with her eyes closed for a moment, the breeze sifting through her hair. She opened her eyes, and her lips parted, moist and soft-looking in the middle, like rose petals wet with dew.

"You ask me why I dwell in the green mountain. I smile and make no reply, for my heart is free of care. As the peach blossom flows downstream and is gone into the unknown, I have a world apart that is not among men."

Russ sat still. He had no idea what she was talking about and was too embarrassed for a moment to admit it. He cleared his throat. "I'm not sure what you said."

The girl laughed. "No, most people would say that. It's a poem by a Chinese man named Li Bai. From a really long time ago. Do you want to hear it again?"

Because he was afraid to say no, and because the sound of her voice was like the music of a violin, he said yes.

She recited the words again. Now that he realized it was a poem and was prepared for it, it sounded pretty. Magical, in a way.

"Yeah, okay. That sounded real nice."

"That's *my* football," she announced. "Poetry. And music. And horses. That's what I like the way you like football."

Russ scratched the back of his neck, looking down at the ground. Helen was sure a beautiful girl, but it was going to be hard keeping up with her. He knew little about horses, and nothing about poetry, and he was too ashamed to admit to her how much he knew about music, mostly because he didn't want it getting around the school that he could play the piano.

"Maybe I better go," Helen said, standing up. "My mom won't know where I am."

"Oh, yeah. Sorry." Russ jumped up too.

"Say, you want a ride or anything?"

Russ sure did. He would have given almost anything to get into the beautiful 1954 Chrysler Imperial hardtop Helen's mother let her drive to school. It was a two-door, rich beige with a black canvas top—the envy of every kid in school, and most likely the adults as well. Helen was one of the few students who had her own ride to school and didn't have to walk or take the bus—even though she lived less than half a mile or so away. But he could never have faced himself after putting his sweaty body all over that fine leather seat.

"Naw, I'd better do some more running."

She giggled. "I guess the girls were right. You really *won't* give up your run."

"Well, no, I just . . . I thought you had to go."

"If you want to go clean up and change, I think I could wait another fifteen minutes. No more."

And with that, the extra run galloped out the window. "I'll be ten minutes," he said.

"Okay. You can come meet my parents."

"Yeah? I'd like that. Where are you gonna be?"

"Right here. I'll stay and look at the mountains or read my book."

Russ bolted for the back door and trotted down the hall to the showers. He was back in nine minutes and five and a quarter seconds, wearing a gray tee shirt, tight Levi's with a rolled up cuff, and tan Chukka boots. The only thing he was missing to be James Dean himself was a pack of smokes rolled up into one of his shirt sleeves—and a shock of daringly long and messy blond hair.

Helen looked over and smiled, standing up to meet him. He would not learn the real reason for her smile until later.

CHAPTER FOUR

They neared the beige Chrysler Imperial, one of only four cars left in the parking lot on the north side at the back of the school. Russ was floored as he touched the passenger door handle and peeked inside at the beautiful tan leather seats. What a ride!

Helen stopped on the other side and looked across at him. "You like it?"

"I sure do. Now *that's* a chariot!"

"Thanks. Mom usually goes with her sister if she must be at a meeting or something, and I get the *chariot.*" She laughed when she repeated Russ's slang. "It's nice to have a set of wheels."

A set of wheels? That's what she called this? This was something above and beyond simply a set of wheels. It was sublime. The thought of taking her anywhere in the car he was stuck driving made him cringe.

When they were seated, and the luxurious leather seemed to enfold them, Russ felt Helen watching him, and he looked over. She smiled. "Look at this." She reached to the radio, one of the most fantastic looking pieces of electronics he'd ever seen, and flipped it on, to the immediate tune of one of his favorite new songs, Bill Hayes singing "The Ballad of Davy Crockett." Had he thought about it a little longer, he would have been miffed at Helen's irreverence when she hit a button, removed her finger, and the radio sought out and found another station playing Rosemary Clooney's "This Ole House." He kind of liked the song, truth be told, but you didn't turn off Davy Crockett! Still, to see a radio that could re-tune itself at the touch of a button was worth the momentary loss of the King of the Wild Frontier.

When she demonstrated the power seats and windows, Russ felt like he was living in another dimension. He was still trying to figure out how to get the radio back to Davy Crockett when she drove out onto Short Street, down to Center, then headed west. As he managed to find the last of "The Ballad of Davy Crockett" coming across the airwaves, she was going over the train tracks and across State Street, and not much later she pulled into the driveway of a beautiful white colonial style home. The graveled driveway made the shape of a fallen rainbow across the front, curving between sections of lawn that even in this part of spring already hinted at the beautiful stretch of green they would be in May and June. Past the two beautiful birch trees in the front lawn, he could see three dormer windows in the home's second story, and pillars holding up an overhanging section of roof over the lower story. A prim and perfect picket fence ran off to the left side of the house.

Helen pulled almost all the way around the rainbow driveway, nose back to the sidewalk, and put it in park.

"Well?"

Russ grinned. "Nice car! But not very far if you had to walk."

She smiled back at him. "Well, so I'm spoiled. Okay, now put your tongue back in your mouth and you can come meet my mom and see if my father's home yet."

They got out, and Russ stood in awe, taking in the enormity of the house, which was kept perfect in every way.

"I'm gonna forget about the car now. This is your *house?*"

"Yes. Do you like it?"

"Like it! Helen, it's a mansion. A masterpiece. Holy smokes! I love it!"

She smiled. "Thank you."

When Helen opened the front door, she hollered, "Mom? I brought someone home to meet you. Mom?"

"Just a minute, honey," the reply floated down from upstairs.

Helen told Russ she would be right back, and then she ascended the stairs. While she was in that act, he had a hard time seeing anything else except her, but after she vanished down the hall, he was left standing stunned, wondering what a man did to amass the wealth it would take to buy and keep a house like this.

Russ had always thought of his father as doing okay at his job. They might not have been rich. They certainly weren't going out and buying a Rolls Royce any time soon. But they had the necessities of life. However, looking around him, he suddenly felt like the Blevins family survived on the edge of poverty.

If someone had asked Russ to write an essay describing the inside—or the outside—of the James home, he would have received a fat one-legged A for his efforts. His descriptions would have been of the rudest sort, for he had no idea the terms used for fancy things like what his eyes beheld. A gold chandelier. White carpet that almost sparkled in its brightness, hugging a curving stairway that went all the way up to an upper landing, covered in the same carpet he imagined must cost the same as his entire house. He knew nothing about woodwork, but the ornately carved, honey-colored railing that curved to match the stairs had been done by a master—that much was plain. And the hundreds of books tucked into built-in shelves to the right of the stairs, all of them dark and luxurious, with gold or silver leaf print, would likely have bought any vehicle the Blevins family had ever owned.

On the instant, Russ felt like a complete fool standing here. He even contemplated turning and going out. But he couldn't. He had never run from anything yet—at least not unless he was carrying a football. And

even then, he was always running *toward* something more than he was running away.

Soon, Helen appeared again at the head of the stairs, and beside her a strikingly beautiful woman perhaps twenty years older, with curves even more voluptuous than those of her daughter.

"Hello, young man," said the woman as she glided down the stairs. He didn't know if he had ever seen anyone move with more elegant, calculated grace, unless it was Scarlet O'Hara in *Gone With the Wind*. She walked with the same fluid motion as a swan navigating a stream.

"Hello, Mrs. James." Russ spoke as he stepped back from the foot of the stairs. He realized his mouth was open, and he clamped it shut.

"Mother, do you recognize who this is?"

The woman turned her eyes again to Russ, studying his face. She had a faint look of confusion, but it was controlled confusion. "Why, no, dear. I'm sorry. Should I?"

Helen laughed. "No, I guess not. But I think Daddy will! This is Russ Blevins!"

The woman's eyes widened this time. "Oh, my goodness. Why, Russ, it is truly a pleasure. I'm sorry I don't follow sporting events very closely, but I have heard your name often—particularly when my husband is reading the newspaper during football season." She held out a perfectly manicured hand. "My closest friends call me Pearl. As we get to know each other better, I would not be averse to that familiarity between us."

Russ took that to mean that for the moment she was still going to be Mrs. James—or "ma'am." He fumbled out his hand to take hers, and it felt tender, and softer than the rabbits his little sister, Kathleen, raised in a cage in the back yard. "Yes, ma'am, Mrs. James."

"His best friends call him Cus," offered Helen.

"Oh, my," Mrs. James exclaimed. "Cuss? Whatever for?" Her eyes widened as a possible explanation seemed to come to her. "My, my. Never mind. You don't have to explain that, young man." But her eyes took on a little bit of hardness, and he realized what she was thinking.

"Oh, no, ma'am! Not like what you're thinking." He blushed. "It's spelled with one S. Short for Custer."

Mrs. James laughed, her eyes sparkling. Her voice sounded like wine glasses jiggling together. "What a delightful young man. I'm sorry I thought anything else."

"That's all right, ma'am. I know it sounds bad."

"Well, don't you worry about it. In all honesty, although I don't approve of . . . *cussing* it is not as if I haven't heard it before. That is the very reason why I stopped allowing Helen's dear father to do any plumbing or electrical work in our home."

Thinking of his own father's bouts of anger while trying to take care of those chores made Russ laugh. But this time he kept his tongue still for lack of anything smart to say.

He heard a noise outside and turned to look, startled. When he looked back at Helen, she said, "That's the garage door. My father is home, just in time."

"Yes, he will be so happy to meet you, Russ—the hero of Shelley, Idaho. So tell me, young man—what plans do you have for after school?"

Russ's feet could not have been flatter. "Uh . . . How's that?"

"After school. After graduation."

"Oh! Well, I think I'm going to go to college and play ball."

The woman's eyes crinkled up once more as she laughed. "Well, I can't say you lack confidence. You do have to be chosen to play, though—correct?"

That comment once again took Russ by surprise. He knew his record. What college scout would *not* want to recruit him?

At that moment, before he could reply, there came the sound of a door opening and shutting at the back of the house, and soon a broad-faced, blond-haired man appeared, the blond hairs disguising the fact that his head was also laced with silver. He carried a briefcase in his left hand.

The man came to an abrupt halt. For a moment, he stared, and then a look of recognition flooded over his face.

"Russet Blevins? You're Russet Blevins, aren't you?"

A sense of great pride came into Russ's chest. "Yes sir. Yes sir, Mr. James."

"Well, I'll be doggoned." The man set down his briefcase in the middle of the floor and practically leaped forward to within a few feet of the

boy, thrusting out his hand. In taking it, Russ was surprised at how firm and powerful it felt, yet the skin was like that of a baby.

"I am honored to meet you, son. Honored! To what do I owe the privilege of having you in my home?"

"I thought you would like to meet him in person, Daddy," cut in Helen. "You go on about him so."

The man scoffed. "Well! I'm not as bad as all that." And then he laughed. "All right, all right. Maybe I do. But this is Russ Blevins, honey! This town has never seen a football player like the lad you're standing with. Believe me, I've watched dozens and dozens of them."

Russ was starting to feel uncomfortable. How did a high school boy act in the face of such praise without starting to look haughty? He decided to play it cool.

"So now we've met, Russ. I'm sorry I seem like I'm in such a rush. Did you two have plans for this evening?"

Russ's mouth came open. He looked to Helen for support. And for rescue.

"Oh, no, not really. Russ asked me to go get a soda with him, but I wanted him to meet you, so . . . Well, that's all."

"All right. Well, I'm sure glad you did. Sure good to meet you, Russ. Really good. I'll be rooting for you in the fall. Sorry, I've got to get on some late paperwork, so if you'll excuse me."

He shook Russ's hand again, then went and retrieved his briefcase and went up the stairs two at a time.

"My father. He's always busy. Hardly a moment to even say boo—unless it's football season."

"Yes, we do miss our daddy," agreed Mrs. James. "It's hard even to get him to the supper table when he has a big deal on the horizon."

Russ stood speechless. He felt small in this spacious house. Too small to have anything of value to say.

Helen turned to him. "Well, Russ, would you like a ride home?"

"Uh, well . . . I . . ."

"Oh, of course he would like a ride home, honey. If you brought him here you mustn't expect him to walk home. You two run along then. But be right back. I want to tell you about my meeting today."

Russ took those words to mean "no sodas or fries," and he was right. Helen took him straight to the white house with the pink trim that he called home on Park Avenue without saying another word, even so much as a comment about the weather.

At his driveway, which she had seen a hundred times or more, she angled up and stopped. She gave the house and yard a once-over, then made a quiet laughing sound down in her throat. Embarrassed, Russ looked at the house and thought of Helen's mansion. He suddenly felt strange even being in the same car as this girl, who had far more money than he or his family ever would.

"Well, I'll see you at school." She didn't call him by name. For some reason, that felt ominous.

"Okay. Well, thanks for the ride."

"You're welcome." Stiff words.

"So I guess I'll see you."

"I guess so." She looked toward the front door of his house. In a way, it was like she threw her glance, symbolically *throwing* Russ that direction by the same act. *You can get out of my car, please,* was the way he took her suddenly cool demeanor.

Without the ability to think of any graceful way to part, Russ threw open the door, stood out of the car and slammed the door. He was about to give the door a pat to let her know he was safely out when the car wheeled about in the wide street, spinning gravel, and sped back the way they had come, halting abruptly at Locust, then zooming off to the west.

Russ was left standing alone in the late afternoon sun.

As he turned, he caught movement down the block, and he thought he recognized the walk of little Isaac Thorpe. He was going up onto the stoop of a house almost directly across the street from his own. As he watched, the door opened, and the boy disappeared inside.

CHAPTER FIVE

Luther Dean loved his car, perhaps more than anything. It was a deep blue 1946 Mercury Eight coupe, and it had sat in his mother's garage in the little settlement of Goshen for five long, solitary years now. As far as Luther knew, the only thing that had been done with it over those years was when his mother would take it up and down Yellowstone Highway ten or twenty miles every few months to make sure it stayed running well. And then she would buy it a few gallons of new gas, to keep the guts free of gunk.

Luther thanked his mother in a chicken-scratch letter he dutifully wrote her every two months—from inside the walls of the Boise State Pen.

Luther stood in the run-down Goshen yard and thought of his mother, a good old lady. Heart of gold. But now she was dead. She had died a mere two months before he finally made parole.

Luther Dean stood five-foot-eleven and three-quarter inches tall. He had always hated knowing he was cheated of honestly claiming to be a six-footer by the width of a pencil. His nearly black hair was tightly wavy, his brows heavy and untrimmed to where sometimes if he looked up he could see hairs hanging down like spider legs. He was lean and tough from doing pull-ups and pushups and sit-ups every other day for those five long years while he waited to hug his mother again and sit in the seat of his beautiful car.

Luther went into the tumble-down shed-garage and climbed into the Mercury, pushing the pedal down to the floor for several seconds, then letting it all the way back up before depressing it halfway again. When he turned the key, it didn't surprise him to hear and feel it rev right up. The wonderful, aromatic fumes of unburned fuel began to fill the tight space, and he leaned his head back against the seat and inhaled deeply.

He was home at last. It was too late for his mother. But at least this old friend was here to cradle his head.

It was a fine automobile. Everyone should own a Mercury, at least once in their lifetime. This one was Luther's pride and joy. After letting it warm up for several minutes, with a feeling of happiness and pride, he backed it out into the yard, then climbed out and shut the door, leaving it running.

Walking back into the house, Luther looked around. It smelled musty and old—much like his mother had smelled. The plaster of the ghost-white walls was cracked, some of it beyond repair. One of the cracks, back in a dark corner of the living room, surely had some big ugly spider backed up deep inside it and staring out at a kaleidoscope world. The web that hung over it and shuddered with the air Luther had caused to move by opening the front door was fresh. He didn't go closer. Luther and spiders were no friends.

The carpet was eons old, it seemed. Originally white, like the walls. Now dingy gray. Where the sofa had been, it was whiter. There was nothing there now. The family vultures had seen to that.

He walked into the kitchen. Dirty dishes were still piled in the sink. New-born flies made the filmy window into a chocolate chip cookie, but without the luring aroma. The cupboards were bare but for a half-empty jar of Adams 100% Natural peanut butter. Some article in Redbook had convinced his mother that natural peanut butter was the only way she could stay healthy, and from then on peanut butter and jelly sandwiches in the Dean home went down the toilet. Luther would rather eat bread only with jelly than to tear his bread into a hundred pieces trying to smear tough-as-mortar Adams on it, or worse yet, soak it down with the fourteen pounds of slimy oil riding on top of a freshly opened jar.

He smiled. *Mom.* She was easy to sway. Just show her something in Redbook. But she was a good egg. He was going to miss her.

And if Sheriff Arch Blevins had not sent him away to prison, for a crime he didn't even commit, he would have been there with her all these five long years. He would never get his mother back. And that filthy dung heap of a cop would not even care.

Nothing in the house was worth scavenging, Luther found. But the only thing that mattered was that Mercury, still in the same place he had

last seen it. He was sure it would be gone, too, if anyone in his family had been brave enough to forge a few names on the title and could have found a key. But his mother kept the key buried in a hole out by the eastern-most clothesline post. He knew it, and she knew it, and maybe God—if there was a God.

Luther Dean looked around. There were the remains of the old swing, now a rotten piece of rope hanging from the gigantic cottonwood tree that, like his mother, had given up hope since he went away. There was the old, rusty, yellow steel drum he used to roll his little brother around in—the very brother who had done the burglaries Luther got thrown in prison for. Nothing was left here for Luther Dean. He had eggs to fry, and they weren't clear out here in the pathetic little wide spot in the road called Goshen.

Climbing into the Mercury, he closed his eyes and shut the door, listening to the satisfying clang of metal on metal. He had spent every dime he owned buying this car when it was one year old. Fifteen hundred dollars and some change. And worth every penny.

Luther backed out of the driveway for the last time and drove out to the main road. Old man Hansen was sitting across the street on a chair on his porch, doing something with his hands—most likely something with leather. When his only boy had died in Okinawa, the old man had given up on everything else in life but his leatherwork. He had turned into a piece of old cracked leather himself. Luther knew how he felt. That war had taken his own father, too, but it was Normandy, not Okinawa. His old man hadn't even made it onto the beach before the bullet took him between the eyes.

Luther nodded sadly and felt something strange in the corner of his eye. A tear. He cursed it and put the pedal to the medal, screaming down the rutted gravel highway toward Firth.

Five miles and a hundred years were not enough between him and Goshen, Idaho.

He drove down and stopped at the Firth river bottoms, to relive some fond memories of him and his brothers and father. They used to catch gopher snakes down there and then fling them out in the water to watch them swim. None of them fished much, but they did like to catch grass-hoppers and throw them way out into the water to see how long it was

before some fish came along and sucked them down. They always had tuna fish sandwiches. His mother hadn't found a way to destroy those! He smiled. That cursed tear tried to come back into his eye, but he growled out loud and chased it away. Then wiped at his salt and pepper whiskers and glanced around to make sure no one had heard or seen.

He sat there and tossed stones into the water—it was too early for grasshoppers—and watched a pumpkin sun melt into the cottonwood trees. The silhouettes of a flock of Canada geese, like black beads catapulted free from a rotted thread, veed across the sky and cupped their wings, making their way down toward the water somewhere beyond his field of view. He sat and smelled the algae and the murky water and the scent of dead suckers someone had left lying around on the shore.

Finally, he got up and knocked sand off the seat of his jeans and ambled back to the car.

It was dark by the time he pulled up at the curb in front of his old friend Billy Earl's house, on Park Avenue in Shelley. Luther let out a long sigh. Good old Billy. He was one thing that would never change—maybe the only thing. He glanced down along the block and to the other side of the street. There squatted that ugly pink and white house that belonged to his most hated enemy, the lawman who thought that he had the right to put people in a cage and destroy their lives.

The waxy yellow light of a dim bulb up under the overhang of Billy's porch sent a weak glow down the sidewalk as Luther got out and walked toward the house. Billy must have been watching, because the door flew open and he appeared on the porch, all one hundred-forty pounds and five-foot-six of him, with his thin brown hair and flabby belly pressing to escape a sweat-dirty white tee shirt.

Billy stepped off the porch and ran to him, clapping his shoulders in his hands. "Hey, buddy! Man, you're a sight for sore eyes."

Luther felt like his face was going to break because he smiled. He couldn't make his prison-haunted face smile as big as Billy did, but for Luther, it was a lot. He slapped his old friend on the side, shaking his head. "So are you, Billy. Man, so are you."

Behind Billy, in the yellow light in the doorway, a form appeared, and Luther started. Then he recognized it as a young boy. "What the heck, Billy? I thought you was livin' alone."

Billy turned, grinning. “Oh, right. Yeah, no worry, Luther. That’s only a friend of mine that likes to come over and talk and listen to my records sometimes and look at my Matchbox car collection. Come’ere, Ikey! Come meet my friend that just got back in town. His name’s Luther Dean.”

The boy came into the glow of the porch light so Luther could see him better, and he had an intrigued look on his face. “Wow, that’s cool. Dean, like James Dean.”

“Yeah, kid, just like James Dean,” said Billy with enthusiasm. “Luther, this is Ikey . . . what’s your last name again, kid?”

“Thorpe.”

“Yeah! Yeah, that’s it. Ikey Thorpe!”

CHAPTER SIX

It wasn’t five minutes after running up the front steps and going into the high school the next morning until Russ Blevins was accosted by his friend Everett Morin.

“Hey, dummy! Your little *date’s* all over school already.”

“Huh?”

“Your date, man. Your *date?* With Helen? Did you already forget?”

“What are you talking about? It wasn’t any date.”

“Okay, okay. So whatever you want to call it. Anyway, it’s the talk of the school.”

“What’s the gag? Why would everyone be talking?”

“Because you won Helen a five dollar bill, that’s why!”

Russ stared his friend down. “Man, you’re drivin’ me nuts.”

Everett grabbed his Russ’s biceps in one hand. “Okay, brother, here’s the deal, according to Johnny Boo. He got it straight from Bobbie Ketchum at the drive-in last night that you gave up your run to go to Helen’s house. Well, dummy, she only took you there on a bet. Bobbie and Lonna had told her there was no way you’d give up your evening

run for anybody, and Helen bet them five bucks she could get you to. Smooth, buddy. Real smooth!"

Russ felt sick to the pit of his stomach. He looked around, hoping no one else was paying them any attention. "So . . . Who all was at the drive-in?"

"Well, Bobbie and Lonna, and of course Helen. Those two wouldn't go *anywhere* without her. And then Johnny Boo and Slick happened down there to grab a burger. Sounds like those girls were laughin' it up to beat the band, you gettin' duped like that."

"I thought you were all for it, dingleberry," said Russ. "What happened to that?"

Ev flushed. "Okay, well, I was. But I didn't expect her to play it that way."

"Ha! You and me both. So don't call *me* dummy. Wow. Well, I'll get square with her somehow."

Throughout the school day, Russ was quiet, brooding. He had adored Helen James for years. Now that he had finally had the courage to ask her out, and she had actually said yes, it all came down to treachery? It was too much for his ego to handle.

He couldn't concentrate on any of his work that day. All he could think of was Helen, laughing at him and talking behind his back. And at track he was sure to see her again. She was the last person he wanted to see today.

But he was not going to miss another workout because of her.

● ● ● ● ●

At track practice, two of the first people Russ laid eyes on were the guys who had spread the word about his being duped the day before, Johnny Boo Fabian and Hank Paterson, who had let the football slip through his fingers so many times one day at practice the fall before that he had earned himself the forever nickname "Slick Fingers," which was usually abbreviated to plain old "Slick." Football friends never forgot something like that.

Russ walked straight out to the two boys, who were in the center of the field watching him. They were both grinning like idiots.

Johnny Boo Fabian was a dark boy a few inches shorter than Russ. The girls called him handsome, but his chocolate-colored eyes were too

close together, and his mouth was too small. Johnny Boo's jawline already had a dark sheen to it from the early onset of a beard, and for that all the other boys envied him. Looking back to grade school, Russ remembered Johnny coming to school one Halloween dressed as a ghost. If memory served him, that was where he got the "Boo" in his name, and unlike most nicknames it had attached itself to his real name and stuck there forever. Russ was pretty sure most people assumed it was the full name his parents had given him.

Johnny Boo was going to be the Russets' star quarterback next fall—a position originally taken from Russ the season before and given to Andy Collins, now a senior, because although Russ had a slightly stronger arm and perhaps an even better eye, nobody could cruise down the field and knock over the other teams' players like bowling pins the way Russ could as a halfback. Russ was also famous for dragging a few of them who had hold of him, from time to time. Russ didn't mind the change too bad, because in that time period, the halfback was generally thought to be the envied position on the team, not the quarterback.

Blond Slick Paterson was a linebacker, wide across the shoulders, broad across the bridge of a nose that had been smashed flat once by a bucking calf, and paunchy as an old man. In spite of his gut size, Slick was a fantastically fast runner, as long as the line he was required to run was straight forward. Like a freight engine, he might as well have been running on rails, because once he had a head of steam he could not turn to one side or the other on a bet, and a three-legged jackrabbit, going in a serpentine, could outrun him by a mile.

"Hey, bean!" greeted Johnny Boo. "How's it going?"

"Jeez, Boo, you tell me," replied Russ, shaking his hand. "Hey, Slick. So Ev tells me you all went down to the drive-in and ran into Helen last night."

"We went to the drive-in, all right! She just happened to be down there. Laughin' her head off, too."

"How bad?" asked Russ. "Was she makin' fun of me?"

"You would have thought you were the class nerd, brother!" joined in Slick in his unfortunate nasally voice, a product of the broken nose. "She thinks she got a real good one over on you."

Russ clenched his jaws. He should have known better than to trust a girl. Even as he thought this, he looked out to the far side of the track and saw Helen and her two friends walking. As his eyes fell on them, Helen was already watching him, and a huge smile came over her face. Russ didn't smile back. He was too sick to smile even if he had wanted to, and her smile was probably more of a laugh anyway.

He jerked his eyes away, but not before her smile transformed to a look of consternation. Russ felt his own kind of consternation when he saw in his peripheral vision a sight he had not expected, and certainly didn't desire at the moment: Helen was walking his way across the field.

From childhood, Russ's parents had taught him chivalry. They had taught him to be polite and to go out of his way not to hurt the feelings of another person, and especially a lady. Right now, he wanted nothing more than a chance to get Helen James back. But instinct and all the years of training took over.

"Hey, I'll check you guys later," he blurted, and he turned, pretending not to have seen Helen, and bolted back to the gravel, then started at a high lope around the track.

It wasn't long before he learned that Helen James was not a mere flash in the pan on the track, as so many said and as he himself had believed. The fact that she had to cut across the grass to do it aside, Helen made a hard sprint across the field and caught Russ rounding the far end.

"Hey!"

Cringing, Russ looked over, unable to avoid the girl without looking even more foolish trying to run away. He knew he could beat her. The fact was, in anything under two hundred yards, there wasn't a soul in that school he couldn't beat—and probably not even in the whole town. But it wasn't worth it. They were far enough away from any of the other students now that anything either of them said to each other would be known only to them.

Russ slowed down as Helen swung to the left to come alongside him, jogging.

"Hi, Russ. Is something wrong?"

"Nope. Just getting my run in."

He had slowed down as much as he was going to. He certainly wasn't going to stop and talk.

"Me too, I guess." Ten yards, twenty. Forty. Fifty. One hundred. Russ was breathing evenly, pacing himself. But it didn't appear that Helen was getting any closer to being out of breath either.

"Are we going to run all day and not say anything?"

Russ looked over at her. She was beautiful in every way. And he hated her for it.

"It's hard to run and talk. Besides, I'm getting ready to do some wind sprints."

"Hey, Russ. Come on. Please stop for a minute."

"Naw, I've gotta go. Sorry."

With that, he took off around the track. He didn't want to look like a show off, especially for Helen, so he started out at a twelve-second pace for the one hundred, then ended up kicking it into medium high gear. He guessed that he made the dash in a little under eleven, if anyone had been timing him. He was aware that several other students had stopped to watch him, and some of them now applauded.

He saw his coach, Dan Nalder, jogging out toward him. He was about to take off running again when the coach hailed him, so he stopped.

"Wow, Russ, that was something! Want to run with me for a couple of minutes?"

"Sure, Coach."

They jogged around the track, passing other students, but now and then being passed by some who were trying for better times in their long runs. Halfway through the first quarter-mile, Nalder said, "Something on your mind, Russ?"

"No, Coach. Why?"

"Buddy, you're one of my sharpest runners, most of the time. You know the score as well as anyone."

"Yeah?"

"So did you warm up and stretch before you did that sprint? I haven't seen you until three or four minutes ago, and I sure didn't see you doing any jogging or stretching to speak of."

Russ looked back at the track. He took in a breath. "Well, probably not enough."

"You've got to get your head in the game, Russ. You get hurt now, it could take a month out of training."

"Sure. Sorry."

"Showing off for Helen James, huh?"

"No!" Russ was mortified. "No way."

"Whoa!" Nalder looked at his star athlete with interest and a little amazement. "You sure? It seems like I touched a nerve."

"Well, it wasn't showing off, Coach. Last night she took me to her house in her car, and . . ."

"Wow, that's a coup," Nalder cut in.

"Yeah, but it wasn't. I found out today she only did it to win a bet. Her friends told her I wouldn't give up my evening run for anybody. She bet 'em five bucks I would. And she won. She was just using me."

They kept jogging for a while as Nalder stewed that information over in his head. "Hey, Russ, you said she took you to her house, right?"

"Yeah."

"And you met her parents?"

"Yeah."

"I know I'm twenty-six, so I probably don't know much anymore, but . . . Brother, when I was your age and a girl took you to meet her parents, that meant something. You sure she was only using you? I mean, maybe she wanted to prove a point, but listen—she could have taken you anywhere else besides to meet her parents and she would have still won that bet, right?"

After a moment, Russ shrugged. "Yeah, I guess so."

"So think about it before you go hating her. And something else."

"Yeah, Coach?"

"You go running sprints again without warming up, and I'll put you through a routine that will curl your hair and have you crawling home to Mommy."

Russ looked over and saw his Coach's mischievous smile, and he grinned. "Okay, Coach. It won't happen again."

When Russ passed Helen James again, he had had a lot of time to think about what Coach Nalder had said. He looked over at her and wanted to accost her, but she was back with her friends, and although both Bobbie and Lonna looked at him and said something to Helen, she did not turn her eyes his way.

CHAPTER SEVEN

Running was Russ Blevins's pastime. Running *hard* was his passion. Running ahead of a pack of high school jackals that thought by some miracle they could catch him? That was the very thing that on certain days seemed to drive his whole existence.

This was supposed to be track practice, and some of the kids who didn't have anything to do with football resented it and thought it diluted their chances of doing as well at future meets. But Coach Nalder couldn't help himself. Sometimes he simply had to put his boys into formation and run them the length of the field. Football season was too far away, and, when it arrived, way too short.

Sometimes—days like today—head coach Ivan Jardinsky would even show up at track practice, although Jardinsky really didn't care one whit about track, other than as another tool for getting his team in shape. Unlike Dan Nalder, there was little finesse in big, gimp-legged Ivan Jardinsky. The big Pole stood six-foot-three, the bridge of his smashed-down nose nearly an inch wide, and the inside corners of his pale blue eyes almost touching it. His trapezius muscles seemed to emerge straight out of his ears and slope down to shoulders that didn't seem as wide as they actually were because of that slope. His impressive hips, however, more than made up for the lack—a sore spot with Jardinsky, and a weak spot that all the players made fun of, but no one—*ever*—to his face.

Jardinsky had once been a formidable halfback himself, playing for the Detroit Lions. But a terrible hit in the left knee by two big Cleveland Rams proved that, at least that year, two Rams could take down a Lion. Jardinsky would never play pro ball again.

Jardinsky taught a token algebra class, not because he excelled at algebra, but because he had a passing understanding of it and because those who hired coaches in Shelley, Idaho, would do anything to keep a man of Jardinsky's giant reputation at the helm of the Shelley Russets.

They seemed to think that if they kept a likable leader like Nalder and a slave driver and genius with a reputation like Jardinsky's on a team that already boasted Russ Blevins, the most celebrated halfback in the entire state, losing was near impossible. So far, in two seasons, that was close to the truth. They had lost their second game out of the gate in fifty-three to the Rigby Trojans, the day Russet Blevins was so sick with the flu he could hardly stop puking, much less run a ball down the field.

Russ had the ball now, and he was driving down the field. This was no football game, in any sense of the word. This was just Russ's chance to tear down the turf with the other guys coming at him from all directions and show them all that he could not be stopped. It was a chance for him to *live.*

At the far end of the field, Russ drove right on past the end zone and over the track. He might have run into some unwary runner, but everyone knew what was going on, and all had stopped to watch the fun. Even those who might not like Russ Blevins would stop and stare at him in awe when he took off down a field. He owned the world.

"All right, Custer!" he heard Jardinsky yell at him from the far end of the field. "Get on back here!"

Russ turned around, amid the whooping and cheering of his teammates, and ran at half speed back to the coaches. The track coach, Miss Brundy, watched them in disgust and walked back to her group of loyal runners, pole vaulters and long jumpers. It was obvious that sometimes Miss Brundy wondered why she even bothered trying to coach a track team when it seemed like Shelley only cared about football, the king of sports.

Russ stopped eye to eye with Jardinsky. "Listen, Blevins—wind sprints every day, boy. Half an hour, no breaks. I'm serious. Last year, some kid named Jim Jackson got nine-point-four in the hundred, out in California. You got that in you. You hear me? Better yet, nine-three."

"Right, Coach!"

"I'm not joking, damnit. If I don't see at least a nine-nine out of you before the end of this track season, I am gonna beat the hell right out of you—and you know I'll do it."

Russ grinned. It was a day and age when coaches really could, and sometimes did, strike their players if they felt they deserved it. But

Yardinsky—they called him that behind his back, referring to his yard-wide hips—was not about to beat Russ. He was too valuable, and in his gruff way he liked him too much.

"Sure, Coach. Got it!"

"What?"

"Got it, Coach!" Russ yelled louder. "I mean, yes, sir!"

Jardinsky nodded, affecting a tough-guy scowl. "All right. You boys get back and do what your track gal tells you to do. You did all right out there."

And he walked off.

When he was a ways off, Dan Nalder slapped Russ on the back. "All right! You did more than all right, Russ boy. You knocked their socks off. This fall is going to be the best Russet season this little burg has ever seen!"

When practice was over and the other athletes were clearing the field, Russ was still stretching. Some of the boys had tried to convince him to catch a train with them down at the depot and go to the Paramount Theater, up in Idaho Falls, to watch Ernie Borgnine in *Marty*. Maybe they had thought because he had skipped his evening run once, they could sway him again. But they didn't know how stubborn he could be. Helen James, his Delilah, had fooled him once. It wasn't about to happen again.

Even as his boys vanished into the school, Russ stood up out of his calf stretch to see Helen James and her two shadows lingering down by the east goal post. She was watching, holding a handful of books, and he shot his eyes away. His glance happened to fall on Edie Russell, who was once again sitting on the bleachers. She had an open book in her hands—although not as open as she herself—but she wasn't reading it. Like Helen, she was watching Russ.

On a whim he walked toward her. When she realized he was on a beeline for her, Edie jumped up, her full, dark, bobbed hair bouncing with the sudden motion, and waited, holding her book with both hands down in front of her like a shield.

"Hi, Russ," she said before he got close enough to commit himself.

"Hi, Edie."

She wanted to say something else. It showed painfully on her face—the desire, the anxiety, then the fear. She dropped her eyes.

"How'd you like to go to the movies?"

Her eyes leaped upward, and she stared at him. "Huh?"

"Hey, dope. I said how'd you like to go see a movie with some of the guys? *Marty* is playing at the Paramount. The guys say it's supposed to be a pretty good show."

"I, uh . . . Russ, are you playing with me?"

"Aw, come on, Edie. Do you want to go, or don't you?"

"Well, yeah! Of course!"

"All right, then. I've got to go clean up, all right? Then I'm gonna have to walk home and get my car, but it's not all that far."

She smiled shyly. "I know where you live, Russ."

"Oh yeah. Right." He almost laughed. He had caught Edie more than once moseying past his house for no apparent reason, acting like she had no idea who lived there. And he had always made sure to be inside by the time she was within speaking distance.

"Mom and Daddy don't know where I am. I don't think they'd really care. Is it okay if I just wait for you and walk with you?"

Wow. She was getting bolder already. "Sure, I don't care. I'll be five minutes. Meet me out front."

As he had promised, he dragged himself away from a locker full of loud-mouthed football players—who could not stop jeering at him for missing this second night in a row of extra running—and met Edie in front of the school.

He couldn't help but notice that Helen was out there too, parked out on the edge of the gravel street with Bobbie in her front seat and Lonna in the back. All of them stared toward him as if waiting to hear the punch-line of some joke.

Edie was holding an armload of books, and Russ motioned at them. "Hey. Let me carry your books."

"What?"

"Jeez, are you going deaf? Let me have your books."

Edie started to hand them over, and one of them slid off the top of the pile and landed on its open pages in the dust and gravel. Russ winced.

He knew without a doubt that Helen and the others were watching, and now probably laughing their heads off at Edie's clumsiness.

He crouched down and picked up the book, whisking gravel and sand off the bent pages. He happened to notice that the book was *Riders of the Purple Sage,* by Zane Grey.

"Hey! You read this stuff?" he asked as he stood back up.

She blushed. "Well, sometimes."

"It's okay. I'm not making fun of you. I do too. My old man has all these books in a bookcase in the hallway."

Edie brightened. She started to say something, then stopped. But he had already noticed. "What?"

"Oh. I was just going to say I already knew you liked him. I've seen you carrying Zane Grey books. And Ernest Haycox."

He grunted. He should have known.

With a feeling half of satisfaction, half of discomfort, he noticed that Helen was still sitting in her Imperial, but now she had started the engine. He should be loving this feeling, the knowledge that he was showing Helen James without a doubt that she had no hold on him. But he wasn't. He was miserable. As much as he had wanted revenge on her, he was still head over heels for her. And that made him madder than anything.

"Come on, Edie, let's get going. Don't want to miss the first part of the film."

They started walking, and about that time the Imperial began to roll as well, its engine purring like a great big, wonderful cat. It pulled up beside Russ and Edie, with the passenger side closest to them.

Helen leaned past her friend Bobbie so she had a straight shot at Russ. "Hey! You two want a ride?"

"What for?" Russ felt Edie move over a little deeper into the protective shadow of his torso.

"So you won't have to walk, I guess." This time Helen's voice was a little petulant. "Where are you going, anyway?"

"Not to run," replied Russ, as he kept walking and the car kept tracking him and Edie.

"Hey!" The car came to an abrupt stop, and the driver's door flew open. Helen got out and leaned across the roof, her glistening copper-

auburn hair looking dangerously beautiful in the late light of day. "What do you mean by that?"

Russ turned fully toward the girl he had been secretly in love with throughout high school, still too hurt by what he thought she had done to care what he said.

"What do you think it means? I hear you won a bet last night by getting me not to run and taking me to your house instead. Well, tonight I'm not running again." He moved enough to the right that he was touching Edie, who had come up beside him now. He could almost feel the fear inside her.

CHAPTER EIGHT

Helen James stared daggers into Russ's eyes.

"Wow," she said, obviously disgusted. She slapped the top of her car. "Fine, then. You can both take a hike."

With that, she dropped back into the driver's seat and burned rubber away from them, spitting flecks of gravel out from under her tires. Saying nothing, Russ started out at a march toward Locust Street, where Helen made a screeching right turn, and once there he turned onto it as well, although by then Helen was long gone. He could hear Edie almost having to trot to keep up.

The girl finally got the nerve to speak. "Russ, can you slow down? Say, are you in a race?"

He spun on her, ready to snap. Then he took a deep breath. Aw, she was only a dumb kid. She was so into him, and she had been forever, he knew. How could he break her heart?

"Sorry. We don't want to miss the movie, do we?" Then he chuckled. "Am I in a race? Wow, Edie. You're feeling kind of spunky, aren't you?"

She offered a shy smile. "I didn't mean to be rude."

"Ha! I don't think it was rude. Kind of funny, actually. Come on."

They started walking, on the edge of the street rather than on the sidewalk. After half a block, Russ heard the hum of a motor, a car turning off Short Street onto Locust. It sounded like a high-end one. Soon, the car came up alongside them and slowed to their pace. Russ looked over and saw Helen in the Imperial again. This time she was alone.

She looked at him for a moment, then sped past by twenty feet and slammed on the brakes with a grind of gravel, throwing it in park. She swung the door open, leaving the car in the middle of the lane, and strode to the trunk, stopping to lean up against it with her arms folded.

"Hey. Russ."

He kept walking until he was standing only four feet from her, Edie to the side but keeping back.

"Can we talk?"

"I don't know what's to talk about. I've got places to go."

"What is *up* with you? Okay. You're right. I made a bet with the girls that you would drop your run and go for a ride with me. So? Is that so bad? Are you telling me you wouldn't have done the same thing if you thought about it?"

Unlike a good ball player or boxer, both sports he prided himself in, Russ was caught flat-footed. In his stubbornness, he wanted to lash out at her, to tell her what a fool she had made him feel like. He had a dozen snide remarks in his head that he had thought out throughout the school day and during track. But almost every one of them might have been a death stroke to any chance he would ever have to get to know Helen James better. As much as his pride wanted him to shame her, there was a deeper part of him that couldn't.

The bad part was, anything he could say or do, while it might reconcile him with Helen, would be in front of Edie Russell. The poor girl was already shy enough, without being embarrassed and shamed that way on top of it.

"Hang on a second, all right?" He was still too miffed, his pride too hurt, to speak Helen's name to her. He turned his back to her so he was facing Edie and blocking her from Helen's view.

"Hey, Edie, I've got to straighten out this thing that happened, okay?"

The girl's reply was instant, as if waiting there on her tongue to erupt. "Oh, yeah! Of course. I totally understand." She put on a brave face. Russ was so in love with Helen James that he tried to fall for Edie's act.

"Yeah, so . . . if it's okay, maybe we'll try to do something some other time." He was sick inside knowing that was a lie. If he made up with Helen, there was never going to be "some other time" with Edie, but he would never tell her that.

"Oh! Right. Sure! It's okay."

"All right. Thanks. Here're your books." He held them out to her, trying to meet her eyes. Usually, she was the one who had trouble with that.

She took the books and said, "Hey, see you later."

"See you later."

Edie started to walk off as Russ turned back to face Helen. But Helen sidestepped so she could see past him. "Hey, Edie! Come here for a minute, okay? Please don't leave."

Russ gave her a confused look, then turned his torso and head and saw Edie paused almost to the sidewalk, looking at them both. Nervously, she came back over.

"What is it, Helen?"

"You're a long ways from home, right?"

"Not too far. I don't really live too far from you."

Helen smiled, her teeth bright, and her face too. Russ was happy to see nothing he would recognize as condescension anywhere in her demeanor.

"Well, that seems like quite a ways to me. What are you doing tonight?"

Obviously stunned and still a little wary, Edie said, "I was just going to read, I guess."

"What are *you* doing, Russ?"

Russ stared at Helen, digging for a hidden motive. How was she going to win a bet off him this time? "I was thinking about going to the Paramount in the Falls to see a show. *Marty.*"

"Oh yes. Father and Mother said it's a wonderful film. I haven't been."

Russ stood still. Edie stood still. Helen stood still. Each was waiting for somebody else to speak. Russ was too used to taking the bull by the horns to stand there consternated, by Helen James or anyone else. He had no idea what this girl was driving at, but somebody had to say *something*.

"Well, why don't you go see it then?"

"What, go by myself?"

A feeling of heat rose up inside Russ's collar that he was not accustomed to. He could not believe what he knew he was about to say. "Well . . . Edie already said she's not doing anything. She was going to read a Zane Grey book, and I can tell her everything that happens in that one. Why don't the three of us head up to the movie together? I mean, none of us have seen it, right? A lot of the guys will be there."

A big smile overcame Helen's face. "Really? The three of us?" She swiveled her eyes over to Edie. "People wouldn't think— Wait. We don't care what people think, right? Let's go."

"I'll have to clean out my car," Russ blurted out, almost mortified to think of Helen seeing the inside of his car.

"Why? Mine's clean. And I'll even let you drive."

On a football field, in a boxing ring, or even in the middle of chemistry or calculus class, Russ was the most confident young man in town, as sure of his prowess at most any skill that he felt he could look *anyone* in the eye, no matter their station in life. But right now his heart was thudding, and he felt like a serf in the presence of a princess.

"Really? You'd let me drive the Imperial? Your dad won't mind?"

Helen laughed. "Well, it is Mother's car, first of all. And second, why should they mind? Father idolizes you, and Mother told me she thinks you're 'dreamy'."

Embarrassed, Russ laughed. "Dreamy? Your mom said that?"

"I swear it. Come on, both of you. Get in and let's go to my house so I can tell Mother where we're headed. Wait—what about you? Is it okay with your parents?"

"I do whatever I want," said Russ. "They've never said no yet. Besides, I'm eighteen."

The three of them got in, Russ at the wheel, and he worked the automatic lever and felt the seat slide backward beneath him. He couldn't help the grin that flooded over his face.

Instead of turning around in the street, Russ kept driving straight down Locust, then made a left on Park, puttering right past his house. Defiant. The truth was, he might be in a lot of trouble with his dad over this move later, eighteen years old or not. But right now he wasn't about to admit that.

As they drove down the block, he saw a shape come out on the sidewalk from the area of Isaac Thorpe's house and walk toward the street. He slowed way down. Sure enough, it was Isaac.

He came to a stop and motioned the boy to cross in front of him. Isaac started across, and when he had passed the car, Russ pulled forward, stopping when he was even with the boy's back.

"Hey!"

Isaac whirled around, a startled look on his face. A big grin broke. "Russ!" The boy's fascinated eyes scanned the car, and he leaned down and looked in, blushing when he saw two feminine faces peering back at him. He jerked upright.

"Where you going, Ikey?" Russ asked.

"Oh. I was just going for a walk."

"Wow. It's starting to get kind of late, isn't it?"

"Sure. I'm not scared."

"Well, heck no! I wouldn't think you would be. Just thought maybe your mom and dad would want you home before dark."

"Oh, yeah. Not really. They don't care."

Russ frowned. "My mom and dad sure would have when I was a whipper snapper."

Isaac smiled shyly, making his greenish-brown eyes sparkle and the deep dimples dent his cheeks.

"Hey, did you get a new car?"

"No way!" Russ replied. "This is Helen's. She's letting me try it out." Feeling suddenly a little nervous, Russ looked up and down the opposite sidewalk, and then the street. "Are you sure it's okay for you to be wandering around out here, buddy? It's gonna be pitch black in an hour."

"Well, I'm just going across the street."

No sooner had he said that than a man appeared from a doorway on the east side of the street and stood holding the door. “Hey, there, Ikey! You comin’ over or not?”

Russ felt a strange little pang of jealousy. The man had called Isaac “Ikey.” For some reason, Russ thought that name was something between him and his friend.

A look of discomfort came over the boy’s face. “Well, I better get goin’.”

Russ gave the man at the house a moment’s scrutiny. “Who is that guy?”

“Oh, that’s Billy.”

“Billy? Billy who?”

“Not sure. He lets me see his model cars sometimes. He’s real nice to me.”

A feeling of real guilt came over Russ. There had been a time when he was that nice guy. But then Isaac became a pest, and he had tried to distance himself. He looked at Billy, then after a second back at Isaac.

“Does he live there by himself?”

“He did, but a friend of his moved in. Luther.”

The whole situation sounded strange to Russ. Moreover, it *felt* odd, deep in his chest. He wasn’t sure why. There was something about it he didn’t like. He made a note to try and treat Isaac better, at least for a while.

“Well, Ikey, if you decide to come over you know where I am!” called Billy, and then he went inside and let the screen door slam.

Russ looked at Isaac, feeling strange about leaving him. “Say, Rusty”—he couldn’t bring himself to call him “Ikey,” now that Billy had stolen it— “you still want to go to a movie sometime?”

Isaac’s eyes got big, and so did his grin. “Really? Sure!”

“Well—”

Another voice cut in on his words, a louder, gruffer voice. “Hey, Isaac. Come on, little man. I’ve got some hot dogs cookin’, and they’re just about done.”

“Oh, hey, Luther! Okay, I’m coming.” The boy turned back and looked an apology at his hero—or his *former* hero, it seemed now to Russ. “Well, I’d better get going. See you later, Russ.”

Russ waved, but the boy was already jogging across the street. Russ put his foot back on the gas and drove the remainder of the block, turning left on Elm, driving one block to Holmes, then turning left again. It wasn't until that point that Helen said, "Who was that little boy?"

Pulled out of troubled thought, Russ looked over at the girls. "Oh. Just a neighbor kid. Isaac Thorpe. He used to come over sometimes. He got to be a real germ."

"Oh. He seemed like a nice kid."

The car was silent for the rest of the block, and Russ pulled to a stop when they reached Locust again. "Do you know those men?" Edie asked.

Russ looked at her, feeling impatient all of a sudden. "What are you talking about? You heard. He just now told me who they are."

"Oh. Right."

"Hey, sorry. I didn't mean to snap."

"No, it was a stupid thing to ask. I knew the answer."

The car didn't budge from the stop sign.

Helen reached out a hand and put it on Russ's forearm. "You seem kind of worried."

"Ha! Not really. Isaac can do whatever he wants, I guess. His folks apparently don't care."

A couple of cars drove past. The second one honked, and someone waved out the passenger window. Russ looked over at Helen, who shrugged.

"You still want to go to the movie?" she asked.

Again flat-footed. Russ stared at her, trying to make sense of what she had asked.

The girl raised her voice. "You know—movie? You seem way distracted."

"Jeez, Helen, I'm sorry. Yeah, I guess I am distracted. I feel strange about letting Isaac go over there with those guys like that. My folks wouldn't have let me do that when I was ten. Holy cow, who would?"

"Listen, Russ, if you don't feel good about it, maybe you should go knock on their door. We can go to a movie any time."

Russ's heart was pounding now so loud he thought both of the girls must hear it. He looked hard at Helen, then past her at Edie. Both of them were watching him with concerned eyes. For a second, he thought he

should do what Helen said. Maybe they should even invite Isaac to go to the movie with them. Then the stubborn rose up inside him, and he scoffed.

"Nah, if his parents think it's okay, they probably know those guys. Let's go see the show."

With that, he gunned the motor and pulled out, right into the lane of an oncoming pickup.

CHAPTER NINE

At the last possible second, Russ whipped the car to the right, slamming it into the curb. The pickup didn't stop, but its driver laid on a weak-sounding horn a second after it had already passed.

Blushing, Russ looked at Helen. "Sorry about that."

"You're way more than a *little* distracted. I can drive if you want."

"Huh? Oh, heck no. I'm fine." He looked carefully to the left, then straightened the wheel, pulled out again onto Locust, and drove to Helen's.

He parked in the crescent driveway, glancing to left and right at the plain-looking homes that surrounded it on either side. That was one thing about Shelley—there was no upper class section of town. The humble lived wherever they could, and the upper crust lived wherever they wanted.

They all went inside, with Edie looking around in awe, and Helen's mother came out in the entryway to greet them, looking every bit as perfect as she had the first time Russ met her—"dreamy", to use her word. She was all smiles and bright eyes, but then she stopped, looking confused. She seemed to be doing mathematics in her head, and the numbers apparently didn't add up, judging by the furrows that knitted her brow.

"Well, hello, dear. Any trouble today?"

Helen laughed, looking over at Russ and then at Edie. "Trouble? No, Mother, why?"

Mrs. James looked at Edie, then darted her eyes away. "Well, just . . . Oh, nothing." She turned to Russ. "Hello, Russ. Nice to see you again." She gave Edie her first direct gaze. "I'm Mrs. James. And you are . . ?"

"Edie Russell, ma'am."

An almost imperceptible change came over Mrs. James's face that Russ wouldn't have caught had he not been looking directly at her. "Oh. Edie . . . Russell?" Her eyes searched the girl's, and then, sounding almost breathless, she asked, "Surely not Frankie's little girl? Oh, sorry—Frank."

Edie's face pinkened, and she hesitated before replying. "Why, yes, Mrs. Russell. Frankie is my father."

Mrs. James lifted her chin a little, for a moment seeming lost for words. "Well, that's nice. So what are you kids up to?" She spun back to Helen. Her face was flushed.

"Mother, we want to go to the Falls and see *Marty*. You and Father adored it, didn't you?"

"It was a nice film," agreed Mrs. James with a prim nod. "Certainly. How late do you plan on being?"

Helen turned her steady gaze on Russ. He guessed now he was expected to be making manly decisions, being eighteen and all. "Uh, well . . . I thought we would watch the show and then maybe get a burger up at Ray's, since we'll be in I.F. anyway. Would that be all right?" He thought he might earn a few points if he pretended he hadn't already made up his mind.

Mrs. James shrugged and turned her head a little to one side. "Why, certainly, kids. Just be careful on that highway, will you? Your father would have an absolute conniption if you wrecked that car."

"We won't, Mother," said Helen. "See you later then."

"No kiss for your mother?" Mrs. James's words stopped all three of them turning, and Helen turned back around, laughing in embarrassment.

"Oh, sorry, Mother. I was a little excited." She took two steps to her mother and leaned close to kiss her cheek. Mrs. James patted her shoulder, which was encased in a soft pink sweater.

"Be safe now. And have a good time."

● ● ● ● ●

When they left the house, Russ couldn't help taking a few streets on his way to Idaho Falls that really weren't anywhere near on his way. But he was driving a shiny two-tone Chrysler Imperial—not just any Imperial, but the Imperial belonging to Helen James. And she was inside with him! This was history in the making. He was not about to speed through his evening.

Unfortunately, when they came around the far end of town and then got back on Fir and drove down to State Street, Sheriff Arch Blevins's black and white Ford was coming in from west of town, on the River Road. He stopped at the stop sign across from the Chrysler, signaling to turn north. Russ froze. *Go, Dad. Just go!* he thought. But he must not have thought it hard enough.

Swinging his eyes this way and that to look for oncoming traffic, the old man's eyes touched upon Russ's face, then swiveled back. He peered closer. Instead of making his left turn, he gunned his squad car across the street, pulling up alongside Russ. In spite of the cool air, Russ already had his window down, and his arm resting half outside. His eyes met his father's.

"Hi, Pop."

"Russ." The sheriff's eyes scanned the length of the car, front to back, then back again to Russ. He glanced past Russ to see the two young women sitting there watching him too, mesmerized. "New car?" asked Arch.

"Uh . . . Well, yeah, sort of. It belongs to Helen's mom."

Arch shook his head, the look on his face saying that name meant nothing to him.

"Oh, yeah, sorry. Pop, this is Helen James." He completely forgot to mention Edie.

Arch continued to look past Russ. "Nice. Hello, Helen. Forgive my saying so, but I seem to be seeing double. You seem to be two people."

A feeling of confusion washed through Russ, and then he felt himself blush. "Oh, jeez! Sorry! Well, you know Edie, don't you? Edie Russell?"

Arch looked back at the far side of the car, focusing on Edie's face in the shadowy interior. "Oh, sure! Edie! Frank's little girl! Well, I'll be. You must be real desperate, hanging around trouble like Russ."

Edie laughed, her face reddening. "No, sir. Russ is real nice."

Arch smiled, but it was a serious smile. “Well, I sure was sorry to hear about your dad. How is he doing?”

Confused, Russ cranked his head around to see Edie. So did Helen. As gloomy as the lighting was starting to get, it was hard to see any big change in her expression.

“He’s okay, Mr. Blevins. Thank you for asking.”

“Tell him I said hello, would you? If your family needs anything, you know where to come.”

Edie’s smile grew. “Thank you, sir. I’ll tell Daddy.”

Arch turned his attention back to Russ. “What’s the plan, Son?”

“What?”

“Where are you headed in the fancy car?”

“To the Falls. To see a movie.”

“I take it you already told your mother.”

A bad feeling began to fill Russ’s chest. He wanted to say yes, he had told her. Perhaps his mother would cover for him. But past experience that wasn’t so good bade him pass up that lie.

“Um, well, not really. It was pretty late, and we didn’t want to miss the start of the show.”

Arch tilted his chin upward. “I see. Well, then, I guess we’ll talk later.”

With that, Arch Blevins nodded at the girls again and said good night, then drove down Fir. Russ pulled right onto State Street, his father’s last words echoing in his head. A farewell salutation that may have seemed casual to a bystander meant a lot more to Russ. When Sheriff Arch Blevins told someone they would talk later, it might mean either of two things. One, a way of saying, “so long.” Two . . . the meaning it held for Russ at that moment. They would indeed *talk later.* And Russ was not going to enjoy what his father had to say. But at least he had the tact not to chew him out in front of the girls. For that, Russ silently thanked him.

● ● ● ● ●

The Paramount was crowded that night for two reasons: One, Ernest Borgnine’s performance in *Marty* was already being applauded by critics, and two, the Paramount had been specially chosen as part of an exclusive period of premier for the movie. The wide release wasn’t even

expected until sometime in July. So the faithful movie-goers of the Idaho Falls area thronged the theater, and the unlikely threesome had to be seated far up in front, where they were sure to have strained necks by the time the film ended.

Luckily, the film was only one hour and thirty-four minutes long, and because Russ spent more time studying Helen than he did watching the movie, while Helen and Edie were massaging the kinks out of the backs of their necks after the show was over, Russ's neck felt fine.

After the movie, Russ drove over to Ray's In and Out, which sat beyond the stockyards on Northgate Mile. He chose that Ray's out of the two locations because past experience told him that the other one, closer to the theater, was going to be packed by now—and because he wasn't in the mood for a grilling from his friends and fellow-students about the circumstances of his strange night out with two girls at once—particularly these two girls, who other than both being female had pretty much nothing whatsoever in common.

They sat eating cheeseburgers and fries in silence for a while until Helen decided conquering the stillness was up to her. "So . . . What did you think of the movie?"

When Russ looked up, Helen's eyes were on Edie.

"I thought it was great."

"Yeah, my mom went on and on about it. I guess Daddy was a little distracted, but mom sure loved it. Russ?"

"It was actually a good show." He didn't dare tell her that his taste usually ran more to John Wayne and Gregory Peck dramas. She obviously liked *Marty,* and it was okay.

"You didn't expect it to be good?"

"Well, somebody told me it didn't have much action in it."

"No, it sure didn't have that. But I thought it was sweet. Here was this lonely man who didn't seem to have anything going for him, really. He was no Gregory Peck, that's for sure. But he still found true love. I like that kind of film."

Russ was taken aback by the girl's mention of Gregory Peck. He asked her about him.

"Oh, I love Gregory Peck! Who could not simply devour *Roman Holiday?* Gregory Peck, Audrey Hepburn. Wow."

Russ was silent, but he smiled. That show was one of the few Peck films he hadn't been that much into. Romances weren't really his cup of tea. He had been thinking more along the lines of *The Gunfighter,* or *Only the Valiant.*

"What about you, Edie? Who do you like?" asked Helen.

"Marlon Brando. Clark Gable. Oh, and Henry Fonda."

"Oh, yes. The real men's men," said Helen, letting out a laugh. "Me too."

"I like Gregory Peck, too," Edie blurted, her eyes darting over to Russ. He averted his gaze. He wanted a shake instead of the iron port and cherry he had chosen. And more than anything he was ready to go. There was a strange energy running throughout his body that he couldn't explain. It might have been in part the thought of what was coming when he got home. But it was also something . . . Well, something he couldn't grab onto.

He looked at Helen. She was deep in conversation with Edie now, about actors and movies that didn't really impress him all that much. As she talked, her green eyes sparkled with a light that made him queasy inside—in a good way. Her fine, glossy hair bobbed up and down with the motions of her head. Her wonderful pink lips moved in a mesmerizing way. Yes, Russ Blevins was smitten. There was no way around it.

But with Helen now engrossed in conversation with Edie, who was actually starting to seem like she was getting comfortable, this wasn't exactly the way Russ had envisioned their first date. It made him resent Edie a little, even though it wasn't her idea to come along in the first place. But under the circumstances, any girl with a lick of common sense would have told Helen no.

Russ saw someone else walking away from the counter with a milkshake, a maraschino cherry perched in the whipped cream on top, and he looked down distastefully at his iron port. "Hey, I'm gonna get me a chocolate shake. Anybody else?"

The girls said no, so Russ got up and made his order, leaving them at the table. When the shake came, he took it and went back to the table, not bothering to sit. "You two ready to go?"

Helen glanced up with surprise at Russ, then looked at the clock on the wall. "It's only nine-thirty."

"Oh, well I didn't know there was a law you had to stay away from home until a certain time," he replied, cracking a smile.

Edie was silent and meek, but Helen was otherwise. "You seriously want to go home this early?"

"I seriously don't," Russ replied. "But what else is there to do?"

Edie fumbled her way out of her seat. She was still looking at Helen, who hadn't moved.

"We could go drive in the country and smell the air," Helen suggested, reaching out to pick up her drink and sipping daintily from the straw. "Come on, Russ, sit back down. Edie and I were just getting into our discussion."

"No, that's fine," Edie cut in, throwing a quick glance at Russ. "I probably should get going anyway."

"Wow. *Two* sticks in the mud." Helen shrugged. "Well, okay." She shot up out of her chair. "Let's go home then. We wouldn't want the roosters to catch us still up, would we?"

Russ felt his face turn hot. "Give me a break. I don't want to take you home late and have your old man holler at me."

"Old man? You mean my father?"

"Oh, yeah. Sorry. Anyway, maybe we can do this again." With that, he reached down with suddenly clumsy hands and helped Helen on with her sweater, and then he picked up his shake again and they walked to the door, which he held open for both of them. As they were leaving, he glanced over to see a table full of guys looking their way and laughing. He frowned, turned, and went out.

In silence, Russ drove the speed limit all the way out of town. There was no more mention of a drive in the country, although he would have been more than happy to if it hadn't been for the third wheel inside the Imperial with him and Helen.

Edie broke the silence. "Hey, Russ, are you getting ready for football?"

What kind of a fool question was that? Russ thought. He was *always* getting ready for football. "Sure."

"Do you guys like the new English teacher, Miss Barnhart?" Helen's question took Russ by surprise. *English* teacher! What?

"I never thought anything about her. Why?"

"Oh, just wondering. She sure is nice."

"Yeah, whatever. It's just English."

"I happen to *like* English."

Russ had allowed his stubborn streak to get to him a lot tonight, but he sensed that he had better stop now if he wanted a chance at any other dates with Helen James. He held back his sarcastic reply.

"Do you do any reading, Russ?" Helen asked.

"Well, not much. I'm usually too busy."

"Not even Zane Grey?"

He looked at her to see if she was mocking him. "Well, I already told you I read Zane Grey. Or at least I used to. My dad reads a lot of Zane Grey. With football practice and running, where am *I* gonna find the time anymore?"

"Well, there's more to life than football."

Russ felt Edie Russell's eyes flicker over at him, but he didn't meet them. He kept driving and staring at the road, thinking it would probably be smart if he did not reply.

The truth was, in Russ Blevins's life, there *was* nothing more than football. And after this failed date with Helen James, maybe there never would be.

CHAPTER TEN

The month of April crept by, but James Russet Blevins didn't. James Russet Blevins ran—until anyone else would have been sick of running.

He ran long distance, miles at a time. He ran short distance, reaching out for sprint records. He laid out old, used-up tires he got down at the tire store, where Charlie Braun worked, in random patterns on the edges of plowed fields of deep dirt, and ran through them with high knees and with fists pumping. And he sometimes spent fifteen cents on gas and drove out to the steep piece of rutted dust they called Presto Hill, out

beyond the settlement of Goshen, where he was born, and did sprints up the hill until he felt like he would throw up—and sometimes actually did.

Then some afternoons he would go out to his friend Mark Knaggs's farm, take fifty or sixty pound bales of hay and throw them up on top of his football helmet, and while balancing them there he would do squats—dozens of them, sometimes without stopping, until his thighs ached, until they lit up with a fire that was the torch that drove him on.

On one of Russ's long runs, he contemplated his return from Idaho Falls the night of his first—and last—date with Helen James. He had been expecting the worst with his father, but it hadn't come. Arch had indeed come into his room to talk to him, but there was no scolding. No punishment. Russ wasn't sure what it was all even about, in fact. He had never seen his father seem as uncomfortable as he had that night. It wasn't until much later that he found out about the murder case.

It felt like his relationship with his father had more and more of those kinds of moments—moments of discomfort, when it seemed Arch Blevins wanted to be anywhere but talking to his son. And, sadly, Russ felt the same.

One Monday, Russ was walking home the half mile from the high school, and he met Isaac Thorpe coming his way. Isaac was blocks from home, but that was nothing for him. Like Russ had done in his childhood days, Isaac sometimes would walk for miles, all alone. No one seemed to notice. And no one seemed to care.

"Hi, Russ," said Isaac as they came up to each other.

"Hey, Rusty," replied Russ, still refusing to call the boy Ikey since Billy, who lived across the street, had picked the nickname up. Russ was still soaked with sweat from his workout, but he had his breath back and felt relaxed. His spirits were high. Even the thought of Isaac pestering him didn't bother him this afternoon.

A light seemed to come over Isaac's face. "What have you been up to?" He turned a little away from the direction he had been heading.

"Getting ready for football."

"This early?"

Russ grinned. "You can't be number one by sitting around till the last minute, buddy."

Isaac lit up like no one else when he was happy, and now his face-wide smile warmed Russ's heart. He hadn't noticed it in a while. Of course, he had been avoiding the little guy as much as possible lately. He had a feeling this time the happiness stemmed from the word "buddy."

"Hey, did you know they're showing *Bad Day at Black Rock* up at the Paramount now?"

Inwardly, Russ groaned. Had he promised to take Isaac to the movies sometime? He honestly couldn't remember for sure, but he was afraid he might have.

"I didn't know that."

Russ resumed walking down Locust, and Isaac rushed to fall in step beside him.

"Yeah." The boy kept walking, trying to match Russ's strides, which in this case wasn't too hard since Russ had just done a hard hour of sprints and calisthenics. "Yep. I hear it's pretty good."

Russ sighed, although trying not to make too big of a production of it. Still a quarter mile to his house . . .

"Did I tell you I saved up a whole buck twenty-five?" Isaac asked.

"You did? You don't say. Good goin', buddy."

"Yeah." Long silence. "It's fifty cents to see a film in Idaho Falls . . . right?"

Even Russ Blevins wasn't totally blind or totally stupid. But he sure was busy—all the time. "Hey, that's great. You could see the movie *and* buy some popcorn with that much. But I wouldn't even worry about the Paramount. I mean, you can walk to the Virginia Theater from your house easy! And they need the money, too. I. F. isn't everything, you know."

"Oh, yeah, that's true." Isaac looked down and seemed to be studying the ground as it passed beneath. Several times, he glanced over at Russ's feet before Russ realized the boy was trying to get up the courage to look up at him.

It was courage he never got, even as they rounded the corner of Locust and turned south on Park Avenue, the last stretch to home for both of them.

The boy was still looking at the ground when he went for his last ditch effort. "Yeah, so . . . Do you ever go to the movies, Russ?"

The boy had asked him the same question many times before, Russ was sure. Or at least once. Sometimes he couldn't keep track. He gritted his teeth, glancing ahead to his house. It was so close now.

"Oh, yeah, sometimes. Not much, though."

Almost there.

"Yeah, me neither. I'm waiting for another cowboy show."

"Yeah?"

"Yeah. Billy says *The Far Country* was good."

"Yeah, prob'ly. Billy said that, huh?"

"Yeah. He talks a lot about movies and stuff. He thinks Jimmy Stewart's cool."

"Yeah, I like him. He's his own man."

The comment seemed to give Isaac new hope, or perhaps the nearness of Russ's house drove the boy to a heightened sense of desperation.

"Hey, Russ, if I save another dollar up to pay you for gasoline, and I pay for your ticket too, do you think maybe sometime we could go to the movie in I. F.?" he asked, using Russ's term for the Falls. "Just you and me, I mean?"

Russ didn't curse very often, but in his head now he wanted to. Thirty feet to his house. Only thirty more feet! And now, when salvation seemed to be in sight, the hammer had come down. Now he was sure he must have told Isaac sometime in the past that he would take him to the show. He was pretty certain he remembered him bugging him about it before.

"We'll see, okay? Summer's comin'."

"Yeah, it sure is." Isaac's voice was hopeful.

"Yeah, so I get pretty busy working and practicing for football in the summer," Russ shot out. He might as well have hit his little shadow in the head with a rock.

They reached the front walkway up to the little white and pink house, and Isaac hesitated. Russ made the mistake of looking at the boy directly, and he could see the hurt in his eyes. His sisters claimed he never paid any attention to other people's feelings, but Isaac's lay on his sleeve like a big black bull's eye.

"Well, I'm glad I got to walk with you, Russ." Isaac sounded broken. The sound of the pain almost made Russ cave in.

"Yeah, thanks, Rusty. So . . . see you around."

"Okay, see ya," Isaac chimed back in a dull voice. The smile he gave Russ back was forced. The pain in his eyes could never be covered with a simple flash of teeth and dimples.

In spite of his rush to get into the house to safety, away from bothersome people, Russ paused on the sidewalk and watched Isaac Thorpe walk away. The boy never even glanced back. Russ watched him all the way to his walkway.

Russ didn't say much at supper that night. In fact, the majority of the conversation was carried by eleven-year-old Kathleen, fifteen-year-old Annie, and their mother. He didn't even notice what they were talking about, only that when one set of lips stopped moving and one tongue ceased to wag, one of the others took over. So he ate his hamburger and mashed spuds in silence—russet spuds, probably—like him. He grinned half-heartedly at that thought. *Mash those Russets.* A famous cheer used by Shelley's rivals, and which had taken on an entirely new meaning now that Russ was the star of the team. *Mash 'em. Fry 'em. Slice 'em up.* Every childish thing that could be said about potatoes was applied to the poor Russets, and sometimes Russ hated the imbecile who had chosen his school mascot. All he could figure was the guy either hated sports altogether, or he believed that by coming up with some stupid, puny-sounding name just one thought away from the "Shelley Fries" he could drive the Shelley teams to fight harder. Well, in Russ's case, at least, it had worked.

"Thanks, Ma," said Arch Blevins suddenly, as he set his napkin down on his empty plate and stood up. He picked his gun belt off the back of the chair and walked down the hall, and for the first time, everyone in the room seemed to notice his silence.

Russ's mom looked after him, losing interest in her conversation with the two girls. Russ caught the concern in her eyes, but she said nothing, and neither did he.

And honestly, Russ didn't care. What adults worried about, or what kept them from talking, was not his concern. Winning football games, and throwing everything he had into doing so, *that* was his game.

Russ looked around the table. "Any of you girls want to go throw a football?"

They all shot him down, some with blank stares, others with comments of derision. "Mom, I'm going to go find some of the guys," he said then. "These girls are a bunch of sticks in the mud. I wish you and Dad could have had at least one more boy!"

"How are you going to get to your friends', Son? Your fan belt is still broken, isn't it?"

"Oh, man!" Russ had forgotten breaking the fan belt on his car a week earlier. "Can you loan me a couple bucks? I'll go down to the auto store and get a belt."

"Russ!" his dad's call came from down the hall.

"Yeah, Pop."

"Get on your studies, Son," the voice came back, sort of quiet and lifeless. "You can throw the ball after school tomorrow."

Russ's mom flashed her eyes over at him. They were full of concern. Russ frowned and lurched up from the table.

"Hey, Son."

He looked back at her.

"Have you practiced the piano lately?"

Russ heard Kathleen giggle. All the girls knew he was embarrassed, now that he was a star football player, that he could play the piano at all. He was even more embarrassed about how good he was at it. A football star was not supposed to know how to play the piano, and he only did it late at night when there was no chance that anyone would be coming over.

"Actually, Mom, I was thinking about giving up the piano."

Russ's mother snapped her fork down on her plate as she fixed her eyes on her son. She eased up out of her chair, supporting herself against the tabletop with firmly planted fingertips. "You don't mean that, Russ."

"Jeez, Mom," replied Russ in a groaning tone. "I'm the only football player I know of who knows how to play the piano."

The house was quiet now. As quiet as death. There were a lot of subjects in the Blevins home on which there were no holds barred. Even football, at times, in spite of all its seriousness to Russ and his father, could become a subject that brought on teasing comments and jabs. But the piano, that was a different story. Eleanor Blevins was pretty relaxed when it came to most things, and for the most part, unlike her parents,

she was very open-minded. But ever since Russ was four years old she had worked with him at the piano, in hopes that someday he would be a young man of the arts, a man of many talents—not only athletically, but at the keyboard.

By the time Russ was twelve, he had mastered so many of the classics, and so many of the contemporary hits, that Eleanor had it in her mind to see him someday playing before crowds of people. The piano and her son James Russet, they were a combination on which Eleanor had no sense of compromise. And everyone in the house with any brains knew it.

"We've talked about this before, James," Eleanor said quietly but firmly. "Please don't do this to me. I have only ever asked one thing out of you. You know I love how good you are at football and boxing. I love the way the crowd cheers you. But all that will be gone someday. The piano can be there forever, when you're way too old for football."

Without saying anything, the girls began to make their getaway, down the hall to their rooms. The entire mood of the house had changed, and joking and teasing would not be welcome in this atmosphere.

When the girls were gone, Russ walked over absently to the piano, running his fingers along the top of the closed keyboard cover. He found not one speck of dust there. His mother would have been mortified if there had been.

Eleanor came close to him and put her arms around his waist. "Will you play 'Moonlight Sonata' for me?"

"Aren't you tired of it?" Agonized, Russ didn't look over at her. He was studying his fingertips on the deep red mahogany wood of the keyboard cover.

"Son, I couldn't get tired of 'Moonlight Sonata' if you played it all day."

Russ looked over at his mother. Their eyes met, and she smiled, giving him a little push with her body. "Come on. Just one time."

So Russ sat down on the bench and uncovered the keyboard, letting his fingers rest on the keys. He hated to admit it to anyone, but he loved the sound of Beethoven's "Moonlight Sonata" too. He didn't like to play it when his father was home because he knew he must think his son was a sissy for giving in like this. After all, how many big, tough boys would

lower themselves to play the piano? But how could he resist his mother when she looked at him like that?

Russ didn't need any sheet music for this song he had played hundreds of times since his childhood. He closed his eyes, and the music began to flow. His mother stood behind him and put her hands on his shoulders, standing there swaying as if she were feeling the music come through his fingers, into his arms, and up his shoulders.

When "Moonlight Sonata" was over, and Russ began almost by natural reflex to play his favorite, "Clair de Lune," Arch Blevins opened the door to the bedroom and walked down the hall, and at the corner he stood, just in sight from the living room. Russ looked up as Arch shook his head and walked away, into the kitchen and then down the back steps.

Russ's fingers faltered on the keys, but he caught himself and played on. He had to, for his mother, who also adored "Clair de Lune".

Eleanor, frowning, looked after her husband and wondered why it was that he would never stay in the house when Russ sat down to the piano.

CHAPTER ELEVEN

The oval track got hard and boring to Russ. He wanted to be on a country road, or running up Wolverine Canyon, southeast of town. He wanted a challenge. A mountain trail. A steep hill. His shoes were starting to make ruts in the track beside the high school. Or at least that was what he dreamed. The track couldn't handle his speed.

One afternoon, Russ was sitting on the grass inside the track, relaxing and visiting with Everett Morin, Pete Basso, and Mark Knaggs, and discussing the boredom the track was beginning to engender for all of them.

Pete said, "There's gotta be some better way to train for football."

Mark pulled out a tuft of grass. "I know, Wop. I'm pretty tired of the same old stretch of gravel, too."

Ev got a bright look in his eye, staring at a row of big cottonwood trees that grew on the outside of the track, in a patch of grass between the track and the gravel road that ran north and south behind the high school, paralleling the irrigation canal.

Russ was watching him when he turned his attention back to the three of them. "What are you cooking up in that pea brain, Ev?"

"I've got a way to keep us from running on the track—tomorrow, at least."

"What? How?" Mark Knaggs was all ears.

"Simple, Spit," replied Ev. "You got an ax?"

"Sure."

"I got one too," threw in Pete Basso.

Ev turned to Russ. "All right, buddy. That makes three axes—me, Spit and Wop. You know how to lop down a tree?"

Russ was looking over at the trees, which were some three feet across. "Are you kiddin'? Those things are huge!"

"So what? There's four of us, right? How long can it take?"

Russ started laughing. "Dang, Ev, that's pretty devious! But funny. You sure you want to do that? My dad might throw the whole bunch of us in jail if we get caught."

"Who's gonna catch us?" asked Spit. "We'll post some lookouts."

"Who?" Pete was all ears.

Russ looked over at Helen, whose relationship with him had been a mix of cool and warm ever since their three-wheeled date at the first of April. "I bet I can find somebody."

Ev followed the trail of Russ's eyes over to Helen, whose hair glistened copper in the late afternoon sun. "Oh, man! You're courtin' trouble, buddy. You gonna trust a girl?"

"Well, who else? If we're all in on it together, we'll be safe. We'll make a pact."

"Call her over here," said Pete.

"Jeez, Wop," said Ev. "You think she'll come over just because he calls her? That dame has too much class to skip to anybody's tune—even our star player's."

Russ took that as a challenge, but he wasn't quite sure he wanted to test it out, not on a field where half of his team mates would see him if

he failed, not to mention the majority of the track team. But how did an eighteen-year-old man who was trying to prove himself turn down so blatant a gauntlet to the face?

Sometimes, one has to take the bait and go for broke.

Russ jumped to his feet and scanned the field and the track until he spotted Helen James again. She and her friends had started walking, and she was some eighty feet away, on the far north end of the track, by the school.

Somehow, Bobbie spotted Russ standing up and looking their way, and she elbowed Helen and said something. Helen's eyes zoomed to Russ, and she gave him a little wave. He waved back, encouraged by the unexpected acknowledgment.

"Helen! Can you come here?" He had worded his request so it didn't sound in any way as if he were giving her an order.

Helen didn't break into a trot, of course. She was much too cool for that. But she did quicken her step, making Lonna and Bobbie rush to catch back up to her. Within twenty seconds, the three of them stood before Russ and his friends.

Russ glanced around at his friends, then decided to make his request a little more private. He beckoned Helen away from the others, then leaned close to her ear.

"You want to get in on something fun?"

Helen studied him, squinting and turning her head a little to one side. "Fun? What exactly is your idea of fun? If you mean me playing tackle football with you and your friends, then no."

Russ couldn't help giggling. "No. Jeez. No, I'm talking about something kind of out there. Adventurous."

"Dangerous?"

"Well, not really 'dangerous'. Or I guess it depends on what your definition of danger is."

"How about 'able to hurt me'? Am I likely to get my leg or arm broken or get eaten by alligators?"

Russ laughed again. "Oh, come on. Get real. Not *that* kind of dangerous. Only dangerous if you're worried about getting suspended."

Helen's eyes got big, and she gave him a look half-dubious, half-scornful. "What in the world are you cooking up, Russ? My mom would kill me if I got kicked out of school."

"So I promise I'll take the fall if we get caught."

"Uh-huh. What's up?"

"Me and the boys are sick of running on the track, see? We're talking about taking down one of those trees tonight." He pointed and swooped his arm out in front of him, palm down, as if mimicking a runner sliding in to home plate. "Right across the track."

Helen looked up and down the huge tree. "Are you kidding? Those trees could smash you flatter than a pancake."

"Aw, come on. I've spent four summers with my uncles taking down trees up in Island Park, Helen. It'll be a breeze."

She looked over at the trees again. "It's kind of a shame, isn't it?"

"What?"

"Well . . . those trees. I mean, they must be a hundred years old."

"Oh, give me a break. This town wasn't even here a hundred years ago."

She frowned. "Well, okay. But still. They've been there a while. Don't you think that's sad?"

"They're stinking cottonwood trees, Helen. Plant a new one and in ten years it will look just like that."

Her lips bunched. She looked at the trees again. Then she met his eyes once more. "So you think that's no big deal? Ten years? I was only seven years old ten years ago, Russ. Think about *that.*"

Those words got Russ a little bit, but he wouldn't admit it. "Okay. Brother! You have to get all sentimental on me? Does that mean you won't help? I guess we can try to find somebody else."

"No."

"No, you won't help?"

"No, it doesn't mean that. I just think it's sad. Listen to this:

I think that I shall never see
A poem lovely as a tree.

A tree whose hungry mouth is prest
Against the earth's sweet flowing breast;

A tree that looks at God all day,
And lifts her leafy arms to pray;

A tree that may in Summer wear
A nest of robins in her hair;

Upon whose bosom snow has lain;
Who intimately lives with rain.

Poems are made by fools like me,
But only God can make a tree.

"Does that sound familiar to you?"

"It sounds like a whole mouthful of words! Wow."

"Well, it *should* be familiar. It's Joyce Killmer: 'Trees'. I think every kid in grade school was forced to memorize and recite it. I guess it didn't stick too well with you, though."

"Aw, come on, Helen. Sure, it's a great poem. I get it. But are you going to help us, or not?"

Helen gave him a sad frown. "What do you want me to do?"

"We need somebody to keep an eye out for the cops, or any nosy neighbor."

"Okay." She tried to give him a smile. "I can do that."

"You will? Great! I just won five bucks betting you would," he said.

"You did what?" She gave him an indignant look.

"I'm kidding. I didn't bet anything."

As if on a whim, Helen reached out and squeezed Russ's fingers. "Hey. Thanks for trusting me with your plan."

"Sure!"

Turning, Russ had to float back down to earth before he could look his friends in the eye.

●●●●●

The stars overhead were like chips of ice in a black velvet sky, seeming to make the moonlight shatter into broken contours. Russ left the house through his bedroom window while his father was in the front room reading a Zane Grey by the light of his favorite lamp and his mom was crocheting an afghan.

Russ, of course, didn't say anything, for it would be hard to come up with any excuse good enough to be leaving the house at 10:30 at night.

He was wearing a black leather jacket that his Uncle Gene had given him as a gift for all his hard hours at the lumber mill in Island Park the summer before. It wasn't enough for the frigid temperatures, but it was the dark shade for which he chose it. Tonight, of all nights, he must be inconspicuous.

Going to the garage, he eased open the walk-in door and went inside, smelling of the oiled metal and the wooden tool handles with linseed oil rubbed into them. He fumbled around in the dark to the tool rack, picking out the double-bit ax. His fingers hovered there, but after some time of considering the ax, he moved on to a two-man crosscut saw his father kept around more as a nostalgia piece than anything else—which was a little strange, considering the fact that his father seemed nostalgic about almost nothing in life.

This was indeed the tool they needed for the job tonight, not an ax. He picked up the saw and left the way he had come.

Having a crew cut sure wasn't the greatest thing on a night like this. The brisk air started turning his ears to ice blocks, but it was too risky to try to go back to the house and sneak a stocking cap out. Fortunately, he had been smart enough to grab some gloves.

In spite of the moon and the stars, something about the night tonight seemed inky black, and he felt like nothing more than the shadow of a tree as he glided along past the silent houses, most of them now dark. At the school, Pete Basso was already waiting. Russ watched the school from across the street, shivering in the dark as he scanned the entire area for anyone who was not supposed to be there. In a final attempt at stealth, he circled around the far side of the big brick school building and came up on the northeast corner of the track. He could see the tan of his Italian friend's coat, with a white tee shirt collar shining through at the top like a beacon.

Russ went over and set his saw by one of the trees, then ambled along the edge of the track to where Pete was standing, fidgeting, at the end of the bleachers. He stopped thirty feet away. "Psst! Hey, Wop!"

Pete whirled on him. "Jeez, man! You scared me."

Laughing, Russ walked the rest of the way toward him. “That was the whole idea. Where’s everyone else?”

“You’re the first one I’ve seen.”

“Great. Well, if it’s just the two of us, then I guess the tree stays.”

It was at that moment they heard the sound of a car flying down the gravel road behind the school, and with a terrible grind of tires and flinging gravel, it slid to a halt not far from the row of trees where Russ had hidden his saw.

Russ and Pete turned to run, but two shapes loomed up out of the shadows in front of them.

CHAPTER TWELVE

An ear-splitting scream shattered the silence of the night, and Pete Basso almost fell backwards. Russ’s reaction was the opposite. He swung out hard and fast with his right fist, and the shape in front of him ducked out of the way in the nick of time, at the same moment yelling out his name.

The raucous sound of Everett Morin laughing registered on Russ’s ears, and he straightened up to see his friend bent almost double, laughing so hard he could not have been aware of anything else that was going on around him. With a grunt, Russ shoved him hard on the shoulder, knocking him down on the grass. Undaunted, Ev continued to laugh, writhing on the ground in his agony of humor.

The other shape proved to be Mark Knaggs. Pete Basso had recovered enough now to swear at him. “Judas Priest, Spit! You scared the hell out of me.”

“Hey, man, watch your language,” Spit growled, then laughed. “Wop, you scream like a girl!”

“Both of you watch it,” commanded Russ. “You’re gonna have the whole town over here to see what’s up. Who’s that in the car? Is that some of our guys?”

Spit started laughing. "No, buddy, that's your Sophie, drivin' her two-tone chariot."

"Say what?"

"Helen, man! Helen! Did you forget asking her to help?"

Russ turned and looked toward where he had heard the car skidding in the gravel. "That was Helen? Driving the Chrysler like *that*?"

"Yeah, man, who else?"

"Boy, if her old man heard that, he'd hit the ceiling. And she's not my 'Sophie'."

"What? That's not how everybody else in school is tellin' it," said Pete, standing beside Russ.

"My Sophie? Give me a break. I went on one date with her, and that wasn't even a real date."

Spit guffawed. "Yeah, man, that was a riot! You, Helen James, and Edie Russell. Ain't my thing, but to each his own."

"Aw, shut up," growled Russ. "So did you guys bring your axes?"

"They're in the trunk of Helen's car," said Ev, getting hold of himself enough to stand back up. "Hey, you're not mad at us, are you? Man, that gag was too good to pass up."

Russ managed a grin now that he could feel his heartrate calming down to Mach one. "Naw, I'm not mad. But you'd better watch your back. Revenge is a dish best served cold, as they say."

Ev and the other boys laughed, and following Russ's lead, they all started east across the field toward the trees. The shadows of three girls approached from the other direction, and Russ could see that Helen had backed the Chrysler up into the shadows of the school.

He recognized her first in the trio. She was the tallest, and her hair the biggest. To her right was Bobbie Ketchum, and he expected Lonna Hansen to be on her left. Only as they came up close, he realized it wasn't. It was Edie Russell! His heart jumped. What the heck was Helen trying to do?

"Hey, where's Lonna?"

"Why?" asked Helen, her voice sounding pert. "You miss her already?"

"Well, no," Russ blustered. "I just figured she'd be with you."

"She couldn't get away. So I brought another friend I thought you'd like to see."

"I see that." Russ noticed that his voice had sounded grumpy, and he tried to cover it up. "Hi, Edie."

"Hi, Russ."

Russ couldn't help but detect a tone of uncertainty in Edie's voice, but he couldn't spend time wondering if he had hurt her feelings. "Hey, what would happen if your old man knew you were sliding his car like that?" he demanded of Helen.

"You mean my father, don't you? Well, it isn't his car in the first place. It's my mother's. And besides, who's going to tell her?"

"You keep driving like that, and the damaged car will tell on you itself. You shouldn't be handling a nice car that way."

"Oh, well, aren't you the wise one?" Helen retorted. This time, Russ was pretty sure she was not happy with the way he had spoken to her. But he couldn't see a nice car like that Chrysler getting messed up simply because she was trying to be cute.

"All right, all right," Ev Morin cut in, always the sage mediator. "We going to cut down a tree, or aren't we? This chopping is going to take half the night."

The words rang true to Russ, but by now he was pretty committed, so he didn't say anything. All he could think of, however, was that in trying to avoid track practice tomorrow they were about to put themselves through more hard labor than all of track! That's what he got for letting a bunch of dumb kids talk him into getting involved in this prank.

"Come on, guys," he said, and started toward the trees. "I've got something that will speed up this night considerably."

When they got to the saw and Russ picked it up, the others seemed elated. "Yeah! Leave it to Russ," said Pete Basso. "The lumberjack!"

"Yeah, Wop—funny," said Russ. "Now come on. Let me show you guys how we have to notch this thing so it goes down right across the track. You do it wrong, and it could go anywhere. Even on top of us!"

Russ got to work with Spit, the toughest of the other boys, one on each handle of the saw, and began cranking it back and forth. Once he got Spit into the rhythm of the strokes, the job went fast, until they had what he deemed a sufficient undercut. They again used the saw for the

top cut, taking a nice big wedge out of the trunk which faced the track. Unfortunately, in the dark, it was hard to tell how deep they had taken the undercut. Also unfortunately, nobody knew that the tree had begun to rot inside.

Russ heard a crackling sound, and he looked up at the looming tree trunk and its branches and limbs, shining in the moonlight. "Guys, everybody needs to move back." Again the tree began to crack. "It's coming down!" he yelled. "Run!"

Everyone took off running in different directions, and some of them kept on going until they were two hundred feet away, three times as far as the tree could reach.

Breathing hard, Russ stood by the wall of the school staring at the tree, which was still standing proud. He waited and prayed for it to come down on top of the track. But without a felling cut on the backside of the trunk, the side opposite of the track, there was no way to know which way it was going to fall.

Even at the distance of seventy or eighty feet, the next crack was loud, considerably more so than the first two. In the dark, it was hard to see what was happening at first, but then it became sickeningly obvious. The tree was toppling straight toward the alley!

With a couple more loud pops, and then a startling, wrenching sound like something tearing in half, the tree tilted straight to the east, and as it landed over the road, clear up onto the bank of the canal, a huge cloud of dust erupted from all around it.

"Come on! Let's get out of here!" Russ barked. "The whole neighborhood's gonna be out here."

The others came running back from all points of the compass they had fled to. Helen had escaped to her car and been ready to fire it up and take off ever since the first command to run. "Russ!" she hissed. "Come on! We'll take you back home."

Russ took off running as lights flickered on in the neighborhood. He reached Helen's car as she was revving the engine. As he piled into the front seat, he landed right on top of someone, and they let out a squeal. The other girls screamed, then started laughing hysterically. Helen managed to compose herself enough as Edie Russell clambered out from under Russ's two hundred pounds of bulk to get the car in reverse, spin

it into a parking place, then hit first and fly off in the other direction, toward Center Street. In a cloud of dust, she was gone, with Bobbie in the back seat, still having a conniption, and Edie Russell in the middle, cold as a stone, and just as silent.

Helen started laughing again as they got to East Center and turned left. After a couple more moments, even Edie was giggling, and Russ couldn't help but join in.

There was going to be a bunch of clean up being done at Shelley senior high school tomorrow, but it sure wasn't going to affect track practice. What a hoot.

On Russ's direction, they drove the long way home, down Milton, then west on Elm. As they passed Park, and Russ looked down the block, he was pretty sure he saw his father's car pull out and head toward Locust.

"Crap!" he said out loud, blushing when he realized what he had said. "Sorry. I was hoping they'd only call out the city cops, but that's my dad leaving to go up to the school. He is not gonna be happy."

He had Helen go north on Emerson, an unpaved street that was more like an alley, and they drove along behind his house, checking to see if there were lights on inside, which there weren't.

Helen pulled right onto Locust, then made the next right, cut her headlights, and pulled up at the curb on Park Avenue, right next to a big old two story house that sat to the north of the Blevins's and which Russ had always said someday he wanted to own.

"Well, you made it home safe, at least," said Helen.

"Yeah," he agreed. "By the luck of the devil."

"You'd better sneak in quiet."

"Oh, yeah. Don't worry about that." He smiled at her. Even in the dark she was beautiful. He hated that Edie was watching him watch Helen.

"Well, good night, Russ."

"Good night. Good night, Bobbie," he said over the seat. He turned and looked last at Edie, and she was trying to meet his gaze, perhaps made braver by the darkness.

"Good night, Russ."

Something came over him, an instinct he might have kicked himself over for days if something much bigger hadn't taken his mind off of his gaffe. He reached out and gave Edie's shoulder a little squeeze.

"Good night, Edie."

Then he got out and shut the door behind him, watching the Chrysler roll south on Park Avenue once again, until it turned east on Elm, its lights flicked back on, and it vanished from sight.

He started home, thinking about how stupid it was to have reached out and squeezed Edie's shoulder. What kind of a message was that going to send to her?

And then that didn't matter anymore. *Nothing* else mattered, all of a sudden. He was thinking about his dad's saw. It was lying on the grass, by the stump of the fallen tree.

CHAPTER THIRTEEN

Even the aftermath of eating five pounds of chili could never have made Russ Blevin's stomach feel the way it did as he slipped resignedly in the back door of the house, up the steps to the landing, and into the kitchen. He crept down the hall to his room and took off his boots, lying down on top of the bedspread. He didn't see much point in getting undressed and under the covers. He wasn't going to be able to take advantage of it anyway.

A bedroom ceiling, viewed by the dark of night, can seem like about the ugliest thing in the universe, especially when that is all one sees for hours on end. Russ lay there, almost hearing his heart pound: dull, like the ponderous beating of a bass drum. A thousand times he closed his eyes. A thousand times, at any stray noise, they popped back open. A car drove down the street. He sat up on the bed. It continued on past the house. It was too loud to be his father's car anyway. His father's was built for stealth.

He began to hear creaks and groans of the house that he had never heard before. He could even hear himself blink. His ears were ringing, even though he could not remember hearing any loud noises recently.

He would have sworn if a mouse was in the corner picking toe jam from between its toes it would have sounded like the chugging of a freight train.

Russ never heard the car come into the driveway. Even the back door opened so softly he didn't realize it. It was the creaking of a big man walking in the hallway that warned him.

Get up, a voice deep inside him said. Get up and face the music. Go out there. Confess to his face. But Russ was paralyzed. Here he was, the big football star—the town's hero. And he could not move. Couldn't even swing his feet over the side of the bed.

The creaking noise continued, then in front of his door it paused. He thought he heard the tiny click of someone trying his door knob. His eyes moved that way. The white door was a deep gray rectangle in the night. He waited for it to move. Nothing happened.

And then, a noise worse than any he had yet to hear, even worse than anything he had yet imagined would finish out this night: the footsteps continued on down the hall. The door to his parents' room opened, and there came one last click as it shut.

Stillness returned to the night. Bed bugs burping and mice popping their knuckles would have sounded like thunder. Russ stared at the hideous black ceiling and waited for sleep, but sleep could not come.

● ● ● ● ●

Russ was sitting in English class the next morning when it came over the loud speaker. It was the thunder he had expected the night before and then never heard.

Attention, please. Attention, please. This is Mr. Ricks. Can we have your attention, please? Would the following students report to the principal's office immediately: Peter Basso, Everett Morin, Helen James, Bobbie Ketchum, Mark Knaggs, Edie Russell—by now Russ was actually starting to sweat—*and James Blevins. I repeat: These students must report to the principal's office at once.*

Too sick to look at anyone else, Russ stood up, feeling like a robot in a science fiction book. He sensed more than saw Edie Russell stand

up, clear across the room from him. She was seated there because at the beginning of the school year he had strategically chosen his desk after waiting for her to choose hers, and then sweet-talked one of the other guys into letting him have the desk farthest from hers. He knew it was childish, but it certainly had made his school year seem more tolerable having her so far away. Remembering that day brought a strange, sudden feeling of guilt over Russ, and he glanced over at Edie, who looked so miserable and forlorn. He wasn't sure now why it had been so important to be separated from her, or why all of this was even coming into his head now when he had things that were so much more important to think about—like marching down the hall to the guillotine.

Everyone in the room was watching Russ and Edie. He didn't need to look at them. You just knew things like that. He walked out of the room without even looking at Miss Barnhart, the teacher, and left his books sitting on the desk.

Once he got outside, he started walking as fast as he could, feeling home-free from Edie. But one last vestige of chivalry made him pause by the door into Mr. Prine's psychology class. Edie came out of the room, turning to click the door shut before looking up to realize he had stopped to wait for her.

A startled look leaped into the girl's face, and she snapped her eyes around to see if anyone else was in sight. She started walking, quickening her step to catch up, until she was almost running.

Russ waited until she caught him and looked down at her, feeling his face redden. "Listen, Edie, I'm real sorry about this. You shouldn't be involved in the first place."

She smiled at him bravely, and he got the feeling that she was almost *happy* to have her name called beside his. "It's okay. I don't mind."

Well, I have the feeling you're about to mind, thought Russ, and then even as he heard another door open farther down the hallway behind them, he started walking, and Edie stayed beside him all the way to Mr. Ricks's office.

Helen James, her face very pale, walked around a corner, on the far side of the office, and Spit was walking in step with her, but three feet away. Russ had never seen Helen looking anything but composed, nor had he ever dreamed she could look so paralyzed with fear. It made him

hurt worse seeing her than all the thoughts of his father coming home had made him feel the night before.

Ev Morin had been coming down the hall behind them, and soon he and Bobbie Ketchum caught up to the whole group as they slowed almost to a stop at the office door.

As usual, Russ was in the lead, and he looked around, feeling like he should apologize to everyone, before taking a deep breath and pushing on inside the office.

Wop was already seated in a chair in the outer room of the office, and as Ev closed the door behind them all, Mrs. Pryce, the school secretary, looked up from her desk and gave them a frown. But it was a frown more of sympathy than of anger, Russ thought.

Mrs. Pryce was a sweet woman. Russ had hardly ever seen her lose her cool, even slightly. She was in her mid-forties, to judge by his parents' age, with slightly strawberry blond hair bobbed short—which in the current slang rendered her a "fuzzy duck"—horn-rimmed glasses, and a stocky build. Her smile was always genuine and caring, but she didn't seem capable of offering it today.

"Are you all here?" she asked.

Russ nodded. "Yeah, I think so."

Mrs. Pryce came closer to them, stopping in front of Russ. Her pale blue eyes were round with worry. "Why, Russ?"

"I don't know. We thought it was cute, I guess."

"Mr. Ricks is madder than I have ever seen him. I'm almost sick to send you kids in there."

"We deserve it. Or at least I do," said Russ.

Mrs. Pryce pursed her lips and nodded. She tried to smile, but it didn't come out right. "Well, you might as well jump in the fire. This is one that isn't going to burn itself out."

Russ nodded. "Thank you, Mrs. Pryce."

He turned and scanned the faces of his fellow criminals. Then he marched the last few feet to Mr. Ricks's office. He started to grab the doorknob, then thought better of it. Raising his hand, he knocked three times, not too loudly, but not meekly either.

"Come in."

Russ eased open the door and stepped in, going to stand in front of the principal's big, blond desk, which was strewn with papers, and one stack of manila folders that were probably filled with the entire school histories of some poor students. He could guess who some of those students might be.

Mr. Ricks stayed seated, glaring up at Russ. Not surprising to Russ, the older man didn't even pay a glance to the others.

If Russ had been asked to describe Mr. Ricks, he would have said he seemed as close to the actor Charlton Heston as any man could have without being Heston himself. The biggest difference was that Mr. Ricks was balding on the top of his head. Otherwise, he had the height of the actor, and the build, and the voice. Oh, that voice. On any normal day, Russ greatly admired his principal and loved to listen to his deep, melodic drawl, but unlike any other day, Russ was not happy to see him or hear his voice.

Even seated, Ben Ricks looked larger than life to Russ, and as he uncurled himself from the chair, he came to stand with his eyes about even with the top of Russ's head—and Russ was no little boy.

The piercing blue eyes of Mr. Ricks were ideal this morning for the task he had undertaken—to pierce through the face of Russ Blevins. Russ was starting to feel like he and Principle Ricks were the only two people in the room.

Ricks raised a hand and scrubbed his mouth, looking down at his desktop for a moment before raising his eyes again. This time, they began to Russ's far right and moved across the entire group of students, landing last on Wop, then coming back, as if magnetized, to Russ.

"Do you know how long it takes a tree to grow?" The booming voice seemed like by itself it could have felled the tree they had sawed at so long. Russ thought back to Helen's words, so much the same as what Mr. Ricks had said.

"No, sir."

"I do."

With those two words, Mr. Ricks turned and walked to his back wall, where a window overlooked the yard. After twenty seconds or so, enough time to let the idea of his impending torture and possible future beheading of the students sink in, he turned back. The move was slow,

almost ponderous—far more ominous than if he had whirled like an attorney in a courtroom drama.

"I have a whole forest of them. Spruce trees, most of them. My father planted them, probably forty or fifty years ago. He babied those things. I swear he was out there every other day with the hose. He didn't trust that job to anyone else. He fertilized them. Brought in loads of steer manure, ground it down into the dirt around the roots. Then he would put shredded wood all around the bases.

"If a limb died, he was out there right away taking it out, and every spring he would prune off any bad tips. Beautiful trees. Not anymore, though. I think there are thirty of them. There might be forty. But so far sixteen of them are dead. Just . . . dead. No obvious reason. I couldn't do a thing to save them, and I tried."

Great. It wasn't bad enough that they had lopped down one of the school's prize cottonwood trees, right out of a matched row. No, wonderfully, it turned out that the school's own Charlton Heston was a tree lover, and currently suffering from the emotional loss of many of his own trees. Russ stood and basked in the heart-warming glow of his driving need to throw up.

Russ didn't know what the ax looked like that was coming toward his own little forest, but it was going to be one ugly sight when it landed.

Suspended? A nightmare. Off the football team? Worse. Fifty lashes with a cat-o-nine tails, staked out naked in the middle of State Street on a Saturday at noon? That one, in comparison, he could handle.

The funny thing was in spite of Mr. Ricks's words, Russ didn't detect the unleashed fury that he had expected. Rather, he began to sense a feeling of sadness. Of loss. It was a surprise, but that hurt Russ worse than any thought of impending danger.

Mr. Ricks studied the group again, and again his eyes settled on Russ. "That tree wasn't anyone's enemy. It was everybody's friend. It gave shade to us all in the hot months, and it kept the harsh wind at bay in the winter. Why would someone do a thing like that to a helpless tree that lived its whole life to make us more comfortable? What was the whole point? Russ?"

It had been plain all along that Russ was the unofficially elected spokesman. He did not shrink from the task.

"We didn't feel like running on the track today."

Mr. Ricks became a carved oaken statue. Seconds ticked by as he stared Russ down. Once, a corner of his mouth twitched. "You're telling me you cut down a thirty or forty-year-old tree to keep from running track for one afternoon? That's what this is all about?"

Russ nodded. The whole thing sounded so pathetic that he couldn't even stand to hear his own voice again.

"So now the tree's across the road, right? It didn't even go on the track."

"Yes sir," said Russ.

"And all those other kids are going to run track this afternoon anyway."

"Yes sir."

"And do you want to know something?"

"Um, no sir. I mean, yes. *Sir.*"

"You are all going to run too, because the tree didn't go on the track, did it?"

"No sir."

"And do you know what else?"

"Uh, no sir."

"You are all released from class this morning."

Russ felt like he had been kicked in the stomach. "Sir? We're suspended?"

"No, far from it. You're only on release from your classes for the day. I have purchased enough axes for the seven of you, and you are going to spend your day chopping that tree into lengths of firewood, then stacking them."

Russ didn't know if the other students realized the monumental task they had all been handed. *Firewood?* Suspension was bad, but perhaps Mr. Ricks had invented something worse. Only it didn't stop there.

"And when you are all done chopping that tree up and stacking the pieces, you are all going to run five miles, on my nice, clean track, where right now I'm pretty sure there isn't even a splinter of cottonwood to be found. Any questions?"

Russ's mind was in a whirl. He thought he could chop wood all day, and he knew he could run five miles, too—with ease. He did more than that most evenings anyway. But what about the girls?

"Sir?"

"Yes."

"What about the girls?"

"What about them?"

Russ froze. Where to run now? Then, the ultimate sacrifice. A lie as big as the school.

"Um, sir, the whole thing was my idea. I kind of forced them into helping us."

Mr. Ricks's eyes scanned the others, pausing longest, for some reason, on Wop. He looked back at Russ. "Your idea, huh? How did you do this coercing?"

"Well—"

"No, wait!" Mr. Ricks held up his hands to halt Russ's words. "If we're going to start into confessions, then I am going to have each of you in here alone, and the rest of you can wait out in the main office."

Russ's heart started pounding even harder. They had discussed nothing like this. There was no way they were all going to be able to back up each other's stories, not without practice. Well, there was one way, and one way only. They had to tell the whole truth.

So the truth was told, and Ev even admitted that he had come up with the plan in the first place and talked Russ and the others into it.

When the last words of confession had been spoken, Mr. Ricks looked over the three girls. "I'm pretty sad, girls. I expected so much better out of all of you."

As the seven students filed out of the office, Mrs. Pryce looking sadly after them, there was one question in Russ's mind, one question besides all of the painful imaginings of a day's blisters from chopping wood: Who had given the principal their names? He had gotten them all correct, and he had not included any innocent parties. His father would have known Russ was involved, because of the abandoned saw. But the others? There was not one piece of evidence to give them away.

Somewhere there was a rat. An evil, vile rat. And Russ was going to have the name of that rat. Come Mr. Ricks or high water.

CHAPTER FOURTEEN

Seven hours in the sun with breaks only for water and to use the restroom—nothing to eat—by itself would have been torment enough for Russ and his friends. But it was when Mr. Ricks came out himself, around ten o'clock, and called Edie Russell away from the group, then took her with him and never brought her back, that Russ's true torture began.

He and the others talked, while still working, of course, about Edie's disappearance. For a while, they assumed it was only temporary, and that before very long she would be back working alongside them. But as hours ran by, and she still had not come, Russ began to realize that something was seriously amiss. And in the end, there was only one thing he and his fellow-delinquents could think of that would have made Mr. Ricks call Edie away and then keep her gone.

The "rat" Russ had been wondering about was now obvious. It was Edie Russell.

The more Russ thought about it, the more he realized it was true. After all, it *had* to be someone from their group of seven students. No one else could have known every student involved. Even if someone else had caught wind of the plan, they would automatically have assumed that Lonna Hansen was one of the group. Everyone at Shelley High knew she, Bobbie, and Helen were joined at the hip. No one who had not been an intimate part of the crime would ever have thought Helen would be there with no Lonna. Yet that morning, Lonna's name had not been called.

Russ was no detective, but some things were as obvious as the harvest moon. No one but one of the seven who had been there could ever have named all of the others. In fact, anyone who knew Russ very well might also have suspected Egg Braun or Nash Wheeler of being a part

of it. But their names weren't called either. It was a simple conclusion. Harsh, but simple.

The question was, why? Why had Edie turned them in? What could she possibly have gained from it? Was she jealous that Russ was trying to date Helen? If she was, it seemed like her jealousy was misguided. Most of the time, that would-be relationship was going nowhere. But in the end, it didn't matter. Edie had fingered all of them in this crime, it was harshly obvious by Ricks pulling her away from the hardest punishment, and Russ would never forget it.

Russ chopped feverishly at the wood, his hands starting to hurt even through his leather gloves, of which he had already worn through one pair. Principal Ricks finally came out and took pity on them, bringing, along with a pitcher of water, three cross-cut saws. From there on, the work was not as difficult, but yet not easy. However, they now had the right tool for the job, and by two-thirty they were almost done.

As he had a thousand times that day, Russ looked over at Helen. Her beautiful hair still shone in the sun, but now some strands of it had come loose from her ponytail, and damp, languid pieces hung on her sweaty forehead. She was sprinkled with bits of sawdust and smaller wood chips, and over the course of the day she had wiped away most of her makeup.

To Russ's pleasant surprise, the lack of makeup didn't hurt her looks any, however. Her eyelashes, unlike many redheads, were dark enough on their own not to need makeup. In fact, he wasn't sure he didn't find her even prettier than normal. Maybe it was because he had never been sure until today that she could actually work. That knowledge added a whole new dimension to the girl who had stolen his heart.

Russ picked up a heavy log and followed Helen, in her now-filthy poodle skirt, to the wood pile. When she threw her log down, exhausted, he eased his up beside it.

"I'll buy you a drink," he said, trying to smile. It was becoming harder and harder as time wore on.

She looked at him and didn't smile back.

"What's wrong?"

She glared at him. For a moment, she seemed about to snap, but then she started to turn away. Before she had gotten halfway turned around,

she whirled back. "What's *wrong?* You want to know what's wrong, Russ?" She grabbed the right side of her skirt and lifted it partway up, showing a place where it had been torn. "See that? My brand-new skirt is ruined." She jerked off her gloves and threw them on the ground. "See that? My hands are about to bleed. See this?" She flipped the hair out of her face but then didn't expound on it. "I shouldn't ever have been here in the first place, Russ Blevins. I have missed all of my classes today, I'm tired and hungry and soaked with sweat, and I'm dirtier than I have been in my entire life. And you ask what's wrong? You stupid oaf. This is all because of you. All of it. What's wrong!"

She turned and stomped over to Bobbie, not even looking back at Russ.

Red-faced, Russ stared at the pile of wood. He sure wasn't going to spend any energy looking at Helen James. Who did that girl think she was, Aphrodite? There were plenty of girls at Shelley High he could date, if he wanted to waste time and money on such pursuits. If she thought she held one tiny bit of power over Russ Blevins, she was mistaken. He gritted his teeth and pulled off his gloves, wiping at the sweat on his face. He glanced over at Wop, Spit, and Ev. All of them were standing still, but not one of them looked his way. Of course he didn't expect them to. Right now, no one would dare.

Russ thought suddenly about Edie. She had betrayed them, and he was still furious over it and couldn't understand why she would do it, but as far as he was concerned personally, it didn't really matter. If it weren't for Edie, he would have been here chopping wood all day by himself. The saw had given him away to his father, so either way, he had been sunk from the start. In a way, she had done him a favor. And that made him stop and think. What if Edie too had remembered the saw? And what if she had turned herself and the others in with the specific thought that it would save Russ from being out there all day alone? It was dishonorable. Unforgivable, even. But at least if it were true it meant she had been thinking of him. And that said *something.*

When the three o'clock bell rang, Mr. Ricks came walking out of the school, Charlton Heston himself, dressed in a suit and tie, stalking toward them and causing the earth to shake, it seemed, as he closed on Russ and his friends with a folder in one hand.

As he reached them, he stopped and spoke, his voice resonating across the field. "Gather up!"

Without hesitation, they all came together before him.

"I trust the wood chopping business was to your enjoyment."

No one spoke.

"I'll bring my truck around, and you can load it full. Stack it nice, too. I don't want any wasted crevices. Tomorrow, if there is any wood left, you can load that in my truck too. Of course, if you know anyone who wants wood and you tell them about this pile, and it's gone by tomorrow, you wouldn't have to load my truck again. I'm just thinking out loud. Any questions?"

There were none.

"Then let me say this. Throughout the day, I have gone through all of your records pretty carefully." He waved a manila folder at them. "And all of you seem to have kept yourselves pretty spotless—up until now. So as far as I'm concerned, this incident is the end of it. A lesson learned for everyone. Now I would suggest you all go get ready for track practice. And people, you had better all be there. I am going to only one track practice all year. And this is the one."

● ● ● ● ●

Russ ran his guts out during track. They all did, but Russ did it with a vengeance. He knew the principal was watching them with expectations that they would be weak, that they would be slower than normal. He sat up on the bleachers with that smug look on his face, his jaw set, staring them down, ready to pounce on the first one who showed any sign of weakness.

Well, he wasn't going to get it out of Russ. No, Russ ran as hard as, or harder than any time before. They were not going to see any weakness in *him.* He ran and ran and ran—*fast*—until he really was ready to drop from exhaustion.

And then, as the hour arrived that they were usually released to go home, he saw a car pull up, in the alley where they had felled the cottonwood. It was the Bingham County sheriff's car.

For a moment, Russ could only stare. He had thought throughout the day about the beating that was coming when evening fell. But he thought he would at least have the chance to ruminate upon it all the way home.

Now it had come to him. And his fellow students, the kids who looked up to him, were everywhere around him. At this moment, for perhaps the first time in his life, Russ suddenly hated his father. Why could he not have made this a private thing, at home between just the two of them?

Mr. Ricks stood up, and in that supremely wonderful, all of a sudden hate-able, way of a big cat that he and Charlton Heston shared, he came down off the bleachers and strode out to the sheriff's car. Russ turned away and started to jog around the track. It was a light, loose jog, not a run, because his mind was on anything but track right now. In a panic, he searched his mind to remember every single face that was out here on this track, the coaches, the athletes . . . Helen James. They were all in for an unforgettable sight: the beating of Russ Blevins.

Russ debated turning around at the end of the track and starting back the other direction, so he wouldn't have to pass too close to his father's car. Maybe he could prolong the next punishment in the string. But for some morbid reason he did not. Perhaps it was Blevins stubbornness. At the end of the track, he paused, but he didn't stop, and he didn't turn around. He kept right on running.

As he came abreast of Mr. Ricks and his father, Ricks called his name. It sounded like the roar of a lion. When he turned, the principal was facing him, his feet braced, like a lawman in a Western movie, facing down the bad man. "It looks like you're released. Your father is taking over."

Taking over. Great. That was a pretty final way to word it.

Soaked in sweat, Russ looked toward the school. He thought about homework, but since he hadn't been in class he didn't have any. He hadn't worn his coat to school either. He had no further reason to stall. He sauntered toward the black and white car, keeping his eyes from any of the other students. His father was not getting out of the car. Maybe that was a good sign. Maybe he was going to save the beating for a private place after all.

When Russ stopped at the driver's door, his father, who had been watching him, turned his eyes away, looking at Ricks. "Thank you for your time, Mr. Ricks."

"Any time, Sheriff," said the principal. He gave one last look to Russ. "I hope you learned something from all this, son. I would sure hate

to lose my football team." Without waiting for a reply, he turned and walked away.

"Get in the car."

Arch Blevins's words were spoken in a low voice, the kind of voice Russ seldom heard him use. The kind of voice no one who knew the man ever wanted to hear Sheriff Blevins use.

He walked around, opened the door, and climbed in. His father pointed to the dash, where two peanut butter and jelly sandwiches sat beside a double package of Hostess Twinkies. "Eat those."

"I'm not really hungry."

His father turned and gave him the look a bear gives to the crow who has ventured too near its food supply. Without another word, Russ reached out, picked up one of the sandwiches, and started eating.

Sheriff Blevins put the car into gear and started driving, bits of wood and small branches crackling under his tires as he drove north toward Center Street. At Center, they turned east.

His father drove on out all the way to Jameston Road, about three miles out of town, and there he pulled off to the side of the road. By then, Russ had dutifully wolfed down both sandwiches and the cream-filled Twinkies he suddenly hated like so many other things he felt hatred for today.

"Get out."

Russ got out.

Arch went to his trunk and opened it while Russ stood beside the car. Soon, he came back over with a strange-looking bundle of leather straps, all hooked together and with a big D ring sewn onto one of them.

"I went out to see old Willis Hansen today," Arch said. "From Goshen. Remember him?"

Russ shook his head. "No."

"Well, he's some kind of a genius with leatherwork. Yeah. And fast, too. He made up this harness—special order. Only took him a couple of hours to do it."

Russ studied the pieces of stitched leather, trying to make heads or tails of them.

"Here. Put it on, I had him make it pretty tight on me. Should fit you about right."

Russ's curiosity was taking him over. "What's it for?"

"Funny you should ask that."

Russ's father worked the harness around his son's shoulders. Then he buckled it tight at the front. The D ring was now on the back, somewhere between Russ's shoulder blades.

Going back to the car, Sheriff Blevins reached into the back seat and withdrew a bottle of Nehi grape soda, from which he removed the cap. He handed the bottle to his son with the command to drink it. Having already lost the battle of wills where the food was concerned, and not interested in losing another such battle, Russ guzzled down the soda pop, feeling the urge to gag, but letting out a huge belch instead. When he was finished, his father nodded, taking the empty bottle and tossing it into the seat before turning his attention back to his son.

"Now, you see those two railroad ties there in the grass?"

As bells began to go off in Russ's head, he looked over to where his father was pointing. In the fresh, green grass of spring, as he had said, lay two beat-up old railroad ties, with a chain that ran through a hole drilled into the ends of them. A loose coil of chain lay there in the grass beyond them.

Russ was a smart boy. He always had been. But figuring out this scenario took no smarts at all. It was obvious that he was about to become a work horse. The only question that remained was: How far?

Arch walked over and picked up the end of the chain, to which was attached a snap ring. "Come over here and turn around." Without questioning, Russ obeyed. He heard the snap ring click into the D ring at his back.

"I'll bet about now you're asking yourself how far I'm going to make you run."

If he wasn't dreading the unknown distance ahead of him so much, Russ would have laughed. His father had read his mind like an old pro. It must have been the long-time lawman in him.

"Well, I'll tell you. You start pulling those ties toward town. And you'd better be *running.* You'd better be running hard. When you collapse, I'll tell you if you've had enough."

Russ wanted to protest that he had chopped wood all day, then had a grueling five-mile run on top of it. But his father was wanting to exact

his revenge for the embarrassment Russ had caused him. That was all this came down to. Revenge. No words Russ could say were going to get him out of it. Words, in fact, could only make it worse.

Russ walked forward until he could feel the chain tauten up behind him. Then he bowed his head and began to run.

CHAPTER FIFTEEN

Russ's shoes thudded on the dusty road. In his mind, he had repeated the words, *I hate my dad* so many times that he started to think he really did. For a long time, he got through the sentence once for every two steps he took. What he was doing was more a plod than a run, but his father had said nothing about it. He could hear the quiet hum of the motor behind him, his father puttering along, watching him like the guard of a chain gang. And right now that was all it seemed like he was. To Russ, his father almost didn't even seem human anymore.

When was this going to end? He had paid for his crime, twice now. He was never one to try and blame someone else for things he did wrong, and chopping down the tree was definitely not the right thing to do. But even so, seven hours of wood chopping was on the verge of inhumane. And at track practice he had driven himself harder than ever before to show them he could do proper penance for what he had done. But now, out here in the country, his father had to carry on the punishment, as if he had not been through enough already. His own father, driving him like a normal, merciful man would not even drive a blockheaded donkey.

Now the railroad ties seemed to be pulling him back. Sweat poured in steady streams down his forehead into his eyes. Down his neck into his shirt, which was already soaked clear through. Down his legs into his socks and shoes. And hatred poured into his heart for his father in a steady stream. After this day, Russ Blevins would never think of Bingham County's number one lawman the same.

Finally, he stopped and threw up. Then he threw up again. He stood there heaving, staring at the ground as purple Nehi drool hung from his lower lip.

His father's car revved, and it pulled up beside him. Russ wiped the spit off his lip and looked over, feeling faint. Arch nodded. "Russ, I clocked two and a half miles out here from when we turned. That's two and a half, plus another half to home. If you start running, maybe you can make it by supper. Either way, those ties had better be with you when you get there."

With that, his father pushed on the gas, and the Ford sped away on Taylor Highway, leaving Russ Blevins very much alone.

●●●●●

The spare bedroom of Billy Earl's house at 377 South Park Avenue had an interesting ceiling. Somebody who knew next-to-nothing about texturing with plaster had apparently done the work, and in some places it was almost completely flat, while others had plaster nearly half an inch thick. It had the awkward appearance of having wanted to be clouds in a still blue sky, but if that were the case someone had thought better of it, for they had painted over the entire thing with pale pink—except for the crevices and low spots where the light gray of the original plaster still shone through.

Luther Dean lay on his bed and stared at the ceiling, trying to make some kind of sense of the clumpy cloud shapes disguised beneath the pale pink. The house was growing warm, although it was only the end of April, so he had the window open and was dressed in faded cut-offs that went to the middle of his thigh. His heavily matted chest was beaded with sweat, and the soft breeze nudging the lace curtains aside at the window felt good on his skin under the faux bear skin rug he had carried with him since he was seventeen.

Luther was powerfully muscular, one of the few things of value he had taken away from the Boise State prison. While there, he had spent countless hours a week doing pull-ups, pushups, sit-ups, and squats, and his sinewy body showed it. Not that it would buy him so much as a sandwich down at Myrt's. But what else had he had to do in the pen to keep his mind off the feet-dragging days besides exercise and think about his mother, his stupid brother, Joe, and about Arch Blevins?

His heart started again to thud heavily, and he felt his blood pressure rise. Those were the reactions his body had learned to live with whenever the name Arch Blevins came into his mind. It wasn't enough that Blevins had arrested him and then helped convict him in court for crimes committed by his brother. To add insult to injury, Blevins's testimony had kept him there long enough for his mother to die, just shy of his parole. That was the deepest cut of all.

All those months in the pen, he had dreamed of only three things: Seeing his mother again, going for a long drive in his Mercury, and beating the hell out of Joe for the two burglaries that had gotten him here. The number three must have been magic, for once his mother died, the desire to see her was replaced by something else, and three remained the number of his goals.

He had driven the Mercury. Check. It was a bittersweet goal to meet, because he had hoped to do it with his mom in the passenger seat. Still, it had been good to feel the wind in his hair again, and the pedals beneath his feet. It had been good to feel the highway soar away beneath him, like the car was a speed boat, and the road a salty marsh.

His brother Joe still awaited him, and he would have to wait, possibly for years, because having Luther put away wasn't enough to teach Joe a lesson about the dangers of breaking the law. After Luther went up to do his time, Joe got drunk and ran a family off the road in Utah, killing a little girl. So Joe was serving time down there, and although he was still on Luther's list, he was at the bottom, unreachable for the time being.

The list contained one other item, and that item was the reason Luther was lying here alone now, waiting for Billy Earl's return from Pash's sporting goods store with a .30/30 rifle, two 1911 Colt .45's, and two boxes of ammunition.

Luther Dean had one careless sheriff to pay for putting him in the pen for a crime he didn't commit, and for taking away the last years he had to spend with his mother, the only person on God's green earth who had ever really cared for him.

● ● ● ● ●

Russ got back after dark with the railroad ties and left them like a rebellious sign in the driveway, but didn't go inside until late that night. Even though he was exhausted from his grueling day of wood chopping

and running, he had no desire to face the heavy atmosphere that would surely be in the house. He didn't want to listen to his sisters' banter, or to his mother badgering him to play something on the piano. And he sure didn't want to breathe in the same air Arch Blevins, his former hero, was breathing out.

He wandered over to Ev Morin's house, where he tanked up on ice water, refreshing himself, and they walked to the city park and threw a pigskin back and forth. There was little talk for a time. Russ reveled in the companionship, and in the cool breeze in his face as he ran to snatch the ball out of the air. He gloried in throwing a perfect spiral out to his best friend and having it nail him right in his out-stretched hands. He pulled in the clean Shelley air, tinged with woodsmoke only now and then, from some die-hard lover of fires in the fireplace.

There was one time of complete peace in life for Russ Blevins, and that was when he had a football in his hands. Nothing else mattered then. His bitterness was gone, along with his hate. He didn't have to think about the cruel way Helen had treated him, or the treacherous way Edie had turned him and all his friends in to the principal. He didn't have to think of his father heaping humiliation on top of torture, and of the devious lengths he had gone to in devising a new and better torture.

Now, it was just Ev and a football, the only two things left in life that he could trust completely.

After half an hour of throwing and catching the ball in the city park, Ev and Russ sat at a picnic table and watched cars pulling in and out of the parking lot at PDQ, the drive-in restaurant, which sat west of the highway. A car would come in and park, and when its occupants were ready to give their order, they would honk and flash their lights. Some of the less lazy ones actually got out and went inside.

Russ watched the activity from afar until Ev cleared his throat.

"What're you thinkin' about, bud? You got a heavy look on your face."

"Heavy? Boy, that's no joke. My dad about killed me after track today."

Ev raised his eyebrows. "He beat you?"

"No. But he might as well have." He went on to tell his friend about the leather harness and the railroad ties.

"Dang. Serious business," said Ev. "And you're still ready to play ball?"

Russ looked down at the ground between his feet. "Yeah," he said absently. "So what do you think of Edie Russell?"

Ev knitted his brow. "Think of her? How?"

"Aw, what do you mean how? She ratted us out to Ricks."

"Naw."

"*Naw?* Hey, blockhead! Why'd you think Ricks came and pulled her out of the torture detail and left the rest of us out there choppin''?"

Ev gave him a blank stare. "Brother, you're wrong. You think a girl that's as sweet on you as Edie would turn you in like that? Not in a million years."

"Then how do you explain her gettin' pulled and not comin' back?"

Ev thought for a moment. "Well, how should I know? But it wasn't that."

Russ stared at his friend. Ev had always seemed so much more mature than most of the kids around him, even clear back in the fifth grade. He always seemed like he had a real head on his shoulders for thinking and reading people. His denial of Edie's guilt gave Russ the first moment of doubt he had had since that afternoon. But it didn't last.

"I don't know where you come up with this, brain, but think about it: There were seven of us, and nobody else got pulled out of work detail. Only one of the seven could have known every name that was involved. You figure it out. Jeez. I thought you were s'posed to be smart."

Ev grunted. This time Russ had touched a nerve.

"Well," his friend said, "I gotta head home before I get my hide tanned. You better think about gettin' gone too. Haven't you had your tail in a crack long enough already?"

Russ nodded and stood up, not relishing the idea of going home any more than he had immediately after taking off his harness and thus releasing himself from his torture on the chain gang. "I guess. I'd just as soon stay here and sleep in the park, if you want to know the truth."

"Suit yourself," said Ev. "I've had enough trouble for one day. And hey— Buddy, I really owe you an apology."

"Apology?" said Russ. "For what?"

"Jeez! For what? For getting you in all this trouble in the first place."

Russ let one corner of his mouth smile and slapped Ev on the shoulder hard enough to make him side-step. "Don't sweat it. I'll get you back somehow."

Ev laughed as they started walking. A short while later was the most convenient turn-off for him to get back to his house, and he stopped. "Somethin' else, Russ: I'm gonna find out about Edie once and for all. I'll bet you a new pair o' jeans it wasn't her that fingered us."

Russ frowned. "You're gullible. And I'll bet you that pair of jeans and anything else you want to throw in that it was."

● ● ● ● ●

With his hands in his pockets, Russ trudged home down State Street. *Blackboard Jungle,* with Glenn Ford and Sidney Poitier, was playing tonight at the Virginia Theater, and cars were parked all up and down both sides of the street, with people filing in to get their seats for the show. A train was sitting at the depot across the street, and there were a few people milling around, embarking or disembarking. The evening light was gray, and a brisk chill had returned to the air. It felt too cold through Russ's damp clothing, but good in his lungs—and in spite of its bite, it still smelled of spring.

As he reached the railroad crossing on Locust, he heard the shrill blast of the train whistle calling for people to board. With his hands in his pockets, he lowered his head, crossed the tracks, and started down the alley behind his house.

He had a feeling it was going to be a long, cold evening, even indoors.

CHAPTER SIXTEEN

Russ reached the point in the alley that was directly behind his house and stopped. He stood staring at the back fence, which his father had painted a deep brick-red color. It looked like all of the first floor lights in the house were on, and he could see people moving around inside. It appeared that life went on as usual, while in Russ's heart the whole world had changed. He could think only of his father's torture and humiliation and how much he did not want to see him.

On a whim, he felt his back pocket, and his wallet was there, as thin as ever, but maybe thick enough for a buck or two. Pulling it out, he flopped it open, and sure enough, there were not two, but three dollar bills inside. With one last look toward the inside of his house, he continued on down the alley.

There were other places he could be this evening.

He went to Myrt's drive-in and took a seat inside. Some younger kids were already there, and all hailed the football hero, lifting Russ's spirits a little. None of them were friends of his, and most kids were a little intimidated by him, so although they said hi or waved, none of them came over, and he had the table to himself.

When shy and plain Leann Stoddard came over, who had gone to school with Russ since the second grade and waited tables here two nights a week, she smiled at him. "Wow, Russ, that was some stunt you guys pulled at the school."

"Yeah. I'd just as soon not talk about it."

She pursed her lips. "Sorry. They came down hard on ya, huh?"

"Yeah, a little. Say, Leann, you used to hang out with Edie Russell, didn't you?"

"Yeah. I still would if she hadn't turned into such a bookworm."

Russ chuckled. "So do you know anything about her dad? Somethin' wrong with him?"

"Oh, wow! You don't know? He lost his hand in an accident at the shop."

"What?" Russ tried to leap up out of his seat, but the tops of his thighs hit the underside of the table, and it shuddered against the force. He sank back down onto the red plastic seat.

"Why'd you think something was wrong?"

"Oh, somethin' that happened at school today, and somethin' my dad said to Edie one day. Said he was sorry about her dad."

"Oh." Leann sighed. "Well, you wanna order? If you're not ready, I'll come back. I gotta go wait on the squirts." She jerked her head toward the booth full of junior high students who had said hi to Russ when he came in.

"I'll have a burger and fries, I guess. And a chocolate shake."

"You got it." She started to turn away, then turned back and gave him a concerned look. "Say—are you okay?"

"Yeah, I will be. Lots on my mind, that's all."

"Okey dokey. I'll be back."

When Russ got home again, it was pitch black out. The first thing he noticed was that most of the lights were still on, and the lovely sound of homemade music emanated through the window screens. That would most likely be Doris, his seventeen-year-old sister, on the violin, and Annie, the fifteen-year-old, on the flute. They were the two most dedicated musicians in the house.

Russ couldn't help smiling. When his mother had decided she was going to have a musical family, she sure went all out. All of them, with the exception of Russ, were singers, and each of the girls played more than one instrument. Russ had lucked out only being forced into piano lessons because it was obvious from a young age that his true destiny was on a football field.

Russ's mother herself played five instruments. Her husband, on the other hand, played only the Smith and Wesson revolver, and one mean razor strap.

Having seen with some surprise, but vast relief, that his father's car wasn't in the drive, Russ went in through the front door. Doris and Annie

were sitting on the couch for their musical recital, and Russ avoided their glances and found his mother in the kitchen.

His burger and fries hadn't sated his appetite, so he glanced around to see what she had cooked.

Eleanor looked over and tried to give him a smile. "Hello, Son. Glad you're home. There's some roast beef in the fridge."

"Thanks. Where's Dad?"

"He had to go back to work. I guess he had a meeting over in Arco."

"*Arco?*" Russ repeated. "What in the world is that about?"

"Who knows? He's been pretty quiet lately. I can't get him to open up."

Too busy inventing tortures for his children, thought Russ. But he knew his mother well enough not to say it.

"You have homework?" asked his mother.

"Nope."

"Really?"

"No, I said. I guess Dad didn't tell you—I was too busy today at school to have homework assigned."

"He didn't tell me much," his mother admitted. "But Doris and Annie sure did."

Russ nodded, a derisive look coming to his face. "Yeah, big surprise there."

"All right now. You would have told on them too," reminded Eleanor.

"Bull. Because I don't care what they do."

Eleanor frowned. "James Russet, I've asked you every day to please watch your language."

"Bull?" Russ said incredulously. "That's bad language?"

"You know what it stands for."

"Yeah, but I didn't say it."

"You thought it. And you made me think it. It's almost the same thing. Come on, Son—at least for me."

"Okay, Ma." He started to turn away.

"You want the roast beef?" Her voice stopped him.

"Nah. I'm not hungry anymore."

Later, while Eleanor and some of the girls were sitting in the front room listening to *Gene Autrey's Melody Ranch* on CBS radio, Russ

heard the back door ease shut. There were subdued voices in the kitchen, where Eleanor must have stepped to greet her husband, and then the lawman's footsteps plodded down the hall. The last clear noise Russ could make out was the *click* of the latch against the strike plate as his father closed himself off from the world. Now there were two males in the Blevins home, and both of them carrying on a solitary evening.

● ● ● ● ●

Everett Morin had earned enough money from three years working at the Virginia Theater to have almost saved up enough to buy himself a car. The car he had his eye on was a midnight blue 1941 Ford that belonged to his father—a Super Deluxe Business Coupe. His father was eyeballing a new Chrysler.

In spite of the story he often told to young Isaac Thorpe to keep from being bugged by him, which was fiction only loosely based on reality, Russ really did like to go to the Virginia Theater, and he could be found there at least every other week when he wasn't working at his family's mill in Island Park—as he did much of the summer.

On Friday, they were playing the new release *Bedevilled,* starring the beautiful Anne Baxter and a new actor Russ instantly took a liking to, a man by the name of Steve Forrest. Russ had paid the full forty cent ticket price for the movie, and he even sprang for a second ticket for his friend Pete Basso.

Now, as he waited patiently for Pete to make his grand entrance, he almost wished he wouldn't. He was really starting to get into the movie, and what he and Pete had planned was going to disrupt the movie's debut in a great big way.

Earlier in the evening, long before the start of the film, Russ had pulled aside a number of younger teens and given them a nickel each. All they had to do was to go one at a time down to the exit door every five minutes or so and walk outside, then use their spent ticket to re-enter through the front. The idea was that eventually Pete Basso was going to be waiting outside that door with a package—a package it was best not to try and smuggle through the foyer, where there were too many eyes of theater employees keeping watch.

Pete would come through the open exit door as whoever the lucky kid was to open it started to go out, and he would deliver his package

nonchalantly to Russ, then go back out the exit and come back in the front door five minutes later, just another late-comer to the film.

The movie had been playing for half an hour, and the fourth kid got up and made his way down the aisle to the exit. Russ wasn't paying much attention anymore. He could hardly keep his eyes off Anne Baxter, up on the screen.

At that point, there were groans from the people in the audience, those who were unfortunate enough to be seated near the exit door and whose exasperation was starting to show because of the constant egress through the door and disruption of their movie-watching enjoyment. But this time, the kid's exit allowed the entrance of one good-looking Italian—Peter Basso.

Pete sauntered up the aisle with a brown paper bag suspended from his right hand, the top portion rolled up to leave a space inside it equal to perhaps half a gallon of air. There was a strange rustling coming from inside the bag, but Pete swung it in such a way that Russ doubted anyone else would notice. After all, the whole entrance on the scene of Pete was enough disturbance in itself.

Pete passed the bag off to Russ as he went by, then continued up the aisle, where he waited for a few minutes by the entryway, as they had planned. Then he walked down the aisle again and went out the exit—a sign to all the young accomplices that no more staged exits were called for.

Five long minutes passed, while Russ tried his best to keep his mind on the story unfolding on the screen. The excitement and anticipation of what was about to happen was too much. Even Anne Baxter could no longer keep his attention.

Soon, the entry door opened for what would be the last time in Russ and Pete's plan, and Pete strolled down the aisle and slid in front of Russ to take the seat he had saved for him.

By now, Russ was grinning so big he couldn't hide it except by putting his open hand over his chin and mouth, pretending to be intent on the movie.

Ten minutes ticked by. The audience forgot about exiting teenagers. They forgot about the strange appearance of Pete Basso, first through the exit door, then through the proper entryway. And they forgot about the

bag in Russ's hand. Anyone who had noticed it surely thought he had simply smuggled in popcorn or Cracker Jacks. It wouldn't have been the first time.

Russ took a deep breath and forced himself not to look over at Pete. Right at the point in the movie where Baxter and Forrest were running down an alley, looking for a place to hide from the police, Russ unrolled the top of the paper bag. The opening soon gaped wide. There was a moment of silence, and then hell began to break loose—or at least *something* did.

Little feathered shapes began to see moving, colored lights streaming down into the paper bag. Beady eyes looked out from the bottom, and little brains calculated chances of escape. The room was soon filled with chirping and screeching, as two dozen captive starlings, held too long in a paper bag, made their escape into a brave new world.

Startled screams and yells began to resonate around the room as freed starlings darted here and there, hitting into and momentarily clinging to walls and exit signs, and landing on the sconces all along the wall. Birds flew like miniature airplanes along the ceiling, looking for a way out into the open air. And also like airplanes, with loads of bombs to drop, some of them did what birds do best, depositing their latest digested meals at random, wherever they would land.

Soon, the startled screams began turning to panicked ones, and people started getting up and streaming up both aisles. It was the attack of the birds! Nature had come for revenge, and the starlings were only the first. Run! Flee!

Russ and Pete Basso were laughing so hard they couldn't have gotten out of their seats had they tried. The only move Russ was smart enough to make was to wad the paper bag into a ball and send it rolling along under the seats down toward the front of the theater, so the presence of the starlings could never be blamed on him and Pete.

CHAPTER SEVENTEEN

The Starling Escapade was all the news by Monday morning at school, and somehow it even made it into the *Shelley Pioneer*. By some miracle, Russ and Pete had not been implicated in it, and no one seemed to have a guess as to how the birds got into the theater in the first place. But the best people in town were scouring the theater's walls and ceiling for any breaches, and they swore to get to the bottom of it and learn how the birds made entry.

In the meantime, the theater lost an entire weekend's sales, and Ev Morin spent the weekend baiting starlings with poison and shooting them with an air rifle, then cleaning up their droppings, until by late Sunday afternoon the theater was almost back to its normal, dark, ominous self—always a little spooky when the crowds all cleared out.

Sitting in government class, Russ smiled at Ev Morin as he came through the door with his books and took his seat across the aisle. "You look beat."

"Jeez! You could say that. Maybe you coulda come down and helped me plugging birds. You're a better shot than I am."

"What would I do that for?" asked Russ, making a confused face. "Shoot! I have important things to take care of."

"Ha. Well, they're all gone now. I hope they find the hole they got in through."

"The hole?"

"Well, yeah—they think there's a hole between the wall and the roof somewhere. They've been scouring that place the whole weekend."

"Yeah, well, a *hole* might have had *something* to do with it, all right." By now, Russ was starting to have a hard time keeping the smile off his face.

Ev stared at him. He glanced around at any neighboring students who were there as early as they were. "What are you grinnin' about? You—"

Ev stopped. He gaped. He shot his eyes left and right and pursed his lips in the angry look of sudden realization. "Russ, you— *You* let those beggars in there?"

Russ let out a laugh, releasing the pressure that had been held in too long. "I never said that."

"You might as well have! What the heck would you do that for?"

"Remember when you and Spit jumped up and scared me and Wop? When you were hiding down in the shadows on the ball field?"

Ev continued to stare. A light dawned over his face. "You . . . You're still mad about *that?*"

"What are you talkin' about, Ev? I'm not mad. I'm just even."

Ev Morin tipped backward in his chair, his hands flopping down to his sides. "Son of a buck."

It became a big advantage to Russ Blevins that week being a popular student. That almost ensured that unless he actually had *wanted* to talk to either Helen James or Edie Russell, he wouldn't have to. Helen passed too close to Russ way too many times between Monday morning and Tuesday afternoon for his comfort. After her angry scolding of him the prior week, on the afternoon of the tree chopping affair, he had nothing to say to her. He was still seething inside—partly at himself, because he was still helplessly in love.

As for Edie Russell, he had seen her several times attempt to approach him to talk, but each time somebody else got to him first, or else he was able to turn and latch onto the closest student—or sometimes even a teacher—and start up a conversation that, because Russ was one of the more popular students and generally gregarious, no one seemed to think of as odd in the least.

The only person who ever questioned his sudden interest in conversation was Miss Barnhart, when Russ saw Edie coming toward him and turned into his teacher abruptly to say, "Hey, Miss Barnhart? Do you think you could spend some time going over the theme of a book with me?"

Miss Barnhart had stared at him blankly. Finally recovering, she had said, "Why certainly, Russ. What is the book?"

Like a coon in the headlights, Russ stared at her, searching his memory banks for the last book he had read. "Uh . . . *Old Bones the Wonder Horse*".

Miss Barnhart stifled a giggle. "*Old Bones the Wonder Horse?* By Mildred Pace? That's the book you want to go over the theme of?"

"Yeah."

By that time, Edie seemed to have sensed that the conversation was going to take a while, and from the corner of Russ's eye he had seen her leave.

Miss Barnhart shrugged and directed Russ to a seat. But with one glance after Edie, he put a disappointed look on his face and said, "Oh! Dang, I almost forgot. I'm going to have to do it later, ma'am. I have track right now."

And with that he was gone.

But the luck held for only so long.

On Thursday morning, a week and two days from the infamous *Day the Tree Fell,* Russ left the house before all his sisters—as was normally the case—but as was *not* normally the case, Edie Russell was standing on the corner of Park and Locust, nearly half a mile from her house, waiting for him.

Russ drew a deep breath as he saw her. His first reaction was to feign forgetting something and turn back to the house. But then he realized that he was the one in the right here, and he was tired of running and ducking her.

Taking another deep breath, he clutched his school books tighter and kept walking. He tried not to meet Edie's eyes directly as they came close together.

"Hi, Russ."

"Hi yourself."

She paused. He could feel her searching his face as he concentrated his eyes on something—or nothing—far in the distance.

He kept walking, and she fell in step beside him, having to quick-step to keep up with him.

"Do you mind if I walk with you?"

"Well, you already are."

"I know, but . . . Russ? Did I do something wrong?"

A feeling of anger and disgust welled up in Russ like he had not felt since Edie was called away on the day of the tree chopping, when he first realized who the stool pigeon was. He gritted his teeth. Even as angry as he was, being mean to other people had for so long been against his nature that he had a hard time saying anything really cross.

"Russ?" she said again, insistently.

Russ jerked to a stop and turned to face her. "Listen, Edie, everybody knows how old Charlton Heston got our names the other day. You seriously think I want to be friends with a snitch?"

Shocked, Edie stared at him. Her mouth opened, but for a moment it would form no words. *"What?"*

"Come on, you heard me."

He turned and started walking again, way too fast—in fact, the same way that used to frustrate him so badly on the rare occasions when his old man used to take him out hiking and he would spend most of the day running to keep up.

Edie caught up and grabbed his arm, making him stop and turn. Her eyes were full of tears, and her face full of hurt anger. "Russ! I didn't do what you said!"

"Oh bull. Come on! Ricks came and got you and took you out of there, and you never came back. We all had to finish chopping that tree without you. That made it pretty obvious when we got thinking about why. Why else would he only take you?"

Russ knew his face was red and full of his indignant anger. He had allowed it to flood over, and now he couldn't hold it back.

Edie almost cried right out loud, as tears welled up and spilled onto her cheeks. "You don't know anything, Russ Blevins. Not one thing!"

Her words were more cried than spoken, and saying them, she threw down her armload of books and ran across the street. It was only thanks to the attentiveness of the oncoming driver in a Ford pickup that she didn't get killed on the spot. The truck's brakes screeched as it skidded to a halt, and Edie kept on running up Park toward its juncture with Spud Alley.

Russ stood there dumbfounded, looking after Edie, while the driver of the pickup stood outside the door of his now-parked vehicle and yelled after her, berating her.

Finally, Russ got tired of the older man's mouth. "Let her alone! Jeez! I don't think she did it on purpose."

The man turned and looked at Russ, his face red. He shook his fist at him and yelled an insult, then got back in the pickup and drove away, after only killing his engine once.

Russ was still standing there when Doris and Annie caught up to him. "What in the world did you say to Edie Russell?" asked his older sister, looking down at the girl's books, then back up at Russ.

"None of your business." With that, he turned and stalked away toward the school. He might have made himself pick up Edie's books, but he didn't have to. He knew Doris or Annie would take care of that.

All the way up to the high school, feeling embarrassed and mad, Russ stared straight ahead. He refused to look to the right or left, and the three times when someone went by and honked, he simply threw his arm up in greeting without seeing who it was.

What was up with Edie? Anyone who had been there that day would know it was her that turned them all in. If she had truly done it because she remembered Russ's saw and figured he was going to get all the blame because of it, that still didn't excuse that she had turned in all of his friends, who would otherwise not have had to be punished—and especially Helen James, who hated him now because he had talked her into taking part in the plot.

But why had Edie reacted so violently? If she had only been trying to save him from taking all the punishment alone, why didn't she just tell him? It would have made everything much easier. He still wouldn't have approved of her tactics, but at least he might feel she had done it for him.

By the time Russ reached the school, he was a block in front of his sisters. He threw open the outer door and started for his first class, but suddenly he looked down the hall. He had to know something first. There was no way he could concentrate on classwork or lectures until he knew.

Russ marched straight on by his class and headed for Principal Ricks's office.

When he reached the desk of Mrs. Pryce, he stopped. She looked up at him and smiled, trying to pretend she didn't remember the events of the week before. "Why hello, Russ. May I help you?"

"Yes, ma'am. I really need to talk to Mr. Ricks."

Mrs. Pryce blinked. “Oh. My. Well, all right. I think you might be able to sneak in a few minutes if you duck in there right now. He has to make his announcements in a minute, though.”

“Okay, Mrs. Pryce. Thank you!” With a quick knock, Russ pushed open the principal’s door even as he heard the man’s voice telling him to enter.

“Good morning, Russ.” The man’s friendly face showed no sign that he even remembered the issue they had been through so recently, and which was still so strong on Russ’s mind. “What can I do for you?”

“Mr. Ricks, I really owe you a huge apology, and—”

Mr. Ricks waved a hand across the front of his face. “Nonsense, Russ. We’re square. You don’t owe me a thing but just to keep being a great student.”

Russ shook his head. “I’m sorry, sir, but I *do* owe you an apology, and I also really have to ask you something. You’re the only one who can help me.”

Mr. Ricks’s brow furrowed, and he shrugged. “Well, sit down, son. Let’s see what we can do.”

Against his will, but because the will of this Charlton Heston-eque figure of a man was more powerful than his, Russ fell into the chair that always sat right in front of the principal’s desk. Mr. Ricks eased his muscular bulk into his own chair.

“What is it you need to ask?”

“Well, sir, I feel like you might think this isn’t my place, but this is really important for me to know.”

“Why don’t you get it out, and I’ll be the judge of whether it’s your place?”

“All right. So the other students and I feel like it must be Edie Russell that squealed on everybody the other day. I mean, there’s no way anyone else could have known exactly who was there, and when you took her out partway through the day and she never had to come back and help…”

Mr. Ricks raised his head in understanding. He sighed out a breath. “I see your dilemma, Russ.” The big man clucked his tongue and turned to look out the window, right down the row of remaining cottonwoods. After a few seconds, he blew a breath out through pursed lips, turned and looked Russ square in the eye.

“I wondered if this wouldn’t become an issue, Russ, but I’m happy to tell you you’re wrong about Edie. Dead wrong.”

“Wait . . . You’re saying she didn’t turn us all in?”

Mr. Ricks shook his head, lifting and letting his broad shoulders fall. He pursed his lips again, deep in thought. He raised one big hand to massage his mouth. Finally, a determined look came over his face.

“Russ, I don’t think it’s my place to tell you very much else. This is a private matter for Edie. But I will say this: If you’re half the man I think you are, you’ll go talk to her yourself. I’m guessing that you and the others have already pretty much let her know what you believe.”

Now ashamed, Russ nodded. “Yes sir.”

“Then it’s time to make amends. What you believe could not be further from the truth. Of course, you know that until I took a certain phone call, you, Russ, were the only known suspect in that incident—you understand: because of your father’s saw you left behind. You would have been the only person called into my office if someone hadn’t called me that morning with the list of everyone’s names—including Edie’s. And you would have been the one on the hot seat to admit who helped you.”

Russ looked down, then back up.

“Oh, I know, I know: You wouldn’t have given me one name, and you would have done all the chopping by yourself. I know you, Russ. I would have done the same thing, at your age. But a phone call saved you from doing it all alone. You should be grateful.”

Russ nodded. “Yes sir,” he said again.

“You know, Russ, we all make mistakes. This isn’t something I should admit to you, but now that it’s water under the bridge, you know what I did when I was a senior?”

“No sir.”

“Well, I tipped the outhouse over on my school principal back in Indiana. And then my friends and I led thirteen cows—lucky number, you know—up to the second floor of the school, along with fifty or sixty chickens and a dozen bull snakes we had caught and were saving up in a gunny sack.”

Russ stared at Mr. Ricks. He managed to choke out, “You’re joshin’ me, right?”

"I wish I were," said Mr. Ricks with a half-grin. "But I'm as serious as the day is long. The difference is no one ever knew. I guess my friends and I are still wanted criminals back in Garry, Indiana."

Feeling shocked and impressed, all at the same time, Russ sank back in his chair with a long whistle and a quiet, "Holy moley."

Mr. Ricks nodded. "Go talk to Edie, Russ. This isn't something you should wait on."

Russ's eyes fell. "She didn't come to school."

"How do you know?" Mr. Ricks asked, after a pause.

"Because she met me by my house and tried to walk to school with me, and I accused her of giving us all up. She threw down her books and ran across the street—almost got hit by a truck."

Mr. Ricks winced. "Russ. This is going to be a first for me, in all my years of teaching and being principal. Who's your first teacher today?"

Russ told him.

"All right. I'll go talk to her, and maybe your second class too, and let them know you're on a special assignment. As for you, I want you gone—now. You get down that hill as fast as you can, and you find that little girl. I'll deny I ever said this, but you have something a lot more important to do right now than to spend an hour or two sitting in a class."

CHAPTER EIGHTEEN

It wasn't all that long ago when Russet Blevins could not have told anyone where Edie Russell lived. But that ignorance ended on the night of his triple date with Helen James, when they had dropped Edie off there.

It was a humble place—every bit as humble as any Russ had ever seen, and in about the poorest part of town imaginable.

Russ paused on the street outside. The place didn't even have an official sidewalk, and the street, such as it was, was still gravel. He looked up and down the street. Was anyone here who might see him? He didn't want to be recognized. The thought of a rumor spreading through town

that he and Edie were more than mere acquaintances at school was more than a little disturbing. But as Mr. Ricks had said, he was on assignment. He couldn't leave now.

Stepping across the dead excuse for a lawn, where patches of grass were trying to struggle for survival, Russ paused at the little porch, which was barely three feet by three, and made of warped and grayed two-by-fours. He looked up at the silver-colored metal door, whose edges were bent and bruised like someone had pried it open more than once with a crowbar. The house itself, blue and white in color, looked old and worn enough that the first stout wind might carry it away into the Land of Oz.

He stepped nervously up the two steps onto the porch, which five men of his weight might have collapsed, and soft-knuckled the door. No answer. In relief, he almost turned to go. Taking another breath, he knocked louder. Still no answer.

He looked at the fifteen-foot two-lane track in the dried mud that some twisted dictionary might have called a driveway. No cars. But that wasn't necessarily a surprise, since many women of the fifties stayed home and didn't own a car. However, there was still no one who came to his knock.

Tentatively, he reached up and turned the doorknob. He knew it wasn't the best-advised idea ever, but he had come a long way for nothing if he didn't at least try. The door was unlocked. He opened it and looked in.

To his surprise, the place wasn't dirty. Although the flooring was old and stained, it appeared to be clean, and all of the flat surfaces were likewise—clean but stained and old.

"Excuse me? Is anyone home?"

Dead silence. Contact attempted—mission aborted. Time to return to home base.

Feeling somehow unsettled, Russ turned and took the long step off the backside of the porch. It seemed safer than taking the stairs.

As he was walking back out to the street, an old man leaning on a cane in the yard of the dilapidated house next door stopped him. He seemed to have materialized out of the air, and now he was doing all he could to pollute it, puffing on a fat brown cigar.

"Yonker. Can I help you?"

Russ looked at the old man, standing in stained cotton trousers, permanently creased down the legs. He wore a white, red, and gray plaid shirt, and all his life's burdens seemed to be weighing his entire face down into his jaw. Even his eyes were slumping down, and the rims inside his lower eyelids showed dark red. His once-bright blue eyes were dull now with age.

"Yeah, maybe. I came here to see the girl who lives here—Edie."

"Gone."

"Gone? Where?"

"Off t' school."

Russ smiled patiently. "Oh, well, she changed her mind and didn't go. I was hoping she came back here."

"No-o. Not here. Mum's gone too, gone off t' find work."

"Her mom's looking for work?"

"Well, yessir. Since Frank's accident, they're gonna lose this place if she don't." The old man scanned the worn-out house from roof to ground and gave out with a chuckle before reaching up to draw the cigar out of his mouth and join his hands on top of the cane. "I know it don't look like much, yonker, but to us folks over here, it's all the castle we got."

"Frank's accident—you mean cutting off his hand?"

"Shoot! Ol' Frank's a tough bird, son. Lose a hand!" He scoffed. "He'd a come back from that. Nope, now I'm talkin' about the car accident."

"Car accident?"

"Yeah! Oh, you didn't hear? The car accident he was in last week in Salt Lake. I'm doubtin' he'll ever be the same."

"Last week?"

"Yep. Yep. Big truck hit 'im while he was tryin' to get across the road in his pickup. Pickup's gone. Both legs broke. Mebbe his back, too. Bad stuff, son. Bad stuff. Well, I better round up the dog," the old man said at last, turning his head with the excruciating slowness of a tortoise to scan the street. "Bud! Bud, come on back now."

"Thank you, sir," said Russ, and as he turned away he saw an ancient yellow lab with a gray face and worn-out, shedding coat, ambling across the street on sore feet, keeping his nose toward the old man.

He had to get out of here. This place depressed him. He thought of his own house, and then he thought of the huge, immaculate James residence. There certainly were no equities in this life.

Hands in his pockets, Russ wandered away. He couldn't help but look back toward Edie's old house three times before he turned the corner and ended up on the highway coming back into town. His head was reeling, and he didn't want to think about why. Edie had been called away and never made to come back to the tree-chopping, all right. But the reason was far from what he and the others had believed.

He had to find that girl. He had to try and tell her how sorry he was. But he had no idea where to go.

Russ found himself back at the school. He thought about going to see Mr. Ricks again. But the principal had better things to do. And anyway, Russ was too ashamed. He had been such a fool.

The principal had sure been right about one thing: Russ had better things to do than sit in class that day. But sit there he did, all while his mind wandered far, far away. And he looked for Edie Russell in the hallways every time he came out of a class, but she was never there.

When school let out, Russ was out on the track, scanning for Edie. She wasn't there either. But Helen was.

From across the field he watched her. It was the first time since being chewed out by her that he had allowed his eyes to remain on the girl for any length of time. And why? Everyone got angry sometimes. Everyone lost their cool and blew their stack. Was he so proud that he couldn't forgive her? After all the years he had been in love with this girl? It all seemed pretty childish now.

But what about Helen? She hadn't made any move to talk to him either. Was she still angry with him for pulling her into the plot to take down the tree? If so, he could deal with that. But one thing was sure: He had to know. He had just three weeks left before school let out, and then he would be headed for Island Park, to work away the summer. If he didn't find out soon, by fall she could well be someone else's girl.

With a new feeling of resolution, he started across the grass, now beautiful green with May.

Bobbie Ketchum poked Helen in the ribs the moment she saw Russ marching their way. She and Lonna both turned alongside Helen, forming an unbreachable wall. But then Russ saw Helen's lips move, and momentarily both girls drifted away.

Russ walked right up to Helen and stopped, with only three feet of space between their noses. "Helen, I need to talk to you."

She searched his eyes. Hers were noncommittal. "Okay."

"I'm sorry for what happened. I should have listened to you. If I have to, I'll buy you a new poodle skirt. I'll do anything you ask. I just don't want us to be enemies."

Helen stared, caught off-guard.

"Okay?"

Her eyes shot to left and right, as if she were looking for a place to run. "Umm . . . Hey, it's all right, Russ. I'm sorry, too." Her smile was small, tentative—but it was a smile, nonetheless.

"I have to tell you something else too. I chewed Edie out this morning about giving us all up."

Helen's face whitened. "What did she say?"

"She didn't come right out and deny it. But she threw down her books on the grass and told me I didn't know what I was talking about." Russ scanned around, noticing several people looking at them. "Hey, can we go for a walk real quick?"

"Sure. Where?"

"I don't know—down the canal?"

She nodded and started walking that way. She didn't even give her friends a backward glance.

When they were up on the canal bank, Russ went on, telling her about his visit to the principal's office, and then out to Edie's house. "I don't know who it was, Helen, but it wasn't Edie who turned us all in."

Helen stared at the ground as she walked. "I feel like a fool," she said. "I was so sure."

"Yeah, me too. It seemed pretty obvious."

"Do you have any idea who it was then?"

"Well, not from Ricks, I don't. And I don't think he'd tell me in a million years. What about Bobbie? Are you sure she's cool?"

"*Bobbie?*" Helen sounded almost indignant. "Yes! She would never do anything like that."

"Well, sorry. I just don't . . ."

"Don't what?"

"Well, I know Ev and Spit and Wop wouldn't have done it. So who did?"

"You sound pretty sure of them. How do you know?" She looked in his eyes, then suddenly threw her arms down in disgust. "Oh, for heaven's sake! Why are we even talking about this? Who cares? Edie's father lost his hand, and now he's been in that terrible wreck, and all we can talk about is who turned us in. It makes us sound like monsters."

Russ was silenced. She was right. He took a deep breath. "Hey, do you think . . . Is there still any way we could go do something?"

"We'll have to see, okay?" Helen's reply was as good as a kick in Russ's guts.

"All right." He wasn't going to beg—Helen or anyone else. "We'd better get back before the coach gets mad."

With that, he turned around and started walking, once again a little too fast. Helen fought to keep up, and he could tell by her silence that she could feel the change in the atmosphere. But why shouldn't there be a change? He had worked so hard to get his courage up, only to be shot down.

● ● ● ● ●

That evening, Russ ran his normal run—ten miles in the country, maybe faster than ever before. Where his fastest ten miles had been an hour and twenty minutes, this time it was closer to an hour and ten. He had good reason, and lots of energy to make him fast.

He got home almost at exactly the same time his father pulled into the driveway. Still not in the mood for any face to face time with the old man, he kept walking down the sidewalk, past the big old house at 118 West Locust, that loomed over its acre of lawn and garden like a gigantic monolith.

To his consternation, when he had gone clear to the alley across from Spud Alley, then turned to walk back to the east again on Locust, and back to its intersection with Park Avenue, there was Sheriff Arch Blevins, rounding the corner on foot.

Russ swore silently. But at that point, there was nothing else to do but keep walking.

Arch met him in front of the sidewalk leading in to the big old brick house.

"Hi, Son."

"Hi."

He couldn't meet his father's eyes. Or maybe he didn't want to.

"Hey, I found out some bad news today, thought you might want to know." Even as he said that, he turned back toward Park and started walking, and Russ kept step with him.

"Yeah, what's up?"

"Your friend Edie, I guess her dad got in a wreck down in Salt Lake last week, the day after . . . Well, the day after the tree thing."

"Yeah, I already know."

"Oh, she told you?"

"No. I went to her house, and some old man next door told me."

Arch nodded. "Well, anyway, sorry about that. She seems like a nice girl."

"Yeah, well, whatever. It's not like she means anything to me."

Arch walked in silence for a few yards. Russ could almost hear the wheels turning in his head as he sought something to say.

"Okay, well, I thought you were friends."

"Not really. She's about like Rusty the germ."

Arch didn't say anything to that. Russ didn't imagine he liked hearing it, but then he didn't care.

"How's the running been going?"

"Great."

Again, Arch nodded. They were almost up to the front sidewalk now. He jingled the keys in his pocket. As they got to the sidewalk, Russ stopped, but his father kept going a couple of steps until he realized Russ wasn't with him.

Working his mouth silently for a moment as he turned back around, his father said, "Say, after supper maybe we could drive over to the park and toss the ball around a little."

"Yeah, maybe," replied Russ. But he had no intention of going anywhere with his father, especially not to do something with him that he

would otherwise enjoy. Did the old man think he could simply toss a ball to him a few times and forget driving him down Taylor Highway like an errant slave?

After another awkward few seconds, Arch nodded again. "Well, we'll see you inside." He walked back to the driveway, turning to go to his car.

As Russ got in the house and went to the kitchen, a glance out back showed him the garage door was up. He didn't know what the old man did in there—smoking cigarettes, probably. Whatever it was, it kept him out of the house.

The sound of the toilet flushing came from the hallway, and then water running. Soon Russ's mother came out and gave him a smile. She searched his eyes.

After a moment, she walked to him. "What's wrong, Son?"

"What?"

"You seem down."

"I'm tired. I just ran ten miles."

"That's good!"

"Sure."

"Well, something else seems wrong. Are you sure everything's okay?"

"Sure, I'm sure."

Eleanor gave him a sad smile and rubbed his arm. "It's starting to seem like the men in this house don't want to have anything to do with the women."

Russ shrugged. "Hey, what are we having for supper?"

"Meatloaf and mashed potatoes," she said, smiling in hopes of getting a smile back. When he didn't give it, she hid her disappointment like a pro. "And the last of the corn I bottled last fall. I even made gingerbread." There was a time that would have made him smile, but this time he couldn't even dredge up a happy look.

"Oh, yeah, that's what I was smelling," he said. "Well, I uh . . ."

"Hey, Son?"

"Yeah?"

"It used to be when I was down I'd play 'Clair de Lune' on the piano. It's so melancholy, you know, but so pretty that it always made me feel better. I'd sure like to hear it."

"Go ahead, Mom. I like to hear you play," said Russ. "I'll be in my room." With that, he turned and made his escape down the hall.

● ● ● ● ●

The girls, who had been who-knows-where, came into the house in a big rush, and instantly the Blevins home was in an uproar. Doris was fending off accusations of being in love with somebody, a name Russ didn't catch right off, and the other girls were relentless, wanting to know all of the details. Finally, he heard the name, and it made him sit right up on the edge of the bed, which he had sworn to lie down on until called to supper.

Andy Collins! The quarterback who had replaced him! He jumped up off the bed and had almost reached his bedroom door when he stopped and stared at it. *Aw, who cared anyway? Andy Collins? So Doris couldn't do any better than that?* Well, it didn't matter anyway. Andy Collins was going to graduate in three weeks, and then he'd be off to college or somewhere. It wasn't like he was going to give Doris Blevins a second thought, not with all the girls he already had hanging all over him.

As the riot went on outside his room, Russ went back and lay down on his bed again, staring up at that ceiling that sometimes could be such a friend, and other times a hated foe.

What was going to become of his team in the fall? he wondered. Collins was leaving—unless by some shot of luck he flunked out and didn't graduate. Russ thought that with a smile. He didn't really want that to happen, but he had to face it: Collins was a great quarterback. He hadn't liked getting replaced by him, but Russ was a better halfback anyway, and the change had released him to show his real prowess on the field, which was carrying a pigskin to the end zone. Everyone knew the halfback was the backbone of the team.

So in the fall, Collins would be gone, and Johnny Boo Fabian would go to starting quarterback. Another year of jokes about the dark-skinned pretty boy with the small mouth and the deep chocolate eyes, who had whiskers on his jaw before anyone else—except of course for Russ, but

his were so light-colored that you didn't see them unless you got real close.

Jack Webber was going to be gone, too, and Tar Durbin, and Scott Christensen. Jamie Kyles, Stan Tharpe, Harrison Long. As far as seniors, those were the seven players Russ could think of right off the bat who would leave a dent in the team. And they were going to be missed. But in all reality, there were just as many good players coming up from the ranks of the sophomores, so there wasn't going to be much pain felt.

Anybody would be making a good bet on Ev Morin ending up being the new standby quarterback, and—

The call of *supper* interrupted Russ in his reverie, and he got up to go into the wild world of only son in a household full of estrogen-Americans—a precarious branch for a high school football player to perch on.

Supper was a little more subdued than Russ had expected. Doris and Annie talked about their music classes, and that made Eleanor smile. Antoinette—who was always called Toni after her starry-eyed mother realized how close her name was to that of her older sister—talked about how happy she was to finally be getting to the ripe-old age of a ninth grade girl. And eleven-year-old Kathleen sat there and smiled and ate her bottled corn, kernel by kernel. Of all of them, Kathleen was going to miss that corn the most.

After ten minutes or so, Kathleen looked across the table to where Russ was pecking at his food with the speed of a tortoise. "You're always the fastest one at the table, Russ. You sick?"

Russ tried to smile. "Naw." He looked down at his plate, realizing how much food he still had left compared to all the girls. "Just thinkin'."

"I saw Isaac Thorpe today. He got a black eye."

Russ jerked his head up. "What? How?"

"Some kids at school."

"You mean more than one? He got beat up? Who did it?"

"Slow down, Son," said Eleanor, then looked over at Kathleen. "Do you know anything else, honey? Is he all right?"

"No, I don't know anything else, not really. Only . . . He seems really sad. He didn't want to be at school."

"He talked to you?" said Russ.

"Yes!" Kathleen replied adamantly. "He always talks to me." She turned back to her mother. "He's always sad, Mom. I feel sorry for him."

Eleanor reached out and stroked her little girl's hair. "You have a big heart, Kathleen. Well, I'm sure your friend will be okay."

Kathleen looked down at her plate. "Yeah." She looked back up, her eyes brightening a little, then going thoughtful again. "He told me to tell you hi, Russ."

"Aw, jeez. Good for him."

"Don't you want him to say hi?"

"He's a germ."

"Stop it!" Kathleen said, then turned and looked at her mom. "Tell him to stop, Mom. I don't know why Ikey even likes Russ."

"Russ, you'd better listen," cautioned Eleanor. "One of these days, that little boy could be the only friend you have left."

Russ frowned at her and wrinkled his brow. "What's that supposed to mean?"

"Just . . . hush now," said Eleanor, glancing over at Arch. Her husband's attention was buried in his food, the corners of his mouth turned down. "All right, children," Eleanor said. "Let's finish up now and get these dishes put away."

With only half the food on his plate gone, Arch Blevins laid his napkin down beside it, his movements small. "Say, Russ—do you want to go throw that ball?"

Russ panicked, then came up with the excuse all parents should be happy to hear: "Naw, I'd better not. I've got a lot of schoolwork to catch up on."

Arch raised his brows and glanced over at Eleanor. She obviously had no better explanation than he did. Arch reached into his shirt pocket and slid out his pack of Chesterfields—advertised by actor Tyrone Power himself!—and a book of matches with the General Electric name emblazoned on the front. "All right."

With only those two words, Arch Blevins got up and walked through the kitchen and out the back door. He seemed to shuffle like a tired old man, not move with the spry strut of a manly forty-five-year-old.

Eleanor studied Russ for twenty seconds, and he felt it the whole time. The girls looked at him now and then as well. He could also feel

that. But not with the same intensity as from his mother. At last, he looked up. "What, Mom?"

"I think you should go after him, Russ. What's wrong? You used to beg him to play ball."

"Yeah. And he was always too busy. Now *I'm* too busy."

"Someday you might regret it," said Eleanor. "Dads don't stay around forever, you know."

"Yeah, right. You couldn't kill that old buzzard with a bomb."

"You hush!" said Eleanor. "That's my husband out there."

"Yeah. And what a husband," said Russ. With that, he got up, leaving at least a fourth of his food un-eaten, and headed for the hall.

"You get back here right now, young man. Russ!"

But he was already down the hall and shutting the door to his room. He heard her house slippers come tromping down the hall after him. At his door, she hesitated. And then, after half a minute of tense waiting, the footsteps retreated, and the house was still.

CHAPTER NINETEEN

Russ didn't have any homework, of course. He simply didn't want to give in to his dad. It would have been tantamount to consorting with the enemy.

The first moment he thought he could get away with it, after he had been in his room for over half an hour and no one had come knocking on his door, he slid the window sash up and dropped out of it into the soft, lush grass of his father's perfectly groomed yard. Going along the house, he made his way to the red cedar basket weave fence dividing their property from that of the big old house next door. With one last glance at the house, he leaped the fence, then made his way along on the other side, right at the edge of the neighbor's garden, reached the sidewalk, and turned north.

He had no idea where he was going, but he sure wasn't going to stay home.

Of all the places Russ could have ended up, he finally landed at the city library, for this was the one night in the week that they stayed open longer—for bored people like him. Not many who didn't know Russ very well would ever have guessed it, and many who *thought* they knew him well would have been shocked too, but he was actually a big fan of books and libraries. It wasn't something he liked to advertise. It wasn't part of the whole aura of being a star football player.

But the truth was that Russ loved the peace he found in the library. He loved the smell of the books, both the brand-new books, and the sweet smell of the glue, and the old books with skin oils embedded in them, and sometimes the scent of tobacco smoke, or the aromas the aging acids used in the process of making paper gave to the brittle, yellowing pages. He liked browsing the new Westerns, or even the old ones by iconic authors like Owen Wister.

But, truth be known, the biggest thing that drew Russ into the Shelley Public Library that evening wasn't the books at all. It was seeing Helen James's Chrysler Imperial parked outside.

Upon opening the door, the first person in the little room who registered on Russ was Helen. She sat primly in a white cashmere sweater and what appeared to be a new baby-blue poodle skirt, and her saddle oxfords, the white portions bleached to perfection because no self-respecting girl of the fifties would ever have allowed the white on her saddle shoes to turn gray. Her eyes were glued in a book.

Russ looked right past the librarian. If she had disappeared five minutes later, he could not have told the police one single thing about her looks. He felt kind of ashamed of himself as he sauntered toward Helen's table, because the only reason he was even in the area was a decision as he got a couple of blocks away from home to go back to Edie Russell's house and see if she had come home yet. He really did want to apologize to her for his erroneous accusation. Somehow, he had to make it better.

But the temptation of seeing Helen's car outside stomped on his magnanimous plans of making amends with Edie, in exchange for the

thought of sharing even a minute or two with the girl he was helplessly in love with.

As he was coming up to the other side of her table, Helen glanced up. Her smile would have made him cross a bed of coals. "Oh, hi, Russ! What in the world are you doing here?"

"Oh, I like to come down here sometimes and browse."

"Oh, really." She looked at him askance. "Since when? I've been coming here for years, and I've never seen you."

He grinned. "Okay, fine. I saw your car outside."

Helen laughed. "Well, at least you can be trapped into honesty."

"Hey! That's not really fair. I would have admitted it on my own—eventually. Besides, the truth is I *do* like it here. I may not come in here as much as you, but I come in when I can. So what's that you're reading?"

She turned the cover up so he could see it, but then told him anyway: "It's called *Another Time,* by W. H. Auden. It's a book of poetry. They're terrific."

"Yeah? Is it new?"

"No, it came out in 1940, right before the War. I think you'd like it."

"Sure. I'd like it if you read it to me." He grinned, but her dubious expression made him wonder if he scored any points or if she only believed him a flatterer. "Hey! You want to go for a drive?" he asked.

"Did you bring your car?"

Russ shrugged. "Well, actually, no. I meant in your car."

"Oh, I see how it is."

Without an invitation, Russ pulled out a chair and sat down on it the wrong way. Somehow, he felt safer having the back of the chair as a shield between him and Helen, a shield to keep from having his pride stomped on.

"Say, Helen, I've been thinking about something."

"Oh, yeah?"

"Yeah. You know, with my first name and your last name being the same name, I think we were destined to be together. I think you should go to the prom with me."

When the whole connection, and Russ's twisted logic, hit her, Helen laughed, making her eyes sparkle. She set her book down on its pages,

and Russ, trying to lighten the mood, nodded at it. "I hear that's not good for a book."

"Is that what you hear?"

He nodded. "So what about the prom? Come on. I'll treat you like a queen."

"Well, I'm flattered, Russ, but aren't you asking a little late? I mean, the prom is next week."

"Oh, sure, I know. I just . . . I got busy and forgot to ask."

"Now I see how I rate!"

Russ felt his face turn red. "Well, I've had some things going on, and . . ."

"Yeah, like big plans to take down helpless, innocent trees, turning starlings loose in theaters—that kind of stuff?"

"What?" Russ whipped his eyes back and forth and leaned in closer to Helen. "Where did you hear that?"

"We girls have our ways. Don't underestimate a woman's intuition."

"Nobody's supposed to know about that."

"Uh-huh. Well, you should be careful who you choose for an accomplice."

"What? Oh, man. That dang Wop."

She nodded with a suddenly informed look. "Oh! So *he* was the other one!"

"Wait—you didn't get that from Pete?"

"No. But I sure got you to admit who helped you!"

After looking at Russ for a moment, Helen burst out laughing. Russ couldn't help but join her. "Well, I guess that leaves the kids I paid to go out the exit door then."

Helen smiled, flashing her beautiful white teeth. "Yes, I guess it does. One of them happened to be Dottie Pearson's little brother—and Dottie happens to sit by me in speech class. *And* has those famous loose lips that sink ships. So you see, you can run, but you can never hide."

Again, Russ laughed. "Oh well. Even if the cops get me, I doubt there's a law against turning starlings loose in a theater."

"Probably not. And it's even kind of funny—except for all those poor people who got . . . the people the birds—" Now it was Helen's turn to blush.

Russ laughed at her. "Yeah, I know what you're trying to say. So what about the prom?" he bulled on.

"Well, I would love to go."

Russ brightened up. "You would?"

"Yes. But Jack Webber already asked me—maybe two months ago."

Stunned, he stared at her. "You're joking, right?"

"I wish I were. But no, I'm not. And I told him yes."

Russ's heart fell. "Wow. Who asks someone to go to a dance almost three months early?"

"Well, someone who really wants someone to go with them, I suppose. And I said two, not three," she reminded him.

Russ regrouped. "Sorry—two and a half. Then what about a movie on Friday?"

Helen pursed her lips. "You're quite persistent, aren't you? You know, I *was* enjoying reading this book before you came in and interrupted me."

Russ looked down at the book, then back up at Helen. For a moment he couldn't read her eyes, but then he saw the twinkle there. "Okay. So . . . a movie?"

Helen's face went serious. "Hey, Russ, can I ask you something?"

Oh great. It was an awkward time to ask a question like that, while he was still waiting for her to tell him yes or no. Usually, this kind of question led to something unpleasant to talk about.

"Uh . . . Yeah, I guess."

"What about Edie Russell?"

"What about her?"

"Well . . . Anyone can see she's really into you."

"So?"

"So . . . Well, before I agree to go out with you, I think you should go talk to her and get all that stuff straightened out."

"Why? What does that have to do with us going out to a movie?"

"Oh, I don't know." Helen shrugged and her movement made the aroma of her perfume reach out to him across the table. Why was this girl torturing him so? "I feel unsettled about all this. I feel like it's something you need to do."

"So you're seriously turning me down?"

"No, not turning you down. I just want to know you did the right thing."

"You think I wouldn't have anyway? Shoot, Helen, the only reason I was even over on this end of town in the first place was to go find Edie. I just saw your car when I was on my way."

"Oh!" Helen searched his eyes, folding her arms, as if she had taken a chill, even with her sweater on. "Are you serious?"

"Well, yeah."

After a drawn-out silence, and an unmistakably puzzled look that took a while to fade from Helen's face, she said, "Then you should go find her. Tell me next time you see me how it goes, okay?"

Now it was once more Russ's turn to do the eye-searching. And in Helen's beautiful blue-green eyes he found no guile. She was serious. With a sigh, he stood up. The thought crossed his mind of saying something again about a date, but his pride took over. A man could only be turned down so many times before he realized a girl was not simply playing hard-to-get.

"Okay. See you later then."

He turned and started walking out of the library. When he was almost to the door, he heard Helen call his name, but he pretended not to hear as he pulled open the door and went out into the cool night air. Sticking his hands in his pockets, he frowned and looked around at the few people in the park. There were two dogs playing on the far side, making him think of his old dog, Chancy, now long-dead.

He waited there for a moment to see if Helen would follow him out. She didn't.

With a deep breath, he started off across the park toward Edie's house.

● ● ● ● ●

Inside the library, behind a shelf of novels, right where the Westerns resided that Russ would have come looking through if he had been in the library for anything other than to see Helen, Edie Russell breathed shallowly. Spellbound, she held a thin hardcover in her hands by an author named Louis L'Amour. *Guns of the Timberlands.* She hadn't even had a chance to open the cover when Russ walked through the front door, and she had been holding onto it tightly ever since. She didn't mean to listen

in on the conversation between Russ and Helen, but it couldn't really be helped. And she couldn't simply walk out and let them both know she was there.

In fact, she had been standing back there when Helen came in, but because she knew that Helen also believed she was the snitch in the tree-felling incident, she didn't step out and say hi. Among the seven people who had taken down the tree, she felt like the enemy—the accused spy in the novel who was innocent but yet had been tried and convicted by her peers.

She wondered now, however, what Helen had meant, telling Russ he needed to go talk to her, that she felt like he needed to do the "right thing." What in the world was the right thing? She couldn't even guess. Russ had told her that all of the others knew she had ratted them out. If that were true, what would he need to talk to her about now?

Pondering the whole thing made Edie think of the books she had thrown down when she was so upset by Russ. She had gone back later to look for them, but they were gone. Could Russ be trying to return them to her? That didn't seem like a good reason to walk all the way across town when he could have taken them and left them at school.

One thing was certain: Even after being accused of being a traitor, Edie still could not get Russ Blevins out of her mind. Even the sound of his voice made her heart start to pound in a way no other boy's voice ever had.

And it made her sick. How could she even like a boy who had treated her the way Russ had, when all she ever wanted was to be his friend?

More to kill time while she waited for Helen to leave than anything else, Edie opened the novel in her hands and started perusing it. It was good writing, she could see right away. Not so detailed as a Zane Grey novel, and faster-paced. It left much more to her imagination—sort of like Russ did. She smiled at the thought, but then forced herself to get angry with her own thoughts again.

She was standing there reading a passage from the book when she heard her name, spoken in a voice full of surprise—the voice of Helen James.

CHAPTER TWENTY

Edie Russell stared at Helen James. Helen stared back. Although it was Helen who had uttered Edie's name, it was Edie who recovered first.

"Hi, Helen."

With a hand to her throat, Helen said, "Uh . . . Hi, Edie. Have you been here . . ." She took in a quick breath. "Of course you've been here this whole time. There's no other entrance to the library."

Edie tried to force a smile. "Yeah. I didn't mean to hear you and Russ talking. I was just looking at a book. I . . . I couldn't think of a way to leave without someone seeing me."

Helen tried to return the smile. It was the first time Edie had ever seen her looking less than confident. "Oh, well . . . I don't even know what to say." Helen gave a little, uncomfortable laugh. "Are you okay?"

"Okay?"

"Yeah. Russ told me about your dad."

"Oh." Edie's mind raced. "How did he know?"

"I think he went to Mr. Ricks and asked him about the other day. I'm really sorry, Edie. About your dad, and about Russ thinking you were the one who turned everyone in."

Again, Edie tried to force a smile. She never had been very good at faking happy expressions—or any other kind, for that matter. She wasn't meant to be an actress. "It's okay."

"Well . . ." Helen's face was still pink. She stepped closer, without warning. "Hey, Edie . . . I think Russ is going to your house right now. He really wants to talk to you. This whole thing is tearing him up."

"You think so? Why would he care?"

Helen smiled. She was beginning to look like her old, collected self. "He thinks a lot of you."

"He does?"

"Well, sure he does! How could he not?"

Edie gave another little smile. "I don't know. Pretty easy, I guess. It's not like I'm one of the popular girls, like you."

Helen pursed her lips, looking at Edie with a certain sadness in her eyes. "Hey! You stop that. Edie, you're beautiful! Now if I were you I'd go run after him. He's got to go home sometime, you know—if you don't hurry, you might miss him."

Edie took a faltering step toward Helen. Suddenly, she reached out and threw her arms around her, making Helen drop her poetry book on the floor.

"Oh, sorry!" said Edie. "I'm a klutz."

"No you're not a klutz," said Helen, in turn. And she leaned close and returned the embrace Edie had offered, only for a few seconds longer. "Now go on and catch that boy," she admonished.

Edie felt tears come into her eyes, and she tried to blink them away as she started past Helen, book still in hand. "Oh! I almost forgot." As she started back over to replace the book, Helen took it out of her hand.

"You go on. I'll take care of that."

Russ Blevins didn't have a clue what to say to Mrs. Russell. He was disappointed when she answered his knock at her door only to tell him Edie wasn't there. But now he felt like he should say *something.* He searched his mind for something his father would have said, not remembering that he was supposed to have no respect for his father right now.

"I was sure sorry to hear about your husband, Mrs. Russell."

Dark-haired Lorna Russell had a slightly up-turned nose and large, dark eyes like her daughter. Also like Edie, she wore eyeglasses. Her mode of dress that evening was a charcoal-gray jumper over a pink, neck-hugging blouse, but she had ditched whatever shoes she had worn that day in favor of some comfortable gray sandals. In spite of the outfit, and her overall attractive appearance, she looked worn-out, and worn-down.

"Thank you, Russ. I really appreciate it."

"Is he home yet?"

"No, they were only able to take him as far as the hospital in Blackfoot, so he could be as close to us as possible. He's hurt way too bad to come home right away."

Russ's heart sank. He didn't intend to be obvious, but he couldn't help glancing around the place once more. The Russells weren't well-off. How were they going to make it with their bread-winner crippled?

Lorna Russell gave a little laugh, following Russ's glance about the place. "I know, I know. It isn't much. Say—do you want to come in? I don't know when Edie will be home, but since you came all this way . . ."

Russ looked about again. "No, ma'am, I guess I'd better not. I kind of left the house without telling anyone where I was going."

A surprised look came over Mrs. Russell's face. "Oh! Then I guess you had better get moving. Listen, I'll tell Edie you stopped by. That will make her happy."

"All right. Thank you, Mrs. Russell. If there's anything I can do for you, will you please call? Our phone number isn't listed—you know, because of Dad—but I think Edie might have it."

"Yes, I would think she very likely does," agreed Lorna Russell. When she smiled, it made her whole face beam, even as tired as she obviously was from her day's job-hunting activities. She was a very pretty lady.

"Good night, ma'am," said Russ, with a little wave, and then he stepped off the back side of the porch straight down onto the lawn and headed east.

Russ had not gone far before, in the gathering blue shadows, he saw the old yellow lab coming toward him, and beside it the shadow of the old man he had talked to earlier.

"Evenin', yonker," said the wrung-out, wrinkled old man as he got closer. "You find the little girl?"

"No sir."

"Not home even still?"

"No sir. But I talked to Mrs. Russell."

The old man nodded. "Pretty lady, Mrs. Russell. The girl, too. You'd oughtta hang onto that one. She'll make some lucky man a great wife one day."

Russ smiled patiently. Who did this old man think he was, anyway? Some kind of match-maker? Adults always seemed to think that being

grown up gave them the right to tell younger people how to live their lives, and how to make decisions.

"Say, what's yer name, boy?"

"I'm Russ. Russ Blevins."

"By damn. You the sheriff's boy?"

Russ smiled. "Yes sir, I guess I am."

"Huh. Well, you tell him old Tupper said hello, would you?"

"Yes sir, I sure will."

The old man stuck his hand out between them abruptly, and Russ shook it, feeling the protruding bone and thin skin of old age. He thought back on this man's humble, run-down home and wondered if he had ever amounted to anything, and how he knew his father.

"Have a good night," said Tupper in parting, smiling a nearly toothless smile. "Come on, Bud." And the old dog did a little skipping step to try and catch up to his master.

With a heavy heart, sad that he had missed Edie, Russ crossed the highway over to the east side and started jogging, afraid of what might await him at home. It was only a little over a half-mile back to the house, but for some reason it had always seemed much farther. This time, wondering where in the world Edie Russell could have gotten to, it felt farther than ever.

The last thing he wondered before he got to the house, and kicked himself for not asking, was if Lorna Russell had been able to find a job. It worried him sick to think of their family losing what few possessions they had, along with their humble home.

● ● ● ● ●

The next night, Arch Blevins didn't come home again for supper. He had called to let Eleanor know he was going out to Arco once more and probably wasn't going to be back until after dark.

Russ was still not over his treatment at his father's hands, with the leather harness and the railroad ties, but even so, it felt strange and quiet without him at the supper table.

He almost said something about it, but then it might have seemed like he cared, so he bit his tongue. Thinking about it, it seemed strange that the sheriff's absence would seem different anyway. He seldom

talked much anymore even if he was at the table. It was almost like a painted statue had taken over his chair.

It should have left a bigger dent not having Doris there, for she had begged out of supper with the family that night and gone to a friend's house to eat. But in all honesty, Russ hardly gave his oldest sister a thought.

When everyone finished eating—and Russ ate more than his share that night—Toni and Annie took their turns washing and drying the dishes, while little Kathleen turned on the first half of a two-night dramatic adaptation of *Frankenstein.*

The show had barely gotten started before Eleanor's voice from back in the kitchen by the refrigerator brought the radio drama to a screeching halt. "Kathleen, honey, can we skip the show tonight? I'm sorry. I'm just really in the mood for some music."

Russ's heart leaped. He had just sat down on the couch to listen to the show himself, and now he wished he had gone somewhere else. The mention of music, since his mother *never* had to bring it up with the girls, could mean only one thing. She was about to come begging him to play—

"Russ, dear?" His mom's silhouette filled part of the wide opening to the kitchen.

"Yeah, Mom?"

"I've really been longing to hear you play 'Clair de Lune,' sweetheart. You didn't do it the other night. Could you, just this once?" The woman turned again to Kathleen. "I'm sorry, dear. I'm sure your program will be on again a different time—or we could even read the book together—but I think it's a little scary for you."

Obviously disappointed, Kathleen hopped up without a word and turned off the radio, then went into the kitchen to be with her sisters. Russ watched her go and wondered when she had gotten to be eleven years old. She was the last little girl in the Blevins household, and now she was not so little anymore. For some reason, it made him feel sad. It was a feeling he couldn't understand and would never have admitted.

Eleanor came over and sat down beside him, reaching over to take his hand. She gave it a little shake as she looked into his eyes. "Please, Son," she said in a quiet voice. "I don't bother you about it very often."

"But, Mom, I'm . . . Why can't *you* play it? You do it better than I do anyway."

She shook his hand again, insistently. "Because I want to hear music coming from the fingers of my big football star again. Is that so wrong?"

Between the look in his mother's big, blue eyes, and the tone of her voice, he couldn't very well refuse. With a put-upon sigh, Russ pushed himself up from the couch and went over to the piano. As he sat down on the padded bench and looked at the keyboard cover, something seemed strange about things tonight. He couldn't put a finger on it. A bizarre feeling of sadness had filled his heart, and he had an unprecedented need to release it. For the life of him, he couldn't understand why.

He opened the keyboard cover and looked down at the black and white keys, so prim and proper, perfectly in their places—so unlike his own life had become, it seemed.

It had been a long time since Russ had needed sheet music to play his mother's favorite song. He started to play, and the magic happened. How could fingers and hands that were made to catch and throw a football, or to hold onto it and charge down a ballfield, be delicate enough to play a song this tender?

Russ didn't want it to happen. He could have wished for any number of other things to occur in his life. But some things simply can't be helped. For no apparent reason, after only twenty seconds or so of the wonderful notes of Debussy's masterpiece resonating through the room, Russ's eyes began to fill up with tears. He cursed himself for his childishness but kept on playing. His mom was behind him, and his sisters safely away in the kitchen. No one would ever see the unexplained tears in his eyes.

At least no one but Doris and her new best friend, Helen James.

CHAPTER TWENTY-ONE

Russ had no idea Doris and Helen had come through the front door until it was much too late, and the damage was done. He had gotten so into the piece, and his back was to the door anyway, and . . . Well, he only expected his mother to be listening and watching, and he knew he could jump up and tell her he had to use the bathroom before she could catch him with any pathetic tears in his eyes.

What in the world was wrong? He was Russ Blevins, star football player! Why would he get tears in his eyes over a silly piece of music? He prayed his mother's emotional side hadn't somehow gotten to him, that he wouldn't get worse as he grew older.

He shut his eyes as he got near the end of the song, gritting his teeth and willing the unexplained tears away. As he finished the final notes, he started to turn back toward the couch. His mother was a ways away and wouldn't be able to see the moisture in his eyes.

"Hey, Mom—"

He couldn't even finish his thought. Startled to see Doris and Helen standing mere feet away looking at him, he lunged to his feet and almost knocked the bench over backwards.

"What the heck? How long have you been there?" he asked Doris, blinking his eyes. He pointedly avoided looking at Helen.

"Long enough to hear you play for the last three or four minutes."

"Wow, Russ!" Helen cut in. "I don't even know what to say. That was beautiful!"

"Yeah, thanks," he said too hurriedly, wiping his hands on his pants out of nervousness. "Say, I need to use the restroom. I'll be right back."

Saying nothing more, and not waiting to be excused, he took off down the hall.

"Wow, that was a sudden departure," he heard Doris say, and then both girls giggled.

He tried to ease the bathroom door shut, playing it cool, then yanked on the light chain, filling the room with light and leaning in close to the mirror to look at his eyes. He let out a curse under his breath. They had seen him. *She* had seen him. What was he going to do? He couldn't hide out in the bathroom, but he wanted to. Of course then he would have the embarrassment of Helen thinking he was stuck in here having another kind of problem. But maybe it was better than facing her.

He could hear his mother and the two girls talking, although he could make out little of what was said. Their tone seemed to be one of excitement. Sure, because they had plotted together and caught him in an evil trap!

He shut his eyes and put a hand to his forehead, rubbing it vigorously. Why was Helen here? She and Doris had never even acted like they cared about each other. Now Doris was going over to her house for supper and then bringing her home?

Again, Russ cursed, feeling ashamed because he knew how much his mother hated it when he did that. "Oh, man!" he said out loud, staring in the mirror as he heard the sounds of laughter in the front room. This was a football player's suicide. Playing the piano! Tears in his eyes! He might as well take up ballet now. Or crocheting. He was going to be the laughing stock of the entire school. Helen and Doris would never let him hear the end of it, and Helen was going to spread the word through the halls of Shelley High like wildfire.

Taking a deep breath, Russ turned on the cold water and leaned down to the sink, splashing his face over and over, then roughing a towel around it as he looked in the mirror. He swore again. He was beginning to appreciate the taste of it—the cursing—like a fine cigar.

He raised his hand and ran it down over his face again, resting it over his mouth as he stared at the mirror and tried to decide what to do. Well, Helen had seen him. That was it. He was doomed. He might as well go face the hunting party now and get the hanging over with.

Swiping his face a couple more times with the towel, he flushed the toilet, for effect, then took another lung-filling breath and stepped out into the hall. When he went to the living room, his mother was still in her place on the couch, only now Helen was sitting near her, and Doris was in his father's dark brown, corduroy-covered La-Z-Boy chair.

Helen and Doris jumped up, while Eleanor rose a little more slowly, trying to act coy, as if she had had nothing to do with setting her son up to look like a dope.

Helen and Doris came to Russ in the middle of the room. Doris was first to speak. "Hey, Russ—that's the first time Helen's ever heard you play. She didn't even know you could."

Russ nodded, glancing over at Helen. "Nice."

Helen's right hand darted out, squeezing his arm. "Wow, Russ, seriously, that was beautiful. I don't even have the words for it. 'Clair de Lune!' Who doesn't love that?"

"Ha. Well, I don't love it all that much right at the moment."

"What?" shot out Doris. "What are you talking about? You've never played that piece with more passion."

"Yeah, great. So what now? I pay you two off to keep this hush-hush at school?"

"Now, Russ," Eleanor cut in, turning back as she was about to walk into the kitchen. "Be nice."

Russ frowned. Before he could say anything, Helen blurted out, "Why would you want to keep that hushed? That was incredible! My dad already idolizes you because of football, and now my mom would drop in a dead faint at your feet if she heard you play the piano. You really don't want people to know?"

This time Russ let out a sigh. He looked from the two girls to his mom, who hovered between going out and walking back into the room.

His eyes settled on Helen's. The look there wasn't quite what he had expected. He thought she would be laughing with delight, talking about how the big, strong football player was only a little girlie boy after all. But she wasn't. She was gazing at him with . . . He didn't know how to describe the look in her eyes, but it most certainly was not one of disdain.

He looked imploringly at Helen. "Hey, seriously, you've gotta keep this out of the school, okay? I'll do whatever you ask."

"Anything?" asked Helen.

"Yes. Well . . . I think, anything." The look in Helen's eyes gave him pause. "But I don't have much money, if that's what you're thinking."

Helen and Doris laughed with glee. He didn't know if they thought he was trying to be funny, or if they still couldn't get over the ammunition they had against him now. It sort of made him wonder, though, why Doris had never turned on him before and spread the word about this through the school. She could have destroyed his tough guy reputation years ago.

"So, Russ, I do have something to ask you, since you said 'anything'." Helen's blue-green eyes were melting into Russ's. He had never seen her look at him quite like this before.

"Okay, fine. What?"

"Can you play other songs?"

"Well . . . Yeah, sure."

"Do you know Beethoven?"

Russ glanced helplessly toward the kitchen only to see that his mother, who should have been his supporter, had vanished.

"Yeah. Not as good as 'Clair de Lune'."

"That's okay. I love two other songs, both by Beethoven: 'Für Elise' and 'Moonlight Sonata'. I would be *so* happy if you can play those."

Russ was still trying to get used to the look in Helen's eyes. Was it real? There was a new light there, a light that . . . If she had looked at him like this years ago, he might have invited her over before!

"Are you for real?"

"What do you mean?"

"Why're you wanting me to do this? I feel like a big fool, you know."

"A fool!" Helen looked astounded. "Russ! Do you know how many people would *die* to be able to play the piano like you? I'm not joking. You were stupendous. *Please?* I'll do anything you want."

Russ laughed. "Wait, that was my line."

"Okay, but I'm turning it around. Please? For me?" She reached out and touched his arm again, and it seemed like electricity came right through his skin.

"You know, Doris can probably play those two pieces way better than I can. Or my mom."

Helen pursed her lips, turning her head a little to the side but keeping her eyes glued to his. "But I want *you* to do it. Come on. Just this once."

Russ realized it took more stamina to get through a tense game against the Rigby Trojans than it did to last through this grueling session of pleading with Helen James. He sighed and looked at Doris, who, in spite of her part in trapping him tonight, had always been very close to him. His sister gave him a warm smile. “You can do it, Russ. It’s time for you to let the world know you can do more than play football.”

So Russ went and opened up the piano bench, and digging around for a while he found his mother’s book of Beethoven, then set it up on the piano’s music stand. Knowing he was doomed, that there was no way out now, he sighed and began to play. And in his own defense, he put his heart into both pieces. That was the only way he knew how to do something.

When he finished “Moonlight Sonata,” he closed the book and let out another long sigh, staring at the closed book. “There. You happy now?”

He turned to look at Helen James, and her eyes were full of tears. He wasn’t the only one! She tilted her head to one side as a smile came to her closed mouth, and she gave him a quick nod. By the look on her face, he guessed she couldn’t speak.

By the time Helen James drove away that night, Russ’s fingers were tired. She had broken her promise and kept asking him for more and more music, getting him to play “The Entertainer,” “Somewhere Over the Rainbow,” “Blue Moon,” “Dancing in the Dark,” and a dozen other well-known melodies from the Thirties and Forties.

When she was leaving, way after everyone’s bedtime, she did something strange. Instead of the normal salute or wave Russ would normally have gotten, Helen held out her hand, like she wanted to shake.

Russ looked down at it and almost laughed, having grown pretty comfortable with her by now. But there was no laughing in Helen’s eyes. He reached out and took her hand, trying to shake it like he would have shaken that of a man. Helen waited through the brusque “shaking” part, holding on like a bulldog—or like one very determined girl.

As she was holding his hand between them, she gave him that look that made him weak in the knees and said, “Russ, I can’t tell you how much I enjoyed the evening. Will you let me come back and hear you again?”

With the look she was giving him, he couldn't have said no. The devil himself couldn't have!

"Sure, Helen. That'd be nice."

And then she said goodbye to Doris, Eleanor, and the other girls, and was gone, and Russ stood there at the door with wobbly knees and watched her until her car wheeled around, drove down to Locust, then turned left and vanished past the big brick house on the corner.

Russ turned around, and Doris was watching him with a mischievous grin. "Wow, Russ. It looks like you've got yourself a girlfriend."

CHAPTER TWENTY-TWO

The next day Edie Russell made it back to school. Russ walked into English class, and there she was, way at the back of the room where his own desk could have been before he finagled his way up to the front in order to avoid sitting by her.

There were only five other people in the class. Russ barely even noticed who they were. With a deep breath to help him get his nerve, he set his books down on his desk and walked straight back to Edie. She was looking down at her books, but as he drew close, she looked up. Their eyes caught and held.

"Hi."

The girl looked at him uncertainly. "Hi, Russ."

Hating the sudden pounding of his heart, Russ threw a quick glance around. Then he looked back down at Edie, who was glued to the seat of her desk. "Hey, are you doing okay?"

"Sure. I'm fine."

Russ knew this was going nowhere. He didn't even know how to go on. He glanced up at the clock. There were still seven more minutes before class would start.

"Hey, I don't suppose you could come outside for a second, could you?"

Edie threw a quick look around. “Uh, yeah, sure.” She pushed up from her desk, and as Russ walked toward the exit door, too hurriedly, she tried to keep pace with him. In the hall, there was a general clamor now as the later-arriving students tried to beat the tardy bell to their classes.

Outside, by the front brick wall, Russ self-consciously tried to figure out a way to talk to Edie without drawing attention to their being together. He sure didn’t intend on starting any rumors around the school about something going on between him and Edie.

“So hey, uh . . . I have to apologize to you, Edie.” He had to throw this right out. There was little time anyway, and it needed to be said.

“Apologize?”

Girls couldn’t make anything easy. “Yeah, about thinking you snitched on us. I know you didn’t do it.”

Edie smiled shyly. “Hey, Russ, you don’t have to say anything else.”

“No, I do! I—”

Edie reached out, seeming bolder than ever before, and laid her fingers on his arm. “Please. Russ, I was in the library the night before last, so I need to apologize too.”

Russ stared at her, trying to process what she meant.

“I’m sorry. I wasn’t trying to listen in. I was only there looking for some new books when you came in. Helen didn’t even know I was there ’til after you were gone.”

“Wait. Now what? You were there when . . . You heard me talking to Helen?” As the truth hit home, Russ didn’t know whether to be elated, or offended that she hadn’t let him know this sooner. He had spent two nights and a day being sick with worry about talking to her. But he might also have been horrified. What had he said to Helen that could have sounded really bad to Edie?

“I did,” Edie replied. “I should have phoned you. But I was . . . I was embarrassed. And yesterday we went down to see my dad, so I didn’t make it to school.”

Russ nodded. “I know. I looked for you.”

“Sorry. I should have found a way to say something.”

Russ was feeling extremely relieved. “Don’t even apologize. Come on! I’m the one trying to say he’s sorry.”

"You really don't have to. After I thought about it, it was pretty obvious why you would have thought I turned you in."

"Yeah. But I should have known you good enough to know you wouldn't ever do something like that."

"It's okay. Really."

Russ nodded. "So . . . what about your dad? Is he doing okay?"

"He's hurt pretty bad," she said with a sober expression. "They aren't sure yet if he'll be able to walk."

"Able to— To *walk?* You mean *ever?"*

Her shoulders bunched upward. "They don't know. He might."

"Yeah, but . . . Wow. I'm really sorry, Edie. I can't even imagine. What are you and your mom gonna do? How will you make your house payment and everything?"

"Don't worry. Mom already got a phone call this morning before I left for school. I think she might have a job as a waitress."

"A waitress! Wow. I don't think they make a lot, do they?"

"I'm sure we'll be okay. Hey, we'd better get into class, huh?"

Shaken back to reality, Russ realized how late it must be now. "Yeah, I guess we better. I'll talk to you later, okay?"

Russ caught her hopeful look as they turned to go back in the school. "Yeah, okay. Later."

As they got to the classroom door, which was already closed, he opened it and started in, then thought better of it and stood aside to let her go first. He realized right then he didn't care what the other students thought. His mother had taught him to be a gentleman, and he was going to be a gentleman.

● ● ● ● ●

When school was out that afternoon, Russ headed for the track. He hadn't made it twenty feet from the door before Edie accosted him. "Hi, Russ."

His heart seemed to skip a beat. Deep inside, his first reaction was worry that he had been too nice to Edie. Was she going to start hanging around and be a germ like Isaac Thorpe now? He chided himself. Was he becoming that big of a jerk?

"Hello, Edie."

"You going to run?" she asked.

A germ! The thought crossed his mind again, but of course he wouldn't let on. What did she think he was going to do, go stand on his head?

"Yeah, it's track."

Blushing, Edie laughed. "Yeah, right. That was dumb."

He didn't reply. He couldn't deny that it wasn't the smartest thing she could have said. "Hey, did you get your books?"

"My books?"

"Yeah. The books you . . . You know, when you stopped me on the corner the other day . . . You know, the books you . . ."

Edie saved him from his embarrassment by turning it back on herself. "Oh, yeah! Yes, I did. Thanks for asking. That was really stupid of me. I just . . . What you said just kind of hurt me."

Russ nodded. He started to say he was sorry, but she raised a finger in mild warning, and he laughed. "Yeah, okay. But I'm still sorry!"

She returned the laugh. "Well, I'm going to be on the bleachers reading my new book if you get bored and want somebody to talk to." She said it with a wink, but he sensed a hopefulness in her as well. The wink was something new for Edie. Somehow, it made her seem cuter than she already was.

"All right. Well, have fun."

Russ ran the track with the feeling that Edie was watching his every lap. He burned it up, turning in some very good times, as good as any he had done yet that year, and better than most. He didn't know why he cared. But something made him feel like he had to live up to her expectations. He had already let little Isaac down, and even as relieved as he was not to have him hanging around anymore, another part of him regretted not being nicer to him when he had the chance.

When the team was released, and the other runners and jumpers had cleared the field, Russ kept running. Of course. That was what he did. It was who he was. He was well aware that he was the only one still training, and that Edie was the only one on the bleachers. He had said hi to Helen when he first saw her, as he rounded the far end of the track and met her with her friends. But he didn't stop to chat with her, and when he realized on his next round that she had departed practice early, he wondered if the hurt he had detected in her eyes the first time might have

been real. But he couldn't give up any more of his training time for her, not if he was going to live up to everyone's expectations on the football field in the fall. It was as simple as that.

Russ ran another hard three miles after everyone was gone. When he was finished, he started at a fast walk one last time around.

From the corner of his eye, on the far side of the track, he saw Edie coming down off the bleachers. He thought about picking up his pace, but for two reasons he didn't. One, he was plain tuckered out. And two, for some reason he suddenly thought it wouldn't be all that bad having someone to walk the track with him a couple more times, assuming she wanted to.

He didn't have to slow down much for Edie. By the time he came all the way around, she was there at the track's edge. "Want some company?"

Inside, he said , *Sure, ya germ.* Out loud, trying to glance as casually at Edie as possible, he said, "Sure, I guess it'd be all right."

She got on the track and started walking with him, and he found himself slowing down to meet her pace. They walked in silence halfway around the track before she said, "Hey, Russ?"

"Yeah?"

She looked thoughtful for a moment, then laughed. "Oh, never mind."

He looked down at her. It was remarkable how much her slightly turned-up nose looked like her mom's. In fact, most things about her looked like her mom. He guessed it was only in her lack of self-confidence that she didn't resemble her.

"Hey, you can't start saying something and then stop. Come on, what were you gonna say?"

"Oh, it was dumb." She pulled her books up to her chest, hugging them like armor.

He walked for a moment. "Hey, what's the new book you said you're reading?"

"It's by a writer named L'Amour. It's French for 'Love'. The book is called *Guns of the Timberlands.* It's actually pretty good."

"Oh yeah?"

"Yeah."

They walked another hundred yards in silence. He looked over a couple of times, and both times she had a little smile tugging at the corners of her mouth.

He came to a stop and looked at her. She didn't realize for a few more steps that he had stopped, and then she turned, still hugging her armload of books.

They stared at each other for a few seconds. He suddenly didn't know what he had meant to say. There was a look about Edie that had caught him by the tongue.

"It's really bugging you, isn't it?" she said, turning her head a little to the side.

"Huh?"

"What I was going to say."

Russ laughed. "It's that obvious, huh?"

"Yep."

"Okay, fine. You gonna tell me?"

"Okay. But stop looking at me like that!" She giggled. Russ couldn't help laughing with her.

"So I feel so dumb saying this, but I already told you I heard you talking to Helen."

"Yeah?"

"Well, I heard your silly thing about how your first name is James and her last name is James, so you're kind of meant to be."

Russ wasn't the type to blush, but he felt his neck grow hot. "Oh, man! You heard that?"

She giggled again. "I did."

"Okay, now I look like a total dope, huh?"

"No. Well . . . Okay, it is kind of silly—but cute." She hurried on before either of them could say anything to make her chicken out. "So that night when I told my mom about it, she said if that's true, then because your middle name is Russet, and my last name is Russell, that might make us a good match too."

Rendered speechless, Russ stared at her. Although not normally at a loss for words, he was too cautious to make a reply.

"I know!" Edie said. "She was just being silly too. Sorry, I guess it wasn't funny."

Russ found his laugh. "No, it was pretty funny. Okay, yeah. You got me. That was pretty dumb. It's not like a girl like Helen would ever go for a meathead like me anyway."

Edie gave him a close-mouthed smile. "I don't think you're a meathead."

With a chuckle, he said, "Well, thanks. But to a rich girl like that, I'm pretty much a nobody."

"I sure don't think you are."

Russ thought, *Yeah, but you're dirt poor. I probably seem like a king to you!* But of course he would never say it.

A bizarre thought came to Russ. If he had had more time to think about it, he would have kept it to himself, but on impulse he said, "Hey, Edie."

"Yeah?"

"I guess somebody asked you to the junior prom a long time ago, huh?"

She stared at him, a rabbit caught out on the lawn by a powerful flashlight beam. "What?"

"Aw, come on! You heard me. Who are you going to the prom with?"

She shrugged, casting her eyes downward. "Oh, I'm not really into that kind of stuff."

Russ studied her for a moment, his heart starting to pound. What was he doing?

"So . . . You're not going?"

"No, not really. I'll probably be pretty busy that night, I imagine."

Russ's better judgment told him to take this gift she offered and run with it—walk away and cool his muscles the rest of the way off and get his better senses back about him. But his better judgment failed to convince him.

"Well, if you had a date, would it be anything you'd ever want to do?"

"I don't know. I'm not really much of a dancer."

"Really?" *Walk, you idiot! Walk!*

Edie stared at Russ. He couldn't find a word for the look on her face . . . Fearful? Hopeful? Whatever it was, it made him go on. His little

guardian angel was trying to grab onto the hair on the back of his head and yank him backward, but he had a crewcut. It must have been impossible to get hold of it.

"Well, if you think about it and decide later that you're not doing anything that night, I wouldn't mind dropping by down there. You know, just to see what's shakin'. Prob'ly a dumb idea, though."

Edie studied him. "Russ . . . You mean like, me and you? At the prom?"

"Well, yeah. I was only thinking out loud." Now he felt like a real fool. He had lost his mind!

"Russ, I would do anything to go to the prom with you."

"You know, it wouldn't be like we're going steady or something, right? I mean, it's only a dance and all."

Disappointment seeped into her eyes. She looked down at her books, then quickly back up. "Helen won't go with you, huh?"

A kick to the belly. He cursed in his head. "Well, yeah, I guess she's going with Jack Webber already."

Edie pursed her lips and nodded. The look in her eyes was almost sad. But her voice hid it. "Oh, sure! I admit, I heard her say that. Yeah, I understand. So we can go hang out if you want. Just friends. That would be great."

"All right," said Russ with a smile. "Well, I'd better get cleaned up. I'll see you tomorrow, I guess."

"See you tomorrow." If Russ didn't know better, he would have said Edie was floating across the school lawn toward home, not walking.

When he was nearly to the corner where he would turn on the final stretch home, knowing he would have to break the news to his mother tonight about his stupid idea to go to prom, he was thinking about both Edie and Helen. It was sure going to feel awkward being at the prom with Edie while Helen was dancing with Jack Webber. Rotten luck!

He came around the corner and stopped. There at his front curb sat Helen's Chrysler Imperial.

CHAPTER TWENTY-THREE

More than a little nervous, and with a rampaging heart, Russ pulled open the front screen door to the house. The weather was warm enough now that the inner door was standing open.

"Hi, Russ!" Helen James had been sitting on the piano bench. She sprang up like a Jack-in-the-box.

"Oh, hi."

He looked to the left, where Doris was getting up off the couch. "How was your day, Russ?"

"Fine." Russ looked cautiously from Doris back to Helen. "How was yours?"

"Oh, fine. We were cruising around, thinking about making it to a movie."

"Oh. That'd be cool. What's playing?"

"Oh, I don't know," Doris replied, looking bored. "Helen got thinking it might be nicer to come and play some more music."

Again, Russ's eyes shot back and forth between them. "Yeah?"

"Yeah. Are you in the mood?"

"What, me? Are you serious? You trying to make a concert pianist out of me?"

Putting both of her hands together in praying fashion, Helen took a few quick steps toward him. "Please, Russ! Pretty please! I really want to hear more. You wouldn't want to break my heart, would you?"

"Hey! Easy! What's the big deal? Can't you put some records on?"

"It's not the same."

"I'm just a yokel," Russ said. "Besides, don't you have schoolwork you have to do or something?"

"No. I just want to kick back and listen to you play."

"Well . . ." Russ made the mistake of letting Helen's eyes draw his in. "All right. But only a few, okay?"

The "few" Russ had sworn he would stop at turned to a solid hour of music. Some of them were tunes Helen could sing to, and she did. Her voice was sweeter than that of any bird. By the time Helen stopped requesting music, all of the girls and his mother were sitting around the room, and Russ's heart was in his throat. Had he finally done it? Had he won the girl of his dreams? And by a stinking piano—and a sheer accident that he would have avoided if he could?

"That was fabulous, Russ," said Doris, coming close to him and putting a hand on his shoulder. "Say, you know, Helen and I had an idea."

"What's that?"

"We were playing around thinking about seeing if you wanted to go on a double date."

"Now what?" Russ's eyes dodged back and forth between the two girls.

"Yeah—like a prom date."

Russ laughed. "Yeah, right! Stop teasing!"

"Who's teasing?" replied Doris.

Russ's eyes jumped over to Helen. "But— Hey, I thought—"

The look Helen James was giving Russ back was hopeful. He was the most confused he had been in some time.

"Let's go driving, Russ," she said. "Can we?"

With his heart pounding, he said, "You mean now?"

"Sure. How about it? It's a beautiful night, isn't it?"

"Well, sure, but—"

"Then come on. Go get your letterman jacket."

Russ was a lot of things, but he was no fool. Jumping up, he went and got his jacket out of the closet. He shrugged into it as he came back into the living room. "Hey, Mom, I guess we're going for a drive." He smiled as he passed his mother and sisters and opened the front door. By that time, Doris was sitting on the arm of their father's La-Z-Boy, and it was only Helen who followed Russ to the door. He looked at his sister. "You coming?"

"Well, no, silly!" replied Doris with a laugh. "Three's a crowd. Helen meant the two of you. I'm going to stay here and bake some cookies."

Russ turned and looked at Helen. She was holding her sweater out to him in one hand, an impish smile on her face. Russ's heart beat fast and hard. Catching himself before he could look unchivalrous, he reached out and took the sweater in both hands, holding it up to help her into it.

Then he turned to his mom again. "Well, Mom, I guess I'll be back later." He never bothered to ask if it was okay.

"All right, sweetheart. Be safe."

At the car, Helen walked around to the driver's door, but when Russ followed her and opened it for her, she held her keys up to him. "Your chariot, my knight," she said with a perfect smile.

"Okay." He watched her slide over to the middle of the seat, then got down in the driver's seat and inserted the key in the ignition. Putting both hands on the wheel, he threw his shoulders back and looked around. As always, this car enthralled him.

He fired it up, checked the rearview mirror, and pulled away from the curb. His heart was beating him up. He was driving Helen James's car, with her beside him, the girl of his dreams, the drive of his dreams.

Helen reached over and hooked her right hand in the crook of his elbow. He looked down at her and took a big breath. "Okay, Helen. So what's the gag?"

"Pardon?"

"What are we really doing?"

"I don't understand."

"Okay, we're going for a drive. Right! But I'm talking about this 'double date' stuff Doris was talking about."

Helen smiled. "Well, I've been thinking about you asking me to the prom and all."

"Okay?"

"Well, you know, I really don't *have* to go with Jack Webber."

He stared at her until he realized he was drifting too far toward the curb and a line of cars parked there. Then he jerked the wheel over and straightened the car out. "Are you . . . So he really didn't ask you?"

"Oh, no! No, he really *did* ask me."

"Oh. So . . . I'm not sure where you're going with this. You told him yes, right?"

"Well, sure, but that was before *you* asked me."

A sick feeling leaked into the pit of Russ's stomach. "Okay, but . . . So what do you plan on telling Jack?"

"I was just going to say I changed my mind. I mean, if you really want to go with me, of course."

Russ sat there, mouth agape, then after a few more seconds laughed helplessly. "Well, sure I want to go with you, Helen! But . . ."

"Okay. But what?"

"Well . . . You don't just . . . You can't just—"

She gave him a little frown. "Can't just what?"

"Well, hey, Jack must have got a suit lined up by now, and flowers, and a car, and . . . I'm sure he's riding on Cloud Nine, looking forward to showing you off at the dance."

"Don't they say a girl can change her mind?"

"Yeah, but— Helen . . . I mean, wow. I'm flattered as all get-out that you want to go with me. But . . . Can you imagine the talk at school if you told Jack you changed your mind and then you and me ended up at the dance together?"

"I don't care what they say. For one thing, Jack's graduating soon. He's not going to hang around this little town. He probably won't think one more thing about it, and if he does, he'll be gone."

The sick feeling had spread all throughout Russ's body now. His heart was still pounding fast, but not in a good way.

When the tension in the car was starting to get too high, he glanced over at Helen, both of his hands gripping the wheel. Right now, he felt strange about even putting a hand on Helen—even if she wanted him to.

"He's going to think about it, all right. And he's going to hate both of us. Helen . . ."

She dropped her hand from his arm. "So are you saying you don't want to go to the prom with me anymore?"

"No! I mean . . . I *do!* I'd love to. I've dreamed of it forever. But . . . I . . . Wow, I just can't stop thinking about Jack."

"Oh, come off it, Russ. Forget about him."

"Why did you change your mind about me?" he asked.

"Come on, Russ, that isn't even fair. If you would have asked me way back when Jack did, I would have told *you* yes. Isn't that good enough?"

"Well, no! He was smart enough to ask you first. What about senior ball? Next year? Could we plan on that instead?"

"A whole year? Are you serious?"

"Well . . ."

"You are," she answered her own question. "Wow. I never expected this to happen."

Russ sighed and sank back in the seat, feeling his pulse in both of his temples. "Yeah, me neither."

His head was still whirling. What was going on? This girl had been playing hard to get with him for weeks. Now it was like he was the only eligible bachelor in the world. What had happened? He couldn't wrap his mind around this change. Was this only because she had heard him playing the piano?

"Do you want to go back to the house?" he asked. The whole atmosphere in the car had changed, and it felt very cool.

"Yeah, sure."

With a heavy heart, he wheeled around at the next intersection and made his way back to Park Avenue. He pulled up to the curb and turned to Helen. "You can come back in the house if you want."

"No, I'd better get home."

Helen wouldn't look Russ in the eyes. He felt like his dream of a lifetime was slipping away, and fast.

"What about a movie Friday? In the Falls?"

"I don't think I can. I'll have to check."

Which flat-out meant no. Russ sighed. He had been hit so hard on the football field before that he had felt sick for two hours. He had a horrible feeling that this was going to last for days.

"Hey, Helen—I'm sorry. I would really love to go to the prom with you—more than you can imagine. I just feel—"

"No. No, you're right," she said. "No, it was a silly idea."

"It wasn't silly, it just . . ." Russ couldn't think of another word to say. Opening the door, he stepped out, and Helen scooted into his place.

"I guess I'll see you at school," said Helen. Before Russ could reply, she sped off up the road, her tires spitting dust and gravel up behind.

And Russ was left to realize that all girls, no matter how much he might adore them, were out of their minds.

CHAPTER TWENTY-FOUR

Russ was on his cool-down walk the next afternoon when he saw Isaac Thorpe leave his front sidewalk and start across the street. The boy was so engrossed in where he was going that he forgot the cardinal rule to always look both ways before crossing.

Fortunately, the only thing that could have hit him this time was Russ.

"Hey, Rusty!"

The boy whirled toward him, eyes large. "Oh! Hey, Russ. How you doing?"

"Great." As Russ got closer, he saw the bruising around Isaac's face that Kathleen had told him about. "What in the world happened to you, buddy? Somebody beat you with the ugly stick?"

Isaac laughed. "Naw. It's nothin'."

Russ stopped, running his forearm across his forehead to smear the sweat away before it got to his eyes. "Nothin'? Shoot! If that's nothing, I hate to see you when you're *really* beat up. Seriously—who did that?"

The boy shrugged. "Oh, just some boys at school. We were all playin' boxing. No big deal."

On a whim, Russ reached out and cupped Isaac's shoulder with his hand. "Hey, bud. This is your old pal Russ you're talking to, remember? None of this secretive stuff, all right? If you're havin' trouble, you've gotta let me know. Another beating or two like this and you could end up in the hospital."

"Yeah, sure. Well, it's all right. I don't hang out with those guys anymore."

Russ frowned. This kid was worse than he was at that age. A thought struck him. Had Isaac completely gotten over the way he used to look up to him? If so, he should be glad. But somehow, he wasn't.

"So where you headin', anyway?"

Isaac glanced across the street at the house Russ had seen him going in before. The boy averted his eyes. "Oh, no place. Just out for a walk."

"A walk?" repeated Russ.

"Yeah, it's pretty nice out."

Russ's eyes roved around, taking in the quiet street and the soft blue-gray sky. The boy was sure right about it being nice. He glanced toward the house across the street, and one of the men was standing back in the shadows inside the screen door, watching them. The man faded back a little when he saw Russ looking. A queasy feeling came over Russ's stomach.

"Hey, Ikey," he used that nickname for the first time since hearing the strange man use it, "I still need to cool off a little bit from my run. Maybe I can go with you. I wouldn't mind some company."

Isaac's eyes flitted toward the strangers' house again, and then away. He didn't say anything for a moment, and that was when it hit Russ hard: He really *had* lost this boy. One of the few sure things in this world, and now he didn't even care about Russ anymore. He was about to tell him he would see him later and head on home. But something wouldn't let him do it.

Isaac shrugged. "Well, yeah. Sure, Russ. You could walk with me, I guess. Where you wanna go?"

Russ returned the shrug, giving Isaac's shoulder an affectionate squeeze. "Shoot, I don't know. I'm just coolin' off. You pick."

The boy scanned both ways along the street, then turned left and started walking north toward Spud Alley. Russ saw his head turn toward the strangers' house, and he looked that way too. The meaner-looking of the two men who lived there was standing partway out of the screen door now, watching after them and puffing on a cigarette. He didn't move even when he saw Russ's eyes on him.

They walked along in silence for some time. The only time Isaac said anything for the first ten minutes was when a big German shepherd came out onto the porch of a house they were passing and gazed at them as they passed. "That's one neat dog," remarked Russ.

"Yeah. Wish I had me one."

Russ laughed. "Yeah? What would you do with it?"

Looking embarrassed, Isaac shrugged. “I don’t know. Maybe train it to attack when somebody wanted a fight.”

Russ walked for a ways without saying anything. Finally, he looked down at his little friend and nudged his arm. “Hey—you wanna tell me yet what really happened? Why you got in a fight?”

“It’s all right,” said Isaac again. He was like a closed book.

They walked all the way to PDQ, and Russ bought them both an ice cream cone. Then they walked back, and when Isaac paused at Russ’s house, Russ kept going for a few steps. He turned when he realized Isaac wasn’t with him.

“Well, what’re you stopping here for?”

“Oh. I thought . . . Where *you* goin’?”

“Going to walk you home.”

Isaac’s gaze flitted toward Russ’s house. He sighed and caught up with him, sticking his hands down deep in his pockets.

When they got to the front sidewalk, Russ looked at the mysterious house across the street. Lights were on inside, but no one was in sight. Isaac had stopped.

“Well, I guess I’ll catch you later,” said the boy.

“Sure. Let’s go on in for a minute. It’s okay if I come in, right? I’ve never seen your place or met your mom and dad.”

“Uh, well . . . I don’t know if anybody’s home.”

“Oh, really?”

“Well, uh . . .” Isaac kicked the toe of his red and white sneaker at the sidewalk. “Yeah, I guess it’s okay if you come up to the door.”

Russ gave the boy a weird look, then started walking. Isaac practically ran to catch up, and at the front door he hesitated again. He turned so he was standing right in front of the door, his back to it. “Well, thanks again for lettin’ me walk with you.”

“You’re not letting me come in?”

“Well, my dad probably wouldn’t— I mean, I don’t know if anybody’s there, and—” His words ended in the obvious indecision of what to say.

Russ laughed, starting to feel a little nervous. “Hey, cool it, buddy. This is me you’re talkin’ about!” With that, he reached past Isaac and

grabbed the screen door handle, pulling it out and forcing the boy to step out of the way or be swept off the concrete stoop.

Russ looked past the boy, into the shadows of the house. He could hear a radio playing.

"Well, it sounds like your folks must be home."

"Oh, yeah! Maybe. I better get goin' then."

Russ detected a bad odor coming from the open door, the mixture of cigarette smoke, stale fried food and maybe even body odor, all melded together.

"Hey! Ike?" The yell came from deep within the guts of the house. "That you, Ike?"

Russ's eyes threw a question at his young friend.

"My brother," Isaac explained.

"Brother, huh? Maybe I could meet him. You know, I've never met any of your family, in all the time you've lived here."

Isaac laughed nervously and looked away. "Yeah, true."

"Ike!" the yell became more insistent. "That you? Don't you be lettin' anybody in this house, you hear?"

Russ looked down at Isaac again. "Wow. He sounds mad."

Isaac's face reddened. "Yeah, he's sometimes kind of grouchy," he said in a quieter voice.

In a moment, two shadows emerged back in the darkness and came forward. As they drew near, their faces got clearer. It was two young men, either a little younger than Russ or perhaps even a little older. Both looked vaguely familiar. They were rough-looking characters, one of them, apparently the older one, with a darkly whiskered face.

The whiskered one shoved the inside door wider, staring a challenge at Russ. He turned half-angry eyes to Isaac. "You ever answer when somebody talks to you? Get in here!"

Isaac did a quick step to get inside the house, and the younger brother kicked at him as he went by. The older brother kept staring at Russ, then glanced both ways out the door, as if to check for reinforcements, before nailing him again with his eyes.

"You want somethin'?"

"No, just walkin' Isaac home."

"Well, you did. Why don't you move on? We're tryin' t' listen to the radio, man. See ya."

With that, the man stepped back inside and shut the door in Russ's face, not slamming it, but definitely in a manner that told him to leave and not bother coming back.

Russ swallowed. With a rumbling feeling in his guts, he turned and cut across the ugly, uncared-for grass back to the main sidewalk. As he walked home, he was starting to think there was a lot more to Isaac wanting to be away from home and hang around at the Blevins home than Russ had ever surmised. He was going to have a lot harder time sending him away if he ever wanted to hang around with him again.

● ● ● ● ●

Supper was late that night, and Russ learned that was because his father had called to say he would be home around seven. The girls had snacked on saltine crackers and peanut butter, and now they were sitting around the living room listening to records. Bill Haley and His Comets singing "Rock Around the Clock" was the first one to greet Russ's ears. His father had been a fan of Bill Haley and his group when they were singing country music a few years earlier, but he made a point of letting everyone know what a traitor he thought the man was for selling out to Rock and Roll music.

Eleanor came in with a plate of crackers, saw Russ and gave him a big smile. "Hi, Russ! Did you have a good run?"

"Yes, ma'am. Say—I ran into Rusty, and we went for a walk."

From the corner of his eye, he saw little Kathleen turn her head toward him, and even in his peripheral vision he saw the flash of her big smile.

"You did, huh? Well, that was nice of you."

"Yeah, sure. But hey, do we know anything about his family?"

Eleanor moved her eyes around as if doing so was helping her think back. She made a facial shrug, mostly with her lips. "I don't know. Why?"

"I don't know. I just walked him back home, and a couple guys came out he said were his brothers."

"Okay?"

"Yeah, and they were pretty rough-lookin'. Talkin', too. They told me to get lost."

Eleanor frowned. "Well, that's not nice."

Russ couldn't help but laugh at the ludicrousness of that statement. "Uh . . . no, I suppose not."

After a moment of consternation, Eleanor returned his laugh. "Okay, that did sound kind of stupid, didn't it?"

"Kind of."

In retaliation for his rude agreement with her self-deprecating statement, Eleanor reached out and dabbed flour on the end of her son's nose. "You don't have to agree *that* fast."

"Rock Around the Clock" ended, and Toni put on a record the sheriff would very much have approved of: "Sixteen Tons," by the wonderful Tennessee Ernie Ford.

Russ waited for the disturbance to end of Toni walking between him and their mother before sitting back down on the couch.

In the background: *You load sixteen tons, what do you get? Another day older . . .*

"When did you say Pop's supposed to be coming home?"

"Soon, why?"

"Maybe he knows something about Ikey's brothers."

Eleanor shrugged. "Maybe." Even as she spoke, they heard gravel crunch against concrete as the car went down the drive and stopped. "Well, now you can ask him yourself."

So Russ took a deep breath and prepared to wait. But he didn't stand there long, because Eleanor herded them all to the table.

When Arch Blevins came in, the females were all sitting there primly, with an upright fork in one hand. Russ hadn't been let in on the joke, and although it crossed his mind to grab up a fork he thought better of it. He still wasn't in the mood to joke around with this master of torture devices. It had taken him long enough to be okay with being in the same room with him again.

Arch could have said thank you to his wife for waiting on supper. But apparently he was too proud, or he didn't care. He looked around the room in obvious surprise, made note of the forks in the poised hands, and sat down. Instead of the laugh Eleanor must have been hoping for, he

grabbed up his napkin and stuffed it into the front of his shirt. "Sorry to keep you all waiting."

He grabbed for a roll, where they sat in a pyramid on a platter in the center of the table, and Eleanor reached out with a remonstrative hand and placed it over his. "Remember the blessing, honey."

Arch sighed. He started to look over at Russ, who had always been the one he turned to for rescue from saying a blessing, and because he knew Russ would save them both from the long-winded ones the girls sometimes felt obliged to utter.

But Arch had felt the coolness in the air between him and his son since the tree incident, and he had yet to ask him to pray again. His eyes scanned the table and landed on Kathleen—still too young to have any great command of all the huge, convoluted words in the English dictionary.

"Kathy, will you bless the food for your mother?"

Russ caught his mother's customary frown at her husband as the girl nodded and they all bowed their heads.

"Our Father," started the girl. "Please bless our daddy. Please bless all the good people who take care of the people and animals that can't take care of themselves. Please bless all the bad people that they won't all want to be so bad. Please bless Jesus for helping us. Please bless Mama and our house. Oh—and bless the food and help it make us stronger. And . . . please bless Daddy to be happy." She ended the prayer, and for a moment the room was dead silent.

Russ waited for the interminable minute before everyone had served themselves and Arch took a huge bite of mashed potatoes. He drew in a big breath. "Hey, Pop?"

His old man looked at him, his face expressionless. One heck of a poker player.

"Yeah, Russ."

"Did you ever know anything about Isaac, the germ?"

"What?"

"No, I mean Isaac Thorpe. Sorry." He knew better than to look at Kathleen, but he had to. The girl was scowling at him. He gave her a sheepish shrug.

"What are you asking?"

"Sorry. I don't really mean about Isaac. But about his brothers. Do you know them? I walked him home tonight, and they were there—two of 'em. They looked pretty mean and told me to get lost. And I think I've seen 'em before."

For a few minutes, Russ had started to fear where he might have seen those two young men, but he didn't want to be the one to say it.

Arch gave his son a level gaze, pulling a roll in half without looking down at it. "I think you're sharp enough to answer your own question. But yes, I know both of them. Randy and Huck. They've, uh . . . spent the night with me, you might say."

CHAPTER TWENTY-FIVE

Russ ran his heart out that Saturday morning. He had skipped the movies or going out anywhere to eat the night before in preference for another run just like it. He didn't have the desire to see anyone.

When Russ was running, he usually thought of football. Or running. He pushed it so hard that there wasn't room in his head for anything else.

But this time, all he could seem to think about was Isaac Thorpe. Both of his brothers—Randy, the older one, and Huck—had spent time in his father's jail. And not only once, but on several occasions.

One of those times must have been a year or so ago, at least, because that was the last time Russ had been in there. He had paid his father a visit, and he would never forget walking past the cells and trying to avoid the stares of the inmates, most of whom seemed to be Mexican or Indian. But two of them he now remembered, and the more he thought back on it, the better he remembered them. He had always considered himself a brave young man. But Randy and Huck Thorpe made the hair stand up on the back of his neck. And there was little Isaac, living right among them. It was no wonder he never wanted to stay home.

Russ pushed thoughts of Isaac out of his head. They returned with a vengeance. He had to stop thinking. Or think about something else. But what else was there? Football . . . running . . . Isaac Thorpe . . . the two strange men across the street . . . Isaac's dirty-looking greaser brothers . . . Edie Russell . . . and Helen James.

On second thought, there was *plenty* Russ could be thinking about.

And with that in mind, he changed course and headed west . . .

In ten minutes, Russ was a block away from Helen James's house, and he slowed down to a walk. Going to a light pole, he put his hands on it and stretched his feet way back, trying to get the kinks out of his calves. He stared at the ominous white house with the rainbow-shaped driveway and thought of Helen James . . . and Jack Webber.

Maybe he should have agreed to go to the prom with her. Jack would get over it. Wouldn't he? And why should he care? Like they always said, all is fair in love and war. Jack might have done the same thing to him.

But he wasn't Jack. And besides, down in his heart he didn't believe Jack would have. Or at least he hoped not. But the fact still came down to his own pride. A man didn't take away someone else's date. That was worse than a thief in the night.

And yet he still longed to be with Helen, or at least to see her. To talk to her. To hold her. He was going to the prom with Edie Russell, but he couldn't get his mind off Helen James.

Russ was still standing there when his shocked eyes saw the front door to the James house open, and two women walked out. It was Helen and her mother, Pearl. A feeling of sickness washed into Russ's chest. He would have loved to see Helen, if he had anything to say. But even if he could think of something, he couldn't have said it with her mother there.

As he continued to stretch, he watched Helen and her mother get into the Chrysler, the older woman getting in the driver's seat this time. The car came around the driveway, and when they entered the street, to Russ's consternation, they turned his way!

He thought about turning and starting to walk east again. But they must already have seen him. He thought about looking straight ahead, pretending not to see them. But his pride was too strong.

As the beautiful beige and black automobile reached him, he froze in place, wishing he were anywhere else, and yet glad for at least a glimpse of Helen as she passed.

The heads of both women pivoted, and as they got close, the car slowed down and stopped in the street. Mrs. James waved out the window.

"Well, hello there, Russ. How are you?"

"I'm fine, ma'am. Thank you. How are you?"

"I'm doing great. Adoring this beautiful weather. I would be doing better if you would start calling me Pearl, though. Remember? That's what my friends call me."

"Uh, yes, ma'am. I . . . Yes, ma'am, Mrs. Pearl."

The woman laughed, letting her arm, clad in the soft pink lace of her dress sleeve, fall down and thump against the side of the car door. "Well, if you're going to say it like *that,* then you may as well just call me Mrs. James!"

She laughed, and Russ forced one in return. "Yes, ma'am. Sorry. Pearl."

The woman's beautiful smile almost made him drop on the spot. He could see that Helen was leaning to look past her at him, and he almost didn't dare even look over, for fear of making eye contact with her.

"Well, we're going into the Falls to do some shopping," said Pearl James. "You have a wonderful day, Russ."

"Yes, ma'am—Pearl. You too." He raised a hand in farewell, and the car rolled toward State Street, picking up speed as it went. Russ felt weak in the knees.

He had pointed his eyes forward and started walking west again when he heard gravel grind on the street behind him. Russ's heart leaped. What was that? It couldn't be the James car. He kept walking.

Soon, he heard the car going into reverse and driving backward up the street faster than his own prudent mother ever would have done. Some ten feet from him, the car slid to a halt in the loose gravel.

Russ heard a car door shut, and he forced himself to turn around. Helen was walking toward him from the far side of the car. From the corner of his eye, Russ saw Pearl James waving at him, and he waved back as she applied the gas and continued toward State Street.

Russ stood there on the sidewalk as Helen James, dressed in a deep olive green blouse and gray skirt, with a small white scarf tied at her throat, walked jauntily toward him. Her auburn hair grabbed the sunshine, pulling the majority of it down into her curls as they bounced against the green of the blouse in perfection like nothing Russ had ever seen. With all that coppery shine in her hair, Russ half-expected the sun to blink out from giving away all its light.

"Hi, Russ," said the girl as she stopped several feet away. "You doing okay?"

He stared at her, trying to find something wise and charming to say. "Uh . . . what?" Evident to both of them, he hadn't found it.

Helen stood there staring at him, looking a little vexed. Then a huge smile burst over her face, and she failed to stifle a giggle. "Wow. One day you're all sophisticated, playing Beethoven, and the next day you make conversation like a caveman."

Russ laughed. "Yeah, jeez. Sorry. I'm good. How are you? What are you doing?"

She walked a couple of steps closer, so dangerously close now that her perfume danced to him on the warm spring breeze.

"I'm well. Say, I was going to go shopping with Mother, but . . . Do you want to go for a walk instead?"

Russ's eyes darted down the road. The Chrysler had reached State Street and was preparing to turn north toward Idaho Falls. "Well, if I'm not able to, you just lost your shopping trip."

"Oh, that's fine. I didn't need to go anyway." She hesitated and put a little smile on her lips, trying to read his expression. "So . . . you don't want to go for a walk?"

"No! I mean *yeah!* Sure. I— Well, you caught me by surprise." He looked down at her shoes, which were white ballet flats with brown heels. "I guess you were already prepared to walk, huh?"

"Well, Mother and I were planning on being on our feet much of the day, so yes, I had to wear something tolerable. *Sensible,* as Mother would say. Do you like them?"

"Yeah! Sure."

"Really?"

"Well, I'm not that much of a shoe guy."

Helen laughed. "There. At least you're honest. What about my outfit?" She swiveled her hips back and forth, making the long, gray skirt sway.

"Yeah, it's pretty." He wanted to elaborate: It was the incredible girl inside it that made it look so wonderful. But he wasn't prepared to be a sap. He was still wondering why she would want to walk with him at all after the other night. *Why do you want to walk with me after you drove off in such a huff the other night?* That was the question Russ wanted to ask. Instead, he only managed: "What's that perfume?"

Helen gave him a big smile. He half-expected stars to sparkle off of her teeth. "It's called Accomplice. Isn't it divine?"

"Uh, yeah, I guess. Divine?"

She giggled. "It's pretty fitting, since I was an accomplice to the infamous Shelley tree chopper."

That made Russ laugh. "Yeah, I guess so." He still felt bad every time he thought back on that tree.

"Where are we going?" Helen asked.

"Want to go up to the canal?" he suggested.

"Oh, I see. You're ashamed to be seen with me in town."

Russ grunted. He was starting to get some of his bravery back, the bravery this girl stole from him every time he laid eyes on her.

"No, we can walk in town—if you don't mind. But I'm kind of scroungy."

"Well, you *are* a football and track star, right?"

Again, he laughed. "Yeah, if you say so."

They started walking past all the houses on either side of them, east up Center toward State. Without warning, Russ saw the girl's left hand come out to the side. Her fingertips sort of brushed against the back of his hand, as if by accident. He looked down at it, and her fist was clenched. He raised his eyes to find her watching him.

"You're gonna trip if you don't watch where you're going."

She took in a big breath and sighed it out. "Well, if . . . If you were holding my hand, you could stop me from falling."

A little stunned, Russ tried to calm his heart back down. What was happening? This was Helen James, the most beautiful and perfect girl in Shelley High. Was she really suggesting that he take her hand?

"What are people going to think?" he managed to say.

She studied him for several more steps. "Do we really care?"

"Well, I don't."

"If you don't want to hold my hand, you don't have to."

Russ was surprised to find he detected a little bit of nervousness in Helen's tone. "Hey, you okay?"

She giggled again. "Okay? Yes, why wouldn't I be?"

"Hey, are you sure you know who you're talking to? This is Russ Blevins, remember? And I just turned down going to the biggest dance of our junior year with you."

Another deep breath filled the top part of Helen's green blouse. Her little, cloud-white scarf fluttered. Her perfect hair bounced and taunted him. She sighed until there couldn't be much breath left in her lungs.

"Hey, Russ, I have to apologize about that."

She turned her head and met his eyes, and her expression was sincere. Or at least he prayed it was.

"You don't have to," he said.

"No, no. I do. That was so selfish and uncalled-for. I told Mother what happened, and she gave it to me good, I'll tell you."

"She what?"

"She was pretty embarrassed I did that. But I . . . I'm really sorry. I guess I let my emotions get carried away. I didn't think how it would look. Mother was totally right—and so were you."

Russ felt like he should say something to rescue her. "Don't feel bad. Helen, can I tell you something?"

"I was trying to tell *you* something."

"Oh, sorry! Go ahead."

"No, I was just having fun with you. That was all I wanted to say. What did you want to tell me?"

"Gosh, it's hard to find the right words, but maybe you kind of already know. Helen, I think you're the prettiest girl in this whole town, and there's no one I'd rather go to the dance with than you. I wish I wasn't so stupid, and I had asked you before Jack did."

"Well, let's face it—he really did jump the gun. Nobody asks anyone to a dance that soon, do they?"

He gave a one-shouldered shrug. "Well, not unless they're asking a girl like you, anyway."

"You are so sweet. Thank you. I think you're really handsome too. I guess I've been kind of a snot."

He laughed. "No, you haven't."

"Now you'd better stop contradicting me. A woman's got to have her own way *sometimes.*"

Russ laughed. "Okay. You've been kind of a snot. Sometimes. But I'd still love to take you on a date."

"Then we will. We will. Promise."

An unspeakable joy filled Russ's heart. He couldn't remember ever winning a football game that made him feel happier than he felt at this moment.

Helen looked over, and almost as if on accident she sort of flicked the tips of her fingers against his hand again as it passed. He looked down at her, and she was watching him intently. His hand was almost shaking when it closed over her fingers. He was glad he weighed so much, or he may have floated away.

CHAPTER TWENTY-SIX

The next day, Sunday, Russ was surprised when the telephone rang, and it was Helen, but she wasn't calling for Doris. She was calling for him. She told him she had just gotten out of church—which made him feel guilty thinking about how long it had been since he was there himself—and she wanted to see if he would like to go for a drive in the country.

The fact that Russ might have done his share of foolish things in his life had no bearing on this moment. He was not *that* much of a fool. He told her yes.

Within twenty minutes, the Chrysler pulled up in front, newly waxed and polished. By then, Russ was dressed up in something nicer than he would normally have worn on a weekend: a gray-blue chambray shirt

covered by a dark blue cardigan sweater, gray cotton slacks with a high, sharp crease in the front of the legs, and his favorite blue suede shoes. He left his jeans and Chukka boots in the closet, knowing that Helen was going to be dressed to the nines.

"See you later, Mom. Pop."

Russ started out the door, but his dad's gruff voice stopped him. "Don't take off just yet, Russ. Why don't you bring her in for a while first?"

Russ's heart fell. Although his dad's words began with the word "why," it was really not a question, but a command. And having Helen come in was the last thing on his mind on a beautiful May afternoon like this. But he knew he couldn't win against his father, the county dictator.

"Sure, Pop."

Walking down the sidewalk, Russ bent down a little to see Helen leaned over in the front seat and smiling up at him. He went around to the driver's door, and she rolled down the window. "You're kind of presumptuous, aren't you? Suppose I wanted to drive this time?"

Russ laughed because he knew she expected him to. His heart sure wasn't in it. "Yeah, that's not why I came around." He reached down and opened her door. "My dad's insisting on me bringing you inside for a bit before we go."

"Oh! How wonderful! I get to meet the famous father of Shelley High School's most famous athlete!" Helen winked at him as she held up a white-gloved hand, which he took to help her stand up.

"Don't be funny," said Russ, frowning. "Believe you me, it's not going to be all that big of a treat."

"Oh! Stop that, Russ. That's not nice." She pretended to swat at his chest. "I'm sure your father is swell."

"Yeah. Swell-headed."

He paused, letting himself notice Helen's outfit for the first time. She was dressed in a white polka-dotted, powder blue swing dress with three-quarter-length sleeves, a white sailor collar, and prim sailor tie that dove down five inches in front. A string of graduating beads obviously made of ivory but supposed to look like pearls hugged her neckline loosely, and her shoes—an item of dress Russ hardly ever looked at because he simply didn't care—he took care to note were white T-straps with three-

inch heels. Like the day before, she was wearing her Accomplice perfume. It had taken him about ten seconds to memorize the scent for life.

Russ looked her up and down while she pretended to brush something off her sleeves. Finally, she looked up at him. "Have you finished ogling me?"

Russ gave her a look of feigned shock, at which she giggled. "Do you like it?"

"Do I like it? Wow! Helen, you're killin' me. You look swell!"

"Oh, really? You aren't just saying that?"

He gave her a frown. "Yeah, come on! You've got a mirror!"

Helen laughed at him again. "Well, thank you, Russ. Now come on—let's go meet your dad."

"I've already met him," said Russ, trying to make himself sound extra grumpy. "And once is enough—you'll see."

As they started up the sidewalk, Russ was proud to feel Helen's gloved hands close around his left arm. She was only seven or eight inches shorter than he was, with her heels on, and her face was very close to his when she looked up and smiled. "You know, everyone else in town seems to think your dad is a cool cat. Why don't you?"

Looking down at the sincere look in her eyes, he knew how she wanted him to reply, so he complied. No sense letting her know what a tyrant his father really was at home.

"Oh, he's all right. He's just been on edge lately, I guess."

"And you too?"

Russ didn't have time to answer that, because they were going up the concrete steps. At the top, they found Kathleen holding open the door.

"Hi, Helen!"

"Hi, pretty girl," replied Helen. "Did you enjoy church today?"

"Yeah! But Russ didn't." The girl looked over with a semi-accusing expression.

Helen didn't have time to ask any more about that, as Russ ushered her through the front door into the world revolving around boisterous Blevins girls and Bingham County's most famous lawman and full-time dictator.

Helen marched right up to Arch and stuck out her hand at arm's length. Her confidence and beauty made Russ tingle with pride.

"Hello, sir. I'm Helen James. You have to be the famous Sheriff Blevins."

The sheriff had stood up to meet her, and he smiled. It was the first time Russ had seen that expression on his face in days.

"I don't know how famous I am, miss, but I am definitely that sheriff. Russ has told us a lot about you."

Behind the girl, Russ looked over at his mother and frowned. That was a flat-out lie; he hadn't told his father one word about the girl—or any other girl, for that matter. When would the old man have taken the time to listen to him if he did? Eleanor shrugged and gave him the "better hush" look.

"Would you like a drink of anything, Helen?" asked Eleanor.

"No, Mrs. Blevins, but thank you."

"Go ahead and have a seat," said Arch, waving at his own favorite La-Z-Boy.

When the girl complied, everyone else took a seat if they could, and the two girls who had been left out, Kathleen and Toni, gathered chairs from the kitchen table and brought them in.

Kathleen volunteered to play some records, but Arch waved her off, a little absently. "No, we're just going to talk for a bit."

Looking disappointed, Kathleen ignored the chair she had brought in and went over to sit on one of Eleanor's legs.

Helen began making conversation with Arch as if it were the most natural thing in the world. She entertained him with stories of her mother and father, made him cluck his tongue now and then, and even made him laugh once, which lately was something he seemed to have forgotten how to do.

During a lull in the conversation, Russ thought of the man who lived next-door to Edie Russell. "Hey, Pop, I keep meaning to tell you, I met some old guy that knows you."

"Oh yeah? Who was it?"

"I can't remember his name. Just some old bum, or at least he looked like it. Smelled like it too. Living in one of those run-down houses way up on the north end of town."

"Next time someone says he knows me, try to remember his name," Arch said.

Russ shrugged. "Sorry. Didn't look like he was worth much, anyway. Maybe some guy you arrested one time or something. Who knows? But anyway, he said to tell you hi."

"Now that isn't nice, Son," chided Eleanor. "I'm sure he was a nice man."

"Oh, yeah! Sure, he was nice enough. Didn't look like anyone that would know Pop, that's all."

"It would sure help if you remembered his name," Arch repeated in a flat tone.

Russ pursed his lips. "Well, I'll try to remember next time." Then he turned to Helen. "So maybe we should go if we're going to see much of the countryside."

Helen smiled at him and looked over at Arch and Eleanor, as if she were about to apologize for their son's impolite behavior.

"Oh, sure!" said Arch, getting up. "Yeah, I guess you didn't come over to hear us yap, did you, Helen?"

"No, I enjoyed it very much, Mr. Blevins. Thank you."

"How long do you expect to be?" asked Eleanor. Everyone knew Arch wouldn't ask, because he wouldn't care.

Russ looked at Helen, then took a guess. "Maybe a couple hours."

"Okay. Have a nice drive. It sure is pretty for it."

Out at the car, they walked around to the driver's side, and Russ opened her door. Remembering what she had said earlier, when she thanked him and sat down, he started to shut it. She stuck out her hand and stopped him, holding up the keys. "I was only having fun with you earlier, you know. Of course I want you to drive."

And so he drove out east of town, toward Mount Taylor and the Blackfoot Range. They had all the windows open, and fresh air swirled around them, or air that sometimes was tainted by the smells of farms. Russ liked those smells, but he noticed Helen brushing at her nose several times, as if to make the odor go away.

"Hey, Russ, I've been wanting to ask you something," Helen said, when they were far out in the country, driving past little homesteads and fields full of bright yellow dandelions.

"Well? Shoot."

"So this is something I've wondered for a long time. And I mean literally years."

"Holy ducks! Must be something big."

"Well, it's about your birthday. You're already eighteen, aren't you?"

Russ nodded. Here it came. "Yeah."

"Well . . . why is that? You're way older than anyone else in the class that I know of."

"Oh, actually, that's a funny story. Well, you know how important football is to me. I plan on playing in college and maybe even the pros, you know."

"Yes, I thought you would. *Everyone* assumes you will."

"So even when I was little, it was pretty much all I cared about. When they tried to make me go to school, I just wasn't into it. All I could think about was ball. Mom and Pop finally decided I wasn't mature enough to start school yet, so after the first three weeks, they jerked me out of there, and I didn't start first grade again until all my class was in school for a year. Which is funny, because old Jack Webber and I started out being best buddies back then."

Helen listened and nodded, looking like the face of wisdom. At last, she smiled. "I get it. Wow. It makes so much sense now. I mean, everything I know about you is upper class. I mean when it comes to your grades. Straight A's, right?"

"Yep."

"That's why I always wondered why a smart guy like you would be so much older. Are you ever sorry—that you couldn't go through with your own age group?"

"Nope. Not once. I wouldn't have been in your grade then, would I?"

Helen gave him a big smile. "No, that's true. You wouldn't have. Hey! So the big dance is coming up this Friday."

A bad feeling surged into Russ's stomach. He had been trying to think of a way to tell Helen that he had asked Edie to go with him. The words wouldn't seem to come.

"Yep, it's comin' up fast. You ready?"

"I guess. I sure wish I were going with you, though."

"It's all right. Jack's a great guy. There's nobody nicer, when it comes down to it."

"Yeah, I suppose. But he seems a little . . . I don't know, maybe a little too wild for me. You know?"

Russ laughed, feeling nervous. "Yeah, I understand. But he's cool. You'll be all right."

Helen sighed, and she laid her head over against his shoulder and put her left hand on his thigh.

"Hey, Helen, I've been trying to think of a way to tell you something."

Helen shot straight up in her seat, pointing out the front window. "Hey, Russ! Look! Look at the piglets."

Out on Sand Creek Road was Ross Stoddard's pig farm, and as Helen pointed out, there in his pens were dozens of the cutest little pink pigs anyone had ever seen. On the moment, Russ's confession was lost in Helen's excitement.

"Let's go see them, Russ. Stop, okay?"

And so the confession that should have been spoken was traded for a visit to Stoddard's pig farm.

CHAPTER TWENTY-SEVEN

Luther Dean drove up to Northgate Auto, in Idaho Falls, with Billy Earl in tow. Billy had found him a motorcycle, an Indian Chief from 1948. That year had been a depressing one for the Indian, because Harley Davidson's new, more powerful cycle was destroying it in the sales department—even shut down the brand for the entire next year altogether. That fact was bad for the makers of the Indian Chief, but good for Luther Dean, because it dropped the value of the Indian quite a bit.

The beautiful motorcycle, with over-sized red and white fenders and an upraised leather seat, was in near mint condition and had only three thousand two hundred miles on it. According to Lonnie, the salesman, some want-to-be rider's wife had forced him to bring it in and trade it, plus fifteen hundred dollars, for a nice, solid car after seeing another motorcyclist get struck on the highway and become nothing but a piece of the scenery.

That man's loss was Luther's gain, and when Billy finished filling out all the paperwork (in his own name because Luther didn't want to have his name associated with the motorcycle or anything else, if it could be helped), Luther Dean was the proud owner of an Indian Chief.

Flying back to Shelley from Idaho Falls down the Yellowstone Highway, Luther relished in the wind in his face. The dealer had thrown in a free pair of huge goggles, which turned out to be indispensable, since there was nothing between his eyes and the dozens of different emerging insects he encountered on the way. But Luther didn't care. He felt free. Not merely free from the penitentiary, but actually *free.*

And he would soon feel avenged as well.

Luther had been formulating his plan, as he lay on the sofa in Billy's house watching endless hours of television, right up until the time the stations went quiet at night and the snow appeared on the screen.

Most of his plan was in place now. He had planned his getaway first—the most important part. He would drive his beloved Mercury 8, while Billy followed him in his own car, out to the remote little town of Soda Springs, toward the Wyoming border. There they would find a quiet street on the edge of town on which to leave the Mercury parked, and they would return to Shelley in Billy's Ford.

Once the plan had succeeded, and Luther was free at last, not only from the pen, but from the haunting memories and the shadow of the man who had put him there, he would flee Shelley on the motorcycle, up into the Blackfoot Range, along the Blackfoot River, and clear to Soda Springs, where he and the Mercury would disappear into Wyoming, cross Nebraska, then shoot up through the Dakotas, eventually making their way all the way up into Canada.

The motorcycle was to be left secreted in a shop in Soda Springs, where in time Billy Earl would have it trailered back to Shelley, there to wait until the day it could be discreetly shipped to the mother of Luther's friend and ex-prison mate, Marty, in Winnipeg, Manitoba.

It was the middle part of the plan that was stressing Luther out. He was going to have to create some major distraction, someplace in the farthest reaches of Sheriff Blevins' jurisdiction from Shelley, something big enough to keep every law enforcement officer in the county tied up. But he would need to make sure that Blevins was far away in the opposite direction when it happened—far enough away that when the call came in for him on Park Avenue, in Shelley, he would be the only one who was able to respond.

After that, he would just have to hope that nothing else happened to cause any other officer to be nearby. It wasn't that he couldn't fight more than one cop at the same time—he just didn't see a need to kill anybody that didn't have anything to do with caging him up without justification.

Luther sighed and revved the bike, almost lifting the front end off the road. How he loved this bike. It was going to carry him away to freedom . . .

●●●●●

Tuesday, after track was done and Russ was hanging out with Helen James and feeling like the biggest man in town, he asked her to get the bicycle he had learned with some excitement she had in her garage and

pace him as he ran his evening ten-miler. Sadly, Helen turned him down, saying she had to go with her mother up to the Falls for some kind of women's meeting.

Edie Russell had heard the conversation, and as Helen said goodbye to Russ and made her way off the field, Edie came down off the bleachers, where she had been pretending to read an Ernest Haycox western novel, and caught Russ before he could finish stretching.

"Hiya, Russ."

"Hi there, Edie," said Russ, trying to act as if she hadn't startled him from his reverie. "How are you?"

"Fine. You?"

"Good. Tired. But I've still got a long ways to go."

"You're going to wear yourself down to nothing," said the girl, looking up and down Russ's two hundred pound frame.

"Why don't you take a picture?" said Russ, with a grin.

Edie blushed. "I wasn't— Oh, stop that! Hey, I heard you talking to Helen. Know something, Russ?"

"What?"

"I have a bike, too. My dad bought it for me."

"Oh yeah?"

"Yeah."

"So?"

"Well, I was thinking if you wanted to run up north instead of to the south, we could go by my house on the way and get my bike. Then I could pace you—you know, since Helen can't."

Inside, Russ cringed. He was doing so well with Helen, it worried him to take any chance of messing it up. However, there was some nice farm country out past Edie's house, and then the Snake River. Maybe it *would* be nice to run on some new road—and he could keep himself pretty invisible out that way, too. It was unlikely that anyone would ever even know that Edie had been pacing him.

"I guess I could go out that way for a change. But how you going to get back to your house?"

"I can run."

"Huh? You, run? You gonna try to keep up with *me?* That's something like a mile from here. Well, maybe half a mile."

Edie tried not to look offended. “Hey! I can run half a mile. Or even a mile. Or you could even run out there, then run around the park until I got there.”

Russ allowed himself a smile. “All right. Yeah, I guess that would be okay. Don’t you have anything else you’d rather do?”

“No!” The girl’s answer was too fast, too adamant. Just what Russ was afraid of.

“Say, did your mom get herself a job?”

Edie smiled. One would have thought Russ had told her she was beautiful, by the expression that came over her face. “She did. They hired her as a secretary at the Bingham County hospital. Cool, huh?”

“Yeah, I guess—cool. Doesn’t sound like much of a fun job to me, but if it keeps you from starving. Better than the waitress job, anyway.”

“Yeah.”

“How’s your dad? He home yet?”

The girl’s face saddened. “No, but I think maybe tomorrow. He’s in a wheelchair until they see if therapy will help him.”

Russ’s frown matched the girl’s. “Hey, Edie, I’m sorry to hear that. That’s tough luck.”

“Yeah. And the police are still trying to talk to the trucking company of the truck that hit him. So far, they haven’t helped with anything except for giving us money for a different pickup.”

“That’s rotten. Maybe my dad could help.”

“Do you think he could?”

“I don’t know. Maybe. I’ll ask him about it.”

“That would be swell. Thanks.”

“All right. Well, if we’re going to get ten miles in, we’d better start. I’ll go slow enough you can keep up with me. You can run in those shoes?” He looked down at her black and white saddle shoes, whose white parts were not nearly as white as style dictated them to be—definitely not as white as Helen’s.

“I don’t know. I guess we’ll see.”

“Okay then. Come on. Oh!” He turned back and reached out his hand. “Might as well give me those books.”

She gave him a big smile, thanked him, and handed her pile of books over to him, with the Haycox novel, *Trail Smoke,* right on top. "Hey! That's a good book," Russ remarked.

The girl beamed. "I like it too."

Russ could not have known it, but the girl didn't jog beside him all the way to her house—she floated.

Russ ended up being far more impressed with Edie's running ability than he had imagined he would be. By the time they reached her house, and she started around to the shed, where she said her bicycle was, he said, "Hey, why aren't you on the track team, anyway? You're pretty good."

"You think so?" Russ was going to end up making the girl break her face if he kept up with the compliments. At the time, he was too stupid to think what hopes it might be building in her.

"Yeah, I think so. There are a lot of girls I see on the team who don't have that kind of drive. But hey—how are your feet?"

"They're fine." He had expected that to be her answer, but by the way she limped off around the house, he knew they weren't.

She came back around with a powder blue and white bike, a Schwinn Scarlet. Russ whistled. "Say, that's a pretty nice bike. Where'd you get that?"

"Don't you remember I told you? My daddy bought it for me—last year," the girl said proudly. "You seriously like it?"

Russ looked up from the bike and saw the glow in Edie's eyes. Not until then did the truth come to him, and he thought to himself, *Cut it with all the compliments, numbskull!*

"Yeah, it's all right," he said casually. "So you ready? What about your mom?"

"She won't be back for a while, I'm sure. She stays with Daddy for a while in the evening."

"All right, then we better scoot."

They took off and ran out into the settlement of Woodville. Going there was Russ's biggest mistake.

Seeing an oncoming Chevrolet pickup at some five hundred yards or so, Russ got off into the green weeds on the left side of the road, while

Edie kept riding on the right shoulder. When it was eighty yards out, Russ recognized the pickup. His heart lurched.

The Chevy was driven by linebacker Bill Jensen, known more commonly as "Sideswipe," or merely "Swipe." Not only was Bill one of the biggest kids in school, but he had a mouth to match.

The pickup slowed way down, then at the last second screeched to a halt. Its gears grinded, and it backed up to where Russ was still running, then even a little farther, so the pickup's occupants could look out at Russ. Bill's little brother, Larry, was in the passenger seat, and at Bill's obvious insistence he cranked down the window.

Bill leaned way over, so he was right in front of his brother. "Hey, Cus! Still runnin'?"

"Hi, Swipe. Yeah, I *was.*"

Bill glanced off to the left, right at Edie. Then his eyes returned to Russ. "Well, looks like you're up to somethin' else, too? New girl, huh?"

"Yeah, right! Cut it out. I have to get on back to town. Better start now."

Bill laughed heartily. "Run all you want, buddy. There ain't no way you're gonna outrun *this!"*

And with that, Bill threw it back into second gear, hit the gas, and sped down the road.

Russ was left on the side of the empty road, and Edie in the far lane. Russ looked at Edie. Edie looked at Russ.

Russ cursed under his breath.

Without a word, he turned and started back the way they had come. He had to find Helen James, as soon as he could.

CHAPTER TWENTY-EIGHT

Helen wasn't home by the time Russ left Edie at her house and got back home to make a call. He was desperate enough he would have stopped at a phone booth, but he didn't have any money on him.

"Do you know when she'll be back, Mrs. James?"

Remember now, Russ—it's Pearl, okay?

"Sorry! Yes, ma'am. Pearl."

That's more like it. So Helen went to a movie in the Falls. I imagine it will be a little late before she's back.

"All right. Would you please tell her I called?"

When Russ hung up, he already had a sick feeling in his stomach. He could feel down deep that this was going to turn out bad. And just when he had started to win Helen over!

He saw Helen in the hall the next day. She was with Lonna, Bobbie, and a third girl, a squatty blonde named Tish McDevitt, who had somehow won her way onto the drill team and thus managed to become a member of Helen's circle, if a somewhat tentative one—a probationary member, so to speak.

Helen happened to glance over at him as he was walking her way, and she turned back to her friends and positioned herself so that there was a little less of her profile, and more of her back to him. It seemed to Russ very deliberate. But he was not in the mood to shrug things off or walk away.

He stopped at the group of girls. "Hey, girls."

The other three girls said hello, glancing at Helen. By the looks in their eyes, it was obvious what they had been talking about. Helen, feigning surprise, turned back around.

"Hi, Helen."

"Hi, Russ."

"Can I talk to you?" He gave a nervous look to the other girls.

"Sure." There was no bright smile. That said it all.

"Uh . . . Well, I mean . . . Not *here.*"

"You can talk in front of my friends. We're all friends, right? Us and more."

He stared at her. "Okay. If by 'us and more' you're talking about Edie, I tried to call last night and explain that."

Helen's eyes flickered. After a moment, she said, "You called my house?"

"I did. I talked to your mom."

"Oh." It was obvious by the fidgeting of her hands and sudden shuffling of her feet that the news caught Helen off-guard. After another long, uncomfortable pause, she turned to the other girls. "Hey, girls, maybe I'd better go. I'll see you later, okay?"

The girls drifted off, and Russ walked with Helen to what amounted to a corner, a space behind one of the large, tiled columns that came partway out of the wall, supporting the roof.

"Helen, I wasn't trying to hide anything."

She seemed to hug her armload of books even tighter. "Hiding anything? I don't know what you're talking about."

"Come on. I know Swipe told you Edie was riding her bike with me when I went running last night."

"Oh. Really?"

"Helen, please." The tone of his voice became even more serious—or at least he guessed she took it that way, by the look in her eyes. He didn't think he could sound much more serious than he already had.

Helen sighed dramatically. "Okay. Yeah, it's kind of funny. I was standing in line at the theater when Bill and his little brother came to get in line. As soon as they saw me, Bill came over and had great fun asking me if I knew that you and Edie were doing things together."

Russ drew in a deep breath. "I didn't go looking for Edie. She heard me ask you to pace me with your bike, and she came and offered to do it when you couldn't. That's all it was. Nothing happened."

Helen threw up a shoulder in a careless shrug. "Well, that's fine. I don't know why you're so worked up. It's not like we own each other, is it?"

Russ started to open his mouth, then clamped it shut, his teeth making a clicking sound. "There's something else I've gotta tell you."

A veil came over Helen's face. "Are you sure? I mean, we're going to be late for next hour."

"I don't care. I've been trying to figure out how to tell you this, but somethin' keeps coming up. Last time, it was Stoddard's pig farm."

A little smile crept to Helen's lips at that memory. "Okay, I guess you'd better hurry and tell me."

"Okay, so I asked Edie to go to the dance with me."

"What? When?"

"A while back. Before you told me you would drop Jack and go with me."

Her face flushed, and she snapped her eyes about. "Why didn't you tell me that when I was making such a fool of myself?"

"I guess I kind of forgot."

"Oh, right. Forgot? How do you forget something like that?"

"Come on, Helen. I asked you to the dance first, remember? What's the difference? You're going to be with Jack. I had no idea you'd be willing to ditch him for me."

"Hmph. Well, for your information, I probably wouldn't have. I was only talking. I would have realized on my own it wasn't a good idea."

"Helen, I don't—"

"Russ, I really have to go. I'm never late for classes."

Russ gave out a disgusted sigh of resignation. "Okay, fine."

"See you later."

Before he could make his reply, she wheeled and walked off down the hall, the heels of her red and white saddle oxfords making fatal clicking noises as she went.

Russ turned and started toward his own class. But he didn't make it. There was no way he could concentrate on schoolwork. He ended up walking out on the canal bank instead.

That afternoon when classes got out, Russ went out to the track. His heart wasn't into running, but he had to do something physical to make him stop thinking about Helen. Fortunately, Helen never showed up for track. It surprised him to see that Edie wasn't anywhere around either.

Russ didn't talk much out on the track or the field. He practiced his heart out, showered up, and then headed out the front door.

When he started across the street, there was Helen's Chrysler, parked at the far curb. He cursed under his breath. The Imperial was right between him and home. And of course she would already have seen him.

He started walking, and soon he realized there was someone else in the car, obviously one of Helen's trio of leeches. As he came abreast of the car, Helen turned her head and looked out at him.

"Hi, Russ. I've been waiting for you."

"Oh yeah? What for?"

"To see if you'd go for a ride."

He looked his confusion at her. "Really? Why?"

"To talk. And I brought someone."

The way she said that sounded strange, so he leaned over to look in the car. As the face registered on him, he was glad he hadn't had a mouthful of food. He would surely have choked, or maybe spat it right out on Helen.

It was Edie Russell!

He jerked back up. "Hey, what is this?"

"Russ, will you please get in?" She scooted over to the middle of her seat.

Russ cast a glance around. Not seeing anyone he knew, he threw open her door and plunked himself down on the seat. He turned so he could see both of them.

"What's the gag?"

"There's no gag," said Helen, as Edie leaned even farther past her.

"Hi, Russ."

"Hi, Edie," he said, trying to relax. "I'm not sure what's up."

"I told you—nothing's up," said Helen, with a sigh. "I have to apologize to you for earlier. I was a pompous . . . fool. I shouldn't have treated you that way."

Russ stared at her, speechless.

"Well?"

"Well, what?"

"Don't you have anything to say?"

"Umm . . . Don't let it get you. It's all right."

"No, it's not. I think it's sweet that you asked Edie to the dance, and I hope you two have a fun time. I'm sure we'll see you there."

Inside, Russ didn't quite believe what Helen was telling him. But he wasn't about to call her a liar.

So he didn't. Instead, they went for a ride in the country. And they actually had fun. Helen and Edie sang with the radio, while Russ drove and listened, amazed.

CHAPTER TWENTY-NINE

When the night of the big prom came, Russ wore his Sunday best, the clothing he almost never wore anymore, because going to church, for him, was about as likely as going to a ballet. Edie was dressed in a high-waisted, soft pink dress, with three-quarters sleeves and a matching pink belt. Her shoes were white ballet flats. Unlike her saddle shoes, the white was exquisite and perfect, as if she had spent the whole day bleaching them—or perhaps they were brand-new. Her dark hair fell against the very top of the dress, and somehow her black-framed "cat-eye" glasses, which were nothing new for Edie, seemed to set off her deep brown eyes. For some reason, Russ had never noticed that before. He had also never noticed her shapely figure.

When she came to the door at his knock, he faltered in whatever he had intended to say. After a moment trying to collect himself, he said, "Wow. Edie, you look great."

She turned her head a little to the side, as if to better catch any joking glint in his eyes. "You really think so?"

"Yeah. Really."

She beamed. "Thanks, Russ. So do you."

Edie's mother, Lorna, appeared over her daughter's shoulder. Russ was once again struck with how attractive she was, and how much they looked alike. He was also aware that he was a little speechless.

"Hello, Russ. Do you want to come in for a minute?"

Russ was going to decline so they could get going to the dance. But the woman's face looked so hopeful he just couldn't. "Um, yeah, sure." He glanced at Edie. "We could do that for a little bit."

With a happy look on her face, Edie stepped against the door, making a larger opening for him to come in.

"Go ahead and sit down, you two," said Lorna Russell. "I'll get you some punch."

"Oh, you don't have to do that, Mrs. Russell."

"Nonsense!" She waved him off. "It'll only take a moment."

Defeated without a fight, Russ walked to the couch with Edie, and a little, barrel-shaped black dog, no bigger than most cats, wandered in, very quiet, and very old. His face was almost more gray than it was black. Apparently, this was the neighborhood for aging canines.

"Oh, Mom, Jet got out," said Edie.

Lorna whirled from the refrigerator and looked in at them. "Oh, darn it! I'll get him in a second. Don't you dare touch him with that dress on."

The dog came over and started sniffing Russ's pant leg. He appeared to be mostly Chihuahua, and maybe the quietest one Russ had ever seen. Russ leaned down and started petting the dog, and it promptly managed to get up on his leg with its front feet, which were too long in the claw.

"Don't let him do that," Edie cautioned. "He sheds like there's no tomorrow."

"Do I look scared?" asked Russ with a laugh. He reached down and cradled the dog's chest with his big hand, raising it up and setting it on his lap.

At first, Edie looked embarrassed. "You're going to regret that."

"Oh, no I won't. I like dogs."

Jet had started licking his hand, and Russ smiled at him. He reminded him of a little gray dog they used to have, which had been dead now for two years. Russ stroked the animal's soft, round head, feeling myriad little bumps under the skin—old age bumps.

In a moment, Lorna Russell came in with two glasses of pink punch and looked at Russ. She shook her head. "I'm sorry about that, Russ. You'll be all covered with hair."

"I don't mind. Dog hair on someone's clothes is the sign of a kind-hearted person—that's what my grandma always used to say."

Lorna's face was overcome with a big smile, and she looked over at Edie. "Wow. Russ isn't like any of the other boys you bring home, honey."

Startled, Russ looked over at Edie, whose face was aghast. "Mom! Russ, don't you listen to her. I've never brought a boy in here—ever!"

When Russ's eyes pivoted to Lorna, she let out a laugh. "I'm sorry, Russ. I'm only having fun with you. You really are the first boy who's come in here."

Russ didn't expect the sad feeling that came over him when he thought about that. Had Edie never been on a date before? And why did he care? To each his—or her—own.

Russ kept petting Jet as he tried to climb his way up his chest, with his obvious final goal being to get that wet little tongue on Russ's face. Russ picked him up and saved him the trouble.

When he was holding the dog up and it was licking his cheek, Edie let out a giggle. "You're something, Russ."

"Yeah, I guess I'm something," he agreed, with a laugh of his own. He put the old dog back down on his lap and looked at Lorna Russell. "Say, Edie tells me you got a job."

Lorna sighed. "Yes, I did. It's such a relief."

"Have you ever worked before? Sorry, I mean out of your home."

Lorna laughed. "Not since I was a teenager. Frank has provided for us."

Russ didn't embarrass his hosts by glancing overtly around the room. But from what he had already seen, it didn't look like Frank Russell had been providing all that much.

"How is he now?"

"He's better." Lorna's face clouded over, belying her words.

"Will he be coming home soon?"

Lorna sighed. "Nobody can tell me for sure."

"With you working and everything, what . . ." He hesitated for a moment, then bulled on. "What are you gonna do with things around here, like the grass and stuff? And I saw there's a big, dead branch in that elm tree out there. The porch steps kind of need to be fixed, too."

Lorna looked sad. "Oh, yes. Well, Frank will get to all that. I have to apologize for those steps. They're really something."

"I didn't mean to sound . . . I'm sorry, ma'am. I shouldn't have said anything."

"No, young man, you didn't say anything wrong. It's nothing I haven't thought about."

They talked for a little longer, and then it was Lorna who shooed the two of them off to the dance, before they could miss anything important.

Russ didn't do much dancing. Of all the things he was interested in, that wasn't one. He was surprised to see that his old friend Jack Webber, on the other hand, was quite an accomplished master of the dance floor, energetic and smooth as butter. With his muscular shoulders and narrow hips, in his black three-piece suit he cut quite a figure. And so did Helen, who had obviously spent a lot of time in dance classes as well. The two of them won a competition, voted on by their peers, while Russ and Edie sat and drank punch and munched on pink- and white-frosted cookies.

Edie spent a lot of time looking down at her hands, which were folded in her lap. In spite of himself, Russ kept thinking how nice she looked and how she should be out on the dance floor, if not with him then with someone else.

Finally, he said, "Hey, Edie."

Her eyes jumped to him, as if she had been waiting for him to say her name.

"Do you wanna try and dance?"

Her dark eyes flitted over to all the couples on the dance floor. "Sure—I guess. Do you?"

"Yeah. Let's give it a shot." He stood up and gave her his hand. She took it, and hers was warm and moist. He smiled and led her to the floor.

The song that was playing, and which Russ realized was what had made him want to get up, was an instrumental called "Autumn Leaves," by Les Baxter. There was no real rhythm to it that made it seem like something a teenage crowd would dance to, and maybe it was that lack which made Russ think it would be a good choice for him and Edie. No one on the floor was likely to be practiced at this song.

Edie only got warmer the longer they stayed on the floor, but Russ didn't mind. He made up whatever dance moves he felt like making up, because with his social standing he knew one thing for sure: No one in Shelley High School was going to tell him he was wrong.

When the song ended, they started playing "Dance With Me, Henry," by Georgia Gibbs, and later it was Pat Boone, with "Ain't That a Shame". To Russ's own surprise, he and Edie stayed on the floor through all three songs. And once they started to relax, he had a feeling they were doing pretty well. There always seemed to be someone looking at them whenever he thought to notice, and the looks in their eyes said it all.

Finally, they went over and got some punch and sat back down. Edie looked at Russ with a huge smile on her face. "That was kind of fun, huh?"

"Yeah, it was. I'm not much of a dancer."

"Me either." Edie shrugged and dropped her eyes. "You sure did good."

He laughed. "So did you! You had a lot of people watching you."

She scanned the crowd as The Four Lads came on, singing "Moments to Remember". There was a look of worry in her eyes. "Were they really looking?"

"They sure were. Edie, I meant it when I told you how pretty you look tonight. Gosh, you're smashing." He instantly wanted to kick himself, as in the background he heard . . . *we will have these moments to remember. Though summer turns to winter, and the present disappears, the laughter we were glad to share will echo through the years* . . . Russ felt foolish when his eyes suddenly got tears in them. Again! What was wrong with him?

"Hey, Edie—you wanna dance anymore? Maybe we could go for a drive instead."

Hopeful, she looked up. "Yeah! I'd like that. It's pretty hot in here."

He smiled understandingly. Edie was not comfortable in this crowd. He shouldn't have told her people were watching her.

They got up, and as they were walking toward the door, Pete Basso accosted them. He had one of the class's prettiest girls at his side, Annette Boring—unfortunate name for a lively girl who wore her dark hair in the same short-cropped style as the much-loved and imitated Audrey Hepburn in *Roman Holiday.* Annette was a perfect match for Pete.

"Hey, Wop! What's up?"

"Man, stop callin' me that. My girl's here." Pete grinned.

"Oh, yeah—sorry."

They talked for a while, until Billy Vaughn's "Melody of Love" came on.

"Say!" Pete cut into whatever Russ was saying. "I think they're playing our song!" He turned to Annette and took her hand, dragging her toward the dance floor as he looked back and waved at Russ and Edie. "See you two later!"

Russ smiled down at Edie. "We could dance to one more before we go," he said, instantly wondering how intelligent it was to ask her to dance to a song with this particular title.

Edie smiled. "Okay." And she stepped close and took his outstretched hand. Somehow, her hand felt natural against his skin, like it fit.

As the song was ending, Russ let go of Edie's hand and looked across the room. His eyes landed on the row of seats just down from the punch table. Helen James was sitting there alone, while Jack must be off seeking refreshments. She was looking right at Russ, but the moment he saw her, she averted her eyes.

Russ sighed. He knew he should try to be the gentleman and take Edie's hand, but he knew the moment he looked away Helen would be watching them. "All right, Edie, let's cut out of here, huh?"

The girl looked down for his hand, making him wonder why she would even expect it. It wasn't there for her, and when he started walking away, his steps too fast, she just followed. At one point, she must have been almost running. But he couldn't feel her embarrassment; he could only feel the gaze of Helen upon them.

CHAPTER THIRTY

The night air was cool. Trying to find a decent view of city lights below, Russ pulled his old Studebaker Champion off a north- and south-running road way up on the Butte, which was southeast of town. Idaho Falls lay about seven miles distant, the closest place for any light show around here. Shelley, basically a village, closed down at night.

Russ tried several times to get Edie talking. But it was only after a few unsuccessful attempts that she really started to open up. However, she didn't talk about anything Russ would have expected a girl to want to discuss. It was as if she had been wanting to say so many things, and now all of them began to spill out in an unchecked stream; a dam had broken.

"What team are you rooting for?" Edie asked, more or less out of the blue. Russ had been gazing at the distant flicker of the city lights and, to his chagrin, thinking of Helen James.

"In football, you mean?" As if she might have been talking about high school debate.

"Yeah. Football teams."

"Uh, probably the Rams, I guess."

"Oh, yes. Don't you think Tank Younger is good?"

Russ looked down at her. "Huh?"

"Tank Younger. The fullback."

After staring at her for a moment more, unable to hide his surprise, Russ said, "Yeah, I know who he is. I'm just surprised you do."

"Oh, I love football."

"You don't say. Really?"

"Sure."

"Who's your team?"

"The Rams. And maybe the Forty-Niners."

"Huh." Russ stared at her, still trying to get over his surprise. "So you just like California, huh?"

Edie laughed. "Well, I guess. It would be dreamy to live there."

"Yeah, I guess."

"What are your dreams, Russ?"

He returned her laugh. "My dreams? That's a silly question. To play ball."

"That's all?"

"Pretty much."

After a long moment of silence, Edie came alive again. She tried to goad Russ into conversations about football, about timber harvest, about Western books, movies, and television shows. With embarrassment, he admitted that his father was too cheap to buy a television, even though they were now priced clear down to around two hundred dollars.

"What makes you so interested in tree cutting?" Russ asked, thinking back with shame on the night of their big adventure.

"Oh, I just like it."

"Hmm. I don't get that. What is there to like about it, especially for a girl?"

"I like to be in the forest. I like the smells, and the sounds. I like the smell of fresh sawdust and pine sap, and the pine needles that have been lying on the ground in the sunshine."

Russ stared at her. If this girl was so interested in all these things, why hadn't he ever known it before? Then he realized he had never known much of *anything* about her. For all he knew she could be a world-renowned trapeze artist or an Olympic marksman.

Russ did not expect that night to go how it did. Although he couldn't stop thinking of Helen James, he found himself starting to kind of like little Edie Russell. It would never amount to anything romantic, of course. They could never be anything but friends.

When they got back to Edie's house, just short of midnight—the time he had promised Mrs. Russell they would return—they sat in the car in front of the house for a while.

Russ found his heart pounding. There was a stupid part, deep inside him, that had been thinking something about Edie. He kept wondering if she had ever been kissed. If she had never even brought a boy over to her

house, and probably had never been on a date, it was pretty unlikely. More than once, he thought about asking her. She was so close, and she smelled so good, and she really was pretty, all dressed up like she was. But he wasn't going to mess up anything with Helen. She had been his dream for far too long.

"Well," he finally said, "I guess you'd better get in before your mom comes looking for you."

Edie shot a glance at him, then looked down at her hands, once again folded in her lap. "Yeah, I guess I better."

Like a good girl, she waited while Russ got out and went around to open her door. It was always stiff, and it took a few good yanks for him to get it open. She slid out, and he held his elbow out to her. It was the least he could do.

They walked to the porch, with Russ's heart inexplicably pounding. He couldn't stop thinking about that kiss. Or maybe at least a hug. But after being caught by Side-Swipe Jensen out in the middle of nowhere, he wasn't about to take a chance here in town. Even as he glanced around, he caught the glow of a cigarette, in the shadows of the house next-door. That proved his own point: Nowhere was safe.

He walked Edie up the rickety porch, where he said goodbye without seeing her mother again. Then he jumped down off the backside of the porch. He didn't like those dilapidated wooden steps even in the daylight, and he had already taken enough risk by walking up them with Edie.

The red tip of the cigarette next-door bobbed toward him in the shadows, with the darkest shadow of all moving with it. Now wearing a fedora, the old man with the yellow lab stopped in front of Russ, swaying. Even from four feet away, Russ could smell the whisky on him.

"Evenin', son," said the man, with slurred speech.

Disgusted by the smell, Russ nodded. "Evening."

"You an' the girl have a nice time at the dance?"

"Sure."

"That little girl's mother sure seems to have taken a likin' to you."

"Really?" Russ was making polite conversation at that point. All he wanted was to get away from the smoke and booze smell.

"Sure. Arch Blevins's boy an' all—who wouldn't, right?" The old man gave what might have been a laugh, but a rough, broken sound it was.

"Hey, I'm sorry, Mister, but I forgot—what was your name again? I tried to tell my dad you said hi."

"Tupper. Barrow Tupper." The old man swayed as if he were about to fall over.

Russ started to reach out to catch him, then thought better of it. Some old guys were pretty proud.

"All right. I'll remember it this time. Where do you know my pop from, anyway?"

The old man took the cigarette out of his mouth and waved it in a wide arc. "Oh, that's ancien' hist'ry." He sounded like an exaggerated wino in a movie. "Hist'ry don't mean nothin' in the life of a man. Right?"

"Yeah, I guess," Russ replied. He had to get out of here. "Well, I better get going."

"Awright. Have a good night. Say—you should come over sometime an' try t' cut some of the dead branches outta that tree. They tell me yer good at wood-choppin'."

Russ could only think old Tupper was talking about the incident at the school. How in the world did he hear about that? If it was supposed to be funny, it wasn't. "All right. See you some other time."

With that, he turned and hurried back out to his car. He heard Tupper mumbling something after him, but he wasn't about to reply. He could be stuck here for another half hour.

● ● ● ● ●

School ended the following week. Russ had mixed feelings. With summer, he was going to be headed up to Island Park to work in the family timber mill. What was going to happen with Helen James while he was gone? Would she find someone else to hang out with? To replace him? And would there be any "replacing" to it? After all, it wasn't like they were officially going steady or anything. He liked her an awful lot, but he still wasn't sure what she thought of him. He had asked her several times to pace him on her bike, and she always had something else she needed to do. All she ever wanted to do was take drives in the country or grab a bite to eat at PDQ or at Jack's Chicken Inn, in the Falls. There

was almost nothing they could really talk about together. So when they went for a drive, he simply listened to her talk about her dreams, or what books she was reading, or listened to her recite poems. One day he even had to listen to her go on and on about a quilt she and her mother were making with some other women from their church.

"Want to hear a poem?" she asked one day while they were driving out on a dusty gravel road east of Idaho Falls.

"Sure." Of course he wasn't going to say no. In actuality, although he wasn't into poetry, it usually sounded pretty when it was coming from her. In fact, almost anything did.

"Okay.

Like a dream, it beckons…
I wake, and the clock is unchanged.
I am walking on a cloud,
Above a city, above a park.

I want never to awake,
For in the waking, there are nightmares.
I long to sleep on, to dream,
And yet morning comes, and tears fall.

"Do you like it?" she asked, after a moment of silence.

"Uh . . . Yeah, I guess. It didn't rhyme, though."

Helen slapped at his arm, frowning. "What? Haven't you ever heard of free verse? You *don't* like it, do you?"

"Well, it's okay. It's just not my style, that's all."

Helen got quiet, and for a while, the only sound was the tires rattling over the gravel. Finally, something dawned on him. He was afraid to ask the question.

"Who wrote it?"

"Oh, it doesn't matter." She turned and looked out the other window.

He sat silent for a while before dredging up his courage again. "Shoot, Helen—did you write that?"

"Like I said, it doesn't matter."

In his head, Russ cursed. Helen had written it.

"Hey, come on. It was pretty good. Yeah, it was good."

"It's too late now, Russ. Okay, it wasn't all that good. I shouldn't have made you listen."

The silence slogged on. How did an eighteen-year-old young man think of anything to break silence like this?

He didn't have to. A horse did it.

He looked out the left window in time to see a white and brown foal frolicking in a grassy field by its mother. "Hey, Helen! Look!"

The girl turned, her eyes looking bored. Then she saw the horse, and those eyes lit up. "Oh, stop, Russ!"

With a sigh of relief, he pulled over, then backed up to where they could look out at the mare and foal. Sitting in a car watching animals was never going to be enough for Helen James. Of course they had to disembark and go closer. And that was all right with Russ. He liked animals, too. It was the one place where they seemed to have anything to talk about.

The next day, on a whim, Russ gathered up some ropes, a couple of axes, wedges, and his father's crosscut saw, and went over to the Russell house. He knocked on the door, and no one was home.

Walking around the back yard, he gazed up at the big old American elm tree. A huge branch on it had died, and it arched out over the house in a very menacing way. He started looking at it from all angles, trying to figure a way to get it to come down without doing any damage to the house.

At last, he concocted a plan. Like a monkey—as he had pretended to be as a young boy—he crawled up in the tree and tied ropes on the limb. He ascended higher, and tied one of the ropes to a higher branch that looked healthy and strong. Then he climbed down and dropped the last eight feet to the grass. He took the ends of the other ropes and bound them around the massive trunk of a neighboring tree. The limb was long enough that he was going to have to cut it in two places, to keep it from falling all the way over and hitting the fence. The intent of the rope being above the branch was so that when it fell, it would, according to plan, dangle there, and then he could ease it straight down. The other ropes were only insurance.

With his plan in place, Russ started sawing. By the time the limb came free and hung there from the rope, Russ looked over and stopped smiling when he saw old Barrow Tupper watching him from next door, his dog, Bud, at his side.

The old man smiled, although the bright sun appeared to be hurting his eyes. He saluted Russ but said nothing. As much whisky as he had consumed the night before, Russ guessed it would hurt too bad.

After another ten minutes, Russ had the whole dead limb down in the yard, and another half hour saw it cut up into firewood lengths. The old man and his dog had gone inside, but when Russ finished and was walking around looking at the lawn, which badly needed cutting, he reemerged without the dog. He was carrying a glass of water.

"You done a man's work," said Tupper, still squinting against the sun. "Better fill back up."

With his thanks, Russ took the water and drank.

"Seen you lookin' at the grass. Yer right—needs cut." The old man waved a hand at his own yard, which was mostly dirt and gravel. "I don't have a lawnmower, myself. It hurts too bad to push one around anymore, so I salted out all my grass an' killed it."

"Do they have one?" asked Russ.

"Oh, sure. Frank used to keep the lawn up. Then a couple summers ago the girl started, when her old man had t' start workin' double shifts t' keep 'em all in shoes. But the girl's been gone to the hospital so much now that it ain't gettin' done."

"Where's the mower?"

"Shed," replied Tupper, nodding toward something that looked more like a mountain man lean-to.

Russ went and pulled out the mower, whose blades turned out to be dull, and he sharpened them up, then began mowing.

As he was finishing up, and when he was at his nastiest, now with not only sawdust, but grass clippings, all over his pants and shirt, the Russells' newly acquired old pickup pulled in and parked.

Russ walked over to greet the occupants, as Lorna and Edie Russell climbed out.

Lorna was staring up at the place where the dead limb had been. "Oh, Russ! You took it down." Tears filled her eyes. "I don't know what to say."

"You don't need to say anything," Russ said, looking over at Edie with an inconspicuous smile. "I had some free time."

"Well, I'm at least going to feed you lunch."

"No, thank you, ma'am. I really didn't do it for anything like that. I just wanted to help."

The woman frowned good-naturedly. "Russ, I made noodles last night, and I took a lot of time cutting up chicken into pieces, and carrots. I am here to tell you that I have a pot of the most delicious chicken noodle soup the civilized world has ever known, and if you turn me down, I'm going to be so offended, not to mention broken-hearted. You wouldn't want that, would you?"

Russ laughed as he saw a teasing light come into the woman's dark eyes. This woman melted him every time he saw her.

"All right. I guess I wouldn't want you to be offended," he said.

"Or broken-hearted," she replied with a laugh. "Come on." She waved him toward the house.

Old Barrow Tupper had disappeared into his house again. So, undisturbed, the three of them, and little Jet, went inside the house and had some of the most delicious soup the civilized world had ever known, and then a big piece of apple pie. By the time Russ finished the last bite, he was thinking he needed to start cutting more trees.

Edie excused herself from the table, only to come back half a minute later from down a dark hall. She was carrying a book, which when she sat down again she placed by Russ's pie plate. It was *Trouble Shooter,* another Ernest Haycox novel.

"I just read this in the last two days. I think you'd like it a lot."

"You think? I don't know if I'd have time to read it."

"You would! Come on. You can't just cut down trees and mow lawns and run every day."

Russ laughed. "I didn't think you saw the lawn."

"Oh, of course we saw it!" Lorna Russell jumped in. "Thank you so much, Russ. I really don't know how to thank you."

"It wasn't much."

"I think that tree branch would have cost me twenty dollars to have taken down, and a dollar for the lawn. And right now, that's a fortune."

Russ nodded. "Sure. How is your husband doing, anyway?"

"He smiled today." Upon saying that, tears filled Lorna's eyes again, and she dropped her glance to her half-eaten piece of pie. She took a deep breath. "Sorry. I don't know where that came from."

Russ nodded. "It's okay." As often as he himself had without reason felt emotional lately, who was he to judge?

"It's just been such a hard time," said Lorna, with a sigh.

With another nod, he said, "Hey, if there's anything else I can do, call me, okay?"

Lorna looked at Russ for a couple of seconds, then turned her eyes to Edie. "Well, there is actually one thing you could do, if you're really serious."

"Oh yeah! Of course I'm serious."

"Well, this coming Tuesday, I have to work, and Edie has a doctor's appointment."

"Oh. In the Falls?"

"No, no. It's here. But it's for her eyes, and they said she will have a hard time seeing when she leaves. They asked me to have someone come who could get her safely home."

Russ looked over at Edie and smiled. "Sure. I was planning on going up to Island Park, but I can wait until Wednesday, or maybe even Tuesday night."

Lorna looked over at Edie, and Russ's eyes naturally followed. The girl was looking down at her plate. When Russ looked back at Lorna, she gave him a sad smile.

"We were sort of hoping you might be around during more of the summer."

Russ shrugged. "I usually spend most of my summers up there. That's how I make all my money for the rest of the year."

Lorna smiled her understanding. "Well, then, as long as we're not imposing too much, I guess we'll see you Tuesday. Or at least Edie will. I have to leave around seven. And the appointment is at eleven o'clock."

Russ's eyes were drawn back over to Edie, and she smiled at him, nudging the novel a little closer to his plate. She spoke again to hide the

look of disappointment on her face because of his revelation. "You'd really like it, Russ. I know you would."

CHAPTER THIRTY-ONE

"Where the hell have you been?"

Russ Blevins stared at his father, who stood in the driveway in his sheriff's uniform.

"You should have had this lawn mowed hours ago."

Russ looked around, then glanced back at his father defiantly. "I went over and took down a tree limb at the Russells', if you have to know. Their old man is still in the hospital. And then I mowed *their* lawn."

Taken by surprise to hear Russ's defiant tone, Arch glared at his son. It took a few moments, but the hard line of his lips began to soften. It almost looked like he was going to speak, but instead he turned away and started fiddling with his keys until he got his trunk open, then made an overt point of checking the operation of one of his tail lights.

At last, looking down at the light, with Russ still waiting behind him dutifully—because to walk away from Arch Blevins without being excused was tantamount to criminal activity and would bring swift retribution—Arch said, "Well, it would be nice if you could get this mowed." No apologies. There never were. Never would be. Arch Blevins didn't know the meaning of the word.

"Yes sir," Russ said, and knew he was excused. He started to walk away, then remembered talking to Barrow Tupper again. "I saw that old man again when I took Edie home from the dance. He's just an old drunk. Couldn't even hardly stand up. Somebody you've arrested, I guess."

"Did you remember his name?"

"No, but I asked him. It's Barrow Tupper. He wouldn't ever tell me how he knows you. That's why I figure you must have arrested him."

Arch paused, resting his hand on the edge of the trunk frame. He nodded in reply, not even looking over at his son. When Russ realized he had no intention of saying anything, he took a chance. "Well, I'm going to get on the lawn." He walked away, and there was no more sound from his father.

● ● ● ● ●

On Saturday morning, Russ called Helen with one last plea to see if she would go pace him on her bike. She said she would rather go for a drive in the country. Although Russ loved Helen, he was not going to give up his fitness, and being ready for football in the fall, simply because she didn't care to ride her bike.

So he turned the tables on her and said no to the ride in the country, then ran alone, a route he knew was going to be extra-long. To the west, out the old river road, past the big gravel pit and over the bridge across the Snake River. He turned north along Cinder Butte Road, made his way, paralleling the Snake, all the way to Woodville Road, where once again he made a turn, this time back to the east.

When he was running through the little settlement of Woodville, his friend Mark Knaggs pulled up alongside him in his father's fifty-two Dodge Meadowbrook, a perfectly waxed deep burgundy, with polished white wall tires. Mark looked very proud, with his left arm hanging out the window, and a straw fedora on his head, tipped at just the right angle. It wasn't lost on Russ that the burgundy hatband matched the color of the Meadowbrook almost to a tee.

Russ was more than happy to stop. He had no idea how long he had been running, but he must have lost eight pounds in sweat by then, and he was soaked clean through. "Hey, Spit!"

"What's buzzin', cousin?" said Mark with a laugh. "Like my cool machine?"

"I like your *dad's* machine."

Mark gave another loud laugh. "Well, it's mine for the day. Headin' into the Falls—gonna cruise the Northgate Mile. If you weren't always runnin', I'd invite you to go with me! But then again, I don't want your sweaty butt all over my dad's nice seats."

"You'd better get rollin', Spit. As slow as you drive, if you give me a head start, I'd hit Yellowstone Highway before you do."

"Oh, right!" With that, Mark spun his tires, flinging gravel and leaving Russ quickly behind.

The rest of the way into town, Russ saw no one he recognized. He ran all the way out Woodville Road until it let him turn south onto New Sweden, where he crossed the river again and eventually came back into town, exhausted.

Thirsty and beat after his run of nearly nine miles, as Russ drew near the Russells' neighborhood, all he could think of was a drink of water. Without compunction, he turned west on Oak and walked on to their house, allowing his body to cool down.

The day was pleasantly warm, and there was a nice breeze flowing, so Russ was halfway dry after making a couple of rounds of the neighborhood. But he was still embarrassed when he knocked on the Russells' door because he was damp enough for it to be seen, and didn't smell much like an iris. Old man Tupper was conspicuous by his absence.

Edie opened the door, and her face showed brief surprise as she realized who she was looking at. "Russ! What are you doing?"

"I was out on a run and thought I'd stop by. I was wondering if I could bum a glass of water off you."

"Oh, yeah! Sure. Come in."

Lorna came in from the back hallway, giving Russ a big smile. "Russ, it's nice to see you. What a surprise. You've been running?"

"Yes, ma'am."

"Listen," said Lorna, putting a hand on her hip. "Why don't you call me Lorna? We're all friends, right?"

"Okay, sure, Lorna." He was amazed how much more natural it felt to call her by her first name than it did Pearl James.

Russ ended up drinking not just one but two tall glasses of ice water before he started to feel rehydrated. When he was finished, Lorna brought a hand towel out and handed it to him. "Maybe you'd like to freshen up a little, Russ. The bathroom is the first door on the right, down the hall."

Russ gladly took the woman up on that, sticking his face down into a sink full of cold water and splashing it over the back of his neck and his throat and hair. When all the salt rime was washed off, he ran the towel over his face and his crew cut—or "lighter," in the vernacular of

the times—and stood back to look in the mirror. Other than a little swelling around his eyes, he was as good as new.

When Russ came out of the bathroom, Lorna invited him to stay and have dinner and then ice cream with them. He was hard-put to turn that down, but he wouldn't do it unless she agreed to let him fix her front steps.

They were finishing dinner, and Lorna had dished up bowls of ice cream, when someone knocked. The two females cast surprised eyes at the door.

"Wow! Grand Central Station today," remarked Lorna with a laugh. "I wonder who this could be."

Setting her napkin down, she walked over to the door and swung it open. For a second or two, she was silent, drawing Russ's curiosity even more and making him scoot his chair to try and see past her. All he could see were the legs of a girl wearing light brown, form-fitting capri pants.

"Mrs. Russell?"

Russ's heart shot into his throat. That voice . . . It sounded like . . . But it couldn't be!

"Yes, that's me," replied Lorna with an obvious question in her tone. "May I help you?"

"I'm Helen James," said the voice. "Edie's friend from school. Is she home?" There was a long, awkward pause from Lorna.

Russ was frozen. His fevered mind thought of going back down the hall to the bathroom. But just as quickly, he banished the thought. There was no getting out of this situation with any grace. His only hope was to play it cool.

He looked over at Edie, and as he had expected, her eyes were glued to his face. He shrugged, knowing the look in his eyes was probably one of bewilderment.

Edie got up as her mom was telling her she had company and walked to the door. Russ noticed that she was trying to position herself in such a way that it would block Russ from Helen's view. What a peach Edie was for that!

"Hi, Helen! What are you up to?"

"Hi, Edie!" said Helen as Lorna backed out of their way. The redhead stepped closer and gave Edie a hug, which it seemed to Russ like Edie returned a little hesitantly. She must be as surprised as he was.

"I was coming from Mallory's and thought of you," Helen went on. "Would you like to go shopping in Idaho Falls with me? It would only be for a few hours."

Edie's hesitancy was blatant. Russ was embarrassed for her. "Well, uh, I'd love to, but . . ."

Russ had to save Edie. It was the gallant thing to do. With a sick stomach, he got up and moved into the room to where Helen could see him. She turned her eyes. Never in Russ's life would he have wanted to see this expression on the face of the girl for which he was head-over-heels. But there it was: sudden, sick shock. It was as if she were trying to digest the news that her mother had been killed.

"Hi, Helen."

"Oh! Hi there, Russ," Helen stammered. It was the first time Russ could remember seeing this stunned look on Helen's face. She was usually as cool as an April breeze. "What are you doing here?"

The truth. The truth would save him!

"I went on a long run, and I was dying for a drink of water. Edie and her mother saved me." He smiled, trying to look casual.

"Oh, that was fortunate." Helen's eyes were unconvinced. Russ didn't know what she was thinking, but a look of belief did not register in her face. She turned back to Edie. "I apologize, Edie. I wish I had known you already had company. I, uh . . . Maybe we can go shopping some other time."

She tried to back away before the sick look on her face could damage her reputation any more.

"No, Helen, I—" Edie was digging for something to say, something that might save them all from this moment. It was her mother who came to the rescue.

"Helen, I am so happy you came by. We'd love to have you come in for a bowl of ice cream. I was just serving it up."

Uncertainly, Helen's eyes jumped from Lorna, to Edie, to Russ, and then back to Lorna. There was no graceful way to escape, and Helen was nothing if not graceful.

"Why, um . . . Sure, Mrs. Russell. Thank you."

And then she entered this realm that Russ had the gut feeling had all of a sudden become the lair of the enemy to her. He smiled, trying to set her at ease. But he knew it wasn't working, and he knew something else: Men were not supposed to be very intuitive in matters such as this, but he was astute enough to realize one thing, out of the blue: Somehow, Helen had decided that she and Russ were an item, for whatever reason, and today, whether by her own choice or not, Edie Russell had declared war.

CHAPTER THIRTY-TWO

The air in the Russell home was cool, and not because of the ice cream. In fact, although the air seemed cool, it was only figurative, and Russ had started to sweat a little once again while Lorna tried to keep an uncomfortable conversation going among the four of them.

Finally, Helen looked around the room. Russ recognized the "time-to-make-a-break-for-it" look in her eyes.

"Well, I should be going. I sure didn't intend to disrupt your day," she said, looking at Lorna.

"Nonsense, Helen. It was a pleasure to have you." Her eyes pivoted to Edie, who smiled.

"Yes, Helen, it was really nice of you to stop. I, uh . . . I'd love to go shopping with you sometime."

She could go with her right now, Russ thought. But he knew better than to suggest it. It was obvious that going shopping was the last thing on either of their minds.

"Of course," said Helen as she stood up, and everyone else stood with her. "That would be fun." The look in her eyes was saying it was now about as likely as seeing an elephant running down State Street.

On a whim, thinking he might be able to salvage something, Russ looked at Lorna, avoiding Edie's eyes as Helen had. "I should get going

too. I need to get home and do some chores my father set out for me. Don't want to make the sheriff mad, you know!" He winked and smiled, but he feared neither looked very genuine.

Lorna and Edie smiled uncomfortably, and the woman spoke. "Okay, Russ. Thank you for coming as well. You're welcome any time."

Russ returned the smile. As he was turning, he remembered cornering Lorna into agreeing to let him fix her steps. Inside, he cringed, but he turned back. He didn't want Helen hearing this, but there was nothing for it now; she was here. "Hey—I'll be back and fix those steps."

"Okay," said Lorna with a smile. "That's very nice of you, Russ."

He nodded and turned, and as Helen was going out the door, he followed her. Both Lorna and Edie had the sense not to follow them outside.

Now Russ was on his final stretch. This was where he either lost the race altogether or at least made a decent showing at the finish line.

"Hey, Helen, could I bum a ride home?"

She glanced over his way as they walked out to where her car was parked but avoided making eye contact.

"I was thinking about going into the Falls by myself. It would kind of be out of my way."

"I, uh . . . Sure . . ." He almost gave in. But giving in was like slipping and falling down in a race and then lying there like a lump and not even trying to get back up and finish. "I just really need to talk to you." His last-ditch effort.

She met his eyes this time, searching them. The expression on her face now was impossible to read. She had had enough time to put on a mask. "All right, I guess I can give you a ride."

They got in the car, Russ knowing without looking back that Edie would be watching them. Before they could pull away, old man Tupper appeared at the end of the street and started walking toward them. He positioned himself right in front of the car as he walked.

"Oh, brother," said Helen with a look of disgust. "Now who's this?"

Russ sighed. "Oh, it's some pesky old man. Lives next door to the Russells."

Helen kept her foot on the brake until the old man walked around to the passenger side, at which time she started to go. Russ stopped her.

"Come on, Helen! Don't take off. He's obviously trying to say somethin' to me. It'll just take a second."

With another sigh of disgust, Helen threw the car back into park. The old man stopped at Russ's window as he was opening it. Tupper leaned far enough down to see Helen on the other side. He nodded. "Miss." Then he looked back at Russ. "Nice car, son," he remarked.

"Yes sir. Real nice."

"You like to play football on more than one field, don't you?"

Russ stared at the old man, confused only for a moment. Then a prideful feeling welled up inside him. "I'm headin' home. I told my old man you said hi." He looked at Helen and motioned for her to drive, seeing her slam it back in drive.

"Just remember," said the old man, and Helen's foot paused on the gas, "you play too many fields you'll never be a winner on any of 'em."

Then he straightened up, and Helen sped away.

After half a minute of silence, but still looking straight ahead, Helen said, "That old man gives me the creeps. Who is he?"

"I don't know. Some old drunk that knows my father. I think he arrested him."

"Hmph." Helen's only reply.

"Hey, Helen, I really need to talk to you."

"Why?"

Her voice was colder than the ice cream.

"Because I have to tell you why I was at the Russells'."

"Oh—you mean at Edie's, don't you?"

"Come on! I stopped for a drink of water."

"You said that. But it's funny how the other day she happened to ask you if she could pace you on her bike, and now you're over there having dinner and ice cream. And you have certainly been over there enough to meet all the neighbors. What's next?"

"Well— Wait, what do mean what's next? I've asked you several times to pace me on your bike and you're always busy."

"So?"

"So . . . I only wanted someone to pace me. Is that so bad?"

"What do you think, Russ? Do you think nobody notices it's a girl—and it isn't me?"

"Well, sure they do, but . . . Helen, it's not like . . ." He couldn't think of the right words to continue.

When his silence went too long, she turned and drilled him with her eyes. "Not like what, Russ?"

"Well, it's not like we're going steady, right?"

She stared at him, and her eyes filled up with an anger he had yet to see from her. "So is that how you want it?"

He tried to stare back. But he was losing. "Helen, what do you want me to do? You say is that how I want it. Is that how I want what? I'm getting confused."

She crossed State Street, driving along ever more slowly as they went. "Yes, I guess you are. I thought you wanted to date me."

"Huh? Of course I do! Helen, I do!"

"Well, you sure aren't proving it."

Russ's head was spinning. He mumbled, "What do I have to do to prove it?"

"You have to be loyal, for one thing."

"Well . . . Helen, I wasn't— I stopped for a drink, and they asked me to stay and eat. Nothing happened. Edie's just a friend."

Helen turned onto Milton. Shelley was far too small for a decent conversation. She drove, then signaled to turn onto Elm. But at the last second she went on past and turned on Fir.

After another minute, she turned on Emerson, heading north, and stopped when she was back at Locust. A long sigh escaped her.

"I don't know what to think, Russ."

"I'm not sure I do either."

She looked over at him. "Wait—what do you mean?"

"I don't know what you want."

"You don't know what I want? Are you serious? Russ, I want to be your steady girlfriend. Can I be any more obvious?"

He stared at her, unaware that his mouth was hanging open. Finally, he clamped it shut. "You want— Helen, that's what I want too! More than anything! I just didn't think— You really want to be my steady?"

"Yes, Russ. Come on. At least meet me halfway."

"Helen, I . . ." He was suddenly at a loss for words. Did going steady mean he would never have anyone to pace him on their bicycle again?

"Are you understanding what I'm saying, Russ?"

"I . . . I'm not sure of anything anymore."

"What? What does that mean?"

"I want to be your boyfriend, Helen. That's *all* I want. But I didn't think you'd care if Edie paced me on her bike, since I couldn't talk you into doing it."

"Russ, I . . . There are things I like to do, but that simply isn't one of them. Isn't that okay?"

He thought for a second, his mind in a whirl. He wanted so badly for her to go with him on his runs—or at least on some of them. But if it was a choice between that and not having her as his girlfriend at all, then there was no choice.

"Yeah, I guess it's okay. I'd like it, but if it's not fun for you then I wouldn't want you to do it."

"So what about Edie?"

"You mean with her pacing me?"

"Yes."

"I guess I won't let her do it anymore."

"And what about going over to her house?"

Russ's heart felt sick. It wasn't like Edie meant anything to him, at least not as more than a friend. But still . . . He felt bad about leaving her and her mother in the lurch, without any man help around the place, when Frank Russell was in such a bad way.

But once again, he wasn't willing to risk what he might have with Helen. And so he swallowed his pride, stomped on his sense of mercy, and nodded.

"I won't go over there anymore, Helen. I promise."

"Really?"

"Yes, really. But is there any way you could at least go check on them until Mr. Russell gets better? They really are in a bad spot."

Helen smiled. "Of course. I'd be happy to do that."

Russ nodded. "Then maybe I could talk Ev or somebody into goin' over there and helpin' them out."

Her smile got bigger, and she reached over on a whim and squeezed his leg. "That's a nice idea. I always thought Edie and Ev would make a nice couple. You're a good person, Russ."

He wanted to thank her, but the moment she said it he had to wonder: Was he really a good person? He wasn't so sure.

CHAPTER THIRTY-THREE

It made Russ sick to have to do it, but he talked Ev Morin into taking Edie to her doctor's appointment on Tuesday. He knew she would be surprised when Ev showed up, but it wasn't like they didn't already know each other, and Edie knew Ev was a great guy. She would be fine with it. To make it easier on everyone, he took off the morning before and headed up to Island Park, to his family's mill and the cabin that sat out behind it, where he would spend much of his summer, as he had for the last three years.

Russ spent a lot of time out in the woods with his uncles, Gene and David. The two were his father's older brothers, Gene being the oldest. They were the tree-fellers in the family, not because they had to do it, but because they loved it so. There was no more exhilarating feeling than making those three perfect cuts and then hearing a monumental tree start to crack and split, yelling out *TIMBER!* at the top of your voice, and hearing and seeing that forest monster land there in the duff, exactly where you had planned it to fall.

So, hot and sweaty, and covered with dots of pine sap and sawdust from all the trees felled during a day's work, Russ, Gene, and David would make their way back to the cabin at the end of the day, driving the big log truck with all the fallen monsters on the back of it, held down with giant chains. The women always had something delicious waiting for them to refuel on.

The end of June rolled around, and Russ had already been in Island Park for a month before he and Gene borrowed a couple of horses from a neighbor Gene had made friends with and went riding through the quiet woods. It was so still and serene there in the evening, and the heat of the day, now dying down, allowed the scents of the forest to seep out into

the air like jasmine. Birds were flitting around the tree tops, and squirrels too. Sometimes they would see deer, moose, or elk, either standing in the gloom where they thought they could not be seen, or bounding away through the sun-dappled shadows.

Altogether, it was simply too beautiful to allow for conversation. But on the way back, when the shadows were growing deep and Gene and Russ had come back into an area of thin timber and meadows, where they were able to ride side by side, Gene said, “That was something, wasn’t it?”

“It sure was. Beautiful. I’m exhausted, but that was worth it.”

“Yep. Say, buddy, how are things going back home these days? I don’t get much word from your folks anymore.”

“It’s all right.”

It was getting almost too dark to see, but Russ felt Gene’s eyes on him for ten seconds or so before he spoke again.

“That’s not much of an answer, Russ. Something troubling you?”

“No, not really. Just tired, I guess.”

Gene grunted. Unfortunately for Russ, his Uncle Gene was a pretty astute fellow, even when he was tired.

“Your mother used to pride herself on getting you kids to play instruments. You still playing the piano? If I recall correctly, it used to be a sore spot with you.”

Russ chuckled. “Yeah, I still play—whenever my mom makes me.”

Gene returned the laugh. After a moment more, he said, “Would you be interested in a little piece of advice from an old man?”

It was funny to hear Gene say that, because he really wasn’t old. Maybe fifty-one or fifty-two was all. “Yeah, Uncle Gene, I’m always interested in what you have to offer.”

“Then listen up. My mother tried to get us boys to play the piano too. Not a one of us took to it. And I know it broke her heart. The day your Uncle Will quit, that was the end of it for Mom. She spent half an hour crying, and that was just when it was loud enough for me to hear her through her bedroom door. Who knows how long she cried quiet after that?”

Russ's Uncle Will was a sad story for the family. Occasions of his mention were few and far between. Will was the only son Russ's Grandmother Ellen had lost in the big war—in the Battle of Garfagnana, in the Tuscan Appenines. Around a thousand Americans were lost in the battle, and Will was reported to be one of the last. The "Christmas Offensive," they called it. That had made Ellen Blevins despise Christmas for years to come.

Russ nodded at his uncle's story. He knew the point was yet to come. Gene didn't disappoint.

"The point is, Russ, I sure do regret not sticking with those piano lessons. Not only because it broke your grandma's heart, but because that would sure have been a nice talent to have, especially at Christmastime."

"Well, Mom likes it when I play. I'll probably keep it up."

"What about your dad?" asked Gene. Russ looked over at him, but now it was too dark to see his expression.

"Ha! Dad leaves the house if he hears me playing—especially when Mom asks me to play certain songs. I don't think that old man really cares what *any* of us are doing. All he cares about is his job."

Gene was uncharacteristically quiet the rest of the ride home. They stopped at the property of Gene's friends and unsaddled the horses, brushing them down good and giving them grain. Then they walked home side by side in the dark, listening to the music of the crickets.

It wasn't until a couple of weeks had passed, when Russ was packing his things to head back down the hill for a few days, that Gene spoke to him again about their piano conversation. They had eaten a hearty breakfast of bacon, eggs, and potatoes, and Russ was feeling pretty good.

Everyone had said goodbye, and they were milling around Russ's old Studebaker to wave to him as he drove away, when Gene said something to his wife, Claudette, then went around and casually opened the passenger door, plopping down for all the world like he was heading home with Russ.

"I'll ride with you out to the highway," said Gene. "I want to tell you something."

"Okay," Russ replied cautiously. He got the car moving, and when they reached the highway, a couple of hundred yards out from the cabin, he rolled to a stop, turning to look at Gene. "What's up, Uncle Gene?"

"Russ, I've thought real hard about this. I always wondered if your father told you this story. Knowing Arch like I do, it would have surprised me if he had. I doubt even Ellie knows, to tell you the truth."

Russ was thinking, *Great. It's one of* those *stories.* He looked at Gene, waiting.

"I finally decided since you're eighteen, and you having the idea that your dad doesn't really care about your piano playing and all, it's probably time you heard this. I'll let you make the choice whether to ever talk about it with your dad, because I'm not sure how he'd feel about me telling you. But it might make a difference in how you look at that 'old man' you mentioned the other day."

Russ was starting to feel uncomfortable. He always did when it came to deep personal stories. He replied, "Okay," and waited.

"Russ, this is real personal, and it makes me sad to have to dredge it up. So I'll probably only tell it once. And I reckon once is going to be enough. When all of us were still pretty young, but me, Will, and David had already left home to join the Army, Arch was stuck around home, trying to be a police officer and trying to take care of our mother by himself. You know your grandfather was hardly ever around—always out gallivantin' around the countryside on a horse, chasin' cows—or helping everyone he knew, except his own family. So after your grandmother got over knowing none of her boys were going to play the piano, she settled down to where she played it herself, sometimes two hours every day.

"Your dad got to where he really enjoyed it, at least according to Mom. She even started to think that maybe someday he'd change his mind and decide to go back to learning to play. So a lot of evenings when it was just the two of them there, Mom would sit on the old piano bench and play to her heart's content, and Arch would sit on the couch smoking and listen to her. It was one of those evenings, when they were all alone, when it happened.

"Mom—I mean your grandmother—was playing a piece. It was your daddy's favorite. He told us she had gotten almost all the way through it when all of a sudden she stopped. He was looking out the window at the sagebrush field behind the house, smoking and listening. When he

looked over at her, she was just sitting there, real still. He said her name, and she didn't answer him.

"He said he started feeling like something was really wrong, so he got up and went over to her. He told me the night before the funeral he would never forget seeing her face. One side of it was all droopy-like—her eye and the side of her mouth. The doctor said it was a stroke. She looked up at Arch when he tried to talk to her, and she looked real confused, like she wanted to say something back to him but couldn't. Arch ran out and pulled the car up, got Mom out into it . . ."

Here, Gene cleared his throat, glancing out his window. For some seconds he sat quiet, until finally Russ heard him swallow. "He drove to the hospital, but on the way there she just kind of leaned over against her window, and when he got there to get her out . . . Ma was gone."

Russ was spell-bound. Where at first he purposely avoided looking over at Gene as he talked, now he couldn't take his eyes off him, and he didn't even think about the tears he saw coursing down Gene's cheek. His big, strong uncle turned to face Russ fully, and both cheeks were wet with tears. He wiped at them to banish them.

"Sorry, bub. Obviously, I haven't told this story to anyone in a long time."

"It's okay, Gene. You don't have to apologize to me. But there is one thing I'd like to know: Do you have any idea what piece of music Grandma was playing when she had the stroke?"

"Yep. Arch remembers that vividly. It was a piece called 'Clair de Lune'."

CHAPTER THIRTY-FOUR

Russ thought about his father all the way home from Island Park. He had a flat tire at the bottom of Ashton Hill, and as he fixed it, he thought of the first time his father had helped him change one, when he was teaching him to drive, out by Presto Hill, near his birth place of Goshen.

He didn't know if the story about his Grandmother Ellen made any of the rest of his relationship with his father any easier, but it sure explained, after all the years of wondering, why the old man wouldn't stay in the house to hear him play. Why didn't Arch tell Eleanor about his mother? Wouldn't it have made everything so much easier if he did? Why did it seem like his father had to keep everything inside?

Russ remembered a feeling of bitter disappointment back when he was eight years old and first getting "Clair de Lune" down, and he had been so excited to play it for the family. Even back then, his first recital, Arch got up and left the room the moment Russ started playing. He had never told anyone how bad that hurt. He had heard his mother later, trying to correct his father's action, but all he told her was she didn't understand, and then he went out in his car and drove away. His father was good at that, when Eleanor tried to talk to him about anything too serious. Russ guessed it was better than a lot of husbands, who instead of leaving decided to slap their wives around.

When Russ rolled into Shelley, he wasn't in the mood to go home. It was a beautiful Saturday, although getting a little on the warm side, and he wanted nothing but to see Helen. As he passed Edie Russell's neighborhood, he looked that way. He wondered what she was doing with herself for the summer. And then he wondered why he should care.

He pulled into the big, rainbow-shaped driveway at Helen's house. He was right behind her Chrysler, and her father's Cadillac was in front of that.

This would be the first time Russ had seen Helen's father since their first meeting. He couldn't even remember his name.

Taking a deep breath, Russ knocked on the heavy oaken door. Soon, he heard faint footsteps, and then Pearl James opened the door.

"Well, hello, Russ! Welcome home! Come in, won't you? I'll go find Helen."

Russ gave her a big smile. How nice it would be if he could get a welcome like this back at home. "Thank you, ma'am—I mean Pearl."

The woman's face grew serious, and her eyes flitted away. The look took Russ aback. Then he heard Mr. James's voice. "Who's there, Pearl?" It didn't sound overly friendly.

"Oh, it's Russ Blevins, dear. He came to see Helen."

The man's voice lightened. "Oh! Russ! Bring him in then." Even as he spoke, his shoe heels were clicking across the tile floor, and soon he appeared in the middle of the room as Russ was stepping inside.

"Hello, Russ!" The man thrust out his hand, giving Russ a hearty handshake.

There was something different about Mr. James from the first time Russ met him. This time, he didn't have about him the polished look he seemed to have fostered before. His hair was in disarray, and he wore a wrinkled shirt, and a tie that was crooked, and very loose. His trousers were also wrinkled, and there was a mustard stain on one leg.

"Sorry about my appearance," said the man as he caught Russ looking him over. "I'm feeling a little reckless today, I guess." He tried to give Russ a laugh, but it didn't feel genuine.

Pearl had waited a few moments, trying to interject something. Finally, she walked away, leaving Mr. James and Russ alone.

For a few minutes, Russ and Mr. James spoke of cutting wood and milling timber, and then of course the upcoming football season, which Shelley was expected to carry all the way to the state championship.

Then Helen appeared at the top of the stairs. "Russ!" Her face brightened, but instead of bounding down the stairs like Russ would probably have done, she descended them in her elegant, well-trained manner, and at the bottom, where he met her, she extended her manicured hand.

Surprised, Russ took it and gave it a squeeze and a little shake. It felt soft in his grasp—soft and unworked.

"Hi, Helen."

"Hi. I thought you told me you were coming home *next* week! What a surprise."

Confused, Russ glanced around. "No, I told you in my letter I'd be home today."

"Oh, never mind," Helen replied with a laugh. "It's just good to have you home."

"Thanks. It's good to be here."

"Hey, Russ, I hate to greet and run, but I have some stuff I have to catch up on," Mr. James cut in. It was a replay of their first meeting.

"Oh, that's all right, sir. It was good to see you."

Mr. James smiled and shook Russ's hand again, then went up the stairs holding a briefcase. His step wasn't as light as it had been the time before.

"Well, Russ, why don't we go in the sitting room," suggested Pearl James, trying to put on a smile, which didn't quite convince Russ. He followed her and Helen into another immaculate room, this one with beautiful carpet and furniture of cherry wood. Here, Pearl stopped him. She gave him an uncomfortable look. "Hey, Russ? I know what I said before, but can you do me a wee favor? Whenever my husband is around, could you please call me Mrs. James? It makes things a lot more comfortable. You understand."

Russ stared at her, momentarily confused. The truth was, he *didn't* understand. But he nodded. "Yeah, sure, ma'am. That's no problem."

She gave him another huge smile—and fake as a counterfeit dollar. "That's a good boy. So . . . I'll go get the two of you something to drink. Sit down, please."

Russ and Helen sat. Russ felt uncomfortable, but he wasn't quite sure why. Something seemed odd about the air in the house all of a sudden. He found himself comparing it to the casual, down-to-earth feel of Edie's. The thought made him frown.

"What's the matter, Russ?" asked Helen.

He looked up. "The matter?"

"You look somewhat sad."

"Oh! No, I'm not sad. I was just thinking."

"Penny for your thoughts?" she said brightly.

"Oh, well . . . I guess I wasn't really *thinking.* I mean, not about anything I can pinpoint." He hated to lie to Helen, but there was no way in the universe he was going to tell her he'd been thinking about Edie. He would rather slap his own father in the face!

Soon, Pearl came back in and brought them root beer in tall, clear glasses, with ice cubes floating on top. Root beer, especially the home-made variety, was his Uncle David's favorite thing in the world, so Russ had had plenty of it since going up to the cabin, and this store-bought kind was nowhere near as good. But after the long drive, it still tasted refreshing. He smiled and thanked Pearl as she went to the doorway. At the last moment, the woman turned and gave Helen a long look and nod-ded toward Russ. The look, Russ guessed, was trying to prod Helen into saying something she would rather not.

When the woman was gone, Helen turned and smiled uncomfortably at Russ. "How has everything been?"

Russ cleared his throat. "Fine, but . . . It seems like there's something more important you want to say."

"Excuse me?"

"There's something going on around here, Helen, and by the way your mother looked when she was leaving . . . What's up?"

Blushing, Helen laughed. "Umm . . . Well, yes, there is actually something. It's funny you should be home right now."

"Funny?"

"Yes, well sort of. I mean, not really *funny,* but maybe fortunate is a better word."

"Fortunate? What's that mean?"

Helen looked around. "Listen, Russ. Would you like to go for a quick drive?"

"Well, I've been in my car quite a while already. I was kind of look-ing forward to kicking back for a bit."

"Oh. Okay." Her shoulders drooped a little. She threw a glance to-ward the doorway.

"Hey. Helen, you're killing me. What's going on? This sure isn't the kind of reception I was hoping for."

Helen tried to give him a smile of apology. "All right. Yes, you are very right, Russ. This isn't how I wanted to welcome you home either. I

am so sorry. But there is something kind of important I need to ask you. A great big favor."

Russ took in a big breath. The way Helen was acting, he had to guess this was not going to be any easy favor. "Okay, shoot."

"Well, something happened down at the office. With my father. There's this silly investigation going, and . . . Anyway it's gotten to be kind of a big mess."

"Investigation? What kind of investigation?"

"Oh, they're saying the books are off a little, and . . . Some people said they think it's something Father did, and . . . Well, I guess he is being investigated for fraud, or embezzlement, or something. I'm not sure I know all of the details. Maybe he hasn't even told Mother."

"So what does all this have to do with me?"

Helen's eyes fell to her hands, which were twisting around each other in her lap. She forced her gaze back up to his. "Okay, somehow I guess your father has ended up being the one in charge of the investigation."

"Dad?" Russ sat up straighter in his chair. "What? How did that happen?"

"No one is really sure, except . . . I guess the police detective and the police chief are sort of friends with my father, and . . . Well, some people thought they weren't qualified to handle the investigation, so the mayor pulled them off. Does that make sense?"

Russ took in another deep breath. He studied Helen's face. He had never imagined her looking and acting this disconcerted. "Yeah, I guess it does. Wow. But I'm not sure what you want me to do."

Again, Helen tried to smile, this time twisting a pearl and silver ring she had on the middle finger of her right hand. She looked so uncomfortable it almost hurt.

"So we were talking about it this morning, and my father . . . He and Mother thought maybe you could talk to your father and get him to drop the whole thing." When Helen finally decided to throw it out there for him to hear, she spoke fast. At the end of her request, she forced herself to gaze into his eyes, but she was only able to hold it for two or three seconds before looking down at her hands again.

Russ was stunned. He stared back at her, his stomach sick. How big was this investigation of his dad's? What had Mr. James done, if anything? Was he in real trouble? And if he was, what was it going to do to Helen? Most disconcerting of all . . . What kind of influence could he possibly have over Sheriff Arch Blevins, the most respected man in all of Bingham County? That man was *never* going to relax his principles. He would take his own life before he did that.

And if he did cave in, it certainly was not going to be for Russ.

Russ was tired of driving, but when he left the James residence, he drove anyway, this time out Taylor Highway. He had to think this thing through. He had told Helen he would try to talk to his dad. But how? He hadn't had to face Pearl or Helen's father. Neither of them had dared show their face again before he left. Now he was left lollygagging down the highway, wondering how in the world he could even think to approach his father with the outlandish proposal that he try to gloss over whatever Mr. James might or might not have done.

But if he didn't do it, what was going to happen with him and Helen? Did he have any choice but to go to his father, to follow through with what the Jameses asked of him? Not as he saw it. His hands were tied.

There was another, even more pressing question that kept coming back to him as he drove endlessly on: Once he asked his father, and his father told him to mind his own business, which was exactly what Russ knew the old man was going to do, was it going to mean anything to Helen that he had at least tried? After all, he was going to lower his father's opinion of him—that thought made him laugh, since it didn't seem like the old man had much of an opinion of him or anyone else lately—so even when his father told him to go away and leave him alone, would Helen accept that he had at least tried?

He had wanted to be where he was with this girl for as far back as he could remember. Now the whole relationship hung in the balance.

CHAPTER THIRTY-FIVE

When Russ got back to the house, he was hailed not as a returning hero, which there was no reason he should be, but as someone who had left behind damsels in distress. Annie and Toni were taking turns at mowing the seemingly expansive lawn, and they stopped when he pulled into the driveway.

"Daddy's making us mow," said Toni. Not a "hi," not a "how are you?" "Can you do it, Russ?"

He looked at her. He guessed he shouldn't expect any better reception from his sisters. He had never had one before.

"Nice to see you too, Toni," he said. "It's Saturday. Where's Dad?"

"Where do you think?" returned Annie as she walked up. "He had to go to work."

"Why's he working on Saturday?"

"Don't look a gift horse in the mouth," quipped Toni. "Just be glad he's gone. He's in a bad mood—again."

Russ frowned. "Wonderful. Then where's Mom?"

The girls looked at each other. Annie returned Russ's frown. "In the house. In her room. Sad."

"Sad? About what?"

"About Dad. He's never home anymore, and when he is he never says anything to anyone—except to be grouchy." Annie looked over at Toni. "I guess we better finish the lawn before he gets back."

Without another glance at Russ, the girls returned to their work, and Russ went up the concrete steps and into the living room. It was empty. The radio was quiet. Russ looked at the top of the big Silvertone console, at the empty place on top, covered only with a doily, where he, Eleanor, and the girls had all begged Arch to put a television for at least a year now. But Arch was too cheap. It was never going to happen.

Russ tiptoed down the hall. The door to the girls' room was closed, as was his. At the very end of the hall, his mother's door was also closed. He put his ear up to it. After twenty seconds or so, he gave it a light tap.

When he did so a second time, his mother replied. "Who is it?"

"It's me, Mom."

"Hold on, Son." There came the sound of bed clothes rustling, and soon the door swung open, and Eleanor threw her arms around him—but not before it registered on him that she had been crying.

"I'm so happy to see you, Russ. Did everything go all right?" She pulled herself away, but kept her hands on his arms.

"Sure. It was a lot of fun."

"Do you want anything to drink? Or a snack?"

"No, ma'am, I'm fine. Say, is Dad going to be home any time soon?"

"Who can say anymore?" Eleanor's hands dropped from his arms, and she looked away. Then she met his eyes again. "Son, I don't know what's going on with your father."

"What are you talking about?"

"He's never home anymore. It's like he doesn't want to be with us."

"You should be glad," said Russ, instantly knowing it was the wrong thing to say.

"He's my husband, Russ. I guess you wouldn't understand."

"No. All I know is he's a grouch, and whenever he's around nobody's even comfortable enough to have a normal conversation. I found out one thing, though." He shouldn't have said it, but as they say, the cat was out of the bag.

"What's that?"

"Oh, maybe I'm not supposed to say anything."

"Well, it's too late now. Tell me."

"Okay, so Uncle Gene told me how Grandma Ellen died."

Eleanor stared. "He did?"

"Yes."

"And?"

"And . . . I think it's the reason Dad won't stay in the house when we play the piano."

Eleanor drew in a deep breath. At last, she reached down and took Russ's hand. "Son, let's go sit in the living room."

When they were on the couch, Russ looked at her earnestly. One glance told him she already knew the story of Grandma Ellen. "You already know, don't you, Mom? How come you never told me?"

"I didn't think it was my place. I hoped someday your father would tell you himself."

"Well, we all know better than that. If he was dying he still wouldn't say anything to us about it."

Eleanor frowned, and a sad look filled her eyes. "Yes, I'm starting to think that's true."

●●●●●

When Arch returned home that evening, after supper, Russ's meeting with him went as he had foreseen. Arch looked him square in the eyes, something he seldom seemed to do anymore.

"Let me tell you something, Russ. I'm the top peace officer in this county. I'm expected to be fair and honest and give the same rights to anyone and everyone who lives here. I would investigate one of my own children the same as I would a total stranger." Now *that* was something that didn't surprise Russ at all to hear—other than to him it seemed like Arch's own children would be judged a little harsher than the rest of the world. "But when it comes to Harold James, I'll tell you right now—he's the last person around here I'd be lenient with. That man is a pompous ass and an arrogant drunk. If I could throw the book at him and make him pay even more than a regular Joe, I would."

And with that, the meeting, such as it was, ended, and Arch Blevins turned and walked out the back kitchen doorway. Russ could hear the heavy plod of his feet, going down into the basement.

Angry, both with himself for bothering to ask, and with his father for his hard, unbending stance, Russ went over and plopped down on the piano bench. It had been a long time—maybe even years—since he had played the piano without being prodded to. But today, feeling as he did, he had a reason to do so, and not an altruistic one.

Opening the keyboard cover, he began to play "Clair de Lune"—as loud as he was able.

Eleanor came down the hall and stood at the corner, looking at him. When Russ turned to her, he saw a tear roll down her cheek.

But even his mother's tears were not going to make him stop playing "Clair de Lune."

A minute later, he heard the closing of the back screen door. The unbending tyrant had left the house.

●●●●●

There was a new show on the television in Billy Earl's house. It was called *Cheyenne,* the first hour-long Western on TV, and the star of the show was a great big, strapping, dark-haired cowboy by the name of Clint Walker. Luther Dean had taken a huge shine to the show, and he enjoyed watching the hero, Cheyenne Bodie, ride about the countryside righting wrongs. But tonight, he had other things on his mind.

With little Isaac Thorpe forgotten in the spare bedroom, where he was busy ogling Billy's Matchbox car collection, Luther sat on the couch, while Billy was on the easy chair, and they were trying to work out the details of Luther's upcoming coup of vengeance. Luther had come up with a way to draw every other peace officer far away from the town of Shelley on the big day. And he was trying to piece together a plan to get Arch Blevins far north of town, far from the scene of where all the other action was going to be. But it was coming up with a sure-fired way to get the sheriff back to town that had Luther stumped.

Suddenly, little Isaac was standing at the doorway to the living room. When the boy's presence registered on Luther, he whirled on him. Had he been listening to their plans? "Hey! You little brat! Get over here."

Shock and fear flared into Isaac's eyes. His glance shot over to Billy, who had also frozen.

"I said come here, boy!" Luther roared.

Unable to withstand, Isaac started forward. Billy finally got his nerve back. "Whoa, Luther! Hold on." Billy scrambled up, and he got to Isaac before he could reach Luther, who was standing now with fists clenched at his sides. "Let's not get too carried away here, buddy."

"You shut up!" Luther roared at Billy. "Stay out of this."

"Luther! Stop, man. You're going to ruin everything."

Eyes wild, Luther looked back at Billy. He took a menacing step toward him, and under the bigger man's baleful stare, Billy cowered back.

Then Luther stopped. He looked over at Isaac. With no explanation at all, the hard look began to melt from his face, and he forced a smile onto it.

"Hey, little man, I'm really sorry. I didn't mean to snap at you. Come on over here and sit with me. I won't hurt you."

Still hesitant, Isaac went forward, until Luther's hand rested on his shoulder. "Come on, buddy, why don't you sit down here? There's a great show on—*Cheyenne.* You're gonna like this one, Ikey. Guarantee you."

As he sat down and settled into the back of the couch, a smile came over his face, and he gave Isaac Thorpe's shoulders a squeeze. "Yes sir, Ikey, we're great pals, you and me. I'd never do anything to hurt you. You know that. You didn't hear anything I was talkin' about with Billy a bit ago, did you?" he asked with forced nonchalance, not taking his eyes off the television and big Cheyenne Bodie.

"No sir. Nothing."

Luther looked over at the boy, gaging him. After a second, he smiled again and patted Isaac's shoulder. "Good boy. Let's watch the show."

And at the same time as Luther settled in to watching *Cheyenne,* a sick look fell over Billy Earl's face while he stared first at Luther, then at Isaac. He closed his eyes and sank back into his chair, for he knew.

The last little piece of Luther Dean's plan had just fallen into place: a surefire way to get Sheriff Blevins back here to Shelley.

CHAPTER THIRTY-SIX

Russ stayed home too long. He should have left Sunday afternoon, or evening, at the latest, to make the drive back to Island Park. But instead, he spent time with Ev Morin, and a little with Pete Basso. He even found an hour to toss a ball back and forth with good old Jack Webber when he called out of the blue on Sunday morning. It had been a long time since they had spent much time together outside of football. Russ was guessing it would have something to do with Helen.

In the city park, Jack caught the ball and smiled. “Good toss!” Instead of throwing it back, he walked on in. “Hey, buddy, I’ve been wanting to ask you something.”

So here it came . . .

“What’s that?”

“What’s up with you and Helen James?”

“What’s up?”

“Yeah. I mean she went to the prom with me, and you went with that Edie chick. So . . . Is there anything serious between you and Helen? Because I’d like to take her out again.”

Russ laughed. “Well, I’ll tell you this, bud. She tells me she wants us to be guy and girl. Steady. But that’s that. It’s not like we’re hitched or anything.”

“But . . . How would you feel about me askin’ her out again?”

“Honest?”

“Well, yeah.”

“Okay. Well, I’d rather you didn’t, if you really want my opinion.”

Jack took a step back. He nodded, musing. “Okay. Okay, then. I won’t. It doesn’t matter. I’m headin’ off to the Navy anyway. Just wanted to see where I could get with her, but not if . . .”

Russ felt the mild look slip from his face, and for a moment he even thought about telling Jack that Helen had tried to cancel their date for the

prom. But he had known and liked Jack much too long to stab him with that kind of ruthless blade. "No, then she's not the one for you. She's not fast. She's a lady. So yeah, let's say she's spoken for."

Jack shrugged. "Well, there's a lot more fish in the sea."

They tossed the ball back and forth a few more times, but the atmosphere had changed, and within fifteen minutes Jack said he had to go, and he did.

Russ started across the park toward home. Halfway across, he thought of Edie and her mother. He wondered if Frank was back home yet. And he thought about the porch steps he had promised to fix and then left without talking about again. He wanted to go check on the Russells, but he had promised Helen he wouldn't be going there. So he headed home.

That afternoon, the phone rang, and Russ's father actually got out of his La-Z-Boy to pick it up. "Hello? Yeah, he's here. Hold on. Russ?" Arch turned and held out the handset.

Russ went and took the phone and answered it, surprised to hear Helen on the other end of the line. *Can I come get you and we'll go for a drive?*

He glanced over at his father, who had settled back into his chair with the Sunday paper open in front of him. The girls were in their rooms napping or otherwise occupied, and Eleanor was in the kitchen cleaning up dishes.

Russ didn't have to think long about going for a drive, although he still dreaded having to tell Helen about his father's response to the idea of helping out her father. "Uh, yeah. Sure."

As Russ started for the kitchen, Arch lowered his paper and pushed his reading glasses down onto the bridge of his nose.

"Where you going, Son?"

"For a ride."

"You just got home from the mill and haven't been here more than a couple of hours all weekend, except to sleep."

Russ stared at his father. Oh, the things he wanted to say! His gun was loaded, but he didn't even dare fire a shot. Inside, he regrouped. "Well, Helen wants to see me. I'm sure we won't be long."

Arch turned his head and looked toward the kitchen, his face impassive. He could have been a world champion poker player. Turning back, he grunted and returned to his paper.

Russ walked into the kitchen. He went up behind Eleanor and hugged her from behind, leaning his mouth close to her ear. "Hey, Mom, Helen's coming to get me. Is that all right?"

With a sigh, Eleanor smooshed the side of her face into Russ's. "All right, Son. I hope you won't be long," she said quietly. Both of them were striving to keep Arch from listening in—as if he would even care enough to try.

"I'll try to be back soon," Russ replied. He hoped it ended up being a lie. He loved his mother, but there was nothing about home right now that tempted him to spend more time here. His father was right: This was only a place to sleep.

Without another glance toward his father, Russ continued on through the kitchen, down the back steps, and out the door into the driveway. Anything to save him having to walk by his grouchy father or feel obligated to tell him goodbye.

He went up to Locust and started walking west, and by the time he reached State Street, he saw the beige Chrysler coming toward him. Twenty seconds later, he met Helen out in the middle of the street, and she put it in park and slid over, letting him take the wheel. "Let's drive out by Blackfoot. We haven't ever gone that way."

Russ was game. Anywhere but home. As he drove, Helen slipped her hand over onto his leg. A chill ran through him. How he wanted to kiss this girl. They still had never done that, and without it his life was not complete.

Casually, Russ put his hand over Helen's and cupped her fingers. Her hand felt cold.

He looked over at her. "Hey, you okay?"

"Of course. Why?"

"Your hand's a little cold."

She sat there thoughtful for a moment, then leaned her head into his shoulder. "Cold hands, warm heart," she said softly.

Russ smiled. He had wondered if she would miss the opportunity to make use of that old saying his mother had worn to a frazzle.

Without any introduction, Helen began speaking: "Faeries, come take me out of this dull world, for I would ride with you upon the wind, run on the top of the disheveled tide, and dance upon the mountains like a flame."

For a moment, Russ sat silent. He was no poet, nor even a student of poetry. But this time her words resonated with him. "Nice! Did you write that too?"

She giggled. "No, silly. That's W. B. Yeats, from the play *The Land of Heart's Desire.*"

Helen wasn't looking up at him. Her head still rested on his shoulder. So she didn't see him smile. He wanted to act like he knew of the play, but he wasn't going to get caught in a lie. "Well, it sounds nice, when you say it."

All of a sudden, she sat up straighter and looked to the east. "Hey, Russ—drive out there, okay?" She pointed toward the Blackfoot Mountains.

"Yeah?"

"Yeah. I don't want to be where there are a lot of people. I have something to show you."

Intrigued, Russ turned on the next road, toward the little settlement of Goshen. When he was quite a ways out into open farm country, with houses scattered around but not many of them very close together, she had him pull off on a farm road that curved along the side of a green wheat field. Two hundred yards in, she put her hand on his, which at the moment was on the wheel.

"Okay, this is good."

He stopped the car. There was really no place to pull it over without being either in sagebrush or in the wheat. He put it in park and looked around. For half a mile in any direction there wasn't a house.

"What in the world do you have to show me that needs showing all the way out here?" he asked. The question was as innocent as could be.

Helen looked up at him. Those bluish green eyes were sparkling, and the copper highlights in her hair framed her silky-skinned, oval face like a masterpiece. She leaned closer to him.

"This."

And with that, she sat up straighter, turning to him as much as she could within the confines of the front seat, and sought his lips with hers.

It was not like Russ Blevins had never been kissed before. His first kiss was at the innocent age of ten, on a dare. Sherlene Bass, the other half of that kiss, had long since moved away to Texas or somewhere. And he had kissed a dozen or so girls since then.

But none of them kissed like Helen James. Her lips were softer, and wetter, than Russ had ever imagined—and he had imagined them a lot. Her hands on his shoulders, on his arms, on his chest, were gentle, yet at the same time stronger than he had thought. He responded to her kiss with the passion he had pent-up inside him from years of watching her, fantasizing about this moment.

Trying to be the gentleman—which was extremely tough—the moment Helen relaxed in her passion, so did Russ. She pressed her cheek down against the top of his chest and let out a long sigh.

"I've dreamed of doing that forever," she said.

Russ was stunned. *Forever?* How long was forever to Helen James? He didn't dare ask.

"Me too. That wasn't what I thought you were going to show me."

Helen looked up. "Oh no? What did you think?"

Laughing, Russ replied, "Well, I didn't have anything specific in mind. But I didn't think it would be that."

Smiling, Helen took his hand and raised it up, dragging slow kisses over his rough palm. She kissed all over it, now and then even touching it gently with her tongue. Now Helen was being a fool. Russ was a gentleman, not a stone.

At last, he pulled his hand back. "Okay, enough of that. Holy cow, Helen! Anybody could come up and find us here."

She glanced around, then looked down coyly, taking his hand again and tracing little patterns on the back of it with the tip of her tongue. She looked up, searching his eyes. "Are you scared?"

"No, but . . . Well, yeah. And you should be too. Can you imagine how this town would blow up if anything happened with us?"

She sighed, and then she brought a hand up and traced his lips with her fingers. "Sometimes I don't think that would be so bad."

Russ's heart was pounding fast. He wanted more of Helen James. But he couldn't. He wouldn't. For too long he had felt her pure and innocent, unreachable. He couldn't pluck that fruit without thinking. He wrapped his arm around her and stared out at the fields and thought what it would be like to marry this girl.

"Do you want to hear another poem?" Helen asked into his shirt.

"Yeah, sure. How many do you know, anyway?"

She laughed. "Too many, I guess."

She sat there for a moment thinking, perhaps preparing herself, and then without introduction she began.

Beautiful must be the mountains whence ye come,
And bright in the fruitful valleys the streams, wherefrom
Ye learn your song:
Where are those starry woods? O might I wander there,
Among the flowers, which in that heavenly air
Bloom the year long!
Nay, barren are those mountains and spent the streams:
Our song is the voice of desire, that haunts our dreams,
A throe of the heart,
Whose pining visions dim, forbidden hopes profound,
No dying cadence nor long sigh can sound,
For all our art.
Alone, aloud in the raptured ear of men
We pour our dark nocturnal secret; and then,
As night is withdrawn
From these sweet-springing meads and bursting boughs of May,
Dream, while the innumerable choir of day
Welcome the dawn.

When Helen finished speaking, the car was quiet. It became even quieter when Russ reached way over with his left hand and turned off the key.

"That was really pretty, Helen."

"It was by Robert Bridges. 'Nightingales'."

"Nice. I wish I could remember all those words."

She squeezed his hand. "You can. You're smart. You just have to want it. *I* want it."

He didn't know if her words had a double meaning. But he didn't intend to find out.

At last, while looking out at the fields, Helen asked a question that Russ had hoped somehow would be forgotten, at least in this idyllic moment. "Russ, did you ask your father about my father's case?"

He froze. Slowly, trying not to let her notice, he filled his lungs with air.

"Uh, yeah. Right when I got home from your house."

"So . . . What did he say? Will Father be all right?"

"Well, Pop wasn't in the greatest mood when I talked to him. I'm still working on him."

"Oh." A sound of flat finality ensued. Russ thought he heard a bee buzz—one hundred yards away.

To break the silence, he said, "How bad does it look, anyway? My dad didn't tell me a thing about what's goin' on."

"I'm not sure. Not super bad. At least I don't think it is. Some little thing, my father said. He wouldn't ever do anything really bad that would hurt anyone. That's why we thought it wouldn't be such a big deal for your father to dismiss it."

Russ cringed. How did he tell this girl his father's *real* reaction? And *why* had he reacted that way? Why was he so heartless? Didn't he know how Russ loved this girl? But then, he wouldn't have cared even if he did know.

"I have to go back to Island Park soon," he said, for lack of something better to say. "I'll talk to him again."

"Tonight?" She gave him a hopeful look.

"Yeah, tonight."

The very thought of bringing it up with his father again made his heart start once more to pound, but nothing like the way Helen had made it pound.

CHAPTER THIRTY-SEVEN

When the silence became deafening while each of them entertained thoughts of their own, they decided they should return to town. Russ dropped himself off, then watched the Imperial drag away and drive on down to Locust, raising a fine cloud of dust. This time, he turned and walked away before it even made the corner.

Russ went in the house, and the whole family was sitting in the dim-lit living room listening to *The Whistler,* a crime drama, on the radio. He cringed. He was hoping to find his father somewhere alone. But he had to bull on. He owed this to Helen—and to himself.

"Hey, Pop." No response. "Dad?"

After a moment, as if the words had to worm their way into Arch's consciousness for a while, he turned and looked up at Russ. "Huh?"

"Can I talk to you for a minute?"

Arch looked over at Eleanor, who sat on the couch between Kathleen and Annie. His eyes flickered back toward the radio, and the soft glow that emanated from its dial.

"Well, couldn't it wait for . . ." A commercial break began. He stopped, glanced back over at Eleanor, then sighed. "All right, just for a minute."

Russ frowned. With the ads on, what in the world was so important? But his father's response didn't surprise him. It had become that way more often than not.

Russ waited for his father to struggle up out of his chair, and then he followed him out through the kitchen and down the back steps to the driveway.

Arch turned and looked at him. "What's on your mind?"

"Pop, I really need to talk to you about Helen."

"Oh yeah. Nice girl."

Russ nodded. Inside, his heart leaped. His father had complimented his girl! Was there hope?

"Yeah, I like her a lot."

"And so what? You're not thinking about getting hitched at this age, are you? What about football?"

"No, Pop!" Russ laughed, embarrassed. "No, nothing like that. I just . . . Well, I told her I'd talk to you. You know, about this thing with her dad."

Arch's eyes went hard, and so did his jaw. "Okay, stop right there."

The heat surged up from Russ's collar. He normally wouldn't think of interrupting his father—*no one* would. But he had to get out what he needed to say.

"Pop, hang on. Please think about this." His father stared at him with bored eyes, his jaw clenched. Russ knew him well enough to see that his ears had already shut down, but he went on anyway. "I really like Helen, but if something happens to her dad, and you're the one that did it, it will be really uncomfortable for us, and—"

"All right, boy, I said *stop,*" Arch cut him off. "That's as far as this is going. *I'm* not doing anything to Harold James. He did it all to himself. Now, I'm the law in this county, and I have to treat everybody the same. You ought to be ashamed of yourself even talking to me about this. If that girl is so shallow that she'd drop you over something her father did, you should start wondering what kind of a girl she is."

Without another word, Arch raised a big hand and put it against Russ's shoulder, pushing him aside to get back to the screen door. It would have killed him to take even half a step to get around him.

Russ clenched his jaws, staring at the big, white-trunked ash tree next door. For a second, his vision seemed blurry. He was so angry he wanted to turn around and punch the side of the house.

He couldn't go back inside. He turned and walked out to the street, then marched south. He had to get away before he did something he would regret.

He kept heading south on Park until a car came up from behind him, slowed way down, then stopped. His first thought was that it was his father, and he gritted his teeth again, walking faster. The car sped up until it was right beside him and laid on the horn.

"Hey, Cus! What's the big hurry?"

Recognizing the voice of Charlie Braun, Russ whipped his head over. Alvin Wheeler's big fifty-one Nash Rambler sat there idling, with a carload of football players inside, Charlie Braun in the front passenger seat.

"Hey, Egg," greeted Russ. "What's up?" He looked past Braun at Al Wheeler, who was leaning forward grinning at him. "Hey, Nash."

The back window rolled down, and Russ heard the discordant, clamoring voices of Johnny Boo Fabian, Pete Basso, and Hank "Slick Fingers" Paterson.

"Hey, boys." The sight of his buddies—his team—made Russ instantly feel lighter.

Charlie thumped the outside of the Nash's door with the flat of his hand. "What'd ya do, bust yer chariot?"

With a laugh, Russ replied, "Nah, it's parked in the driveway. I just needed to stretch my legs."

Charlie jerked his thumb toward the three in back. "Well, we were tryin' to get up a quick game t' clear out the cobwebs. Funny we should run into you out here! Wanna come along?"

Russ glanced at the crowd in the back seat and laughed. "Yeah, and ride in the trunk? Or on the roof?"

Charlie echoed his laugh, as did the others. Nash yelled out past Charlie: "Come on, bud! We're just gonna head out in a wheat field or somethin'. We hardly see you anymore."

"I'll walk. Maybe I'll catch you there."

Giving up, Charlie threw him some general directions to where he thought they'd end up, and then they all hurrahed him as the Nash sped off down the road.

As Russ walked, pulling in the warm, almost perfumy air of the June day, he decided it might actually be nice to get his hands on a pig skin again, so he started to jog, and in ten minutes he reached the specified wheat field. The Nash was parked at its edge.

He walked out to the boys and caught a surprise spiral from Johnny Boo. Johnny laughed. "Dang, bud, you ain't lost it yet."

Russ scoffed. "Oh yeah, like that was some tough throw!"

Alvin, walking up, said, "Hey, did you guys hear what happened with those Thorpe boys?"

Pete replied, "My dad said something about it. I didn't catch the whole thing."

"Yeah, bro, it was crazy! I guess some bunch of white guys jumped 'em. Tried to knock 'em around."

Intrigued, Russ had perked his ears to the conversation. "What happened?"

"Oh man! Those two boys busted 'em up! Bad."

"Good for them," Pete said. "What were they jumpin' 'em for in the first place? Because they're Indians?"

"Exactly!" said Slick. "What are you, some Injun lover?" He jabbed Pete in the ribs.

Pete smacked his hand. "Yeah, I guess! You oughtta try growin' up a stinkin' Wop like me. I feel sorry for a lot of people you guys don't think about." Pete sounded pretty light-hearted, and he probably was, but the words of both of them struck Russ hard.

"So wait, guys . . . You saying the Thorpes . . . They're Indians? Are you talkin' about Isaac Thorpe's family?"

"Oh yeah!" replied Pete. "What rock have you been livin' under, bud? Real live Nez Perces, from what my daddy tells me."

Russ looked from Pete, to Slick, and back to Pete. Then his eyes skimmed the others. "Are you guys pullin' my leg?"

"Honest Injun!" said Slick Paterson, then let out with a big laugh. "Serious! Well, they're half, anyway—from their mom, I guess."

Russ felt like a fool. He had known Isaac Thorpe for . . . How many years *had* that kid been hanging around, anyway? How had he never found out he was part Indian?

He thought back to the recent time when Isaac had gotten beaten up. Had that beating had anything to do with this? And why? What did guys have against an Indian? Nothing more than his skin color? If that was all it came down to, it really was a sad world. And the Thorpes weren't even all that dark.

They played ball for a while, but Russ couldn't get his mind off Isaac Thorpe. How was that little kid doing, anyway? Had he had any more trouble since his fight? He thought back on all the times Isaac had asked

him to go to a movie or play ball, or even go for a walk—all the times he had thought of some excuse to turn him down, some excuse that at the time sounded perfectly valid. Now, none of those excuses seemed good enough. Isaac hadn't come to bother him for a long time now. He had finally driven him away.

Russ at last made an excuse and headed home. He had too much to think about to want to be tossing a ball around. Besides, he needed to pack his things to be ready to head back to the mill.

Instead of returning home, Russ ended up turning west onto Fir Street. He walked down to where Yellowstone Highway became State Street, wandering more or less aimlessly, enjoying the pleasant afternoon air, which was starting to cool down as a gentle breeze began picking its way in from the southeast.

While deciding which way to walk at the corner of Fir and State, he saw a pickup coming in from the south, and he recognized the Russell rig. It slowed when they got close, then came to a stop and backed up. You could do that on the main street of Shelley on a Sunday afternoon—it was that dead.

Russ walked over, more glad to see the Russells than he would have expected. As he got close, it dawned on him that it wasn't Edie in the passenger side, but Frank, her father.

Frank was a solid-looking, handsome man, with greenish-blue eyes and a head of short-cropped, coppery brown hair that shone in the sun. He had the look of an actor from Western movies.

Edie leaned past her father. "Hey, Russ!"

Russ waved at her. "Hi, Edie." He smiled at Frank. "Hello, sir."

"Hi, Russ. Good to meet you. Edie has told me a lot about you. Well, I've actually seen you and maybe met you before, but it's been years."

Russ politely replied to Lorna's salutation, then looked back at Frank. "Is this the first time you're coming home?"

"No, I've been back for a couple weeks now."

"Oh, that's great."

"Yeah, I'm glad we saw you," said Frank. "I've been wanting to thank you for helping out while I was in the hospital. Especially cutting out that bad branch."

Russ felt a surge of guilt, thinking about the rickety steps he had never followed through on. "Oh, yeah, don't worry about it. I was glad to help. Sorry I didn't make it back to fix up those steps."

"Oh, no worry there. Your friend Everett came and did that. They're solid as concrete now."

"Oh, wow! Ev, huh?"

"Yeah. He's been a real big help around the place."

"He has?" Russ was almost shocked, and he didn't even know why. Russ was, however, the one who had asked Ev to take Edie to the eye doctor the day he had promised he would do it. He should be happy that his buddy had gone the extra mile.

Russ heard Lorna saying something from the driver's seat, too quiet for him to make out. Frank looked at her, then turned his face back to Russ. "Yeah, Russ, we were thinking about having you over to the house for a steak dinner some night. You game?"

"Well, sir, I, uh . . ."

"Sounds like a yes to me," said Frank, with a grin. He slapped the truck door with what Russ realized was the stump of his missing hand. It sickened him to think about it, since a missing hand would end for him so many of his own life's dreams.

He tried to think of a reply to the dinner invitation. He couldn't take them up on it. He had promised Helen he wouldn't go over there. But how did he turn Frank Russell down, when he looked so enthusiastic?

"Okay, well, I'll let you know when I'm going to be back in town," Russ said, hating himself for the lie. He had no intention of calling them when he came back. But hopefully they would forget, and it would never happen.

"Great," replied Frank. "You want a ride anywhere?"

"No, sir. I'm just taking a walk to enjoy the town a little bit before I have to head back up to Island Park."

"All right. Then you take care. Sure was good to see you."

Russ waved at them as the pickup rolled north. His thoughts were on Ev Morin, his best friend. What was his buddy doing? Had he found something that really drew him back to the Russell home? Or was he only going because he was a nice guy?

Ev was indeed a good guy, but he had a job, and a lot of chores to do at home, and . . . Russ couldn't stop thinking about his friend, and the Russells, all the way back home.

CHAPTER THIRTY-EIGHT

Russ returned home again two weeks later, and this time he had made sure that Helen James understood the exact date he would be there. He had even ended up rendering her a little petulant over the phone by making her repeat back to him what he had said.

He went to Helen's house first thing, and because it was a Saturday again, both Pearl and Harold were home. They greeted him with big smiles, and Harold gave him a slap on the back. But like the visit before there was something different in the air. And Harold, unshaven for more than a couple of days and once again in a wrinkled shirt, this time in jeans, without a tie, did not look well. His eyes were red-rimmed and appeared swollen. He and Pearl quickly made an exit, but not before Russ caught a meaningful look in Harold's eyes that was meant for Helen, and a nod toward Russ that he suspected he wasn't supposed to catch.

Helen took Russ into the parlor again, and they sat and sipped on lemonade Pearl brought them before once again making herself invisible.

After initial pleasantries, all of which seemed to have taken on a superficial ring, Helen went straight for the throat.

"Hey, Russ, I was wondering, have you had a chance to talk to your father any more about the thing with my father?"

"Uh . . . No, I haven't spoken with him since I left two weeks ago. Dad isn't much for talking on the phone or any of that jazz—especially as expensive as it is for long distance."

"Oh. Well, maybe you could ask him again today."

"Yeah, sure." Russ made a face as if he was surprised she would even question the thought. "I meant to as soon as I get home." But really he hadn't meant to. He had been trying to put the entire thing out of his

mind. It made him cringe even thinking about bringing it up again with his dad, who had made it plainer than his hard, cold heart that his sense of justice was not going to budge.

He decided right then and there that like it or not, he was going to try again. He would simply take a different strategy.

An uncomfortable air hung in the Blevins home when Arch returned that evening, in time for supper. The sheriff again seemed to make a point not to ask Russ to pray. This time, he went to Doris.

When her prayer was finished, they ate mostly in silence. The only sounds were of silverware clinking against plates, or someone quietly asking someone else to pass something. Russ kept on eating and eating until he realized he had gulped down way too much. Now his guts hurt, but he kept nibbling at a roll. One thing he had noticed tonight was that his mother wouldn't seem to make eye contact with his father, and it had been that way on his last visit as well.

The one thing he did know was that it was going to be a really bad time to talk to his father.

The more he thought about it, the more worried he got. Finally, he decided it would have to wait until tomorrow, while his mother and the girls were all in church.

● ● ● ● ●

Sunday came and went, and Russ never worked up the guts to talk to his father. It was sometime during the day, while he was over spending a little time with Helen after church—which turned out to be almost as uncomfortable as being at home—that Russ came up with the plan to ask his father if he could go to work with him. Maybe the thought of his wanting to spend some quality time with his old man would soften Arch up a bit.

When he returned home that evening, and his father was sitting in his La-Z-Boy reading the Sunday paper, in spite of the radio program going that all the females of the house were glued to, Russ popped the question.

Arch lowered his newspaper and gave Russ a blank stare for several seconds. "What was that again?"

"I wondered if it'd be okay for me to come ride with you at work tomorrow."

Arch's lips thinned out as he continued to stare at Russ. His mind was obviously more on whatever he had been reading in the paper than it was on Russ's question.

At last, he shrugged. "I don't understand why. It's not that exciting."

"Just wanted to spend some time with you, Pop."

Arch seemed to have a hard time digesting this idea. At last, he shrugged. "Well, if you really want to, I s'pose that would be fine."

Russ smiled. He had made his first score—and it wasn't even the end of the first quarter.

In the morning, Russ was up early, dressed in a red and gray shadow-plaid Western shirt, tan slacks, and his chukka boots. He didn't know if he was overplaying his hand, but on a whim he had cooked bacon, eggs, and toast. When his father came down the hall, freshly shaven, in his uniform and carrying his hat, he lurched to a stop at the kitchen doorway. He saw Russ standing at the stove, then let his eyes scan the room.

"Where's your mother?"

"I think she went back to bed."

"Huh?'"

"Back in bed, I think."

"Huh."

Arch walked closer, his nostrils working overtime, and glanced over the skillets where the last of the cooking was taking place.

"You cook this?"

"Sure, Pop. I knew you'd be short on time."

"Huh." No thank you, no smile—everything Russ was accustomed to.

They sat down at the table, where Russ had set the skillets, a couple of plates, and forks, and they ate ravenously. Russ knew he had to get his fill fast, because the moment his father was finished, he would be up and ready to go.

This morning, without any of the girls about, there was of course no time wasted on a prayer.

As Russ had expected, the moment his father was done, he threw down his napkin, got up and grabbed his fedora. Russ threw the last piece of bacon into his mouth and lurched out of his own chair, not bothering to wipe his mouth.

They walked out to the Crown Vic. Arch started the engine, and while it was idling, trying to warm up and lubricate itself, he fine-tuned Ernest Tubb on the radio, singing "Walking the Floor Over You."

At last, they backed out of the driveway and drove off, and in no time they were heading south down Yellowstone Highway. In the excruciating quiet, "no time," to Russ, seemed like eternity. They were listening to the Andrews Sisters singing, ironically, "Can't We Talk It Over?" when Russ got bold enough to break the silence with something he had studied out for long enough to feel it sounded innocent.

"So are you working any big cases now?"

"Sometimes."

Russ frowned. *Sometimes?* What was that supposed to mean? Had his father even heard his question?

"Like what?"

Arch kept staring at the road. After a while, he glanced over at Russ. "Did you say something?"

This was going to be a long day.

"Yeah, Pop, I was asking what kind of big cases you're working. Will they let you talk about it?"

"Sure, I don't see why not."

Silence. The tires rumbled on the primitive asphalt. How did he even keep a conversation like this alive? Five minutes slogged by. His father had lost track of whatever they had been talking about, and he was swept up with his own thoughts. Maybe it was time to try another tack.

"What do you think about football this year?"

Arch looked over. "Football? Why?"

"What do you mean why?" Russ had to battle hard to hide his frustration.

"What did you ask about it?"

Enough.

"Hey, Pop, is something goin' on? It doesn't seem like you're hearing anything I say."

Arch stared at him for a long several seconds, long enough for Russ to get nervous about the impending direction of the car. At last, his old man sighed and looked back at the road.

"Oh, yeah. Well, we've had some rough things to deal with at the office lately. Unsolved crimes—you know. Same old stuff. Same criminals, coming back again and again."

"Anything you want to talk about?"

Arch drove for a long time. "One of the Blackfoot city councilmen got drunk and ran over a farmer's cow. Crippled the cow. Almost killed himself. Now they're trying to decide who was at fault—the councilman for driving drunk, or the farmer for letting his cow wander loose."

For some reason, the ludicrousness of the idea made Russ laugh. "Or the cow, for wanting to wander in the first place."

His father looked at him, then after a moment let out a chuckle himself.

"The things we have to deal with," he said. A smile stayed upon the corners of his wide lips for quite some time after that, while Russ sat back and soaked in the silence, thinking about his father, and about Helen James.

They arrived at the Bingham County jail without much more talk passing between them. Inside the jail, they were greeted by Deputy Mark Daniels. Mark, who stood a couple of inches shorter than Russ, was in his late thirties, and one of Sheriff Blevins' good deputies—one of the few that he talked about at home in good terms. He had a friendly smile on his face, but behind his eyes there was often a look of sadness.

The day at the office was slow and routine, and during a stretch when Arch had to leave to confer with the coroner, he asked Mark to take Russ out on patrol with him through some of the farm country.

Mark and Russ had a nice conversation as they drove, but it eventually came out that Mark's wife had been very sick. Their medical bills were stacking up, and the Daniels family, Mark, his wife, and five children, were down to eating beans and ketchup, and sometimes bread that kindly friends and neighbors would bring over because they felt sorry for them. Mark didn't like to talk about it, but Russ apparently said something that touched a nerve and made Mark break down and spill his guts.

When he finished telling his woes, he said, "I hope you won't say anything to anybody, Russ. I'm trying to keep it quiet if I can. You understand? I just needed to tell somebody, I guess."

For a while, Russ was silent. Then at last he asked, "Hey, Mark, are you going to be all right? I mean with money and stuff?"

Mark stared out the windshield. Once, he looked over at Russ, but he returned his eyes to the road when he saw that he was being watched. Finally, he said, "Yeah, I've had a little help. I think we'll be okay."

When they returned to the jail, there was a note on the desk. A very cryptic note saying simply: *Mark, I had to go back to where I've been conducting that investigation. Will you please give Russ a ride home?*

CHAPTER THIRTY-NINE

It was a quiet ride back to Shelley. Russ tried half-heartedly to get Mark Daniels to tell him what his father's note meant, and what investigation he was working, but Mark shut him down, telling him it was something he didn't feel comfortable talking about and that if his father ever wanted his family to know about it it was going to have to come from him.

That evening, Russ drove with Helen to the Falls, where they ate at Jack's Chicken Inn. It was one of the more expensive places in Idaho Falls, the kind of establishment Russ would take a date if he wanted her to know she was special. Tonight, it was also to make up to Helen for not yet being able to get through to his father.

To Russ's chagrin, talk was sparse. Helen wasn't rude, nor even cold. She was simply distant. Her thoughts were obviously elsewhere. Even when she was ordering her meal, she didn't seem to be listening to anything the waitress said, and she had to repeat almost everything twice.

Toward the end of their meal, when Helen was to the point of picking at the remains of her already-tortured food, she looked up at Russ and took a big breath. "Hey, Russ?"

"Yeah?"

"Do you think your father will ever soften up on mine?"

Helen didn't mean it this way, but to Russ it felt like a punch to the guts. "I don't know, Helen. I hope you know I'm trying my best to work on him. But he's gotten to where he's like a wall."

He sat there for a few seconds after saying that, watching Helen's reaction, before a realization came to him. Without thinking about it, he voiced his thoughts. "Actually, you know what? My dad's always been hard to talk to. I guess I never thought about it until lately. It seems like he'd rather be anywhere else but home, and if he is there all he does is sit around with his nose in the paper. He doesn't say much to anyone. He comes home mostly to eat and sleep, and maybe to work in the yard."

Watching Russ as he talked, Helen's face softened. She reached across and squeezed his hand. "Hey, Russ, I'm sorry. That sounds hard."

Embarrassed, Russ jerked his hand away and rubbed it across his mouth. "Hey, don't worry about it. I don't really care." He realized he was lying through his teeth. He tried all the time to tell himself he didn't care what his dad was doing or thinking. Sometimes he was even able to make it work, if he tried hard enough. But then other times, when he was all alone, lying in bed, or even out on a long run, he would think back and remember throwing the ball with his dad, or even working, maybe raking leaves with him in the yard, when it seemed like they were really a father and son—almost friends. Sometimes his father even used to go not only to his football games—of which Russ had to admit he had never missed one at home—but even to his practices.

Now those days were gone.

Without warning, Helen got up and came around to Russ's side of the booth, scooting in until their legs were touching. She put an arm around his waist and gave him a squeeze, not saying a word.

Before going home, they drove out to the east hills and parked, up on a high bluff where there were nothing but far-scattered farm houses. Down below them in the distance, the lights of the city sprawled out, sprinkled in the blackness like little hard candies on top of a deep chocolate cake: white, orange, and pale yellow. For some reason, a distant city always looked sort of magical and homey to Russ, even if in reality it had its dirty, poverty-stricken places. At night, from up above, it all looked something like the Emerald City, in the Land of Oz.

Helen reached over and took Russ's right hand in hers, then leaned into him and lay her head on his shoulder.

"What do you want out of your life, Russ?"

He sat there thoughtful. "To play ball," he said at last. He knew what a lame, canned answer it was.

"Nothing past that? You don't think of anything else at all?"

Russ's heart was pounding. When it came right down to it, he and Helen hardly even knew each other. As much as he would have liked to claim otherwise, he was savvy enough to see they had a long time ahead of them if they were really going to know each other inside and out. And yet he did have other dreams, beyond football. But that was a realm that scared him to talk about more than anything else he had ever known.

"I do think of something else." He stopped. How did he dare go on?

She squeezed his hand a little harder. "What, Russ? What else do you think about?"

"You."

She raised her head and looked up at him, trying to read his eyes. "You do, really? What about me?"

Talk about feeling cornered! Russ should have kept his mouth shut. "Oh, I don't know. Just . . ." He had to think fast, and talk fast. How did he give her even the slightest hint of where his thoughts about them went without saying too much and embarrassing himself? "I guess sometimes I wonder what's going to happen to us after school. It's only one more year till we graduate. I never thought school would be done."

She leaned her head against his shoulder again. "I know. Russ, it scares me really bad. Does it scare you?"

He had to stall. What was a big halfback football star going to do, admit that something scared him? "Well . . . Not really. I mean . . . What do you mean by scare?"

"I mean life seems so uncertain. When you're in school, everything is laid out for you, and even at the hardest nothing really seems hard, when you look back. But the next thing you know, you have to think about college, and who you'll marry, and raising a family, and maybe getting a job. You have to be the grown-up, even if you still feel like a dumb kid. I'm scared. One more year, Russ. Just one more. And then

everything changes. Every secure thing in our lives, every little thing we took for granted—it's all gone."

She stopped talking and was quiet for a long time. Russ was frozen. He wasn't ready to talk about this. Never in his entire life had he been forced into a place where he had to discuss personal things like this. He had always kept a hard shell over his emotions. Helen was trying to break him!

A full two minutes passed before Russ felt Helen's body shaking. It hit him like a truckload of coal that she was crying. Panic almost set in, but then he reminded himself again that he was a big, muscular football star. Afraid of nothing! Yet scared all the same.

"Hey, Helen! You okay?"

Caught in her weak moment, Helen turned so she was facing Russ more fully and threw her arms around him, letting herself start to cry in earnest. Startled, Russ wrapped her in his arms and held her, afraid to speak.

Some time passed before Helen sobbed herself to silence, except for an occasional sniffle—and even her sniffles were lady-like.

"I'm sorry," she said in a soft voice. "It's just so much. I'm overwhelmed. Thinking about school ending, having to grow up, and now this whole thing with my father, and wondering what's going to happen. It's tearing me apart, Russ. I don't know where to turn anymore."

With his heart pounding, Russ drew in a deep but silent breath. He steeled himself to enter this realm of trying to comfort a girl he was afraid he was in love with. He held her away from him and looked into her eyes.

"Hey, it'll be all right. I'll keep working on my dad. How bad is that thing, really? What's the worst that can happen?"

Helen was quiet for a long time. "I think it's way worse than they led me to believe before. I'm not sure, but my mom is in a dither, and Father spends so much of his time in his room now, or drinking. He never used to drink like this before, Russ. I'm scared. I think he could go to prison."

"What? Prison?" he echoed. "No way. It can't be that bad."

"Really? You don't think so?"

Although he was afraid to commit himself for fear he would be wrong, Russ couldn't help trying to comfort Helen. He hated to see her sad. "Yeah. How bad could it be?"

She gave out with a sobbing sigh. "Yeah. Maybe you're right. But Father seems almost as scared as I am. I've never seen him like this before."

Russ swallowed. That statement quieted him. Maybe he should stop before he got in too deep. He couldn't make any promises. It wouldn't be the first time some businessman had gone to prison for wrongdoing. He took her in his arms again, and this time neither of them spoke. Helen was right: Their future was so uncertain.

Without getting the guts to talk to his father again, Russ packed his things that night in his silent, shadowy room, and the next morning, after waiting for his father to go to work before leaving his room, he went out and said goodbye to his mother and drove back up to Island Park while the girls were still asleep.

The honey-sweet scent of the lodgepole forests of Ashton Hill and Island Park coming in through his wing windows was refreshing after leaving the lowland farm country. If it weren't for football, he would love to live up here forever. This was closer to heaven than any place he had ever been.

Russ didn't return home this time for a full month. By that time, the summer was drawing to a close. It was a time he always hated to face, in some ways, but particularly this year. This was his last summer up here at the Park. Like Helen had said, after this school year, everything about life was going to change. Since that night with Helen, he had thought an awful lot about it. One more football season. One more winter shoveling snow and driving on the icy roads of Shelley, Idaho. One track season. One Senior Prom. And then he was going to walk up on stage and accept his diploma, a little piece of paper telling him it was all over. The idyllic, simple part of life that was childhood and young adulthood would have reached an end. The serious, difficult part of life, where all big, hard decisions were up to him, would begin. The thought sometimes left him short of breath.

Russ had spent a lot of his spare time up in Island Park running. At least twice every week, he would drive down to the bottom of Ashton

Hill and run as far up the hill as his strength would allow. Those were the best workouts he had ever had—except perhaps for the day after the tree felling incident, and the brutal workout his father had concocted for him, pulling the railroad ties.

When that thought first had come to Russ, while he was driving home past the little town of Saint Anthony, it was almost jarring. He had never stopped to think about that day as anything but a punishment. But all of a sudden he realized maybe there was more to that railroad tie torture than he had thought. Maybe it was more than a mere punishment. Maybe he should have taken it to heart and followed the routine even after that day. For quite a while after that, he thought about his father. Was there more to his old man than met the eye?

A strange thought hit Russ in Shelley. He had just left the James house, where there were no cars in the driveway and no one answered his knock at the door. He started to head straight home, but then he thought about the Russells. Would they be home? He had the feeling that he should go see them. He even turned his car that way. But then he thought, *Why?* Why would he want to open that door again when he had so artfully closed and locked it? Chiding himself, he turned on the next street and made for home. He was better off without Edie Russell in his life—and she was better off without him.

Russ was only home for a one and a half-day stay, and then he headed back up to Island Park for the last time. He worked three more weeks at the mill, got a handful of cash in payment, and packed his things that last morning in late August.

Before he left, his Uncle Gene took him to the side and shook his hand.

"It's been good having you up here with us, Russ. As always. So I guess this is it, huh? Probably your last summer in the Park."

"Yeah." A feeling of overwhelming sadness washed over Russ. A part of his youth was fading away forever, a part he could never reclaim. It was jarring to think about.

"I want you to remember something about your dad, all right?"

Here goes. "Okay."

"It's just this. He's a tough bird. He's had to be. A tough life has molded him. But even when he acts his toughest, that old bird still loves

you and those girls and your mom—more than you'll ever know. He'd throw himself in a fire before he'd let anything happen to one of you. Someday you'll see that."

Russ frowned. "It sure doesn't feel like it."

"No? Then you're not feeling for it deep enough. Do us both one favor: Think about what I said. And watch your dad carefully. It's there. You'll see it. You guys are his whole life. I promise you that."

Russ tried to believe it. But he didn't. He knew his father better than Gene did.

"All right, Uncle Gene. Thanks."

"No, thank *you,* son. It really has been a pleasure to have you. Good luck with your football season."

Russ said goodbye to the others, and Gene got in the Studebaker and rode with him again out to the road. Toward the end of the lane, he put out his hand and squeezed Russ's leg. "Hey." He acted like he was going to say something, but then he stopped and looked away, and down the highway. He gave a couple of brisk nods of his head, then, without looking at Russ, said, "All right, buddy. Drive safe."

He got out of the car before Russ could see into his eyes and gave the roof a couple of hard pats.

Russ drove away with a knot in his throat. He was going to miss Gene and the rest of the family there. It felt like he was leaving a huge part of his heart here in this lodgepole forest, and one of the most meaningful pieces of his adolescence.

● ● ● ● ●

The first evening back in Shelley, with a fresh promise to Helen on his tongue to talk to his father about the investigation, things came to a head in the Blevins home.

Sitting next to Arch, little Kathleen knocked over her glass of lemonade, and part of the flood washed up onto Arch's plate, mixing with his mashed potatoes.

"Sorry, Daddy!" said Kathleen. But it wasn't enough.

Arch jumped up. "Damnit! What is wrong with you people? Clean that up now." His face was unreasonably scarlet.

Eleanor got up and threw down her napkin. "It was an accident, Arch! What are you doing?"

"Hush!" he shot back.

The woman stared him down. Tears had filled her eyes. Russ couldn't take his eyes off her. He had never seen so much fury in his mother's face.

"We need to talk—alone," she said, her voice barely controlled.

"Well I don't want to," Arch shot back, his eyes flashing at Kathleen. He looked like he was about to yell at her again, but he held it in.

"Arch. *Now.* We have to talk."

"I'm done," he growled. "I'm going for a drive."

He turned and headed out onto the porch and down the back steps. Undaunted, Eleanor rushed after him. She caught him in the driveway at his driver's door. Russ had followed partway. He stopped at the top of the stairs and heard every word of their exchange.

"What's going on, Arch?" He reached for his door handle, but she blocked his way.

"Move."

"I *won't* move! Tell me what's happening! I'm sick of you treating us this way. Are you seeing somebody, Arch?"

"What?"

"You heard me perfectly well. I think you're having an affair."

"You're crazy! I ought to—"

"You ought to what, Arch? Hit me? That's how you handle everything, isn't it? Just tell me if I'm right. You owe me at least that."

"You're wrong. Now get out of my way." With that, he shoved her to the side and threw open his door. Sliding in, he fired up the engine and sped backward out of the driveway. Eleanor knew at least enough not to try and stop him.

She wept after her husband drove away. She sat in her room with the door shut, and neither Russ nor any of the girls dared even approach her, in her grief and anger. It was an intolerably long evening.

And Russ found himself really starting to hate his father.

CHAPTER FORTY

Senior year for the Class of '56 began, and Russ buckled down for the ride. It was rough for the first while, because he wanted nothing more than to think about football, not school work. Football, and Helen James.

Russ avoided going to the James home like the proverbial plague. His father was distant and taciturn, and he still had not worked up the courage to talk about Harold James with him again. So when he spent time with Helen, it was right after school, only for a few minutes, or after football practice. She seemed happy when they were together, and they still shared as many laughs as serious moments. Russ listened to Helen talk about her dreams, while he held his own inside. He was pretty sure she didn't care to hear about football. And it didn't matter. He only wanted to know more about her.

But at the end of the second week of school, the bomb hit. Helen had come to the house for supper, in spite of Russ's wishes to the contrary. Fortunately, it was one of the many nights recently without a father in the home.

The girls laughed and talked about school, while Eleanor tried to look and sound interested, in spite of the pain etched all over her face. As soon as the dishes were in the sink, Russ took Helen and bolted to the car, and they drove south, with long, full rows of potato vines in fields on every side, soon ready to harvest.

Russ sensed what was coming. The feeling was emanating from Helen like her perfume on the air.

"Russ, have you talked to your father?"

"No."

"Can I ask why?"

"I don't know, Helen. Something's goin' on. Nobody can even get close to him, not even my mom."

"I'm sorry," she said quietly. She folded her hands in her lap and studied them for a long time, like some world-renowned sculpture.

Gravel rattled beneath the tires, and a steady plume of dust funneled up behind them.

"I don't know what to do," Russ said, breaking the long dearth of speaking.

Helen looked over at him and drew in a deep breath. She sighed it out and was silent. And then, after two minutes, she said, "Russ, I have to tell you something."

"Okay."

"But I can't. I'm scared."

"What?" He turned and stared at her, veering off onto the edge of the road and swerving back to right the Chrysler. "Sorry. What's going on?"

"My father. He . . . he's worried sick, and he's so mad at your dad."

"Okay. A lot of people are, I guess."

"Yeah, but not like my father."

Russ's heart had really begun to pound now. His guts were telling him something dreadful. He didn't want to hear the rest.

"You've gotta tell me, Helen. Keeping it to yourself isn't going to help." He tried to run through scenarios in his head, but he couldn't find but one. And it was the worst case.

A tear fell down Helen's cheek, and she slapped it away. She took a quick, deep breath, closed her eyes, and lowered her head. Russ drove. And waited. But he was only waiting for the sound of her voice. He had already read her mind.

"Father won't let us be together anymore."

After spitting out the words, Helen whipped her face the other way and stared out at the passing potato fields, the sugar beet fields, and the already-harvested fields of grain stubble.

Russ looked straight ahead, hardly able to breathe. He tried not to think. But thoughts kept raging through his head. He kept trying to believe that by "us" she must be speaking of someone else. But there was no one else.

Then he realized something. It didn't matter what Harold said. First of all, he would get over his anger in time. And second, Helen was her

own woman, wasn't she? They could still be together. They would simply have to hide it a little better.

He drove in silence for five minutes or more before reaching out and putting his hand on Helen's leg. It stayed there for only a few seconds before Helen, without looking over, put her hand down as if to lay it over his, but then gently removed it from her leg and set it back on the seat between them.

"We'd better head back to town. Father is expecting me not to be very long."

And that was that. On the way back, he timidly brought up the possibility of their still seeing each other on the sly. He was met by a brick wall.

"I can't, Russ. That's all. Let's don't make this any harder than we have to."

So Russ drove himself back to the corner of Park and Fir, and pulled the Imperial over to the curb. He put it in park and let out a sigh. He couldn't look at Helen, at least not right now.

"What are you doing?"

"Getting out."

She scoffed. "Oh come on, don't be silly. It's only a couple more blocks. Just drive home. I have to go past there anyway."

He still didn't look at her, but drawing in a big breath, he put it back into drive and spun it around in the street, made the corner onto Fir, so the car was facing west, and parked once more.

"There, now you don't have to go past there. Better?"

Helen looked at him for a long time. He should have gotten right out. It would have made it easier for them both.

"Russ, it's not like I want this. Please talk to your dad. I'm sure my Father is only blowing off steam. He'll change his mind once he has his head about him again. He's just under a lot of stress."

Russ bunched his jaws. "It doesn't matter. I know my dad well enough to know he isn't going to change his mind. Until something changes with your dad, I guess I can't see you anymore."

The sickening finality of those words struck Russ hard in the chest. He threw open the door and jumped out, then started for Park. He never

looked back, although he didn't hear the Chrysler pull away and assumed Helen was still sitting there.

He didn't have the strength to look at her again.

When he got home, he headed through the living room and straight for the hall. He had seen his father's car out in the driveway, but he hoped he didn't have to see him.

"Russ? Are you okay?" It was Eleanor, who had walked in from the kitchen. Russ started to look at her but then saw the looming form of his father appear behind her.

"Yeah, Mom, I'm fine." He headed down the hall and escaped into his room as fast as he could shut the door.

● ● ● ● ●

Time passed. Russ buried himself in his studies and lost himself on the football field. Their first game was looming now, with Firth. He homed in on his goal to crush the Cougars. He ran harder, caught more passes, knocked more teammates flying than ever before. In his barely controlled rage and pain, he was unstoppable. But once, when both he and Slick Patterson went after the same pass from Johnny Boo Fabian, and big, heavy-bodied Slick managed to get there first and make the catch ahead of Russ, a fight ensued.

The coaches, young Dan Nalder, and hulking Ivan Jardinsky, saw the fight, and they stopped it right as Russ ripped the ball out of Slick's hands.

"Hey!" It was the deep, ragged voice of head coach Jardinsky. "Custer! Cut it out *now!*"

As Slick grabbed for the ball, Russ leaped at him, throwing the ball down and going into pugilism stance. He threw a right that hit Slick in the right cheekbone, knocking him back. Before he knew what was happening, he felt a heavy hand on the back of his neck, and someone jerked him backward.

Whirling, he tried to find his new opponent through the red rage clouding his eyes.

He heard his name again. "Russ! Hey!" He sucked in a big breath. This time he recognized assistant coach Nalder's voice. He whipped his head back and forth, looking from Jardinsky to Nalder.

"Russ," came Nalder's warning voice. "Come on, buddy. It's only a practice. Settle down."

"In the locker room!" roared the voice of Ivan Jardinsky. "Move it!" The coach sounded like drill sergeants Russ had heard in the movies. Starting to realize the mistake he had made, he headed for the school. He started off too fast and had to force himself to slow down his pace before Jardinsky yelled at him, which he knew was coming.

In the locker room, followed closely by the coaches, Russ felt a powerful hand clutch his upper arm, and he was slammed against a locker. Shocked, he turned his head and looked into the furious eyes of six-foot-three Jardinsky, the former Detroit Lions halfback.

"What the hell are you doin', Blevins?"

Russ stared at him, his eyes flitting toward Dan Nalder, looking for support. It was just a little fight over a ball! "What?"

"What? You're out of control, boy! You wanna get kicked out of the game? I said *what the hell are you doin'?"*

Russ blinked his eyes, clearing them of sweat, anger, and a gathering feeling of what he could only call fear. He didn't know if he had ever seen Ivan Jardinsky this angry—and Jardinsky was well-known for his bouts of rage. What was all this anger over? Teammates fought over the ball all the time.

Russ drew in a big breath, trying to think back on the details of the little struggle with Slick. Was he that out of line? Okay, so one punch. And it wasn't even that hard. He had started to drum up a reply when Nalder stepped in.

"Hey, Ivan, do me a favor, huh?"

The raging bull spun on his assistant coach and roared, "What!"

Calmly, Nalder held up his hands. "Let's uh . . . Let me talk to Blevins alone for a minute, all right? One minute," he repeated when Jardinsky opened his mouth to yell again.

Blowing air out his nostrils, Jardinsky glared over at Russ. His pale blue eyes, almost touching his nose on the inside, looked icy, yet the whites were engorged with red vessels. The coach jerked a finger up in the air between himself and Nalder.

"One. Just one, Nalder."

And then he turned around and gimped out of the room. His limp didn't seem as severe as normal, probably because, as some of his players surmised, he tried his best to hide it when he was at his angriest. At those times, he wanted attention drawn to his ire, not his weakness.

When the door to Jardinsky's office clicked shut, Dan Nalder remained staring after the man, and he let out a long sigh. After a moment, he turned his attention back to Russ and rubbed a hand down his lower face.

"Holy cow, buddy! You woke up a sleeping tiger."

"He was a Lion," said Russ. He had settled down a little and was trying to bring some humor to the situation.

Dan Nalder let a smile start at one corner of his lips, but then he squelched it. "Good try, Russ. But this isn't funny. What's goin' on with you?"

"I'm not sure what you mean."

"Not sure what I mean! Buddy, you've been a real bear the last few practices. Ivan and me've been watching you, and so have the other players."

"Huh?"

"Come on! Russ, are you tellin' me nothing's goin' on? You're not feeling any different from normal? Because to everyone else, it's bad."

"It was just a little struggle over the ball. And one hit."

"Huh. Yeah, well he wasn't doing anything drastic enough to get hit at all, and you swung *after* we told you both to stop. Besides, this isn't only about the thing with Slick. It's just the straw that broke the camel's back. This has been building up for the last several practices. Anyone could see it coming."

"Are you serious? I didn't think I was any different than ever."

"Well, you are. Way different. You used to be pretty even keel. Never used to fly into a rage like you've been doin' lately. Something's gotta give. You know you're our best player. Not the whole team, obviously, but you sure are one huge part of it. I honestly don't know if we could win half our games without you. And this is your year! This is the year you're gonna shine! But Russ, you've gotta change something, and you've only got four days right now. This could be a no-loss season for us. But you're not going to win any games acting like this. I promise you.

You'll be lucky if the refs don't flat-out pull you out of the game. Is that what you want?"

"Of course not!"

"Then you've gotta start actin' like it, bud. I'm worried. And so is Ivan."

"Worried! He looks mad."

Nalder chuckled. "That may be true, but it's because he doesn't know any other way to show concern."

"Concern? About what?"

"About you boys, of course. You're his whole world."

Russ turned his head to look incredulously after Jardinsky, then looked back at Nalder. "That old jerk? He wouldn't care if all of us died, as long as he won his season."

Russ had never seen an angrier look than the one that flared in Nalder's eyes. He jabbed his finger in the direction Jardinsky had gone.

"Listen! That old *jerk* in there was a big hot-shot ball player just like you. Halfback. Maybe the best the Detroit Lions ever had. It took *two* Cleveland Rams to take his knee out, you know. And he lost everything. *Everything,* you hear me? All he has left is you boys. Do you know his wife left him last May? Yeah. Second week of May, she just up and left. Even took their dog with her. He's got nobody, Russ. Only us. And I don't care if you want to hear it or not, but that *old jerk,* as you call him, loves you boys as if you were his own sons. And yes—he'd pummel me if he ever knew I told you that."

Nalder heaved out a fiery breath. He stared at Russ, his face flushed. Russ tried to stare back. He knew all of a sudden that Dan Nalder was right. So was Ivan Jardinsky. Something *had* happened to him. It was Helen James. And he didn't know what to do to change it.

"I'm sorry, Coach."

Nalder stared at him, reading the truth behind his eyes. Seeming satisfied, he put out a hand and clasped Russ's shoulder.

"This is only a game, buddy. A sport. They call it *sportsmanship* for a reason, and that's how you should be treating it. I'm glad you give it everything you've got. Believe me, so is Coach Jardinsky. But if you keep goin' down the road you're on, you're going to lose all the friends you have out there, the respect of everyone who knows you, and most

likely your place on the team. You've gotta rein it in. I can't say it any plainer than that."

Russ's world came crashing down—the pain, the anger, the frustration. Helen was gone. His team feared him and didn't want anything to do with him. He had seen it in the last few practices, and he had been pushing the thought aside. But yes, Dan Nalder was right. He and Jardinsky were right about everything.

When Nalder stepped closer and wrapped his arms around Russ, he met him all the way. He had to fight back tears, because no coach would ever see Shelley's star Russet cry.

● ● ● ● ●

Russ had been avoiding Edie Russell since classes began, and she knew it. Often, when he saw her she was walking somewhere with Ev Morin, and that was good, although there was a place down deep in Russ that felt slighted. He had no right to feel that way, but he did. Ev was *his* friend. And Edie liked *him,* not Ev. Yet the pairing was the best thing that could have ever happened. He should have been nothing if not ecstatic.

When he walked out of the locker room that evening, there stood Edie, holding her armload of books. Inwardly, he groaned. Why did she have to be here? This was not the time!

He took a chance as he reached her. "You waitin' for Ev?" He knew she wasn't. Ev had bolted before even showering, without saying a word to Russ.

Confused, she looked at him. "No . . . I was waiting to talk to *you.* Is it okay if I walk with you?"

"It's not like you're going my way," he said as he continued toward the front door, making her hustle to catch up.

"I know. It's okay. I just wanted to see if everything's all right."

Why did she care? What business was it of hers?

"I'm fine."

They went on in silence, out the front doors, across the street. Edie had to walk fast, but she managed to stay with him.

"Russ?"

"What?" He kept walking and avoided looking at her.

"You seem mad about something. Is everything okay with Helen? I haven't seen you together for a while."

Russ jerked to a halt, whirling to face her. "Listen, Edie, that's nobody's business, okay? I said I'm fine. Isn't there somebody else you can talk to? Where's Ev?"

Her eyes filling with shock, Edie stared up at him. In a moment, the shock was replaced by tears, and she whirled away, headed north.

A pang of shame came over Russ, and he took a step after her. He had to stop himself from yelling out. But why was he worried? He should be glad she was gone. He didn't need any girl bugging him around football season, and especially not Edie.

Turning, he strode downhill, past the old LDS tabernacle, and toward home. All the way there the self-loathing built up inside him.

What had Edie Russell ever done to deserve Russ Blevins?

CHAPTER FORTY-ONE

As Russ was walking home, a car pulled up to the intersection at Holmes and stopped at the stop sign. Not wanting to have to greet anyone, he tried to avoid looking at it, but he couldn't. In spite of himself, the look of the car registered in his peripheral vision.

It was a fifty-three Crown Vic, white with black doors, on its side the legend ***Bingham County Sheriff.*** A car Russ had seen more times than he cared to think about.

As Russ passed in front of the car's hood, not because he wanted to but because his pride wouldn't let him cross to the other side of the street, his father got out and towered behind the shield of the door.

"Hey, Russ."

"Hi, Pop." He stopped because there wasn't a choice. No one walked away from Sheriff Arch Blevins unless he told them they could.

"I've been waiting for you."

"How come?"

"Wanted to see if you'd like to go grab an ice cream."

Russ looked closer at his father. *Ice cream!* That sounded way too friendly. And friendly, considering how things were right now with Helen, was about the last thing he wanted to be with Arch Blevins.

"Not really, if it's all the same to you. I'm pretty loaded down with homework."

Russ had touched off a stick of dynamite right there between them, and they stared each other down. Arch was looking for words, and Russ was hoping to avoid them.

"Okay," the sheriff said. "Yeah, that's good. You probably should make sure not to get behind." Russ couldn't help seeing a strange look in his father's eyes, a look he had never seen before and one he couldn't place.

"Yeah," he replied. "Is that it?"

"Yeah, that was all."

"Okay. See ya." Steeling himself, Russ took a big breath and continued walking. He knew his father stayed at the intersection for a long time after he was gone. He didn't look back, but he could feel it.

And he didn't care.

● ● ● ● ●

That night, Russ ate supper with the females again. His father didn't come home until well after dark, and this time he hadn't even called to warn them. When he finally pulled into the driveway, Russ bolted out of Arch's La-Z-Boy and headed down the hall to his room.

He heard the old man go past not five minutes later, his steps almost shuffling in their slowness. He could hear low voices in the bedroom. Between the fact that he needed to use the bathroom, and his sudden urge to see what his father was going to say about him, he left his room and crept down the hall, praying none of the girls caught him listening to his parents' door.

He heard his father's voice: *Yeah, it's a lot worse than anyone even imagined.*

Oh, dear! Does Russ know? replied Eleanor.

Well, no. I don't see how he could. I didn't even get all the details put together until today.

Is he in jail?

He was. His wife came and bailed him out earlier, to the tune of five thousand dollars.

Russ's mother must have been as stunned as Russ was as he put two and two together, because for a long time she said nothing in reply. It was his father who broke the silence again.

I'm pretty sure he's going to prison, depending on the jury selection. I mean, I've never seen a case much more cut and dried. He stole money from an awful lot of people—and some of them pretty important folks. Tens of thousands of dollars, Ellie. I don't see how he can get out of this.

Oh, that poor girl! came Eleanor's voice again. *And his wife! How will they live if he's gone to jail? What are they going to do?*

There was a long silence. It lasted so long Russ began to fear his father opening the door. So he turned and tiptoed back to the bathroom, went in, shut the door, and sat down on the toilet in a daze, staring at the door.

Harold James was going to prison! Russ's mother immediately started thinking of Pearl and Helen, and she was right to do so. They couldn't make it without him! They certainly couldn't keep paying for the huge, fancy house and the nice cars. Russ felt like he had been kicked in the stomach.

Why did his father try to sound like he even cared? He could have dropped the case any time, like Russ had asked him to. If he had, Harold James could have given all the money back that he had stolen, Russ would be even more like a hero to Helen's father than he had been as a plain old football player, and Helen would still be with him. His father's sheer stubbornness had done this. Now it could never be undone!

He used the toilet, only half aware of his actions, and flushed it as he heard his parents' bedroom door open. He waited and heard his father's footsteps go by, then steeled himself and cracked open the door. When he saw that no one was in the hall, he went out and slipped back into his room.

A moment later he heard the back door open, and then within a couple of minutes he could smell cigarette smoke coming through his window. That meant his father would be out in the driveway in his lawn chair, smoking a Chesterfield.

The next day, during lunch break, Russ saw a sight that startled him and made him stare. Up along the canal bank, some distance away, he could see two people walking. He first recognized his best friend, Ev, and in another moment he realized the other one was Edie.

What was going on? Was his buddy falling for Edie? It was great if he was. Good for them. A little pang of regret hit him from out of the blue then. It hadn't been that long ago when Edie was following him around, acting like a lost puppy. It sure hadn't taken her long to move on. Was he really that forgettable? But he didn't care. He had Helen. Or at least he had until his dad's stubbornness ruined everything.

He couldn't take his eyes off Edie and Ev, but in a moment more he wished he had. All of a sudden, they stopped, and Ev's arms went around the girl. She met his embrace, and from this distance it appeared that she did so pretty eagerly. With a frown, he turned away. He didn't need to see that kind of stuff.

He walked north down Short Street and turned west on Center, walking along with his hands in his pockets, kicking gravel. Soon, he reached State. Only a short distance away was the James house. He didn't even look that direction. He had enough reminders of Helen James without seeing her house.

Aimlessly, he strolled until it was almost time to be back in school, by which time he had made a big loop and was back on Short. A stream of students was trickling toward the front doors.

Of course fate would have it that the first two people Russ saw as he passed through the front doors were Edie and Ev. Ev didn't see him, but the girl did. He gave her a smile, but she whipped away and hurried down the hall, squeezing her ever-present stack of books to her body.

Quickening his step, Russ caught up to Ev. As he got beside him, he said, "Hey, buddy."

Ev whipped his head around. "Hey! Man, you scared me. What's up?"

"Nothin'. Just out walking. Hey, so . . . What's up with you and Edie Russell?" His question was meant to sound casual, but apparently it didn't come out that way.

"Huh?" Ev stared at him, taken by surprise.

"Aw, come on! I saw you out walking."

"Oh! Jeez, man. We were only talking." His friend wouldn't meet his eyes. And some of his normal friendliness wasn't there. The realization was jarring to Russ.

"Hey, Ev—everything all right?"

Ev shrugged. "Yeah, fine."

"How come you're so down?"

"I'm not down." Ev had come to a stop at the doorway of his next class.

"You don't seem too happy."

Ev turned and looked at the classroom door, where a plaque said *Miss Pettit.* "Hey, Russ, maybe we oughtta talk later. I gotta get in class."

Russ frowned. Once again, Ev's glance was furtive. "All right, man. See you later then."

Ev turned and bolted through the doorway.

Heading for his class, way at the other end of the school, Russ came across a cluster of ball players. He said hi, but they hardly even seemed to notice him. Charlie Braun even seemed purposely to turn away. What was going on? Russ walked on to his class, and he slumped into his chair. Glancing around the room, he saw that nobody was even looking at him. There was no reason they should, he guessed, but generally at least someone did. He usually got a hi from at least one person everywhere he went. Come on! He was Russet Blevins! He was the entire football team at Shelley High! With a quiet grunt, Russ reached into the desk and pulled out his book, waiting for Mr. Hanson to start his lecture on chemistry. He had better things to do than think about the other kids in this school. In fact, he really didn't care what they thought anyway.

But he couldn't get it off his mind.

● ● ● ● ●

After school, Russ made practice, and just like in school the air seemed cool, even though the sun was out. He started toward where a group of his friends were huddled up: Pete Basso, Mark Knags, Alvin Wheeler, Johnny Boo, and Charlie Braun. Ev Morin was on the other end of the field.

At the last second, he realized that Slick Patterson was standing in the group as well, but had been hidden by Charlie. Inside, Russ cursed. It was obvious that he had been headed for the group. What did he do

now, turn and walk off? He couldn't save face doing that, so he took a big breath and continued on. Maybe this was the best time for a confrontation anyway.

He walked right up to the group. "Hey, guys."

Every eye turned to him, but most of them were quick to flicker away. There were a few greetings, most of them half-hearted.

"What's up?" asked Pete.

Russ wanted to make small talk. He didn't want to do what he knew he had to do in order to keep this team together.

"Guys, I've been wanting to talk with you."

"All right—*Captain.*" Slick Fingers Patterson had a purple bruise on his cheek. His voice had a surly, sarcastic ring to it, and Russ couldn't blame him.

Assistant coach Dan Nalder came walking up, and he must have caught something in the wind, for he looked around the group uncertainly. "You boys ready to hit the field, or what?"

Russ stood there and looked at him. It felt like all the boys' eyes were on him. He realized that what he had to do was something much bigger than just with this group of his team mates. This was going to be a big step in his life. But he had to get the respect of his friends back. He had been a real ass.

"Hey, Coach, before we start, do you think we could round up the whole team? I have something I need to say."

Nalder stared at him. At last he nodded. "Well, Russ, that sounds like a great idea. Maybe Coach should be out here too. You think?"

Russ nodded. A hopeful feeling had come into his chest. "Yeah, Coach. Yeah, I think that's a good idea."

Ten minutes later, they had the entire ball team standing in a crescent shape, with Jardinsky off to one side. Dan Nalder came over and leaned close to Russ's ear, where he stood separated from the others on the end of the crescent by several feet. "Buddy, are you sure this is what you want to do?"

Russ nodded, his stomach tight and full of acid. "Yes sir. I have to."

Nalder clapped him on the shoulder a couple of times and gave it a squeeze, then turned to the group. "Guys, I brought you all in because one of your captains has something to say to you. Russ?"

Nalder turned and looked at Russ, and there was a look of pride glowing in his face—or at least that was how it looked to Russ.

Realizing he was starting to shake, Russ found himself wondering how he was going to get through this. He had grown up through all his school years with a lot of these boys, playing catch, baseball, basketball, running races—and of course, hitting the grid iron. Now he was realizing that in the last while he might have permanently damaged his relationship with some of them. It made him ache.

Russ walked to where Dan Nalder had been standing as Dan went over to be beside Jardinsky.

"Guys, I don't even know how to say this. I'm supposed to be one of your captains. I'm the old man of this ball team—the greatest football team in the whole state of Idaho, I have to add." This statement got a lot of nods from the team. Seeing that gave Russ the strength to forge on.

"You guys and the coaches put me in as a captain I guess because I'm supposed to know the score, and kind of know what's going on out here, and maybe I'm supposed to be respected. I'm not sure if any of you ever really have, because we grew up together, but I think a football captain ought to live his life and treat other people so they can look up to him too."

He paused and looked around him, bunching his jaw muscles to try and strengthen him at this point of weakness. These were his buddies. They had fought and bled together, lost games that never should have been lost together, seen each other cry, even given each other hugs—which wasn't something tough boys were supposed to do. But they were a family. At least he prayed they still were.

All eyes were upon him now, even the guys he had abused the worst, like Slick Fingers Patterson.

"Since this practice season started, I haven't been that guy at all. I've been acting like a real jerk. I let some stuff that's happening in my private life take me over on the field. You guys didn't do anything to deserve any of that. I owe you all a huge apology—some more than others. Especially you, Slick—take the ball away from me any time, man—if you can." He laughed, and the whole group laughed with him.

Some of the boys started forward, their faces filled with sudden emotions, but Russ's voice stopped them. "I promise you guys we're going

to take State this year. And I also promise you I'm gonna be the kind of captain you deserve. No more being surly. I hope you'll forgive me for anything I did this last week or so."

That was the unofficial release, and the wave of players surged forward, engulfing Russ in their camaraderie. They were a team, and they were one—a family. Russ knew in his heart he had just made the biggest play of all.

When practice was over that day, Ivan Jardinsky gimped over to where Russ was standing with Pete Basso and Johnny Boo. The one person on the whole field who hadn't come over to talk to Russ was Ev Morin, his best friend. He didn't know what he had done to Ev, but whatever it was, the meeting with him was going to have to be alone.

Jardinsky looked at Pete and Johnny and jerked a thumb downfield. "Hey, boys—take a lap, huh?" They stared at him, as a smile almost overcame his hard face. "Please?" he said gruffly.

With big smiles, Pete and Johnny Boo turned away and jogged off to some of the other players.

Jardinsky turned to Russ. He took a deep breath. "Think yer a pretty big deal on this field, don't you, Cus?"

Russ stared at him, searching his expression for a hint of how he should take that comment. "Um, no sir."

Appearing to chew the inside of his lips, Jardinsky started nodding briskly, as if he were trying to shake something off his head. He looked down at Russ's feet as he took a step forward and slung a big, once-muscular arm around Russ's neck.

"Well, son, you are. That was a hell of a speech you gave out there. I couldn't be prouder of you, Cus. Honestly." Jardinsky's voice broke on that last word, and he gave Russ's neck a rough squeeze, then turned before Russ could see his eyes and bolted at a fast limp toward the school, his clipboard swinging at his side.

CHAPTER FORTY-TWO

There were a lot of fences in Russ's life that needed mending. He didn't know for sure what he had done to his best friend, but Ev was too good of a pal to simply let him go. He had bared his soul in front of the whole world, it seemed—or at least the entire world of a Shelley Russet.

Ev Morin might as well be next.

He showered in a hurry, trying to make sure Ev didn't escape before he could get dressed. But when he came out of the showers and looked at Ev's locker, it was shut, and there weren't any clothes lying in the area.

Pete Basso, seated on the bench a couple of spots down from where Ev should have been, gave his friend a grin.

"Hey, Pete—where's Ev?"

"He took off, man. He's gonna be one stinky cat—didn't even hit the showers."

Russ frowned. Wow. Ev really *didn't* want to see him. He wasn't normally a guy who would let himself stink.

"Any idea why he left so fast?"

Pete shrugged. "Not sure. He's not been real talkative today—to me or anybody else."

"All right." A thought hit Russ, and he sat down astride of the bench, facing Pete. "Hey, Wop, have you ever done any more thinking about who could've ratted us out about that tree thing?"

With a frown, Pete shrugged his shoulders again. "Wow! It's crazy you'd even think about it after all this time. No, I don't have a clue. I'm not sure I'd want to find out, either. You should just let it go."

"Huh. You think it could be Bobbie? Or Spit?"

"Jeez, Cus! Come on! I said I have no idea. But Spit? Man, why would you even say that? I'm gonna start suspectin' *you* if you keep up with crap like that."

"So you think Bobbie then?"

Pete lurched up off the bench. "Russ, I'm leavin', man. You've lost it. I told you, I don't know, and I don't want to know. What if I up and said it was me?"

Mouth open, Russ stared at his Italian friend. "Wait . . . What?"

"Oh, for— Russ, for the love of Pete! It *wasn't* me! I'm just tired of talking about it. Give it a rest. It doesn't matter, man. It's done."

Russ stared at Pete, gaging him. Finally, he scoffed. "Well, you're a lot easier going than I am. I'd love to get my hands on 'em. I used to think it was Edie, but it wasn't. It had to be Bobbie."

"Great." Pete threw down his hands in disgust, picking up his helmet and slamming it against the back of his locker, then slamming the door as well. He snapped his padlock shut with an exaggerated motion and turned back to Russ, still holding his towel, which he tossed toward the bin and missed. "Why don't you go find Bobbie and give her hell, Russ? Beat her face in. Maybe that'll make you feel better."

Russ stared at Pete Basso. He had a sick feeling in the pit of his stomach. All of a sudden, he knew. The snitch wasn't Bobbie Fletcher. It really *was* Pete. Why else would he react like this? Spinning around, he left the room without another word, walking past three other teammates without even looking at them. He could hardly even see where he was walking.

● ● ● ● ●

Russ didn't go home after he left the school. He wished he had the Studebaker, but he didn't want to go home to get it. So he walked all the way down to State Street and turned north, crossing the street partway down. He stepped into Mallory's, on a whim. Mallory's, on its south side, was a grocery store, while on the north they carried dry goods.

In the back of the store was the meat department, and Russ traipsed through with purpose until he hit the sawdust floor where the meat was sold. With mild disinterest, he scanned all the cuts of meat in the big glass case, as a woman he recognized as the mother of one of his classmates was ordering some hamburger down the case to his right.

Russ unscrewed a jar that stood about eighteen inches tall and sat on top of the glass counter and fished out a pickled pig's foot, setting his

nickel on top of the counter and waiting until the clerk looked over, so he could point to it.

"Thank you, Russ," said the clerk. "Enjoy your disgusting snack."

Grinning, Russ walked off, eating the whitish foot, which was pink inside. It tasted somewhat like a mixture of Jell-O, raw chicken, and vinegar. But for some reason, he had gotten a taste for it.

Leaving Mallory's, Russ decided to go in the Virginia Theater. There was a gentleman sweeping up the lobby, Hank, by name, and he grinned at Russ. "You come in for a job, Russ?"

Russ laughed. "No, Hank, actually I was wondering if Ev came in. Is he working today?"

Hank nodded and started to reply, but all of a sudden the front door opened again, and Russ turned to look. It was Ev.

"Well, there's your answer," replied Hank. "Hey, Ev. Just in time to take over sweeping. *After* Russ has a word with you, apparently?" He looked the question at Russ.

"Yes sir. It won't take long. Can we go outside for a second, Ev?" Russ asked as he turned back to his friend.

Ev shrugged. "Yeah, I guess so." Without waiting, he went back out on the sidewalk, and Russ followed.

Ev didn't smile. "So what's up?"

"Why're you avoiding me?"

"What?"

"Aw, come on, buddy! Why'd you leave school without even saying anything? You steamed about something? Did I do something wrong?"

Ev drew a deep breath. "Man, this isn't the best place to talk. Plus, I've gotta get to work. Hank'll get mad if I don't hop in there and take the broom from him."

"Jeez, Ev. Man, give me a break. In school, you said we could talk later, but then you bolted out of the locker room while I was showering. Somethin's eating you. What's goin' on? I apologized to everybody else, and that meant you too. But I thought we were getting along fine."

Ev seemed to find strength inside. "Russ, come on. I don't even want to talk about this crap. But you're forcin' me into it."

"Yes. I am."

"Well, it's about Edie."

Russ sighed. "All right. All right. Buddy, there's not one thing you've got to explain to me about that. She's not my girl, Ev—she never was! You know me better. You worried you're stepping on my toes, or what?"

"Shut up already!" Ev cut in. "Man, you must love the sound of your own voice."

"What?" Russ started to get angry on the instant. *Shut up?* Who said that to a friend?

"Be quiet. Man, just zip it. I don't have a lot of time anyway. I already told you that. So let me finish."

Russ sighed, calming down. "All right, go ahead."

"Like I said, it's about Edie. And it's nothing like what you're thinking. Man, you're a dope, Russ. I used to think you were so smart."

"What are you talking about?"

"You think this is about me and Edie? Well, I'll flat-out tell you, she doesn't care one little bit about me—not as a beau, anyway!"

"But I saw you hugging up on the canal bank!"

"Oh, please. That's rich, man. Are you serious? For your information, I was comforting her—but maybe you wouldn't know about something like that."

Ignoring the jab, Russ jumped to conclusions. "Is her dad okay?"

"Her dad? I don't know what that has to do with anything. He's not really okay, no, but what I'm talking about doesn't have a stinking thing to do with her dad. It has to do with *you!*"

"Okay, now you're starting to make me mad. Just spit it out."

"Spit it out? Okay. I'll spit it out. I'll spit it out, all right. That little girl is head over heels for you, Russ. Holy crap! I think she's an idiot and a half, if you want to know the truth. You don't do anything but treat her like the scum of the earth, and she keeps on worshiping the ground you walk on. I'll never understand girls if I live to be a hundred."

The two stared at each other. Russ could have taken offense to any number of things Ev had said, but he was still trying to digest the main message. He stammered, "So you and Edie . . . There's nothing going on with . . . You guys aren't going steady or anything?"

"No! Jeez. I took her to a movie and dinner, yeah. And when it was over I felt like a total ass."

"Why? I think it would be cool."

"Yeah? Well she doesn't. I think that girl is swell, Russ. Way too nice to be treated like you treat people. But she sees only you. She told me nicely that she loved having me as a friend but her heart was taken. Man. What a slap in the face."

With that, Ev let out a frustrated grunt and turned, threw open the theater door and stomped inside.

Feeling red-faced, Russ stood on the sidewalk, staring into his reflection in the glass. He had to get out of there. He had to escape.

Without thinking about what direction he was heading, he spun on his heel and started north. He had to walk. He had to clear his mind. And most of all, he had to get far away from Everett Morin.

● ● ● ● ●

North was the direction of the Russell house. Russ didn't think about it until he was already way up by the park. He had, however, thought unceasingly about the girl. What was she thinking? They weren't a fit for each other. Anyone could see that! And she knew how he felt about Helen. Didn't she? It should have been obvious.

Still needing to cool down and think, Russ kept walking way beyond the edge of town, toward Idaho Falls. He went out two miles before he even realized it, then turned and headed south again.

When he got down to the turn-off to the Russell house, he stopped. He looked that way. Dumb girl. What was she thinking? He had to set her straight. Shouldn't he? Or did he let it ride? Outlast her.

What was he going to do? He couldn't go around with some dumb girl talking about how she was in love with him, when he wanted nothing to do with her. Yes, that was it. He had to go talk to her. He had to make sure she knew where his heart lay.

With that determination, he headed west. He got to Edie's neighborhood, and he was almost to her house now. It was late evening, and shadows were falling fast. Street lights had already started to flicker on.

He spotted a shape on the sidewalk, right in front of old Barrow Tupper's house. Slowing down, he tried to make it out in the half-light. Was it a dog, lying there waiting to waylay him? He got closer, cautious. Then he realized it was a man!

With alarm, Russ almost ran to the man lying there, recognizing Tupper. He knelt and felt for a pulse on his neck. His heartbeat was there, and it was plenty strong. But Tupper reeked of alcohol.

With a sigh, Russ shook his head. How did somebody ever get to a state like this? Looking around, he saw no one, so he got behind Tupper and pushed him up to a sitting position, then got his hands under his arms while the old man started muttering something nonsensical.

He dragged the old man back to the stoop in front of his house, then set him down while he opened the front door. He pulled him inside and got him onto his couch, where he lay him on his side, so if he threw up it would be on the floor, and not back down his throat. He had heard his father talk about people dying that way.

The place stunk of cigarettes and booze, and there were beer cans and whisky bottles lying around, all clean as a whistle—this fellow obviously wasn't one to waste alcohol.

Russ went into a bedroom down the hall and got a blanket, which he hated even to touch. Bringing it back, he laid it over the old man, glancing around the room again. Tupper was gone out like a light once more, and it didn't look like he was going to wake up any time soon.

That meant it was time to escape. Suddenly, he thought about the ancient yellow lab, Bud. Great. The dog must still be out walking, and now he wasn't going to get let inside when he came home tonight. Oh well. There was nothing Russ could do about that. He sure wasn't going to wait around until the dog got home.

He walked to the front door and pushed it open. His eyes were drawn to the Russells'. What was he doing here? He didn't have any business talking to Edie. He had hurt her, and it was for the best. Let her stew about it and realize what a great guy Ev was. He was the one she really needed, not Russ. Russ's heart was taken, and he could never get it back.

Glad that common sense had finally found him, he headed for home.

CHAPTER FORTY-THREE

The next day at school, Ev Morin managed to avoid Russ, and Russ made it easy for him, at least until football practice. He had made up his mind to let his buddy simmer for a few days. They had fought before. It was mostly years ago, but every time it happened, Ev just needed time to cool off. It was usually something stupid anyway.

He didn't know how long it might take this time, but he had faith that Ev would cool off the same as always. In the meantime, he wasn't going to push it. He would cut a wide swathe around his friend and let him sulk. Maybe it would do him good—knock his pride down a few notches.

Edie avoided him as well, but every time he saw her, he either caught her looking at him, or he had the feeling she had just looked away. Down deep in his heart, he felt bad about Edie. She really was a nice girl. But she didn't stack up to Helen. He probably should break down and apologize to her—tell her how things stood. She was cute enough, if it got right down to it. Somebody would eventually be attracted enough to her to take her out. Look at Ev! He had already as much as said he would be her steady.

But he couldn't quite dredge up what it took to talk to her. And so he let her avoid him, which made it look like the entire thing was her choice, and he went on about his day.

The hardest person not to talk to was Helen. And it seemed like she was everywhere. One time, right after lunch, their eyes met, and she gave him a sad smile before averting her eyes. It was all he could think of the rest of the afternoon.

On the football field, Ev managed to keep away from Russ, which meant he spent most of the time alone, because the rest of the team seemed to be glued to Russ. Other than Ev, things were back to normal—back the way they should be.

They ran some skirmishes, Johnny Boo Fabian's arm was in fine form, and Russ caught most of his passes and ran the field, demonstrating over and over why he was the top football player who had ever played for the Shelley Russets. Almost no one could catch him. And if they did, half the time he would drag them down the field for several yards, sometimes even escaping their clutches altogether and making it all the way to the end zone. This was going to be a fantastic year.

He was too busy to think about Everett Morin or Edie Russell. He hardly even thought about Helen James. Football meant everything to him. Nothing was going to ruin this season. Nothing.

● ● ● ● ●

Later that afternoon, Russ avoided going home, as he had been doing a lot lately. Instead, he went with Mark Knaggs, Pete Basso, and Charlie Braun down to Pash's, which sat right next to the Virginia Theater.

Pash's was one of the favorite local hangouts for teenagers. It had an excellent soda fountain on one side, where they sold all kinds of ice cream, malts, and shakes, and usually one of Russ's favorite things, an iron port and cherry. Down the center stood a long magazine rack, with magazines specializing in every popular topic imaginable, and it divided the soda fountain half of the establishment from the other side, which was a sporting goods store. Because one of Russ's other loves had always been hunting and fishing, at least back when his father had time to take him, Pash's had the ideal environment.

When they went in, three girls Russ recognized as sophomores were seated at the soda counter, sipping on sodas, while two junior boys were flirting with them and trying to regale them with tales of their glory. The boys weren't ball players. They weren't anyone who would normally even draw Russ's attention. He only knew who they were because Shelley was so small.

"I'll be over in a minute," said Russ to the others, and went over to the sporting goods side to see if they had anything he hadn't already seen. When he was satisfied that he had already browsed all of the wares before, he went back over to where his teammates were already starting to get their orders.

As he reached them, and his attention was on the cute blonde clerk behind the counter, he heard the front door bells jingle, and Charlie

Braun said, "Oh crap! Don't look now, Russ, but you're sugar pie's comin' in."

As the words registered on Russ's preoccupied mind, his heart jumped into his throat. He whipped his head over to see Edie Russell pushing her father into the store in his wheelchair, while Lorna Russell held the door.

Inside, Russ cursed. "Cut it, Egg!" he said. "Why'd you say that? You made me think it was Helen."

Charlie laughed, raising a hand to rub it down the back of his bald head. "Well, they're saying all around school that you like 'em both!"

Russ hardly heard him. He was too busy looking for a hole. But there was no escape in Pash's. Only a blind person could miss seeing everyone there.

Lorna Russell saw Russ, and a big smile came over her face. The same expression took over Frank, although not as expansive. Edie, on the other hand, was not smiling.

"Aw, crap," said Russ, under his breath. But he smiled as big as he dared. "Hello, Mr. and Mrs. Russell. Hi, Edie."

The girl's parents greeted him back. No one but Russ seemed to notice that Edie said nothing in return.

"Hey, we never did hear back from you when you got into town," said Frank. "Still up for supper sometime?"

"Yes," Lorna chimed in. "I got a new recipe out of *Woman's Day* that I've been dying to try out."

Russ felt like a rat caught in a corner holding a piece of cheese. The only hole he could have escaped to was out the front door, right past all three of them. His eyes ducked over to Edie, then bumped away from her back to Frank, then Lorna. "Uh . . . Well, yeah, sure. Sorry I lost track of time. Everything got pretty hectic when I got back. You know, with my last year of school and all—and football season." He was careful to itemize every reason he might be too busy to come to their house.

But it didn't work.

Frank looked up at Lorna, then back at Russ, taking the bull by the horns. "So how about Monday? No football that day, for sure."

Russ was roped and tied. He looked at Edie. A sick feeling swept over him. What did he say? She surely didn't want him there any more than he wanted to be there.

His eyes returned to Frank, then raised to Lorna. Their hopeful smiles were too big. They obviously didn't know how he had treated their daughter. Russ's leg was in a grizzly bear trap. And when he glanced over at his friends he realized there was no help. He was on his own.

"Oh, yeah. So . . . Monday? I don't think I have any plans—at least not after ball practice."

"All right then," said Frank, slapping the arm of his wheelchair. "It's a date."

The word choice made Russ cringe.

When Frank told Russ to go ahead and not let them interrupt him, he numbly ordered a chocolate shake. He didn't even want one. In fact, he had lost all of his appetite, for a shake or for anything else.

While Frank and his family were ordering their beverages, Russ went over and sat on the far side of his friends. Charlie was trying not to be too obvious while he laughed his head off at Russ. Mark Knaggs practiced looking studiously mature. Wop was the only one who actually seemed to have any sympathy for his buddy.

Downing his shake way too fast, Russ leaned past the backs of his friends and eyeballed the front door. Twenty feet away. It was an easy touchdown. But he had to get past hell to get there. He glanced in the mirror behind the soda counter. Okay. They weren't looking toward him. This was his chance. His friends were on their own.

Getting up, he started down the room past the bar stools. As he got to where Frank and Lorna sat, he knew he had no choice, by common etiquette, but to tell them goodbye.

"Well, it was good seeing you folks. Guess I'll see you Monday then—if you're sure it's not too much bother." *Please, oh please—tell me it's too much bother!*

"No bother at all," said Lorna happily, turning partway around on her stool to squeeze Russ's forearm. "It will be nice to have you over again."

Russ said thanks, and then, like a star halfback, he bolted for the door and made it across the line. Essentially, however, he had left the ball on the field behind him. Everyone in that room was a winner but Russ Blevins.

Outside, the air was cooling down, because the sun had sunk in the west, and the street was bathed in blue shadow. But it still felt warm and welcoming. One of the best times of the day.

Not even thinking of waiting around for the others, Russ started walking. He had no desire to go home, even if he did have homework he needed to do. He didn't want to be around his father—on the off-chance that he came home, that is.

He headed south, so he wouldn't be walking north when the Russells left Pash's. The last thing he needed was for them to see him again.

He walked clear out to Baseline Road, beyond the town limits, then turned east and went past the cemetery. He thought about going in, but by then it was past dark, and there was no point in being in there. He would have liked to see his grandparents' graves, but it would have to wait for some other time. He found himself missing those two old folks. He had fond memories of spending time in their home, and being out with his grandfather riding horses in the hills.

When he had passed the cemetery and got to Park, he turned north again. It was well after dark, and his mother would be starting to worry about him. It was only another ten or twenty minutes back home.

He had passed Elm Street, and was almost back home, when he saw a dark shape crossing the street from his right. He paused, and watched it materialize into young Isaac Thorpe. Russ's heart jumped. The boy was coming from the strange house where he seemed to spend most of his time now.

"Hey, Rusty."

"Oh, hi!" The boy didn't even speak his name. That fact was ominous, because there was a time when the boy seemed to love the sound of it coming from his mouth.

"You okay?"

"Sure."

"Really?"

"Yeah, I'm fine. Gotta get home, though."

Something overcame Russ, something he could never explain, right then or later. He was great at acting on gut instincts on the football field, but not so much with people. This time was different.

"Hey, buddy, you sure you have to go home right now?"

Isaac paused. "Yeah, prob'ly."

"I was going to see if you wanted to come over to the house."

Again, Isaac paused, only this time for another several seconds. At last, his voice full of uncertainty and hope, he said, "Really? You mean it?"

"Well, of course. I wouldn't have said it if I didn't mean it."

The boy seemed to be gathering his nerve, wanting to say yes but perhaps afraid Russ would tell him he was only joking. Had this boy lost that much faith in him?

"Yeah, sure, Russ! I'd like to."

"Well, come on then. I haven't had anything to eat yet, except a shake down at Pash's. Let's go see if my mom has anything good to eat."

Russ reached out and put his hand on the boy's shoulder. A warm feeling went all through him as the boy moved over closer to him, as if trying to get under his shelter, to feel his warmth. It was a feeling he hadn't felt in a long, long time. Maybe he hadn't lost his little buddy yet.

As they reached the house, and Russ saw his father's patrol car parked in the driveway, he had the sudden, sick feeling that maybe he was only using little Isaac as a kind of protection. If that was the case, it wasn't something he had done consciously. But even so, it might be the perfect way to get out of being yelled at by his father for not telling anyone where he was. One way or another, he was about to find out.

CHAPTER FORTY-FOUR

Walking in through the back door, Russ smelled the wonderful aroma of fried potatoes, his favorite food. It still remained to be seen if the family had left him any, but he was willing to bet they had. Little Kathleen and his mother were both pretty good about making sure he was covered, even on those days (of which there had been many lately) when he didn't come home or give them any reason why.

Russ could hear *Gunsmoke* on the radio in the living room, with the very recognizable voice of William Conrad, as Marshal Matt Dillon. That was a huge boon! Even at his angriest, Russ couldn't see his father getting out of the La-Z-Boy to deal with him while his favorite radio program was on.

He led Isaac up the back steps and into the kitchen, seeing his father sitting in his chair, and his mother not far away. He gave them both a wave but didn't interrupt their show.

His mother started to get up when she realized that Isaac was with him, but he motioned her back down and put his finger to his lips. Eleanor sank back onto the couch, giving him a little frown.

Clicking on the light, Russ went to a covered frying pan on the stove and lifted the lid.

His first reaction was to feel sick. There were potatoes left, sure enough, but barely enough for one. And he was so hungry! He looked at Isaac, who was watching him nervously. A little hopeful smile came to the boy's lips, and he stared at Russ. "Is there any left?"

"Well, yeah, but only enough for one person."

The boy's face fell, and Russ clapped him on the shoulder. "But hey, buddy, it's just fried potatoes, all right? I'm not really much of a fan. Do you like 'em?"

"Well, yeah, sure," said the boy, with a shrug. "They're okay." His face said a lot more. Isaac licked his lips and gazed at the cast iron pan.

"They're yours, then. I'm going to find some real food." He suddenly thought better of what he was saying, knowing how the boy liked to ape him. "Not that they're too bad, mind you. They were my first choice when I was your age, but I started to not like them as much a few weeks ago."

The boy gave him a huge grin, and Russ knew it was a good save. Pulling out a plate, he shoveled all of the potatoes onto it with a pancake turner and handed it to Isaac, then got a fork out of the dish drainer for him. He pointed at the table. "Go on and eat that, all right?"

While the boy obeyed, sitting down at the table, Russ rummaged in the cupboard for a loaf of bread. He watched Isaac from the corner of his eye, and he couldn't help the lump that rose in his throat. There was one contented face. Russ felt good. Better than he had felt about anything he had done in a long time. Shoot, maybe potatoes weren't that great anyway. Not as great as seeing Isaac happy.

He slathered peanut butter on a piece of his mom's homemade wheat bread and then went over and sat across from Isaac, munching on his simple fare. It tasted better than anything else he could think of.

"You like the spuds?" he asked.

Isaac gave him a happy smile and a nod.

"What do you wanna bet they're russets?"

The boy laughed. "Yeah!" he spoke around a mouthful.

When they finished eating, Russ took Isaac's plate, washed it and his fork and set them in the drainer. No reason to give his mom or dad any more reason to yell at him.

"You wanna go to my room for a while?" Russ wasn't sure what he and Isaac would do in his room, but the idea of making the kid feel good made him feel warm inside, something he hadn't felt much lately.

"Sure!" said Isaac with a shrug. The kid should have been expecting some kind of trick, but it was obvious he wasn't. He was loving the attention. As they walked back to Russ's room, Russ seemed to float. It had been so long since Isaac had been in here that he couldn't even remember the last time. Now that he was, it was like stepping back in time, back to when he and little Isaac had first become friends.

Russ let Isaac look over his toy car collection, which wasn't much, because he had gotten rid of many. He let him run his fingers over his

Western novels, and Isaac was especially interested in his favorite, a signed copy of *The Virginian* that his Uncle Gene had bought for him when he was little.

Isaac was of course interested in Russ's guns, a Winchester shotgun, a .30/06 Springfield, and a Marlin lever action .22. Russ patiently talked to the boy about gun safety and responsibility, and he smiled as the boy caressed the smooth, beautiful metal and stocks. He even seemed interested in each scar and dent.

Finally, Russ got out his football card collection, and they sat back on the bed, where Russ leaned his pillow up against the headboard to let Isaac use as a headrest.

As the boy was thumbing through the cards, his eyes big, Russ asked him something he had been thinking about for a while but never thought he would have a chance to ask.

"Hey, Rusty, I'm curious about something. Do you mind if I ask you a personal question?"

The smile vanished from the boy's face. He looked up at Russ, his eyes flickering around as if he didn't dare meet his gaze. "No, I guess not."

"All right. Maybe it's none of my business, but . . . Your mom doesn't live with you, does she?"

"What?"

Russ gazed at him. "It's okay, buddy. I'm not tryin' to be nosey. You don't have to tell me if you don't want to."

The boy was frozen, staring down at a 1953 Doak Walker card. For a while, he didn't even seem to be breathing. Russ waited until the boy took a big breath. He set the card back on the stack and folded his hands in his lap.

"When I was five years old, my mom died. My dad says it was from drinking."

Russ stared at Isaac, his heart thudding dully. His mind ran to his own mother, sitting safe and sound in the living room listening to *Gunsmoke.* He couldn't imagine losing her at the age of five.

"I'm sorry to hear that, bud."

"Yeah. It's okay. I don't hardly remember her now."

"Sure you do! She's your mom!"

"Naw. She wasn't never much. She used to fight with Pa. She'd fight hard. Hit him with stuff. He would put his arms around her and try to hold her till she quit fighting. Then he'd go out in his car and drive off and leave me and my brothers there with Ma. She would usually drink some more, then pass out on the floor. We never woke her. We were afraid of her wakin' up."

Russ was almost sorry he had brought this up. But it was the most words Isaac had ever spoken at one time. Maybe he had needed to talk.

"Hey, Rusty, my buddies told me you're part Indian. Is that true?"

Isaac's eyes jumped up. He met Russ's gaze square-on for two or three seconds, and then looked away. "Uh . . ." He was frantically seeking a way out.

"It's okay, bud. I think it's neat."

Isaac looked up again. "You do?"

"Sure."

"Why?"

"Why? Shoot, Rusty, the Indians were the first people here when the Pilgrims came over, right? Nobody else lived in Idaho but them. Don't you think that's cool?"

Isaac looked down and studied his hands. He reached out and picked up the Doak Walker card again, turning it over in his hands as if to find something of great importance written on it. "I don't know. I guess. But nobody else seems to think so."

"What do you mean?"

"Well, they call me names. Like redskin, and Injun. And war whoop. And sometimes they push me around."

"Yeah?"

"Yeah."

"Is that how you got those bruises I saw on you that one time?"

Isaac nodded.

"What happened?"

"Nothin'."

"Come on, buddy. Something happened, or you wouldn't have had bruises."

Building up his courage, Isaac said, "Okay, Tommy Holmes pushed me down, and another boy named Sam kicked me."

"Did you run away?"

"No!" Isaac averred.

"You didn't?"

"No. I fought with 'em. And my teacher got mad and made me sit in a corner."

Russ was quiet for a long time, lost somewhere between sympathy for his little friend and wanting to punch Tommy and Sam—and Isaac's teacher.

"Sorry to hear that, buddy. I'm real sorry."

"It ain't much being an Indian, Russ," said the boy, still staring at the card, although a glance at his eyes said he really wasn't seeing it.

"You're wrong about that, Rusty. Know how I know?"

Isaac shook his head, not looking back up.

"Well, let me show you something."

Russ got up and went to a little wooden box he had on top of his dresser. It had a padlock on it, and he reached in his sock drawer and rummaged to the back to find a little brass key. Opening the lock, he set it aside and eased back the box's lid. There inside was a short stack of football cards that he kept separate from the others. These were his special cards, or at least some of the ones he cherished the most.

He went back over and sat down on the bed. He started fanning the cards out with a thumb, so Isaac could see them. "See these guys? They're the best of the best. The greatest."

He showed Isaac the cards one by one: a Jim Lansford oversized card from fifty-two, a Thomas Landry from fifty-one. Otto Graham, from fifty; Bob Waterfield, Sammy Baugh, Sid Luckman, and Charles Bednarik, all from forty-eight.

The card that was second-to-last was of a startlingly white-skinned player, Chicago Bear Bronko Nagurski, from 1935. Russ smiled at that one. "That was one tough guy. Somebody once said the only way to stop him was to shoot him before he left the locker room."

Isaac giggled. "He was a good one, huh?"

"Yeah. Tough guy."

Isaac looked up at Russ with a question in his eyes. Nagurski's skin color and his name both pointed him out as one of the whitest guys in football. Why was Russ talking about him?

"You're wondering why I'm talking about this Nagurski guy, aren't you?" Russ asked.

"No, I guess it's 'cause you like him."

Russ laughed. "Well, he was pretty great. But have you ever heard of a guy named Jim Thorpe?"

Isaac shook his head.

"You're kidding! You've never heard of Jim Thorpe? For real?" He slid Nagurski's card away, and the last card in his hand was of a tough-looking, dark-skinned man with a sharp nose, and a wide, full mouth that seemed to be smiling naturally. "That's Jim Thorpe. The greatest athlete that ever lived."

Isaac searched Russ's eyes. "Gosh, really? He had the same name as me!"

"Sure did. You wanna know more about him?"

"Yeah. Who was he?"

Russ smiled. "Well, buddy, I can tell you an awful lot about Jim Thorpe. A lot of people can. Back when this card was made, in nineteen thirty-three, Jim was already done in sports. In fact, he died two years ago. That was a sad day.

"But back in 1912, Jim Thorpe was everything. Man, he won two gold medals in the Olympics. He played pro basketball, and for a while he was playing part-time baseball for the New York Giants at the same time he was playing pro football! And in nineteen twenty, when they first started the National Football League, they elected him as president. Not bad, huh?"

"Yeah," replied Isaac, staring at the card. "That's pretty cool."

"Cool! I'll say! In nineteen fifty, Jim was voted the greatest male athlete of the first half of the 20th Century. So it's not just me saying that.

"Jim was the All-American halfback at Carlisle for two years straight, in nineteen eleven and nineteen twelve. That's the position I play! And then in nineteen fifteen the Canton Bulldogs signed him up as both a player and a coach at the same time, and he was making two hundred fifty bucks a game! No other football player before him had ever made money like that."

Isaac smiled. "He sounds like a cool cat."

Russ laughed and ruffled the boy's hair. "Yeah, he was a cool cat!"

"Did you show him to me just because he has the same name as me?"

"Nope. I showed him to you for another reason."

"What?"

"Well, buddy, look at this guy's face. Take a real good look. What do you see?"

"I'm not sure," replied Isaac after a moment.

"Well then I'll tell you something else. Jim Thorpe had a different name too. They called him *Wa-Tho-Huk.*"

"Huh? What does that mean?"

"Well, it's got a long meaning and a short one. The long one is 'Path Lit by Great Flash of Lightning'. The short one is 'Bright Path'. Now does this photo mean anything?"

"Uh-uh." It was obvious that Isaac was a little embarrassed that he had no smart answer.

"So I'll tell you. Jim Thorpe was like you. He was an Indian, born in Oklahoma."

"Uh-uh!" Isaac's eyes grew huge. "He was?"

"He really was. He was listed as Sauk and Fox, some tribes maybe you never heard of. Most people wouldn't have if it hadn't been for Jim Thorpe. He had Irish and French in him too, like you have some other blood in you. But he was an Indian, sure enough. The first Indian ever to win a gold medal for our country in the Olympics. And Burt Lancaster was even in a movie about him, four years ago. I wish you could have seen it with me."

Isaac's eyes were glowing. He stared at the card, beginning to understand all that Russ had shared with him.

"That's my favorite card in my whole collection, buddy," said Russ proudly. "Worth the most, too. But I'd never sell it off to anybody, ever."

"It's a good one, Russ," said the boy, turning the card over and then back to the front. He let out a big sigh. His face was lit up in a way Russ hadn't seen it in months.

"I won't sell it, but I'll give it away. That card's yours, Rusty. To keep. Something to remind you that being Indian is a proud thing. And something for you to remember me by, when I'm gone away."

Isaac's eyes jerked up to Russ's face. "I don't want you to leave, Russ."

On a whim, Russ reached over and put his arm around the boy, pulling him close and squeezing him hard. "I don't want to leave you either, buddy. But I won't be able to stay here forever."

A tear jumped down Isaac's cheek, and he dropped his eyes, trying to pretend nothing was wrong. It took half a minute, and a number of hard swallows, before the boy said, "Russ? Thanks for telling me about Jim Thorpe. I'll always keep this card safe."

CHAPTER FORTY-FIVE

At football practice the next day, Mark Knaggs, Pete Basso, and Charlie Braun caught up with Russ before the coaches came out. Pete said, "Holy cow, buddy, that was sure awkward yesterday! What's up with you and Edie Russell?"

Russ frowned, not wanting to talk about this. "What do you mean what's up?"

"I don't know, man. She used to act like you walked on water. Now she acts like you're a piranha! She didn't even say one thing to you down at Pash's."

"Well, how should I know? Maybe she finally got smart. Come on! Let's play ball."

"Oh, jeez," said Pete. "Don't get sore. I was only wondering."

"Boy, she sure doesn't look a thing like her old man, does she?" cut in Mark Knaggs. "He's got that red-brown hair, and hers is almost black. She looks a lot like her mom, though."

"Yeah," Russ agreed. "I guess her mom had all the strong genes in that family."

The others laughed, and then the subject was dropped. They hit practice hard that day, but nothing they did seemed to be enough. Jardinsky

drove them like rented mules. He had sworn they wouldn't lose one game this season, and they were to face the Bonneville Bees Friday night.

They won the game, twenty-four to twenty-one—far too close for comfort. It was the first home game Russ had played in that his father didn't make.

Later that night, when Russ got home from celebrating with his friends, Arch was eating a late supper. Russ went into the kitchen, saw him, and walked back out without saying hello. He went down the hall to his room. Luckily, he had eaten an order of fries in Idaho Falls at Ray's In and Out. It would have to be enough for tonight.

● ● ● ● ●

The next morning, Russ rolled out of bed early and mowed the lawn. His father's car was still parked in the driveway—fairly strange considering his work habits of late—and he must be sleeping in, because Russ hadn't seen him.

Russ's father was too cheap to buy the family a television, but he had bought the first Victa lawnmower he could find, which boasted of its powerful motor. Fortunately, it was also very loud. That fact gave Russ great pleasure each time he passed beneath his parents' window—although he felt a touch of regret that his mother had to hear it too.

When the lawn was finished, he went in, and his mother had made breakfast: bacon, eggs, and toast. But most important of all, she had fried some potatoes. Smelling like gas fumes and grass, Russ went to the bathroom and cleaned up, then sat down at the table at his mother's command.

"Where's Pop?"

She gave him a sad frown and shrugged a shoulder, brushing hair out of her face. "Oh, he had to go to work again."

Hearing that made Russ furious. His father must have left while he was in the bathroom. But he decided not to say anything about his anger. His mother brought the food, last of all dishing up the potatoes.

"I peeked in on you and your little friend last night, Russ."

He looked up at her. "Huh?"

"When you were eating."

"Oh yeah? That's creepy, Mom," he said, grinning.

"I'm glad I did." She put a warm hand on his shoulder. "You gave him your supper, honey. That was such a sweet thing to do."

Embarrassed, Russ looked down at his plate. "Oh, yeah. Well, you know—it was already cold anyway."

She patted his shoulder. "Yes, well cold or not, I was very proud of you."

Before he could get any more embarrassed, she turned and walked back to the sink, and Russ ate with a glow in his heart. He forgot all about his dad.

Suddenly, the sound of a car pulling into the driveway registered on Russ. He was curious, but more hungry, so he didn't go look. It sounded like his father's Ford, but he couldn't conceive him coming back so soon.

The back door opened, and he heard his father's footsteps. He frowned and kept eating. He simply wouldn't look over.

"Hey, Russ. Have you seen old Tupper anymore?"

Cursing because now he had to interact, Russ looked over. "Not for a few days."

"Huh. Somebody in town told me he was sick."

"Yeah. Sick. Well, you could say that. Sick drunk."

Arch shrugged off the comment. "You care to go for a drive?"

Russ couldn't believe he was even in the position to have to answer that. "Not really. I got a lot goin' today. I already mowed the lawn for you."

"Yeah, I heard you."

Looking down at his food, Russ took another bite of potatoes. But the little smile on his face wasn't from the delicious food.

"You know, it's getting a little old having you gone all the time." Russ's father walked closer.

Russ couldn't believe what he had heard. He looked up. "What?"

"I think you heard me. You're hardly ever here anymore."

Russ glanced around incredulously, looking for his mother. She had left the room.

A dam burst inside him, something he didn't know could happen, because of his natural trepidation when it came to this man. *"Me?* What are you talking about? How would you know whether I'm here or not?

You're never here either!" Having said this, he lurched out of his chair, expecting his father to grab him or even maybe try to strike him.

Arch stood there staring, the top dog lawman in Bingham County, who took grief from *no* man. Finally, he turned away and made a big deal of getting a drink of water from the sink, which he sipped slowly, his back to Russ.

"I know because your mother tells me," he said at last, in a subdued voice. He was speaking as if to the sink.

Something about the confrontation had ended too soon for Russ, who had taken years to build up the courage to speak back to his father.

"I'll tell you something, too, about that old Tupper. I found him passed out on the sidewalk the other night—dead drunk. I had to drag the worthless old wino into his house and put him on his couch, and he didn't even wake up."

Arch whirled, his face suddenly red. "You watch your mouth, boy. That old wino you're talking about is worth ten of the kind of so-called men you're turning out to be."

Leaving Russ stunned to silence, Arch Blevins turned and stomped out of the house and to his car. In a moment, Russ heard the engine fire up, and it sped backwards out of the driveway into the street, its tires spinning as it pulled away.

When Russ turned around, his mother was standing by the refrigerator with a hand over her mouth and her eyes full of tears.

● ● ● ● ●

Russ walked around town for hours. He couldn't remember ever walking so much of this town, so much that he was seeing some houses three or four times when the sun had passed its zenith and started making its way along the western sky.

All he could think about was what his father had said to him. That was really it as far as he was concerned. His father had told him exactly what he thought of him. And what the heck was it about Barrow Tupper that fascinated his old man so much? He was a worthless, filthy old man who didn't even serve a purpose in life.

Russ felt his body relaxing. He was still angry every time he thought of what his father had said, but it didn't matter. When it came right down

to it, he didn't think that much of his father anymore anyway. So why should he care about his opinion?

He ended up walking out north of town, once he had seen all the rest of it too many times. As he got to Center, which led to Edie's street, something drew him to turn there, and he trudged westward.

As he turned on their street and neared the house, he was disappointed not to see any vehicle near it. He sighed. He didn't know what he would have said to them even if they had been home. Their dinner date wasn't until Monday. They would wonder why he had come around now. He was wondering the same thing.

Regardless, he kept on walking, and at their house he stopped to look over the steps Ev Morin had fixed. He had done a great job. They were as solid as anything Russ had seen. He glanced around the yard, and it was being well-kept. There were delphiniums and dahlias growing along the front wall, and they brightened the place up considerably. Well, he needed to get out of there before they came home, now that he had gotten his senses about him.

As he turned to head out of the neighborhood, he couldn't help but glance into Barrow Tupper's back yard. He spotted the old man kneeling on the ground, his hands in front of him. What was he doing?

Curiosity made him walk closer. Then he got a start. The old man was kneeling in front of a mound of dirt, and at the end of it was a homemade cross.

In bold strokes were carved, and then painted, the letters B-U-D.

Old Tupper's yellow lab had died.

His mind flashed back to the night he was here. He had thought about Bud, wondering where he was. He felt sick. He remembered too well the day he had lost his own dog, Chancy.

With his feet frozen to the sidewalk, Russ stared at the old man. He wanted to turn and leave. He meant to with all that was in him. But he couldn't move. Something held him there.

Barrow Tupper turned his head, for no obvious reason, and their eyes met. Still, Russ didn't move.

Tupper seemed as surprised as Russ was. He started to struggle to his feet, and Russ waited. There was of course no way he could leave now, not until this all played out.

The old man stood slightly bent, and he started brushing at his eyes and cheeks. After half a minute or so, he limped over to the side of the house and picked up his cane. He came out to Russ, more at a totter than a walk. As he got close, he raised his free hand to give him a little wave.

"'Lo, boy. Good t' see you."

Russ nodded. "Hello, Mr. Tupper."

"You fine'ly get smart an' decide t' come see that little Edie girl?"

Russ whipped his face over toward the Russell house, then back to Tupper. "Well, they invited me to supper with them, that's all."

"Well, make the most of it. But I didn't think they was home. Fact, I thought they was gone all weekend."

"Oh. Yeah, actually, the supper isn't today. I only happened to be walking by."

"I see." The old man's face crinkled up, in a grin or a grimace.

Russ motioned toward his back yard. "Hey, uh . . . I saw you back there. I guess your dog died, huh?"

"Yeah. Yup. Ol' Bud's gone. Good fer him. Yup." The old man's eyes filled up with tears, and he looked down and acted like he was looking for something in his pockets. Finally, he raised a battered hand and wiped at his eyes.

Russ was embarrassed for the old guy. He knew he should leave him in peace. "I had a dog too. His name was Chancy. He died a couple years ago."

"Oh yeah? Well, those little rascals . . . They shore don't hang 'round long enough, do they? But heck—they're an awful lot o' trouble, so . . ." Tupper's eyes misted over again, and it must have been too much. "I better git on in. I'd invite you in, but the place ain't real presentable right now. Be seein' ya, son." He turned around and headed for the house.

Russ watched him go, thinking about the inside of his house. As long as either of them lived, old Tupper was never going to know that Russ had to drag him off the sidewalk and settle him down for the night.

CHAPTER FORTY-SIX

Russ went to church on Sunday. It was either that or stay home alone with his father, and he still hadn't gotten over what the old man had said to him. He had a slightly different understanding of Tupper after learning that his dog had died. Maybe he had reason to drink himself into a stupor and pass out. But what his father had said, that Tupper was worth ten of him, was unforgettable. And unforgivable.

After church, Russ changed clothes and told his mother he was going to Pete Basso's house. Basso's family lived up to their Italian countrymen's legend as great chefs. Russ had never had a mediocre meal cooked by Rosetti Basso.

Thus, the day part of Sunday passed, and Russ stayed to have supper with the Bassos as well. When he went home, everyone but his mother was in bed, and she was sitting up in the living room with only a lamp on to light the room, reading the newspaper—or at least pretending to. Russ knew she didn't normally like to read the news.

"Hi, Mom."

"Hi, Russ. How was your day?"

"Good, I guess. Pete's mom said to tell you hi."

"Oh, that's nice. Hey, can you sit down here with me for a bit?"

Russ looked at the couch. He liked the soft way it looked, but he hated the tone of her voice and the look in her eyes.

"Sure, Mom." He went and sat down next to her, their legs touching. "What's up?"

"Russ, I'm sad. I don't know what's going on with your dad."

"I heard you ask him if he was having an affair."

A sad look overcame her face. "Yes, I did. I apologized to him for that. I know he's not seeing anyone. But he keeps telling me nothing's wrong. And if I push him he goes outside and smokes—or drives away."

"Okay, well . . . I don't know how I could help."

"It's not help with that I need, honey. It's . . . Russ, I hate seeing you and your father treat each other this way. When did this all start? It's like you're in a war."

"It's not a war, Mom. He just doesn't seem to like me much anymore, and I don't like him too much either."

Eleanor's eyes filled up with a sudden rush of tears. "Please don't say that, Son. You don't really mean it."

For a moment, Russ wasn't sure. He did mean it, didn't he? But his mom sounded so certain. "Okay, Mom, sure. But he sure isn't any fun to be around—that's when he's actually here."

"You're sad he missed the Firth game, aren't you?" She reached over and patted his hand.

"Heck no! I don't care one way or the other about him coming to a game. I don't care if he ever goes to another one."

His mom frowned. She looked back and forth in his eyes. "I want you to think about that, Russ. When you go to bed tonight. Think about whether or not you really care if he never goes to another game. You know, until Friday, he went to every game you ever played in town, and a lot of your practices too. He was your biggest fan."

A strange pang of sorrow shot through Russ, and he drew in a quick breath. "Yeah." He tried to smile. "I remember that."

"Do me a big favor tonight, Son. Say your prayers. Okay?"

Her eyes were so big and pleading he couldn't deny her. "Okay, Mom. But why this all of a sudden?"

"It isn't all of a sudden. I've begged all of you kids to say your prayers since you were old enough to understand. But tonight I want you to pray about you and your dad. Whisper it out loud, honey. A prayer said out loud will mean a lot more to you than one you say in your head. And think about your father. Think how you would really feel if he never went to another game."

After Russ's mom went to bed, he helped himself to some punch from the fridge, used the bathroom, then walked down the dark hall, lit only by a plug-in nightlight, and went into his room. He pulled off his shoes and lay down on his back on top of his covers, staring up at the ceiling.

He lay there, and he prayed. And in the silence of his room, as he thought about his father, and the fun they had shared throughout their lives, the tears began to course down the sides of his face.

Russ Blevins had not allowed real tears to flow in so long he couldn't even remember the last time.

●●●●●

The next day was Monday, and Russ saw Edie walking in the hall. He had seen Helen, too, but she had whirled away without even acknowledging him.

He slowed down so that when Edie reached him, embracing her books like she always did, he was almost at a stand-still. She was looking more at the floor than she was at anyone in her way, so it was obvious when she looked up that she had had no idea he was even there.

With a start, Edie came to a stop.

"Hi, Edie."

"Hi." Her face was noncommittal.

"You won't even say my name anymore?"

She pursed her lips. "Why does it matter?"

"Edie, please. I'm coming to your house for supper tonight, remember?"

"How could I forget?" she asked with a one-shoulder shrug.

He stared her down until she dropped her eyes. "Hey, where you going? Can I at least carry your books?"

"Russ, I'm a big girl. I can carry my own books. I always have."

"Hey! You said my name."

In consternation, she looked up at him, her eyes telling him she was trying to think of something to say. At last, a little smile came to her lips. "Okay. Russ, Russ, Russ. Is that better?"

"It's a lot better. Now, where you going?"

"Typing."

Reaching out, he pried the books out of her vise. "Come on then. I know you probably don't want to walk with me, but you've gotta follow your books to class."

And so they started off down the hall.

When they made the next corner, into the hall at the end of which sat the type classroom, Helen was standing there talking to her friend Bobbie. Both of them stopped talking when they saw Russ and Edie.

Helen looked up at Russ, but only for a few seconds. Her eyes went to Edie, and she stared her down.

"Hi, Helen," Edie greeted as they came to within a few feet.

"Hello." Helen's eyes were cold. She moved them to Russ. "Hi, Russ."

"Hi, Helen." He stood there uncomfortably for another few seconds, then motioned with his head toward the type room. "Hey, I was carrying Edie's books to her class for her. We'd better get going."

Helen shrugged, and her face looked for all the world like she didn't care if he fell into a pit and died. "Okay. See you."

Russ started walking off, realizing how stupid he was to say what he had. He must look like the biggest dope in the universe to Helen and Bobbie right about then.

At the classroom door, Russ stopped and glanced back. Helen and Bobbie were still in the same place, and although Helen was trying to pretend she wasn't looking, it was obvious she was. She jerked her glance away and faked a yawn.

Russ frowned. He glanced into the classroom, and it was already filling up with people. One of them, to his dismay, was Bill Jensen, the linebacker who had gone tattling to Helen that he had seen Russ on his country run being paced by Edie on her bicycle. He shoved Edie's books at her. "Hey, I better scoot before I'm late for class. See you tonight."

Edie looked up at him and pushed her glasses farther up the bridge of her nose. "Okay."

He started to turn, and she said his name, so he turned back.

"Hey—thank you for carrying my books."

All of a sudden he didn't care what Bill Jensen said or did. "It's okay, Edie. I was happy to." She smiled up at him, and he turned with a smile on his own face.

And there was Helen, still standing where he had last seen her, standing like a gargoyle. Only this time she was alone.

Russ started walking. He had to go right past Helen to get to his science class. The farthest he could squeeze away from her would have

been some twelve feet or so—the other side of the hall. But he wasn't going to give her the satisfaction. Instead, he walked right down the middle.

As he got within ten feet of her, still trying to pretend he didn't know she was staring at him, she stepped away from the wall and stood in his path, hands crossed in front of her.

"Hi, Russ."

He stopped. His only other choices would have been to run her over or go around.

"Hi."

"How've you been?"

He studied her face. Oh, how beautiful she was! He wondered if she had a real motive for stopping him. He was afraid it had something to do with Edie. In fact, he would have bet money on it.

"I've been all right. Hey, did you see my first game?" He knew she didn't. She had already told him she wasn't into football. He was only trying to draw her away from the obvious subject of interest.

"Actually, I did."

"Wait. What? You went?"

She smiled. "I did. I had to see what it was all about."

"Really? How'd you like it?"

"I enjoyed myself a lot, Russ. I really did. I was surprised."

"Wow. Are you a fan now?"

She smiled mischievously, turning his heart into new butter in the sun. "Of football—or of you?"

He smiled back, starting to warm up. "Uh . . . Okay, either one."

"So what if I said yes to both? But I was already a fan of one, and that's what made me a fan of the other."

He laughed. "So what parts do you remember about the game?"

"Well, that's a hard question," she replied. "I mean, I don't know all the rules of the game and so on. But what I really found remarkable is how there were some times when two, and one time even three boys from the other team had hold of you and it took them forever to take you down. You were like a machine."

He laughed again. Wow! He liked it when she decided to find something to compliment him about. Being unstoppable was something he

prided himself on. That was why he looked up to Bronko Nagurski so much. Unstoppable—like a bull.

"Thank you, Helen. Think you'll go again?"

"I know I will. When's your next game?"

"This Friday—against Saint Anthony. But it's away."

"Oh. Yes. I . . . I'm sure I can't take the car that far. There's no way my father would . . ." She didn't finish.

"He still hates me, huh?"

"He doesn't hate you, Russ!" she corrected him. "He never hated you. In fact, he even went to the game too—he and Mother. Please don't be mad at him. He's under a lot of stress, waiting for this thing to be settled."

Russ started to say something about the conversation he had overheard between his father and mother. But looking into Helen's eyes it struck him like the kick of a mule. She had no idea what was coming. She still believed her father might get off. A sick feeling engulfed him.

"Hey, Helen, it sure is good seeing you, but I guess we'd better get running. I'll see you later, okay?"

He started to turn, but she caught the sleeve of his letterman jacket. "Russ, wait! What are you doing tonight?"

"Why?" he asked, his evening plans flying out the window of his mind.

"I thought we could go do something."

"Uh, I guess we— Oh!" A memory of Frank and Lorna Russell's faces went through his mind—and the happy smile of Edie as they parted at the doorway to her class. "Hey, Helen, I won't be able to tonight. I already made plans. But uh, maybe tomorrow?"

"Oh. Okay, So what are you—"

"Hey, we really need to get going, Helen. I'm going to make you late for class, and you'll never forgive me. I'll see you!"

Having dodged that bullet, he turned and walked away as fast as he could.

CHAPTER FORTY-SEVEN

Russ left his last class a little early, so Edie wouldn't beat him out of the building. He really needed to talk to her before going over to her house for supper. Nervous, he watched Helen's car, parked across the street. He waited and waited, but there was no Edie. He couldn't wait anymore. He had to get to football practice.

Turning around, he almost knocked Helen over backward. He actually had to reach out and grab her shoulders, as her eyes flew open and she tipped back.

"Oh! Hey, Helen, I'm sorry."

She laughed. Her teeth were perfect. Her nose was perfect. Her eyes were perfect. Even her laugh was perfect. Part of him wanted not even to notice her, but how could he help it?

"It's my fault, Russ. You don't have to apologize. I was trying to sneak up on you."

He smiled. "Sneak up on me! What for?"

She shrugged, holding her books against a snug white cashmere sweater. "I was trying to surprise you."

His smile grew. He had not lost Helen James! "What if your dad saw you talking to me?"

"Oh, Russ. I think he was just upset and growling because he was worried. He doesn't seem worried anymore. He has a really good lawyer."

Russ pushed his memory of his father's words to his mother to the back of his mind. "So you think he'd let us see each other again?"

"I don't know. Only one way to find out, right?"

"Yep."

"But not tonight," she threw in.

"Yeah, not tonight."

"Can I ask what you have going on?"

Now she had him. There was no way he could lie to her. That was no way to build a relationship—and especially in a town like Shelley, where it would be so easy to find out the truth.

"Yeah. Hey, Helen, I didn't have a choice about this, okay?"

She cocked her head to the side, looking concerned. "What? Russ, what is it?"

"No big deal!" He held up a placating hand. "It's just . . . Well, Frank Russell wanted to pay me back for helping out Mrs. Russell while he was in the hospital. So he invited me to supper tonight." There it was between them—flat and ugly.

Helen forced a smile, but he read her feelings in her eyes. "Oh. Well, that's okay."

"Hey, Helen, I know I told you I wouldn't go over there anymore. But they kept asking me, and . . ."

"No. No, Russ." She held up her hands and canted her head down and away. "No, I am not going to tell you what to do. I was the one who said I couldn't see you anymore, remember? I don't expect you to keep waiting for me your whole life."

"Yeah, but—"

"No. Please don't say another word. Go over there tonight and enjoy your supper. I know it will be a nice evening for you. I'll see you a different day, right? Maybe tomorrow?"

His face brightened. "Uh . . . Really? Yeah, sure!"

"Okay." The real smile was back on her face, and she drew in and released a breath in the same second. She suddenly looked very much at ease. Releasing her all-important books with one hand, she reached out and touched him on the sleeve. "I'll see you around."

And then she walked around him and headed out to her car.

Russ was a little later than everyone else for practice, but he didn't care. He was floating by the time he got there.

Edie was sitting on the bleachers with a book.

She pretended at first not to see him, and Russ was going to play it that way and keep walking. But it was obvious she wasn't reading. She was watching his every move. He stopped at the bottom of the bleachers as he was taking off his jacket.

"Hey, Edie! Good book?"

Caught in her ruse, she looked all the way up, feigning surprise. "Oh! Hi there, Russ! Yeah, it's pretty good. It's *The Last of the Plainsmen,* by Zane Grey." She smiled, as if very proud. Russ had never noticed how perfect her teeth were.

"Good." On a whim, he said, "Hey, if you're going to be up there a while, would you mind holding onto my jacket? I don't want to set it on these dirty bleachers."

She stared at him as if trying to process his request. "Really? I mean— Sure! Yeah, I'll hold it." She leaped up off her seat, but before she could come down, Russ bundled it up. He was taking a chance, but there was something about Edie he knew he could trust.

"Here it comes then." And he threw his precious coat.

Like a pro, Edie caught it without it touching the dirty steps. He had gambled right.

"Good catch, Edie!" Her smile was like the sun coming up.

Russ turned and trotted across the field toward his team mates, knowing he was being watched all the way. That Edie Russell was a nice girl.

The practice was shorter than normal, but fast and hard. Knowing Edie would be watching his every move somehow made Russ run harder, hit with more force, catch the ball with a surer eye. He had never noticed himself caring before. In fact, in the past, knowing she was there only made him nervous. Maybe the girl was good for his game.

Russ made a touchdown, with three of his opposing players hot on his trail but nowhere close enough to have a hope of catching him before the end zone. It felt exhilarating.

"All right, men, gather up here!" he heard the stentorian voice of Ivan Jardinsky pound down the field.

He jogged back, beside Pete Basso, still holding onto the ball. They got into their typical crescent-shaped group, with Jardinsky and Dan Nalder in the middle. Russ couldn't help but notice that Ev Morin made sure to get as far away as possible from him before taking his stance.

"You guys are lookin' real good out there. If it was only the Los Angeles Rams we were gonna be facing Friday night, I'd be scared for them. But you guys are going up against the Saint Anthony Cougars! Not just some NFL team. This is the real deal."

The sarcasm in Jardinsky's voice couldn't be missed by anyone, but he kept a straight face, which was more than most of the team.

"Seriously, I hear those Saint Anthony farm boys are pretty tough this year. Can't catch or throw a ball, but they're tough."

Another laugh rippled through the players.

"Cougars!" he then said derisively. "We already beat the Firth Cougars, and now it's the Saint Anthony Cougars. Cougars everywhere! I hope you boys appreciate the fact that somebody down the line wanted to be original and named you after some awesome, awe-inspiring beast like a russet potato. All dirty and round and fat and soft inside. The epitome of mascots to strike fear into the heart of a mountain lion!"

When the ensuing laughter died down, Jardinsky let the half-grin that had come to his face slide away. "All right. That's why we've gotta prove we're faster, stronger, and able to take more punishment than anybody else. Nobody's taking the potatoes to harvest this year, guys. We're not going to let ourselves lose one game. You hear me? We're going to walk all over those Cougars like they're the Los Angeles Rams."

A cheer went up. Something about Ivan Jardinsky was able to infuse even the meekest of his players with a feeling of power and pride.

"All right. Practice is over for today. Why're we ending early? Because it's Monday night, and we just had a victory. You need the rest. And I want you boys to go home and have some good family time. But if I hear you didn't spend the evening with your families, there'll be hell to pay."

A twinge of shame went through Russ. He really didn't have much intention of spending time with his family tonight—and as little as possible any other night. He loved his mom, but his sisters he could do without most days. And his dad, that went kind of without saying. There had been way too many wedges driven between them—from both sides.

As Russ walked off the field, Edie stood up and walked down the bleachers to meet him. He was smiling, at first, but then it struck him that with Side-Swipe Jensen and some of those other boys out on the field, it was a sure thing it was going to get back to Helen James that he had been letting Edie hold his letterman jacket for him. For a moment, he thought about having Edie throw him his jacket, then turning and leaving without saying much more to her. But why did he care? Maybe the story would

serve to make Helen jealous and she would try harder to find time to spend with him. Maybe this would be a good thing.

"You were fabulous, Russ," Edie said, holding his jacket out to him at arm's length.

"You really think so?"

"Oh, yes! You were unstoppable."

That made Russ grin as he took the jacket out of her hand. Unstoppable. That was the word he hoped would be on his tombstone.

"Thanks, Edie. And thanks for holding my jacket."

"Oh, that wasn't anything." She stepped off the last step on the bleachers, so now the top of her head came even with the bottom of Russ's chin. Looking down shyly, she said, "It smells good."

Knitting his brow, he looked at her. "What's that?"

"Your jacket," she said too quickly. "I said it smells good."

Russ laughed. "Well, thanks, Edie. I think you're the first one who ever said that."

She giggled, and her cheeks turned pinker.

He stood there as the other boys streamed by, some of them making comments that were quiet yet still obviously intended to be heard by him. He ignored them.

Waiting until she looked back up at him, he said, "Hey, Edie, I want to tell you something."

"Okay."

"I'm really sorry about how I talked to you the other day. You've been a swell friend. I was a real jerk to hurt your feelings."

"Oh, Russ," she said, looking back down at the ground and squeezing the life out of her book. "You don't have to say anything. I shouldn't have talked to you when you were in a bad mood."

"Like you'd know if I'm in a bad mood," he replied.

"Well . . . Okay, you're right. But you still don't have to apologize."

He turned straight on to her. "Yes, I do, Edie. You've been a loyal friend, and there aren't very many of those around."

Now Edie couldn't meet his eyes at all. She gave a tight little nod, staring at his knees. "Thank you."

"You're welcome. So hey—I have to go shower up, but I was thinking maybe we could walk to your house together."

"Aren't you going home?"

"Nah. No reason to."

"You don't want to tell your family what you're doing?"

"Hey, Edie, I'm a grown man. They'll see me when they see me. Besides, I'm sure I must have already told my mom about it."

The look that came to her face was sort of a thoughtful frown. "Okay. Yeah, if you want me to I'll wait for you back here."

"All right. I'll be quick."

He came out the back door of the school seven minutes later, wearing his chukka boots, 501 Levi's, and the letterman jacket.

Edie was dressed in Levi's that day as well, with sneakers and a navy blue blouse that was tied at the bottom, with its two ears hanging down in front of her jeans.

"That's a nice look on you," Russ said, instantly wondering why he did. Except, of course, because it was the truth.

"Oh, thanks. It's not much."

They walked to Edie's house side by side, talking about football, and Western books and movies, even about music. It turned out that Edie loved The Sons of the Pioneers, Marty Robbins, Eddy Arnold, and Elvis Presley, like Russ did. But her love of Gregory Peck and Henry Fonda really cemented it all: Edie Russell was a cool kid—even if she was way too shy and unsure of herself.

Frank and Lorna Russell were surprised to see Russ and Edie coming through the front door.

"Hi, honey!" Lorna greeted. "Well, hello, Russ. Why, it's only five o'clock."

"Yes, ma'am. Sorry, I hope I'm not too early."

"Well, of course not! We're glad to have you any time."

Russ walked over to Frank, who sat in his wheelchair, and held out his left hand. Frank shook it. "Great to see you, Russ. You want to see what I can do?"

Russ's eyebrows went up. "Yes sir. Sure."

Without waiting, Frank leaned forward in his chair and pushed first one, then the other of his foot rests aside. He grabbed onto the left arm of the chair, and eased himself up out of it. Then he stood there, perfectly balanced. "What do you think?"

“That’s fantastic, Mr. Russell!” Russ said, his face breaking into a grin.

“All right,” said Frank, feigning disappointment. “We’ve got to get something straight right off, or you’re not gonna be welcome in this house. The name is Frank, okay? Frank, Lorna, and Edie. There aren’t any ‘Misters’ or ‘Missuses’ in this house. Fair enough?”

Russ smiled. “That’s fair enough. Sorry. Bad habit.”

“Nope. No, it’s a good habit. But only until you’re told it isn’t acceptable.”

“Got it—Frank.”

Frank grinned.

Russ mentioned that he had noticed the grass was getting a little long, and since he was early for supper, he asked if he could mow it. Of course Edie being Edie tried to dissuade him, but Russ wouldn’t be turned aside. So the two of them went out together and worked in the yard, enjoying the cool fall evening. They both loved the smell of the new-mown grass, and they loved the color of the maple leaves in the yards around them, which were starting to change.

There was a bench in the back yard, and Edie asked Russ if he wanted to sit for a while. A back yard was a good, safe place, where no other nosy students could see them sitting side by side and report back to Helen. So Russ agreed.

And really, what harm could there be in sitting on a bench next to a girl who had proven for a long time now that she was not only a loyal, but a very forgiving friend?

CHAPTER FORTY-EIGHT

Dinner was ready at seven o'clock, and when Russ and Edie went inside, the house smelled so aromatic it made Russ almost want to run straight into the kitchen. He commented upon the aroma.

"I think you'll like it," replied Lorna. "It's Scotland's most traditional meal. I don't know if you realized it, but the name Russell—at least our line—comes from Scotland."

"No, I didn't know that."

"Well, you're in for a treat," Frank added. He was already seated, but now in a regular dining chair rather than his wheelchair. That made Russ feel good, like there was hope for the family in spite of all their setbacks.

They sat down, and both Lorna and Edie served the men their meal. Edie deposited a large portion of some kind of brown, meaty-looking substance on his plate, and when he looked up at her questioningly, she said, "It's called haggis."

Before she could say any more, her mother chimed in. "Yes, and when you're all finished we'll tell you how it's made." She winked at Edie.

When Lorna came around with a big bowl and dished a portion of what obviously was mashed potatoes onto Russ's plate, he smiled. "Are they russets?"

"Technically, yes. But in Scotland they're called tatties." As Edie spooned something else that appeared to be stewed in butter next to the potatoes, Lorna added, "And those are neeps. Turnips, in this country."

"Wow. You folks know a lot about Scotland, huh?"

"Yes," said Lorna. "From lots of reading. We'd love to go there someday."

"It sounds nice—and green," Russ commented. Inside, he was sad, because he knew there was no way they could ever afford that trip. It would always be merely a nice dream.

For a while, amid the oohs and ahs coming from Russ while he was getting used to the delicious dish called haggis—as well as some fantastic mashed potatoes spiced like none he could remember ever eating before—they discussed Scotland, and the origins of the Russell name.

Then the conversation turned to Western music, and movies, and even television programs, although Russ had only seen those in the homes of his friends.

When they started discussing literature, Russ was surprised to learn that in spite of Frank's great love of the West, he had an expansive taste for books of all kinds.

One of Russ's greatest surprises was when Frank revealed how much he loved *Charlotte's Web,* and the revelation touched Russ because that book was one of his guilty pleasures. They spoke of Steinbeck, particularly *East of Eden,* and Hemingway's *Old Man and the Sea.* Then *Inherit the Wind* and *Twelve Angry Men.* By that time, Russ was really thinking how he needed to stop judging people by appearances, for he would never have pegged Frank Russell to be so well-versed in literature. He seemed like a much simpler man.

"What do you plan to do with your life after high school, Russ?" Frank finally asked that dreaded question all fathers had to ask of young male visitors.

Russ almost hated to say it, because he knew how canned it was starting to sound, but it was the truth: "Play football in college, and then in the NFL."

Frank nodded to himself, and he took a sip of punch—their replacement for the traditional Scotch whisky that should have gone with this meal. "I'm a football fan myself."

"Oh yeah? Who's your team?"

"I guess I'd have to say the Forty-niners. But I like Baltimore, too."

"Wow! I don't hear Baltimore much around here."

"Yeah, I know. But I kind of like Alan Ameche."

"Yeah, he's good."

They talked then about some of the game's greats, names like Tony Canadeo, "Bullet Bill" Dudley, George McAffe, and Tom Fears. Frank liked Joe Perry, Hugh McElhenny, and Norm Van Brocklin. But Russ really sat up to attention when Frank mentioned Bronko Nagurski.

"Man, he was unstoppable."

Russ laughed. "I was just talking about him a while back when I was looking at my football cards. That guy was incredible."

"You remind me of him—unstoppable."

Russ felt a glow of pride inside. "You really think so?"

"I've watched almost every game you've played here, Russ. I think you'll make your dream of going pro."

"Thank you. I sure hope so."

Frank then took in a deep breath and sighed it out. He scooted a fork full of turnips—*neeps*—around on his plate for a moment, and Russ could tell he was contemplating how to word something. He waited politely.

"I've been thinking a lot about something, Russ. Like I said, I think you can make that dream. But I want to tell you about a dream I had myself. Actually, a couple of big dreams. There was a time I wanted to go off and play the guitar. I did play, at least until the accident, but nothing like what I wanted. I wanted to do it professionally. I also wanted to be a woodworker. There wasn't anything that interested me much more. But now?" He held up the stub of his right hand.

When Frank said nothing more, Russ nodded sadly. The sight of Frank's blunt, scarred wrist was sobering. Russ said, "What will you do now?"

Frank shrugged. "I'm really not sure. I'll have to go looking at new options. Maybe I can be an actor, huh?"

Russ laughed. "Well, you could be! You look a lot better than a lot of other guys in the movies."

With a laugh to meet Russ's, Frank tapped his wrist on the edge of the table. "Well, it's not really my bag. Seems like a pretty silly way to make a living, doesn't it?"

"Yeah, I guess so."

"One thing, Russ—one thing you should think about: No matter what you decide to do, think long and hard about each move you make

in your life. It's a lot easier to think things through extra-long before you do them than to spend the rest of your life trying to undo them or wishing you could travel back in time." He glanced over at Edie. "That goes for you too, Sis. Think long and hard before you make choices that will affect your whole life. I sure would like to go back now and make some choices different." As he said those words, he reached over and took Lorna's hand, giving it a loving squeeze. The woman smiled at him and tilted her head to the side, patting his hand.

"Everything happens for a reason, honey," she said. "You know that as well as I do."

Frank nodded, and Russ caught an unmistakable hint of sadness in his eyes. "That's what they say. But there sure are some things that I can't see a reason for, and I guess I'll never know the whys until I get to the other side."

Russ was left wondering about that statement a long time after the meal was over, and after Lorna had revealed the somewhat disgusting ingredients used in haggis, and the way of making it. Frank Russell had some kind of ghost haunting him—a skeleton in his closet, as the saying went. Russ wondered what he had done that he regretted so much. But at the same time, he didn't care. Frank seemed like a great man, and one who cared deeply for his wife and daughter. If it was the two accidents, they were only that—accidents. There was nothing Frank could have done differently. If he was speaking of a choice he had made, Russ didn't care about that either. He had made plenty of wrong choices himself.

● ● ● ● ●

Three weeks later, many people were calling it a miracle. Frank Russell was up and walking, and seldom did he even get tired enough to make use of the wheelchair with which he had built a love-hate relationship. There were some things he could do around home, and many more that he was learning to do with his left hand. Her father's progress wasn't the only thing Edie talked about the times she and Russ were together, but it was certainly at the top of her list.

As for Helen, she had started coming around once more, and she never said any more about whether her visits with Russ were "father-approved." Even as Russ became closer and closer friends with Edie

Russell, and concerned with her well-being and that of her family, he fell more and more in love with Helen.

And yet he was starting to see some things about her that bothered him. She still treated Edie politely whenever they were all together, but Russ wasn't sure her demeanor was genuine. Her smiles for Russ whenever Edie wasn't around were very different from the smiles for him or Edie when she was. Those smiles seemed to be only with her lips, and never with her eyes.

Helen had come to Russ's next two winning games after the embarrassing walloping they gave the Saint Anthony Cougars—thirty-one to three. But she seemed to stay at the game only long enough to make sure he saw her there, and at the end of the second game she was nowhere around for him even to say hi to her and thank her for coming.

But Edie Russell and her parents were.

When the Virginia Theater decided to bring back the movie *East of Eden* for an encore showing (it had premiered the March before), Edie begged Russ so energetically to go to it with her that he agreed in spite of knowing that Helen might find out. However, since the book was one of Frank's avowed favorites, Russ managed to convince him to bring Lorna to the movie as well. A close study of Edie's face when she learned of this development might have shown an astute friend her disappointment, but she was good at masking it.

Russ and Ev Morin had slowly begun talking again, but their friendship didn't seem to be what it once had been. Russ mourned knowing this, for he had never had a greater friend than Ev. He wished if Ev really liked Edie they could somehow hit it off. It would be great to settle down to going out on double dates with them. But Edie seemed content to be friends—with both Russ and Ev. And who was Russ to try and change her mind?

Russ and his father continued to drift further and further apart. There were times when Russ was alone that he admitted to himself that the emotional distance made him sad. His father had once been his greatest champion at his football games. He was the one who had gotten him interested in football in the first place. And although Arch hadn't missed one home game since the Firth match-up, he, like Helen James, was

never around for Russ to see when the grass clippings on the field all had settled.

Russ wasn't even sure anymore why he and his father had first stopped interacting like loving father and son. It all seemed like jumbled, senseless memories. But even though he felt angry every time he saw his father now, he sometimes wished he could go back in time and they could throw the ball back and forth again.

A father and his son, in the park, acting like a father and son should act.

But Arch didn't seem to care, so Russ would keep on pretending that he didn't either.

<p style="text-align:center">● ● ● ● ●</p>

Shelley's famous "Spud Day" that year was on October first. Many people looked forward to Spud Day for the entire year, a day celebrating the final harvest of all the potatoes out of the fields. It was the town's biggest draw of the year.

Many hundreds of people turned out for Spud Day, even people from other towns. The whole town was dressed up, with flags and banners up and down State Street.

There was a huge blow-up potato down by the train depot, and a Ferris wheel, and impromptu food booths were set up all around.

The day began at ten o'clock, with a huge parade down State Street, led by Uncle Sam, in a beautiful white fifty-five Cadillac convertible. The horse club, the Riding Russets, followed. All the school bands from up and down the valley participated, with drill teams and cheerleading squads in full force and battle array. Dozens of riders on horses of every color and several breeds were represented, along with people on bicycles, and even kids on trikes. And of course all of the local politicians, both from Shelley and from all the neighboring towns and the county, had to make their presence known, with their candy-throwing and their fake waves and painted-on smiles.

The big man on campus, Russ's own father, Arch Blevins, brought up the tail end of the parade, driving his Ford and smiling out the window at his legions of fans. There was a time when Russ had been one of those fans. Now he agreed to leave that to those who didn't know his father like he and his family did.

CHAPTER FORTY-NINE

Russ met up with Pete Basso, Charlie Braun, and Mark Knaggs while walking the parade route, picking up wayward salt water taffy that some little kid had missed.

"Hey, Cus!" Charlie sang out. "Wanna make a bet?"

"A bet? What now?"

"First guy to get a kiss today gets a free shot to the other guy's arm. What do ya say?"

Russ thought about that for only a second before laughing. There was no way big, silly Egg Braun was going to make such a bet without having some girl already lined up—maybe even his little sister!

"Nothing doing," replied Russ. "I already know I'm way more selective than you."

Pete turned and gave Charlie a punch to the shoulder. "Ha! See, I told you he wouldn't fall for it."

"Aw, you guys are a bunch of stick-in-the-muds."

"Wouldn't that be 'sticks in the mud'?" rejoined Russ.

"Man, stuff it," said Charlie, and as he said it he turned to a ten-year-old obvious female member of the Braun clan across the street and waved her off. The girl put her hand to her mouth and giggled, then ran after a couple of other girls her age.

"You're one rotten egg, Egg," said Russ, clapping his friend on the shoulder. They all had a good laugh.

Picking up a couple of fresh donuts each at Mallory's, they sauntered on down the sidewalk, shouldering through the post-parade crowd, most of whom were also headed toward the city park, where later a big freebie football game had been set up between Shelley and the Rigby Trojans, the Russets' toughest rival. The real game against the so far-undefeated Trojans wasn't for three more weeks.

At the park, there were booths set up everywhere, and here they held sack races and spud picking contests. Only in Shelley!

The whole town was like a carnival, and even many of the local farmers and their families were in attendance, glad to be out from under the stress of bringing in the potatoes before any chance of nasty weather.

After wandering around the park, visiting with friends, and watching some of the guys make their girlfriends sick by pushing the merry go-around too fast, they headed south again, ending up at Nalder's funeral home and furniture store, where music was playing and people were dancing to the beat of rock and roll—with a polka thrown in now and then for the older set.

Finally getting hungry enough for something besides donuts and cotton candy, Russ and the others crossed over to the train depot, on the east side of State Street, where every year they gave away free baked potatoes. It wasn't really much. They never offered enough butter, and the only seasonings were salt and pepper. But it was food, and it was free, and for the football crowd those were the only two requirements.

They had been served, and Russ was forcing down his dry potato, along with copious amounts of water, when he turned and saw Ev coming in the front door. To his shock, he was closely trailed by Edie Russell!

Russ almost choked on a mouthful of spud. He stared at the two of them before they turned and saw him, not realizing that Pete Basso had seen them together as well, and was now staring at Russ to catch his reaction.

A jumble of thoughts bombarded Russ at once. The first was jealousy, which didn't fit at all with everything he had been telling himself. The second was the realization that this pairing was what he had been telling himself all along he wanted for Edie and Ev—two great people and great friends to him. Lastly, he wondered if he was missing something—had Edie and Ev stumbled into each other outside and happened to be walking in together out of chance?

"What's goin' on in that head of yours, Cus?" It was Mark Knaggs, not Pete, who had spoken. "You look like somebody walked on your grave."

Russ tried to force a laugh. "What? I can't look at somebody without gettin' comments?"

"Depends on how you look," cut in Pete.

Standing six-foot-one, as well as being near bald-headed Egg Braun, who was six-foot-four, didn't allow Russ to be very inconspicuous in a crowd. Edie spotted him almost instantly, and a huge smile jumped onto her face. She turned and said something to Ev, which made Ev's face darker, not lighter, and then made her way through the crowd to Russ and the others.

"Hi, Russ!"

"Hi, Edie," he said, a little self-consciously, knowing every eye was on them. "Did you see the parade?"

"Of course. Didn't those horses look incredible?"

"Sure," he replied. It must be something about girls—was every one of them drawn to horses?

"Your father looked really dashing."

"Huh?"

"Your father? In his sheriff car?"

"Oh, yeah." Russ let out an embarrassed chuckle. "I guess it was the word 'dashing' that threw me off a little. I've never heard anyone call him that before."

"Well, it's true. He cuts quite a figure. Even Daddy says so."

Well, what would they know? thought Russ. He had to *live* with that dashing peace officer.

"Are you ready for your big game?"

Wow. Edie was really a chatterbox this morning. Had she decided to come out of her shell?

"Oh, sure. That'll be nothin'."

"Really? Nothing? It's the Trojans!"

"Okay, well, they might play it up big when they're with other schools, but they don't stand a chance against us."

Edie laughed. "Okay. I believe you."

By this time, Ev had made his way over and was talking with Pete and the others. He said hi to Russ, but without any of his former friendliness. Seeing that was heartbreaking to Russ. What could he do to get

inside Ev's head? How was he ever going to get his friendship back? What was the big grudge all about?

He was thinking about that when he heard Edie's voice, as if from a distance. "You didn't hear one thing I said, did you?"

"What?"

She giggled, reaching up to push her black-rimmed glasses farther up her nose. "I said maybe later we could go for a ride on the Ferris wheel."

Russ let out a laugh, reaching out to squeeze her arm. "Sorry! Yeah, I was thinking about something else." He glanced over at Ev. "Say, I'd love to, but . . . didn't you come with Ev?"

"Oh, no! I just ran into him after the parade."

One question answered.

"Want me to go get you a spud?" asked Russ.

"Oh, would you? Thanks! I didn't want to get into that crowd."

"Well, maybe you could walk with me. It looks like it could be a while."

"Okay. I'd like that."

They got in line, side by side, and suddenly, without asking if it was okay or even saying she was going to do it, Edie reached up and took Russ's arm. He looked down at her hands and smiled. Right now, he really didn't care what his friends thought. Anyone with half a brain could see he and Edie were only friends.

The front door of the depot opened again, and Russ looked over, as was his habit. Helen James, standing beside her mother, was staring right at him, her lips parted in surprise.

For a second, as they stared at each other, Russ could read the girl's face, and he was positive she was going to turn and beat a retreat out of the building. But then a look of resolve came over her face, and she turned and said something to Pearl, who looked Russ's way then as well. Pearl's eyes met Russ's, but then they dropped to see Edie standing there, oblivious to their presence, her hands still holding tight to Russ's elbow. Pearl looked up at Russ again and gave him a reserved smile. Then she patted Helen's arm and said something, turned, and left the station.

Helen made her graceful way through the crowd. Today, her beautiful red hair was up above her head, leaving her long, slender neck exposed but for a few wayward wisps of hair that hung down, accentuating its slenderness.

"Hi, Russ," she said, making her smile big and bright. Then her eyes dropped a little. "Oh—hi, Edie. I didn't see you there."

Edie smiled uncertainly, dropping her hands away from Russ as if suddenly he was made of molten lava. "Hi, Helen. You really look beautiful today."

Helen tried to smile. "Thanks."

"Hey, Helen," Russ said. "You want to cut in line with us? If you don't, it's going to take you forever."

"No, I'm not that hungry."

"You're not? What'd you come in for then, a train ride?" Russ was trying to lighten a moment that even through the eyes of a dense football player was obviously tense. He gave a little laugh, but Helen didn't match it.

"Well, yes . . . I *was* wanting a potato when I came in. But they look really dry."

Russ chuckled again. "Well, they're always dry. Not everyone can afford to put four tablespoons of butter on a spud."

Helen's attempted smile was a miserable failure. "So hey, Russ, I tried to call you at home this morning. You must already have come down here."

"Oh, yeah. Sorry! What did you need?"

"Well, I wanted to see if you'd come to the parade with me and Mother. But . . . I see you're already busy."

"Oh, no! No," repeated Russ, looking at Edie. "No, Edie came in with Ev. I just told her I'd help her get a spud."

"Oh, really? Okay." She gave Edie a big smile, the kind of smile Russ wished she had given the girl when she first saw them together. Now, it seemed like too little too late.

"Then maybe when you're done you'd like to come with me and go dancing," Helen suggested, now ignoring Edie.

"Uh—sure. Maybe we can meet somewhere in a half hour or so, when I get out of here."

Helen looked over at Edie, giving her another smile, once again with no substance. She might as well have voiced the thought that showed plainly in her eyes: *Isn't Edie big enough to get her own potato?* She looked toward the front of the line, seeing several girls there who couldn't have been more than eleven or twelve.

"Well, then maybe I'll be over at Mallory's. But you have to get ready for your game soon, right?"

"Oh, shoot. Yeah. We might have to wait until after the game to dance, but the dancing goes really late."

Again, the door opened, and by now it was starting to make Russ nervous. But then, what could be worse than having Helen walk in?

This time, to Russ's big surprise, it was Frank and Lorna Russell. They made him and Edie out in the line and started to work their way closer. When Helen noticed Russ staring that way with a smile, she also turned.

Frank Russell froze. His eyes were locked on Helen. Lorna took a moment longer, but when the girl registered on her, she too, stopped walking. To the Russells, it seemed like there was no one else in the room but Helen James. Russ knew how that felt, but the look in their eyes wasn't like the look that came into his whenever he saw her.

At last, composing himself, Frank took Lorna's hand, and they kept on coming. Russ was baffled. He couldn't see Helen's expression, because she was turned away from him. But Edie looked as confused by the silent interaction as he felt.

Frank and Lorna reached them and stopped, both trying to keep their eyes off Helen. Russ, putting a smile on his face, said, "Hi, Frank. Hi, Lorna. Have you met Helen James? She goes to school with us."

Frank looked more nervous than Russ had ever seen him—more nervous than he could have thought possible. His hand almost seemed to be shaking as he put it out toward Helen.

"No, we haven't actually met in person. Hello, Helen. I'm Frank Russell. And this is my wife, Lorna."

Russ was stunned to notice that Frank's eyes seemed to be shining. He couldn't swear to it, but they almost looked misted over with tears.

Russ took a couple of steps to the side, to place himself in a position where he could better see Helen's face. Something strange was going on here, and he felt completely in the dark.

Helen graciously put her left hand into Frank's and gave him her winning smile—this one genuine. "It's nice to meet you, Frank. My mother knows you, I think she said. Maybe you went to school together?"

"Yes. Yeah, we did. A long, long time ago."

"I think I heard her one time slip and call you Frankie."

Frank laughed. Russ saw then that there really were tears in his eyes.

"Do you not like that name?" Helen asked innocently.

"Oh, it was only your mother's name for me. Nobody ever . . . Yeah, it was just what she called me. I never let anybody else use it. You know—kid stuff."

Frank held onto Helen's hand for a long time before letting it slip from his fingers. She turned then and put her hand out to Lorna. "It's nice to see you again, too, Mrs. Russell. You sure do have a nice daughter."

"Oh, thank you, Helen. Thank you very much. And it is so good to see you again too."

The doorbell jingled again, and the door came open to reveal Pearl James. She saw Russ and started toward him. Frank Russell followed the line of Russ's eyes when he saw that something had drawn them to the opening door, and as he turned, he froze.

But this time his recovery was fast. He turned back to Russ. "Well, Lorna and me better get going. My back isn't ready to be standing up and walking around so much yet. Hey, Russ—we'll see you later at the game, okay?"

"All right, Frank. Sounds good."

Frank waved goodbye to Edie without another word, then turned and started for the door.

The look of consternation on Pearl's face when the sight of Frank Russell registered on her could be felt clear across the room.

CHAPTER FIFTY

There was no avoiding a collision, at least an emotional one. Pearl was making her way down an aisle between human bodies, and Frank and Lorna Russell were in that same aisle. None of them could escape it.

Pearl stopped. Dressed in a light blue, sleeveless swing dress in a beautiful floral design, a tiny white “fascinator” hat perched aslant on her head, with a small mesh screen hanging down before her eyes, demure-looking Pearl James could have dropped any man in his tracks. She was as polished and perfect as any actress Russ had ever seen on the silver screen.

Russ couldn’t see Frank and Lorna’s faces—only the backs of their heads. The thought of Lorna Russell ran through his mind, and in spite of the fact that she would be no Hollywood beauty, her warm, genuine good looks would stand up to any test, at least in Russ’s mind.

“Hello, Frankie.” Pearl blushed and laughed. “I’m sorry—Frank.”

“Hello, Pearl. It’s been a long time.” Frank’s voice was muffled, because he was facing away and because the crowd in the room was noisy.

“I don’t know if we’ve actually ever met,” said Pearl then, turning her eyes to Lorna. “You’re very beautiful, Mrs. Russell. I’m Pearl James.” She put out a white-gloved hand, palm down, and Lorna took it and gave it a firm squeeze.

“Thank you, Pearl. So are you. I really love the dress. And no, I’m quite positive we’ve not met.”

Pearl smiled. “You would think this town had a million people in it, wouldn’t you?”

“Yes, I agree. I’ve only had a chance to admire you from afar.”

Pearl cocked her head to the side. “That is a sweet thing to say.”

“But easy to say, as well. You really are breathtaking, Mrs. James. I have to say it.”

Pearl gave Lorna a warm smile. "Well, in my opinion beauty is only skin deep." She looked over at Frank and offered him the same smile. Taking in a deep breath, she said, "I must say, Frank, you did very well for yourself. Your wife is truly lovely."

"Thanks for saying that. I agree. Hey—it's been good to see you. Maybe we'll see you around again." Frank gave a little nod to the woman, then held out his hand to Lorna. She took it, said so long to Pearl, and they walked past Pearl and out the door. Pearl turned partway around, and for a long time stood gazing after them.

Looking somewhat disconcerted, Helen looked up at Russ. "Hey, I guess I'd better go. I'll see you at the game."

"What about dancing?"

"No, forget it. Well, I don't know. Maybe after the game?"

"All right. See you later, Helen."

He watched the girl go to meet her mother, and Pearl turned as if in a daze to give Russ a wave before turning again with Helen and following the Russells out of the station.

Forty-five minutes before the game, Russ went home and got the Studebaker, then drove up to the school and changed into his uniform. He stayed at the school for a while and did some warm-ups and stretching before meeting his teammates and the coaches back at the city park.

The Rigby Trojans were warming up on the other side of the park. Big Troy Ridley was their star player, a boy who was sure to go on to great things if he kept going as he was. They had other phenomenal players as well—Sparks, John, Holloway, Briggs, Walhouse. Those were the names Russ knew well, but there were others whose names he couldn't recall who were just as good. It was a tough, rugged team of farm boys. But they could not compare to the 1955 Shelley Russets.

The Russets were in fine form. Tossing the ball back and forth, Russ had full confidence—in everyone. Even Ev Morin, while so aloof toward Russ lately, was a tiger once he had possession of the ball. They were going to take this fun little game—the only question was by how much.

Before the start of the game, Russ scanned the crowd. Everyone he cared about was out there somewhere. All three of the Russells, Pearl James and Helen. Russ was happy to see that Harold had made the game

as well, and when he caught Russ's eye he raised his fist in the air and pumped it encouragingly.

It warmed Russ's heart to see his mother and all of his sisters, and even his Uncle Gene and his wife Claudette were there. And there, walking in from the street, came his father, big Arch Blevins. Russ felt a warm glow pass through him that he couldn't understand, since he didn't care if his father was there or not.

The coin toss went to the Trojans, which pleased Russ fine. He was great with letting the Rigby players think they had a leg up on Shelley.

A couple of mistakes on the part of the Russets, and some fast footwork, plus an excellent throw by Trojan quarterback Bobby John, got the Trojans their first down fairly quickly. After that, the Russet defense held them until they almost ran out of downs.

Then Troy Ridley took the ball from his quarterback and made a run downfield, dashing some thirty yards between Russet players before Mark Knaggs brought him to the ground.

Russ was stunned when, in three more minutes, he saw Ridley cross into the Russet end zone and score the first touchdown of the game. Only five minutes into the game, and the score was already six to zero in favor of the Trojans. Soon, with the conversion kick, it was seven.

With the ball now in the hands of the Russets, Russ was full of confidence once more. First down was easy. Then another first down. On the next play, Pete Basso took the ball and ran, but he was cut off by a swarm of Trojans and had to backtrack. By the time Trojans Bud Holloway and Myrt Walhouse dragged him to the ground, Pete had lost two yards.

Russ got his team together in a huddle. "Don't sweat it, guys. This is nothing. We're just getting warmed up, and I can already see they're wearing themselves out. They've got a lot to prove, and they know it. But they won't prove it here!"

He called the play—actually two different plays, a Plan A and a Plan B, and they broke. Mark Knaggs snapped the ball to Johnny Boo Fabian, who turned and tried to spiral it in to Russ. But Russ was the Trojans' main target, as everyone had known he would be. When he couldn't get

open, and two Trojans broke free and were closing in on Johnny Boo, he switched to Plan B.

Tucking the ball, Johnny Boo took off running, dodging around the two descending Trojans. But when Myrt Walhouse and Jud Anderson were zeroing in, he hooked to the left—straight into Nate Sparks.

Johnny Boo went down hard. By the time they got the pile cleared, he still had possession of the ball, but he looked pretty shaken.

Before Russ or any of the Russets could reach Johnny, Trojan Nate Sparks put out his hand. Johnny looked at it for a second before accepting it and letting Sparks hoist him to his feet.

"Hey, Johnny. You all right?" Russ heard Sparks ask as he was coming up with Slick Patterson and Mark Knaggs.

"Yeah, man, I'm okay—I think."

"Good," said Sparks with a big grin. "And hey—that was a great play. I think I would actually have rooted for you if you made that run all the way in."

"Thanks—it's Nate, right?"

"Yeah. Nate Sparks." They shook hands, and Sparks turned and started to go, then spun back, seeing Russ.

"Hey! Man, I gotta tell you somethin'! You're some player, Blevins. It's an honor to be out here on the field with you."

Russ was taken aback, but he grinned. "Well, thanks, I appreciate that. It doesn't take long to see you're pretty good yourself."

They shook hands, and then Sparks ran back to his team.

Russ and Johnny Boo walked back to their team together. As they walked, Russ tried to study Johnny without looking at him outright. Before they reached the others, he asked, "You really all right, Boo? You need to sit for a few?"

"No, man. I'm great."

"Promise?"

"Yeah. Promise."

They all came together, and Bill Jensen piped up, "Hey, Blevins! Hobnobbing with the enemy out there, huh? We gotta kill those guys, you know! We can't be pattin' 'em on the head before we pull the trigger."

Russ ignored him. He was still shaken by his quick interaction with Nate Sparks. He hadn't been expecting anything of the kind.

"All right, boys. I've got one mission for you this time: Keep Johnny Boo safe! At least let him catch his breath, all right?"

The others whooped and hollered out their agreement, and some of them gave Johnny rough slaps on the shoulders and back, which he most likely could have lived without.

Russ called the play, and they started out onto the field again, lining up on the line of scrimmage. Mark Knaggs snapped the ball to Johnny Boo, who with perfect precision spiraled it into the arms of Russ as he was running fill-tilt for the other end zone.

This time, there was no stopping the Russets. Two Trojans Russ didn't know got hold of him seven or eight yards from the line, and his momentum and strength helped him drag all three of them on through into the end zone for a touchdown.

The Russet kicker was a kid named Scott Leader, a sophomore Russ didn't know well but didn't like all that much. However, this particular time his foot was magic, and he put the ball right down the center, giving them a full seven points now, and a tied game.

By halftime, Russ had worked up a good sweat, and he was thankful for his crewcut. Some of the other boys still had regular haircuts, the kind a businessman might wear. The score now stood at a respectable twenty-seven to twenty-one, and of course the Russets were ahead. Things were going nicely, and if they kept their heads the Russets were in for a tidy win. Scott Leader was the only one Russ was worried about: He had missed his second kick by inches, and they didn't get the conversion.

Russ saw Ev Morin sit down on the grass twenty feet away from him, and he frowned. He needed to talk to that boy. Obviously, whatever was eating at him wasn't going away until Russ took the bull by the horns. Johnny Boo came and plopped down next to Russ, while the band was playing a rousing marching tune and the cheerleaders were going crazy.

"Hey, what do you think about that Nate Sparks fella?"

Russ looked over. "Crazy, huh? Nice kid."

"Kinda makes you think."

Russ knitted his brow. "Oh yeah? What about?"

"Well, dang, I don't know. Here we are knocking ourselves out to slam all these other guys, and we're so het up to take State, and then you

get thinkin' about it, and all those guys are prob'ly thinkin' all the same stuff. It sort of takes some of the fun out of beatin' 'em, doesn't it?"

Russ laughed. "You crazy? It doesn't take any of *my* fun away!" He cuffed Johnny playfully on the top of the head and gave another laugh. "Don't go gettin' soft on me now, Boo! We got a game to win!"

When halftime ended, the Russets ran into the game full-force. The score was soon upped by another touchdown, that one run in not by Russ, but by Pete Basso. A cheer went up, and Russ could hear Pete's mother screaming above the crowd. He looked over to see the dark-haired woman jumping up and down. She always made him laugh. She was bigger around than she was tall.

But then, within minutes, the Russets and all their fans had a huge jolt when the Trojans tried a trick play, and before anyone knew what had happened, Troy Ridley had waltzed right into the end zone for another touchdown.

Nobody managed to score for quite a while after that. Both defenses were on fire, and they held the offense at bay. At last, tall, scrawny Rigby player Hy Miller managed to slip through the Russets' defensive wall, and the next thing Russ knew the Trojans had another touchdown, and then a good kick. The Trojans were ahead by one point!

When the Russets got the ball again, Russ forced himself to be supremely confident. But he was starting to realize what an incredible force this year's Trojans had become. Right out of the chute, Russ got his team a first down. Then he got them another, before Troy Ridley and Bud Holloway helped Darwin Janikowski take him to the ground.

After that, they couldn't seem to gain a yard. They would pull ahead, only to be driven back. They made it to their fourth down and decided to kick a field goal. They were about to lose the ball anyway.

Russ walked out to Scott Leader, putting a pleasant smile on his face. "Hey, bud, don't let these guys sweat you. We're counting on you for these three points. Give 'em heck!"

Every player and every onlooker watched with bated breath. Leader went in for the kick, and Russ studied him. His pace was perfect. He was going to make it!

Leader's shoe against the ball made a tell-tale *thump,* and the ball sailed free. Every eye was on it. It was going to hit the bar!

Then, to everyone's surprise, the ball skimmed the top of the bar and went in. The Russets were once again ahead—but only by two points.

Both teams were showing wear now. Most of the players were on both the offense and the defense, and there was very little chance to rest. Russ pushed his men as hard as he could, trying to build them up to create a wall in front of their end zone. But somehow it didn't work.

Troy Ridley blew through their defenses once again, for another touchdown. And the conversion was beyond easy, sailing at least seven feet above the center of the goal post.

Russ felt sick. There was one minute left now until the end of the third quarter, and the score was forty-two to thirty-seven, and not in their favor. He didn't understand what was happening, but for some reason his team seemed to be falling apart.

Coach Jardinsky called a time out, and he and Dan Nalder met their boys on the edge of the field. Russ could feel his family and friends watching, mere yards away behind him. He was doing the best he could! He hoped they all could see that.

Ivan Jardinsky put his right hand on Russ's left shoulder, and then, to Russ's astonishment, Jardinsky pointed his heavy index finger at Ev Morin, who stood in the crowd across from him. He didn't say a word, just motioned Ev over with a flick of his fingers, then put his left hand on his shoulder. Best friends, separated now by only a coach.

"I'm damn proud of you boys. You're more like men than boys. That right there—" he jabbed a finger downfield "—is one of the toughest teams in this entire state right now. I'll bet you all a dollar that's who we face when we go to State."

Russ noted the fact that Jardinsky didn't say *if,* but *when.*

"You boys're givin' them hell, and it's wearing them down. I can see it. It reminds me of my game against the Forty-niners, in forty-six. Tied thirty-five to thirty-five, half a minute on the clock, and we took 'em. Yes, we did, boy. Scored a touchdown right in the last three seconds of that game. We took 'em! Like you're gonna take the Trojans. Now go out there and knock their heads off!"

He started to turn away, but then he paused and yelled out again, "Hey! One thing." He grabbed Russ and Ev with a great big, gnarled hand by the sides of their necks and drew them in close. "You just

remember that this game is all about building friendships, more than anything else. There's nothin' else more important. No matter what happens out there. No matter who wins or loses, you've still got your friendships. Some of those will last your whole lives. Don't lose that, boys. For nothin'."

With big, powerful arms, he drew Russ and Ev around in front of him, so he could switch his glance only a little to look each of them right in the eye.

"Remember what I said, Russ. Ev. Nothin' else matters like a true friend."

CHAPTER FIFTY-ONE

Russ got his team in the huddle. He looked around at each of them. "You guys are pretty all right," he said at last. "I don't care what all the girls say about you." Everyone guffawed at his joke.

Then he stopped grinning. "Seriously, I've had a great time playing ball with you boys. Football is an awesome game, but remember, like Yardinsky says—that's all it is. That's something I have to keep telling myself over and over. We're going to go out there now and win a game. That's all there is to it. But even if we didn't win, I'd still think the world of all of you. Now enough mush. We've got one minute left. That's plenty of time for a touchdown." He called the play. "Now on three. One-two-*three!* Break!"

The team walked to the scrimmage line, faces grim. At the last moment, Russ looked over at his best friend. "Hey, Ev!" When Ev looked at him, he said, "Good luck out there."

Ev smiled. It was the first spontaneous smile he had given Russ in weeks. "You too, bud."

Fifty yards. An easy fifty yards. Before the start of the fourth quarter, the Russets were going to tie this game. One minute? A cut and dried touchdown, for a team like the Russets.

They made an easy first down after Johnny Boo passed off the ball to fullback Pete Basso. He was sacked hard by Rye Sparks and Bobby John, but bounced back up, spry and ready to go again.

On the second play, Rigby's Shane Hudson managed somehow to slip through the line and took out Johnny Boo before he could even find an open receiver. At least Johnny held on stubbornly to the ball.

They only made one more yard, and a third down, with the next play. Russ had let Pete carry the ball, and the Trojans' Darwin Janikowski piled in front of him and took out his feet.

In the huddle, Pete told Russ, "Hey, man, you've gotta run it this time. Thanks for the tries, but brother, we need some yards."

They broke with the understanding that Russ was going to pick up a short left pass from Johnny Boo and run down the center of the field, with Pete and two ends running interference for him.

Russ was really starting to need the help, as most of the Trojan force made a point now of concentrating their efforts on bringing him down.

Russ caught the pass and took off sprinting, hoping for a good, straight line. He had it, and he had made seventeen yards, and another first down, when Troy Ridley hit him out of the blue. Ridley, almost as big as Russ, drove him so hard that his feet crossed, and down he went, in a major roll that set his head spinning.

Still holding onto the ball, Russ had to sit there for several seconds and get his bearings. It was Ridley who put a hand down to him. "Good play, man," said the farm boy from Rigby.

Vaulting up, Russ clapped his opponent on the shoulder. "Thanks, Troy. You guys are in great form today."

But inside he added, *Too bad it's not going to help you!*

They didn't make the whistle. They were five yards from the end zone when the clock ran out—and still forty-two to thirty-seven.

Between the third and fourth quarter, Russ got his boys together in a loose half circle, every last one of them. He slowly looked from one to another of them, until he was pretty sure he had made eye contact with every one. "All right, guys. I remember the moment I realized I had lost my last game. Last October. The day before Halloween. Some of you guys remember. The only game we lost last year—to the same guys

we're facing right now. The Trojans. I swore I'd never lose another high school football game. Some of you remember that, too.

"But this isn't about me. It's about all of us. We're in the middle of the biggest celebration Shelley has, in our own hometown. The Trojans might be one of the toughest teams around, but they're *not* the Russets, right? And they're on *our turf.* On our terms, too.

"So I know this game doesn't mean anything in the standings. It's supposed to be for fun, right? Wrong! If we let these clowns win this game, it's going to be nothing but a huge confidence boost for them. So if it's only for that one reason, we've got to crush them. I know they really want to win State this year. And they've tried hard. But they don't want it like we do. Do they?"

A chorus of "no's" went up from the team.

"That's what I want to hear. The Russets are taking this game, and then we're going on and taking State. And *nobody's* going to stand in our way. All right. Let's get out there."

The offense met out on the field, and Ev suggested a strategy that Russ liked and everyone else agreed to. They had to get another touchdown, and then the conversion, and they would be back on top, forty-four to forty-two. Easy!

Break!

They took their places on the scrimmage line. Pete Basso took off paralleling the line of scrimmage, behind Johnny Boo Fabian, and when the ball was snapped he shot for the end zone. A Trojan was instantly covering him, running right with him, and no matter what he tried, he couldn't break free.

Johnny Boo turned and zapped the ball in an arrow-straight shot toward the waiting arms of hard-running Russet end Anthony Wayne, but at the last second, Trojan Troy Ridley leaped up into the air, like a cat swatting at a bird. He tipped the ball so that Wayne had to veer sharply to the side to catch it. In the process, he ran out of bounds, and the pass was incomplete.

They ran it again, and this time Wayne got away from Ridley, by a sudden J-hook, but Trojan Rye Sparks had already taken up Wayne's path.

Johnny Boo was hit by Rich Wheatley, the Trojan nose guard, and knocked flying, barely managing to hang onto the ball.

Second down.

On the next play, near-disaster struck—or at least it seemed that way to Russ. Johnny had zipped a close-up spiral straight at Russ, but Trojan linebacker Jud Anderson made a spectacular leap through the air toward the ball. It looked like a sure catch, but apparently Jud Anderson was the "Slick-Fingers" Patterson of the Trojan team, and the ball spun out of his fingers and up into the air, where Russ caught it in a desperate dive that landed him on the ground and wound up with his being dropped on by a ton of Trojans.

Third down. They had only made it seven yards.

Breathing heavily, Russ leaned down in the huddle, looking around at the guys as he wiped sweat out of his eyes. "Guys! We're coming up on a fourth down. We can't let this happen. Ten yards this time. That's all I'm asking." He looked over at end Darren Holm. Darren wasn't a huge player. But he was well-built and fast, and he had good hands. "Darren, let's shoot this one to you. Get downfield as fast as you can, at least ten yards, then zap to the right. Boo, you concentrate on him, all right? Hit him with the ball when he whirls. We'll have your back."

Johnny nodded. "Got it."

"Now, Egg, and Nash—I want you boys on top of Boo. Kill anybody that comes after him, got it?"

The boys nodded and smiled.

"Break!"

They got into position. Mark Knaggs snapped the ball into Johnny's hands, as Russ took off at a diagonal run, almost right through Troy Ridley, who tried to stay with him but lost him when Russ whirled as if to catch a pass.

Russ looked over in time to see Holm make a picture-perfect catch and whirl to run. He only made it fifteen yards before Trojan Bud Holloway brought him down. But it didn't matter: They had a first down!

The Russets were back in the play.

The crowd of onlookers was going wild. Now and then, Russ thought he heard his name, and whenever he took the time to look he could see his people, at various points, up in front of the crowd of fans.

The recovery was temporary. Johnny Boo's next spiral was meant for Russ, but Troy Ridley hit him hard as the ball was nearing him, and it grazed off his fingertips and into the air.

In a moment that left everyone dazed, and a much smaller contingent of fans screaming with elation, Trojan Walter Briggs had ripped the ball right out of the air and was headed toward the Russet end zone.

With a growl like a wild animal, a sound that barely even registered on himself, Russ took off at a sprint, outrunning the two Trojans who tried to cut him off. Briggs only had a five yard head start on him before Russ recovered. Five yards might as well have been an inch.

Russ drove into Walter Briggs's back with all his force, sending him sprawling, but another Trojan, Darwin Janikowski, fell on the ball. Russ had made the tackle, but the ball was still in Trojan hands.

First down. Second down. Then a twelve-yard run by Troy Ridley. First down. The next run was made by Myrt Walhouse, but the Russets drove him off his course, and when Nash Wheeler grabbed him like a bear and threw him to the ground, he had lost three yards. Second down.

The Russets were losing steam. The Trojans were losing steam. There was enough sweat and spit on the field to wash a car, if they could have gotten it all into one place. There was also more than a little fresh blood, and a few torn-off scabs.

Time was running out. The Russets held the Trojans back, but every time they would start coming up on a fourth down, one of them would get just enough yardage to put them back in the play.

Finally, the Trojans didn't make enough yardage on a play, and the ball went back to the Russets, to the sound of a legion of fans cheering.

But not gaining enough yardage proved not to be a market the Trojans had a corner on, when to everyone's astonishment the ball went back again to the Trojans after a fourth down.

Now they were coming down to the wire for time. Players were hot and tired, and tempers were stretched. Ev Morin said something he shouldn't have to one of the Trojans, Douglas Hudson, who decided to run over and give Ev a punch right in the face. That set Russ off, for there was one thing he didn't put up with, and that was one of the other team hurting his best friend.

He rushed in and took Hudson down, but before he could do anything worse than put him on the ground, Johnny Boo Fabian and Pete Basso were dragging him off, and the refs were in the middle of everything, blowing whistles and screaming.

The whole affair could have ended badly, but after a consultation of several minutes, the refs decided that since Ev had called Hudson a name, starting the whole mix-up, but Hudson had resorted to his fist to finish it, that Russ was only protecting his team, and if both sides agreed this would be their one freebie—no penalties for either side.

Taking a deep breath, Russ looked around. For a moment, the whole park seemed dead. It seemed no one was making a sound. All he could hear was the ringing of his ears. His eyes fell on Helen James, who must have been waiting for that moment. She put her hands together in praying fashion and shook them, giving him a hopeful smile.

Russ's energy seemed to leap back into him, maybe double what it had been five minutes before. He smiled back at her and held up a finger. *Number one,* he meant to say. The Russets were number one!

He was going to make a touchdown. He was going to make it for Helen James. There was only a minute and a half left in the game, and the Trojans, who were five points up on them, now had possession of the ball. But Russ didn't care. They were going to win this game!

In the huddle, Russ drew a deep breath, and once again he scanned his team. "You boys have fought a hard battle. You've earned a good rest. But we have one more play in us—the one that will get that ball back in our hands. You all understand me? We're taking the ball back, guys. Now. I'll give twenty bucks to the guy who can intercept this next pass. And I'm not kidding. Don't let me down."

After calling the play, they went out to the line. The ball was snapped, and it was in the Trojans' hands. Every Russet had his man, had him good and tight. Troy Ridley whirled, opening himself up away from Russ. The distance was twenty yards—hardly a throw at all.

But Troy Ridley, right then, was hardly a player at all. Russ was doing this for Helen.

With an athleticism he didn't even know himself he had, Russ launched himself through the air, right in front of Ridley. One moment he was up there, feeling like he had taken flight, and the next, the ball

struck him right in the chest. He heard Troy Ridley swear. He struck the ground hard, and daylight disappeared as eight or nine bodies landed on top of him, crushing the wind from him.

When the grass clippings and the blue air from the cursing Trojans cleared, Russ Blevins was found to be in possession of the ball.

And there was one minute and seventeen seconds left in the game.

CHAPTER FIFTY-TWO

One minute and seventeen seconds. To Russ Blevins, it seemed in one way like hours, and in another way like an eye-blink.

The fifty yard line felt like it was a mile away. Once they started shooting for it, it seemed even farther. Nobody trusted anyone but Russ to run the ball now. Russ was their team. He was the guy who was going to lead them to State. Every time Russ suggested passing the ball off to someone else, or making a long run downfield and having Johnny rocket the ball way out there, they shot him down.

You gotta run it, Cus! they said. *It's too risky for us.*

Russ fought them. They were a team! Each of them should be as good as the next man. Down deep, he kind of agreed with them. It was only right that he run the ball. He was, after all, the halfback, and the halfback was the backbone of a team. But there was a big problem with that: The Trojans were all over him! They weren't about to let him out of their sight, and at times they even dedicated *two* players to keeping him handicapped.

At last, after a hard battle and two downs, it came to the final huddle. There were twelve seconds left in the game. The fans were eerily silent. Russ couldn't even hear the birds chirping in the trees. He looked over to scan the crowd, his support group. He picked out Helen by her glistening hair. She blew him a kiss, and Russ saw her mother, who stood behind her, clutch her shoulders.

Russ grinned at Helen, Pearl, and Harold, and bent into the huddle. "Guys, you heard the ref—twelve seconds left, and we're still down by a touchdown. But only one! One touchdown will win this game by a point, even without the conversion. Got it? Easy. We've got this in the bag."

"The second Spit hits me, I'm going to be looking for you, Russ," said Johnny Boo. "Get out and run for all you're worth for three seconds, then turn. I'll hit you square."

Russ stared at Johnny, trying to decide if he should let him have the power to call this one. Well, why not? Johnny was their strong arm, after all. And his eye and arm were impeccable.

"Fine, Boo—have it your way. I'll run it, if the guys can keep me clear. But if I can't . . . Hey, Ev?"

Ev Morin's eyes snapped up to his pal. "Yeah?"

"I need you to back me up, buddy."

"How?"

"You get downfield, okay? Run as fast and hard as you can. Maybe clear into the end zone. Those jerks are gonna be on me like fleas on a dog. If I can't get open, you've gotta take it. It's only twenty yards—easy money."

Ev looked toward the end zone. It seemed so far away. "All right. I'll try."

"No, you'll do it, man. I know you will."

"All right," said Ev, clenching his jaw. "I'll be down there."

"You hear me, Boo?" Russ said. "If you can't get a hole to throw to me through, you aim for Ev. And Wop, you try to get over to the far left and stay clear too.

"I've been trying, man! They're all over me."

"Well, do your best."

"If I make the touchdown, you have to quit callin' me Wop, all right?"

Russ straightened up, knitting his brow. "Huh?"

"Stop callin' me Wop."

"Jeez, man—great time to tell me you don't like Wop. Shoot, if you make this touchdown I'll start callin' you King Pete, if you want."

Pete grinned, his ivories shining like the sun. "That's a deal."

They broke.

Everyone walked to the line with determination. Mark Knaggs leaned down to the ball. Johnny dried his hands on his towel. He called for the snap.

Sure and true, the pigskin found his magic hands. He stood up and looked around. Russ was running full-tilt. Two Trojans were on him. He feinted a step to the left, spun in a circle and bolted back to the right. Troy Ridley stuck to him like a dog on a bone, and Bobby John wasn't far behind.

There was no hole.

Russ spun to look downfield. Pete was blocked by big Rye Sparks, the older of the Sparks brothers. A throw to him was suicide.

But Everett Morin was open as planned and five feet from the line. Ev whirled. Bud Holloway ducked in for the kill on Johnny Boo, but Nash knocked him to the side and to a knee. Trojan Rich Wheatley came in low and fast. He was almost to Johnny when Egg Braun came down on him like a ton of sandstone.

Johnny licked his lips. He zeroed in on Ev Morin, and he made the throw. It was a long one, but it wasn't. It seemed like he was throwing half the football field.

Ev had to dart out to meet the ball. He was right on the line. One catch and a whirl, and he would be into the end zone.

Russ didn't see where Rigby's Nate Sparks came from. Ev was wide-open one second, and the next, Nate was closing on him like a greyhound.

Ev reached out his hands for the perfect catch, just as Nate Sparks made his leap. The ball was sailing right for Ev's fingers. But it never made it.

The point of the perfectly spiraling ball hit the web of Nate Sparks's hand and did a somersault.

Startled, with eyes and mouth wide-open, Ev spun. Both hands grasped for the ball. He could still make the catch.

And then Nate Sparks touched the ball again, and it spun away, and downward.

Pete Basso, the would-be King Pete, was sprinting along the edge of the goal line. There was nothing more he could give. The run was Olympic-class. But he was too far away.

With a thud like a cannonball, the football hit the turf, three feet inside the end zone. It bounced off to the side, back the other way, then rolled to a stop.

Ev landed on his back. He lay a forearm over his eyes, shading them from the sun. It was obvious he had no desire to move.

A roar went up from the small but exuberant crowd that had come down from up north to watch their Trojans do battle. Russ stood there in shock. He had lost a game. The perfect season was gone. His fans were standing with their mouths open. He saw Edie Russell, her hands over her mouth. Frank had wrapped an arm around her shoulders and was saying something to her, and Lorna was patting her other shoulder.

Some distance from Edie, Helen stood in her red and black sweater with her arms hanging limp at her sides. Her father and mother were standing behind her, as if afraid to move.

The world of the Shelley Russets had stopped.

Gathering himself, Russ trotted toward the end zone to check on Ev. As he reached him, Nate Sparks leaned down and offered Ev his hand, but Bill Jensen stepped in and slapped it away.

"Leave 'im alone, ya puke! Get back over to yer own team."

"Hey!" Russ barked as he saw Pete Basso about to open his mouth. "Leave 'im alone, Swipe." He looked at Nate. "Sorry, man."

Nate nodded. "It's okay. I understand."

By that time, Ev had gotten up on his knees. He couldn't meet anyone else's eyes.

Russ walked over and put his hand out to Nate Sparks. "That was a heck of a game."

Nate smiled tentatively and shook his hand. "Thanks. You too."

"Hey!" Russ heard the voice off to the side, and turning, he saw seniors Troy Ridley and Rye Sparks loping up.

Troy stopped and nodded at Russ. "Hey, man. You guys played a great game."

Russ was aching inside. But he couldn't let on. "You too, man. That was some real ball." When Troy's hand came out between them, he

forced himself to shake it, as much as it hurt. But when their hands were clasped, he realized it actually felt good. He shook Rye Sparks's hand, too, then jerked a thumb over at Nate.

"Hey, Ryan, it looks like your spot's gonna be well taken care of when you're done."

Rye grinned. "Shoot, Nate? Yeah, he's all right, I guess."

"Congratulations," Russ forced himself to say. That was a lot harder than the handshake had been. "I guess we'll see you at State, huh?"

The others laughed, and dark-haired, dark-eyed Troy Ridley pointed his finger at Russ like a gun. "I'm expecting we will," he said. "But we got one more game before that."

And then the Trojans walked away, and the defeated were left on the field of battle to nurse their wounds.

In scattered clusters, the Russet supporters ventured out on the field of sick and wounded troops.

Russ stood there with Ev, not knowing what to say. Side-Swipe hadn't walked off yet, and he looked over at Ev. "Well, nice catch, Ev."

Before Ev could respond, Russ balled up his fists and stepped in front of the bigger boy. "Shut your damn mouth, Swipe, or I'll knock your stupid block off. Get out of here!"

Side-Swipe smirked and walked away. He was three inches taller than Russ and at least thirty pounds heavier. But nobody would be taking any bets on him in this fight.

Russ turned to Ev as his mother and sisters were coming up to him. He glanced around, and his father was nowhere in sight.

"Hey, buddy," Russ said to Ev, clapping a hand on his shoulder and resting it there. "You all right?"

Ev grunted, looking up for a moment at his friend. There were tears in his eyes. "Man, I had that ball right in my hands. If that kid hadn't run in when he did . . ."

"Dumb luck," said Russ. "Nobody could have made that catch with him comin' out of nowhere like that."

"Yeah, sure." Russ knew what Ev wanted to say. He wanted to say Russ would have made the catch. But Russ was pretty sure he wouldn't have. Nate Sparks didn't only have dumb luck. He was one good ball player.

Russ turned to his mother, who came and gave him a big hug, overriding his protests. "Mom, jeez! I'm all sweaty!"

"I don't care, Son. It's family sweat," she said with a smile. "You boys sure played a great game."

"No, we didn't," Russ countered. "We lost."

"It was still good!" insisted little Kathleen, putting her hands on her hips. "You were everyone's hero, Russ!"

When she said that, he saw Ev lower his head again. "Naw, I wasn't anybody's hero. We were a good team, that's all." He glanced over at Ev and wished he could say something that would make him feel better.

He glanced around. "So . . . where did Dad go?"

Eleanor pursed her lips sadly. "Oh, Russ. He felt so bad. He didn't know what to say, and he didn't think you'd want to see him."

"What? He said that?"

"He did."

Russ swiped the inside of his cheek with the tip of his tongue, glancing around at the crowd, trying to catch a fleeting glimpse of his dad. But even as tall as Arch was, he was nowhere to be seen. "Well, that's fine with me. I don't know what I would have said to him anyway."

He had been waiting for Helen and her parents to come over, but when he looked their way they were walking off too. Helen was looking back, and she gave him a sad little wave, but then kept going.

Edie and her parents were left standing when the rest of the crowd had drifted away except for the other families of the Russets and the defeated Russets themselves.

Edie's eyes were full of sadness.

CHAPTER FIFTY-THREE

Edie walked over to Russ as his sisters were taking their turns trying to think of something to say that might be comforting. Surprisingly, Russ wasn't devastated. He could only keep thinking that at least this game didn't count toward the standings. It was just a Spud Day match-up for fun. Maybe the loss itself didn't bother him so much because he had something else to think about: He was worried about Ev.

Edie stopped close to Russ, and Dorothy cut short whatever sage thought she had been sharing, of which Russ hadn't heard a single word.

"Hi, Russ."

"Hi."

Silence. Russ was rescued by his mother. Moms were good at filling voids.

"Who's your friend, Russ? I don't think we've met her."

"Oh! Sorry." Russ looked around. "Hey, everyone, this is Edie Russell. Frank and Lorna's daughter."

"Oh, yes! Of course," said Eleanor. "I should have known. You're the spitting image of your mother. Such a beautiful face and complexion. How did you get so lucky?"

Edie laughed, and blushed. "Thank you. I'm not sure."

Russ introduced his mother and the girls, reaching out and pinching Kathleen's cute button nose. "Stop it, Russ! I'm too old!" the girl protested.

Russ laughed all the more. "Too big for your britches, Little Britches! That's what you are!"

Ev was standing there looking uncomfortable, but it was obvious that he didn't want to walk away without saying anything.

"Hey, Russ, I prob'ly oughtta get going."

"No, man. Don't go yet, all right?"

"No! Boys, I'm sorry," Eleanor cut in. "I didn't mean to interrupt. I'm sure you'd rather be with the team."

"Not really," replied Ev. "I'm pretty sure that's the last place I want to be."

"Hey . . ." Eleanor walked over and gave Ev a warm, motherly hug. "Chin up, Ev. That was a great game, and you did a superb job. There's no way in the world anyone could have made that catch. That was nothing but luck of the draw. That boy came out of nowhere."

"She's right, man. Don't even think about it again," Russ agreed.

Ev nodded, trying to smile. "Yeah. Well, when you miss the catch that lost probably the only game we're gonna lose this whole year, that's easier said than done."

"Well, I thought you were great!" Toni cut in. "Next time you'll catch it!"

"Thanks, Toni," said Ev. "Hey, I really oughtta be goin'. I think I'm gonna run up to the Falls and have some lunch or something."

"You gonna be okay, buddy?" asked Russ.

Ev smiled at him and reached out to shake his hand. "Oh yeah, man. Yeah, I'll be fine. I just wanna be alone for a while."

"All right. All right." On a whim, Russ threw an arm around Ev and gave him a squeeze. "Thanks for a great game, Ev. I'll talk to you later."

When Ev started walking away, head down, Edie turned to Russ. "Hey, Russ, please don't leave yet, okay?"

"Huh?"

"Please wait a minute for me. I want to say something to Ev."

Russ agreed, and the girl ran to catch up to Ev. They stood talking for a few minutes, and finally Edie enclosed him in a long, warm embrace. That little, shy girl from yesteryear was growing up, thought Russ. Maybe she and Ev would make a pair yet. And even as he thought that, a strange, sad feeling welled up inside him.

Soon, Edie returned, and Ev kept on walking. Russ followed him with his eyes, knowing how he must feel.

Frank and Lorna Russell had been lingering thirty yards away, but at last they walked over, greeted Eleanor, and met the girls. "I want to thank you for raising up such a great kid, Mrs. Blevins," said Frank. "He's sure been a big help to us."

"Well, thank you, Mr. Russell. I think you see more of Russ than we do." She laughed, but something about her face made Russ study her longer. Did that bother her, not having him at home all the time? He was, after all, a grown man, and he had things to do. He wasn't some little kid anymore, who needed to be hanging around home pestering his mother.

Frank and Lorna ended up inviting Russ over for dinner, and he gladly accepted. He would enjoy some more time in the park, visit with his friends, and maybe even with some of the boys from Rigby, who, even though they were his rivals, were pretty good boys, as long as they weren't battling him for honors on the field. He was also hoping to find Helen and do some dancing in front of Nalder's, where the records would be put out of commission and they would soon have a band set up.

Much to his chagrin, Edie asked if it was okay if she hung around with him for a while. He couldn't very well turn her down, especially not with her parents and his mom right there, so of course he said yes. But it would seriously cramp his style. What was Helen going to think?

They wandered down to Pash's, by the Virginia Theater, where Russ treated Edie to an iron port and cherry and a cheeseburger and French fries.

When they came back outside, Russ saw Ev's car parked in front of the Virginia Theater. His friend hadn't made it too far. He must be hiding out inside, since he had free run of the place. There wouldn't be any movies going until later.

They wandered down and around the corner, where the band was getting set up. They were all dressed up in blue suits, and wearing black and white saddle oxfords. Every one of them wore duck butt haircuts, which made Russ chuckle. Some of the styles guys got caught up in!

All of a sudden, Russ caught a wave out of the corner of his eye. He looked over to see Helen hurrying his way, still wearing her school colors, the red and black sweater and a white skirt with a black poodle embroidered on the side.

"Hi, Russ."

"Hey! I thought you went home."

"I did, for a while."

"Where's your mom and dad?"

"Oh, they stayed home. Dad's a little uncomfortable being out in public right now. You understand."

"Oh, right. How's he doing?"

"Well, he already had his preliminary hearing."

"Yeah? Did they decide to do a plea bargain?"

Helen sighed, glancing over at Edie. "Well . . . Hey, sorry, Edie—could you let me talk to Russ for a minute by ourselves?"

"Oh, yeah! Sorry. I'll be over here." Obviously embarrassed, Edie rushed away and stood looking in Nalder's front window, ten feet away from them. Russ looked at her. Poor, awkward girl. What was she even doing here? She should have been hanging around with her friends. And then he realized he wasn't all that sure she had any real friends. He never saw her with anyone else.

"What's so interesting?"

Helen's voice drew Russ's eyes away from Edie, who was dressed in her drab gray sweater and navy blue blouse, with an olive green skirt and scuffed ballet flats. He felt bad seeing how almost impoverished Helen made Edie look.

"Huh?"

"I'm right here, Russ. Aren't you interested in what I'm saying?"

"Oh, yeah. Sorry. Of course I am."

"Well, it looked like you were a little more into Edie."

"Sorry."

"Okay. So I guess Father has to go to trial. We thought the prosecuting attorney might drop the whole thing or maybe just put him on probation, to keep it all quiet. But that man is really mean. He's making Father go to an actual trial."

Russ was sick. He still didn't have the heart to tell Helen what he had overheard his dad telling his mom.

"When's that going to be?"

"It starts next Tuesday morning at nine."

"Wow. That's fast."

"Yeah. I guess they don't have anything better to do than harass innocent people. My dad didn't even do anything wrong!"

Of course, he didn't, thought Russ. *They never do.* He instantly realized he was starting to think exactly the way he had heard his father talk for years. He couldn't stomach that thought!

"I'm sure it'll work out, Helen. They'll figure out he's innocent, and then they'll have to set him free, and your life will be back to normal." He said it, but down deep he had a gut feeling it wasn't true. He sensed that Helen and Pearl James's lives were about to completely unravel—the way his mom and dad had been talking about.

If his father had only listened and had some mercy on Harold James! Why did he have to be so hard with people? Everyone made mistakes. But Arch Blevins was unbendable. The thought of him right then disgusted Russ.

"You know what, Russ?" Helen said. "I just want to dance. Okay? I want to forget about all this." She turned to see that Edie was watching them, and she gave her a forced smile that to Russ was almost shocking in its insincerity. She spoke loudly enough for Edie—and anyone else standing nearby—to hear: "Do you mind, Edie? I'm going to steal Russ for some dances."

Surprised, Edie looked at Russ. "Oh no! That's fine, Helen. Sure," she stammered. "I'm just . . . Yeah, that'll be cool. I'm going to go in and look at the furniture for a while."

Edie walked into the store with Russ watching her, feeling guilty because it was obvious she was hurt and embarrassed. As the band started to play their first number, Helen held out her hand. Russ only saw it from the corner of his eye.

"Russ! I'm right here. Why do you keep staring at her?"

He turned back to Helen. "What are you talkin' about?"

"Edie, silly! Why do you keep staring at her? Don't you want to dance with me?"

"Yeah, of course. It's just . . . I think you hurt her feelings."

Helen slammed both of her hands to her hips. "Well, I'm sorry. My feelings are hurt too. I want to forget about everything and dance. Don't you want to be mine, Russ? Just mine?"

"Yeah! Of course I do. That's all I've *ever* wanted."

"Well, I don't want to be rude, but remember when you promised me you wouldn't even go to the Russells' anymore?"

“Sure I do, but—”

She waited, watching him. “But what? Do you try to find excuses to break your promises? Come on, Russ. Please dance with me. You can go find Edie later if you really need to make her feel better. But right now I need you. Is that so much to ask?”

“No, it isn’t.” Russ took Helen’s hand and put a hand on her waist, and they began dancing. He stepped on her toe once and apologized as she frowned down at the scuffed toe of her saddle shoe. She didn’t say anything at all, even to accept his apology. She just leaned closer to him, and he guessed that was her way of saying she didn’t hold it against him.

As they came around, Russ looked toward Nalder’s, and through the reflections on the glass he saw Edie. She was inside the big front window, watching them.

Helen saw where he was looking, and he moved his eyes away. She didn’t say one word, but suddenly she stopped their movement, and looking up into Russ’s eyes she said, “You know what I want?”

“What?”

“I want nothing more right now than for you to kiss me. Right here, with everyone watching. I want the whole world to know that Helen James and Russet Blevins are together.”

CHAPTER FIFTY-FOUR

Russ stared at Helen, frozen in his tracks. She took both his hands, and her lips parted expectantly as she looked up at him. But he couldn’t move. An offer he would have jumped at the spring before now left him feeling confused. He couldn’t even call it tantalizing. Here they were, in the middle of a crowd, some of whom he had known for years, and others who of course would know who he was, if from nothing more than seeing his picture in the *Shelley Pioneer.*

Helen James was standing in front of him. *The* Helen James! The girl he had dreamed about as far back as he had had the hormones of an

adolescent. And she wanted him to kiss her. The whole world would then know that HELEN JAMES BELONGED TO RUSS BLEVINS!

And that Russ Blevins belonged to her . . .

"Are you sure?" he finally stammered. "I mean, in front of all these people?"

She frowned. "Why not? Are you ashamed of me?"

"No! Of course not! But . . . Well, it just seems like . . . It seems kind of out in the open."

She frowned again, cocking her head to one side. "Well, that's the whole idea, isn't it? You know what? Forget I ever said it." She dropped her hands away from his.

"No!" he said. "No, hang on. I'm game."

She smiled, as if she knew all along that he was mere putty in her hands.

Bending down, he kissed her on the mouth. One peck, the way a grade school kid might do on a dare.

Helen frowned once more. It was starting to seem like her normal expression. "That's it? That's what you call a kiss now? It isn't how you've kissed me before."

Russ glanced over to Nalder's huge picture window. Edie was still standing there in the exact same place, but now her head was turned away. Helen followed his glance. She stared at Edie for several seconds, then looked up at Russ, who by then was looking at her.

"So that's it. You and Edie?"

In shock, Russ said, "What are you talking about?"

"I saw how you were looking at her. Is that why you didn't give me a real kiss?"

"That was— Okay, come here. I'll give you a real kiss."

By now, Russ was aware that several people in close proximity were looking on, even if they pretended not to notice what was happening.

"Are you serious?" asked Helen. "Don't patronize me. Come on. The moment is passed. Let's just dance."

The band was playing "Love Is a Many Splendored Thing," made popular that year by Sammy Fain and used in the movie of the same name. At the moment, the irony of the title was not lost on Russ. He could have re-written it: "Love Is a Very Confusing Thing."

Helen stepped into him, and he took her in dancing stance. They started to move around the street. But she was stiff, and wouldn't even look at him. He had the feeling they were only dancing because she was trying to save face with those around them.

When the song ended, Helen said, "Hey, sorry about making a scene. You know, I just remembered I told Mother I wouldn't be gone too long. I'd better go."

"Okay. Are you coming to the game Friday? It's here."

"Sure, I imagine. Father wouldn't let us miss one."

"All right. I'll see you Monday at school." She started to turn, and trying to salvage something, he said, "Hey."

She turned back.

"Are you mad at me?"

"No. Why would I be mad?" She tried to smile. It was a pathetic effort. "I'll see you Monday."

Russ watched Helen walk away. He saw someone striding toward him from the area of Owen's Hardware, which sat on the northeast corner. The way they were walking made him look over to see Pete Basso and Johnny Boo Fabian headed his way.

They stopped in front of him, and Pete reached out and shook Russ's hand. Then he jerked a thumb after Helen. "Hey, man, what's up with that, anyway? She get mad because you kissed her in public?"

Russ turned and looked after Helen as she crossed State Street toward where her car was parked.

"Ha. Not even close. She didn't think it was enough of a kiss."

"Huh?" Pete looked shocked. "What are you talking about?"

"She asked for a kiss, Pete. Jeez. Right here in front of the world."

Pete and Johnny looked at each other incredulously, then back at Russ. Johnny laughed. "Man, last spring that would have been like you struck gold! You feelin' okay, brother?"

Russ frowned. "Hey, guys, I gotta go, all right?"

"What's the big hurry? Your Sheila's gone now anyway! Let's hang out," said Pete.

"Well, hang on . . ." Russ turned toward Nalder's. Edie had come outside, and she was standing there alone, pretending to look at something on the front of her skirt, which she seemed to be picking at. There

was no one else around, and no one was waiting for Edie. "No, guys, I really need to go."

Pete and Johnny stared at Edie, then returned their attention to Russ. "Hey, bud, are you goin' nuts?" asked Johnny. "That's Edie. I thought she was a germ."

"Cut it out!" Russ said defensively, standing up straighter. "Come on. She's a nice girl."

Pete laughed. "Okay. Nobody ever said she wasn't a nice girl. But since when does that mean anything?"

"All right, Pete, cut the gas. I like her, all right?"

"What?"

"Not like that. Come on, give me a break. She's by herself. Besides, her dad invited me over for supper tonight. You guys go bug somebody else, huh? I'll see you later."

With that, Russ walked over to Edie. He could tell by her eyes she was well aware of his presence all along, but she looked up at the last moment, feigning surprise. "Oh, hey!"

"Hey."

"Where did Helen go?"

"Oh, she had to take off."

"You mean . . . So she's not coming back?"

"No. She said she told her mom she wouldn't be gone long. Where'd your mom and dad go, anyway?"

"Oh, back home, I think. Daddy was getting tired out, and I think they were going to start on supper."

"Cool." A thought struck him, and he glanced around. He hoped he wasn't about to make a huge mistake, but Edie looked so out of sorts that he thought it wouldn't hurt to ask, just this once. "Hey . . . Listen to the song." The band was playing "Moments to Remember", one of the songs they had danced to at the prom the spring before.

Edie's face brightened. "Wow! Yeah."

"You remember?"

Her dark eyes met his, and she smiled. It was a heart-warming smile. "Well, of course. I'll never forget."

"So, do you want to dance—you know, for old time's sake?" he quipped.

"Sure. For old time's sake."

And so they danced. And Russ thought about Helen, and hoped she wasn't too mad. And he thought about how white Edie's teeth were whenever she smiled that great big, heart-warming smile.

The big trial of Harold James began on Tuesday morning. Russ was on edge because of it, and because Helen had seemed so preoccupied the day before that she hardly even had time to say hi. This was another full day of her being distracted, and although she hung around with her friends Bobbie and Lonna, Russ never once saw her laugh, or even smile. He went to football practice without having said one word to her all day, because she seemed unapproachable.

The next day wasn't any better. If anything, it was worse. He saw Helen in the halls a few times, but unlike the day before, today she wasn't even with her friends. She walked crushing her books to her chest, and her eyes concentrated only on where her feet were going.

By Thursday, Russ couldn't take it anymore. He found Helen sitting by herself in the empty English classroom during lunchtime, eating a tuna fish sandwich out of a brown paper bag. Glancing around through the door's window, he couldn't see anyone else inside, so he eased open the door. The room was indeed empty, except for Helen, who at the moment was staring out the window.

"Hi."

She whipped her head over at his voice and tried to smile. "Hi."

"Can I keep you company?"

She shrugged. "Sure, if you'd like to. I probably won't be very good company."

He came over and sat down. Helen took tiny bites of her sandwich and divided her time between frowning down at it and glancing out the window at what had proven to be a glum, gray day.

"Any news on the trial yet?" Russ dared to ask.

Helen whipped her eyes away. For a long time she stared out the window before looking back down at her sandwich and pulling in a deep breath. She blinked quickly, as if trying to clear tears from her eyes.

"No big news."

"No idea how it's going?"

Helen bunched her lips and looked away again. She started to put down the sandwich nervously, then brought it back up, clutching the little bit that was left in both hands. Another deep breath.

"Not good, I think."

"What's happening? Last time we talked you said your dad was pretty confident nothing would happen."

"Yes, well . . . I guess he was wrong."

"But it's not over yet! Until the jury comes back, there's no way anybody can guess."

Helen pursed her lips again, and her chin began to quiver. She took another dainty bite of the sandwich, then finally gave up and put it down. When she swallowed, it was with great effort.

Without warning, she got up, banging her legs against the underside of her desk, and came toward Russ. He leaped out of his chair to meet her, and she threw herself against him.

"Oh, Russ. I'm so scared. They're going to find him guilty. I just know they are. What are Mother and I going to do?"

He was speechless. How could he respond to that?

He held her tight and patted her back. Since he didn't dare speak, that was the only way he could think of to comfort her.

● ● ● ● ●

The Russets won their game the next evening. Russ was angry, and that made him focus. It wasn't even a game, really. It was a slaughter. The Salmon Savages died thirty-nine to seven. And when the game was over, Russ didn't even celebrate. He went looking for Helen.

She was nowhere to be found. But Edie and her parents were there. Russ walked out to them, mostly ignoring the excited congratulations of his teammates. It had been a stupid game anyway. Who could really celebrate over a score like that? It was like the Savages were playing in wheelchairs.

"Hey, Russ," greeted Frank. "Great game."

"Thank you." He was too polite to say what he really thought.

"How are you, Russ?" asked Lorna. Her smile brightened him up a little.

"I'm good."

"Yeah?"

"Yeah."

"I hope you'll forgive me for saying so, but you don't seem yourself."

Russ smiled with one side of his mouth. "No, I'm okay. Just worn out, I guess."

"Well, you'd better go rest up," suggested Frank. "And me, too. I have a job interview tomorrow."

"That's great!" said Russ with a smile. "Good luck."

"Thanks, buddy."

Lorna and Frank said goodbye, and Frank put his hand on Edie's shoulder to guide her away. "Hey, Dad?" She stopped him.

"Yes, honey?"

"Can you hang on for a minute?"

Frank looked at her, a little confused, then over at Russ. "Well, sure."

Edie walked to Russ. It seemed to take all her strength to look at him. With her hands clasped down in front of her, she met his eyes. Russ smiled at her, feeling the second wave of warmth he had felt that day. He found it cute how much she resembled her mother.

Edie pushed her glasses up on the bridge of her nose. "Hey, what are you doing now?"

"Oh, just going to go shower."

"Can I . . . I mean, would it be okay if I wait for you?"

Taken off-guard, he looked over at her parents, who were judiciously looking the other way. "What do you mean? Wait for me for what?"

"I don't know. I thought maybe we could sit on the bleachers for a while after everybody's gone."

What did a guy say to something like that? He hesitated. Edie knew Russ's normal routine after a game was to go out on the field and do some more hard sprints, and then cool down with a slower jog. But he wasn't up to it today anyway. What the heck? What else did he have to do? He didn't dare even make an appearance at the James residence.

"Yeah, I guess that'd be fine."

And so, fifteen minutes later, he came out the back door of the school, and there was Edie, seated way up on the top bleacher, facing the field, and the western plains beyond.

Stiffly, he climbed the bleachers and stood there looking down at the girl for a moment.

"Do you want to sit?"

He smiled. "Sure."

He sat down by her. Neither one spoke. They stared out at the silvering western sky. The distant mountains were melting into a smutty blue line on the horizon, and streaks of purple-gray cloud made streamers of themselves, angling from behind the mountains up toward heaven.

The surprise came when the already-vanished sun shot a brilliant burst of color up, like one last gift to mankind, and painted all the cloud streamers in a brilliant hot pink that set the sky's silver-blue off perfectly and made the two of them stare. They were beyond words.

When it was over, and the graying of the skyscape released them from their need for reverence, Edie said, "Wow. Wasn't that beautiful?"

"Yeah, that was pretty cool. I'm glad I was here to see it."

"One time I wrote a poem about sunsets," Edie volunteered.

"Oh yeah?"

"Yeah."

Silence. Finally, Russ felt obliged to say the obvious: "Well, let's hear it." And then he realized that he wasn't obliged at all. He actually *wanted* to hear it. He was starting to appreciate poetry—especially if it rhymed.

"Really? You want to hear it?"

"Well of course. I wouldn't ask if I didn't."

"Okay. I hope I can remember it. It's not free verse. It's kind of old-fashioned, I guess. It rhymes."

He laughed. "Well, you know something? I don't know if I'll ever get used to poetry that doesn't rhyme."

"Okay. So here goes . . ."

He smiled at her discomfort. She was so cute and innocent. Edie had really turned into a sweet friend. The way a really close sister should be.

I know that God's alive, when I see the colors there.
I see the clouds all glowing—heaven's soul laid bare.

I've often wondered, when I see a sky so bright,
If wishes do come true, and if I'll know tonight.

I don't know how they do it, those angels in the sky,
But the colors that they show me make me want to cry.

But it isn't a cry of sadness, for my soul sings like a bird,
Repeating back to me the melodies I've heard.

Tears of joy have filled my eyes, and will stay until the end,
For I see there in that sunset, the promise of a friend.

Russ sat quietly after she stopped speaking. He wanted to say something. He wanted to tell her how nice her poem was. But he didn't have the words. Something about it had touched him down deep. There were always things about Edie that surprised him.

"It was kind of silly, huh?" said Edie at last, looking down at her hands.

"Not even! Wow, Edie. It was really pretty. I'm very impressed."

"Yeah? Thanks." A shiver suddenly shook her whole body.

"You gettin' cold?"

"Yeah, a little."

Like an idiot, Russ said, "Here," and he shrugged out of his letterman jacket and laid it over her shoulders.

She was barely able to get out the word "thanks."

He wanted to reply, *No problem. That's what brothers do.* But the words caught in his throat. *Brothers don't sit on top of bleachers all alone with their sisters and watch sunsets,* he thought to himself.

CHAPTER FIFTY-FIVE

Russ happened to be sitting across the room from Helen in speech class when a student aid came for her. He was busy penning his first required speech of the year, as were the other students, when the girl he only knew as Brenda, a sophomore, came in with a note and spoke to the teacher. The teacher went to Helen's desk, and Helen listened to something she whispered, then picked up her books and started out of the room.

Russ jumped up and went after her, but the teacher stopped him. "Russ? Where are you going?"

"I have to talk to Helen real quick."

The teacher started to protest, then sighed. "All right. But don't take too long."

She had to be smart enough to know Russ was going to be worthless now anyway.

He caught Helen halfway down the hall. He didn't have to walk very fast, because she certainly wasn't. She traveled with the pace of someone on their way to the gallows.

"Helen!"

She turned to him. There was real fear in her eyes.

"Hi."

"Hi. Did they say why you got called out?"

"No."

He paused. "You're going to the office?"

All she could do was nod and clutch her books.

"So . . . Hey, I'll wait out in the hall, okay?"

"Okay. Please don't leave me, Russ," she managed to get out. And then whirling around, she continued on to the office.

It was only five minutes later, and Russ was leaning against the outer wall, when Helen stepped back out, shutting the door with extreme care.

She looked up at Russ, and the books plummeted from her hands to the floor. Her eyes were already red and puffy.

"Is your dad . . ." He stopped. The girl was already nodding in answer to the question he had started to ask but couldn't finish.

"Oh, Russ. What are Mother and I going to do?"

He didn't speak. He couldn't. He had thought a lot about this eventuality, and he had no answer for her. He thought of their big, beautiful home, and their cars. He thought of many things. Last of all, he thought of his father, who could have made this all go away.

When Russ got home, his father was in the driveway standing by his car, smoking. Russ tried to walk past him. Arch put out a hand and stopped him.

"I don't know if you heard, but—"

"Heard?" Russ cut him off. "Of course I heard. I was in class with Helen when they called her out."

"Oh." Arch's face looked grave. "Well, sorry."

"Sorry?" Russ snapped. "You could have stopped the whole thing."

Arch's face hardened. "Don't you even think of starting back on that, boy."

"Helen and her mom are probably going to end up on the street now. You never even stopped to think about them!"

Face turning red, Arch threw out a hand, palm out, and hit Russ's chest, slamming him up against the wall of the house. "Keep a civil tongue in your head when you're talking to me!"

"*You* keep a civil tongue!" Russ yelled back. Turning, he got to the back door and flung it open. There was a time not too long ago that he would have known his father was fast on his heels if he acted like this—which was why he had never acted like this. But his moment of apprehension fled, for somehow this time he knew Arch wouldn't follow him.

Going through the kitchen, past his mother, Russ headed down the hall and into his room. He heard Eleanor call after him, but he had no intention of replying. He shut the bedroom door behind him, then stood looking around the room, trying hard to catch his breath. At last, he went to his closet and pulled out a duffle bag, which he started shoving clothes into from his dresser. He took out his chukka boots and tied the laces together, then flung them over his shoulder. With one last look around

the room, he turned and stepped back out and went down the hall. A part of him wanted to walk out the front door, but he couldn't go without any parting words to his mother.

Eleanor was leaning against the kitchen entryway. The look on her face was one of devastation.

"Five to ten years, the judge said."

Russ stared at her, the words hardly registering. At last, he said, "What?"

"The judge told Harold James he was probably looking at five to ten years behind bars. I guess it was pretty bad. He gave him a few weeks to get his affairs in order before the final sentencing."

Russ felt like someone had kicked him in the guts. "Yeah. I guess it must have been pretty bad. Sorry, Mom, but I'm gonna go see if I can stay with Pete or Ev or somebody. I can't stay here with *him* anymore."

Eleanor pursed her lips and fought back tears. "I know. I knew this would happen." She pushed away from the wall and sprang forward, throwing her arms around him. "Don't give up on your father, Son. I don't know what's happening around here. I don't know if even he knows. But he still loves you."

"Right. He's got a funny way of showing it."

She pulled away from him, holding the lapels of his letterman jacket. "Yes. He does. A very funny way."

Russ felt too much emotion in his chest. "Hey, Ma, I have to go."

He turned and got to the front door, and as he was going out he heard her tell him she loved him. His answer was the clacking shut of the screen door.

Going out to the Studebaker, he didn't see his father in the driveway anymore, but he could still smell the telltale cigarette smoke. He got in and started up the car, then had to sit there while it warmed up enough to drive. He kept waiting to see his father come around the back corner of the house, but he never did.

At last, the motor was purring nicely, and he put it in reverse and backed out of the drive. It wasn't until he was on the street that he looked back to see Arch Blevins standing by the garage pinching his cigarette between his thumb and forefinger as he held it to his mouth and watched him drive away.

Helen didn't come back to school for the whole remainder of that week. Edie tried to hang around with Russ, but he was intentionally brusque with her, so she began to make herself scarce. Russ was spending all of his nights now with the Morins, who seemed happy to have him even though they were obviously worried about him.

On Friday, the Russets' game was out of town, and once again Russ's anger and frustration drove him to new heights of fury on the field. It was another embarrassingly easy victory, and the other team might as well have stayed in their locker room. They scored only three points in the game, from a desperate field goal. Russet felt no joy in winning. He almost didn't even feel joy in the sport at all anymore. He couldn't get Helen James out of his head.

And then, the following Wednesday night, Russ's mom called him at the Morins' with frightening news.

Russ parked in the driveway back home. He was happy to see that his father's car was gone. He went in quietly, and no one was in sight. Going back to the girls' room, he found all of them and their mother gathered around little Kathleen, who lay in bed.

When Kathleen saw him, her face brightened, although it was very wan, and she could barely lift her head off the pillow. "Hi, Russ."

"Hi, little girl. What are you doing getting sick on us, huh?"

She tried to smile at him. "I don't know. Maybe I just wanted to make you come home."

He smiled back, then looked over at his mother. "What does she have, Mom?"

"We aren't sure. So far, she is really weak, her muscles hurt, and she's running a high fever. Oh, and headaches. The doctor said to give it another day or so and then bring her in if it doesn't get better."

"Aw, it'll get better," said Russ, trying to act confident. "Shoot, if I have to I'll bring over the whole team, and we'll scare whatever it is out of here forever."

Kathleen tried to laugh, but it looked like she almost cried instead. He gave his mom a sad look, which she returned ten-fold. When the other

girls and his mother finally left the room, Russ stayed. He sat in a chair beside the bed and held his little sister's hand. She fell asleep that way.

That evening when Arch pulled into the driveway, Russ waited until he was coming in the back door, and then he went out the front and drove back to Ev's.

Each day that Kathleen was sick, Russ went back to visit. It was during that time that he became distracted enough that he and his team won their away game with Rigby by only three points. That was their vindication against the Trojans, but three points was hardly anything to crow about. Russ couldn't even celebrate the victory. He only wanted to get back home and check on Kathleen. He was aware that, other than the Spud Day game that didn't count in the rankings, he still had a no-loss season, but until Kathleen got better it was hard to concentrate on that coup.

Saturday morning, the Morins' phone rang, and Mrs. Morin came in to tell him it was for him. Expecting one of his friends, or maybe his mother, he went and answered. On the other end of the line, he heard: *Hi, Russ! Guess what.*

It was Kathleen! "Hey, little sis—what?"

I'm all better!

"You are? Really? Wow! How did that happen?"

I woke up this morning, and I wasn't hot anymore, and my headache is gone. Now Mom's taking us all down to Pash's for ice cream!

"That's great! I'm glad you called me. I've been worried sick about you, you know."

I know. Mom told me. Can you come for ice cream with us, Russ?

He paused. "No, maybe some other time, all right? But thanks for asking."

When he caught the huge sound of disappointment in the girl's voice as she was saying goodbye, he almost called back. But he had other things to do.

With a big load now lifted off his mind, Russ went out and ran wind sprints for half an hour, followed by a half-hour jog, then got Ev and ran through some plays and tossed the ball back and forth. He felt light and free.

CHAPTER FIFTY-SIX

On Sunday evening, the Morins' phone rang again, and to Russ's surprise it was once again for him. Two phone calls in two days!

Clive Morin, Ev's dad, handed the phone to Russ with a grin. "You're quite the popular fellow!"

Russ laughed. "Who is it?"

"Some guy named Mark."

Taking the phone with a *thanks,* Russ answered. On the other end, he heard, *Hey there, Russ. Mark Daniels here.*

It took Russ a moment for the name to register. "Oh! Hi, Mark. How'd you find me over here?"

"Easy. Your mom."

"Oh. So what's up?

Well, that's the funny thing. Now, you've got to swear yourself to secrecy, all right? If your dad knew I was talking to you, he'd kick my butt. Got it?

To himself, Russ frowned. "Sure, Mark. Got it."

All right. So your dad's been having some rough times lately.

"Lately? What do you mean lately?"

Honest? Four months, I guess. Maybe more now. Hard to keep track.

Russ was silent. He didn't know what Mark wanted him to say.

Hey, Russ. Listen. I think I've been where you are, buddy. And I hate to see it happening to somebody else. Do you think if I drive up there tomorrow you could get out of school for a bit? I think it's important for us to talk. We'll go for a ride, all right?

Russ felt his heart pounding. What was Mark going to reveal about his father? Was it going to be something earth-shattering? Was it going to be something he and his family could handle? One way or the other, he had to know.

"Yeah, I'm sure if we both went to Mr. Ricks's office he'd let me go. He's a pretty square guy."

All right then. I'll be there right after the start of school tomorrow. See you then.

In the morning, as he had promised, Deputy Mark Daniels arrived at Shelley High. A student came looking for Russ and got him released from class, and he went to the principal's office. Mrs. Pryce smiled at Russ with a touch of worry in her face.

"Good morning, Russ. Hey, is everything okay?"

Russ grinned. "Deputy Daniels must be here, huh?"

Mrs. Pryce was taken aback. She leaned her head back and squinted her eyes at him dubiously. "Why, yes, he is. You knew?"

"Yes, ma'am. It's nothing bad. I was expecting him."

"Oh, good!" A look of relief washed over the woman's face. "Well, go on in then. He's in with Mr. Ricks."

Russ tapped on the principal's door and was bade enter. He walked in, and Mark Daniels stood up from his chair with a friendly grin. "Hi, buddy."

"Hi, Mark. It's good to see you."

"You too, Russ." Mark shook his hand.

Since handshakes were going on, Mr. Ricks also offered his to Russ, and he shook it warmly. "I haven't had a good chance to congratulate you on how the season's going, Russ. You're burning a hole in the entire football district."

"Thank you, sir. I have a good team."

"They have a good halfback," countered Ricks. "And yes, yes. You're right—your team is fantastic as well. Way to be humble. So Deputy Daniels tells me you need to go for a ride with him. Is everything all right at home, son?"

"Yes, fine." Russ didn't think a small lie would burn him.

"Well, I'm going to sign you out for two hours. Is that enough time?" he asked Daniels.

"Oh, sure. You bet. I'll probably have him back sooner."

Russ and Daniels headed out of the school without speaking and got into Daniels's patrol car. Car radios were very expensive and hard to come by, so Daniels's car, like those of all other deputies and all law

enforcement officers in the area except for the sheriff and chief of police, were not cluttered with unnecessary items like that. Instead, his car was equipped with a shotgun, a couple of extra pairs of handcuffs, and one tough deputy who could never allow himself to need backup, for he would never get it, unless it was from a passing citizen.

Daniels took off driving down Locust, toward downtown. He didn't say anything, so Russ drew in a deep breath. "So what's going on, Mark? You seem pretty quiet. I thought you were gonna tell me all about my dad's tough times."

Daniels seemed to catch the hint of sarcasm Russ couldn't keep out of his voice. He looked over and gave Russ a level gaze. "Hey, buddy, you don't have to be tough with me, all right? This is one place where you can let down your guard. Anything we say won't leave this squad car—at least not by me."

Russ nodded, a little disquieted. "Okay. Sorry. So what's up?"

"First off," countered Daniels, "what's up with you? How come you and your dad aren't gettin' along?"

"Ha! Because he's a selfish jerk. And he's never home when anyone needs him."

The car cruised past Park Avenue, and with a glance that way Russ could see no movement around their house. Daniels drew in a deep breath and sighed it out as they were bumping across the rough railroad crossing—three rail lines that ran much of the way through town.

They stopped at State Street, and after all crossing traffic passed, they turned north. "Heading out this way so we don't run into your dad," explained Daniels. Once they were rolling up State, he looked over at Russ again.

"So you think your dad's selfish. And never home. Well, I'm glad I came and got you today. I almost don't know where to start. But I'm going to start with my part in all this, because you mentioned your dad being selfish. We must be talking about two totally different people. So do you remember when I told you about all the financial trouble I've had—the medical bills and everything?"

"Sure, Mark. Everything all right?"

"Yeah. Well, it is for me."

"What do you mean?"

"Well, remember when I told you I'd had a little help?"

"Uh-huh."

"That was your dad."

"Huh?"

"Yeah. Your dad gave us some money."

"Where'd he get any extra money?"

Daniels sighed. "That's the hard part. Please don't ever tell your dad I told you this, but I feel like I have to. It might help explain a lot. Originally, he went to the county clerk and tried to get a raise for me. They flat-out turned him down and told him I could go work somewhere else if I needed more."

The only sound for a while was the hum of the white wall tires on the highway. "And?" Russ prodded Daniels on.

"And . . . well, your dad got pretty steamed, and he took some money out of petty cash. It wasn't a lot. Just enough to buy us some food and tide us over for a while."

"Okay. I don't think that's so bad."

"Me either. But apparently the county does."

"Huh? He got caught?"

"Yeah. They found out, and they're all up in arms. Your dad's been under investigation for a while. Some of the county officials think he needs to be gone. He's been under their thumb since that happened, clear last May."

A sick feeling had filled Russ's stomach. "So . . . when does he find out anything?"

"I don't know, Russ. There are some other things going on at the same time that need to get ironed out. I think they're waiting to see what happens before they make a decision. But anyway, as you can see, when you say your dad is selfish, that sure isn't a side of him I see. He's put his job on the line because he cared so much about me and my family."

Russ was dead quiet. He looked away from Daniels and out the windshield, watching the countryside roll by. He was having a hard time digesting this new information about Arch Blevins.

They had gone two or three miles in silence before Daniels looked over at Russ again. "Sorry for being so quiet, Russ. I've been mulling

over something else you said, tryin' to figure out how to tell you something without breaking a confidence."

"A confidence about my dad, you mean?"

"Yeah. It's complicated. I guess I'm probably not at liberty to tell you all of it, but I really need to give you a hint. Something about why your dad hasn't been around much lately. Son, your dad . . . Well, first off, I can honestly tell you he has always thought you were made of pure gold. I've never heard any man talk with as much pride about his son as Arch does."

His jaw slack, Russ stared at Daniels. "I'm sorry. I have a hard time believing that."

"I'm sorry too. But it's true. And your mother too. He thinks she's some kind of angel on earth."

"Mark," Russ said, turning in his seat to face the deputy as squarely as he could, "you've got to level with me. If this isn't true, you can't be saying it." He felt a lump in his throat he had to fight back.

"It's true, son. I wouldn't make it up."

"Then why is he always gone? Why doesn't he do anything with us anymore?"

"Son, it's . . . Oh, man. I'm going to be in big trouble if it gets out I ever told you any of this."

"I won't whisper a word."

Daniels ground his teeth together. "All right. All right. My job is in your hands, Russ. But I sure can't see a family getting torn apart over a misunderstanding. Your dad is working a big case. A case so big . . . Well, it's probably the biggest case we've ever had around here."

"What case?" Russ thought of the Harold James thing. Just how big *was* that?

"That's what I can't tell you. The only person who maybe can tell you is your dad."

"Oh, yeah! Like old steel jaws is going to let anything out! What is it, Mark?"

"Buddy, I really can't tell you. I can only tell you this: If you knew the case, and if you knew what it's doing to your old man, you would be begging his forgiveness right now. There's not a question in my mind it's the hardest thing he's ever had to do in his law enforcement career.

Believe me when I tell you, Russ: Your dad loves his family as much as any man I've ever known. And it's tearing him apart to have you two at odds. But he doesn't know how to fix it."

"He told you that?" Russ asked incredulously.

"Not in those words. But I've known him for a long time, in a whole different way than you do. Believe me, son. He would die for you any day. And the same goes for your whole family."

Mark Daniels had turned around and was headed back toward Shelley when Russ thought of something that had been driving him crazy since seeing his father's reaction. This was something he had to know, and short of his father telling him—which wasn't likely—there might not be a better source of information than Mark Daniels.

"Hey, Mark?"

The deputy looked at him, his eyes soft. "Yeah?"

"I need to ask you about somebody."

"Okay?"

"All right. If you don't know anything about this, I'll understand, but . . . There's this old guy I met. As far as I've ever seen, he's just a used-up old drunk, pretty much good-for-nothing. I even had to drag him into his house one time, he was so drunk." He felt guilty after saying that, because now at least he understood that on that night the old man was mourning the loss of his dog, Bud.

"Okay, who is he?"

"His name's Tupper. Barrow Tupper. And when I said something about him being a drunk, my dad got pretty mad and told me that old man was worth more than I was. Ever since, I've been wondering who that old man is."

For half a minute, Daniels didn't say anything. But the moment he found a side-road that left the highway and went into a wide gravel yard near some spud cellars, he pulled off.

The deputy looked down at the steering wheel, where both of his hands rested. He drew in a lung-filling breath and swallowed a couple of times. With another breath, he looked over at Russ as he cut the engine.

"Barrow Tupper, an old drunk, huh? I guess it might seem that way now. But I'm kind of surprised you haven't heard about Barrow Tupper before—somewhere."

"I haven't. I never met him until last spring, when he said he knew my dad."

"Well then let me tell you about that old drunk. First off, he was a lieutenant in the Battle of Tardenois—in the First World War. They say he saved fifty men from sure death there, and he saved ten lives by dragging wounded men off the line while half his squad was running. He got more medals there than most people have ever seen."

Russ was stunned. Were they talking about the same man? But how many Barrow Tuppers could there be?

"And then that drunk came home and became a police officer. Best one they ever had around here, some people still say. He spent years at it. And for you, I guess I'd have to say this: There wouldn't be a Blevins family if it hadn't been for Barrow Tupper."

After a moment of quiet surprise, trying to digest those words, Russ let out a long breath. "Can you tell me the story?"

"I guess I have to," replied Daniels. "It's obvious your dad's never going to. So I guess it was back in the early thirties sometime—not too long before you were born, I guess. Tupper was the police chief then. And your dad was a Shelley cop, and hadn't been on the force very long, if I remember how the story goes.

"There weren't too many cops back then. Shelley really didn't need 'em. It was even quieter then than it is now. So Tupper, even being the chief, went out and trained your father up as a policeman. Taught him everything he knew, I guess—about dealing with all kinds of people, about how to shoot, about how to drive. Your father pretty much thought Barrow Tupper walked on water.

"One day they were both down at city hall when a call came in that a car had crashed in the river. Tupper was tending to something else, so Arch took off to the call and got there first. I guess there was a car out there teetering on the ice. The driver was still in there, yellin' that he had a baby in the back. Your dad couldn't watch without trying to help.

"So he tried to get out to the car, but the whole thing broke through the ice right before he got there, and it pulled him down with it. He was able to catch himself on the edge of the ice, but the current was pulling his feet underneath, and he couldn't get loose. Tupper came along in his

car and got out, and I guess there were people all over the place, all yelling at Arch, but nobody knew how to help him—or else they were too scared.

"So Barrow Tupper grabs a shovel out of his trunk and heads out to get your dad. He got almost out there before he started to go through the ice too. But he had that shovel held horizontal, just in case, and when he went down the shovel caught him. I guess your dad couldn't hold on anymore, because he let go and went under the ice."

"What? Dad went under?" Russ was up on the edge of his seat. "What happened?"

"I guess Tupper was watchin' where your dad went, and when he came by, he reached down in the water and got your dad by the coat collar. He pulled him up so they were both there in the same hole in the ice. By then, a couple of farmers threw out a rope, and Tupper got it around him and Arch so they could pull them in to shore."

After listening to the story, Russ was almost breathless. "So . . . Tupper was a big hero—again. Then what happened? Why did he end up like he is now?"

"That's the saddest part. It's the part that makes me sick to tell. Why I had to pull off the road to tell you. It chokes me up when I think about it."

"What, Mark? What happened?"

"Well, Russ, your dad came out of the river okay. He might have had a cold or something—I can't really remember what he said about that. But Tupper, he ended up in the hospital with pneumonia. And it was bad. Real bad. His family had to leave him in there for a while, and when he was in there there was a great big snowstorm. Before they could get it cleared, there was ice all over all the roads. It was the worst storm and the slickest roads of that whole winter, I guess. I even remember it from when I was in school.

"When Tupper's family tried to drive back up to see him after a few days in the hospital, a big truck lost control on the highway and ran right into them. Knocked their car off the bridge into the river. They went under, and there wasn't anything anyone could do. They lost 'em. The entire family. Drowned in the river. The last thing that man did as a cop

was saving your father from dying and your mother from becoming a young widow."

It seemed like quite a while before Russ could take a real breath. He thought back to the night he had to drag drunken, shriveled up old Barrow Tupper into his house. He realized there was no way he would ever be able to look at a human being again and judge him for whatever he might see on the surface.

CHAPTER FIFTY-SEVEN

Tuesday after ball practice, Russ needed to get some clean clothes, so he got in his car and drove past the house. His father's car was in the driveway already.

Disappointed, he drove on past and continued up Park until it merged with Spud Alley and canted to the northeast. Eventually, he passed Oak, then made the last left that took him over to Yellowstone Highway, beyond the north end of town. He drove on up toward Idaho Falls, thinking about his father.

Why couldn't he go home? Why wasn't he man enough to go face to face with his father? What case was he working that was more important than his family? Why was he never home? Did he really love his family as much as Mark Daniels claimed, or was the deputy only trying to make Russ feel better?

Somehow, he had to at least talk to the old man. But the truth was he didn't know how. Arch Blevins had never been one for serious talks with his family. And Russ had grown up that way too. It was so easy to talk to other people, to have meaningful conversations with anyone but those who should matter most. Russ had a sinking feeling in his guts that he and his father were going to go through his entire last football season in high school without exchanging a meaningful thought between them. He would never have admitted it. Not to Ev, not to Helen, not even to Edie—

but the thought of going to State without being friends again with his father was tearing out his heart.

It took him several minutes before another thought struck him. He was thinking back on the thoughts that had consumed him for over half an hour when he realized that he had put Edie, not Helen, at the top of his list of people he would have shared something personal with. The thought baffled him. But he guessed it made sense. Where he and Edie were just friends, and he wanted something more with Helen, of course he would still be trying to put forth his best face for her. Showing any kind of weakness at all, any kind of confession that might make him look like less of a man, was not something he would risk with the girl whose hand he hoped to someday win for life.

Making a big loop, east out Cotton Road, then south on Jameston, then west on Taylor Highway, Russ finally found his way back to Shelley, going south on Short Avenue, past the high school, and west again on Locust. He turned south on Park for the final leg of the drive, hoping to find his father's car gone.

Russ was in luck, and the driveway was empty, so he parked and went inside. It turned out that not only was his father gone, but all the girls and his mother as well. He went down the hall and looked in the girls' room, just to be sure. He was astounded. The door was standing open, and the place was a big mess. It looked like the girls hadn't picked up in a while. Knowing what his father would think of that if he saw it, he drew the door shut. No need making the old man any surlier than he already was of late.

Russ went back to his room and started putting some of his things in a paper bag—his only excuse for a suitcase. Before he had finished, the shutting of the back door startled him. He waited, hoping for some sign of who had come in. Soon, he cursed under his breath, hearing the slow steps of his father, but no others. Where were his mother and the girls?

Knowing he was in the house alone with Arch now, Russ thought how perfect the moment might be to approach the old man, to try and make amends. But he couldn't bring himself to do it. He wouldn't even know where to start.

Russ sat on the bed. With any luck, his father would go in his room and shut the door, and Russ could make his escape. Arch had to know he

was here, because of his car outside, but if he was tired enough to go lie down for a nap, maybe he wouldn't even care to check. Or maybe he believed Russ had left again with friends since parking his car.

He heard his father plod past, down to his bedroom. Yes! He was going to get out without a confrontation. Waiting for a safe amount of time, he opened his door and started out. He was startled to see his father standing there at the doorway to the girls' room. He had opened *their* door, not his own bedroom door, and he was looking inside, shaking his head.

Russ might still be able to escape down the hallway and get outside before Arch saw him. That was his first thought, and turning, he started to put it into play. Then something came to him, and he stopped. He couldn't leave his sisters in the lurch this way. Even as terrified as he was to interact with his father right now, he had to say something.

"Hey, Pop."

Arch turned slowly and looked at him. He didn't act startled to hear him, or even the slightest bit surprised. "Hello, Son."

"Hey, don't worry about the mess in there, all right? I told them I'd clean it up for them."

Arch knitted his brow. He had obviously been thinking about the girls' cluttered bedroom, and it took him a moment for what Russ had said to register. "You told them that? Exactly when was that?"

Russ froze. How did he answer? Suddenly, his father's question felt like a trap. Was he trying to catch him in a lie? That was something Arch would never tolerate. "Uh . . . Well, last night I came by after the game, and . . ."

He stopped. Arch was staring at him, taking in his reply. His father didn't believe him for a second. He must know something Russ didn't. "Sorry, Pop. I didn't really tell them that. But I *will* clean it up. Right now."

When Russ started toward his father, the old man straightened up from leaning against the doorframe. "No, it doesn't matter, Russ. Let it be."

With that, he started forward, and his broad frame scared Russ to death. This was one man he couldn't buck. In fact, no one in their right mind would have taken Arch Blevins on.

As it registered on Russ that his father had no plan to stop, he turned to the side, putting his back against the hallway wall, and Arch stepped past him and into the kitchen. Russ went back into his room and sat on the bed. Was his father going to leave? Maybe he could wait him out. Stubbornness made him not want to be the one to drive away first. He wanted to be the one with the ability to say his dad was never home, not the other way around.

It was only a few more minutes before he heard his father's steps again. This time, they were very hushed, almost as if he were sliding his feet. What was going on?

His curiosity getting the better of him, Russ got up and opened his door, looking down the hall. His father's bedroom door was still shut, and the girls' was open. With a bad feeling in his chest, he crept that way. He hesitated outside the door. One part of him wanted to step into the doorway and take his father by surprise. Another part wanted to slip away. What was his old man doing in there?

Finally, he couldn't hold himself back, and he took another step. His father was sitting on the edge of the bed Kathleen and Toni slept in. It registered on Russ's confused brain that his father wasn't looking angrily at the mess in the room, but at something in his hands. It was an old Teddy bear Kathleen had owned since she was a little girl.

With tired, worn-out eyes, Arch looked up, and his eyes met Russ's. They looked at each other for several seconds. Holding the bear in one big hand, Arch thumped it a couple of times against his leg.

"I guess you should know your mother tried to reach you at Ev's earlier. They said you might be on your way over here to get some things."

"Oh. Yeah, I took a drive out in the country."

Arch nodded, blinking his eyes to clear his vision. "Sure. Sure. Anyway . . . Well, it's probably nothing, but Kathleen's fever came back."

"Huh?"

"Yeah. Pretty bad. It's up to one hundred-five."

"*One hundred-five!* That's really high, right?"

Arch nodded again, seeming distracted by the bear, whose eyes he seemed to be staring into. "Uh . . . yeah. I've never seen over one hundred-six, and not for as long as hers stayed up high."

"Where are they?"

"I took them all up to the hospital in the Falls. I have to make some phone calls here in a while, and then I'll get some hamburgers or something and go back up there."

"When can Kathleen come home?"

Arch shrugged. "They couldn't say. The doctor said he thinks he'll have to admit her while they do some tests."

Later, when Arch left the house in his Ford, Russ followed him up to Idaho Falls in the Studebaker. He had to see his little sister. He had to know she was all right. Why hadn't he gone out for ice cream when she asked him? He couldn't stop cursing himself. For never being there for the family, he had become worse than the man he was so angry with for doing the same.

Kathleen was asleep when they got to the hospital. Eleanor was still waiting for the doctor to return. While she and Arch talked quietly in the hallway, Russ went into Kathleen's room, where the girls were also sitting. Dorothy, whose face was wet with tears, starting crying again when she saw him, and she got up and ran to him, throwing her arms around him.

"She's gonna be all right," Russ said, patting her back. But the way she was acting scared him.

"She's really bad," replied Dorothy, sobbing. "They think it could be meningitis."

Meningitis! Everyone had heard of that dreaded, deadly disease. "They can't be right," Russ said. "I bet it's something else." But now his heart was beating double-time, and his breaths came with difficulty. He looked past Dorothy to see Toni and Annie staring him down. They, too, had been crying, and they sat close together, the two girls who were closer than any sisters Russ had ever seen, holding onto each other, afraid to let go.

Russ felt tears of fear coming into his eyes. Or maybe they were tears of sadness. He hated to see his sisters cry. It had been a long time since he had felt so close to his family.

The doctor walked past, down the hall toward Arch and Eleanor, and they all talked in quiet tones for five or ten minutes before the doctor, dressed in white, hurried away.

Russ took one last, long look at his sleeping sister, whose face was bright red and beaded with sweat, and he and the girls went out and huddled around their parents, Russ putting his arm around his mother.

Eleanor did the talking. Arch seemed deathly pale, and he had no voice. He would hardly even look at the other children.

"The doctor says it's something really strange, something he doesn't think he's ever seen before. It's a bacteria, and he has studied it under a microscope, but it isn't familiar. Someone is driving a sample to Salt Lake City, to the University of Utah. He thinks she has meningitis, but he doesn't know what caused it. It's this bacteria."

"Why did it go and then come back?" Toni asked.

"I don't know, sweetheart," said Eleanor, reaching out and squeezing her daughter's hand. "Nobody knows yet."

● ● ● ● ●

And so the long wait began. They managed with medication and a lot of cool baths over the next few days to keep the girl's temperature in check, but it never dipped much below a hundred, and always managed to climb back up again in time. It never made it up to one hundred-five again, but it was never far off.

Arch was silent on the subject, but Eleanor begged Russ not to miss any of his practices, after all the hard work he had put into his football career, and all of his dreams. So Russ fought as hard out on the practice field as ever, and sometimes maybe harder, because he was doing it to take his mind off Kathleen. Coach Dan Nalder and Ev Morin were the only ones who knew about Kathleen and her illness. Russ didn't have the heart to tell anyone else.

Every night after practice, Russ would speed back up to the hospital to see Kathleen and see if she was awake. Usually, his mother and sisters were there, if they had been able to get a ride from a neighbor. Sheriff Blevins was only there now and then.

On Thursday evening, Russ couldn't hold his thought inside anymore, and he caught his mother alone in the hall. "I don't think our father even cares about any of us anymore, Mom. Why isn't he up here?"

Eleanor looked sadly at her son. "Russ, please try to understand. Your father owes something to this entire county, not only us. Everyone relies on him. He can't walk away and be gone whenever he wants."

"But once a day? Mom! You're letting him off too easy."

Eleanor squeezed Russ's arm. He had half-expected to see her get angry, but she didn't. "I know why you'd be angry, dear. I know why you'd think these things. But you didn't see the fear in your father's eyes that first night. You've got to give him another chance. He has spent most of his life holding his feelings inside. That's not something you can brush off overnight."

That night, Russ lay in bed pondering his mother's words. He wanted to believe them. But this was Arch Blevins's youngest daughter! What if she were to die, and he was so busy holding his emotions inside? When was he ever going to let them show?

Before he could quite fall asleep, a thought hit Russ hard: When was *he* ever going to let his emotions show? Sometimes he was as bad at that as his father. Maybe he had no room to talk at all. Was he becoming his old man?

Friday night, they played the Firth Cougars again. It was the loneliest game Russ had played in his entire life. Nobody from his family was there. They were all at the hospital. And Helen wasn't there either. It was only Edie and her parents, and a flock of people Russ didn't even care to see tonight.

He ran three touchdowns himself that night, plowing Bo Hansen, the biggest linebacker in southern Idaho, into the grass on one of the plays, right at the sixty-yard line, and then running unobstructed the last forty yards while three Cougars tried in vain to bring him down.

One of their toughest opponents, the Cougars, scored two touchdowns, two conversions, and a field goal that night, while the Russets ran home five touchdowns with conversions. Russ was unstoppable. And it was all for little Kathleen.

CHAPTER FIFTY-EIGHT

On Saturday morning, the doctor called from the hospital. As was the custom lately, Arch had received a phone call earlier and had to go in to work. The call was from Sheriff Turnbull, from Butte County, where Arco was the county seat. Being his usual secretive self, Arch refused to say anything about the phone call, but at least it was a relief to Eleanor to have answered the phone and to have heard the voice of a man on the other end of the line. Anyway, she had long since lost any notion that Arch might be seeing someone else. For one thing, he really was not the type, and for another, no woman but Eleanor would have put up with his moods.

Russ had been planning on going for a long run along the river, but when the call came in from the doctor, he changed his plans. He would take his mother up to the hospital to meet with the doctor, while the other girls would stay home and try to catch up on some long-neglected housework, waiting impatiently for Eleanor to call them with whatever news the doctor had to give. It was a heart-breaking farewell for Eleanor and the girls.

"What if something's really wrong?" asked Annie.

The other girls stared at their mother, waiting for a reply, hoping it would somehow comfort them.

"We'll have to have faith," Eleanor said. The girls looked at each other. Russ couldn't tell if the answer satisfied them or not.

"What if . . ." Toni stopped, looking over at Dorothy, who was her rock.

"What, Toni?" asked Eleanor.

"Well, Mom, what if . . ." Toni couldn't finish. She started crying and stepped to her mom, throwing her arms around her.

"She's trying to ask you what if this is our last chance to see Kathleen," Dorothy finished her sister's thought soberly, just before her chin began to shake.

"Let's not think that way, girls," Eleanor said, rubbing Toni's back. "God won't let her leave us without a good reason, okay? I promise."

She and Russ went to the beat-up old Studebaker and waved goodbye to the girls after Eleanor told them several times how much she loved them. Russ wished those words would come as easy to him as they did to his mother. He guessed, like it or not, he was too much like his father.

It seemed like a long drive to the hospital. Russ stared at the road, his hands moving mechanically on the wheel. It was Eleanor who broke the quiet.

"I wish your father were with us."

"I don't."

"Russ!"

"Well? I don't. He'd always rather be somewhere else, even when he knows how bad this is." He suddenly felt guilty, for the thought of his father sitting on the girls' bed holding Kathleen's Teddy bear came back to him. He had never told anyone about that, but even now, after what he had just said, his pride wouldn't let him bring it up. He couldn't shake the memory, however, now that it had come back to him.

"Russ, I have to tell you something," said his mother after another few minutes of silence.

"Okay."

"I know you think your father doesn't care. But I think he does. I think he is under so much stress at work, and so much of his time is demanded from every person in the whole county, that he has drawn inside himself. I think he wishes down deep he could talk to us. But he doesn't know how."

Russ reacted with: "I just think he doesn't care about his kids." And again he had the guilty memory of his father and the Teddy bear. Was he the one who was being unfair? Was he every bit as bad about opening up?

He was finally getting to the point of swallowing his pride and talking about what he had seen that afternoon in his sisters' room when he saw the hospital on the horizon. His heart fell. His moment had passed.

They parked out in the lot and went inside, asking for Doctor Gates, who had been working Kathleen's case. When he came to the nurse's call, Doctor Gates, a man in his mid-fifties, with an unruly shock of pure white hair that did not want to lie over flat, stared at Eleanor and Russ in confusion. His hands hung at his sides.

Finally, Doctor Gates came to them and held out his hand, enfolding Eleanor's in it when hers came out between them. "Hello, Mrs. Blevins. I didn't know you were coming."

"I—I don't understand. Didn't you call for us?"

"Yes, but . . . Mr. Blevins came in shortly after, and I . . . I'm sorry, I assumed he would pass on the news."

"Arch was here?"

"Why yes, not twenty minutes earlier."

Eleanor and Russ looked at each other in surprise.

"But don't worry, Mrs. Blevins. Since you're here, let's go into my office. I might be able to explain what I've found a little better, and I'll be able to answer any questions. Your husband seemed . . . Well, forgive me, but he seemed very shaken. I'm not sure how much of what I told him he really took in."

Those words made Russ feel instantly sick, and he knew they did the same to his mother by the way she looked at him. "Come on," said Doctor Gates. "Let's go into my office for a few minutes, and then you can go peek in on your girl."

In the office, Eleanor and Russ sat like statues while the doctor told them of the rare disease eleven-year-old Kathleen was suffering. It was called leptospirosis, and he had personally never seen a case of it until now. It was spread generally in hot, wet areas, which Shelley was not, but typically through the urine of rodents, and most often through a break in the skin or contact with the mouth or mucus membranes.

It was typical of this disease to manifest itself as it had done for the first several days, then go away for several, and then, if it came back, come back with a vengeance. The second phase would consist of a high-grade fever and other things, but in Kathleen's case it had brought on meningitis—something known to be potentially deadly.

They were doing everything they could now to treat the meningitis, and by a stroke of good fortune there was a doctor visiting from Houston

who had had some experience with both leptospirosis and meningitis, and he had decided to stay on for a few more days to see what he could do for Kathleen. He was a younger doctor, perhaps in his mid-forties, but according to Doctor Gates, he had had huge success in Houston with such cases, and he cared very deeply for people, as proven by his desire to remain at the hospital to see Kathleen's case through. This information gave Russ and Eleanor both great hope.

Once Doctor Gates had assured them they were doing all they could to help, and that Kathleen was sedated and sleeping comfortably, he encouraged them to go look in on her. Doctor Gates offered them both a warm handshake, and they walked away from him and headed upstairs still feeling that strong sense of hope, in spite of the strange, unknown qualities of the rare disease.

Upstairs, the nurses' station was temporarily abandoned, so they didn't check in. They hadn't come this far only to wait longer, so they started down the hall. The charge nurse might be in with Kathleen anyway.

As they got to the door, Russ could hear a voice inside, and he paused with his hand on the knob. Putting his ear up to the door, the sound of the voice inside startled him. It was somebody singing! He turned and looked at his mother, who had heard it too. She was giving him a strange look.

Unable to hold back his curiosity, Russ gently turned the doorknob, and eased the door open a crack. The voice inside kept singing, and Russ felt a puzzled look come over his face. It sounded like . . . It couldn't be. This was impossible.

He eased the door open a touch farther. After a couple of seconds, he whipped his head to the side to look at his mother. Was this registering on her like it was on him?

"It's your father," Eleanor whispered, putting a hand on Russ's arm. She was staring at the door, and tears had come into her eyes.

On the other side of the door, and now as plain as anything, they could hear big, tough Sheriff Arch Blevins singing, "I'll Take You Home, Kathleen."

I know you love me, Kathleen, dear;

Your heart was ever fond and true.
I always feel when you are near
That life holds nothing dear but you.

The smiles that once you gave to me
I scarcely ever see them now;
Though many many times I see
A dark'ning shadow on your brow.

Arch stopped singing for a moment, and then, as Russ and his mother listened, spell-bound, he went back to the song's beginning and started it again without having finished the last verse.

I'll take you home again, Kathleen,
Across the ocean wild and wide,
To where your heart has ever been
Since first you were my bonnie bride.

The roses all have left your cheek;
I've watched them fade away and die . . .

Russ had pushed the door open a couple of feet now, and he and his mother were looking in, both with a perfect view of the man who had for so many years made their home a safe place. Arch Blevins was seated at Kathleen's bedside, holding her hand in both of his.

As he pronounced the word "die," his voice broke, and as he bent down his head, his body began to shake.

Eleanor turned her head in shock and looked up at Russ. As he pulled the door mostly shut, she whispered, "We need to go in to him, Son."

"No, Ma, I can't. You go. I'll see you back home."

Before she could even try to protest, Russ turned and hurried down the hall. The vision of his father, being destroyed at the thought of his daughter's dying was too much for him. He had never seen his old man cry. He had to get away. He had to leave here as fast as he was able.

He was suddenly seeing and feeling something that made him sick. Was it truly Sheriff Arch Blevins who cared more about himself and his

own worries than he did about anyone else, as Russ had been thinking? Or was it Russ?

CHAPTER FIFTY-NINE

After going home to talk to Dorothy, Toni, and Annie about Kathleen's prognosis, Russ made the decision to go back to Ev's house. He was still so shaken by what he had witnessed at the hospital that he couldn't handle the thought of being in the house with his father. He had a lot to process, a lot to digest. For so long now he had been harboring resentment against his father for never being there, for obviously not caring about his family, that it was hard to let go of it and think of anything else. Only now the whole microscope was turned back on him. Was it true, after all, that he, Russ, was the one who needed to repent? The very thought of it was so brutal he didn't want to contemplate it, but it was all he could think about.

He was thankful when the phone rang later, and Ev's father came seeking him out where he and Ev were idly admiring Ev's knife collection in his room.

Mr. Morin was grinning when he cracked the door open far enough to insert his face and scanned the room until he saw Russ in the far corner. "You guessed it, buddy. It's for you again!"

Trying to match Mr. Morin's grin, Russ got up, not feeling in the mood to smile but knowing he had to. "Hey, Mr. Morin, I'm sorry. I didn't expect for you to have to answer the phone for me all the time when I came to stay with you."

Mr. Morin laughed. "Oh yeah. All three phone calls, right? Hey, son, I'm just giving you a hard time, all right? If I can't get up three times and answer phone calls for you during your stay, then I'm not much of a host, am I?"

Russ smiled. "Okay. Well, thanks." He went and picked up the handset, which was bold red because that was the favorite color of Ev's mother.

On the other end, Helen's voice came over, sounding meek. She *had* to talk to him, she said, and could she come over?

Of course he wasn't going to turn her down. He had been missing her, missing their drives and their visits. But he was politely trying to give her and her family as much time together as he could.

Helen drove herself over and pulled up in front of Ev's house. Russ was looking out the window, and he went out to meet her and got in.

The girl turned her head and tried to smile at him, but her chin was quivering. "Hey."

"Hey," he replied. "Are you okay?"

Stoically, she forced the smile. "Sure. I just needed to see you."

She reached out and laid her hand on top of his. "I've missed you."

"Yeah. Me too."

"Then why did you stop coming around?"

"Hey! I sure didn't want to. Helen, I figured you'd want as much time with your family right now as you could get. I would have been over every day if I thought it was all right."

She smiled again, her eyes wet. "So . . . Tomorrow my father goes in for his sentencing with the judge."

Russ stared at her. This day had been looming now for some time. But now it had been so long since the jury pronounced him guilty for his crime it seemed like all was in limbo, like it was all a dream, and like maybe Harold James would never have to serve time at all. Russ didn't know what to say.

Helen seemed to understand, and finally she squeezed his hand. "We've been selling a lot of things," she said. As she said it, she pointed a finger at the back window, and Russ's eyes followed where she indicated. There was a big FOR SALE sign taped in the back window of the Chrysler. The sight of it made him sick. It brought everything home.

"Helen, I can't tell you how sorry I am."

"Yeah. I wish . . . Well, it doesn't matter what I wish." A tear escaped and rolled down her cheek and she uttered what for her was probably a drastic curse—"Oh, darn it!"—and brushed it away with a fingertip.

"What about the house?" asked Russ.

She tried to be brave and smile again, and her eyes filled with so many tears that Russ knew she couldn't even see him. "We were going to try and sell it, but the bank repossessed it before we could."

Someone might as well have kicked Russ in the stomach. "Where will you go?"

Helen shrugged. "Mom has an apartment picked out. It's okay."

"An apartment? But . . . how will you pay for it?"

Helen dropped her chin on her chest, and Russ saw her squeeze her eyes shut. She stayed that way for a moment, silent and still, until she composed herself and sniffled. "Mother's trying to find a job. Oh, Russ—she's never had to work a day in her life."

"What about your grandparents?"

"Oh, they want us to move in with them, of course. But Mother doesn't want to."

"Why?"

"Russ! Why? They live in Moscow! Do you know what that would do to me if we had to move that far from you?"

Russ didn't believe he could feel any worse. But when Helen said that, he felt two things at the same moment: Worse, for one, and like he had just won a million dollars. Did Helen care so much about him that she and her mother were willing to stay in Shelley now, under the scrutiny of all high society—not to mention a lot of *low* society—to be near him? The idea was unfathomable. A regular Joe like Russ was nothing to a girl like Helen!

If ever there was a proper moment to give someone a comforting hug, this was that moment. Russ leaned closer to Helen and put his arms around her, and she began to cry. To her credit, it was a soft cry. Maybe all of her most shocked wailing had already passed, in the privacy of her own room.

"I'd better get going back home," Helen finally said, after getting herself under control. "I told Mother I wouldn't be gone very long."

Russ nodded. "Okay. I'm glad you came."

She nodded back. "Me too."

Leaning in, Russ gave her a soft, lingering kiss. He wanted to tell her he loved her. Because he did. He *loved* Helen James, and no one could

ever stop that love! But he didn't know if she was ready to hear it, and the last thing he wanted to do was to scare her away.

● ● ● ● ●

The next day when the phone rang after football practice, and Mr. Morin came to the bedroom looking for Russ, the typical grin was missing. He looked back and forth between Russ and Ev, who were sitting on Ev's bed playing cards. His face was flushed.

The look made Russ's heart leap. "What's wrong?"

"It's . . . it's for you again, Russ. It's . . ."

No! Russ immediately thought of Kathleen. He hadn't checked in when he got home from school. He had completely forgotten. Don't let them say . . . He couldn't even think beyond that. He was jumping up off the bed, his stomach sick, before Mr. Morin could even finish what he was trying to say.

"It's a young lady, Russ. Maybe the same one who called yesterday. Just a warning, buddy—she sounds extremely distraught."

"What? It's not my mom?" Russ said, standing in front of Mr. Morin in sheer panic.

"No, no! Nothing like that. I'm sorry if I frightened you."

"No, it's okay. Thank you, sir." Russ said the words, and he was already moving past Mr. Morin, his mind on a new dilemma.

Helen's voice on the other end of the line was nearly unintelligible. She was trying to talk and sob and sniffle, all at the same time. She sounded terrible.

The first words she got out that Russ understood clearly were: *Please, Russ! Please come get me. As soon as you can.*

And as soon as he understood them, he promised he would be right there, and he dropped the handset on the base. In his panic, he forgot even to tell the Morins where he was going.

It was only a little over a mile to the James house from the Morins'. But it seemed like a half-hour drive. Russ screeched into the driveway, where today there was no other car.

He ran up and was set to pound on the front door when Helen threw it open. Two things registered at the same moment on Russ—the sight of Helen with her face all red from crying, and her makeup smeared everywhere and hair in disarray, and her mother, standing behind her

with her hands up to her mouth. She had also been crying. She started forward with one hand outstretched as Helen whirled and saw her.

"No! Get away from me!" She stepped out onto the porch and slammed the door right in Pearl's face, falling against Russ and nearly knocking him backwards down the concrete steps.

"Hey!" Russ tried to grab Helen's shoulders and hold her away from him so he could look into her eyes. But she was clutching him too tightly. "Hey, Helen! Hey, take a breath, okay? Whatever it is, it'll be okay."

"No!" she screamed. "It won't. It won't be okay, ever!"

From the corner of his eye, Russ saw Pearl peer out through one of the tall, slender windows beside the big white door. The poor woman, like Helen, was in a shambles.

"Helen! Helen, what's wrong? Did something happen to your dad?"

"No!" He understood that clearly, but he didn't understand the words she screamed at him next as she raised a fist and started pounding down on his trapezius muscle.

"Hold on! Hey! Slow down. I didn't hear you."

"I said he's not my dad!" she screamed, looking up at him with what almost amounted to a snarl on her lips. "He's not my dad!" she screamed once more. And then she broke into a crying fit and would have fallen to her knees right there on the porch if Russ hadn't been holding her up.

"Is he okay?" Russ barked again. "Helen, is your dad all right?"

"He's not my dad, damn it!" Her voice was a snarl. "He's not my father! They've been lying to me. They lied to me my whole life. Oh, Russ!" She stared at him, the expression on her face almost ugly. He stared back at her. Suddenly, she found her strength and ran down the steps, nearly collapsing on the drive.

Russ ran after her and caught her arm, whirling her around to him. She screamed in his face like a panther he had once heard at the zoo. Only Helen was much more frightening. "Take me out of here! Russ, please don't leave me here."

"Okay! Okay, come on. Go get in the car." He hurried to the car, feeling his pocket to make sure he still had his keys, and threw open his door, letting her fall down on the seat. "Hey, Helen, I'll be right back."

"Why? Where are you going?" Her voice was frantic.

"I have to go tell your mom."

"No! Don't you talk to her. I hate that woman! Russ, stay here!"

Ignoring the girl's pleas, Russ ran back to the house and shoved open the door. Pearl had seen him coming and was standing a few feet back from the door, her hands over her mouth. She spoke right through her hands. He had never seen a more horror-stricken face on anybody. "Russ, I'm so sorry. Please tell her how sorry I am. Oh, Russ, please help us."

"Hey!" She was asking for Russ's help, when he himself had never felt more helpless. "Ma'am, I don't know what to do. I don't even know what's going on."

Before he knew it, Pearl was holding him, weeping against his shirt. He stood patting her back, embracing her. She said something, but he couldn't understand a word of it. "I didn't understand."

The woman took a deep, sobbing breath, trying to calm down. "Please help her understand. Please! I'm so sorry, Russ. I'm so sorry for making you part of this mess." With those words, she collapsed away from him before he could react, folding down to the floor so she was sitting on her lower legs.

He went to reach for her to help her up, but she waved him off. "No," she cried, her chin shaking. "No, you just go on. Go to my little girl."

Baffled and scared, he started to turn away, but she reached out and grabbed the lower part of his jeans. "Please, Russ. Please, if you can, tell her how much I love her. And tell her how sorry I am."

On a whim, he reached down and got hold of Pearl by her upper arms, forcing her to stand. He couldn't leave her like that. "I'll tell her, ma'am. Now come on, all right? At least come sit down."

He guided her to a big, soft chair and, feeling like a fool, reached out and patted the side of her head, much the same way he would have patted a four-year-old, or a dog. "I'm sorry, ma'am. I'll bring her back as soon as I can. I promise."

Pearl started crying openly again, and, shaking her head, she buried her face in her hands. It was going to be some time, Russ judged, before the woman could force intelligible words out again.

Turning, he went out and shut the door, striding out to the car. Helen was sitting in the middle now with both feet up on the seat, hugging her legs to her body. Sobbing, she rocked back and forth, staring at the dash but seeing nothing.

Russ threw it in gear and drove out of the driveway and onto the street, spinning his tires in his hurry to get away. He drove out to Center Street, turned right and went flying east, where Center turned into Taylor Highway. A mile out, going at his car's top speed, he passed a farm road that turned and went out through the middle of a harvested wheat field. He skidded to a halt, threw it in reverse to back up for twenty feet, then turned into the field and drove until they were well off the road.

He turned to Helen and threw his arm around her. She made no response. She was quiet now, except for sniffling. But there was snot running down onto her lip that she didn't even have the presence of mind to try and wipe away. Using his sleeve, he did it for her.

The girl, a shell of her beautiful self, kept staring at the dash—actually at the silent radio, he realized. Her eyes were vacant. Her cheeks were lined with streaks of black mascara, and her skin was puffy and splotchy red.

He started to smooth back the hair on the far side of her face, that beautiful chestnut hair, now looking like she had slept on it for the past ten hours. She began to cry again, but softly this time, and leaned her head over against him. She stayed that way for twenty minutes, weeping. Neither of them spoke.

Finally, he heard her whisper, but the words were muffled and broken. He pulled a bit away from her and looked down, hoping if he could see her lips that he could discern what she was saying by a mixture of sound and sight.

"I'm sorry I didn't understand, Helen."

"He's not my father," she said a little louder, continuing to drill holes into the broken radio. "He isn't my father. They lied to me, Russ. Why? Why would they do that to somebody? Why?"

"I don't know, Helen. Hey, listen to me—I'm not sure what you mean when you say he's not your father. Help me."

Like a robot, she tilted her face upward and met his eyes. As if in a trance, she looked back and forth between his eyes for several moments before speaking again, in a voice that had lost all life.

"Harold James isn't my real father. Mother just now told me. After seventeen years, she finally decided to tell me, but she waited until after they took him away to prison."

"Helen! What are you talking about, he isn't your real father?" Russ had heard the words, but he couldn't grasp their meaning.

She raised her dull-looking eyes to look into his. "My real father is Frank Russell."

CHAPTER SIXTY

When they left the wheat field, Russ asked Helen where he could take her. The place he *wanted* to take her, and the place he felt she needed to be, was home to her mother. His guts told him that Pearl was as broken up right now as her daughter. Sure, she and her husband should probably have found a way years before to tell Helen the truth. Or perhaps at this point it was better never to let her know at all. Russ had no idea what had prompted the revelation now, other than maybe the woman had been waiting for years for a "right time," and now, with Harold gone, she had decided it was that time. Thinking about it, he was able to put himself in Pearl's shoes, and he knew one thing without thinking about it: For something as big as this, there would never have been a good time.

Russ had some money in his wallet, so he did the only thing he could think of to do. He couldn't stand the thought of anyone interrogating Helen, and he couldn't stand the thought of having to leave her alone in some strange bedroom for the night even if he could find one of his friends to take her in. This was not a good night for Helen to be by herself, and she had told him she didn't want to be with either Lonna or Bobbie. That left one choice he could see, and it was a choice that frightened him beyond words: Helen would have to spend the night with him.

Driving to a motel on the southern edge of Idaho Falls, Russ left Helen curled up on the front seat of the idling Studebaker and went inside. He had never rented a room before, but it proved to be pretty easy. He paid them three dollars in cash, got a key, and went back out to the car.

Helen still sat in the position he had left her, her knees drawn up, stocking feet on the seat, and arms wrapped around her legs. She stared blankly at the instrument panel, a real-life girl hardened to a statue.

Russ drove around and parked on the side of the motel. He wasn't about to leave the car out where any of his friends or family could come by and wonder why it was sitting there. With his heart pounding to the point he could hear it making whipping noises in his ears, he got out, went around front, and opened the motel room door. The room was dank and dark, and it stank of stale cigarette smoke. There was one queen-size bed almost in the center, a desk, a broken-down, thread-bare arm chair in a corner, and a closet with five hangers. About as simple as it came. Pulling a chain, he turned on a sickly yellow light bulb hanging over the foot of the bed, then went back out to the car.

Opening the door, he reached his hand out. Helen continued to stare straight forward. It was as if she was aware of nothing. He tapped her left hand, which was wrapped around the right one, and both of them holding her knees together.

Mechanically, Helen turned to look at him. "Come on, Helen. I got a place you can stay."

Helen suddenly seemed to become aware of her surroundings. She glanced around, half-confused, at the brownish-pink bricks on the side of the motel. "Where are we?"

"Idaho Falls. A motel. Come on."

She scooted over, then under the steering wheel. He slipped her ballet flats back on her feet, then took her elbows and helped her stand up. She almost fell; her legs must be numb.

"Where are we?" she repeated.

"I told you. Idaho Falls. Listen, you okay?"

She stared at him, a bleak look in her eyes. "Fine," she said at last. "But I still don't understand where we are."

"Helen!" He had raised his voice a little, but hopefully not enough to upset her. "You've gotta snap out of it. Come on." He reached out and took her hand.

"Okay. I'm fine, Russ. Just tell me where I am." Bewildered, she glanced around again.

"All right, I got a room for you. A motel room. If you want, I'll let you stay here, and I'll come back and get you tomorrow."

Her eyes grew large, and she stepped closer to him. "Russ, you're not leaving!"

"Okay. Okay. I'll stay right here. I won't leave you. Come on. We need to get inside."

He led her around to the front of the motel, glancing at a passing car when he should have been ducking his head. Luckily, he didn't recognize the driver. They hurried into the hotel room. Helen looked around and made a face, brushing at her nose with a sleeve. "It smells."

"I know. Everybody's gotta smoke everywhere they go. There's not much to do in here. You want me to go get a paper?"

She shook her head robotically. "No. I wouldn't read it."

"Well ... Hey, I'll tell you what. The bathroom's right over there, okay? You go do whatever you need to do to clean up. I promise I won't be far. I'm going to go get a couple of soda pops and something to eat. When I leave, you put this chain here in this hole and slide it over." He showed her the chain lock on the door; living in her nice home, he would have been surprised if she had ever seen such a lock before. "I'll probably be half an hour, but I promise I'll be back. I'll knock three times so you know it's me."

Her eyes full of fear he couldn't grasp, she looked over at the door. Finally, she nodded. "You won't leave me, right? You'll come back fast?"

"I promise." He leaned down and gently kissed her. She didn't turn her head away, but neither did she do anything to meet the kiss. She looked up at him when he stepped away almost as if she didn't even understand what had just taken place. Helen was a mess. It made Russ's heart ache to see his beautiful, normally calm and collected princess this way.

As soon as he shut the door, he waited for the chain lock to be put in place, and then he went to a phone booth that was attached to the front wall. He dropped a dime in the slot, calling Ev Morin's house.

As usual, Ev's father answered. Once Ev got on the phone, he told him in as little detail as possible that Helen was in some kind of trouble and that he had brought her to the motel. Good old, faithful Ev said very

little, but when Russ was finished, he asked if he could bring any of Russ's things up. Russ told him no, that it would only be one night, but he begged him to call the front desk and ask for him if he received any other phone calls, especially any from home.

Okay, buddy, Ev replied. *Hey, Russ?*

"Yeah?"

Man, be careful, okay? I'd hate to see you get in any kind of bad trouble.

Russ smiled. Ever since they were little, Ev had been watching out for him, like the sensible little brother watching out for his reckless older sibling.

"Yeah, bud. I'll be good. Thanks."

He hung up, and with an almost trembling hand, he dialed another number, that of Pearl James. It took one ring before it sounded like somebody jerked the phone off the base. *Yes, hello?*

"Hello, Mrs. James. It's me, Russ."

Russ! Russ! Oh, thank you for calling. Is she all right?

"Yes, ma'am. She's okay. I wanted to make sure and let you know she'll be safe. I'll bring her home as soon as I can."

Tonight? Pearl's voice was hopeful.

After a moment of hesitation, Russ drew in a deep breath. "No, I don't think she'll be ready until morning. Will that be all right?"

Long silence. Then: *Yes. I understand. But, Russ? I'm begging you to keep her safe. I would die if anything ever happened to my little girl.*

"I promise you, ma'am. She'll be safe."

He hung up and went out to find the nearest Foodtown, where he decided rather than soda pops to buy a half-gallon of milk, a bag of potato chips, and a bag of Oreos. On the way up to the checkout stand, he saw a newspaper and decided to buy that for himself, even if Helen wasn't interested. He had a feeling he was going to be looking for something to do this evening.

When he got back to the room, he glanced around, saw no traffic, and knocked three times. The door opened too fast, as if Helen had been standing there waiting.

He slipped in, shut and locked the door once more. Helen had washed off all her wayward makeup and tried to fix her hair. Other than

her red, puffy eyes, she still looked incredible, even though completely undone emotionally and without any makeup as a crutch.

He tore open the potato chips and handed the bag to her. She took one chip out as if she felt obligated and nibbled at it. When it was obvious that she didn't intend to take any more, he set it over on the dresser. "Want an Oreo instead?" She shook her head. "Milk then?" Another head shake. "It might help you sleep." She didn't respond. "Come on then." He led her to the bed. Pulling back the covers, he said, "Sit down and hold your feet up, and I'll take off your shoes for you. Then you won't have to touch this filthy floor with your bare feet, just turn over and get under the covers."

Helen complied, and once she had laid down her head and then turned to watch him, he said, "Don't worry, I'll sleep on the floor."

"No, Russ. Please . . ." She held out her hand to him.

"I can't get in bed with you, silly girl! What would people think?" He was trying to lighten the mood by teasing her, but it didn't work.

"Russ . . . There's nobody else here. Nobody will ever know. And I can't sleep in here alone."

Now, very much against his will, his heart started to pound once more. This girl had a way of making him feel either at the top of the world, or very uncomfortable.

"Hey, Helen. You know we shouldn't be here in the first place." He looked down at the place on the bed next to her, and the waiting pillow. "You really should have gone back home and tried to talk to your mom."

In a quiet, almost calm-sounding voice, with a face that looked as matter-of-fact as if she were reporting the weather outside, she replied, "No, I don't want to talk to her. I hate my mom."

Russ stared at her. Words he had told himself time and time again came back to him: *I hate my dad.* But he didn't. Right now, out of all the times he could think of in the past several months, he knew he didn't hate his father. He loved him. He was only angry with him for his choices, and wishing things could be like they were before. He knew that was all Helen meant, but there was no way he was going to argue with her, not considering her mental state right now.

"Hey, I'll sit in the bed with you for a while, all right? How's that? I'll read the paper, and you try to go to sleep."

Looking defeated, she nodded. Apparently, that was better than nothing. He went to the other side of the bed and pulled off his letterman jacket and his boots, then fluffed his pillow up against the headboard and got on the mattress, pulling the blankets up to his hips. As he snapped the paper open, Helen rolled over onto her side, and he felt her hand settle on his thigh. Trying to ignore it, he glanced over the headlines. It took a moment to realize it, but he hadn't seen much of the front page, so he flipped it back over. The first headline to catch his eye read **"Butte County Murder Investigation Still Ongoing".** Curious, Russ started reading, managing to get Helen out of his head, at least for the moment.

The article spoke of a story that had been circulating through the halls of Shelley High since the May before, lain dormant throughout the summer except in the homes of abhorred citizens, and then cropped up again throughout the school system with the start of the new year.

A girl about the age of Annie had disappeared from an Idaho Falls home toward the end of May, and a rancher in Butte County had discovered her mutilated body out in the lava beds three days later. Her arms were tied behind her back, she had been stabbed repeatedly, and her throat had been slashed. There was a handkerchief stuffed in her mouth.

The crime was horrendous, like nothing the students of Shelley High School had ever heard of taking place in their lifetime, and the scariest thing was that no one had ever been accused of the crime. Of course, the boys of the school, trying to act tough and untouched by the crime, took great pleasure in using the story to scare the girls into holding them tighter, or simply to scare them, period. After all, what if the murderer was still stalking the streets, hungry, looking for his next victim?

With his heart pounding now for a different reason, Russ read the article all the way through. The last part was taken from an interview with Jeremy Turnbull, the sheriff of Butte County. It told how Turnbull was using a skilled investigator from elsewhere who had been a mentor of his to go over the crime scene and all of the facts with a fine-tooth comb, and how they had several details put together and felt certain of finding the killer before the onset of winter.

As Russ finished reading the story, something drew him back to the words of Sheriff Turnbull. He remembered not that long ago—no more than three years, in fact—when Turnbull had taken over the job as sheriff

of Butte County. He remembered it well because Turnbull had been one of his father's best deputies back then, and that was one period when his father had actually let his feelings show, if only as much as the tip of the iceberg. He was devastated to lose such a fine deputy, but at the same time happy that one of his best men could find a better life for himself and his family.

The truth can sometimes slap you in the face when you least expect it. That was how it happened that night with Russ. He was staring at the paper, reading through the Post Register's quotations from Turnbull once more, when it all came together with complete clarity: the words of Arch's deputy Mark Daniels, of how his father was working some big case he couldn't talk about yet; the fact that his father was gone so much of the time when he had never been away from home that often at night and on weekends before, coupled with the blatant fact that he had told them several times he had to go to Butte County; his father's often taciturn mood that seemed much worse than it had been even last April when Russ was starting his track practice in earnest. Even his father's huge concern over Kathleen's sickness seemed to take on new meaning all of a sudden.

The man who was running that investigation, but had been trying all of this time to keep the gruesome details to himself, hoping to save his family from the savage picture of the crime, was Bingham County Sheriff Arch Blevins.

Suddenly, Russ understood a lot more about his stoic father than he had for the past five months.

Helen fell asleep before Russ even finished the paper, much to his surprise. The way she had been staring at him while he read, he was sure she would be awake all night. Thankful that he hadn't decided to read the stories in the paper out loud, he folded it up and lay it face-down on the floor by the bed. Looking down at Helen and wishing he were comfortable enough to lie on the floor as he had first suggested, he fluffed up his pillow once more, then went and turned out the light, leaving the one in the bathroom on. He came back and scooted down under the covers, laying down his head and looking up at the ceiling.

The girl moved, and it startled him. She wasn't asleep at all, at least not anymore. She rolled over onto her stomach and pulled herself over

until her upper body lay on top of his. Lowering her face, she began softly to kiss him. There was a moment when Russ felt his hormones rage up inside him, and he realized how alone they were here, and how easy it could be to let himself go. But it wasn't. It would *never* be easy, not after the promises he had made Pearl James and Ev tonight.

Russ didn't stop Helen from kissing him for several minutes, as her intentions got bolder and bolder, and she began kissing his ears, and then the sides of his neck. At last, he reached up and put his arms around her, drawing her tight against him.

He spoke into her ear, his voice soft. "Helen, I need to say something."

She worked her hand free of his grasp and laid it alongside his face, but because he held her so close she spoke into his shirt. "What?"

"I already made up my mind about this whole situation before I ever walked in here and rented this room, and now I'm glad I did. If I hadn't, I'm afraid what would happen tonight. Over eighteen years ago, I guess it would be, your mom made a mistake that affected the rest of her life—and now yours too. She finally got to release what has been haunting her all these years, by telling you today what happened back then. As long as I live, I'm never going to allow you to look back on this night, and me, and regret doing something you didn't think through—something you didn't have a right to do. Understand?"

Helen's body slowly went limp. She took in a deep breath and let it sigh out. It was a long time, and a breathless one for Russ, before she said, "I do. Thank you, Russ. Thank you so much."

He breathed a sigh of relief, loosening his grip on her and wishing with all his young hormones that things could be different.

"Don't think a thing about it, Helen. I just don't ever want to be the mistake you're having to explain to your kid someday."

He didn't realize at the moment how much that made it sound like he didn't believe they were going to have a future together. "I know. I know. You're stronger than I am. Thank you again. Russ?"

She raised up on her elbow again and looked down at him, although even in the dim light spilling in from the bathroom he could barely make out her eyes.

"Yeah?"

"I do love you."

CHAPTER SIXTY-ONE

In the morning, it took Russ and Helen a long time to decide what they had to do. Russ had enough to pay for another night at the motel, or even two—and probably enough to cover food for both days as well. But besides the obvious moral dangers of two people their age staying one or two more nights in the same room, there was the fact that they needed to be in school, Russ needed to make it to football practice, and one, two or two hundred more days were not going to do one useful thing toward reaching a solution to this situation.

Russ finally talked Helen into going home. He knew she could never face the school without being dolled up, and especially while wearing the same clothes she had worn the day before. For that, he didn't blame her. He dreaded seeing her mother, knowing Pearl was going to be remembering her own youthful mistakes and, knowing human nature as she did, dreading the worst. But that couldn't be helped.

He pulled into the rainbow-shaped driveway and up to the front of the big house that would soon belong to someone else, with every intention of going inside with Helen to back her up as she tried to explain where they had spent the night. But the girl was adamant about not getting him involved in that.

"Please stay out here and wait for me, Russ. You owe me that much. Don't come in. It will only make things worse. No matter how it goes, I'll come back and let you know."

And so he watched his girl disappear behind the big white door, and he began the eternal wait—or at least it *seemed* eternal.

At one point, about two minutes after Helen had gone in, the front door flew wide, and Russ saw the terrifying sight of Pearl James, her hair in a mess and dressed in a bathrobe and slippers, trying to stomp outside. He heard her and Helen screaming, and somehow Helen got the door

away from her mother, but only after Pearl had gotten one good glare in at Russ. The door slammed shut, and the waiting began again—but this time it was harder.

It was a full half hour before the door Russ had been staring at almost non-stop cracked open again. Expecting Helen to be the one standing there now, because of the slowness of its opening, he waited, almost dreading to hear what had happened inside those walls.

But it wasn't Helen who emerged. It was Pearl. With Helen standing back in the shadows, arms folded across her chest and looking out the door, Pearl stepped out on the porch, her lips pursed, looking into the front of the Studebaker. She came slowly down the steps, and Russ was smart enough to throw open his door and get out. At least he had better get himself in as defensive a mode as he could.

Pearl didn't say anything. She walked straight out to the car and crossed around in front of it, her eyes on him the whole time, and an inscrutable look on her face.

She stopped shy of him, looking more broken and more taken apart than he could have imagined a woman who was so proud of her appearance. She looked up into his eyes. Like Helen, her arms were folded, making her seem like she wanted no one getting inside her defenses.

Suddenly, she gave a little shake of her head. "You dear, sweet young man. Thank you, Russ." Had she read something in his eyes? "Thank you so much for keeping my baby safe." She stepped in closer, and to his surprise, her arms folded around his middle, and she hugged him tight, holding on past that point of a nice, grateful embrace, into that time of youthful discomfort, and beyond it to that strange point where discomfort breaks over into a strange sensation where one person realizes they mean the world to someone else. Russ suddenly felt very close to Pearl James, and not in a physical way. This was the opposite of the feelings he had expected to leave here with.

Pearl stepped away from Russ, wiping her eyes and clearing her throat. She put out her hand and squeezed his. "Young man, you are one-of-a-kind. I owe you everything this morning. Everything."

Russ gave her a close-lipped smile. "It's okay, ma'am. I mean Pearl. I just didn't want to leave her with any regrets."

Pearl gave him a little shake of her head as tears welled up in her eyes. "Your parents should be incredibly proud of you."

● ● ● ● ●

That afternoon, after classes let out, Russ had a strange request for Coach Jardinsky: to be excused from practice, something he would never have dreamed of asking for in the past. The big, gruff coach was alone when he caught him in his office, so there was no need to put on a front for anyone watching.

The big man searched Russ's eyes. "Must be somethin' perty important, you askin' out of practice. You okay, Cus? Anything I can do?"

Russ shook his head, gratitude filling his heart. He hadn't expected this moment to go like this. He wished he could tell Jardinsky all about what was on his mind. But he couldn't. He wasn't the kind to talk with another man about something like this, first off, and second, it wasn't his place to let out the Jameses' secret. He stood there long enough that Jardinsky seemed to read his mind. The coach stuck out a heavy, battered paw, and Russ shook it. Jardinsky was still, all these years after the pros, one powerful man.

"Thanks, Coach."

Jardinsky could have made some wisecrack. If anyone else had been around to witness it, Russ knew he would have. "Don't worry about it, bud. I know you'll make up for any practice you miss. Take care of whatever you gotta deal with and I'll see you tomorrow."

Russ left the school with a full heart and drove straight over to Ev's, letting himself in. Ev's mother was in the kitchen sweeping, and she looked up in surprise. "Hey, Mom," he said for fun. He had grown very close to Ev's parents during his stay here.

"Hey, Russ! Aren't you missing practice?"

"Yep. But no, not really." He forced a grin.

After showering and changing his clothes, he went out to the car. He drove straight to the Russells' and parked the car on the edge of the street. The new family pickup was in the driveway, which meant not only Frank would be home, but Lorna as well. Edie was the only wild card. But he hadn't seen her on the way over here, so he assumed she would have had enough time to walk home while he was cleaning up at Ev's. Surely, once she discovered he wasn't at practice, she wouldn't

have had any reason to remain late at the school. Then again, he hadn't seen her in school at all that day, so he wondered now if something had kept her home.

For ten minutes, he sat in the car. Several times he reached for the ignition key with the intention of starting up the car and driving away. He felt like a complete fool. What was he doing here? He needed to talk to someone—and Edie Russell was the only person he could think of who was a good enough listener for this, at least right now while his mother had more important things on her mind, like the life and death struggle her daughter was going through. As he thought of that, it was with an immediate twinge of shame. Maybe instead of being here he should have driven straight up to the hospital to check on his little sister. But it would be okay. He would go there from here.

Once again, he reached for the key. What was he going to do here anyway? He was a fool to think he could talk to Edie. She was going to be as distraught about this as Helen was, and he sure couldn't go through that a second time.

Russ's head was in a whirl. But it didn't last long before he was out of choices. The front door of the Russell home opened as he was turning the engine over, and as it roared to life Lorna Russell appeared in the doorway of the home. Their eyes met. He looked at the gear shift. He should throw it into first and peel out. He should drive as fast as he could away from here. But he was too late, and he knew it.

Lorna stepped down the wonderful, solid wooden steps Ev had made and bent down a little to see into the car. She smiled uncertainly and gave him a little wave.

Reaching out, Russ shut off the ignition and took a deep breath. He wasn't ready to greet Lorna, but now he had to. What was he going to say? It wasn't his place to bring news that could shatter this family forever.

With another deep breath, he got out of the car.

"Hi, Russ. What a surprise." She gave him a bigger smile. "Did you have any reason for stopping there? Just resting your foot?"

He grinned. "Oh, sorry for just sitting out here. Probably a little weird. No, ma'am. I . . . Well, I forgot why I came over."

"Oh? Not to see Edie?"

"Well, yeah, it was, but . . ."

She raised her shoulders with her next sigh and walked out to him, looking almost strikingly beautiful this afternoon. He was more amazed every time he saw her, and somewhat ashamed to think of her that way. But he couldn't deny it or ignore it, any more than he could a wonderful sunrise or sunset.

Russ met Lorna in the middle of the yard. He searched his head for something to say, but there was nothing. He had never been more at a loss for words.

She smiled at him again. "I think I know why you came over, Russ."

"You do?" *Right! If you knew why I was here you wouldn't be smiling, lady!* Of course that was only in his head. He could never have said those words to this kind, wonderful woman.

"I think so," she replied. "Do you want to come in?"

"Uh . . ." What did he do now? How did he get out of this? How was he going to walk into that house, with a family that might be destroyed by the revelation he had at his fingertips, and try to pretend everything was okay?

"Come on." She smiled again and reached down for his hand. Like a dumb brute, he let her take it, and she led him across the strip of lawn to the steps. Of course she had to point them out as they went up.

"Ev did such a nice job, didn't he?"

"He sure did." They had talked about the steps almost every time he came over, but he was glad to have some other topic of conversation than the taboo one he knew now he could never bring up.

Lorna opened the door, let go of his hand, and ushered him inside. Frank was sitting at the kitchen table, and he struggled up off his chair and walked over, shaking Russ's hand. Edie came down the hallway from her room. Even as light-footed as she was, somehow her steps sounded as ominous as thunder before she appeared from around the corner. She smiled at Russ, but it was the same expression her parents had given him in name only. The look on her face made it obvious that something was wrong.

"Good to see you, Russ," Frank said, covering the uncomfortable silence from Edie.

Prompted, the girl said, "Hi, Russ." She attempted a brighter smile.

Frank and Lorna looked at each other, a question in both of their eyes. Edie looked ill. Russ wanted to run.

It was Lorna who had the boldness to go on in the face of such tension that seemed to fill the room. "Hey, Russ, I know what you're going through, and I think it's best if we all go through this together."

He glanced around at the three of them, his eyes lingering longest on Edie. He didn't want to hurt this girl! He didn't want to see her hurt, either. She was already so shy and introverted—such a sweet, gentle person. She didn't deserve what was coming. He wished she could be gone. He wished if ever he had to come here it had been during a time when she was in school and he could have spoken with her parents alone. He had only wanted to warn them that bad news was likely coming their way. Now he wanted no part of it. Why should he even be in the middle of this? He hadn't asked for any of it.

All of a sudden, Lorna's words registered on him, and they locked eyes. *Go through this together?* What was she talking about?

Before he could even form the words, Lorna explained: "We got a call this morning from Pearl James."

A mule kicked Russ low in the gut—or at least it might as well have. Maybe it would have felt like an improvement.

"Pardon?"

"Pearl called," Frank said, to reinforce what his wife had said.

The words and their meaning began to register on Russ. Startled, he looked over at Edie. She must have been waiting for that look from him, because she walked forward and embraced him, her demeanor calm. She didn't seem to care that her parents saw her with her arms around him. He patted her back, trying not to meet the eyes of Frank and Lorna.

It seemed improper to speak until Edie stepped away from him, so Russ held his tongue, wishing her mother and father were worlds away right now. So many things he wanted to say to Edie, but he couldn't form any of the words. Mostly, as the realization struck him that she already knew the truth, he wanted to ask her if she was okay.

Lorna walked over to Edie and started rubbing her back with one hand as she looked at Russ with a sad smile.

"There are some things you need to know, Russ. It might help."

"Okay?"

"So I've known about Helen from the very beginning—even before she was born. Frank told me about her on our second date."

Startled, Russ looked over at Frank. It struck him how hard that must have been.

"Yes. Our second date. I could have run right then, you know? I'm sure a lot of women would have. I mean, it wasn't like Frank was set to be a millionaire. He didn't even have those kinds of aspirations. He was a simple man. A simple, honest man. A simple, honest man with a huge regret and a great big, loving heart. That's why I stayed. He could have hidden Helen from me. I could be finding out about it right now, like Helen and Edie have. But I've known all along."

Almost without thinking about it, Russ started stroking the back of Edie's hair, gently pushing her head closer into his chest. "Can I ask you something?"

"Of course. I hope you will."

Frank stayed silent. He knew this was a conversation for his wife, not him.

"Why didn't someone tell Edie?"

Lorna gave her daughter's shoulder a squeeze. "Protecting Helen, I guess. Now it seems foolish. But we assumed Pearl would never whisper a word of it, and it didn't seem like our place."

"Edie wouldn't have told anybody," Russ said, as sure of that statement as he was of anything.

"I know," said Lorna, blinking her eyes. "I know. It was stupid of us. I wish we could go back now. But it's like admitting there is no Santa Claus—you know? There comes a time when you have pretended for so long that you simply don't know how to break the news. And then you finally decide that what they don't know won't hurt them and that maybe it's best if they go their whole lives without knowing. Does that make any sense?"

A memory came back to Russ, not of the first time he knew there was no Santa Claus, but of the first time he realized that other children thought the chubby old elf was real. His own mother and father were not fun-loving that way. They had made sure from the very beginning that he knew any Christmas gift he received was purchased with his father's hard-earned cash, not brought by some mystical elf from the North Pole.

He nodded at Lorna. "Yeah. It makes sense, I guess."

Like with Pearl James that morning, this embrace with Edie had passed beyond that point of being too long to be simply comfortable to the point of feeling completely natural now. It was like the two of them had become one, and it was a startling realization to Russ. When had he first started to feel so close to Edie, closer in a way than he did to his own family? It was something he would never have expected, especially considering how annoyed she used to make him not all that long ago.

When Edie looked up at Russ and stepped back from him, she kept her hands boldly on his arms. Even with both of her parents watching, Russ no longer felt any embarrassment or discomfort.

"Russ, do you think we could do something together?"

"Um . . . What's that?"

Her next words were like a land mine he had stepped on and was scared to pull his foot off.

"Do you think we could go over and see Helen together?"

CHAPTER SIXTY-TWO

Edie's reception at Helen James's was not what she had anticipated. In truth, it was nothing like Russ had expected either.

It wasn't Helen, but Pearl James, who opened the door when Russ knocked, with Edie standing behind his left shoulder.

With a smile on her face, Pearl looked at Russ. Then it registered on her that he wasn't alone. She dropped her eyes to Edie, and the air changed.

Other than the one flinty-eyed glance, Pearl didn't acknowledge Edie's presence. "Hello, Russ. May I help you?"

Russ took a moment to adjust to Pearl's suddenly cool demeanor, after her warm smile as she was opening the door.

"Sorry, Pearl, I hope it isn't a bad time. Edie and I wanted to see if we could visit for a little bit."

Pearl tried to smile again, but it was a pathetic attempt. "You mean with me? Or Helen?"

Russ wished he had not only one but three football teams bearing down on him with blood in their eyes. It would have been preferable to the way he felt right now. The way he had been foreseeing this visit was him, Edie, and Helen. He hadn't thought about what it would feel like with Pearl included as well.

"I guess we were thinking just us and Helen, but you'd be welcome to sit with us if you want."

"That's kind of you," Pearl said stiffly. "You know what? Wait. Hold on a moment and I'll check with Helen. Just a minute."

With that, she closed the door in Russ's face. After a second to compose himself, he turned and looked at Edie. She was already staring up at him.

"Maybe this wasn't such a great idea, huh?"

"Oh, it'll be okay," Russ assured her. But inside he wasn't so sure.

It seemed like Russ stood there with Edie, fidgeting, for some five minutes, when in reality it was more like two. Then the door opened again, enough for Pearl's face to show.

"I don't think this is really a good time, Russ."

"I, uh . . ." If ever the cat had someone's tongue, it had Russ's now, with both paws.

"Please call another time," Pearl said.

Russ didn't know how to respond, but he knew he had to say something to alleviate the strain. "Okay, ma'am. I will. Is Helen all right?"

A look of hurt flashed through Pearl's eyes, and she glanced past Russ, then back to meet his gaze. "I'm sure she's fine. She just . . . I'm sure she's fine." With that, she shut the door.

Embarrassed and feeling sick to the pit of his stomach, Russ looked at Edie. He wanted to find something to say to her, because it was obvious why Pearl had treated them the way she had, and Edie couldn't possibly not know. Here she had wanted so badly to talk to Helen and somehow try to make her feel better, and Helen might as well have spat in her face. Russ felt so bad for this girl. Hadn't her self-confidence already suffered enough?

He wanted to speak, but he didn't, other than to say, "Come on, Edie. I'll take you home."

They had made it halfway to the Studebaker when Russ heard the door to the house open behind them, and he turned, startled. Helen was partway out the door, but it was still shut most of the way.

"Wait, Russ."

"Hi, Helen."

"Hi." The girl didn't look at Edie.

"Can I talk to you?"

Russ glanced over at Edie. "Both of us?"

With a fleeting glance toward Edie, but as if she couldn't even see her there, she said, "No, just you."

Russ cringed inwardly. He wished Helen hadn't even come out. Were Helen and her mother absolutely trying to crush Edie?

Well, he wasn't about to walk away and leave Edie standing without at least saying something to her. He turned and tapped her arm. "Hey, can you wait in the car? I'll be back as quick as I can."

Edie, her hands now clasped in front of her, gave a brisk nod, trying not to look at him. Her eyes shone with wetness.

Russ went back to the house and up onto the porch, and Helen moved out of the way and let him in, casting a quick look toward Edie.

When he got inside, Pearl was standing in the entryway to the kitchen, her arms folded and staring toward him and Helen. Her lips were tight.

"Russ," Helen said, trying to keep her voice down. But Pearl was too close not to hear. "You shouldn't have brought her here."

"It was her idea to come, Helen," he protested. "She wanted to talk to you about all this. You know, she didn't know anything either."

Helen turned and looked over her shoulder at her mother. Her mother folded her arms tighter.

Helen turned back to Russ, seemed about to say something, then looked again at Pearl. "Mother, could you please leave us alone? Just for a minute?" Her voice sounded desperate.

With a huff, Pearl turned and left the room.

Helen sank against Russ. "Oh, why did you bring her here?" she asked in a whisper. "Why?"

"Helen, she's . . ." He started to say that Edie was Helen's sister. But his gut told him reminding her of that would only make things worse.

"She's what?" Helen looked up, pulling away from him.

"Nothing."

"Russ, I don't know what to do!"

"Hey!" He put his finger over her lips. "Helen, I love you. I'm sorry, but I have to tell you that."

"No, Russ. No, you don't. I'm not the girl for you."

"What?" He was stunned by her words. "What are you talking about? You're perfect for me!"

"Come on, Russ. My parents weren't even married—ever. How is that going to look to your mom and dad? Or did you already tell them?"

"No, I haven't talked to them. I won't ever say a word if you don't want me to."

"Right!" A dark look came to her face. "There's no way to keep that kind of secret now."

"Why not? It's been kept for eighteen years."

She must have known he was right, for she didn't argue the point.

"I don't want Edie looking down on me. We're losing everything. Can you imagine how happy that's going to make her, after spending her life poor and seeing how rich we were? And now I'll be just like her."

"What are you talking about? Helen, Edie's not like that."

Helen looked bitter. "Oh, Russ, you don't know anything about girls. She's like that, all right. She's probably out there rubbing her hands together right now with glee. I'm falling, and she's there to see it. How lucky can she be? And now she's going to catch you, too."

"What the heck are you talking about? I don't *want* Edie! I want *you!* Why are you talking like this? Edie's only a friend. That's all she could ever be to me."

Helen stared Russ down. At last, a light of hope came into her eyes. "Are you sure? After all this?"

"All what? You didn't do anything, Helen! Nothing has changed for me! Why would it? What kind of guy would I be if I dumped you over something you had no control over?"

Helen seemed breathless. She fell against him again and embraced him almost fiercely. Russ looked over to see Pearl watching them from the kitchen doorway. The woman's face had softened.

"Hey, I have to take Edie home," Russ whispered, trying not to let Pearl hear. "I'll see you as soon as I can."

"Why?"

"Why what?"

"Why do you have to take her home? She walks all the time."

"Helen, come on. She came here with me, and her mom and dad are waiting."

Pursing her lips, Helen stared up at him. Finally, her face relaxed. "Okay. Yes, you're right. Take her home. But Mother and I are going to be out of town for a couple of days. I'll see you back at school."

Russ felt an impulse to lean down and kiss Helen, but her mother was still looking on, pretending to be dusting a marble-topped table that sat up against the wall by the kitchen entry.

In fact, the girl didn't look very kissable at the moment anyway. Her lips were too tight.

"I'll see you at school then," he said, squeezing her shoulder, and he turned and went out. Helen didn't follow him.

When Russ got outside, he looked at the car. It was empty!

Rushing out, he looked down inside, hoping Edie was lying down. But she wasn't there.

Glancing wildly around, he saw no sign of her. He jumped in the car and fired it up, killing it the first time he tried to drive off. Then he had to crank it for ten seconds before it would start again. He drove toward Edie's house, searching for her. He was only a few blocks away when he realized she couldn't have come this way. There was no way she could have traveled that fast.

He drove back slowly toward the James house. She was nowhere in sight! What were Frank and Lorna going to think if he didn't bring their daughter home?

On a whim, and frantic, he drove up to the school, searching the area. He spotted her sitting up on top of the bleachers, this time looking east, rather than west, as they had done when they watched the sunset.

Sliding the car to a stop, he turned it off and set the brake, jumping out. He was mad! Why would she do something like that? Russ ran to the bleachers, intent on chewing the girl out.

But as he came around the end of the bleachers and made to run up them, he saw that her shoulders were shaking, and her head was down. Edie was crying her eyes out.

He ascended the bleachers, getting slower and slower with each one. At last, he stood beside her, looking down. She was hugging herself, and her face remained downcast. He sat beside her. What did he do now?

For a long time, they sat that way, Edie with her hands hugging her body, weeping now in silence, Russ with his hands in the pockets of his letterman jacket. Finally, he pulled his right hand out and put his arm around her back, pulling her close to him. The move made her cry even harder, but now she leaned close to him.

What were people going to think if they saw him with Edie like this? Everyone was going to get the wrong idea, and he couldn't even blame them. He would think the same thing they were going to. But he couldn't let Edie cry without trying to comfort her. She was such a sweet, innocent girl. Why did the innocent people always get hurt?

As soon as he thought this, it reminded him of Isaac, and then of Kathleen. His sister! She was suffering in the hospital, and the whole family must think he didn't even care! Why had this thing had to happen now, of all the times it could have come out? What was he supposed to do? Where did he turn?

Family . . . He should be with his family. But his father would be there. He was man enough to make up for Russ's absence. They didn't need two males in the same place—especially not two males who couldn't stand to be in the same room with each other.

He felt a surge of sadness. Was it mere contagion? The feeling of sadness being absorbed from Edie?

What had become of Russ's life? It seemed like everything had become about him. Russ and football. He had been going around for as far back as he could remember acting like the world owed him a living, like everyone should practically bow to him when he entered a room. Helen should fall into his arms, and anyone else he meant anything to should

wait their turn for his attentions. And most of the time, those attentions never came—not unless he needed something from them.

What had he become?

Russ raised the arm that was behind Edie's back and began to caress her hair. It was so soft. He had never thought about her hair before. He thought of the tears on her face—he couldn't see her anymore, for her cheek was against his chest. He wanted Edie to be happy. He wanted her to find someone she could call her own. She was a lonely girl, and no one had ever seemed to look at her, all through school, as far back as he could remember. And he knew deep inside that she had always liked him, in a way he wasn't ready for. But he had almost come to expect that for so long. While he had never been turned down for a single date, Edie had probably never even been asked. She seemed lost in her books. She seemed like she didn't care about anyone else. But she did. It was so plain now, as her mask slipped away.

He kept stroking her hair with his right hand until she unfolded her arms and tried to dry her cheeks with her left hand. He carried a handkerchief in a pocket of his jacket, and it happened to be clean—for once.

"Hey. You need a hankie?"

Edie nodded but didn't look at him. He pulled out the handkerchief and handed it to her. She blew her nose, trying to be lady-like. He smiled to himself. Poor thing.

"I ruined it," she said, sniffling.

"Oh yeah!" he agreed jokingly. "You know, that toxic snot won't wash out."

Edie was helpless to keep a little giggle from escaping her. She leaned over and bumped her head against his chest. "You know what I mean."

"Well, you can keep it. I think I prob'ly stole it from my dad anyway."

She smiled and looked up at him. Her glasses were fogging a little.

He reached out and tugged them off, thinking he would clean them on his shirt. Edie was looking up at him. Her cheeks were ruddy from crying, and her eyes a little puffy. But the red seemed to make the deep, dark chocolate of her eyes stand out even more.

She smiled at him. He held her glasses in his left hand and smiled back.

"How good can you see me?"

"I can see fine. Put them on. They aren't very strong."

Russ put her glasses on the tip of his nose and glared sagely over the top of them at Edie, making her giggle again.

"Do I look dignified?"

"Yes. Very. No," she corrected herself. "You look silly."

"You sure don't."

"I don't?"

"No."

"How do I look?"

Russ's heart was pounding. He and Edie were sitting too close to each other. What if someone saw them?

"You look . . ." *Don't be stupid, Russ!* Inside, it was like he was yelling.

Edie searched his eyes.

"You look really pretty." Somebody should have kicked him. Lightning should have struck him. What was he doing playing with this poor girl's heart? "You look beautiful."

Tears flooded Edie's eyes. She swiped at them, then looked back up as if to see if he were still looking at her the same.

"You really think so?"

"I do. Who wouldn't?"

And then something was happening, something Russ didn't want to happen. His face was getting closer, and Edie was raising hers to him. Too close! *Too close!* He needed to jump down and go home. If she wanted to stay here alone, she could! He had to go. He had to check on Kathleen. He had to . . .

Edie's lips were parted, and moist. His mouth touched them gently. Her shoulders started shaking, and her eyes closed. She turned and put her arms around him, and he put his around her. He kissed her in a tender way he didn't remember kissing anyone before. Not a sexual way. Not a hungry way. And she kissed him back, in that same gentle, caring way, as if hurting him were the last thing she could ever do.

And that was the same thing in Russ's heart: He never wanted to hurt this shy, innocent girl, whose lips felt so tender and warm, and who held onto him like her last breath of life.

CHAPTER SIXTY-THREE

Russ had to push all thought of Edie and Helen out of his mind as he drove away from Edie's house. The taste of Edie's kiss still lingered on his lips. It had been so different from the kisses he had shared with Helen, all of them so full of passion and desire. The kiss from Edie had been soft and gentle, slow, easy, and natural. And for all its gentleness, it shook him right to the core.

He drove straight to Idaho Falls, not caring whether his family was already there at the hospital or not, but assuming they would be. When he told the nurse who he was there to see, she smiled at him.

"Okay, young man, go ahead and go on in. Visiting hours will be over in about half an hour."

Russ hustled down the hall, trying to take the nurse's smile as a good sign. He saw no one else in the hall. No sign that Kathleen had any other visitors. He got to the room and eased open the door, peeking in. Kathleen was lying there alone, her head turned the other way.

He crept in, ready to sit on the chair that was always beside Kathleen's bed. Before he could reach her, her head whipped over his way. Kathleen was awake!

A huge smile broke over her face like a sunrise, a face whose color had gone back to its normal pink. "Russ!"

"Hey, little girl!" he replied. The unexpected tears that welled up in his eyes embarrassed him. "What are you doing awake?"

"I'm getting better. The doctor said my temperature is all the way back to normal, and all signs of infection are gone."

Grinning, Russ looked up and down the length of Kathleen's bed and the austere looking white sheets and blankets that covered her. "Whoa! That's some big language for a punk kid like you."

Kathleen frowned. "Stop it!"

Russ laughed. "You know I'm kidding. Wow, Sis. I'm happy to hear that. Everybody was pretty worried about you."

"Even Dad?" Kathleen asked.

Russ felt his heart drop. "Hey. Hey." He didn't know how he was going to tell her. He wasn't sure what to think about *anything* anymore. He plopped into the chair, conscious of Kathleen's big eyes concentrating on him, waiting for whatever he was going to say.

"So . . . Yeah, Sis, even Dad. Mom and me came up one day to visit you, and you know what? Dad was already up here. He was singing you a song."

"Daddy?"

The girl seemed as shocked as Russ had been. "Well, of course, *Daddy!* No, I'm talking about Charlie Chan."

Big tears suddenly rolled out of Kathleen's eyes, and down her cheeks. "Are you really serious?" she asked. "Daddy sang to me? What was he singing?"

"'I'll Take You Home, Kathleen'. And yes, he was really singing to you. Mom and me both heard it. If you don't believe me, you can ask her."

"Daddy never sings anymore."

An empty feeling filled Russ's chest. "Nope. But he sure was singing for you. Hey, kid—I think Dad has had some really hard stuff on his mind lately. Maybe we should go easy on him."

Kathleen stared at him. Again, tears squeezed out and ran down into her hair. "Are you and Daddy talking again now?"

Russ frowned. "Well, not much. I just found out some stuff, that's all."

"How come you don't talk to him?"

He sat there for a long time. He had a great big urge to hug this sister of his, but he held it back. "I'm not sure why, I guess."

Kathleen smiled sadly. And Russ knew that somehow she understood.

They heard voices in the hallway. "Oh, great!" Russ said. "I think I heard Toni."

"Yeah!" Kathleen gave him a huge smile and tried to sit up. "They're all coming to see me. The nurse said Mommy called."

Russ stood up abruptly. "All of them? You mean Dad too?"

Kathleen nodded, smiling. Russ's eyes darted around for a place to escape. But there was nowhere.

The door clicked open, and Eleanor's eyes met Russ's. By the look in them, he knew the nurse had already told them he was here. "Hi, Son!" She hurried to him and threw her arms around him. "We've been really worried about you."

"Don't worry, Mom. Everything's okay. I have a lot to tell you, but it can wait." In the back of his mind, he was aware that Toni, Dorothy, and Annie had come in behind his mother, but his father wasn't there. As usual.

"Dad didn't make it, did he?"

Eleanor met his eyes, and hers shifted to the side. "No, he did. He's in the hall."

Russ had wanted his father not to be there. He had wanted to be justified in his anger with his father for deserting the family. Now that justification was torn out from under him. He sighed. "Well, I gotta get."

Eleanor reached up in a sudden motion and put the palm of her hand on the side of Russ's face. "Son, you're growing up fast. You have a few more games to go, and then you'll probably go to State with your team. Don't let this all go by without trying to make friends with your dad again. You'll always be sorry."

No, I won't, Russ thought. *Dad's the one who chose to be gone.* "Okay, Mom," he said. "Anyway, I'd better get going."

Eleanor gave him a sad smile and patted his cheek. He said goodbye, turned and walked out of the room.

Arch Blevins was standing in the hallway, seeming to take up half of it with his big frame. Arch Blevins, the sheriff who stood ten feet tall but was too little to be there for his family.

"Hi, Pop." Russ didn't have a choice but to speak. His dad was like a wall keeping him from going out.

"Hello, Russ." The sheriff's chin seemed to quiver, but Russ pulled his glance away.

There were several moments of uncomfortable silence. Arch's mouth opened as if to speak. Russ didn't look up at him, but he waited. Then, finally, "Hey, Pop, I'd better get going. Looks like Kathleen's feeling good, though." He tried to look bright. He didn't feel it.

His father took a side-step, and Russ walked past. Something made him want to turn around, one last time. But he couldn't. He kept on walking, and on the way down he took the stairs two at a time.

Russ fought an urge to stop at the Russells' on his way by. He wanted to tell someone about Kathleen. But he had another call to make first. When he got home, he went right in and dialed the sheriff's office.

To his happy surprise, the phone was answered by Deputy Mark Daniels. "How long you working, Mark?" he asked after initial cordialities.

Three more hours.

"You got anything goin'?"

Going? Not really? What's up?

"I need to talk to you."

That's a serious tone to your voice, Russ. Everything okay?

"I don't know. I just need to ask you something."

You can't say it over the phone?

"I'd rather see you."

Okay then. Want to meet me in Firth? I'll just park down on Main and wait 'til I see you.

"Sounds good. Thanks, Mark."

Russ drove the old Studebaker as fast as he could. He ended up being the one waiting for Deputy Daniels, for at least five minutes, which seemed like sixty.

He was standing by his car when Mark pulled up. "Hey, can I ride with you?" he asked through the deputy's open window.

"Sure, hop in."

Russ got in, and they drove west into farm country. After a long few minutes of heavy silence, Mark said, "Just talk whenever you're ready, buddy. I'm not in any hurry."

Russ chuckled uncomfortably. "Okay. Yeah, sorry, Mark. Well, you know how you told me Dad's working a big case?"

"Sure."

"It's the girl who got killed over by Arco. Isn't it?"

Mark's face went even more serious. He looked at the road as he went around a sweeping curve. "How'd you know that?"

"I was reading the paper last night. I just put two and two together."

"Nobody's supposed to know about it—especially not the county. They're mad at your dad already for giving me that petty cash. If they ever found out he was giving all that county time to Butte, when he could be working on our own caseload, they'd have his hide. And . . . Well, there's something else, too."

"What?"

Mark took a deep breath and slapped the steering wheel. "Shoot, Russ. Your dad would kill me. But I've gotta tell you something. This is eating your old man alive."

"What do you mean?"

"I mean . . . Well, you know, that old sheriff is one tough bird. He never lets on if something bothers him. Or at least he never did."

A long minute of silence passed. Russ waited, just beginning to wonder if Mark needed prompting when Mark took another big breath.

"Well, he's talking now, bud. A lot. He can't stop talking about it. That girl was about the age of your sister Toni, you know. So now after seeing all the photos, and seeing that girl's body . . . Hey, kid—sorry if this is too much."

"No, Mark. No, I need to know."

"All right. Well, the short of it is your dad's been talking to me a lot—opening up like I don't remember him ever doing before. I've never seen him be affected this bad by something. He has . . . He's been having dreams, you know? Nightmares. He thinks something bad's gonna happen to one of you kids."

"So when Kathleen got sick . . ." Russ's voice trailed off.

"Yeah, when that happened, I think he was pretty sure she was going to die. I could hardly even get him to eat. And then there's something else, too."

By Mark's expression, Russ was afraid the "something else" was going to be pretty bad. "What is it?"

"Son, I don't even know how to tell you this. And I don't know how you could even change it anyway, not if you're anything like your old man."

"What?"

"You swear you'll find some other way than to tell Arch we talked, right?"

"Sure."

"Then Russ, that feller you call your 'old man,' he's tough as nails. He could take on most any two or three men single-handedly and walk away the victor. But he can't walk away from what's ailing him now. And that's you."

"Me?"

"Yeah. You. All the years I've worked with your dad, half of what he talks about is his big hero of a son. Russ won this game, Russ won that game, Russ intercepted a pass and ran eighty yards, and nobody could bring him down. Now, mind you, I never got sick of him talking about you. It always made me happy, because you could tell he was on Cloud Nine when he'd talk about you."

Mark paused for a long time, while Russ's heart got more and more full thinking about what he had said.

"I don't know what happened with you two, buddy. But somebody better figure it out. I don't know if you ever felt like your old man was a friend to you, or only your father. But that tough old bird worshipped you. I don't know any other way to put it. Like I said, I don't know what happened, but here's something to think about: You look at your coach, Jardinsky. And look at your dad. He played college ball for a year, you know. Got busted up real bad, just like Jardinsky. You know, football is there, and then in a flash it can be gone. One bad injury. Or the scouts just don't like you. And it's all over. No career. No more ball. No more hero.

"But family, Russ—family should always be there. Don't ever forget that. You won't be a young man forever. If you burn all your family bridges now, they could take a long time to rebuild—and they might never be as strong again."

They drove for a long time after that without saying anything. But the inside of the squad car was full of energy, two men's thoughts going crazy.

"What do you think, Russ?" Mark asked as he was pulling back up to the curb behind Russ's car.

"I don't know how to start, Mark. I don't know what to do."

"Then you know what I'd do?"

"What?"

"I'd pray about it."

Russ chuckled, thinking back to the simpler days, back when he and his father used to make a joke of prayers over supper, back when his father used to pick him specially to give the prayer, because they had a deal: He would give a very fast, succinct prayer, and they could both go to eating. He also thought back to the time not long ago when his mother had asked the same thing of him—to pray.

"I don't really know how to do that either," he replied.

Mark gave him a long, serious look. "Well, I'd say that's something you'd better figure out. I know your mother sure is."

Russ nodded. About that, there was no doubt.

CHAPTER SIXTY-FOUR

Arch Blevins managed by some miracle to take Wednesday off and go with his wife to bring Kathleen home from the hospital. She spent that day in bed, resting, but at least she was home. Russ thought about his little sister throughout the day, knowing she was coming home, happy to think of her greeting him there, but somehow feeling sad and left out to know he couldn't be there when she was checked out of the hospital. He had never cared about anything like that before, but before this he had never faced the thought that one of his family members could actually die. That stark realization had changed a lot for Russ.

Russ hit it hard at football practice, making up for lost time. Down deep, he wondered if he wasn't running extra fast, hitting with compounded force, to try and chase away his jumbled thoughts, now mostly about his father. He wanted to be friends with his old man again, the way it used to be—except that even back then there had always been a distance between them. One was obviously the father, the other the son, and there was no blurry line between them. Yet at least they had enjoyed going places and doing things together. And now his father was always gone, and what could Russ do about that anyway? If they were going to become friends again, why did it have to be up to Russ? Couldn't his father meet him at least halfway?

Russ caught a pass while running full sprint. Two of his team mates tried to catch him, but their attempts were laughable. He was Russ Blevins! Good luck to any mere mortal who wanted to bring him down.

Strangely, right after he thought that and was prancing in the end zone, a strange twinge of guilt struck him. He remembered when he first started having thoughts like that. It had been all in fun. But now . . . Had he come to believe his own legends? He was only a man. A man who had lucked out with his genetics and then worked hard to polish his game. Probably much the same as Coach Jardinsky had done in his younger days. What was there that set Russ Blevins apart from the rest? Besides genetics, which was nothing but a game of chance, and his own hard work. And maybe the grace of God.

That thought struck him hard. He didn't remember even thanking God for any success he had out on the gridiron.

Russ avoided talking to Edie Russell that day. He got something like a gut ache every time he even thought about her, and once when he saw her he even started to break out in a sweat. That one time, he caught her looking his way, but he quickly averted his eyes, and when he looked back she had her head down in her usual manner, reading, or at least pretending to read, some book.

What had he done? Why had he kissed that girl? How was he going to tell her it meant nothing, that he was only trying to make her feel better? He could never leave Helen, especially not now. He had been in love with her for too long, and now she needed him. He finally had what he had always wanted, right in the palm of his hand.

So he spent the day avoiding Edie, and he noted with gladness during mid-practice that she hadn't made it to the bleachers, the way he had thought she might on this beautiful afternoon. At least he thought it was gladness. But then, looking at that empty place on the upper bleachers where the girl liked to sit and watch the boys practice, he felt lonely again, like there was a piece missing from the day.

He shrugged it off and tackled another runner to the ground.

Helen James didn't return to school until Friday morning. When Russ saw her walking in the hall, his heart leaped. There she was, back in his life again! He pushed through the between-class hallway crowd and caught her by the arm just as she reached her biology class.

"Helen!"

She turned. "Hi."

Russ enfolded her in his arms. But something was wrong. She felt stiff. As he pulled away, she looked up at him.

"It's good to see you," he said. But for some reason, it didn't feel like the fulfilling, wonderful reunion he had been imagining.

"You too. I'm glad to be back." Helen tried to smile.

"Is everything okay?"

"Sure. Why?"

"I don't know. It seems like you're distracted or something."

"No, just thinking about class, I guess."

"Did your mom get a new car?"

"Yeah. A forty-seven Ford sedan. It's not much. I'll be walking to school from now on anyway."

Russ felt an ache for her. Helen had never had to live like this. How were she and her mother going to adjust? Well, he would keep her safe. Inside, he promised her that.

"I guess I'd better get in," she said before he could think of anything wise and comforting to say.

"Oh yeah. All right, I'll see you later."

And he did see Helen later. Two or three times, in fact. But each time it seemed like she saw him first, and somehow she evaded him. Something was wrong. Had something happened to her while she was gone?

That afternoon, Russ went to football practice, and he was a few minutes late. As he ran out on the field and happened to glance over at

the east bleachers, his heart sang. There sat Helen! She had come to watch him practice. It was a sure sign that everything was going to be okay.

Russ made a perfect catch on the first pass Johnny Boo spiraled his way. He ran it into the end zone with three boys playing the other side doing their best to catch up. As he turned, a jolt went through him. There, in her normal place high on the west bleachers, sat Edie! He looked back over to the east bleachers, and Helen was still there as well.

This could be a real train wreck! But then he had never given Edie any real hope. Or had he? He had never told her there was anything but friendship between them, but he had never gotten around to telling her what he thought about their kiss, either. Well, one thing was for sure. Edie was a kind girl. She wouldn't tell Helen about their kiss, not in a million years. If there was one thing he knew about her, it was that.

And then he thought of Helen. If the tables were turned, he could not have said the same thing for her.

After running the ball several times and going through some plays, Coach Nalder set his boys to running wind sprints on the track, and after twenty minutes of those he told them to run two more miles at a moderate pace before cooling down with a slower half.

As Russ came around on his second-to-last lap, he saw Helen coming down the bleachers. She was heading home! And he hadn't even had a chance to talk to her.

But he couldn't just peel away from the track now. Nalder would be on him like a tarantula. Maybe it was for the best. He didn't want to see her right now anyway, as sweaty as he was. He could clean up and then go see her at her house later.

He was coming around the track for the last time when he looked up to see if Edie was still sitting in her place. When his pace faltered, Pete Basso almost ran right into him, having to shove off his shoulder to keep from colliding.

"Hey, bud, don't stop in the middle!"

"Sorry," Russ called after him as he stepped to the side of the track. He had another half-lap to go, but his mind was far from the track now. Helen James had not gone home at all. She was standing up in the west bleachers in front of Edie, who had set down her book.

Russ wanted to run over there and sprint up the bleachers. He wanted to be in on whatever conversation they were having. Edie wouldn't turn on him . . . would she? No. That was a sure thing. So what was going on? He had not been invited, but he had never wanted to be in on something more—or at least to be close by, and invisible, to hear what was passing between them.

As he was about to turn away, he saw Edie stand up. Before he could even think what was happening, they leaned closer, and the two of them were sharing an embrace!

Russ was stunned. He didn't even notice that Ev Morin had stopped beside him and was also watching the two girls.

"What the hay, man? Are they that good of friends?"

Bewildered, Russ shrugged. He couldn't begin to think what was going on. But whatever it was had his stomach in knots.

Trying to calm down, Russ started a light jog around the track. By now, everyone else was done sprinting, and they were moving around the track at a lazy jog. Russ slowed to a walk and looked at the bleachers. The last thing on his mind was exercise.

Edie and Helen were slowly walking down the bleachers. At the bottom, Edie turned and gave Helen another hug. Then she hugged her books to her (they seemed to be her best friends), turned, and walked briskly away toward the street. Helen sat down on the bottom bleacher and folded her arms, bowing her head.

When the coach released them to shower, Russ headed straight for Helen. Whatever had just happened, he couldn't leave to chance that if he went and showered she would be here when he came out. He didn't want a confrontation, but some things had to be handled immediately.

He walked up to Helen, and by the time he got there she had her face up and was looking past him at something—or perhaps at nothing.

"Hey," he greeted.

"Hey." Her voice was quiet. She was still beautiful, and the same sun glistened in her hair. But something was missing in her eyes.

"How's Edie?"

Helen looked up at him, shrugging with her face. "Good. Really good, I think. It's still so strange to think we're sisters."

"Yeah," he agreed. "I'll never get used to it."

Russ wanted to ask flat-out what they had been talking about. He hesitated. How did he ask that without sounding like a controlling jerk?

Helen stood up. She folded her hands behind her back. "Hey, Russ, we need to talk."

"Okay." The look in her eyes scared him.

"What do you really think of Edie?" she asked.

Oh no! Edie had spilled the beans! He knew it. She had told everything. What was he going to say? How could he possibly excuse what he had done?

He asked cautiously, "What do you mean?"

"I mean, don't you think she's a sweet girl? She has a lot going for her."

Russ laughed. It sounded forced because it was. The sound of his own voice almost made him nauseous, because he was trying to sound so cool, and he knew he was failing.

"What brought all this on? Yeah, she's all right, I guess. She's a nice kid."

"She's more than a nice kid," said Helen.

"Hey, I thought— You were pretty mad at her the other day." Russ was still thinking about the kiss. Something about Helen's voice and demeanor told him Edie hadn't said anything after all. What a great friend!

"Yeah. I was angry. But I've had time to think about it. A lot of time."

Helen turned her head and looked down the track, where Coach Nalder was picking up a towel and Jardinsky was jotting notes on a clipboard.

"Russ, we really need to talk about some things."

Jeez! So had Edie told on him, or hadn't she? He was in a dilemma. He had to play it close to the vest.

"Okay, I'm still listening. What's up, Helen? What's wrong?"

"Russ . . ." She looked up and met his eyes. "You're a great guy, you know? A super guy. Any girl would be lucky to have somebody like you."

His heart was starting to pound in a way he didn't like. It felt as if it were sending him a message by Morse code, and the message was not one he wanted to decipher.

"I'm glad you feel like that." His voice was cautious.

"But a good girl with a conscience would know when . . ."

She paused too long. "When *what,* Helen?"

"When a guy is too good for her." The words raced out of her mouth, as if she had to hurry them out to make sure they got said.

"What are you talking about?"

"Russ, I'm not the right girl for you."

It was like someone had dumped a bucket of ice water over Russ's head, and in the middle of January. *"What?* Why would you even say that? Come on, Helen! If it's about . . ." He started to bring up the kiss, then stopped.

"You know Edie has always thought you were Adonis."

He almost blushed. "Okay, so? I don't care about that."

"Well, you should. Russ . . ."

"Helen, what are you trying to say? Come on! We love each other. What are you doing?"

Her hands came from behind her back, and she took Russ's. "You're right." Tears filled her eyes, and she started to speak, then had to swallow before she could form words. "You're right. I do love you. You're everything I could ever want. But . . . This isn't right. I have to let you go."

"No, Helen. Stop this right now!"

"No, Russ, listen . . . I've seen Edie looking at you. And I've started to see you look at her too—in a certain way."

"What the heck are you talking about? Helen, that's *Edie!* She's just a nice girl! She's like my sister! She's nothing I'd ever be interested in."

"Please forgive me." She squeezed his hand. "But I think you're lying to yourself. I think on the surface you really mean that, but down deep you know better. Edie is a much better person than I am. You need to go to her. I could never be the good person she is."

"Please don't do this." Russ's guts were churning. "Come on. Let's give it a few days. We'll go to a movie and dinner tonight, maybe go up in the hills and look at the city lights. You need to clear your head, that's all."

"No, Russ. That's what I've been doing for these last two days—clearing my head. And now it's the clearest it's been in a long time—

longer than I can remember. It's you that needs to clear your head now." Without warning, tears spilled out of her eyes and rolled down both cheeks. She rushed them away with the sleeves of her sweater, looking down to avoid his eyes. "Sorry," she spoke to the ground. "I swore I wasn't going to do this."

Russ grabbed her by the upper arms. "Then why are you? You're not giving us a chance! Is it because I didn't do anything with you at the motel?"

Her eyes jumped up to his. "No! Russ, no! No," she said in a softer voice. "That was just . . . That was when I started to get confused. When I started trying to think through this whole thing—to really see. Russ, I may not be the smartest girl in the world, and you sure aren't the smartest guy, at least not about this kind of stuff. But anybody can see that you and Edie are meant to be together. Anyone can look at her and see how much she adores you. And you love her too."

"No, I don't! Where in the heck are you getting this? Helen! I want *you!* You're all I've ever dreamed of."

"Russ, let me tell you something. Something I've kept inside for a long time. Something I did. Something Edie Russell would have never done. She would have died first, before hurting you."

"What?" He was beyond confused.

"I have to say this. I don't know how but simply to say it. You know the tree, Russ? When you cut down the tree?"

"Huh?"

"Come on! Are you even listening? The tree!"

"Oh, yeah. Okay. What about it?"

"It was me that told on you. I was the one that got all of us in trouble. Not Edie, not Pete. Not anybody else. *Me!*"

Russ stared at her. The words didn't want to register. "What are you saying that for? I already know Pete did it. He told me so."

"Did he? Did he really? Then he lied."

Russ thought back on the day of his conversation with Pete in the locker room. The truth was Pete had denied doing it, right after saying he did. He had only said it out of frustration in the first place. It was Russ who had convicted him, on the moment.

"But . . . Why?"

"Because . . . somebody called my father and said they saw my car in the alley behind the school when it happened. I could tell he was adding everything up when it came out about the tree the next day. He confronted me. I knew it was just going to be me in trouble, and I caved in. I didn't want it to be me by myself, so I gave him every name. He said I would be punished alone if I didn't go tell the principal. So he made me do it. But I didn't *have* to give everyone else up. I didn't have to. My dad would never have known who else was involved. I just didn't want to take the fall alone. I caused everyone a lot of pain and suffering, and then I kept it from you. And even when you were suspecting Edie, and then Pete, I didn't say anything. I could have exonerated them at least to you any time, but I was so scared of what you would think."

Russ stared at her, his mind churning. The whole idea of being turned in by the girl he loved the most was startling. But then, it was so long ago and far away. Did it even matter now? It sure wasn't going to change his love for Helen, especially when he had left the saw there and would have been caught anyway. Besides, at least she had come clean about it now. Who hadn't made mistakes before?

"Well, I don't care about that," he finally said. "That's old news."

"Not for me, Russ. I'm sorry. You need to go find Edie. Maybe not right now. Maybe you need some time to think about all this. But one day you'll see I'm right. I promise you."

"No, I won't. I'm not giving up on us, Helen." Russ took a stubborn stance. He knew what was right for him.

Helen drew in a deep breath. "Well, I'm going to make it easy for you." The tears started to flow again, this time in earnest, before she could go on. Russ reached out to hold her, and she let him. She even met his embrace.

But at last she drew away again. "We're moving up to Moscow to live with my grandparents. Mother got a job as a receptionist in a dentist's office."

The shock hit Russ like a strike to his belly. "Helen, no! Why? Can't you tell her you want to stay, at least till we graduate?"

Helen searched his eyes. She sniffed and tried to dry her cheeks with her fingertips. "No, Russ, I can't. No. I'm the one that asked her if we could go."

CHAPTER SIXTY-FIVE

Their first Saturday game was the following day. Russ lay awake most of the night, thinking about Helen. When sleep did find him, it was fitful, filled with dark, frightening, hopeless dreams. In one of them, he dreamed that Kathleen, Helen, and little Isaac were all kidnapped and taken away. He tried desperately to get them back, but all to no avail.

He awoke soaked with sweat and got up to peer out the window into the back yard. The big spruce trees loomed there like giant sentinels, a barrier against the evil of the world.

He wanted to tiptoe down to the girls' room and look in, to make sure Kathleen was really there. It was funny how even with three teenage girls still in the house, it had seemed empty without Kathleen.

Pulling on his Levi's, he left the room and padded down the hall, through the kitchen, and down the back steps into the driveway. His father's sheriff car was there, its white body and the letters on the door gleaming silver in the starlight. It had been a long time since he stayed here in this house. Perhaps that was why he felt so restless. But his mother had called him at Ev's that evening after practice, telling him she made Sloppy Joes, one of his favorite meals, and asking him if he would come home, at least for a night. With the pleading in her voice, coupled with the sadness of what had happened with Helen, it hadn't taken much talking to get him here.

Now he didn't know if it was such a good idea. He hadn't felt so nervous at night in a long time, like he had to be so quiet or risk waking a sleeping giant. It wasn't like he was afraid of his father, and there were things he understood about him much more clearly now than he ever had before. But he still didn't have the strength to talk to him. At least not about anything of importance.

Saturday dawned cool and cloudy, smelling like distant rain. He didn't want to wake anyone, but he had noticed the lawn needed mowing

one more time before putting away the mower for the year, and he decided he should get to it before stormy weather set in.

As he started up the mower, going first to the back of the house, the farthest from his parents' window, he thought of the game that afternoon, away at Bonneville. He hoped it would be a success. He wanted to crush someone today. He wanted someone to know they might as well have stayed in the sixth grade to play ball, if they thought they could get anywhere against the Shelley Russets.

A light mist, almost more of a wet fog, was in the air by the time Russ turned off the lawnmower in front of the house and then went back by the garage to get out the hose, spray the damp new grass out from under it, then empty out the oil and the last of the fuel, the latter of which he ran through a funnel into his fuel tank after pouring it out into a bucket.

As he opened the side door that led up to the first floor of the house, or down into the basement, he could hear pans clunking in the kitchen, and he could already smell meat frying.

There was no way to get through to his room without being seen, at least without going around to the front door, and he wasn't about to cross the forbidden territory of the living room carpet with grass clippings on his sneakers.

Taking a deep breath, he took the few stairs up and made the corner. His father was sitting at the table with his back turned to him, a newspaper opened in front of him. But his mother was at the stove, and her left side faced him. She turned as she saw him and gave him a tentative smile and a wave. Russ waved back and started across the room for the hall that led to the bedrooms and bath.

Arch heard him, and he jerked his head around. He must have seen a glimpse of him, but Russ was already on the other side, so Arch cranked his body halfway around the other direction, looking up at him as he tried to pass.

"Russ?"

With a sinking feeling, Russ looked down. "Yeah, Pop?"

"Thanks for getting that lawn. Looks like it's going to rain."

Russ tried to smile. "Yeah, sure."

"Hey, did you clean the mower and get that oil and gas out of it?"

Russ had already turned to go, but he turned back. "Sure, Pop. Got it all, and the mower's back in the garage."

Arch looked like he wanted to smile. Russ felt a surge of hope.

"Okay, Son. I appreciate it." It looked like Arch wanted to say more. Whatever words were in there, they didn't come out. After a couple more seconds, he jerked the paper to straighten it out, then dropped his eyes back down to the words.

Russ went on down the hall and into his room. He could hear the girls stirring around, so he got into the bathroom as fast as he could and cleaned up, then got dressed. The bus would be leaving soon for Idaho Falls, so he had to eat and run.

He went back to the kitchen. His mother had three pans covered on the stove, now with all the burners off. "I made you a big breakfast. Did you sleep okay? You sounded sort of restless."

"I guess. Hey, Mom? Oh, never mind. It's not important."

"What, Son?"

"Nothing. Really." He was thinking about Helen. He hadn't told a soul about yesterday, not even Ev. He had to talk. But he didn't know how. "I wanted to see if you bought any new Tabasco. We were out."

Eleanor gave him a strange look. "Tabasco? Well, yes, I did."

Russ thought he had dodged the bullet. He got a plate and filled it with hash browns, sausage, biscuits and gravy. One of his favorite breakfasts, if not number one.

"Thanks, Ma," he said quietly. He sat down and bowed his head to the task.

His mother was watching him, and she interrupted. "Maybe you should bless the food. And you could say a little prayer to keep you safe today too."

He looked up at her questioningly.

"Don't you think?" she asked, cocking her head a little. "It wouldn't hurt, right?"

He forced a smile, glancing over at his father. Arch still had the paper up, but he was surreptitiously watching his son over the top of his reading glasses. The moment Russ looked over, he dropped his eyes again. And then, without being nudged, he lay the paper down and bowed his head.

With his heart pounding, Russ lowered his head. He wasn't prepared to speak to God out loud yet, because he wasn't ready for his father to hear anything of true importance he had to say. But whenever he ended up praying silently, part of it was for his own stubbornness. And he just as quickly brushed the prayer away and assumed it wouldn't work. He was his father's son. This prayer was quick and meaningless.

Russ ate, then went and picked up Ev, Pete Basso, and Mark Knaggs. He had called them all the night before to ask if he could get them.

When they were all in the car, Russ pulled over. Mark's eyes darted around, and he scooted forward on his seat, as if that would help him see better. "What's up? Your car okay?"

"Cool it, Spit. I just have somethin' I gotta tell you guys, all right?"

Ev glanced back at the others. "All right, bud. What's up?"

"Hey, uh . . . First off, Pete—I owe you an apology. I thought you were the one that turned us in for cutting down the tree."

"What?

"Yeah. Sorry. But you said you did it!"

"Huh? When?"

"When we were talking about it in the locker room."

"Oh, jeez! Man, I was being sarcastic."

"Yeah, I know now. I know who it was. But I don't want you guys to be mad, all right? I'm only telling you because I guess it's probably still bugging you pretty bad like it was me."

"Come on, man!" cut in Ev. "Who was it already?"

"Promise you won't be mad at 'em?"

"Whatever," shot back Mark. "Just spill the beans."

Russ told them the story, exactly as it had been told to him the day before. Everyone was silent for a long time. For a while, nobody would even look at one another.

"That's heavy," Ev finally said. "You okay? You're the one that got it the worst, because of your old man."

"Yeah." A little chuckle escaped Russ. "That actually turned out to be a pretty good workout. I've yanked those railroad ties around quite a few times since then. Yeah, guys, I'm fine. I just thought you should know. And something else—only for you guys." He took a big breath. "Helen's moving to Moscow to live with her grandparents."

It took all the strength he had to get out the words. Then he threw the car back into second and pulled away from the curb, driving slowly away. Nobody said a word. With a car full of football players on the way to a game, Russ had never heard the car so silent.

They pulled up on the street in front of the school and got out. Ev waited by the front bumper for Russ to come around, as the other two boys cast them furtive glances but hoisted their duffel bags and fled for the waiting bus, and safety.

"Hey, bud."

Russ stopped, fidgeting with the handles of his bag.

"You doin' okay?"

"Sure. Why?"

"Aw, come on, man! We've been friends our whole lives. I'm no idiot. You've been in love with Helen forever. You gonna be able to be in the game?"

Russ clenched his jaw. "Heck yeah. It's nothing but life, right?"

Ev searched his friend's eyes. "Come off it, Russ. This isn't just life. This is the girl of your dreams."

The words echoed hollowly in Russ's head. Yes, there was a feeling there, but it wasn't the pain he would have thought he would feel. It was something else. Just . . . emptiness.

"I'm gonna be all right, buddy. Thanks for asking." He clapped his friend on the shoulder. "Really."

And then a picture of Edie Russell came into his mind, smiling and looking at him through those silly, black-rimmed glasses. Suddenly, he wanted to see Edie, more than anyone else in the world. But it was a desire he wouldn't have told to anyone else, not even Ev.

On the bus, they were talking about crushing the Bonneville Bees. It was mostly Russ, trying to give the boys a pep talk. The coaches were up front, going over plays, where Russ should have been as well.

After a while, Russ heard one of the sophomore players, Tige, talking about one of the Bonneville Bees.

"Yeah, they've got a player named Norman Barrett—a new halfback. Young kid. Do any of you guys remember his big brother, Joe?"

Russ scooted forward on his seat. He remembered Joe Barrett. They were the same age and had met many times on the field. He was a funny-looking kid, but he sure could tackle, and he could really run the ball.

One of the other kids egged Tige on.

"Well, so I guess Joe got killed two weeks ago in a farming accident. Tractor rolled over on him."

Russ's heart leaped, and without thinking he blurted out a curse. "What? You said Joe's dead?"

"Yeah," said Tige, seeming a little intimidated that Russ would talk to him personally.

"Man, that's rough stuff," said Nash Wheeler after a moment of quiet awe. Nobody else had found their tongue.

Russ sank back in his seat. Joe Barrett was gone. It was hard to fathom. He was one of the few Bees Russ would have cared to see again—a good, level-headed player who always kept his team squared away. Russ wasn't able to talk to anyone for minutes after that.

This was a sure example of what Deputy Daniels had told him: Football was great, but from one day to the next it could be gone. He had to live his life while he could, and above all, he had to recognize the things that were most important.

CHAPTER SIXTY-SIX

They pulled into the parking lot at Bonneville, and everyone piled out, tired of the stale air in the bus. It was overcast here, but not misty like it had been back home. Russ scanned the sky. It was going to be a good game. At least he guessed it would. In reality, where earlier all he could think about was crushing the Bees, now he could think only of Norman Barrett, playing without his big brother in what would have been Joe's last season on the gridiron, even if nothing had happened to him. But no one could have expected it to be this way.

Russ was quiet in the locker room, working his shoulders to loosen them up, then his back, his hips, and his knees. Lastly, he worked on his arms and wrists. Edie and Helen flashed through his mind now and then, but mostly he couldn't stop thinking about that poor kid, Norman Barrett. He had to get back in the game! They were going to crush these guys!

Taking several deep breaths, he got up and let out a roar. Several of the other players, after getting over him startling them, echoed him. He did it again, and they *all* joined in. He looked over at Ev and nodded. He sure did love that kid.

The crowd was all out there already. Their pep bands were playing, and drill teams were working the spectators up to a frenzy. It was a pretty quiet frenzy whenever it came the Russets' turn. Very few people would drive all the way from Shelley, even for a football game. Russ certainly wasn't going to have anyone there.

At last, they ran out on the field. The cheers were louder than Russ had expected, which made him smile in happy confusion. They ran in a big arc and came back to join their coaches, huddling up.

Nalder, and then Jardinsky, worked them up with patriotic words. The boys were all excited. Russ wondered if anyone here could possibly be going through what he was right now, the gamut of emotions that were tearing him in every direction.

After the group huddle, Russ went over to Coach Jardinsky. "Hey, coach!"

"Hey, bud! You ready for a great game?"

"Yeah, but . . ."

Jardinsky read something in Russ's face. As gruff as he liked to act, this man knew all his boys well. "What's up, son? Something on your mind?"

"Yeah. Hey, did you hear about Joe Barrett?"

"That the big fullback? Oh, wait—yeah, I heard he got killed a couple weeks ago, yeah. Tough luck, huh?"

Tough luck! Those weren't the words Russ would have chosen. "Yeah, I guess."

"What about him?"

"So I guess he's got a little brother on the team—a halfback."

"Oh. Okay?"

"And . . . Man, Coach, I don't want to play him right now."

"Huh? What are you talking about?"

"I don't want to play him."

"I'm not gettin' you, Russ. Lay it on the line. It's almost tipoff."

"I can't tackle him."

"Hell, you can't! You can tackle anybody out there! Russ, what's up? I've never heard you talk like this! You've gotta get your head in the game." All of a sudden, Jardinsky stopped. "Hey, son, are you doing okay?"

"Yeah, coach, I just . . ." He couldn't finish.

"Listen, buddy . . . So you're telling me you want the Bees to have a sporting chance. Well, that's kind of up to them, ain't it?"

"What do you mean?"

"It's not up to you to hand them a game."

"I know, but—"

"Listen, Russ. We've only got a couple seconds. I want you to imagine how you'd feel if another team heard something bad had happened to you, and they started feeling sorry for you. So they let you win a game. Maybe handed you a few touchdowns. It would be pretty obvious to you, right? You'd know they weren't playing their best. It would be a slap in

the face. Who'd want to win something that didn't really belong to them?"

Russ swallowed hard. He realized he had made a major mistake. He should never have talked to Jardinsky about something like this. And in the second place, Jardinsky was right. He would be furious to win a game that some other, better, team had handed him.

He forced himself to grin. "Yeah, I was just having fun with you, Coach. I'll knock him down!"

"There you go!" Jardinsky growled. "Jeez, kid, this isn't any time to be clowning around. Now get out there!"

Russ ran out, feeling a glow of warmth for his coach. That big, tough bird knew him. He knew he hadn't been joking. But his mistake was just as soon forgotten. Now they would have a game.

Hell or high water.

The coin toss went to the Bees. Russ had his eye on Number 42, Norman Barrett. He prayed he wouldn't get the ball. Barrett got the ball.

First play out of the chute, and Norman Barrett had the ball. He was running his heart out for the end zone. He was in the open. Russ got away from his guard and roared like a freight train across the field. He struck Barrett from the side, raising him off his feet with the force and sending him flying. Barrett lost the ball, and a Russet picked it up.

Less than a minute into the game, and Russ's team already had the ball back in their possession. He couldn't help thinking back on the game with the Bees last fall. Fourth quarter, the score was thirty-five to zero. The Russets roared with delight. They had sworn that this time the Potatoes were going to lick the honey-makers, and they did. They made two more touchdowns and won the game forty-nine to zero. And how they had crowed and strutted as they walked off the field that day.

By the end of that one, Joe Barrett was sitting on the sidelines because of a bad limp—thanks to Russ.

Now Russ's head was back in today. They scored a touchdown like strolling past babies, and the conversion was good as well. The ball went back to the Bees, who couldn't hold it. They tried for a field goal on the fourth down, didn't make it, and the ball reverted to the Russets. Seven to one, and the game had just got going.

Russ ran it in again, this time for a forty-yard touchdown. His team cheered, the coaches cheered, and the few Russet fans who had made the trip cheered. Russ looked around until he found Number 42. Norman Barrett was loping off the field with his head down. Any spring was already gone from his step. Fourteen points to zero, four minutes in the game. Russ had a sour taste in his mouth. He had sworn to have a zero-loss season. But suddenly it scared him. He didn't want to win like this. The 1955 Bees were helpless.

Russ looked over at the Bees, and somebody was working them up into a frenzy. That gave him hope for them. Russ didn't want to crush them anymore. He wanted them to score, at least once. And in particular, he wanted Norman Barrett to score.

A Bees fullback, Number 28, got the ball and ran. Russ could have stopped him sooner, but somehow he slipped past his defenses. Finally, Russet safety Number 65 took him to the ground, but not until he was only fifteen yards from the end zone.

In an angry voice, Russ heard Jardinsky yelling. He had called for a time-out and he got the team together on the sideline. The coach turned all his fire straight on Russ. "What the hell was that, Blevins? You had that guy and let him slip past you."

Russ cringed. He hadn't thought it was so obvious. "Yeah, sorry about that, Coach. My foot twisted on the grass."

"Huh?" the big coach bellowed. Then he yelled, "Never mind! Just don't let that crap happen again. Get your head in the game!"

But it didn't matter. Even with his head in the game, Russ was too far away from Norman Barrett the next time he got the ball in his hands. Barrett ran for all he was worth. And made it. All the way to a Bees touchdown.

Russ wanted to leap into the air and cheer, but he managed to hold his excitement in. He would have liked to run over and congratulate the boy on his touchdown, his first ever against the Russets, but even as dumb as Russ could be, he knew that was bad decorum. Until the game was over, going out of one's way to go over to the other side and tell them they did a good job was tantamount to suicide—at least in the eyes of his team and coach.

He was walking back to his huddle when he happened to look over in the stands where the Shelley fans were gathered. It was only a casual glance, not in search of anyone in particular, but a familiar face caught his eye. Jerking his head back to scan the crowd, he couldn't believe his eyes. There sat Edie Russell! He couldn't have been happier to see anyone. And seated next to her was little Isaac Thorpe. They were soon joined by others, a line of people coming up the bleachers in single file. Frank and Lorna Russell, his sisters, Dorothy, Annie, Toni, and even little Kathleen! And behind them came his mother, and then . . . Russ froze. His father had come, all the way from Shelley! His father had come to his game. Russ wasn't sure why, but it felt as if he floated back to the huddle.

They won the game thirty-five to seventeen. It wasn't easy. They had to work for it. When it was over, and the Russets were screaming in the delight of victory, Russ ran over and caught Norman Barrett.

"Hey! Barrett!"

Helmet hanging at his side, the sophomore turned to see who was hailing him. Sweat plastered his hair to his forehead.

A surprised look came over his face as he saw Russ coming up. Three of his teammates stopped nearby, all watching Russ warily. Did they think he was coming over for a fight?

"Hey, man, I heard about Joe."

Norman nodded. "Yeah."

"Well, I wanted to tell you how sorry I am. He was a dang good player—and a good man. I always liked meeting him on the field."

The words seemed to catch Norman Barrett off-guard, for his eyes filled with tears, snapped downward, and blinked a couple of times.

"Hey, man, thanks. He would have liked to hear that."

"Yeah, no problem. Good game, huh?" He walked close, on a whim, and thrust out his hand. Barrett shook it and gave him a smile.

Russ nodded and looked around at the other boys, giving them a nod as well. "See you all around."

With that, he turned and trotted off. When he got close to his team, he slowed to a walk. They were still celebrating, and their families had come down among them on the field.

Russ looked over to see all his people gathered at the base of the bleachers. There was Edie, right in front, holding Isaac's hand. Russ nearly lost it then. He started across the field, with no idea that there were two other fans standing there as well, two who had been there since the very start of the game, seated way up on the far end of the bleachers.

Russ couldn't help but think of Norman Barrett as he strode across the field. If Barrett had won this ball game, it would have to have been fair and square. That was only right. And Helen hadn't given the game to Edie, either. Edie had been working at it for a long time, and she had been winning Russ Blevins for weeks.

Holding himself in check for a moment, trying not to look at Edie, Russ scanned his group. "Hey, everybody. Wow! I'm glad you came." He looked down at Isaac. "Hey, little man!" He squeezed the side of his neck. "I'm glad you're here!"

Then, with all his heart, he turned and threw his arms around Edie Russell and squeezed her to him. Until today, he had never realized it, but he loved this girl, more than anything. He was never going to let her go, not in a thousand lifetimes.

Up in the stands, Helen James's hand came up to her mouth, and she started to cry. Pearl James turned to her and put her arms around her, like a hen settling its wings over one of its chicks to keep it safe.

CHAPTER SIXTY-SEVEN

Luther Dean got on his Indian Chief motorcycle and launched himself out of Shelley, Idaho. He found himself heading south on Sugar Factory Road, and in time he turned on Goshen Road and made his way back to his old home place. There was nothing here for him anymore, of course, but he had to see it one last time.

It appeared as if no one had been here since the day he picked up his car. He parked the bike on the sidewalk leading up to the front door and strolled around through the brittle, yellow grass. Had there been anyone

walking on grass this dry during the summer, the lawn would have been dust by now.

He took a last walk through the house, glancing around. The memories flooded back over him.

"I meant to be there for you, Mama. I would have been too."

He thought of Sheriff Arch Blevins, and of his plan . . .

Getting back on the Indian Chief, Luther drove out past Presto Hill, then up into Blackfoot River country, making his way along the dirt and gravel road past sagebrush and harvested grain fields.

His plan was in place. It was in place, but even more perfectly than he had imagined. As everything came together, it had worried him that he was putting his buddy Billy Earl into the middle of everything—an accomplice. The whole thing was going to culminate right there at Billy's house. But then, on a walk of the neighborhood one night, he realized there was a house farther up the street that had stood abandoned all summer. And it was poetically right across the street from the sheriff's house. So why was there any need, after all, to point a finger at Billy? They would simply do everything in that abandoned house. Billy could help him do what needed to be done, and then when Luther fled town for the last time, Billy could go out the back door and make his way back to his own safe little abode. It was perfect.

The bomb in Blackfoot, and the bomb scares in Idaho Falls, that was another story. There was a strung-out old World War II vet years ago who had fallen on hard times and stolen a car, which he tried to sell in Nampa. But that vet was captured and sent to the pen, and it was there that Luther Dean made his acquaintance. The old vet had been out of the pen for some time now.

Luther knew the man lived in the Blackfoot area, and with a little work he had located him. They had a nice reunion. And the vet was every bit as down and out as before, and gaunt to the point of looking like the proverbial toothpick. Luther offered him a little money. All his friend had to do was light off a fuse at the back of a building off Main Street in Blackfoot, and do it at just the right time. Simple. That would set off an explosion, which in turn would ignite nearly a whole block of buildings, and require so much help from the fire, police, and sheriff's departments

that there would be no one to spare anywhere else—no one, that is, except for one who was already far away. And the vet was bitter enough with the world that he didn't need much of a payment to take part in the plan.

Feeling the wind in his face, Luther smiled. The puzzle was almost finished. It was a huge boon that very few lawmen had car radios, but he knew for a fact that Sheriff Blevins did—he had gone to his house late one night and made sure. And then, pretending to be a radio salesman, he had called around to the other law enforcement agencies, and in every instance was told that they couldn't afford anything like that.

So while Arch Blevins could be called to the scene of an emergency, very few other peace officers could. Blevins would be alone . . .

And then there was that one loose end. And as far as that thing was concerned, there was no choice. Other than Blevins, Luther didn't want to kill anyone, but with that one person he wasn't going to have any choice.

He had to keep Billy Earl safe, at all costs. He was the only true friend he had in the world.

● ● ● ● ●

The next morning, the phone rang, and Eleanor Blevins answered it. Russ was watching her, and a disappointed look came over her face. She called Arch to get the phone.

It was obvious to Russ what the conversation was about, and as his father hung up the phone and turned to his mother, Russ knew what he was going to say before he said it.

"Hey, I have to go out of town after work tonight."

Russ saw the sadness in his mother's eyes. He heard the gruffness in his father's voice, and saw the set of his jaw. Right then, he didn't really care about anything but making his mother happy. If his father felt compelled to go to another county and work a case because they were too inept to do it themselves, that was his business. But it was time he changed the way he went about it. And it was obvious that no one but Russ would ever say a word.

"Hey, Pop?"

Arch turned and looked distractedly at him. "Yeah?"

"You got a big case, don't you?"

Arch's gaze faltered. "Uh, yeah. Something like that."

Russ knew by the look on his father's face that he was on thin ice. But he had to bull on, if only for his mother.

"Why don't you at least tell Mom what it is?"

For a moment, Arch looked confused. "Huh?"

"Why don't you tell Mom where you're going when you're gone all the time? We're not little kids, you know."

Arch Blevins stared at his son while the words were trying to register. His eyes jumped over for a second to his wife, but then they drilled Russ once more.

"Don't you think you're a little out of line?"

"No! Pop, you gotta stop treating us like children. We'd understand if you just said what you're doing."

"NO YOU WOULDN'T! NONE OF YOU WOULD!"

It had been a long time since Russ had seen his father lose his cool so completely. But there he stood, his face dark red, his eyes looking swollen, staring Russ down with an open hand partway raised.

"What are you gonna do—hit me?" Russ glared back at his father. Eleanor was too spellbound to act one way or another.

Like a huge, angry bull with too many opponents to face, Arch stared first at Russ, then at Eleanor, and last at Toni, who had heard the anger in her father's voice and run down the hall to see what was happening.

At last, Arch turned to his wife, blinking his eyes with exaggeration. "Forget breakfast. I'll get something somewhere else."

With no more acknowledgment of Eleanor, Russ, Toni, or the other three girls, who had now come into the room, Arch picked up his hat and gun belt and stomped through the kitchen and down the back stairs, out to the driveway.

After a sufficient period for his car to warm up, they heard it back out of the driveway. The entire time, no one else moved.

Late that night, Arch Blevins returned home after Eleanor and the girls were in bed. There was no Russ. He had gone to stay with Ev Morin, and he had no hard plans of coming back before he headed off to find an apartment in whatever town had a university with enough sense to pick up the fastest, toughest halfback in Idaho.

Arch had not seen Russ's car in the drive, but even so, he knocked lightly on his door. No answer. He pushed open the door and glanced about the room. His son was no more of a nostalgic person than he was, but for some reason there were certain things he had kept all these years. One was his first football.

Crossing to Russ's dresser, Arch picked the battered old football up in one big hand. Not that it was difficult—it was only a child's ball. He stood there looking at that ball, a ball he still remembered buying, down at Woolworth's. He slapped it back and forth between his hands, drew a deep breath, and looked one more time around the room. It felt like his heart was trying to burst.

Before he could feel any foolish emotions, he left the room and eased the door shut. He plodded on down to his own room, thinking briefly about looking in at his girls. With an aching hand—because Arch Blevins ached all over—he eased his door open. There was a lamp on by his side of the bed, and Eleanor lay there with her face the other direction, the covers pulled up tight around her.

He felt his big frame begin to shake as he walked around to her side of the bed and sat. Eleanor dragged her eyes open and looked up, "Hi, dear."

"Hi."

"How was your day?"

"About the same as always."

She brought herself partway up on her elbow. "You okay?"

She could read him. He knew it. Too many times throughout their marriage she had read him, although during this particular time of trial he had tried harder than ever to keep a mask over his face.

He thought of the Idaho Falls girl, lying there dead. Mutilated. He thought of his girls, especially Annie, who was the same age and could so easily have been that girl from Idaho Falls. He thought of Eleanor's great big, unscarred heart. How could he ever involve the women he loved in something like that?

But he had thought all day about what Russ said to him, and maybe Russ was right. It would relieve so much stress if someone else in his tight-knit group knew what he was going through.

"Talk to me, Arch," said Eleanor. By the look in her eyes, he could see that she was getting frightened by his demeanor. And he didn't blame her. He wondered if he had looked like this in years, because he certainly hadn't felt this way in that long.

"She was such a sweet girl, Ellie."

"Huh?" Eleanor stared at him.

"That girl. Janet Hartford. From Idaho Falls. Such a gentle-looking thing. She—"

He stopped. How was he going to go on? How could he do this to his family?

His chin started to quiver. He had to forge on, fast.

"Her mother and father had these big dreams for her. She played the piano, and danced, and . . ." Somehow, a smile came to his face. "She kept this Teddy Bear—like Kathleen. Now her room just sits there, empty."

He couldn't stop the flow. Arch Blevins couldn't remember crying in front of someone, about anything. But the tears surged up in his eyes and began to tumble down, and as Eleanor struggled under the covers to come up and embrace him, he began to sob out loud, and his head felt as if it would burst. If Russ had been sleeping across the hall tonight, he would have heard him. His big, dauntless football star would have heard him weeping like a little, lost girl. It was already too much for him knowing all four of his daughters were over there, and that they could never possibly think of their father the same way after this.

Arch Blevins was thankful his son was not in the house that night.

CHAPTER SIXTY-EIGHT

The Idaho high school football season flew by, and the State championship game came down, to the surprise of no one, to the Shelley Russets and the Rigby Trojans. The big game would be on Saturday afternoon, to begin at two o'clock.

Friday, November twenty-fifth, was a light practice for the Russets. After it was finished, Coaches Jardinsky and Nalder called their team together in the locker room, which after months of practices smelled so bad no one but a football player would willingly have set foot in there.

In spite of an overriding feeling of excitement about tomorrow's State Championship, which would be held right there on Shelley's field, there was also a sense of awe in the room. This would be the Russets' fourth shot at a state title in as many years. They had taken State two years earlier, against the Firth Cougars, but lost to the Trojans when Russ was a freshman, and once again in 1954. Now, as luck would have it, they were facing the Trojans once again. And it would be Russ's last time.

But this time, the Russets had enjoyed a no-loss season, while the Trojans had lost once—to them. And now, the rumor had it that they were hot for revenge. Russ would have been surprised had it been otherwise.

The team quieted down more quickly than normal. There was a feeling in the stale-smelling, echoey room, a feeling of reverence. For a long while, Jardinsky didn't say a word. He glanced about the room with a sense almost of reverence about him, his hands not fisted on his hips, in his normal pose, but folded down in front of him. Dan Nalder's were folded behind.

"There's not gonna be any yellin' in here tonight, boys."

The big coach's words were followed by moments of silence, and a few flickering eyelids. What was the catch?

"I don't want to yell at you tonight. No, I don't. I know that probably surprises most of you. All of you, maybe."

The boys laughed politely, glancing around at each other, still waiting for the joke.

"No, boys, what I want to say tonight," he went on in his deep, gruff voice, "is how damn proud I am of you. All of you. And you can go run home and tell your mommies I said a cuss word if you want to. That's okay. But I've never been much prouder of a ball team than I am of you boys this year."

As he finished that statement, his eyes were settling on Russ, and he gave him a wink.

"You know, boys, we all have our funny nicknames for each other. There's Cus, and Nash, Spit, Slick Fingers, Egg, Side-Swipe, and Wop. Johnny Boo." As he ticked off each pet name, he swapped glances with its owner. "Might surprise you all that I've known all along about your 'Yardinsky' name for me." Surprised looks. Jardinsky laughed. "Hell, I don't care! I know I've gotten pretty wide—a yard wide, at least! It's all in fun. But tonight? Tonight, and tomorrow, and for the rest of your lives, the name you all should be known by, first and foremost, is Mister. Or Sir. Because you boys have earned it. You've stuck together, you've watched each other's backs. Even those among you who believe you're some kind of superstar, or a football god," —he glanced at Russ— "you've played this season for your team. And that's why we're number one."

He jutted his big, crooked finger up in the air. "Number one! You hear me? That's something to be proud of, boys—*men.* Somethin' to take home and set up on the mantle: A big sign that says 'WE WERE A TEAM'. Boys, if I were your families, I would be bustin' buttons off my shirts thinkin' about you. You've shown fire and fight, but even with all that, you've shown some compassion to the other teams you've fought—no, *played,* with. And that right there is the mark of a great man.

"But I've gotta tell you all a story. I haven't told it in a while, so I hope you'll bear with me. Back on November twenty-second, 1945, I was standing on the scrimmage line right where you men are gonna stand

tomorrow. I was a Detroit Lion. Maybe the toughest, cockiest ball player alive. There we were, facing the Cleveland Rams, in Briggs Stadium. Forty thousand people in the stands!

"I was up on top of the world. On *top!* Then, right at the middle of the third quarter, I had the ball. Had what I thought was a clear shot to the Rams' end zone. Had it made. But Tom Fears and Luke Higgins had other ideas. Them two Rams came out of nowhere. I swear I never saw 'em. Slipped past their guards, came at me. Fears hit me up high, Higgins down low, right below the knee.

"Shattered me. I never felt a worse pain in my life. And as I lay there on that field, looking up at the sky, I knew it was all over. Football was done. Nobody had to tell me. I heard the sound, and there's nothing like it in the world. Nothing. Luke Higgins, a good old boy out of Jersey, he felt real bad. His coach couldn't hardly drag him away from me. He kept tellin' me how sorry he was. I believed him, too. But it didn't make it any easier.

"Yep, football was over. A whole new life was begun that game. Boys, they say we get to make our own destiny. Well, I'm here to tell you that ain't always true. Sometimes there are things that happen that simply aren't ours to control.

"What counts is playing it clean. All right? You play it clean. You play it square. You play it like you know God's watchin' you. You play for all you're worth, and then if it turns out that God has somethin' different in the cards for you than what might have been your first choice, you roll with it.

"I might not ever have met you boys if I hadn't got hurt that day. I mighta kept on playin' pro, mighta made a helluva lot of money, mighta retired and been livin' high on the hog in some mansion right now. And you know what? That would have been a real shame."

There was dead silence in the room. Some of the boys had tears in their eyes. Great big Charlie Braun reached up with a paw and swept both of his eyes, looking down at the floor and trying to pretend he was removing something from his eye.

"Wouldn't that have been a shame, Morin?" Jardinsky zeroed in on Ev, leaning down closer to him.

"Yes sir."

"*What* would have been a shame?"

Ev stared at him, confused. "I'm not sure what you mean."

A corner of Jardinsky's mouth came up. "It would have been a shame not meetin' you boys."

Jardinsky let his words settle on the boys for several seconds.

"Yeah. Not meetin' you boys. That would have been a shame. If I hadn't got my leg hurt, I would never have gotten to meet this room full of great boys. That's right. Now, whatever happens tomorrow, we're done doing this thing together. Some of you might go on and play in college, and maybe even go pro." He looked right at Russ. "But a lot of you seniors are going to go off into the real world, get married, and get other jobs, and this is it for you. Tomorrow afternoon. The end. Win or lose. But I have to tell you no matter what happens tomorrow, for me and the Russets, as a unit, football is over."

Russ stared up at his coach. He glanced over at Dan Nalder, trying to see if he could read anything in his eyes. This little speech was like nothing he had ever heard from Ivan Jardinsky in four years of football. What was he trying to say?

Nalder gave a sad little smile to Russ. A sick feeling came into Russ's chest. This was it? Jardinsky was leaving!

Russ straightened up on his bench. "What are you trying to tell us, Coach? You . . ." He couldn't finish his thought.

"Yep." Jardinsky nodded. The tears that suddenly flooded his eyes must have surprised him as much as they did everyone else. He looked over helplessly at his assistant coach and drew in a deep, broken breath. "Sorry, boys. I didn't know a better time to tell you. I'll be going to work for the Los Angeles Rams this year." He tried to grin. "Yeah, ain't that somethin'? The Rams! The team that crippled me up ten years ago, and now I'll be going out to help coach them. Life's a funny thing."

Jardinsky stood there for a long time and looked over his boys, meeting the eyes of those who were able. The not-so-dry eyes in the room must have overwhelmed him, for suddenly he swore. "Well, I wasn't expecting a bawl baby session, here. Come on, guys!"

The team began to stand up, and they grouped around Jardinsky, shaking hands and patting him on the back, telling him congratulations. Russ and Ev were the last two waiting. Russ's heart was breaking for this

team. The Shelley Russets would never be the same. What a way to end his four-year run.

While the other players were wordlessly going about showering and getting dressed, Ev walked right up and gave Jardinsky his biggest hug, unable to stop the tears that were flowing down his cheeks. Russ's embrace was stronger, but not by much. Coach Dan Nalder had become a good friend to him, but Ivan Jardinsky had become like the father Russ should have had, unlike the father who had grown too distant to reach. He was glad he would not be around for next year's season. He could not imagine the Shelley Russets without Ivan Jardinsky.

● ● ● ● ●

Luther Dean sat in front of the television, with no idea what program was playing. That was the farthest thing from his mind. He had worked long and hard. His buddy, Billy Earl, was an integral part of the plan, but not the planning. Oh, he had been fine for running ideas off of, but Billy didn't have the kind of sharp mind needed for planning big jobs like what Luther had planned. So Luther had gone it alone. While Billy was gone to work, up in Idaho Falls, working at the mechanic shop, Luther spent many hours lying on the couch, the record player or television droning in the background, while he scoured maps of Idaho Falls, Blackfoot, Firth, and Shelley, while he figured out what places were most likely to have the greatest crowds, and when.

His first plan had involved setting off an explosion at a local school, probably in Blackfoot. Then a well-planned phone call warning the authorities that there were two or three more such explosions set to go off at other locations in the area. Simple. He had only to get Arch Blevins to a far-away area before the explosion and the phone call that promised more, to get him in some place where he would be all alone.

But the final plan came down to something less deadly for the school children. It came down to the downtown area of Blackfoot. The bomb there was going to wreak havoc, but hopefully not kill quite as many people.

Getting Arch Blevins to a remote location was easy. All he had to do was to start calling the Bingham County sheriff's department, pretending to be a reporter, to find out that he was working on a big murder case. From there, it was a short ride to the discovery that there had been only

one murder in the area of late, and that was not in Bingham County, but Butte. An article in the Idaho Falls *Post Register* claimed there was an outside source helping solve the grisly murder of a local teen, and *bam*! Arch Blevins was nailed down.

If Arch Blevins had been the legendary alert lawman he was famed to be, he might have seen Luther Dean follow him away from the sheriff's office, not only once, but many times. He might have seen Luther Dean's Indian Chief bike behind him on Saturday mornings, shadowing him out of town on his long rides out to Arco to visit the Butte County sheriff.

But Arch Blevins was not that man. He never noticed Luther Dean on his motorcycle, and had never suspected a thing.

Arch Blevins had been sly enough only to put a man behind bars for crimes he didn't commit, crimes committed by that man's brother, and to keep him in prison until his mother died. And now, at last, Arch Blevins was going to pay.

CHAPTER SIXTY-NINE

Russ and Ev were quiet that afternoon on the way home. When Russ pulled up in the Morins' driveway, he threw it into neutral, then put both hands back on the wheel and drew in a big breath. Ev sighed and leaned down a little to look out the windshield at the front door of the house. Surreptitiously, he looked over at Russ. After another moment of silence, both boys knew one of them had to speak.

"You're pretty quiet," said Ev.

Russ nodded soberly. He wanted to say something. He really needed to talk. But he didn't know how to start.

"What's on your mind, buddy?"

Russ gave a sigh of his own. "Oh, man, I don't know. Thinkin' about Coach, I guess."

"That all?"

As always, Ev was too smart for his own good.

"No, not really." *Take the chance, Russ! Talk, for cripes' sake!* "Hey, Ev?" The cat got his tongue again. He looked out his window, avoiding his friend's eyes.

"Jeez, what's up? It must be a big one."

Russ looked back at his friend. His heart was throbbing. "Yeah. I guess. So I got a question for you: How do you and your old man keep gettin' along so great?"

Ev frowned thoughtfully for a few moments. "Heck, I don't know. Maybe because we're nothing alike."

"Huh?"

Ev laughed. "Sorry. I know that sounds stupid. But seriously, me and my dad have a lot different personalities. We don't butt heads much. We sure don't do any wars of silence."

"Wars of silence?"

"Yeah, you know what I mean. Where you go a long time and don't talk because you're mad at each other."

Russ sat thinking for a moment. "That's like what you and me did for a while, huh?"

Ev smiled ruefully. "Yeah, sort of like that."

"And . . . like me and my old man."

With a nod, Ev said, "Yeah, sort of like that too."

Russ gripped the wheel. He hadn't yet shut the car off; now he did. "So about that . . . I don't know how to change it. What do you have to do when months have gone by like that?"

"You haven't talked in months?"

"Well, you know. It's not like we haven't talked at all. Just seems like it's about anything but what's the matter. And if one of us touches on any subject that's important, we end up in a fight. Well, not a real fight—he blows up, and I *shut* up. He'd clean my clock in a fight."

Ev chuckled. "That's one thing I never had to worry about with my dad. He's too mellow to fight, or even hit anybody. Besides, I'm bigger than he is."

Russ matched Ev's chuckle, ruefully. "Yeah, I guess I wouldn't know for sure. Nobody ever tested my dad that far."

"I know one thing, bud," said Ev. "I have a feeling you're always going to regret it if you can't do something to make up with your dad before the game tomorrow. He's the one who got us into football, remember? Back when we were little."

Russ nodded. His throat became too tight to speak. Of course he remembered! How could he ever forget?

"He used to seem like he lived for our games. Coached us, got us all keyed up, excited to play. We're gonna take State this year, Russ. Everybody knows it. It's as good as in the bag. And why? All because of you."

"Oh, give me a break! What about you?"

"Come on! Russ, this isn't my game. I was never even close to as big and fast and tough as you are. That team doesn't need me one way or the other. You're the one they need."

Russ was quiet for a moment. There was a time that, at least down deep inside, he might have agreed with that. Now, that part of him was gone. And he was glad. The Russets were a team. That team wasn't about any one person. They had gotten where they were because they worked together, and played together.

"You're as important as anyone, buddy. Why are you even saying that?"

"You can say whatever you want, man. We both know I'm telling the truth. We could never have beaten the Trojans without you, not to mention some of the other teams. We probably wouldn't even be going to State."

"Okay, have it your way," Russ gave in. "What'd you even bring this up for?"

"To tell you how important it is for your old man to be a part of that game tomorrow. He got us into football, coached us along, made us all we could be, and now . . . If you two aren't gettin' along, is it even going to be worth it? I mean yeah, it'll be great and all, but without you and your dad bein' friends . . . It sure doesn't seem like the game will be complete. That's all I'm saying."

Russ drew in a big breath, his tight throat causing it to make a chattering sound. He slapped the wheel. "You're right, buddy. You're

right. Okay. Hey, if you don't mind, I'm gonna get my stuff and go home tonight."

"I don't mind. I think that would be cool."

● ● ● ● ●

No one was expecting Russ home for supper, so everything was gone when he got there, and the dishes cleaned up. The family was gathered in the living room listening to the radio when he came in the back door, and his mother got up to meet him in the kitchen.

"Russ! I didn't think you'd be coming home!"

He tried to give her a smile. He didn't care that all the food was gone. All he could think about was the lump in his throat and the pounding in his chest. The fact that his breath was so hard to draw in. There sat his father, mere feet away, and he needed so bad to talk to him. But everyone was there, all sitting around. How did he do it?

Eleanor made Russ a sandwich. It was obvious she wanted to talk to him, every bit as badly as he wanted to talk to his father. She kept looking over at him, but then it was like she would lose her nerve. He almost smiled, because she reminded him so much of himself.

His mother never did say much of any import, and he didn't press her, mostly because he was too concerned with figuring out how to approach his father.

When she gave up and went to sit back down on the couch with Kathleen, he took his sandwich and stood in the doorway, ostensibly listening to the radio. In actuality, if anyone had asked he couldn't even have told them what was playing.

But the moment a commercial came on, he swallowed what he was chewing.

"Hey, Pop?"

With a look somewhere between being startled and confused, Arch looked over at his son.

"Yeah?"

"How's it going?" *What a stupid thing to say!* This commercial break was only going to last so long. He had to move fast!

"Fine. You?"

"Uh . . . I wondered if I could talk to you for a minute."

"Sure, go ahead." The look in his father's eyes was veiled, but behind it was something else, or maybe Russ only imagined it. Maybe he simply wanted for it to be a look of hope—the same hope he was feeling inside.

"Well, I mean somewhere else."

"Oh?" Arch glanced around. Russ had no idea what he could be looking for, other than perhaps a way out. "Uh, yeah. Sure."

As he started to get up, the phone rang, and Dorothy answered it, after one ring. He heard one of the girls whispering that Dorothy must have been expecting a call from her "boyfriend."

As his father came into the kitchen and motioned toward the back steps (his favorite talking place in temperate weather was the driveway), Russ heard Dorothy say into the phone, "Oh, yes, he is. Just a minute. Hey, Dad? The phone's for you."

Russ's heart fell. So close! He had worked so hard to a place where he could say to his father what he had needed for so long to say! Now it was going to have to wait, for at least a few more minutes. It was a cruel blow.

With a discouraged-looking frown, Arch turned around and came back past Russ, going to the phone. "Hello, this is Arch. Yes . . . Yes, I have been. Who is this?" Silence. Arch's face looked intent. "Okay. That's all right. Where?" Another stretch of silence. "Wait. What time again? Could we do it later? Maybe in the evening?" This time the stretch of silence while a hard look was forming on Arch's face became almost interminable.

Finally, Arch drew in a big breath, obviously trying to calm himself. "You had better be there. You've got to promise me. No, I'll be alone. Ray's In and Out, by the stockyards. Between twelve and twelve-thirty. And I won't be able to stay much past that. I have another appointment right afterward."

When Arch hung up and turned to Russ, Russ was already staring at him. He felt like someone had kicked him in the stomach.

"Is that about tomorrow?" He didn't know why he asked. He already knew.

"Yeah. It's—" Arch stopped himself and looked over at Eleanor, his eyes helpless and without hope. "It's that thing I've been working."

Russ nodded. He felt numb all over. The big game was going to begin at two o'clock, and now his father had an appointment clear up in the Falls, right before that. Russ had been around long enough to know what those "appointments" led to. His father wasn't going to be there for the last game of his high school career.

"It's . . . I'll be quick, Russ. I promise."

"Sure, Pop. Hey, it's all right." Russ was holding himself back.

Arch looked at him inquisitively, seeming afraid to say what was now on his mind. "Uh, we better go have that talk, huh?"

"Ah, no, it's all right. It's wasn't that big of a deal," Russ said, his chest all the while feeling almost too tight to draw another breath. "No, I think your program's almost back on now. It can keep. Besides," he tried to force a grin, "I have to use the bathroom anyway."

Arch nodded and tried to give him a smile. "All right then. Yeah, we can talk when you're done."

But at the height of the radio program's climax, which Russ timed just so, he nonchalantly walked out the back door, without saying anything to anybody, then headed out the back gate. He guessed there really was no reason to talk to his father after all. Anything he might have said would have made no difference anyway, in the face of his father's call to duty.

It was time to take a walk, and think about his future.

CHAPTER SEVENTY

Luther Dean awoke on the morning of the big day with his heart pounding. He pulled the Winchester .30/30 out from under his bed and jacked the lever. He bent and sniffed inside the receiver, relishing the smell of the solvent he had used to clean it. He slid seven cartridges into the magazine, jacked one into the chamber, then slid another into the magazine. He then proceeded to load both of the Model 1911 Colt .45's Billy had purchased for him.

He went in the kitchen and made himself a pot of cornmeal mush, ate it with half and half and brown sugar in it and savored every bite. There was an excited feeling in his chest that he could barely hold back.

He returned to his room, and laying a blanket out on the bed, he set the rifle on it and made one roll, then set both pistols there and continued rolling the blanket until he had one long tube. He looked around the room. Last night was the last night he would ever spend in this bedroom. He gave a nod of satisfaction. It had been a good place to stay. Now it was time to move on.

Stepping out into the frosty morning air, he made his way down the sidewalk, the blanketed bundle under his arm. It was early Saturday morning, and the town, as he had expected, seemed to be asleep. He went to the house two lots north of Billy's, and up the front sidewalk, walking on in as if he owned the place. He had gone the night before and picked the lock to make sure that in the daylight there would be no issues.

Setting the guns on a dusty brown couch in the front room, he walked through the house. He had never seen the inside of it in the daylight. He peeked out the back, at the long expanse of dry lawn that ran clear back to the alley. There was a kitchen on the south side, and a bedroom, farther back, on the north. But the front room, the living room, that was where he would make his stand.

He walked back to Billy's and flipped the television on. Morning cartoons were playing. Going to Billy's room, he roused him from sleep.

"It's time to get moving, bud." Billy rolled over, blinking his eyes. He stared up at Luther as if he didn't know quite where he was. "You ready?"

"Huh?"

"Get up, man. I said 'you ready'?"

Billy blinked again and looked around. He flung his legs over the bed and set his feet on the floor. "Oh, yeah, man. Ready."

"All right. You told Ikey noon, right?"

Billy rubbed at his eyes, still trying to chase sleep. "Yeah. Noon. I think."

"You think! Better be sure."

"Okay, I'll ring him in a while. Dang, it's still early, ain't it?"

"Early bird gets the worm," quipped Luther. "Yeah, it's early. I already got the guns down there. In a while, I'll ride the bike over there and put it in the backyard. Now, once you get inside I want you wearin' a hood, okay? I don't want anybody to recognize you so you can get back here safe after everything goes down. When it's all done, you go out the back with that hood on, run over to Locust, run east, and then when you get to the corner up there you take the mask off and stuff it in your pocket. Come all the way around the block and come back in through your back door."

Billy smiled and nodded. "I know, I know. I got it. I will, Luther. Thanks for thinking of me."

"What are friends for, bud? You've done right by me, I sure can't leave you to the wolves. Now we've gotta make sure Ikey's gonna be here on time. Got it?"

"Got it. Hey, Luther?"

"Hey, Billy?"

"I don't know if I'll get much chance later when everything start's goin' down, but I wanted to tell you—it's been great having you stay here, man. I hope Canada's good to you."

Luther clapped his friend on the shoulder and gave it a squeeze. "Don't get all mushy on me, bro. We'll see each other again, you know. This ain't goodbye."

● ● ● ● ●

Russ got up early and took a light jog around the neighborhood, more to get rid of nervous energy and loosen his joints than because he needed the exercise. He managed somehow to get out of the house before his mother and father even got out of bed. But he returned home after they were up, and his mother was cooking breakfast.

"You're going to need to eat a big, hearty meal, Son," Eleanor said when Russ came up the back steps. She glanced nervously at Russ's father.

"You bet, Mom. Thanks."

Russ was trying to debate the best way to say hello to his father, or whether to say anything at all. Arch took the dilemma out of his hands.

"Morning, Russ. I'm sorry we didn't get to talk last night." He rustled the morning paper. "Did you . . ."

"No, it's all right, Pop. Actually, I forgot what it was about. I got thinking I needed to get some fresh air and didn't expect to be gone so long."

Arch stared at him past the once all-important news. "Well . . ." That big, strong man was struggling for something to say. Russ almost hated himself at the moment, but he had no idea how to make it easier for his dad even if he wanted to. He still could not come to grips with the fact that his father was going to miss what up until this point was the most important game of his entire life. No one had come out and said that, exactly, but he could read the writing on the wall plainly enough.

"I have a few more hours home before I have to drive up to the Falls for a meeting. If you happen to think about what you were wanting to say . . ."

"Okay, Pop. That'll be great." He went down the hall and showered, then didn't come out of his room until his mother had called everyone in for breakfast.

Even as delicious as the breakfast was, and even as much of it as Russ put down, it was only for the sake of energy later in the day. He didn't remember enjoying a single bite.

Throughout breakfast, he kept thinking that even if his father couldn't see his big game, maybe he could at least ask him to go toss the ball around for a while. But the words kept getting stuck in his throat. Why couldn't he and his father talk to each other? It had been so long since they shared a real talk.

In despair, after breakfast Russ asked Toni to throw the ball with him. She wasn't any superstar athlete, but of all the girls she was the most athletic. They went out on the lawn and tossed the ball back and forth, and Toni threw a few impressive spirals. He made sure to tell her, even though normally he would not have mentioned it. His own need for some kind of praise from his father seemed to be driving him to go out of his way in making sure others knew when they did something right.

The day was idyllic. The possibility of snow the weather guesser had predicted turned into nothing, and it got up to fifty-one degrees, with a bright sun shining and almost no wind. Where did all of those phantom storms go? That was a good thing about percentages: As long as the

weatherman wasn't fool enough to shout out one hundred percent anything, he would always have something to fall back on!

Around eleven o'clock, Toni wanted to go in, and Russ guessed he had had enough too. Maybe it was time to go hunt up Ev and get some *real* practice in before the game.

He plopped onto the couch in the living room in time to see his father cross through the room in his uniform pants and shoes, with a white undershirt on. He went into the kitchen and rummaged around in the refrigerator for a while, then came back past peeling an orange.

Russ's heart was pounding. He still wished he could talk to his father. What if there were at least a part of the big game to salvage? This was it! After today, Russ would never play high school football again. Although once you were part of a team, it was in your blood, the reality was that other than boxing, and perhaps track, he would never again be a Shelley Russet—at least not when it came to football. The thought jarred him clear down to his toes. No matter how this game ended up, his life today was changing forever. And his father would not be there to see it.

Arch loomed large in the doorway, buttoning his shirt at the collar. He looked at Russ as he was clipping on his tie and trying to straighten it. His gun belt and .38 Special Colt revolver were already strapped around his waist. He stared at Russ as he reached over and took his fedora from its hook by the entry to the hallway. It was obvious he wanted to say something, but until Eleanor came down the hall and nudged him, then walked on by, the big lawman couldn't find his voice.

At last, he drew a big breath. "Hey, Russ?"

Russ pretended only now to notice him standing there. "Yeah?"

"Hey, do you think I could see you for a minute outside?"

The request caught Russ flat-footed. If he had had time to think, he would have had a parry, but he didn't. "Uh, sure, Pop. Now?"

"Yeah."

Russ was starting to hate this feeling he always had now when he was about to have a conversation with his father. He hated to feel helpless under any circumstances, and with his father it seemed like that was all he felt anymore.

They walked out into the driveway, and Arch threw a notebook into the front seat of his car. He seemed to be stalling for time, and Russ understood. He probably would have done something similar.

Arch turned to him straight on. "Hey, Son, I . . . I'm on a big case. Well, I guess you know about it. Mark apologized to me about this. He knew he wasn't supposed to tell, but he did."

Inside, Russ cringed. "Yeah." Now it was time for his father to admit he couldn't be at the game.

"Well, I have to go meet with someone in the Falls, and it's about this case. I guess you heard that too. It could be really important for me catching a really bad person. But I . . . I'm not going to miss your big game."

Russ stared. He had heard the words as plain as anything, but the flat finality of them took a moment to register.

"Okay," he said dully. "I understand."

"No, I don't think you do," said Arch a little louder. "Son, I want to ask you a big favor."

"Okay."

"I'd like you to go to Idaho Falls with me."

"Huh? Pop, I can't! The game!"

Russ knew his father well enough after eighteen years to know what his normal reaction would have been. He would have said something along the lines of "fine, maybe another time," and that would have been that. But this time, his father looked at him with a look of what could only be called desperation, to anyone intimately familiar with the ways of Sheriff Arch Blevins.

"I know, boy. I know. But . . . I'd really like to have you go. I'll make you a deal."

"What's that?" asked Russ, feeling sick at the very thought of what was coming.

"If you go with me, we'll be back here by one o'clock. I don't make too many promises, but I'll promise you that. Come hell or high water, we'll be back."

"But . . . Pop, what about your case?"

"I don't give a damn about that case right now, Russ. Just ride with me. Please?"

There was no way a son who loved his father, in spite of all their differences of late, could have turned down that plea, and the hopefulness in his father's eyes.

"Okay, Pop. I'll go."

And thus began the most grueling, terrifying period of Russ and Arch Blevins's life.

● ● ● ● ●

As Arch drove to Idaho Falls, he and Russ were silent. But it was the loudest silence Russ had ever been a part of. A voice cried out inside his head, telling him that it was all right to be the one to break the silence. *Someone* had to, after all. And if he knew his father, it was not going to be him.

And yet the raging quiet wore on, complete but for the sound of the tires on the road and the beating of Russ's heart, like the sound of a ticking time bomb.

"Russ?"

The sound of his father's voice was like the blast of a shotgun in the confined space of the car.

"Yeah, Pop?"

"I've been trying to talk to you . . . for a long time."

"All right."

"But now that it comes down to it, I'm not quite sure what to say."

Russ looked over at him, feeling a lump rise in his throat. "Yeah. I know, Pop. I know the feeling."

Arch let out a chuckle, an actual chuckle. "We're sure a pair, Son."

"Yes sir."

"Well," Arch forged on. "I got you here, and our time's running out to have this talk. I lay awake all night trying to think of the right things to say. Now they all seem sort of foolish, like something someone else would say to each other, but not us."

Russ let a grin onto his face, and unwanted tears moistened his eyes. "Yeah, me too."

"I want to tell you . . ." Arch stopped and jerked his head the other direction. Watching him, Russ saw his old man's jaws working, and he mercifully turned his eyes back toward the front. Arch was working at blinking his eyes back to normal. Russ could see that much even with

peripheral vision. The whole notion brought the tears back to Russ's eyes and made him feel stupid. What were they, two babies sitting here? They were supposed to be grown men! But the thought that this was his own big, brave father, the man he had worshiped for as far back as he could remember, somehow gave him strength.

"Dad? Are you okay?"

Arch said a clipped "Of course," and gave a brisk nod. He swallowed and looked back at the road. He took a deep breath.

"Sorry about that, Russ. No son should ever have to see his father like that."

"No, Dad. It's okay. Sometimes I feel like that too."

His father nodded again, clenching his jaws. After several seconds, he had himself under control enough to look over at his boy. "You do?"

"Yeah."

Arch fought back a smile and blinked at more tears that he refused to let spill.

"So I guess what I'm trying to tell you is something my own father never said to me, not in all the years we lived together. I just don't want you to ever have to say that to your own children. Understand?"

"Sure, I guess. But . . ."

"Yeah. So I want to tell you how proud I am of you, Son. From the bottom of my heart. I don't know why this is so hard. I've told grown men I'm proud of them. I've said a lot of things that were harder to say. But I'm proud of you. I couldn't be happier about how you've turned out, Russ. And I don't think I've ever told you that."

Russ was fighting for all he was worth to hide his emotions. He had waited most of his life to hear such words from his father, the kind of words he only could remember hearing from various coaches throughout his life, and maybe from a church leader or school teacher along the way. Even the Shelley police chief had told him something similar one day after Russ had stood up to a crowd of bullies who were picking on a retarded boy.

"Thanks, Dad. I've been wanting to say the same things to you. I'm proud to have you for my dad."

"I'm not even sure what happened with us," Arch said. "I've been kicking myself for months. Was it those railroad ties? If so, I want you

to know I regretted that ever since. I did stupid things when I was in school myself. There was no reason for me to be that harsh."

Russ laughed. "No, I deserved it. And you know what? I've used that harness quite a few times since then, too. It's a good workout."

Arch let out a laugh. A real laugh. For a moment, while Russ was looking at his father, he saw a young face, a face that was all of a sudden free of stress. A face like one he remembered from long before this sad and lonely spring, summer, and fall. This was the father he always wanted to remember. Arch Blevins, his dad.

With what must have been a sudden surge of emotion, a feeling of release like the one Russ was feeling, his father raised that big right paw, the one that was so used to firing a gun or putting handcuffs on someone, and clapped Russ on the leg, giving it a squeeze.

Russ had something to say, and he had to say it in a rush or he might never find the courage again. "I love you, Dad."

CHAPTER SEVENTY-ONE

They got to Ray's In and Out and found a booth to sit in and wait for Arch's informant. Russ knew he was going to have to leave when the man arrived, but until then Arch wanted him to sit with him. Neither of them was very hungry, but they ordered chocolate shakes and sipped on them quietly, both basking in the afterglow of the confessions they had shared. Although Arch's reply to the three most important words Russ had to tell him was a simple, "I know you do, Son," that was enough for Russ. He knew his father loved him. He didn't need to hear the man break a lifelong habit for him to recognize the truth.

The time ticked by, and Arch kept looking at his watch. Finally, he said, "Well, I guess that's it." He started to stand up.

"Wait, Dad!" Russ stopped him. "This is something pretty important, isn't it?"

"It is. This guy said he has something that will button up this murder case."

"Then we'd better wait."

Arch drilled his son with his eyes. "Russ, I made you a promise to get you back for that game. And there's no way I'm going to miss the biggest game of your life either. If this guy needs to talk to me so bad, he should have been here when he said he would, and he'll call me back."

"But what if he doesn't?"

Arch looked into his son's eyes. "Then I guess he probably didn't have anything as important as he thought he did anyway."

● ● ● ● ●

Little Kathleen Blevins was roller skating on the sidewalk, heading down the block toward Elm Street, where she had every intention of turning around and skating back. Her mother had told her to make sure she didn't cross any streets.

As she reached Isaac Thorpe's house, the dark-skinned ten-year-old was coming out, and he shut the screen door behind him. Kathleen felt a huge smile come over her face, and she waved excitedly. "Hi, Rusty!" She had loved this little boy for as far back as she could remember. It didn't matter that he was only a fifth grader, and she was a big sixth grader. With his black hair and mischievous greenish-brown eyes, and that impish grin he got every time he saw her, he was the cutest boy in her whole school.

"Hi, Kathleen," said Isaac, waving back. "Where you goin'?"

"Just to the end of the block," she said, planting the toe of her left skate and standing there expertly balanced. "Hey, do you want to come skating with me?"

"Oh, no, I can't. I told Billy I'd come over."

"Oh. You go over there a lot," she said.

"Yeah. Billy and me are best friends."

"That's nice. But I thought you and Russ were best friends."

Isaac gave her a shy laugh and shrugged. "Yeah, but he's too busy. I don't see him so much anymore."

Kathleen nodded. "That's what Mom says too. I guess he thinks he got all grown up."

"Yeah. That's okay. I still like him and all. But Billy's a grown up too, and he has a lot more time than Russ."

Kathleen looked across the street. She thought of her mother's order not to cross the street. But didn't she really mean in her roller skates?

"Can I come with you? What do you do over there?"

"Oh, we just look at his cars, and listen to his records and stuff. Sometimes we just watch TV."

Kathleen wrinkled her nose as she laughed. "That's funny! You could do that at home."

A serious look came over the boy's face. "Naw . . . Not really. My brothers . . ."

She caught his meaning. "Well, it's okay if you like to go somewhere else. But can I go? And then maybe in a while we can go to Russ's big game. It's going to start at two."

He shrugged. "Yeah, I guess you could come. And I sure don't want to miss the game, either."

"Okay! Hang on. Here, help me." Saying that, she reached out and put one hand on his shoulder, raising a foot to unbuckle and take off her skate. She did the same with the other one, not noticing the proud, big-boy look that had come over Isaac's face to be called on to support her.

Kathleen buckled the skates together and hung them from one hand. "Okay, let's go." She reached out and took Isaac's hand.

With that lovable grin coming over his face, and color to his cheeks, Isaac folded her hand in his, they looked both ways along the street, then ran across, her skates swinging from her fingers.

They walked up the sidewalk, and the boy knocked boldly on the door. They stood there waiting for what seemed forever.

Kathleen looked at Isaac. "Do you think he's home?"

"Well, yeah, I think so." He knocked again.

Finally, the door swung open. Billy was standing there with a strange look on his face. It must have been hot inside, in spite of the cool temperatures out, because Billy had droplets of sweat on his cheeks, chin, and forehead.

"Hey, Ikey." Billy Earl stared at Kathleen, even though he was speaking to the boy. His eyes landed at last on Isaac. "What's up?"

"You said to come over now, right?"

Billy's eyes flickered over at Kathleen, then back. "Well, yeah, but . . . I meant just you."

"Oh." Isaac looked openly surprised. "Well, I thought maybe it would be okay if I brought my friend over too. She wanted to see your cars."

Billy looked at Kathleen and licked his lips. "Uh . . . Hey, buddy, I was going to see if you'd go walking with me, and . . . Well, her mom probably wouldn't want her to go."

A look of disappointment came over Isaac's face. For some reason, he was still holding onto Kathleen's hand, as if he had forgotten he ever took it. His grip tightened, rather than letting go.

"Oh, well maybe I can come over a different time."

"What?"

"Is it okay if I hang out with Kathleen for a while? I don't get to very often, and we were going to go up to her brother's football game."

Billy swallowed hard and once more licked his lips. There was something about his face that Kathleen could only describe as fear. That notion started to make her nervous. "Hey, buddy, but we had plans and all." A drop of sweat came to the tip of his nose, and he wiped it away as if it were a fly. "Couldn't you be with your little friend some other time?" He looked over and tried to smile at Kathleen, but his face made more of a grimace.

A look of determination came over Isaac's face. He squeezed Kathleen's hand even harder. She sensed that it was very hard for him to tell Billy no. "Is Luther with you?"

"No, not right now," Billy sputtered.

"Well, maybe . . . Can I come over later, after the game?"

"No. Come on, buddy. We had plans!" Billy was starting to look desperate. "Hey, how about just for a few minutes? A quick walk."

"What about Kathleen?"

Billy stared at the girl, his face blank. It was almost as if he were staring at a grizzly bear about to devour him.

"Um . . . Yeah, but . . . I don't think . . ." Billy's eyes darted around. His face twitched, and his tongue swirled around the inside of his cheek. To Kathleen, he looked as sick as anyone she had ever seen. He glanced down at his wristwatch. Something seemed very wrong, and suddenly

Kathleen only wanted to go home. But something told her to take Isaac with her.

"Hey, Rusty, come on. Let's go to my house and get my family." She tugged at his hand. "Come on." She didn't dare look up at Billy anymore.

Isaac seemed trapped between the desire to be with Kathleen and the fear of upsetting Billy. Even a child could sense the tension and the strange need Billy had to keep him there.

"No, Kathleen, come with us, okay?" She stared at him, realizing he didn't want to be alone with Billy.

"Okay, but just for a minute." She glanced down the street, toward her house. It was so close, but it might as well have been blocks away.

His face pale, and sweat running down his temples, Billy stepped out of his house and shut the door. He gave the knob a couple of jerks, looking down at it for a second as if it wasn't registering on him that it had already latched. His hand on the doorknob appeared to be shaking.

"Hey, let's walk down this way," said Billy, setting out at too fast of a pace and cutting across the edge of his yellow lawn, which hadn't had near enough water that summer and fall.

The children almost ran to keep up. "Hey, Billy, what are you goin' so fast for?" said Isaac. His words made Billy slow down, and he turned and tried to grin.

"Oh, sorry. I knew you didn't have long."

The man kept his pace slow, looking down now and then to make sure the children were still right beside him. They were walking north, toward Locust Street, and Kathleen couldn't help letting her eyes cross the street. There was her house. Something told her to run for it, but Isaac was holding so tight to her hand.

There was a house that had stood empty all summer, straight across from her house. Here, Billy veered off without warning, going up the sidewalk.

"Where we goin', Billy?" asked Isaac, towing the girl with him as he followed his friend.

"Oh . . . I was gonna show you something here."

As the door to the empty house came open, Kathleen heard her mother's voice calling her from across the street. A man appeared in the doorway, staring down at Kathleen.

"Billy! What the hell?"

"Kathleen!" her mother called again from across the street.

Billy glanced that way, his expression turning to panic. He started fumbling for something in his pocket, tugging out a wad of dirty gray fabric. "Hey, I couldn't get the kid here without her. I—"

Luther looked across the street at Eleanor Blevins. He stared at her, then snarled. Without warning, his right hand shot out, and he lunged forward to grab Kathleen by the arm and drag her toward the house. "Get that kid in here!" he ordered Billy.

Eleanor screamed out Kathleen's name as the door was shutting.

Kathleen was too scared to cry, too scared to move. Nothing in her young childhood had prepared her for a moment like this. But Isaac Thorpe had grown up in much harder circumstances.

"Hey! Let go of her!" he yelled at Luther. For which he won a hard backhand that knocked him into the door.

"What're you doin'?" yelled Billy. "You said you wouldn't hurt him."

Luther, still holding onto the girl's arm, turned and glared at his friend. He didn't even waste his time with a reply.

"What the hell did you bring the girl here for?"

"He wasn't gonna come without her. Come on, man! I had no choice."

"Well, I guess it's done now," growled Luther. "The other thing's done too."

"Huh?"

"The explosion. The fire. It's going. The other bomb threats. Everything. It's all in motion. It's too late to turn back. I disabled the police chief's car radio last night, and now there's only one radio in this stinking county, and it's in Arch Blevins's car. Throw these brats in the bathroom!" He whirled on the children. "You try to come out, I'll slit both your throats. Now *move!*"

Almost running, in their terror, Kathleen and Isaac went to the bathroom with Billy, and he pushed them inside. He looked back at Luther,

then down at Isaac. "You keep quiet, Ikey. You hear me! Don't say a word. Don't say nothin'!" A sudden sob escaped Billy's lips. "Ikey, I'm so sorry." He shut the door with a click.

Kathleen threw her arms around Isaac, squeezing so tight she must have been shutting off his breath. Both of them were crying now, the shock worn off enough to let emotion past. Through the bathroom door, Kathleen heard Luther's voice. It took but moments to realize he was on the phone.

"Yeah. This is your worst nightmare. I'm at 341 South Park Avenue, and I've got a boy and a girl here with me. This girl belongs to Sheriff Blevins. I want Blevins here, and I want him by himself. *Now.* If he isn't here in twenty minutes, I'm killing one of these kids, but I haven't decided which one yet. Call him on the radio. I want to hear it!"

● ● ● ● ●

Arch was driving toward Shelley, going over the speed limit. He had promised Russ he would get him home for the game, and he was going to, and with plenty of time to warm up and get himself together.

A strange-sounding voice came over the radio, and he fumbled to answer it, realizing at the last moment that it was his dispatcher. Something was wrong.

"This is the sheriff."

Sheriff! Listen, something really bad is happening.

"Hey, Heather, slow down, all right? Just slow down. What's wrong?"

Sheriff, we couldn't get you on the radio. I tried.

"It's okay, Heather. I was out of the car, but I'm here now. What's wrong?"

The voice on the other end came back on, but this time it began with a sob. *Sheriff, a bomb went off in Blackfoot, and it set off a bunch of fires, right downtown. Someone called and said there are five more bombs just like it, and where they are.*

Arch's face went white. He glanced over at Russ, as if somehow he could get comfort from him. "Five more bombs went off?"

No, they haven't gone off yet.

"Where's everyone else?"

They're gone! the voice came back. *I sent them all to the fire and to the places where the other bombs are. Now I don't have contact with any of them!*

"Okay, Heather. Okay, good. Where do you need me most?"

This time the woman's voice came back with an outright wail. It sounded like she was on the verge of crying out loud. *Sheriff, you have to go to 341 South Park in Shelley. There is a man there who says . . .* Her voice broke again.

"Says what, Heather? He said what?"

He says he has one of your daughters and a boy, and . . . Sheriff, he says he's going to kill one of them if you don't get there in twenty minutes and come alone!

Arch froze. He stared at the microphone. "Who is it?" he yelled back.

He didn't say, she cried. *But . . . Wait. He's on the phone, and he wants to say something.*

Russ had never seen fear on his father's face before, at least not as far back as he could remember, even during the two times when Russ himself had been scared half to death. One of those times, they were lost out in a blizzard, and the other they were surrounded by a group of angry migrant farm workers, upset that he was taking one of them to jail. Even in those scariest of times, Russ had never seen his father scared before. This was the first time. Arch glanced over at his son, and there were tears in his eyes.

Big Sheriff. This is an old friend. I got yer little girl by the hair right now, and a friend's got this boy from down the street. I'm gonna slash one of their throats in twenty minutes—you hear me? Twenty minutes! You get here fast as that old tub will fly, or the blood starts runnin'.

"I'm on my way," said Arch dully. The dispatcher, too stunned to think what she was doing, answered a question that must have been posed over the phone by hitting the radio call button instead.

Yes, he's on his way. In a moment, she got back on the radio. *Sheriff? Sheriff? Sheriff! Can you hear me?*

As Russ was reaching for the microphone, Arch picked it up.

"Yes, Heather. I can hear you."

The whole downtown is burning up, Mr. Blevins. And there are other bombs . . . And . . . I won't be able to find any help for you.

Arch frowned, taking a deep breath. He gathered himself together, then pushed the mic button. "Thanks, Heather. Just say some prayers, okay?"

It was the only time Russ could remember his father asking anyone to pray without being prompted by his mother.

CHAPTER SEVENTY-TWO

It took half a minute for Billy to get up the strength to go back in where Luther was. His friend was kneeling on the couch to look out the front window, the two .45's Billy had bought him tucked behind his belt, and the .30/30 in his hands.

They both saw Eleanor Blevins running across the street, and Luther started to aim the gun through the glass at her.

Billy ran close to him. "Hey! Luther! Man, come on! You said nobody else!"

"Get away from me and shut up, you idiot! I'm runnin' this!"

"I know, but— Man, please don't kill her!"

By that time, Eleanor had passed out of their sight, and there was a loud banging on the front door. "Open this door now! I know you're in there. Open it up!"

"All right," Luther growled, mostly to himself. He threw the rifle down on the couch and drew out one of the pistols, then stalked to the front door, jerking it open. He met Eleanor with a gun barrel sticking almost in her face, extended to arm's length.

"All right! It's open! Now what?"

Eleanor's hands went to her mouth to stifle a scream. Her knees almost buckled, and she fumbled behind her as if searching for some kind of support that wasn't there.

"What did you do with my daughter?"

"What do you think, you stupid slut? She's locked up."

Eleanor's face couldn't have been any paler. "You… You let her go! Why are you doing this?"

"I'm keeping her! Want to do something about it?"

"You let her go! My husband is the sheriff!" she cried.

"Well, isn't that a coincidence, lady?" said Luther with a hate-filled sneer. "And that's just who I wanted to see. But don't worry—he's on his way."

"What?"

"The sheriff's already on his way—you deaf? Now you get your ugly witch face back across the street before I blow your brains out. *Go on!*"

Terrified beyond tears, Eleanor stared at him in horror, then whirled away and stumbled down the steps, up the sidewalk, and out into the street, her hands to her mouth. She ran across the street, to be met by the girls, who had all come out of the house and stared at her in alarm.

Eleanor cried out something to them that couldn't be made out from across the street, and they all piled through the front door and slammed it. Within a moment, the curtains began moving, and Billy saw a strange smile come to Luther's lips. "Man, that woman's got guts," he said as if to himself.

Billy stared at his friend. For half a minute, he was speechless. Luther put the pistol back in his belt, then returned to the sofa and picked up the rifle.

Billy continued staring. Finally, he held up the hood and said, "Hey, Luther, you want me to put this on now?"

Luther whipped his head to the side, fire flaring in his eyes. He eyed the formless mass in Billy's hand until it registered on him what it was. He took in a deep breath and let it seep out. "Well, yeah, I guess. If it ain't too late. Did you let that woman see you?"

"No. I don't think so, anyway."

Luther drew in and released another big breath, trying to calm himself. He blinked his eyes with exaggeration to clear his vision. "All right. Then, yeah, put it on. Should have already had it on."

With fumbling hands, Billy managed to pull the hood down over his face, but he hadn't even looked at it before doing so and realized suddenly that he couldn't see a thing. Shaking, he jerked it back off again and stared at it like he had never seen it before, or like it had ended up

being a live rat rather than a hood. The second time, he managed to get the eye and mouth holes in front instead of in the back, and he pulled it on with jerky movements. He had tried so carefully to cut the eyes and mouth just right, but somehow when it was drawn down tight the hole only let his lower lip poke through, and most of his chin.

"Maybe you oughtta go watch that back door," said Luther after a while.

"How come?"

"Well, dummy, there's no law says that fool has to come up to the front of the house, right?"

"Oh. Yeah."

●●●●●

Arch Blevins' gas pedal stayed most of the way to the floor all the way into town. But when he came in on State, he turned east on Center Street.

"Dad! What are you doing?"

Arch didn't look over at him. "Son, you're going to play the hardest ball game you ever played. I promised you were going to be there, and you're going to be there."

"No! Dad, I can't. You can't do this."

"The hell I can't. I'm the boss around here, right? There's nothing you can do to help me. You're only going to get in the way and get hurt. Now you go up there and play ball." He turned and met Russ's eyes as he slammed on the brakes at Short Avenue and made the corner. "You got it. Buddy, you're gonna win this one for both of us, all right?"

Tears filled Russ's eyes as he stared at his father. Numbly, he got out of the car. He couldn't even speak.

"Son?"

His father's voice called him to lean back down and look inside. "Russ, what you said earlier? Son, I love you, too. Don't you ever forget how proud you've made me. Now go and win your biggest game."

He stared his father down until he motioned for him to shut the door. Without uttering a word in reply, because all words were caught in his throat, Russ closed the door, only making it latch partway.

The tires spun gravel as the Ford peeled away, raced down the street, and made the corner onto Locust almost on two wheels. And then Arch Blevins was gone.

Numb all the way through, Russ started walking toward the ball field. Other people were already gathered there, many of those being from Rigby. Members of both teams were gathered in clusters outside the area of the field.

A face turned toward him from one of those clusters, and that person made a little, excited jump and came running his way, a football in one hand. It was Ev Morin. Ev waved as he came close.

"What the hay, buddy! Kind of cutting it close, aren't you?"

Russ didn't reply. He kept walking until they stood together. By now, Ev's face had an alarmed look.

"What's goin' on, Russ?"

"Ev! Man, my dad's gone down to meet some guy."

"Huh? What are you talking about?"

"Ev!" Russ reached out and grabbed his friend by the arm, looking beyond him at the other players. They had all turned and were facing him and Ev expectantly. "Some guy grabbed my little sister. Kidnapped her!"

"Bull!" Ev shot out. He searched Russ's eyes, and a sick look washed over his face as his notion that his buddy might be pulling his leg vanished in smoke. "What the heck are you talking about?" he repeated.

"I gotta go help my dad," Russ cried, a huge chill running throughout his body. "There's no other cops. He's all by himself."

"I'm comin' too!"

Russ didn't even fight him. He started walking in the direction his father had driven while Ev ran back to the other players. As he walked, he turned his head to see Ev go through the same motions Russ had with him, trying to convince them that he wasn't joking. Then Ev ran back over to him, and they started running.

They had made the corner onto Locust before Russ got his head together, and he put on the brakes. "Hey, wait! Wait, Ev."

As he came to a stop, so did Ev, and Ev had to backtrack to him. "What? What are you doin'?"

"Buddy, you can't go. They need you to play."

"Screw that game, Russ! Screw it! What if I don't even like football?"

They stared each other down.

"You get back up there, Ev!" he growled. "Win that game for us!"

"Come on. I'm not winning any game for anybody. You know that as well as I do. But even if I was the best ball player on the earth and would make all the difference in that game, I'm not letting you run off alone like this. I couldn't keep my head in that game anyway."

Russ took a deep breath. He felt a rush of love for this boy, his brother. He wished he had a way to tell him. "Okay then, come on."

They ran all the way down Locust and were within a block when they heard the first shot—the sound of a big rifle.

Billy Earl had gone to the back door like he was ordered. He felt almost like he had to swim through the fear and tension that filled this house. He stood at the back window and thought of Ikey and the little girl. And he thought of them. And thought of them. And then thought some more. And in the muddle of his terror, his mind began to churn things around that had been at the back of it for a long while but were only now surfacing.

A sick feeling washed over him, even sicker than the feeling that had plagued him since breakfast that morning, which he had eaten at Luther's insistence, then promptly gone and thrown up.

He turned toward the front of the house. Luther was out of his sight. Trembling all over, he heard Luther say, "Oh. Well, look at that. He really is coming to the front door. Just for me."

Billy kept walking, his mind in a whirl. He got to the living room in time to see the black and white sheriff's car pull up, the car he had been seeing ever since he moved into his house, parked in the driveway across the street like a sentinel, a wall between evil and the absence of it.

And until Luther's release, it had stayed that way.

The car had pulled up quartering toward the house, with the driver's door angled away. Luther swore. Billy cringed.

But what Billy had to say couldn't wait.

"Hey, Luther. You're gonna shoot him and then go, right? And you'll call me when it's time to bring your car, right?"

"Right," said Luther tightly, without looking back. He had the Winchester clutched in his hands, and one knee on the couch with the other leg stretched out behind him.

"Well . . ."

"Well, what?"

"I been thinkin' of something." He saw the driver's door come open on the car, and Luther tensed up like a big cat ready to spring. He started to bring the rifle butt to his shoulder.

"What you been thinkin'?" Luther growled. Billy was surprised to find his friend had even heard him.

"So I got this mask on and everything, but . . ."

"But what? Speak up!" Luther moved around, trying to get a better angle. Under his breath, he said, "Come on, you old piece of scum. Get out of the car already!"

"But Luther, what about Ikey? And now that girl? I got this hood, but . . . What about them?"

"What about 'em?"

"Well, they both seen me."

"Here he comes . . . *Here he comes . . .*" Sheriff Blevins had appeared to be stepping out of his car, but then he dropped down to one knee. Luther growled out a curse. He whirled on Billy. "Yeah. So they seen you. You think I don't know that?"

"Well how do I keep them from tellin'? We just threaten 'em?"

"Come on, you stupid oaf. You can't be that dumb. Billy! I can't do *everything* the way you want. There's only one way them two kids are keepin' quiet."

A chill went over Billy. "What do you mean?"

Luther stared at him. "You know good and well what I mean. Now why don't you get out that back door right now? Get back to your house before anybody else sees you. I'll do what has to be done with those kids. Now you listen to me and *get!*"

CHAPTER SEVENTY-THREE

Two things happened at once then. As Arch was getting into a position of safety behind his car and readying himself to yell out to whoever was inside the house, a door slammed behind him, and his wife screamed hysterically, "Arch! Somebody has Kathleen!"

Arch lunged up and whirled. "Ellie! Get back inside *now!*"

In the same moments, the thought of Luther Dean killing Ikey and the girl flooded through Billy Earl's mind and made him go nearly blind with panic. As Luther saw his chance for a lethal shot, he stood up straighter, sucking the rifle butt against his cheek, and aimed at Arch Blevin's chest. Billy grabbed his arm and jerked it down, not even seeing, or caring, that he had the perfect shot. All he wanted was to plead for the children's life.

The rifle went off, and the explosion seemed to shake the little house to the rafters. Arch yelled out and fell down behind the car, out of sight, as Eleanor, screaming, turned and fled into the house again.

Luther whirled around. Still holding the Winchester in one hand, he struck out savagely with a fist, hitting Billy in the face and knocking him back. "You idiot! You made me miss! What are you doing?" His words were more screamed than shouted.

Billy felt tears in his eyes. "Luther, you can't kill them kids!" he blubbered through the cloth mask.

"You don't have any say in it, you dumb hick! Billy! If those kids are left alive, they're gonna turn you in, and you're goin' to the pen! Now get out of here while you can. Stick to the plan!"

"Luther, the plan wasn't to kill nobody but the sheriff. You promised!"

"Get out of here! You don't know what it's like inside those walls! *Get!*" Luther was ready to explode. He whirled back to search for the

sheriff. The lawman was out of sight. Maybe he hadn't missed him after all!

Billy Earl stood at Luther's back. Luther was his best friend. He knew what was best. But . . . Those children! Billy didn't know the little girl. He had seen her many times, but they had never exchanged one word. But Ikey—little Ikey! He was such a nice kid. Trusted everybody. Just wanted a friend. Those eyes. That innocent mouth. How could anyone kill a nice kid like that?

Luther whirled around and saw the look in Billy's eyes. Something in him seemed to soften. He reached out and grabbed the shoulder of Billy's Levi jacket. "Come on, buddy. You've gotta listen to me and get goin'. Nobody else has seen you yet. Get out of here. You wouldn't survive one day behind those bars, believe me! Please, man, go! When I get long gone, I'll call you—like I said I would."

A voice rang out from the street: "Who's inside there?"

Luther whirled away from Billy. It had been a long time since he had heard that hated voice.

"It's Luther Dean, Sheriff! You remember me? You should—you sent me up to the pen to pay for burglaries my brother did. You destroyed the life of an innocent man! And now I'm gonna destroy yours!"

● ● ● ● ●

Inside the house, Eleanor's mind was a-whirl. As her girls gathered around her, she hung up the phone once again. Dispatch couldn't help her. All other officers were either at an explosion-caused fire in Blackfoot, or at various other places around the area, trying to keep people back from other locations where bombs had been called in. There was no one to come to her husband's rescue.

Eleanor could think of only one man. With shaking hands, she picked up the phone book and thumbed through the pages. Locating the number, with a shaking hand she began to spin the phone dial.

● ● ● ● ●

Russ and Ev reached the corner of Locust and Park Avenue shortly after the rifle shot. They saw Russ's mother scramble back inside the house, then watched his father, with blood around him on the ground, get to one knee beside his car, his revolver in his hand. Russ's first instinct

was to yell out. But something stopped him. No one could know that he and Ev were here. *No one.*

He turned to Ev and pointed at the back of the corner house, and they turned that way. As they did, they saw movement, and a cluster of white-suited figures running their way from the east. It took but a moment for the sight of six of the Russets to register on Russ.

"What are you guys doing?" he hissed as Pete, Johnny Boo, Charlie, Mark, Slick, and Nash ran up. "You guys can't be here! Get back to the game!"

"We're not leaving till you go with us!" Mark shot back. "Come on. We gotta get outta here. Where are the cops, man?"

"There aren't any," Russ said, almost reverting to panic. "Dad's it."

"What's goin' on?" shot out Pete Basso.

"Some guy kidnapped my sister—and I think Isaac Thorpe. He's trying to kill my dad! Guys—I gotta go!"

In spite of their pale faces, Mark said, "Then we're goin' with you. What are we gonna do?"

Looking around, Russ saw a pile of decorative rocks lying around the base of a cutleaf birch tree on the corner. They were the perfect size for his fists, and he picked two of them up.

"I don't know," he said, straightening up. "But I've gotta try something."

He turned and ran along the back of the closest house. The fourth house on the street was the one his father was parked at an angle in front of—a white-sided house that had been abandoned for some time. He could hear his friends coming behind him, and as he stopped within sight of the house he turned and looked at them. Looking scared but fierce, all of his friends had their fists full of stones.

Russ had no idea what they were going to do with them.

They all heard the screaming of a vehicle's engine, clear over on State Street. It squealed as it made the corner, then bounced recklessly across the rough train tracks, spewing gravel as it headed their way. As its brakes screeched at the corner of Park, another rifle shot exploded from inside the house. This time it was answered by two spiteful ones from his dad. Russ settled on a plan. Whoever was in the vehicle that had

just arrived, he couldn't wait to see what side they were on or what they were going to do. He had to move *now!*

"Guys, I'm goin' in the house!"

"What?" shot back Ev. "No, you aren't, Russ! You're gonna get killed!"

"That's my dad out there!" He knew his voice sounded angry, but he didn't have time to regret it. "Come on. You guys all get to the back of the house. I want you all to start throwing rocks at the back windows, and make all the noise you can. I'm gonna break out one of the side windows and try to get in there with that guy."

Ev and the others stared at Russ, then at each other. There were tears in Ev's eyes.

"Okay, go on."

The boys knew he wasn't backing down. They had all known him too long. And they had all grown up looking up to Sheriff Blevins. There was not one of them who could have faced himself later if he ran now.

When the gang got to the back of the house, they all looked at each other, then over at Russ. He returned their gaze as chills ran over his body. He knew with all that was in him that none of them might see him again. He nodded and turned, and as he heard glass start to shatter at the back of the house, he broke out the glass of what appeared to be a bedroom with one of his rocks.

Taking care to clear away all the glass he could, while in the background he could hear his team screaming and yelling, to create the biggest distraction possible, Russ took off his letterman jacket and threw it over the windowsill, dropping both rocks inside, in case he needed them. He launched himself up onto his stomach and scrambled into the room. He knew he had cut his hands, but there was nothing to be done about it now.

He could still hear the boys yelling at the back of the house, and then he heard a pistol shot from that direction. His eyes leaped that way! Had one of his friends been shot?

Shaking as if he were sick, he started out of the bedroom, expecting the gunman to be to his left, since that was where the shot had come from. But from the corner of his eye he spied Luther Dean at the front

room window, crouched with a rifle in his hands. There were two of them!

As his eyes fell on Luther Dean, a couple of shots rang out from the street. Luther yelped and threw the rifle down, clutching at his left hand. He swore and grabbed for something in his belt, pulling out a Colt auto. As he cursed again and raised the pistol out straight, taking four quick shots, Russ came up with one of the rocks and let it fly. Years of throwing baseballs and footballs paid off. The rock struck the back of Luther's hand, making the gun fall from his helpless grasp.

Without having to think, Russ charged across the room. He hit Luther Dean like a sledge hammer, down low in the abdomen, and his momentum carried them both forward and over the couch. Russ had only enough time to duck down behind Luther's head as he saw them heading for the plate glass picture window, which already had several bullet holes through it.

The sound of shattering glass was usually music to a young boy's ears, unless it was one of those times when it was caused by a stray ball. But this had no musical sound for Russ.

He and Luther Dean landed in a heap on the grass below the window, and Russ came up alone. The air had been knocked out of Luther by the fall and by Russ's shoulder.

Lying on his side, Russ saw Luther fumbling around at the front of his belt. Even as he realized there was blood all over his own arms, he reached for Luther's hands, trying to pin them. There was so much blood running off his hands that he couldn't keep hold of the other man's right wrist, and he managed to yank it away. Russ jumped on him with his knees and drove a bloody fist into his face—one, two, three times, as hard as he could strike.

Then a voice sounded behind him. "You get off him! Get off, or I'll shoot!"

CHAPTER SEVENTY-FOUR

Luther Dean, his face running with blood from at least one cut on his forehead and another deep, ugly one on his cheek, managed somehow to suck in a breath as Russ shoved up and away from him. He stared up at Russ, then threw a glance behind him—a glance of recognition.

"Billy . . ." he croaked.

"I got you, buddy," said the voice of Billy Earl.

Suddenly, there was another voice. It was Isaac Thorpe's. "Don't hurt him, Billy. Please!" Russ turned his head to see Isaac with his arms wrapped around the waist of the masked Billy. Billy was holding the forty-five that Russ had knocked out of Luther's hand. "Please don't hurt Russ. He's my friend," sobbed Isaac.

"Somebody help me," came a weak call from the street. Russ's eyes flew that way. A quick glance showed his father on the ground. His leg was moving around, and maybe an arm, but he was making no progress if he was trying to rise.

Looking up weakly at Billy and Russ, Luther started to gather his strength, and he managed half a grin. As Russ stood helplessly, he fumbled the other forty-five out of his belt and lurched to his feet among the shards of glass lying all around.

Russ lunged forward and grabbed Luther's gun hand. Luther tried to strike him with his left, but it had been rendered useless, apparently by a bullet from the sheriff. They struggled, and Luther cried out: "Billy, shoot him!"

Only Isaac's pleading voice came in reply.

"You gotta get goin', Luther," Billy managed. "Go on, man, run!"

But Russ had gotten both arms around Luther, and he had a hold on him like he was trying to squeeze out of him the last breath of life. With his face turning red, Luther looked helplessly beyond Russ's shoulder. "Come on, Billy! Shoot him! They're gonna send me back up!"

As Russ saw his friends edging closer from the back of the house, someone else registered on him. A dark-clad form had moved up alongside the neighboring house, not far from where the ball team was closing in. It was old Barrow Tupper! And he was holding an Enfield rifle in his hands, its barrel leveled at Billy.

"Better drop the gun there, Billy. This rifle'll blow a hole all the way through you 'n' out th'other side. Yer still a young man. You ain't ready t' die." The old man's words were rough, but surprisingly calm.

Frank Russell emerged from behind a tree. He held a revolver in his hand, and it was also pointed toward Billy.

A vast feeling of relief washed over Russ. Tears flooded his vision, and he blinked them back. They were safe! The cavalry was here after all, right at the last second, like Marshal Dillon on *Gunsmoke!*

Slowly, but without faltering, Billy began to lower the forty-five. Isaac let go of him as he went to bend down, and he set the weapon on the ground.

Luther watched the gun moving in slow motion. As it touched the ground and then came free of his friend's hand, a broken look overtook the ex-con's bloody face, almost as if he would start to cry. "No, Billy," he said softly. "No-o."

A hideous old 1947 Buick station wagon that served the area as an ambulance came racing up and skidded to a halt, and two men and a woman piled out. The man who had been in the passenger seat yelled out, "Hey! Everything safe here? Can we come on in?"

Barrow Tupper turned his head. "Yeah, boys. Come on, quick. The sheriff's down over there, and we don't know how bad."

The ambulance attendants raced to the fallen sheriff, one of them carrying a jump kit. As they knelt around him, Russ looked over at Barrow Tupper. The former lawman seemed to read his mind, and he gave him a reassuring nod.

"You can let 'im go now, boy. You did good," he said as Russ's arms released.

It was like Russ alone had been holding Luther Dean erect, for as his arms came away, the other man wobbled down to his knees, then sank onto his elbows, the crown of his head touching the grass. He was a picture of utter, bloody defeat.

Eleanor came running across the street, leaving her daughters gathered in fear on the porch, and clutched Kathleen to her as the girl ran out of the house crying.

She could only comfort the child for long enough to send her on her way to her waiting sisters, however, because Eleanor had to get to her husband.

While Barrow Tupper and Frank Russell held Luther and Billy at gunpoint, Russ and his friends gathered with Eleanor near the ambulance attendants. The men were trying to bandage a wound in the sheriff's leg that had lost a large amount of blood, while the woman held a stack of blood-soaked bandages on a wound in his ribs. She looked up at Russ and Eleanor, her face nearly as pale as Arch's.

One of the men glanced up. "Can anybody run and get that cot out of the back of the ambulance? We've gotta move fast."

Russ made to go, but his friends were already running for the wagon. Russ turned back and tried to make eye contact with his father. He was looking around, but he didn't seem to have any idea where he was. He acted as if he had just awoke from some bad dream. Eleanor was on her knees by his head, oblivious to the sharp gravel and her gentle hands settled on either side of his face. She began talking to him softly.

Russ glanced at all the blood on the ground. It was everywhere. No one could lose that much blood and survive.

He looked again at his father's face, and at the tears dripping from his mother's eyes. He remembered his father's last words to him before he drove away from the high school.

Russ, I love you. Don't you ever forget how proud you've made me. Now go and win your biggest game.

He could remember each word as clearly as if it were only a minute ago.

Russ stared as the ambulance crew loaded his father up, and he watched old Tupper handcuff Luther Dean and the now unmasked Billy Earl with his father's handcuffs and load them in the back of the sheriff car. They were going to have to go to the hospital too. With his pistol held in the one hand he had left, Frank Russell got into the front passenger seat of the car, kneeling down and facing backwards at Tupper's request. The gun pivoted back and forth between the two felons.

Suddenly, there was somebody standing next to Russ, more felt than seen. He turned and looked down at Isaac Thorpe. The boy was gazing up at him, his chin quivering, his face covered in tears. Without thinking, Russ dropped to his knees and clutched the boy to his body. Isaac was too shocked even to speak.

"I'm glad you're safe, buddy," Russ said. "I'm sure glad you're safe. Do you want to stay with me?"

Isaac shook his head. "I do, but I gotta go see my dad."

The words surprised Russ. He hardly ever gave a thought to Isaac's father. He stood up and tousled the boy's hair. "That's a good idea. Go give him a hug and make sure he knows you're okay."

Trying to give his friend a smile, Isaac's whole body shook with a sob, and he swiped at his nose. With grim determination, he turned and walked stiffly toward home. It looked like it was all he could do not to break into a run.

It wasn't until then that Russ realized there were two other people here that he had neither seen nor expected. One of them ran to him and threw her arms around him. With shocked eyes, he looked over the top of her head to see her mother, Lorna, smiling at him, her hands pressed palm together in front of her mouth.

There wasn't any room in the ambulance for Eleanor to ride with them to the hospital, so she was going to need a ride, but luckily several passing cars had stopped, and most of them were friends of the Blevins family. Eleanor would have plenty of willing people to take her in their car.

Eleanor, her face still white with shock, turned from the ambulance as they shut the door. One of the attendants smiled at her reassuringly and patted her arm, but then Russ saw him look at the other one and give a discouraged little shake of his head.

When Eleanor's eyes fell on Russ, she walked over, acting like she barely had strength to move. "Hey. Bonnie Stutes said she'd take me and the girls up to the hospital. You have a big game to play."

Russ stared at her, his father's words ringing in his head. *Now go and win your biggest game.*

"But Mom, there won't be anybody there to watch." The other players were all standing a ways back, glancing anxiously back up the hill toward the school. Russ looked over at them, then back at his mother.

"Dad wants me to go play," he said. "He said to win the game for both of us."

Tears flooded Eleanor's eyes as she threw her hand up to her mouth. She dropped it and gave him a sad smile. "He *would* say that. Russ, you go get your arms and hands bandaged and taped up, all right? And then you go play that game. Play for all you're worth!"

His mother looked down. She had her husband's blood on her skirt and on her hands and one sleeve, and her knees were bloody where the gravel had scuffed them. She looked at all the blood on Russ and smiled again, leaning in to give him a warm, loving embrace. Stepping back, she took his hands. "You know where we'll be, honey. We'll listen to you on the radio."

Russ could only manage a nod. The lump in his throat wouldn't let him speak.

They all watched the ambulance wheel away, and the reckless speed with which it accelerated north up State Street was lost on no one. In a minute, the only thing left of it was the settling dust.

Barrow Tupper looked in on Frank, who still watched his prisoners grimly. He came over to where Russ and his teammates had gathered. They were ready to start up the hill and see if they could salvage a game.

Tupper looked at Russ and nodded. "You did good today, son. I'll be looking to hear the whole story of what happened in there, but you got places to be right now. You gonna go win a game?"

"Pop told me to." Russ felt like he was making excuses.

"You gotta do what you believe is right. That's all any of us c'n do."

"Yeah," Russ agreed. "The last thing Pop said before he drove off was to go win my biggest game." After hearing the words from his father and repeating them so many times, they were starting to sound almost hollow, robotic.

Tupper nodded and looked toward Russ's team. "I'll tell you something before I take these yahoos up to the hospital and then to the jail. No one but a peace officer will ever understand the things that go through

another peace officer's head. Sometimes I don't think he even understands what's in his own head—like what your father told you today. Times like those, sorting things out is up to God.

"But son, I want you to think about one thing. Football's been good to you, and it might take you far. But that 'biggest game' your dad mentioned? Well . . . that don't have to mean football."

Barrow Tupper's piercing old eyes shot through Russ. They had never seemed so wise and all-seeing. He reached out his hand, and when Russ shook it the grip, in spite of the emaciated, wrinkled hand, was warm and firm. Russ could see how Barrow Tupper had been so revered.

"Good luck, Russ Blevins. Whatever it is you decide."

With that, Tupper walked to the car and got in, and he turned around in the street and followed the ambulance, in a much more sedate manner.

Russ was left standing with Edie and Lorna, and his teammates gathered all around.

"We can give you a ride in Mr. Tupper's truck," said Lorna Russell, offering Russ a smile.

Pete stood there impatiently. He couldn't hold his worries in any longer. "Hey, bud—we gotta get to the game. You're comin', right?"

"Yeah, sure. I gotta go get all taped up first, though. They're not gonna let me play like this."

He held up his hands and arms. The bleeding had stopped, but some of the wounds were ugly.

"Can you still play like that?" asked Charlie Braun.

"You bet I can!"

"I'll help you clean up, Russ," said Lorna. "You boys go on. We'll bring Russ up."

Pete looked to Russ for approval. "You gonna be okay, bud?"

"Yeah, man. We're gonna take those Trojans. Guaranteed."

"Hey, Wop," Ev cut in. Pete turned to him. "I'm gonna come up with Russ. You boys run for it."

Pete and the others nodded. Spit pointed a finger at Russ and shook it, almost warningly. "We'll see you up there, Russ. Right?"

"Yeah, man," Russ tried to grin. "Go on already!"

The four of them went into the house, and Lorna and Edie helped Russ wash his wounds with soap and water while Ev waited outside.

Russ couldn't tell the girls how bad this hurt. He had to be a man about *something!* "You're lucky you didn't cut anything important, like big blood vessels or tendons. You really are lucky, Russ," said Lorna, cringing. "Oh, I am so sorry. This must hurt."

He smiled at her. "That's only a scratch." And then he thought of his father. His father hadn't fared so well.

They wrapped his forearms with gauze, taped them up with adhesive tape, and then Edie took her turn cleaning the lesser wounds on his face and hands. Only one of the facial wounds needed a bandage.

Following a mother's instinct, Lorna left them alone in the bathroom, and Russ leaned down and gently kissed Edie's mouth. He pulled away, looking down at her and wondering how he had ever not realized she was the prettiest girl in town.

"You aren't really going to the game. Are you, Russ?" she asked.

The words startled him. He searched her eyes, knowing that whatever he decided she would support.

His eyes misted. "I can't, Edie. I've gotta be with my dad."

Edie smiled and leaned into him to squeeze him hard.

She said in a whisper, "Russ, I think you already won your biggest game."

They all went out and crowded into Barrow Tupper's pickup. Russ started it and drove up to the school. He didn't park. He only stopped in the roadway.

"Who's getting out?"

The car was silent for a moment. Ev's voice broke the quiet. "Hey, bud—what are you doin'?"

"I have to go to the hospital."

"But . . . You said your dad . . . Your dad asked you to win the game for *both* of you . . . Right?"

Edie and Lorna were watching Russ. Neither spoke.

Russ threw the emergency brake and got out, walking around to the passenger side and jerking the door open. "Come on, Ev."

Ev climbed out. Russ put a hand on the door of the pickup, supporting himself. His face was mere inches from Ev's. "You go give 'em hell, brother."

"What? What are you doin'?"

"I can't play, buddy."

"What? Why?" The look on Ev's face was one of panic.

"I've gotta go be with my dad."

Resignation spilled over Ev's countenance. He knew Russ was right. "We can't win without you."

"Yes you can. You just have to believe in yourself. In *you.*" He jabbed Ev in the chest with his finger. "You, bud. And the greatest team of Russets ever."

Without warning, Ev Morin threw his arms around Russ as if he didn't intend ever to let go. He stepped away with tears on his face. He couldn't look Russ in the eyes. "It won't be the same without you," he said in a husky voice. "But this game's for you. All right?" Now he looked up, and Russ smacked him on the side of the face and held his hand there for a moment, then gave him a couple more taps.

"Tell all the boys I wish I could be there. I hope they'll understand."

CHAPTER SEVENTY-FIVE

When Russ walked into the hospital, the first person he saw in the waiting room was his mother, sitting with her arm around Kathleen's shoulders. One of the other girls must have seen Russ and spoken his name, for Eleanor's face snapped his way. Her hand leaped up to cover her mouth. On the instant, she started to cry. And that scared Russ to death. Was his father already gone?

She jumped up and almost ran down the hall toward him, while Russ, Edie, and Lorna were frozen in mid-stride. As she got close, Russ managed to blurt out, "Mom! What's wrong?"

All his mother could do was shake her head as she threw her arms around him and tried to crush him to death. He held her close, and waited.

Finally, he managed to whisper in her ear, "Mom, please tell me what's wrong."

"Nothing's wrong, Son," she whispered back. "I'm just so glad you're here with us."

Russ felt like his knees were going to give out on him. He had never felt such relief. He hugged his mother tighter. "I love you, Mom. I'm sorry. I couldn't play knowing Dad's lying in here."

Those words made Eleanor weep harder.

Later, as they sat all together in the waiting room, one of the nurses came in holding a wood-case Motorola tube radio. She looked around the room. "Hi, everyone," the young lady smiled, standing there in her Audrey Hepburn hair-do, white dress, and little white hat. "The doctor wanted me to bring you this. The game's on."

A feeling of hopelessness surged up inside of Russ at the thought of listening to the game. The boys were playing the big game without him. Steeling himself, he stood up and took the radio from her, and they plugged it in and tuned in to find local celebrity Mel Richardson doing the announcing. The reception was staticky, and sometimes the sounds of the crowd were not unlike the static, but it was the best they could do.

Once the game was going, and he could hear the sounds of the crowd and the play by play in Richardson's deep, mellow voice, perfectly suited to be an announcer, Russ was happy they had the radio. It let him feel like he was still some part of what was going on, and for the moment it took his mind off his father's life and death struggle in the operating room.

Edie was sitting right next to him, their legs touching, and her mom was on the other side of her. Russ would never have guessed how dear this girl would become to him.

Kathleen came over and got on his lap, making Russ well up with emotion as he pulled her to him. He thought again of Isaac and ached to know the boy was all right.

The first quarter of the game was four minutes in. They could hear Mel Richardson yelling excitedly: *Wow! What a catch! What a catch. Trojan Number Fifteen, Bobby John! Catching the ball just inside the Russets' end zone, for the first touchdown of the game!* In the background, the crowd roared.

Russ swallowed sourly and frowned. The Trojans. Already scoring. Soon, Richardson announced the kick, and it was good. Seven to zero, Russets down.

He listened dully to the game for a while, his thoughts running back and forth between the game and his father. Kathleen got off his lap and went walking the hallways, exploring. Russ was proud of her lack of fear, after what she had been through. The game hardly seemed to matter right then. He had seen the amount of his father's blood on the ground. He had caught the discouraging looks of the ambulance attendants. There was no doubt his father was hovering between life and death.

Mel Richardson kept getting so excited over the game that in Russ's mind his voice began to drone, and his thoughts went in and out, so that by the end of the first quarter, when the Trojans scored a field goal on the fourth down and Richardson proceeded to announce the score as seventeen to zero, Russ realized he had missed a whole touchdown.

His boys were behind by seventeen points! He bowed his head and buried it in his hands, and feeling his mother pat his back didn't make him feel any better.

Then right off the bat in the second quarter, the tide began to turn. The Russets got a first down, then another, and another. On the next play, it sounded like Mel Richardson was out of his chair. *Russet Number Six, Johnny Fabian sending a lateral pass to Number Thirty-Seven, Everett Morin, and Morin . . . Wait . . . Wait! He's running it! He's running it! Would you look at that boy go? He's on fire! Oh, no! Trojans tackle Number Forty-Five, Myrt Walhouse bringing Morin down, but wait! Wait! Wow! Russet tackle Bill Jensen picked the ball right out of the air, and . . . He's in! He's in! Bill Jensen, with a first touchdown for the Russets!*

The crowd went wild, and Russ managed a smile. How about that? Old Side-Swipe had made the first touchdown. He looked over at his mom, and she gave him a weary wink. The girls were smiling too. For a moment, they had been able to take themselves out of this place, out of these circumstances, for a fleeting glimpse of glory.

In moments more . . . *The Russets, lining up for the kick. Sophomore kicker Scot Leader, Number Fifty-Two, getting ready to strut his stuff. And . . . oh, it could be wide . . . No—no! Wait! It's good! It's good! It*

just barely squeezed by the left upright. The Russets have the conversion, for a score of seventeen to seven, and the ball goes back to the Trojans! He went on to talk about how Leader had better watch his tendency to kick to the left, and Russ leaned back in his chair and closed his eyes.

When half-time came, the score was nearly neck and neck, now at twenty-four points for the Trojans, and twenty-one for the Russets. His boys were doing great! Even without their so-called star.

Eleanor looked at her son and rubbed his back. "What are you thinking, buddy?"

Russ shook his head. He wanted to smile, and he wanted to cry, all at the same time. "Nothin', Mom. I just wish I was there. I wish this whole thing had never happened. This was going to be my last high school game, and Dad would have been there, and . . ." He bunched his jaw muscles and bowed his head. He couldn't let go of his emotions now.

Eleanor leaned close. "Son, we all have to let go sometimes. Why don't you go use the restroom?"

He knew exactly what she meant. She was trying to save his pride. He squeezed her hand with a warm smile.

Half-time passed, and he was finding himself getting more and more into the game. He felt guilty when his mind went back to his father. They should turn this game off! The real game, the one that mattered, was being played out on an operating table. What happened on that ball field didn't mean a thing, not in the real world.

But he couldn't take his mind away from his boys.

In the back of his mind, he heard Richardson proclaim a first down for the Trojans. They lined up on the scrimmage line. *They're getting ready for the snap. And it's off! It's in Dean Murphy's hands. He's looking for an open receiver . . . And . . . No, it's a hand-off! Number Seven, Troy Ridley, has picked up the ball, and he's running all-out. No, wait—bam! He's down! What a hit! Wow! What a hit, from Russets Number Thirty-Two, Alvin Wheeler. Oooh, I wouldn't want to be Troy Ridley right now. That was some hit! I think he shook my teeth loose clear up here. But Troy held onto that ball, and he's up and jogging off. He's okay!*

Russ smiled. He didn't mind one bit thinking about Nash knocking Ridley for a loop, but he was glad at the same time that he had been able

to get up and wasn't hurt. There was a time when pain and destruction for the other side was a welcome thing to him. But for some reason, that had all changed this season.

The quick break was over, and Richardson was on a roll again. *Dean Murphy has the ball again, looking for an open player. It's a toss. Great spiral! Oh, wow! Right out of the air! Nate Sparks has picked up the ball, and he's running straight for the end zone. And look at this! Look at this, folks—his big brother Rye is running with him side by side. Watch . . . Watch! Slam! Another touchdown for the Trojans!*

By the end of the third quarter, everyone in the room was spending half their time on their feet. Russ had broken into a sweat from jumping up and down and yelling, and people had started to come and peek around the corner, wondering if there was a riot going on in the waiting room.

His boys were down by two touchdowns now, thirty-eight to twenty-one, and it was looking grim. Ridley and the Sparks brothers were on a roll, crushing out the opposition, and Bud Holloway was knocking Russets down left and right. Johnny Boo was cool, and whenever he got the ball in his hands he was nailing the Russets right down the line. But the Trojans were brutalizing the receivers once they had caught a pass, and the Russets' chances of coming back were beginning to look about as likely as butter staying solid in the August sun.

Russ could do nothing about it now. He had made his choice, and he was where he needed to be, with his family. The rest of life, ball playing included, was only fluff. He knew that now. And he was praying with all his might that no matter how this game ended, he and his father would soon be able to sit out in the driveway talking about this great football season, with the wonderful smell of his father's cigarette smoke drifting all around them.

Then something happened. The Russets had barely started out with the ball before it was intercepted by Myrt Walhouse, who only made a run of five yards before Slick Patterson brought him shatteringly to the ground. This time it was bad, and they had to carry Walhouse off the field. It looked like his last play for High School, as he would graduate this spring like Russ. Sad.

Trojan quarterback Dean Murphy had the ball, and he rocketed a chancy bomb straight out to Rye Sparks, a throw that should have been a sure thing. Mel Richardson's voice went as crazy as those in the crowded waiting room felt now. *No! No! Oh, boy! What an upset! Russets Number Forty-One, Hank Patterson, snatched that ball straight out from in front of Sparks, and he's running. What a bull! He's pushing the Trojans down like candle sticks, headed back for the Trojans' end zone. Thirty yards. Now it's forty-five! Here comes . . . Oh, he's down, down! But what a run. Wow-ee! Brought down by Trojans tackle, Number Twenty-Two, Bud Holloway, but holy! What a run! I hear a rumor they've nicknamed that boy "Slick Fingers," but maybe they'll have to rename him "Sticky Fingers!" What a run! What a crowning moment for Hank Patterson, Russet Number Forty-One!*

Russ turned in time to catch Edie as she threw herself against him in her excitement. The room was in an uproar. The Russets had the ball back in their possession!

Russ stood holding onto Edie for the next play. He couldn't even bear to sit down. His boys were only yards from the end zone, with a ball that by all rights shouldn't even have been theirs.

Richardson was talking on the radio, saying something about Coach Jardinsky. The words filled Russ's eyes with tears, as Richardson announced publicly for the first time that this would be Jardinsky's final year before going off to coach in the pros.

Edie looked up at Russ and gave him a sad frown, patting his chest. She had long known how Russ felt about his big, gruff coach from the Detroit Lions.

Oh, they're out of the huddle, lining up now, ready to make the thunder roll again. And there's the snap! Johnny Fabian has the ball, and . . . Looks like he's got Anthony Wayne open, but no, NO! He's handing it off again! The ball goes to Peter Basso, and the tough little Italian from Shelley is off. That's it, Number Twenty-Five, running like a real freight train. And . . . He's . . . Yes! He did it! He did it! Incredible! He's over the line, with two Trojans trailing him! Another touchdown for the Shelley Russets!

Russ's cheer rocked the room. And then the doctor stepped in.

CHAPTER SEVENTY-SIX

The doctor's eyes went right to Eleanor Blevins. She was smiling, but the smile went away from her face when she saw the grim look on the doctor's.

"Ma'am, could you step out here with me for a minute? Do you have any other adults that are family?"

"Yes, my son."

The doctor looked at Russ and motioned him over with a flick of his fingers. They went out into the hall, and the doctor turned to face them. He spoke in low tones.

"Your husband has lost a great deal of blood. Almost enormous, I would say. I'm talking something over three pints. Now, I think we've got the bleeding stopped, and everything patched up. But with the kind of penetrating trauma he's suffered, we've got to get some more blood in him. Do you happen to know what his blood type is?"

"Yes. It's O negative."

The doctor stared at her. He clenched his jaw, then took a big breath. "You did say O negative, right?"

"Yes."

"Okay."

"Is that a problem?"

"Well, it can be. That . . . Well, a person with O negative blood can only receive O negative blood. If there isn't any on hand . . . Does anyone else in your family have this blood type?"

Eleanor looked around. "Yes—Kathleen." She pointed the girl out through the window.

"Oh. I'm afraid she's too young to give blood. No one else?"

Eleanor shook her head. The doctor put the top of his balled-up fist to his forehead. "All right. Let's not panic. I'll make some phone calls and—"

They heard footsteps, and Russ looked over to see Frank Russell and Barrow Tupper coming into the hallway. The two men couldn't help but catch the concerned look of the doctor, Eleanor, and Russ.

"We got here quick as we could," said Frank. "How is he?"

The doctor glanced over at Eleanor. "Family?"

"They're good friends. It's okay." She looked back at Frank. "Arch needs blood."

Tupper Barrow squared himself with the doctor. "Arch and I have the same blood type."

"You're kidding!" said the doctor. "Really? O negative?"

"Yes sir. Really."

The doctor looked him up and down. Even at a glance, the old man was dangerously thin, but choices were slim. "Would you be willing to give blood—just one pint, even?"

"I've tried t' give my own life for that boy before, Doc. Yer darn right I'll give him blood—all of it, if he needs it."

Forgetting all about the game, Russ and Eleanor went with Tupper to get ready to give blood. Once they had him in a room, and a nurse was getting ready to put a needle in his arm, the old man looked up and glanced back and forth between the woman and her son. "So . . . what are you two doin' here?"

Eleanor's brows went up. "I'm sorry?"

"What are you doin' here? That game's still on, ain't it?"

"Yes, but . . ."

"When's the last time a seventy-two year old man needed a woman and her snot-nose kid to hold his hand so he could give one or two little pints of blood? You two get goin'! Least you c'n do is tell me all about the game when this is over!"

After a moment, Barrow ended his tirade with a wink at Russ. Tears flooded Eleanor's eyes, and she leaned down and kissed Tupper on the cheek. "Thank you, Mr. Barrow."

"Dang!" he exclaimed. "If I'd known I'd get that, I'd be in here givin' blood all the time."

Eleanor and Russ hurried back down the hall to find the score standing now at thirty-eight to thirty-four, still in the Trojans' favor. But the

ball was in the Trojans' hands, and there were only forty seconds left in the game.

Russ looked over at his mother. He knew they would have won that game if he had been there. He knew it with everything that was in him. But there was no way he was ever going to say that to a soul. Ev Morin, in his absence, would in all likelihood have stepped into the position of halfback, and what Ev had said to Russ earlier was right: He was a great kid, no doubt. But he had never been cut out to excel in football. It simply was not in the cards. It made Russ sick to think about how Ev was going to feel after this day. He had been so sure they were going to lose without Russ. Maybe he had willed it.

Eleanor patted her son's arm. "They sure gave it a good shot, Son. You have to give them that."

He put a good smile on. "Heck yes. They did great. I'm proud of 'em."

Edie came over and reached out to take Russ's hand. It made him smile to see how she had come out of her shell. He didn't want to embarrass her in front of the others, but he wanted so badly to lean down and kiss her full, red lips right now. He wouldn't care who saw, but he knew she couldn't handle it.

He could hear Mel Richardson on the radio.

Okay, it looks like time-out has ended. The teams are huddling up. The line of scrimmage will be just ten yards off the Russets' end zone now, and those Trojans are looking tough. And I mean tough, *now. This has been one great game. Those game Russets gave it all, even without one of their best players. Let me take a moment here to say from the announcers that we all wish Russ's father well. He's a great man, and a great sheriff, and he would be an insurmountable loss to law enforcement. So when you are all getting ready for bed tonight, please include Sheriff Arch Blevins and all of the Blevins family in your prayers.*

Russ looked over at his mother, realizing that at some time during the game Mel Richardson must have told the story of the near-disaster on Park Avenue. There were tears rolling down Eleanor's face.

All right, they're toeing the line now. Trojans' center, Darwin Janikowski, is getting down on the ball. Dean Murphy's ankle injury is keeping him out of the play, so Bobby John has stepped in as quarterback.

Waiting for the snap. And it's off! Bobby John has got it in his hands, looking for an opening . . . Those Russets are all over the place, I'm telling you! Wow! Oh! It looks like Charlie Braun's comin' at Bobby John, and he'd better lose that— Oh, he threw it, right out to Nate Sparks. But— Oh, my gosh! OH MY GOSH! I CAN'T BELIEVE IT! I CAN'T BELIEVE IT! The Russets' stand-in halfback, Everett Morin, just came flat-out of nowhere. He snatched that ball right out of the air. With one hand! ONE HAND! He's running . . . He's running . . . No way . . . There is no *way . . . This can't be happening! How many seconds in the game? Twelve seconds! Twelve seconds to the whistle, folks, and Everett Morin is still running. Still running . . . I've never seen anything like this! He's . . . He's . . . Oh my— No way! NO WAY! WHAT IN THE— No way, Idaho, no way! Everett Morin just ran straight into the Trojans' end zone for a touchdown—to WIN THE GAME! I can't believe it! I can't believe it! What an upset!*

The room was in chaos all around him, but Russ didn't even move. He stared at the radio. Had he heard Richardson right? Was he talking about Russ's boys? His team? Was he talking about Russ's best friend, Ev Morin? Was this a dream? Had Ev really snatched the ball out of nowhere and made a nearly one hundred yard touchdown? Or had Mel Richardson finally gone all the way crazy?

Trying to pull himself out of a state of shock, Russ looked at Edie. She was jumping up and down and screaming, and both Eleanor and Edie's mother were laughing, out of control. Edie jumped up and threw her arms around Russ's neck, and pulling him down, she kissed him right on the mouth.

Apparently, Edie didn't care if anyone saw them after all.

● ● ● ● ●

Later, Barrow Tupper came shuffling back to the room, looking wan, and sat down across from Eleanor. She was sitting there with her eyes shut, but it was as if she sensed him, for she opened them and got up, walking over. She crouched down and put her arms around his neck and gave him another kiss on his cheek, and he fumbled up off his chair. He put his arms around her and patted her back, saying soft words to her that no one else could hear. The picture made Russ smile. He remembered one night, carrying Tupper into his house and putting him to bed, playing

his angel. This night, Tupper had played the angel to Arch, and to all of them.

Into the evening, and then through part of a long night, they waited. Edie leaned way over on Russ, fast asleep. Her glasses were in his pocket for safe-keeping. Lorna also leaned to the left, asleep on her daughter's arm. And Frank bent forward with his elbows on his knees, staring at the floor.

Around midnight, a nurse came in and looked around. Even at the late hour, her eyes looked bright.

"Mrs. Blevins? Mrs. Arch Blevins?"

Eleanor left Tupper and went to her. This time, Russ stayed seated. He couldn't bear to wake his sleeping angel. As the nurse spoke quietly, Russ saw his mother's hands come up to her face, and he jumped. Was something wrong?

His involuntary jerk woke Edie up, and she looked around disconcertedly until he handed her glasses to her. She put them on and smiled at him, then saw where he was looking.

In a moment, Eleanor turned around. There was a look of sheer hopefulness painted all over her face as she searched the room, seeking out someone to talk to. Of course that someone would be Tupper, Russ, and Edie, because everyone else was asleep.

Russ and Edie got up to meet her halfway. "Mom?" said Russ. "Is he okay?"

She gave him a great big nod up and down. "Yes, honey. He's okay. They said nothing vital was hit. The rifle shot in his leg nicked the bone, but it mostly only damaged muscle, and the pistol shot in his ribs did puncture a lung, but he's breathing fine from the right one. It might be a couple of months, and a lot of rest, but they expect him to make a full recovery."

Russ felt tears come into his eyes, and he tried to wipe at them before they got to his cheeks. He threw his arms around his mother, and Edie hugged them both. The excitement of those three must have filled the room, for something began to awake the others. And that was the picture they woke to.

CHAPTER SEVENTY-SEVEN

The following day was Sunday, and the doctors believed there was nothing better to do for Arch Blevins than to let him sleep away as much of the day as possible. Eleanor wanted to be beside him, of course, but something else compelled her as well, so she took her family and headed home. Russ did the same, after a quick stop on his way to drop off Edie, her mother, and Frank on his way. It was dark and cold by the time they reached Shelley, and brilliant stars beamed across the black sky. Lorna Russell turned before going in the house and gave Russ a big hug.

"Russ, you are a brave young man. I'm so happy our daughter has found herself a hero."

Russ grinned and looked over at Edie. "Yeah, me too. Now that her hero finally got his head on straight and saw the light."

Frank shook Russ's hand and held on tight. "My wife's right, son. There aren't many eighteen-year-old men without any kind of training in combat who would have gone into the situation you did. I think you saved your father's life. I'm proud to know you."

"Thank you, sir. Thanks a lot. And thanks for coming to help. I can't even tell you how good it made me feel to know you and Mr. Tupper came."

"Your family means a lot to us, Russ. Anything I could ever do to help, I would."

Frank and Lorna said good night after a glance over at Edie made them realize, as they had suspected, that she wasn't ready to go in.

After the door shut, Edie looked up at Russ. "You really are my hero. I wish we could have gotten to know each other sooner."

"That wasn't your fault, Edie. I had my head caught up in thinking I was some kind of super star. I was the worst one for not seeing the forest for the trees. So now we're going to make up for lost time."

Edie nodded and gave him a big, innocent smile. "Yeah." He bent and enfolded her in his arms, and for thirty seconds they kissed and held on.

After saying goodbye, Russ drove to Ev's and sat out front, looking at the house. He wished he could go in and see his buddy. He had a lot of heroes himself, and Everett Morin was not the least of them.

● ● ● ● ●

When Sunday morning came, snowflakes like gentle leaves were drifting down from a windless sky. The ground was white, but it wasn't deep enough yet to be measured. Only deep enough to be starkly beautiful.

Russ didn't feel completely rested from the stresses of the day before, but he knew he could never go back to sleep. And the place he knew his mother was headed today, he had to go as well. It was another place he had years to make up for forsaking.

Pulling out a white shirt and black, severely creased slacks he hardly ever wore, he got dressed and even put on a tie. He polished his shoes, and when he got them on and headed out through the kitchen to warm up the car his mother saw him, and a look of shock came over her face and the faces of his sisters. No one spoke. Even as he went out the back door and down the stairs, the room remained silent. He started the car and kept pressure on the pedal until he knew it would stay running.

He came back in, and his mother was sniffling. He walked over to where she stood turning hash browns at the stove and put his arms around her. She whirled around and hugged him, but still she didn't say a word. None needed to be spoken.

When breakfast was served, Russ sat in Arch's place. He looked around solemnly as his sisters folded their hands in front of them, and last of all he looked at his mother.

"Mom, if it's all right, could I say the prayer?"

With tears glistening in her eyes, his mother could only nod.

After a long and thoughtful blessing on the food, everyone began to serve themselves—all except Kathleen, who was staring at her big brother.

"Russ? Are you gonna come to church with us?"

"I sure am, Sis. And I think I might bring someone else too."

During breakfast, after he knew the Studebaker would be good and warm, he went out and shut it off and stood with the flakes of pure white snow drifting down and sticking to his shirt. It was an almost soundless Sunday, and up and down the street the parked cars were growing white like his own. It reminded him of the James Stewart movie *It's a Wonderful Life.* And indeed, it *was* a wonderful life.

He walked down the block until he reached Isaac Thorpe's house. He stood there on the front sidewalk for fifteen or twenty seconds, a little nervous as he remembered the reception he had gotten last time from Isaac's brothers.

At last, he bowed his head and went up the walk, and he knocked on the door and took one step back. It was a full minute, and one more knock, before the door cracked open. A face looked out, a lined, weary-looking face with eyes that had blue bags under them and brown hair sticking in all directions.

The man who owned the face studied Russ, and then threw the door open wider. "Are you Russ Blevins?"

"Yes sir. You must be Rusty's father."

The man managed a smile, wiping at his mouth. "Yes, I am. I am! I wish . . . That is, I meant to come to your home today with my boy."

When he didn't say anything else, Russ said, "Is he here?"

"He sure is." Mr. Thorpe nodded. "He is, and it sounds like it's because of you. Now, I ain't always been much of a father to that boy, but . . . Well, I'd like to shake your hand, if you'll let me. It would have killed me to lose that little guy's smile around here."

Russ grinned and took Thorpe's outstretched hand. Before the man could even call for his son, Isaac was there, and his sleep-deprived eyes managed to focus on Russ. He yelled out his name and came running, and his father was apparently sober enough to back away.

Isaac threw his arms around Russ, and Russ returned the embrace. No words needed to be spoken.

They stood that way for twenty seconds, and finally Isaac stepped back and looked up at Russ, his dimples showing. Russ looked at Mr. Thorpe. "Sir, I'm going to church today for the first time in a long time. I'd sure like it if you'd let me take Rusty along with me."

The man nodded briskly. "Oh, you bet you can. We don't have much in the way o' any church clothes, but we'll get him the best we got."

Russ looked down at Isaac. "Is that okay with you, Rusty? I'd sure like to have you with me to get me used to goin' again."

Isaac grinned. "Sure. I never been in a church."

"Well, you're in for a nice time then. We'll stop and pick you up in about half an hour if you can be ready."

Russ thanked Isaac's father again and started to turn when the man's voice stopped him.

"I was thinkin', it's gettin' close to Christmastime. I wonder . . . You think it would offend anybody if I came along too?"

"Really? No, of course not. We'd love to have you. I'll tell you what: I'll take my mom and sisters, then come back and get you."

The man nodded and thanked him, and Russ nearly floated back to the house. Back home, he started the car again five minutes before they were going to leave. He wasn't going to make his family sit in a cold car.

That day, for the first time in many months, the entire Blevins family, minus the head of the household, attended Sunday service with Mr. Thorpe, and a young boy who had never set foot inside a church house.

After church, there was an inch of powder snow on the sidewalks and out on the street, where tire tracks ran through it and made it look like an old Currier and Ives Christmas print. The snow had stopped now, but the sky, although it had lifted high, was still white with cloud.

Eleanor made a nice meal, and then Russ drove everyone back up to the hospital, where they stayed with the sleeping sheriff until being advised that visiting hours were over. When they got home, there was a note taped on the back glass door, and Eleanor was first to see it. It said simply, PLEASE CALL EV WHEN YOU CAN.

Of course, Russ ran right in and called his friend, who had only cryptic words for him on the phone. He stayed on just long enough to make sure Russ wasn't going to leave again, and then excused himself and hung up.

Forty-five minutes later, they were sitting listening to records on the phonograph. Everyone had to take their turn getting up to put a new record on each time one ended. Toni was up and had just put on Bing Crosby

singing "White Christmas" when she turned around and got a strange look on her face.

Outside, it was dark, but it had started to snow again, and the snow reflected street lights and the lights from people's houses. "Look outside!" she exclaimed. "Something's happening."

Alarmed, everyone got up and looked out. It seemed like an army of cars was gathering up and down the street, their headlights reflecting yellow in the snow, and the snowflakes visible as they fluttered down in front of the lights.

People started emerging from the vehicles, and even in the darkness it only took Russ five or six seconds to start recognizing the shapes of people who stood out in a crowd: Charlie Braun, Alvin Wheeler, Coach Ivan Jardinsky . . . The list went on and on. There must be more than twenty people out there, and all gathering up to walk his way.

"Well, they can't all fit in this house, Son," said Eleanor, giving him a broad smile when he looked over at her. She motioned sideways with her head. "You best open the door and greet them."

Russ went over and threw open the door, as all his sisters and his mother looked out through the curtains.

The coaches and what appeared to be the entire football team gathered on the lawn and sidewalk. A cheer went up for Russ as he stood there not knowing what to say. He had never wanted more to be able to speak, but never felt more unable.

Ev Morin came out of the crowd holding a great big gold trophy. As he came close, Russ looked down at him from the porch, his chest full of emotion.

"Since you weren't there to see it all, buddy, we wanted to bring this over in person." Ev walked up the two steps and handed the trophy to Russ. "You helped build this team, and we won that game for you."

Russ still couldn't speak. He stood there nodding, looking at the beautiful trophy, which shone even in the dim light and which would grace the glass cabinet in the hallway of the high school for years to come. He finally handed it back to Ev, and Ivan Jardinsky and Dan Nalder walked over.

"We held a vote yesterday, son," said Jardinsky. "I wanted the boys to pick their most valuable player, the one who best represented the Shelley Russets of nineteen fifty-five. I probably don't need to tell you, it was unanimous. Everyone wanted you. So as luck would have it, I know the trophy engraver personally, and he made me this plaque. This is for your wall."

Jardinsky reached way up toward Russ, on the porch, Russ reached down, and a twelve-by-twelve oak board exchanged hands. Russ held it up in the porch light and scanned the simple words engraved on a black metal plate in gold letters: JAMES RUSSET "CUS" BLEVINS 1955 SHELLEY RUSSETS MOST VALUABLE AND MOST BELOVED PLAYER.

Russ stood there shaking his head.

"I guess when they talk about the cat getting someone's tongue, they aren't kidding around," shouted Dan Nalder.

Russ laughed, and the sound of his voice released the swarm. Every football player clambered to get close, to shake his hand, and pat him on the back. More than a few of them exchanged hearty hugs with him.

When they were all done, Jardinsky walked up the stairs and threw his big arm around Russ. He turned his head, and their faces were very close together, while the Russets' head coach gave Russ Blevins a living eulogy, speaking loudly enough for everyone to hear.

"We all know what you did, buddy. We all know that the actions of you and some of your friends most likely saved the lives of your father, your little sister, and one of the neighborhood kids. That kind of bravery goes far beyond anything that can be done on the gridiron. We also know that you had a big choice to make yesterday. You could have left your mother and your sisters to go to the hospital without you and wait for word about your father, about whether he was going to live or die. You could have come and played ball, and you would have been an important part of the biggest game you probably would ever have played in your high school career. But you chose something else a lot more important: family. And that will last you a long ways past football.

"You did us all proud, buddy. And I want you to know something else. This wasn't on the radio. I guess they only had a certain amount of

time on air. So you wouldn't have heard it, but it's something that's gotta be passed on.

"When that game was over, those Trojans could have screamed and yelled and cried. That was the biggest game ever for a lot of them, too, the same as it would have been for you. But they didn't. You know what those boys did? They came to me with their coach, and they asked if they could give a tribute to you. And then while all those boys held their helmets and stood at attention, Troy Ridley came and handed me this."

He motioned toward Dan Nalder, who walked up the steps with one hand behind his back. As he reached Russ, he brought his hand around, and in it rested a football.

"This is the game football, son. The football your buddy Ev intercepted and ran all the way to the other end zone to win that game. It's signed by every single Trojan player and all of your own boys too. It's yours, buddy. Your spirit was there at that game, and everyone agreed this belongs to you."

CHAPTER SEVENTY-EIGHT

A week passed, and Arch Blevins was awake for most of it. Although he had a slight difficulty breathing, while his collapsed lung was making a recovery, he wasn't moving around much, so it wasn't a struggle.

The family spent as much of their time as possible with him, and especially his loving wife was there nearly every waking hour. Often, the girls cleaned the house and cooked, but there must have been two dozen friends, neighbors, and members of their church who kept coming over to help keep things up and to bring in meals. When Arch received that news, he went very quiet, and after a while Russ realized he was fighting back his emotions. His father was a proud man.

Russ went in a few times and played inane card games with his father and sometimes would sit and listen to the radio with him. But something

was strained—not between the two of them, but simply in the way Arch reacted to everyone around him.

One day when Russ peeked in, while Eleanor was down the hall using the restroom, he found Arch staring at the blank wall, lost in thought. His face was bland—not frowning, but not smiling, either. It was Sunday afternoon. It had been a week and a day since the incident on Park Avenue, and even to this moment Russ and his father had said very little about what had happened.

Arch must have been extremely preoccupied not to know the door had edged open. But it was obvious he had no idea. As Russ watched his old man, he saw him swallow hard a couple of times, and then a great look of sadness swept over his face. As tears began to roll down his father's cheeks, he bowed his head to his chest.

Russ let the door shut and stood in the hall. He had no idea what to do.

His mother came back five minutes later, while Russ was leaning up against the wall with one foot propped behind him. He looked over at her and put his finger to his lips.

With a concerned look, Eleanor stopped in front of him. "What's wrong?"

"Mom, Dad was crying."

Eleanor's head whipped over, and she stared at the door. "I guess maybe it's finally hitting him."

"What?"

"How close it all was. You know."

Russ nodded.

"Russ, I think you should go talk to him. He's in a funk, and it doesn't seem like anyone can get him out of it. He's got another week in here at a minimum, and then a long road of recovery at home before he can even think about going back to work."

"Mom, I don't know what to say."

Eleanor frowned sadly, putting her hand on one of Russ's folded arms. "Honey, you are a man now. You're truly grown up. I know you can talk to all of your friends. It's time you learned to talk man to man with the most important man in your life."

Russ stared at her. His heart had begun to thud in his chest. He knew his mother was right. He had been feeling the need for a week to have a serious heart to heart talk with his father. But where did one begin a talk like that?

He guessed he would have to follow his heart. His mother was right. Of course. She always was.

He nodded and took a deep breath. With no verbal response, he turned and eased the door open again. Arch's head was resting back on the pillow, and he was staring the other way. Russ walked in and let the door shut soundlessly.

"Hey, Dad."

Arch turned his head. His eyes and cheeks were dry. As far as he could know, his sadness was only between him and God.

"Hi, Son."

Russ walked close. "So . . . how are you feeling?"

"Good."

"Are you breathing okay?"

"Sure."

This man was worse than Russ at talking. How could he make him open up?

"When do you think you'll be coming home?"

"Oh, they said maybe a week."

Russ nodded. He felt a strange panic closing over him. In his head and his heart, he asked God for help.

"Hey, Pop?"

Arch looked up. Their eyes held.

His father broke the spell. "What is it, Russ?" Was that fear or worry Russ saw in his old man's eyes? He was a great poker player. Maybe Russ was reading something that wasn't really there.

"I just want to say how glad I am you're still around."

Arch stared at him. His lips parted, but no sound came out.

"And . . . I want to tell you how glad I am—and how lucky I feel to have you as my father."

Even as he spoke, he felt like he was being unfair. His father would not know how to handle these words, any more than he would have himself. And here Arch was, trapped in this bed where he couldn't walk away. It must be sheer torture.

His father's chin started to tremble, and he blinked his eyes rapidly several times and looked down. His jaw was clenched so hard he could not have spoken if he tried. His chin stopped shaking, and he drew in a breath and worked his jaw muscles a couple of times, looking down at his hand—his gun hand.

Arch wouldn't look at his son. Russ figured that was what he had to do to gather his courage. "I messed up. I think Luther Dean was telling the truth. I think maybe his brother really did do those burglaries, not him. But I was so sure."

He looked away toward the other wall again. He was struggling to keep his composure. Russ knew better than to speak.

At last, Arch returned his eyes to his hand, which rested on the top of the bedspread.

"I almost got myself killed out there. But it's worse than that. I almost got Kathleen killed, too, and right after she barely went through that hard sickness. And we were so happy to have her back." His eyes squeezed shut, and a tear escaped. Almost savagely, because he knew Russ had to have seen, he pushed it off his cheek. "I almost got Isaac killed too. And I couldn't even handle getting out of it."

Arch lay there in utter silence. Russ stood there the same. This was his father's time. He wasn't going to alter the course of what his old man needed to get out. That was at least one thing he had learned in his life.

Arch's chest filled with a great big breath. It seemed like he would keep inhaling until he exploded. He glanced furtively up at his son, then once more away.

"Russ . . . I don't really know how to say this."

Why couldn't his father meet his eyes, at least for this earth-shaking moment?

"Just say it, Pop."

A smile raised one side of Arch's wide, thick lips. He sighed, a self-strengthening sigh. "I will. You saved my life, Son. I don't think I'd be here right now if you hadn't stayed with me."

Arch made the mistake of doing what Russ had wanted: He tried to meet him eye for eye. And then his big face began to redden, and his great big, tough lawman of a father began to sob.

Russ was petrified. And neither of them realized that Eleanor had cracked open the door and was fighting to keep herself back. Her mother and wife's need to comfort was tugging her into the room.

Russ reached out his hand and squeezed Arch's shoulder, and Arch's shaking hand came up and gave his son's hand what amounted to a hug.

"I love you, Dad," he managed to say. He wanted to tell him he was his hero. Somehow the words wouldn't come out.

In reply to his son's words, Arch, with his eyes still clamped shut, could only give a vigorous, wordless nod.

● ● ● ● ●

Visiting hours were over and the Blevins family sat with the radio on in their accustomed places in the living room. Accustomed places, that is, except that Russ sat right next to his mother, with his arm around her shoulders. If everyone else in the room was like Russ, they weren't even hearing the drivel on the radio. Each of them was lost in his or her own thoughts.

A knock came on the door, and everyone looked over at Eleanor in surprise. It was well after dark! Who would be coming unannounced at this time of night?

Russ jumped up, always wanting to be the protector, and parted the curtain an inch or two, looking out into the shadows. He recognized Barrow Tupper's car parked at the curb, and he told the others.

Eleanor got up and answered the door. "Hi, Mr. Tupper." She stepped forward and threw her arms around the old man. "Do you want to come in?"

"I sure do. It's cold out here."

Using his cane again, as if the day of the shoot-out he had become a young man, and the aging Barrow Tupper had since returned, he walked into the room, glancing around.

"Hello there, Russ. Hello, girls. You're all sure growin' up. I got somethin' to say to all of you. Somethin' important for you all to know."

Eleanor touched his arm. "Come in and sit down then. Do you want something to drink? Maybe something warm?"

"No, ma'am. Thank you. Just had coffee before I got here."

Eleanor showed him to Arch's chair, which for the most part the family had reverently left sitting empty in their father's honor. Russ made Tupper wait while he repositioned the chair so that the old man could see everyone as he spoke.

When they were all seated, the old man leaned forward, clutching his cane in both hands.

"I came to tell you this: A lawman thinks different than anyone else in the world. He wants to think he's a big, tough sheepdog. The rest of the world is either his flock, or they're hungry wolves. And he's the only thing that stands like a wall of protection between the two. He takes great pride in that. Especially a man like Arch. I know. I was the same way, and I trained him. I saw it in him, and I can see it now. But . . .

"Well, now your father thinks he almost got some of his flock killed, because he made a mistake. He doesn't think he's valuable as a sheepdog anymore. Arch wants to step down from being sheriff."

Russ almost jumped forward on the couch. *"What?* Why would he think that?"

Tupper looked squarely at Russ. "Think about it, son. You were there. As far as he's concerned, it was you that saved everyone, not him. He let himself be ambushed. He's sure everyone in the county is talking bad about him now and that no one could possibly want him tryin' to protect them. He's one step away from givin' up that badge forever—at what, forty-five years old? Seems a great big shame, to me."

The girls were looking around at each other, and at Russ and their mother, with horror in their eyes. To all of them, Arch Blevins was a hero!

"What can we do?" Eleanor asked. "You know Arch and his pride. It's hard to talk to him about anything big."

Tupper chuckled. "Yep. I was the same way. When you're wearin' that heavy badge, you think it's part of your job to hold everything inside. It eats away at the insides of you and ages you, while on the outside you go around lookin' like a rock wall. But I'll give you an insight: That tough man lyin' in the hospital ain't as tough as he makes out. And he sure ain't any rock wall. Let him pretend if he wants to, but he's not.

"To answer your question, I wish I knew. I really do. I don't know how to help him. The only part I can play is lettin' you know what he told me. And he only told me because he knows my story, and he knows how I gave up too. He wants to step down, and he told me why. And I don't know if he'll ever admit that to another soul but me. So now you know . . . But I hope you'll never tell him I was here. I hope you'll never tell that big, tough cuss that I ratted him out."

CHAPTER SEVENTY-NINE

Two or three times during the first week Arch Blevins was in the hospital, Edie had asked Russ to take her with him on his visits. Arch had a hard time showing it, but it was obvious to Russ that his father was happy to see him. Yet when Edie would come in with him a huge smile would break over his face, changing Arch's entire countenance. The first time she bent down and kissed him on the cheek, he blushed fiercely and couldn't even keep eye contact with her.

Once, after Russ had been in the room for a while, on one of the nights when Edie wasn't there, Arch said, "Say, Son, this little Edie girl you're bringing around is tough and smart—and she's about as cute as they come. No surprise—her mother always was that way, and she's her spitting image."

Russ smiled. "Thanks, Pop. Edie's pretty special."

"I would think so. What did you ever do with that shiny, polished redhead you had?"

There was a time when mention of Helen would have made Russ want to leave, out of anger. Not because his father hadn't liked Helen, because he obviously had, but because of the part Arch had played in putting her father in prison. Now, although he still felt a certain sadness for Helen and wished the best for her, thinking of their split never made his heart hurt the way he once had thought it would.

"She moved on, Dad. I guess she finally realized I'll never be much but a hick."

Arch managed one of his rare grins. "You're pretty all right, Son—for a hick."

The day after Barrow Tupper's visit to the Blevins home, Russ and Edie went walking along the now-empty canal behind the school, where white fish that had been trapped in deep holes when the water flow was stopped could be seen lying dead in the ice. The air had a bite to it, along with that wonderful aroma of late fall that comes just before the snows begin to fly. Russ confided in Edie about what old Tupper had revealed to the family, and Edie reacted the way Russ had known she would.

"Oh no! Russ, that's terrible! My mom and dad love your dad being the sheriff. I think it would be a huge loss for *everybody* if he gave up. I'll bet there aren't very many people in the whole county who wouldn't want him to stay."

"Yeah—except maybe Luther Dean and Billy Earl, huh?"

Edie laughed, but Russ could tell she was distracted. They walked a few more minutes before he felt like he had to ask her: "Is anything wrong?"

Edie seemed to come out of deep thought, and her eyes popped open wider when she looked at him. "What?"

"Are you okay?"

"Oh, yes. I was just thinking."

Great. Another girl who wanted to let her mind drift off while he was talking to her. "Thinking about what?" He figured he might as well know.

"Well, about your dad, silly!"

"Oh. Well, what about him?"

"I don't know. It seems like there's something we could do to make him see how important he is to the people in this area."

Russ sighed. "Yeah. I don't know what it would be. Maybe get him a nice card or something and have a bunch of people sign it?"

"Hmm." She stared at her feet as they stepped along the now-dead grass on the canal bank. "I'm sure he'd like that. But it doesn't sound like very much."

Again, Russ sighed. "Well, we'd better get back to school. Lunch is about over."

"Okay. I'll see you after class. Can I come see your dad with you again?"

He laughed. "Sure. You're a glutton for punishment, aren't you?"

When classes were over for the day, Russ went out into the hall. It was a sea of faces and bodies, anxious to get away and go home. But somehow, even though she was only five-foot-four or so, he spotted Edie, far down the hall. Even at a distance, and among the crowd, there was a glow about her that seemed to light the hall. Eager to see what was on her mind, he started pushing through the crowd toward her. The whole while, she was doing the same.

He couldn't help smiling as she ran up to him, almost breathless, and grabbed his hands. Before she could speak, he said, "What in the world happened to you? Did you just find a million bucks?"

She laughed. "No! Better! Russ, I thought of something. I thought of something we can do!"

"Do? You mean like a movie or something?"

She stared at him for a second, then let out another laugh. "No, funny! Not like *that!* Something about your dad!"

"Wow! Okay. It must be good!"

"Believe me," she replied, "it's *good!* And if you'll take me over to PDQ for some fries and a cheeseburger, I'll even tell you. Oh—and a strawberry shake!"

"I don't know if it could possibly be worth a strawberry shake too. But fine. We've gotta get out of this hall anyway. I feel like a fish swimming upstream!"

Later, after their meal, and after Edie had laid out her big plan before Russ for his inspection, she poked one last fry in ketchup and stuck it in her mouth, looking like a sailor smoking a cigarette. "So. What do you think?" she asked around the fry.

Russ laughed at the picture before him, and at Edie acting so serious in spite of it. He took a big breath. "Wow. That's huge. Lots of work too, but if it works . . ."

"It *will* work. I promise!"

Russ grinned. "Okay. It was worth everything except the shake."

Edie giggled. "And now I have something a little smaller to tell you."

"What's that?"

"You know the company that has the truck that hit Dad in the wreck?"

"Yeah?"

"Fifty thousand dollars."

"*What?*"

"Fifty thousand dollars! Aren't you listening to me?"

"Well, yeah, but . . . I still don't know what you're talking about."

"Fifty thousand dollars. That's how much they're paying Mom and Dad for the settlement."

It was a good thing Russ wasn't holding his shake at the moment. He would have dropped it to the table the same way he lost the bubblegum he had just put in his mouth.

●●●●●

One week later, the doctors allowed Arch Blevins to go home and finish recuperating there. In his doctor's words, there was no longer anything he and even a thousand other doctors could accomplish in the hospital that God, some homemade chicken soup, plenty of rest, and a loving family could not do at home.

Edie accompanied Russ home from school, and to Russ it felt all the while like they were floating. He kept looking over at Edie and thinking how beautiful she was, and how sweet and incredibly smart. There was no other girl in the world he could adore like he did Edie Russell. Every time he thought about the years he had been oblivious her, he felt like a fool.

Eleanor was watching out the window when they arrived, and she had already started up Russ's Studebaker to make sure it was nice and warm for the trip. The last thing before walking out the door, she turned to the girls. "Okay, girls, you'll be there on time, right?"

"Yes, Mom," they all replied, almost in unison.

"Okay. Bundle up nice and warm."

"Just go on," said Dorothy, throwing open the door. "See you soon!"

Russ had a hard time not keeping the gas pedal to the floor on the way to Idaho Falls. All three of them rode in the front seat, and Russ was wishing Edie could sit in front on the way home, too.

They found Arch looking a little down in the mouth, staring at the wall as he listened half-heartedly to someone talking on the radio. He smiled at Eleanor and Russ, but when he saw Edie, his smile grew bigger. "Well, hi there, young lady!"

"Wow," said Eleanor with a laugh. "It isn't hard to tell who your pet is!"

Arch grinned. "Oh, come on, honey. You and I have been looking at each other for… Wow, about twenty-one years now! What's new?"

Again, Eleanor laughed. "So are you ready?"

Arch chuckled. "Am I ready?" He threw off the sheets to reveal the red and gray flannel shirt they had brought him and gray slacks with a cuff and a sharp crease down the middle of the legs. The left side barely fit over the heavy bandages on the lower part of his leg. "Do I look ready?"

"You sure do, Pop. Let's go then," said Russ. "I want to show you something on the way home." Saying this, he reached down and grabbed his father's shoes and handed them to him one at a time.

The charge nurse had seen them come in, and she appeared in a moment with a clipboard and paperwork for the sheriff to sign.

"Okay, Sheriff. It sure has been a pleasure to have you, but it looks like you have a few people anxious to get you home. So if you'll sign on the bottom of the two top pages, we'll have you on your way. Do you want a wheelchair to go out in?"

"No thank you, Pam. I have to learn how to use those crutches somehow," Arch said as he sat on the edge of the bed and signed the papers. Pam gave Eleanor a carbon copy, and as Russ handed him two crutches that had been leaning in the corner, Arch stood up and situated them under his arms. He turned and looked at Eleanor and the others. "Okay. I'm ready. Let's go home and get some home cooking!"

The snow that had fallen the week before was all melted off now except for a little of it in the mountains. "Looks like it might be a late winter," Arch commented.

"That's true," agreed Eleanor. "We only had one inch of snow. But you're coming home just in time for Thanksgiving, and a lot of people are predicting that will be our first real storm of the year."

"Guess who's coming to eat Thanksgiving dinner with us, Pop." Russ looked away from the road.

"I don't know, Son. Maybe Gregory Peck?"

"Funny! No—Edie and her mom and dad!"

Arch's face lit up, and he tried to crank around to see the girl in the back seat. "Well, isn't that nice? It will be great to have you, Edie."

Edie gave him a huge smile. "We're bringing Mr. Tupper, too."

"We have a lot to be thankful for this year, don't we, dear?" Eleanor said.

Arch was silent for a bit. His face slowly became more and more serious, and he started fidgeting with his hands. Finally, he pulled in a big breath.

"Hey, Ellie? Russ? There's something I should tell you. I've been thinking a lot about this."

"What?" asked Eleanor.

"I'm thinking about resigning from my job."

Eleanor, Russ, and Edie froze. Russ glanced at his mother, and she stared back at him. After a few moments of silence, she looked over at Arch. "Wow. That would be pretty big, hon. Why?"

"Oh, it's time, I think. Time to move on." He looked away from her prying eyes, pretending to be interested in something off the side of the road ahead.

As they were getting close to Shelley, Russ turned off Yellowstone Highway and headed east on Christensen Road. Arch looked at him, surprised. "Hey, Son! Where are you going?"

"Don't you remember I told you I wanted to show you something?"

"Oh. Okay. I hope it won't take long, will it? I'm ready to fall down and sleep for two days."

Russ shrugged. "Naw. It shouldn't take long."

Silence filled the car. The rattle of the gravel under the tires seemed to make Arch nervous. At last, he looked over again. "Nobody said anything. What do you think?"

"About you resigning?" asked Eleanor.

"Well, yeah. About that."

"I think it would be sad. I think the people in Bingham County must really have wanted you bad or they wouldn't have voted you in again.

You know, Mark's been doing a great job while you were gone, but he said he's anxious for you to be back too."

The ensuing silence was broken several times by Arch sighing. For five minutes, no one spoke. Russ made a right turn on the next road, now heading south. Arch looked around, but he didn't speak, and neither did anyone else.

At last, on the corner before turning west on Taylor Highway, Russ pulled over and stopped. "Look over there, Pop." He pointed at a big house with pine pole fencing around it, several dozen full, beautiful trees, and a green pasture.

"Well, that's nice, Son."

"Yeah, isn't it? Edie's mom and dad are getting a bunch of money from the trucking company that was involved in the wreck. They're thinking of buying this."

Arch twisted around again and looked at Edie. "Is that right?"

"Yes!" said Edie, feigning excitement. "Isn't it gorgeous?"

"Sure. Well, good for you folks. A real nice place."

Russ smiled. "Yep."

"So . . . this was the thing you wanted to show me?" asked Arch.

"Yep."

"Okay. Well, maybe when I can get around better we can come back and walk around it. I'd sure like to get back home now, though."

"Okay, Pop. We're going." Russ looked in the rearview mirror, and Edie was watching him, as he thought she might be. He gave her a wink, but held back a grin.

They turned east on Taylor Highway and headed back toward Shelley.

When Taylor Highway turned into Center Street, Russ slowed way down. Arch cleared his throat, and Russ felt his sideways glance. Where they should have turned south on Milton, which would have taken them down to Locust and gotten them more quickly back to Park, Russ kept on going.

Arch cleared his throat again, obviously wanting to say something. But to his credit, he held his tongue, and letting out a sigh, he sank back in his seat.

As they neared State Street, it began to be very noticeable that for a day that couldn't be much more than fifty degrees, there was a large amount of activity in town. The sidewalk was packed, and people almost seemed to be simply standing, watching—waiting for something.

Arch bent over a little, to clear the car's roofline, and scanned the street. There was a car stopped facing them at the stop sign across the street, and Russ gave three loud blasts of his horn, then waved. It was a county sheriff's car, and a big smile came over Arch's face. "Hey! I think that's Mark!"

"Huh," responded Russ, and he turned south on State.

"Hey, why don't you stop? I think . . ." His voice tapered off.

Russ brought the Studebaker to a halt, as people began filtering off of the sidewalks and right out into the street. "What in the world? What are they all doing?" asked Arch. He didn't notice that Mark Daniels had pulled Arch's own sheriff's car up behind them and turned it sideways in the street, flipping on his overhead lights.

Something began to rise up off the street, something that stretched nearly the width of it, and appeared to be attached to a building on the right and to a street light pole on the left. People were standing all around, and Arch began looking about, squinting in confusion.

"What's going on here?" he asked, almost to himself. "It almost looks like they're redoing Spud Day!"

Teenagers were materializing out of the crowd with band instruments, both brass and drums. Arch looked over at his wife and Russ in confusion, then scanned the street again.

By now, the thing that had been lying across the street had come all the way up, and it spanned the street fifteen feet above them, but Russ had stopped far enough away for them to read the great big red letters sprawled across it:

WELCOME HOME TO OUR SHERIFF, ARCH BLEVINS

"I don't—" Arch started, then stopped. He looked over at Russ and Eleanor again. His wife had tears running down her cheeks, and Russ was grinning.

"Don't what, Pop? Cat got your tongue?"

"What is this?"

"Why don't you roll down your window? I think I hear something."

Looking like he had been blind-sided, Arch complied. As the window came down, and Russ's did as well, they could hear the band blaring, "He's a Jolly Good Fellow."

The crowd parted down the middle, and at the far end there was another squad car, that one belonging to Shelley's chief of police.

Russ put the car into low gear and started rolling down the street, as slowly as possible. People yelled greetings as they passed. Russ could make out some of the words: "We love our sheriff!" "Shelley loves Arch Blevins!" "Welcome home to our hero!"

The band kept playing, and soon it melded into a second band, this one from Firth. After theirs dwindled down, the Blackfoot High School band took its place.

As Russ putted by, they recognized dozens of faces, and there were many Russ didn't know. But they obviously knew the most famous lawman in Bingham County.

There were smaller banners everywhere, all sporting words similar to what the citizens of Bingham County were shouting out.

At the end of the line, when Russ was forced either to stop or broadside the police chief's car, all three of Bingham County's sports teams were gathered and cheering: Shelley, Firth, and Blackfoot. In the crowd, Russ could see all of his sisters, every one of his best friends, the police chief, the mayor, the city council and county commissioners. Frank and Lorna Russell were smiling at the occupants of Russ's car, standing beside old Barrow Tupper, whose big mouth and loose lips had caused this circus. The last person Arch stopped to stare at was standing beside the county coroner, a personal and close friend of his, and this was a face even Russ had never expected to see.

"Is that—?" He stopped and looked into the rearview mirror. "Edie, is that— Did you—?"

"Yes, Russ, I think the mayor made a little phone call. That's the governor."

Russ looked over at his father, whose mouth was now ajar as he stared around him and listened to the crowd.

"What do you think, Pop? Should we get out?"

Mechanically, Arch turned his head and looked at Russ, then at Eleanor. "Is all this . . . Did you all do this?"

Russ grinned. "The whole county did it. But it was Edie's idea."

Arch was overcome. His eyes went red, and tears streamed out of them as he fumbled for his door handle, pushing the door open, then swatting the tears away before anyone else could see them.

Russ turned off the car and jumped out, running around to help his father if he needed it. But Arch didn't need it. By holding onto the door and using his good leg, he stood up fine, and his smoky blue eyes scanned the crowd that surrounded them. There were easily three thousand people on the street, probably many more than that.

Arch stepped out of the way and held his hand down to his wife, who climbed out to stand beside him as Russ opened Edie's door and let her out too.

The four of them stood there, with Russ, Eleanor, and Edie grinning, and Arch dumbfounded, unable to utter a word.

The mayor, chief, and governor walked forward, and the governor held out his hand. Dumbly, Arch shook it, looking like he needed to catch his breath.

"Hello there, Sheriff Blevins. Someone had a feeling you might be thinking about stepping down from your position. I think that would be a very sad day for this county. There are a lot of people who would rather you stayed on."

Arch met the governor's eyes, then once more swept the crowd around him, and he couldn't hold at bay the tears that filled his eyes. This time, he seemed to realize it was pointless to try.

He gave a nod, and as he turned and met Edie's eyes, and then Russ's, his son smiled. "Nobody wants you to go, Dad. You're our sheriff."

With his chin quivering, Arch gave his boy a smile. He had not put his arms around this young man in years while he told him how proud he was of him and how much having him for a son had meant.

It was time to change that.

THE END

AUTHOR'S NOTES

It was my desire to write a second novel about my childhood home of Shelley, Idaho, about a boy who got too self-important and proud to realize what the love of his father meant to him. It seemed only natural to model my protagonist after my uncle, Burdette Hess, who was the true hero of the Shelley Russetts in the early 1950's, and who went on to play college ball, then was drafted by the San Francisco Forty-Niners and went on to play for the Calgary Stampeders.

My second thought was that it would be fitting to have his father be modeled after his father in real life, my grandfather, Arch Hess, who was the police chief in Shelley, then Bingham County sheriff for over two decades before retiring in the seventies.

As usual, I have used a few names in these pages that are real people. Retired Officer Mark Daniels of the Pocatello Police Department graciously allowed me to make him a deputy to Arch Blevins. Jack Webber, Harrison Long, and Stan Tharpe are three firefighters I worked alongside in the Pocatello Fire Department. All of these men I have used fictitiously, and nothing they do in these pages should be construed as anything they have done, or might do, in real life. The only historical character I have used as he really was is sports announcer Mel Richardson.

I have taken some large liberties with the sports scene of the 1950's. Many of you may remember that the "State football championship," at least in Idaho, did not come about until 1979. Also, football games were usually a once-per-season thing against each rival school. But to make the rivalry with Rigby be a bigger part of this story, I used my literary license to create a State championship long before it actually existed. I hope this fictional leap isn't too jarring to those who lived and played ball in that time period.

To the best of my ability, I have tried to re-create the town of Shelley

as it was in 1955, and to this end I extensively used the high school memories of my mother, Cherie Hess Jonas and her three friends, Alene Huntsman, Carol Thompson, and Karen Likes. I also had help from my friend Todd Christensen and other people who called Shelley home.

Within the pages of this book there are some things that actually happened in Shelley, although most of those have been changed in some way to meet the needs of the story. The starlings-in-the-theater incident was real, as was the felling of the tree over the track that went awry. I am told that the incident of near drowning under the ice is also factual, but it happened to my Uncle Burdette, rather than to my grandfather.

The names of the Shelley businesses are all real, and as far as I could learn all in the original places they would have been in 1955.

As a note of possible personal interest, the Blevins home on Park Avenue was in real life the home of my grandparents, and the home next to it, on the corner of Park and Locust, was my childhood home of the 1970's and 80's, which was also used as the home of the protagonist, Samuel Jordan, in my 1977-based novel, *Samuel's Angel*, and will be the setting of other novels in the future.

About the Author

Kirby Frank Jonas was born in 1965 in Bozeman, Montana. His earliest memories are of living seven miles outside of town in a wide crack in the mountains known as Bear Canyon. At that time it was a remote and lonely place, a place where a boy with an imagination could grow and nurture his mind, body, and soul.

From Montana, the Jonas family moved almost as far across the country as they could go, to Broad Run, Virginia, a place that, although not as deep in the timbered mountains as Bear Canyon, was every bit as remote—Roland Farm. Once again, young Jonas spent his time mostly alone, or with his older brother, if he was not in school. Jonas learned to hike with his mother, fish with his father, and to dodge an unruly horse.

Jonas moved to Shelley, Idaho, in 1971, and from that time forth, with the exception of a couple of short sojourns elsewhere, he became an Idahoan. Jonas attended all twelve years of school in Shelley, graduating in 1983. In the sixth grade, he penned his first novel, *The Tumbleweed,* and in high school he wrote his second, *The Vigilante.*

Jonas has lived in six cities in France, in Mesa, Arizona, and explored the United States extensively. He has fought fires for the Bureau of Land Management in five western states and carried a gun in three different jobs.

In 1987, Jonas met his wife-to-be, Debbie Chatterton, and in 1989 took her to the altar. Over some rough and rocky roads they have traveled, and across some raging rivers that have at times threatened to draw them under, but they survived, and with four beautiful children to show for it: Cheyenne, Jacob, Clay, and Matthew. Middle son Clay has now taken up the writing of fiction himself, and is writing a series of fantasy-science fiction novels, so the legacy will live on.

Jonas has been employed as a security guard and Wells Fargo armed guard in Phoenix, Arizona, a wildland firefighter, Pocatello, Idaho, police officer, and municipal firefighter. After a full career, he retired from the Pocatello Fire Department in 2017 and is currently employed once more in armed security, guarding federal facilities.

Books by Kirby Jonas

Season of the Vigilante, Book One: The Bloody Season
Season of the Vigilante, Book Two: Season's End
The Dansing Star
Death of an Eagle
Legend of the Tumbleweed
Lady Winchester
The Devil's Blood
The Secret of Two Hawks
Knight of the Ribbons
Drygulch to Destiny
Samuel's Angel
The Night of My Hanging (And Other Short Stories)

Savage Law **series**
Law of the Lemhi, part 1
Law of the Lemhi, part 2
River of Death
Lockdown for Lockwood

The Badlands **series**
Yaqui Gold (co-author Clint Walker)
Canyon of the Haunted Shadows (in electronic format only)

Legends West **series**
Disciples of the Wind (co-author Jamie Jonas)
Reapers of the Wind (co-author Jamie Jonas)

Lehi's Dream **series**
Nephi Was My Friend
The Faith of a Man
A Land Called Bountiful
Shores of Promise (forthcoming)

Gray Eagle **series**

The Fledgling (electronic format only)
Flight of the Fledgling (electronic format only)
Wings on the Wind (electronic format only)

Books on audio tape

The Dansing Star, narrated by James Drury, *"The Virginian"*
Death of an Eagle, narrated by James Drury
Legend of the Tumbleweed, narrated by James Drury
Lady Winchester, narrated by James Drury
Yaqui Gold, narrated by Gene Engene
The Secret of Two Hawks, narrated by Kevin Foley
Knight of the Ribbons, narrated by Rusty Nelson
Drygulch to Destiny, narrated by Kirby Jonas

Available through the author at www.kirbyjonas.com

To order books, go to www.kirbyjonas.com or write to:

Howling Wolf Publishing
1611 City Creek Road
Pocatello ID 83204

Or send email to: kirby@kirbyjonas.com

RUSSET

I0665745